Remembrance OF THE *Past*

LORY LILIAN

Meryton Press

REMEMBRANCE OF THE PAST

Copyright © 2011 by Lory Lilian

ISBN: 978-1-936009-10-7

Book and cover design by Ellen Pickels

Acknowledgments

Special thanks to Ellen Pickels and Margaret Fransen for their
support and assistance in publishing this book. I would also like
to add a word of appreciation to Jane Austen fan fiction readers for
their constant encouragement during the writing of this story.

Chapter 1

"You must allow me to tell you how ardently I admire and love you."

Three months had passed since those astonishing words erupted from the last man in the world from whom she would expect to hear them. Three months filled with tormenting uncertainties about herself and her abilities to judge people. Three months of self-reproach and self-censure, not because she had refused his marriage offer — no, in this she had no doubt about the justice of her decision, and not for a moment could she repent her refusal — but because Elizabeth Bennet knew she had been blind, partial, prejudiced, and absurd in his regard.

In the succeeding months, she had yet to recover from the surprise of that singular day at Hunsford parsonage. Even now, walking with her aunt in the paths of Hyde Park, her thoughts travelled back to the torment of that moment. That he should have been in love with her for so many months — so much in love as to wish to marry her in spite of all his objections against her and her family — was still incredible to Elizabeth.

"You could not have made the offer of your hand in any possible way that would have tempted me to accept it."

It was true; nothing he could have told her at that moment would have induced her to marry him. Still, the expression of mingled incredulity and mortification that overspread his face at hearing her words had haunted her restless nights ever since. His disappointed feelings became the object of her compassion.

Yet, she could not approve his manner nor forgive the offenses he heaped on her family, regardless of how merited the reproaches had been. She only wished she had not allowed rage and prejudice to cloud her judgment nor refused him in such a despicable manner.

Most of all, she could not think without shame and humiliation of her lack of discernment and her poor abilities to see the truth behind the appearance of both Mr. Wickham and Mr. Darcy.

Fortunately, the regiment had departed for Brighton, and she likely never would see Mr. Wickham again. Elizabeth's relief was overshadowed by her distress that her father had allowed Lydia to accompany Colonel Forster's wife on their journey to the Brighton encampment. She had tried to convince Mr. Bennet to keep Lydia at home, but he refused to see the reason of her arguments and met her concerns with wry amusement. Consequently, Lydia was off, and Elizabeth struggled to subdue her vexation by not dwelling on the situation. She only hoped her father would prove to be right in this instance.

"Elizabeth!" Mrs. Gardiner's voice brought her back to reality. "My dear, I am truly worried about you lately. You seem so...unlike yourself."

"Do not trouble yourself, Aunt. I was thinking of Longbourn and especially of Jane." She blushed, ashamed to deceive her affectionate aunt. She always had complete confidence in Mrs. Gardiner and shared many secrets with her, but she could not divulge this one.

"Jane is not well, either, but in her case, I know the reason that prevents her being happy. I only hope in time that she will find the strength to put aside her regrets before they become injurious to her health."

"I had hoped she would join us; I feel sad to know she will be mourning in the solitude of her room while I enjoy the many beauties on our tour."

"Well, my dear, she offered to remain at Longbourn and take care of your little cousins, and you know she could not be persuaded otherwise."

"Yes, I know, Aunt. You have been very kind both to Jane and to me. We shall never be able to repay your kindness."

"Oh, do not say a word more, Lizzy. Besides, I feel guilty; we promised you a two-month tour to the Lakes and instead we returned to London without a certain date for our departure. I hope your uncle can solve his urgent business matter soon so we may leave as planned."

"My dear Aunt, while I confess I am anxious to start our tour, it is such a rare pleasure to enjoy your company for an entire day; I truly do not mind."

"I am glad, my dear, because I also enjoy your presence here exceedingly. And this morning was very productive, was it not?"

"Yes, very productive," laughed Elizabeth. "Two new dresses ordered at the modiste, visits to every shop in Covent Garden, and now a long walk in Hyde Park."

"Well, your uncle insisted on our doing so. I hope you are not fatigued."

"Oh, I am not at all fatigued, Aunt — quite the contrary. You know I am fond of walking, though I have to say I prefer country roads to over-crowded, fashionable London streets."

"My dear, the disadvantage of walking in those secluded places of yours is that you may not have a carriage following you that you can simply enter when your feet refuse to obey you anymore."

Good humour seized Elizabeth again, and she succeeded in putting aside any disturbing thoughts. Warmed by the powerful June sun, she continued to enjoy their walk through the park and the chat with her aunt, making plans for their long-awaited trip to the North.

It was past midday when the heat finally drove Elizabeth and her aunt to the park's exit. Their animated discussion occupied Elizabeth's full attention, and she startled in utter surprise when a familiar voice called her name. She stopped and turned back, only to see the jovial face of Colonel Fitzwilliam.

Memories of the last time she had met the gentleman instantly invaded her mind, and her cheeks burned crimson as she forced herself to smile and greet him with the same openness he displayed. He was as charming as ever, unable to conceal his pleasure at seeing her again, and she was content not to notice any change in his behaviour toward her, which only proved, she hoped, that he remained oblivious of the events preceding his departure from Kent. *Would he be as jovial if he knew? Likely not.*

A moment later, her newly formed smile faded, her heart nearly stopped, and her face turned white when her eyes met Mr. Darcy's intense gaze from a short distance behind the colonel.

Her eyes remained imprisoned by his, and no word escaped her lips, nor could she hear what the colonel was saying. It took her several moments to distinguish the young lady who was staring at her as she clutched Mr. Darcy's arm, her blue eyes filled with curiosity.

Elizabeth's first impulse was to hide or run. Yet, she could not have done so had she wanted; the shock of seeing him had anchored her feet in place.

The colonel's voice turned her eyes again to him, and she returned his greeting. Her mind instantly discerned the circumstances: The colonel had seen her and hurried in her direction, unaware of the great distress the encounter would cause her and his cousin. Mr. Darcy looked stony and immovable, not taking his eyes from her until she could feel his intense stare burning her profile. She cast another glance at him only to see his countenance as severe as ever.

She could not run from him, but she was certain *he* would soon turn and depart, together with the beautiful young lady, and she could not blame him. Why would he show any enjoyment in seeing her again? Why would he desire even to speak to her?

For a moment, Mr. Darcy recovered himself enough to move, but instead of turning away, he advanced towards the ladies and bowed to Elizabeth, greeting her, if not in perfect composure, at least with well-bred civility. His cheeks were slightly coloured and his tone hesitant.

"Miss Bennet, it is such a pleasant surprise to see you again."

"Mr. Darcy," was all she could manage to say, curtsying to him. Her eyes lowered to the ground and then returned to the colonel who was smiling at her, well humoured.

"Miss Bennet, how are you? Very well, I hope. Have you been in London long?

Are you residing in the neighbourhood by any chance?"

"No, I have not been in London long, sir; I left Hertfordshire only a week ago. I am visiting my aunt and uncle." Only then did she remember Mrs. Gardiner, who was patiently waiting a few steps behind her. She looked from her aunt to the colonel and then to Mr. Darcy and his companion. How would he respond to the revelation that this was her aunt who lived in Gracechurch Street? And what of the young lady? He had not yet introduced her to them; perhaps he was protecting her from their inferior company. She certainly did not look as though she were accustomed to mingling with the inhabitants of Cheapside.

As he guessed the reason for her hesitation, Darcy stepped closer and slightly bowed to Mrs. Gardiner in acknowledgment; the colonel, easier in manner, directly asked for the favour of an introduction, and Elizabeth obliged, casting repeated glances at both gentlemen.

While the colonel's countenance displayed nothing but delight during the introduction, Darcy was undoubtedly surprised, but his attitude remained polite, and he expressed his pleasure to meet Mrs. Gardiner.

Then, to Elizabeth's utter shock, he turned and gently took the young lady's hand until he brought her in front of him. He met Elizabeth's eyes and, with a gentleness she had never heard from him before, spoke more to her than to her aunt. "Miss Bennet, Mrs. Gardiner, allow me to introduce my sister, Georgiana."

Elizabeth's eyes opened wide at such a request so humbly addressed — surprisingly relieved at the revelation that she was his sister — and she tried to understand the reason for his unexpected change in manners. She was certain he would make his escape as soon as possible, avoiding her as he would his greatest enemy. Instead, he was kind and polite, extending the introduction of his sister to her and her aunt. Her colour changed, and she stood mute for a few moments.

The formidable presentation took place, and Elizabeth dared to shift her gaze to Miss Darcy. With astonishment, she noticed that the young lady's embarrassment and uneasiness were greater than her own, and her long silence was not due to aloofness or pride — as she previously had been led to believe — but to profound shyness. The girl managed with difficulty to say a few words to Mrs. Gardiner, and when her brother introduced her to Elizabeth, she forced a smile while curtseying elegantly. These efforts garnered Elizabeth's good opinion immediately; with an open smile, she returned the curtsey, expressing her delight.

"Miss Darcy, I am honoured to meet you. I have heard so many wonderful things about you."

"And I about you, Miss Bennet. I have long desired to make your acquaintance." Georgiana's tentative smile and the deep blush that accompanied those few words were further indications of how unaccustomed she was and how uneasy she felt to have a conversation with strangers.

Elizabeth's cheeks coloured, wondering *what* Miss Darcy had been told about her and from whence came the wish to make her acquaintance.

In a desperate attempt to control her emotions, Elizabeth tried to lighten the tension and, consequently, her spirit. "Thank you for your kind words, Miss Darcy; I can only hope that not *everything* you have heard about me was frightfully bad."

She smiled fleetingly, as the effect of her words seemed to be the opposite of what she intended. Miss Darcy instantly frowned, and she looked with visible worry from her brother to the colonel. The latter started to laugh and finally intervened.

"Well, Miss Bennet, to be completely honest, Georgiana did hear some *mixed* things about you, which is understandable considering the various sources of her information. However, I assure you that nothing she heard was *'frightfully bad'*."

Elizabeth laughed softly. Miss Darcy, however, obviously not accustomed to this kind of teasing exchange, startled at her cousin's statement, which sounded offensive, and turned to her brother as if silently asking for his assistance. Elizabeth was about to say something to alleviate her distress when Mr. Darcy's voice settled the situation; and indeed, a moment later, the young lady's face lightened in relief.

"Georgiana, our cousin speaks in jest. I am also certain Miss Bennet knows that neither the colonel nor I could have done anything but praise her. As I said some time ago, no one with the privilege of knowing Miss Bennet could find anything wanting."

His words made Elizabeth reel while her cheeks coloured and her eyes locked on his. She tried to catch her breath for a moment, shocked to hear him declaring his admiration so publicly in front of *his* relatives and *hers*.

Of course, he had told her almost the same thing one night at Rosings as he stood near the piano while she played, the colonel at her side. Nevertheless, to reiterate the statement after everything that had happened — to admit his continued admiration in front of her and the others — what could he mean by this? Was she perhaps wrong in her judgment again? That night at Rosings, she failed to understand the true meaning of his words. Was she presuming too much again? Was it possible he only meant to relieve his sister's discomfort by repeating in jest one of their earlier debates?

"My brother is right, Miss Bennet. I have heard nothing but wonderful things, I assure you." Miss Darcy's voice sounded more confident and managed to return Elizabeth's thoughts to the present. Avoiding Mr. Darcy's gaze, she smiled at his sister while trying to control the tremor in her voice.

"I thank you, Miss Darcy, and I thank you, gentlemen."

She noticed from the corner of her eye that both Mr. Darcy and the colonel returned her smile, and she hoped the entire incident had ended. Decidedly, she kept her attention focused on her new acquaintance, sharing a few more polite exchanges.

"Miss Bennet, Mrs. Gardiner, do you have an appointment to attend or were you just enjoying this beautiful day in the park?" asked the colonel as the group started to walk toward the exit. Miss Darcy was on Elizabeth's left, holding tightly to her brother's arm while the colonel politely offered his arms to both Mrs. Gardiner and her niece.

"No appointment, sir — merely concluding a morning of shopping with a pleasant walk," answered the elder lady. Their conversation turned to the warm weather, and they discussed the advantages of leaving London at that time of year. The colonel's conversational skills perfectly matched those of Mrs. Gardiner, and they easily conducted and sustained the discussion.

Still not completely at ease, Elizabeth remained less talkative than usual, rather listening to the conversation than contributing to it.

"Miss Bennet, I hope your family is in good health?"

Mr. Darcy's deep voice startled her, and she lifted her eyes to meet his for a moment. "Yes, thank you; they are in excellent health." She did not feel easy enough to say more.

"When did you leave Longbourn?"

"Only a week ago, sir."

"Yes, you already told us that. Forgive me."

She only smiled as did Miss Darcy.

"Will you remain in London long?" This time their eyes met and locked briefly, but it was enough for her to see that he was as embarrassed as she was by his direct question. She could not read in his glowering countenance whether he was truly interested in her plans or merely being polite, and she answered as neutrally as possible.

"I am not certain at the moment. Our plans are not fixed. At least a few more days, I imagine."

The colonel intervened. "Only a few more days? Such a pity! I do hope we will have the pleasure of seeing you again."

Elizabeth made no reply as Mrs. Gardiner answered, "Indeed, sir, we would be very pleased to enjoy your company again. However, we cannot make any plans for the moment and Elizabeth even less so. She is entirely at our mercy — a prisoner of our busy schedule."

Following the colonel's polite but curious inquiry, Mrs. Gardiner explained the delay in their plans for departing London and their hope that they would be able to start the journey as soon as possible. The mention of the Lakes as their destination animated the conversation once more.

"I hope you will enjoy the trip, Miss Bennet. In fact, I daresay I am certain you will." More than Darcy's words, the tone of his voice and their implication only disconcerted and confused Elizabeth more. He was addressing her with more warmth than ever, and he even suggested that he was certain she would be pleased with the trip. Did he presume to know or take a sincere interest in what would please her? Happily, she had not much time to remain mired in her confusion as Miss Darcy suddenly became daring enough to share her opinion about the new topic.

"I have always liked the Lakes very much. My brother has been so kind as to take me there twice, and except for Pemberley, it is one of my favourite places." She paused a moment, smiled to Elizabeth, and then continued, slightly embarrassed. "Oh... Forgive me, Miss Bennet, I should have told you; Pemberley is our home."

"I know," answered Elizabeth, smiling back. "From what I have heard, it is a most wonderful place."

"Oh, did my brother tell you of Pemberley?" Her innocent question made them lift their eyes at the same time; their gazes met, a deep redness spreading over both their faces.

"No, Georgiana; *unfortunately,* I did not find the opportunity to tell Miss Bennet much about Pemberley."

"I...I had the pleasure of spending a few days in Mr. Bingley's house when he resided at Netherfield, and during that time, I heard both Mr. Darcy and Miss Bingley talking of Pemberley. Miss Bingley was very generous in her praise and showed the deepest admiration for the beauties of Pemberley; I am sure she was not exaggerating."

Elizabeth did not waste the opportunity to search Miss Darcy's face with great attention when she mentioned Mr. Bingley and his home in Hertfordshire, trying to find a sign of emotion; she found none. However, when she mentioned Miss Bingley, Georgiana's lips unconsciously lifted in a slight grin. Elizabeth's smile grew more open, and she almost chuckled.

"Miss Bingley is very generous in her praise," added Darcy somewhat neutrally, "though she has visited Pemberley on only three occasions. To my recollection, many of its beauties remain unknown to her."

His statement increased Elizabeth's amusement, as she was certain it was meant to clarify Miss Bingley's pretensions of being *intimate* with the Darcys and their home. She rejoiced in the newly discovered pleasure of talking with him without *quite* talking, the others not fully understanding the hidden implications of their exchange.

Mrs. Gardiner then offered, "I did not have the pleasure of talking to Miss Bingley about Pemberley, but I can well testify that her praise could not have been exaggerated. Indeed, I do not think I have ever seen a place more happily situated and more beautiful than your home, Mr. Darcy."

Mr. Darcy's surprise was even greater than his sister's was, and he turned to the lady without concealing his eager curiosity. "Mrs. Gardiner, thank you for your approval, but may I dare ask when you visited Pemberley? I do not remember having the pleasure of meeting you before."

"Indeed we did not meet before, sir. I cannot say I actually visited Pemberley, but I did see it various times when I was younger. And I had the honour of meeting Lady Anne a few times — the most wonderful lady I have ever met." At their wondrous looks, she smiled and added, "I grew up in Lambton, which is only five miles from Pemberley."

With increasing surprise did Elizabeth witness Mr. Darcy's face lighten by a smile more bright than she had ever seen; Miss Darcy could not refrain from asking hastily, "Oh, Mrs. Gardiner… did you really meet my mother?"

"Yes, I did, Miss Darcy. My father had a shop in Lambton, and my mother — who had been a governess before marrying — used to teach the children in Lambton School. Lady Anne was the most fervent supporter and generous patroness of the school; there was nothing needed for the children that she did not provide. She also purchased quite often from my father's shop, so I had many opportunities to meet her."

Miss Darcy abruptly left her brother's side and moved closer to Mrs. Gardiner, listening with such rapt attention to every word that she barely breathed. This change of positions put Elizabeth near Darcy, and as she was listening attentively to her aunt's words, her heart skipped a beat when her hand brushed against his as they walked. She shivered at their brief touch, barely able to follow what Mrs. Gardiner continued to relate.

"She was very kind, was she not?" asked Georgiana..

"Indeed she was," agreed Mrs. Gardiner. "And very beautiful, too. I must say, Miss Darcy, you bear a striking resemblance to her."

"Do I?" Her eyes opened widely in disbelief.

"Yes, most certainly. If I had not the pleasure of being introduced to you and had only seen you from afar, I could still tell with certainty that you were related to her."

"Thank you, Mrs. Gardiner, but I know I am not at all as beautiful as she was — not hardly so." The emotion seemed to leave Miss Darcy with little strength, and her last words were mere whispers.

"I must disagree with you in this respect. I am only speaking the truth."

"I…I am very happy that I met you, Mrs. Gardiner," was her only reply. Miss Darcy resumed her place on her brother's arm, and this time she seemed to need his support. Elizabeth's heart melted as she saw the girl fighting back tears. She dared to lift her eyes to Darcy, only to see the emotions changing his own countenance. She wanted to say something, but she dared not, nor could she find the proper words; even more, the siblings' closeness and shared comfort proved to Elizabeth that they needed no stranger to help them with their grief.

"Well, Mrs. Gardiner," spoke the colonel, in an unsuccessful attempt to hide his own emotion, "this meeting has proved to be a wonderful source of surprise for us. It was fortunate that Darcy noticed Miss Bennet as we were about to leave the park. If not for his attention, I would not have recognised her, and we would have missed the pleasure of this delightful meeting."

"Thank you, sir," replied Mrs. Gardiner. "The feeling is mutual, I assure you. We are very happy to have met you."

This new revelation that Mr. Darcy was the one who saw her and acknowledged her presence to the others threw Elizabeth into a new torment. He could have left the park and avoided her; instead, he made the decision to approach her on his own and then introduced her to his sister. *What might be the significance of all this?*

She *felt* before she noticed his stare upon her but did not dare to meet his eyes at that moment. She vaguely heard her aunt, together with the colonel and Georgiana, talking about Lambton and Derbyshire. From time to time, *his* deep voice intervened to add a few words, and the sound startled her each time. Be it from the pleasure of talking about his home or her aunt's easy and pleasant manners, never had Elizabeth seen Mr. Darcy so open in talking about a subject, and never had his voice sounded so gentle. Nothing in his attitude indicated any sort of disdain for his new acquaintance — one of those whose situation in life he considered so decidedly below his own.

Elizabeth was the only one to remain quiet and disconcerted; her emotions still overwhelmed her. Her eyes were drawn continuously toward Mr. Darcy, and she had to fight the impulse to stare at him. Several times his quick glances met her eyes and locked with them momentarily, colouring her cheeks crimson. Each time their eyes met, he smiled at her — a small, hidden smile — but it was a smile he extended to her nevertheless.

After almost half an hour, they finally reached the exit of the park, and the separation of the parties became inevitable. Elizabeth knew she would likely never see him again, and to her utter shock, she discovered she was already feeling the loss of his company.

She dared lift her eyes only to meet his dark ones staring intensely at her; this time, although cold shivers travelled wildly through her, she did not avert her gaze until hearing the colonel's voice taking his leave of them.

"Miss Bennet, Mrs. Gardiner, it was a pleasure to meet with you today." I hope you have your carriage close by; it is very hot — quite unpleasant I might say. If not, I would be glad to accompany you with my carriage."

"Thank you, Colonel Fitzwilliam, our carriage is waiting."

"I hope we did not delay you too much, Mrs. Gardiner." Elizabeth turned to Mr. Darcy. Could she really detect a sort of regret in his voice?

"No indeed, Mr. Darcy. We were in no hurry at all. Mr. Gardiner will return home later this afternoon."

"Then...if I may..." Miss Darcy stopped for a moment, looking at Mrs. Gardiner, then at her brother, and finally at Elizabeth. "Mrs. Gardiner, I was wondering...our home is nearby in Grosvenor Square. If you are not in a great hurry, would you like to join me for tea? I mean...if you have no other engagements. I would dearly like to resume our earlier conversation."

She blushed as if suddenly realizing the impetuosity of her invitation. Her eyes turned to her brother as though she were asking for his late agreement. Mrs. Gardiner, surprised and honoured by the invitation, did not formulate an immediate answer, as she was concerned that the master of the house might not be in complete agreement with his sister. She delayed her answer, trying to ascertain her niece's opinion, but Elizabeth's cheeks had lost their colour, and she had lowered her eyes.

"Miss Darcy, I thank you for your kind invitation, but we do not want to intrude on such short notice."

"Oh, no. It is no intrusion at all — quite the contrary. Your company would be a delightful addition."

Mr. Darcy stepped in. "Mrs. Gardiner, Miss Bennet, please forgive my sister's insistence. I dare say she surprised me as well; it is not her habit to bestow such impromptu invitations, I assure you." Darcy's voice was lightly polite, but the subtle censure of his sister did not go unnoticed by anyone, making Georgiana blush even more. Yet he continued, leaving no room for misunderstanding regarding his opinion. "Indeed it would be a pleasure to have your company longer, but we understand if you have other appointments or, perhaps, feel too tired for a visit."

Elizabeth felt Darcy's gaze and dared to lift her eyes to his. She could easily understand his intervention mostly had been meant to ease *her* discomfort. While assuring her of his approval of his sister's invitation, he also offered her the opportunity politely to refuse. What his *true* wish was she could not tell.

She was brought out of her preoccupation by Georgiana's shy voice.

"Miss Bennet, Mrs. Gardiner, please forgive me. I now realise I have been improper in my insistence." Her face displayed a deep distress that Elizabeth could not ignore or neglect.

"Miss Darcy, there is no need to apologise. As my aunt said, we are honoured by your invitation. We hesitated only because we were afraid to intrude on your or Mr. Darcy's schedule. As for us, I believe we have no fixed engagement, have we Aunt?"

"No, indeed."

"Very well, then; it is settled," Mr. Darcy hurried to conclude. "We shall tell your coachman to follow us; he will be taken care of by my servants. Please allow me to show you to my house."

He walked ahead of the group, arm-in-arm with his sister, while the colonel again offered his arms to the other two ladies.

From time to time, both Mr. and Miss Darcy turned their heads as to be certain the rest of the party were following them. Elizabeth could not hide her smile at this somewhat eager gesture, though many questions were still spinning in her head. A few hours earlier, she was certain she would never meet Mr. Darcy again and was quite content as she imagined he would not harbour kind feelings toward her should they meet. She had treated this man abominably in her refusal and misjudged him so grossly that she knew she deserved no kindness from him; yet, his opinion seemed different.

She did not even notice when they stopped in front of an impressive building, and Darcy showed them in.

"Miss Bennet, Mrs. Gardiner, welcome to our home."

Georgiana entered first, followed by the other two ladies and the gentlemen. Then, just inside the grand hall, as the colonel accompanied Miss Darcy and Mrs. Gardiner, Elizabeth suddenly froze and was unable to go any further. She had no right to be there. She could feel it with every fibre of her body. *"You are the last man..."*

What am I doing in his house? She felt as though she would not be able to gather her courage to enter. Was it too late to retract her acceptance? Perhaps there was still time to feign tiredness and leave before exposing herself to even more censure. How could she accept his hospitality after everything she had said to him?

By this time, Georgiana and her aunt had entered the salon, and she could hear their voices together with that of the colonel. She startled when she felt Darcy's presence near her. "Miss Bennet, are you unwell?"

"No sir, I am quite well."

"Miss Bennet." He lowered his head a little and unconsciously she lifted her face so their eyes met; she felt her cheeks burning as she waited for him to continue. "Thank you for being so kind to my sister. Indeed, she surprised me. She seemed so open and friendly with you, though she is usually very restrained with strangers. Apparently, it must be a family trait."

He forced a smile, adding some playfulness to his tone, but her embarrassment increased as she remembered her previous accusations. "Oh...forgive me, I did not mean to —"

Before she could answer, he took a step forward and frowned as he continued in earnest: "Miss Bennet, forgive me if I am presuming too much, but I can see you do not feel easy being here. While I can understand my sister's desire to be in your and Mrs. Gardiner's delightful company, I hope it did not create any additional distress for you. If you would rather leave, please tell me, and I will find a way to explain it to Georgiana. However, if *my presence* bothers you, I would gladly allow you to enjoy your visit and remove myself to the library as I have some business needing attention. One word from you and I will comply with your wish."

His eyes became darker as he spoke, and she felt herself trembling from his nearness. She could not find the words to answer, as she did know what she wanted. Her face and neck flushed with embarrassment as she tried to swallow the sudden lump in her throat. Someone's voice — or was it her own — whispered, "I should not be here."

His voice lowered and softened to a caress, while the expression of his eyes changed in a way she had never seen before.

"Miss Bennet, if it is your *desire* not to be here and you are only here at my sister's insistence, then allow me to remedy the situation at once."

"Sir, it is not my *desire*, but my *conviction* that I should not be here; I do not deserve your generous hospitality." She could no longer speak or bear the intensity of his gaze, and she was angry with him for forcing her to humiliate herself to such an extent.

"You do not *deserve* my hospitality? Miss Bennet, never has my hospitality been more happily or more deservedly bestowed upon a guest — of that, you may be certain."

Her brows knit as she tried to understand fully the meaning of his words; his nearness did not help her in the slightest.

"Elizabeth, is anything wrong?" Mrs. Gardiner's appearance in the doorway startled them both; she finally gathered her thoughts enough to assure her aunt that she was well and would join them in an instant. Mrs. Gardiner hesitated a moment and then returned to the salon with a last glance toward her niece. The two of them followed her, but before reaching the door, Elizabeth stopped and turned to him, finally offering her answer.

"Mr. Darcy…I thank you, sir — for your concern and for your kind invitation. I am sure we will enjoy Miss Darcy's company very much during this visit, as well as the colonel's and *yours* — that is, if you gentlemen have no other more important duties?"

Darcy's surprise was as obvious as was his delight, and his countenance lightened in an instant; even more, a smile graced the corner of his lips. "The pleasure would be mine, Miss Bennet. Please allow me to show you in."

Their late entrance drew three pairs of eyes toward them, but no comment was made. Elizabeth sat near Georgiana while Mrs. Gardiner and the colonel sat opposite; Darcy chose an armchair a little apart from the rest.

Tea and sweets were ordered, and as the time passed, Elizabeth felt her spirits rising again and her fears dissipating one by one until she could almost enjoy the visit. The room, as did the rest of the house she had seen, heightened Elizabeth's admiration for the exquisite taste of the owner. Together with her aunt, she expressed her admiration and delight to Miss Darcy, but then she remembered the master's presence and the words *beautiful* and *charming* died on her lips, fearing her praise would be misinterpreted as presumptuous.

At some point, the names of Mr. Bingley and his sister entered the conversation, and Elizabeth was told the whole family had been out of town for the last couple of months; however, they were expected to return in a fortnight. Again, she searched Miss Darcy's face as she spoke about that gentleman, and her opinion remained the same in that regard. No visible emotion affected the young lady when Mr. Bingley was discussed.

Colonel Fitzwilliam retired after less than half an hour, as he had a previous appointment, but not before asking for permission to call soon at Gracechurch Street.

After his cousin's departure, Darcy participated even less in the conversation. Despite this, it was obvious that he encouraged any attempt at conversation between Elizabeth and his sister and approved their animated talk about music and theatre. The mention of their music room at Pemberley apparently brought new recollections to Miss Darcy as she addressed Mrs. Gardiner with a new plea.

"Mrs. Gardiner, I was wondering… If I am not asking too much, could you please tell me a few more things about my mother? I used to talk to my brother and even to my father about her, but it is so wonderful to hear the opinion of someone outside the family."

"Gladly, Miss Darcy; I will tell you everything I remember." For almost half an hour, Mrs. Gardiner continued to relate her memories. Several times Elizabeth turned her eyes to Mr. Darcy, and each time the picture he presented was more of a young boy fighting to look brave and conceal his sadness than of the proud, haughty, unpleasant man she had known. Moreover, the pretty face of Miss Darcy, wearing the love and longing for her mother, made Elizabeth's heart melt with tenderness and ache in grief and remorse for her previous behaviour and complete lack of fairness in judging them.

She also remembered Mr. Wickham's words about Miss Darcy's pride and cold manners; how easily she had given him full credit in this. She never took the trouble before to consider that the young lady Wickham was speaking of was almost still a child and could not be so vicious in character at such a young age. Not once while listening to that gentleman's stories did she consider how difficult it must have been for the Darcy siblings to deal with both parents passing and how intensely that loss affected not only their private deportment but their public interactions.

"As for your father, the late Mr. Darcy," concluded Mrs. Gardiner, "I did not meet him more than three or four times, I think, but I remember him being a handsome gentleman and that he was considered by many people as the best master and the best landlord. My father used to say that he did not hear anybody ever complain about Mr. Darcy's generosity and fairness."

"And my brother is the same, Mrs. Gardiner, I assure you." Both Elizabeth and her aunt smiled at the expression of love and pride on Miss Darcy's face; it would have been difficult for anyone to doubt for a single moment the young lady's adoration of her brother.

"I am sure he is, Miss Darcy," offered Mrs. Gardiner. Then she leaned toward Miss Darcy to whisper. "I confess I have heard nothing about Mr. Darcy's abilities as a landlord, but I can heartily testify that he is one of the handsomest young men I have ever seen. Would you not agree, Elizabeth?"

Miss Darcy quickly hid a chuckle behind her hand. Elizabeth blushed and nodded in agreement, trying to conceal her laugh and her mortification as three pairs of eyes turned to the subject of their conversation. Mr. Darcy could do nothing but wonder at the reason for the ladies' sudden amusement. Yet, none of them seemed inclined to share it with him, so his only alternative was to smile sheepishly at them.

Shortly thereafter, the visitors took their leave. Miss Darcy promised to return their visit the next day or the day after as soon as her brother could find the time to accompany her. Elizabeth had to bear another surprise when she understood that Mr. Darcy intended not only to encourage the growing closeness between the ladies but also to return the call himself. New questions made her head spin as she attempted to maintain her countenance on her way out of the house. Fortunately, the warm — hot — air of the June day provided a legitimate explanation for the redness of her cheeks.

The master of the house handed both ladies into the carriage. When her hand entwined with his, Elizabeth shivered and unconsciously tightened her hold, seeking support. She could not be certain whether in the next moment his fingers gently squeezed hers or if it was only her imagination. However, there was no doubt that his hand lingered against her palm a moment longer than propriety dictated.

The carriage departed, but after a short distance, Elizabeth braved a look back and saw Mr. Darcy still in the street, his eyes following her as though trying to hold her presence in an extended farewell.

THE RIDE HOME WAS SILENT. Elizabeth could not find the strength to speak and was grateful to her aunt for not requesting details.

The interactions between Elizabeth and Mr. Darcy did not escape Mrs. Gardiner's notice. It was obvious they were not mere acquaintances, but the nature of their relationship was more difficult to gauge. Yet, she was almost certain she noticed Mr. Darcy's admiration for her niece, though about Elizabeth's feelings she could not be certain. She had learned in Hertfordshire of Elizabeth's dislike for Mr. Darcy, but the interaction she had just witnessed was by no means dislike. She reserved her assessment for the future, as it was likely they would all be in one another's company again.

Later that evening when Mr. Gardiner retired to his library, Mrs. Gardiner finally approached her niece with great gentleness and equal determination.

"My dear, you have been very quiet this evening."

"Have I? I am sorry, Aunt; I am not quite myself these days. I think I should go and rest. I am sure tomorrow I will feel much better."

"I think you should tell me what is bothering you so, for I am now preoccupied with both you and Jane."

"There is nothing, Aunt, believe me. Or actually, there is nothing that can be solved for now."

"As you wish; I will not force your confidence — for the moment."

She watched Elizabeth's sigh of relief carefully and smiled. *Not too hasty, my dear; we are not done yet.*

"We have had an eventful day, would you not agree? As the colonel said, it was very fortunate that Mr. Darcy noticed your presence."

"Yes, indeed, Aunt." Elizabeth forced a smile, but she was clearly flustered as she played with her cup of tea.

"And I have to say I very much liked Miss Darcy and the colonel — and Mr. Darcy even more. He was nothing but polite and amiable. Which makes me wonder at how you ever came to tell us he was so disagreeable. I should have known that the son of Lady Anne could not have been as bad as you proclaimed."

"I admit I was wrong in my estimation of Mr. Darcy's character. On the other hand, Aunt, his manners at the beginning of our acquaintance were utterly different. I never saw him as amiable and polite as today; he truly astonished me. I do not know how to explain it, but perhaps it was due to his sister's presence; he is obviously very fond of her."

"Yes — that must be the explanation — his sister's presence, indeed."

Elizabeth could not be certain, but she thought she detected a trace of mockery in her aunt's voice; however, she had no time to dwell on the subject overmuch as her aunt continued.

"What do you think? Will they call on us as they promised? I would not be surprised if they changed their minds about coming tomorrow. Such important people as Mr. Darcy may be a little whimsical in their civilities."

"Do you think so, Aunt? I... I would say that Mr. Darcy will not break his word. I mean, he would not promise so earnestly if he did not intend to do so. He is a man of his word."

"Yes, so he seems. Well, you must be correct; it appears you are better acquainted with Mr. Darcy than I am. We shall see."

"Aunt, I have to tell you I am so looking forward to tomorrow evening. My uncle was so good to procure tickets for my favourite play."

Mrs. Gardiner chose to indulge her niece's desire of changing the topic — at least for the moment — and for another half an hour they talked of the coming evening at the theatre. They retired rather early though neither of them fell asleep for several hours.

In the privacy of their rooms, Mrs. Gardiner shared her impressions with her husband. Surprised and intrigued by his wife's suspicions of a possible relationship between his niece and Mr. Darcy, Mr. Gardiner insisted he be informed whenever any of the gentlemen happened to call, as he wanted to meet them personally and form his own judgment.

Sleep eluded Elizabeth for a time as her mind was not ready to rest. She recollected and twisted in her head every moment of their meeting — every word, every gesture — continually wondering about the reasons for the alteration of his manners. She did not dare to admit to herself that it was for her — that her reproofs at Hunsford could have worked such a change in his character. Moreover, she dare not ask herself whether the meaning of his attentions might be that he still loved her.

Miss Darcy's friendly behaviour also must be a result of his kind words about her; she said as much. Of course, Miss Darcy clearly had been taken by Mrs. Gardiner's pleasant manners and by her connection with the late Lady Anne as well. Still, from the first moment they met, it was obvious that Georgiana already knew about Elizabeth and showed an inclination to make a friendly acquaintance; no doubt, her brother had said much in her favour.

The way he spoke to her when she entered the house — his concern for her well-being and the gentleness in his voice — were recollections that increased Elizabeth's distress. What could be the meaning of it? Why was he disposed to encourage an increasing closeness in their relationship? Was it possible he did so only to indulge his sister's wishes? Undoubtedly, a future friendship between her and Miss Darcy might generate a difficult situation for the two of them after their tumultuous history; he must be aware of that.

Finally, she decided there was no point in increasing her torment by speculating so after only one meeting with the man. It was likely they would be in each other's company again, so she would have time to discern his true motivation.

Suddenly, the idea of being in his company again consumed her mind, and for a few moments, she thought only of that. She could not deny that a friendly, polite Mr. Darcy was rather pleasant company even if he spoke little. After this first meeting, being in his company again would be neither as awkward nor as difficult, so she had reason to await the Darcys' visit eagerly.

Finally, she indulged the sleep that threatened to overwhelm her, and full of restless dreams, she greeted the dawn unsettled and still tired.

Neither the Darcys nor the colonel indicated their intention of returning the call the next day. In fact, Mr. Darcy had said he had previous engagements. Thus, her good sense told her it was unlikely they would visit her so soon, but she found herself still waiting and looking anxiously out the window at every passing carriage. She was quite amazed at her own discomposure and eagerness, yet she did not feel courageous enough to question the undoubted reason behind those feelings.

As time passed, she finally ceased her waiting: firstly, because it was not a proper hour for a call without notification and, secondly, because she needed to prepare for the theatre and found herself grateful for something to distract her from disappointment.

MR. GARDINER'S BUSINESS, THOUGH TIRESOME, demanding, and often interfering in his vacation plans, truly gave him little reason to complain — quite the contrary. It helped him make a more than comfortable living for his wife and their four children, comfortable enough to secure their future and sustain their hope of eventually purchasing a small estate.

Indeed, he considered himself a fortunate man, but he knew his greatest fortune had been in his choice of wife. He believed that a man never had been more blessed than he had in his family: his astonishing wife and their wonderful children. From the first blush of married life ten years earlier, Edward Gardiner's love, respect and admiration for Marianne Gardiner only grew stronger and deeper with each passing year. He knew he had every reason to be proud of his wife — and so he was.

Enjoying a glass of port, he was anticipating her descending the staircase

— together with Elizabeth — to attend the theatre. Truth be told, he was tired and would have preferred to stay home and enjoy the benefit of a quiet evening. However, complying with one of his wife's wishes was more important to him than his own comfort, and considering that his favourite niece was equally fond of the theatre left him little choice. So there he was, ready to accompany them.

When their carriage reached its destination, Elizabeth noticed, as did her aunt, that they had been wrong in assuming not many people would attend the Little Theatre that evening. The season was ending, and many of the fashionable families were leaving town for the comfort and gentle air of their country estates. However, to their utter surprise, a crowd was gathered in front of the theatre.

It was still early, and many people seemed inclined to linger outside the entrance. Animated conversations were carried on in low voices as propriety demanded. A parade of the latest fashions and jewels — worn with grace by young ladies attempting to draw the attention of eligible gentlemen — made Elizabeth's lips twist in a hidden smile. Her mother was not so different after all from the ladies of the *ton* — at least in this regard.

Mr. and Mrs. Gardiner exchanged greetings with acquaintances on their way inside the theatre while Elizabeth could feel a few gentlemen's eyes scrutinizing her with what her mother would call admiration; yet, she knew it was mere curiosity at an unknown face, and she smiled again.

Their party had almost reached the entrance when Elizabeth's attention was drawn by a lady's laughter — open, full of joy, and unrestricted. She could not help turning her head, and her eyes fell upon a young lady whose stunning beauty made Elizabeth stop for a moment to admire her. She was taller than the other ladies, and her hair — light brown — was masterfully arranged. Equally impressive was the evident costliness of her elegant gown; she also wore a necklace and earrings set with diamonds and emeralds, which increased the brightness of her green eyes. She looked around and then down the street, clearly waiting for someone and being inattentive to her companions. Her entire demeanour demonstrated self-confidence, and the condescension with which the others were treating her indicated to Elizabeth her noble breeding. Her companions called her "Lady Cassandra."

For a moment, the lady caught Elizabeth's eyes, and her inquiring look was not friendly. She did not seem pleased to find Elizabeth staring at her nor did she find it necessary to hide her displeasure. Yet, instead of being offended by that look, Elizabeth smiled at her with unconcealed admiration; in the next moment, the lady's eyes widened in surprise, and then she returned the smile as Elizabeth passed by her and entered the theatre.

Elizabeth and the Gardiners took their places in a small box on the second level, some distance from the stage.

In a short time, the arena grew crowded. Elizabeth noticed the lady from the entrance hall alone in a large box — the third from the stage — and it was obvious that her presence drew numerous eyes and prompted various comments. Elizabeth heard people nearby talking loudly enough about "Lady Cassandra" to be a subject of great interest; she could easily understand the lady's cold and annoyed gaze earlier. No doubt, she had been the subject of whispers and stares from the moment she arrived. Elizabeth felt suddenly inclined to sympathise with Lady Cassandra without even knowing her.

The bells rang for the last time; the play was ready to start, and the theatre patrons were taking their seats. The theatre seemed filled to capacity. While Mrs. Gardiner was relating to her what she knew of the actors, Elizabeth, with a smile, cast her eyes around the beautiful theatre once more and abruptly caught her breath in a quiet gasp.

On Lady Cassandra's left, closely engaged in a private conversation with her and oblivious to everything around him, sat Mr. Darcy. A disquieting chill travelled along her spine and down her arms to her fingers, which became as cold as ice. She struggled to turn her eyes away, but, mesmerised, they remained fixed on the couple until the performance began.

Startled by music from the orchestra pit, her head turned abruptly, and her absent gaze followed the action on stage as she was engulfed by new and disconcerting emotions she could not understand. Elizabeth struggled not to return her attention to that box, so she failed to notice the gentleman's surprised eyes staring back at her or the expression on his face the moment he recognised her.

Chapter 2

So that is why he did not call today, was the first thought that came to Elizabeth's mind. Less than a moment later, she felt her cheeks burning in mortification at such an outrageous statement. Surely, she had no right to question Mr. Darcy's reasons for doing whatever he pleased, whenever he pleased, and certainly, with whomever he pleased.

Struggling to keep her eyes focused straight ahead and to pay attention to the performance met with little success as did an attempt to regain her composure. An uncomfortable sensation of being watched made her restless, and she wondered who else might be in that box. Did someone in the party recognise her? As far as Mr. Darcy was concerned, if he noticed her presence, she fully expected he would not be pleased to socialise with her and her relatives from Cheapside in the presence of his titled friends. This, she understood, was unlike their meeting in the park — but what of the others in the party. Was Miss Darcy in the box, too — or the colonel? Had they noticed her? Would they see her during the intermission?

She startled a couple of times under the impression she heard his voice, though she knew it was not possible. Mr. Darcy, a man who was highly proper at all times, certainly never would speak to be heard from such a distance. Then again, she could be wrong. Mr. Darcy's recent behaviour seemed to be completely different from what she formerly knew of him. Based on their previous encounters, she never would have believed him capable of being as...*animated*...as he was that evening and certainly not in a crowded room under the scrutiny of countless curious eyes.

"Neither of us perform to strangers."

The recollection of his words during an evening at Rosings brought back other unpleasant and embarrassing memories. She now spent countless minutes reflecting on their past interactions; an inner smile unconsciously lifted the corner of her lips as she recalled their sparkling verbal duels. How could she have been so thoroughly blind as to misinterpret every word, stare, smile and approach — she, who prided herself on her talent for observation and discernment?

He had always been so serious, stern and haughty with others but not with her — at least not *all* the time. Mr. Darcy did smile at her — and quite often. More-over, he singled her out more than once during those weeks in Hertfordshire; he danced with her at the Netherfield Ball even though she had previously refused him in the presence of Sir William Lucas. Then, there had been all their talks at Neth-erfield about accomplished ladies and the *"improvement of one's mind by extensive reading"* while *she* was reading, about his faults and hers, his reference to his sister's height in comparison with hers, and his plea that she not *"sketch his character at this time"* after their harsh talk during the dance.

Everything seemed to her now to be cast in an utterly different light.

Of course, her friend Charlotte Lucas had been perceptive enough to notice the truth almost immediately and, most likely, so had Miss Bingley, which explained the lady's rude dismissal of her.

Why am I thinking of all this now? No good will come of these belated revelations; indeed, these thoughts are not helping me. I must be grateful for Mr. Darcy's civility, politeness, and apparent acceptance of a future acquaintance between us. Who knows? Perhaps I will have the chance to see Mr. Bingley again and he might —

An increase in the music's tempo startled Elizabeth and brought her back to the reality of her surroundings. The seeming irrationality of her speculations caused her to censure herself again instantly. She must not entertain any certain hopes of Mr. Bingley for Jane or *anything* for herself.

She steeled herself to think of nothing but the exquisite performance on the stage and her long-awaited tour of the Lake country. If only they could leave sooner... Had Mr. Gardiner not been forced to return to town, they would have been far away by this time. Then, of course, they would not have encountered Mr. and Miss Darcy at all, and she likely would have had no occasion to meet Mr. Darcy ever again.

It might have been better if we had not met again.

Only a moment later, Elizabeth again questioned herself, laughing at her own folly. *Better? Easier perhaps. Compared to what? I am so ridiculous! Truthfully, did anything of significance happen? Not by design but by simple chance did we occasion upon Mr. Darcy and Colonel Fitzwilliam, and out of courtesy, Mr. Darcy introduced us to his sister. That is all. Things are no different now than they were a week ago.*

Yet, in retrospect, things were quite different, and Elizabeth knew it. She not only had met Mr. Darcy but also had the opportunity to witness an utter change: a significant softening of his manners and a completely new aspect of his character in his affectionate care toward his sister. He had been more than just polite; he had been gracious and, indeed, friendlier —with both herself and her aunt — than she ever had witnessed before.

He had invited her to his home and declared her to be a welcome guest. In addi-tion, he offered to do whatever she required to assure her comfort and enjoyment during the visit. To her greater surprise, he had encouraged a further acquaintance between her and his sister, promising to call on her in Cheapside, an event she never would have considered possible.

Chills shivered down her spine as her mind admitted the implications of her thoughts. She could not deny the truth any longer — at least to herself: Her torment was due to the presence near him of the beautiful Lady Cassandra and his warm behaviour toward her. Obviously, they were more than mere acquaintances, and this realisation greatly affected her, throwing her into a storm of anxious speculations.

"*...the last man in the world...*"

She never had desired his good opinion nor had she welcomed his declarations. She was content to know she would never see him again after the unfortunate day at the parsonage. Then why did the mere presence of another young lady near him bother her so? She was not jealous — no, that was not possible and could not even be taken into consideration! But she admitted she was...*distressed*, a sort of distress she never before had experienced and that made her think herself a simpleton.

Furious to feel her cheeks burning, she sighed deeply, drawing Mrs. Gardiner's attention. She met her aunt's inquiring look and forced a smile to calm herself. Then, with great determination, she kept her gaze fixed upon the activities on stage for that part of the performance. However, it was fortunate that she knew the play by heart, or she never would have known what transpired during the remaining minutes.

The sudden activity of those around her took Elizabeth by surprise. She had been so caught up in her thoughts that she failed to notice the end of the first act.

Mrs. Gardiner asked her opinion about the performance, and she tried to formulate a polite, neutral answer. The voices around her — complimenting the actors' performances and the excellence of the play — helped her express a favourable opinion; however, she could not deceive her perceptive aunt who looked with doubt upon her answer. She considered herself fortunate that Mrs. Gardiner did not question her further; instead, they all rose from their seats, and a moment later, the inevitable happened.

As she was facing her aunt, Elizabeth saw the elder lady's countenance lighten as she curtseyed discreetly and addressed both her niece and her husband. "What a delightful surprise! Mr. and Miss Darcy are here too! And so is Colonel Fitzwilliam — just to your left, Lizzy!"

Elizabeth was forced to turn by her aunt's command and her own curiosity. Mrs. Gardiner would not have greeted the Darcy party had the gentlemen not acknowledged her presence first.

She hesitated a few moments, causing her aunt to raise her eyebrow in wonder. "Lizzy, what is the matter with you? Are you not turning to greet Miss Darcy? Is everything well, my dear?"

She nodded in agreement, forced a smile, and then turned to the place she had tried so hard to avoid; yet, by the time her eyes settled on the box, no gentlemen remained — only Miss Darcy and Lady Cassandra. The former smiled openly at her, the discreet move of her head accompanied by a small gesture with her hand.

Elizabeth returned her warm greeting with real pleasure and an equally warm and genuine smile.

At the same moment, she sensed Lady Cassandra's insistent, piercing gaze upon her and could do nothing but meet it. Elizabeth did not fail to comprehend that this second wordless encounter was utterly different from their earlier one when both were oblivious of the other's identity. *My identity? It must be of little interest other than one of curiosity for her ladyship,* Elizabeth thought as her smile faded and her countenance changed from one of friendly warmth to one of demure, though distracted, politeness.

"Well, my dear," said her aunt, "apparently the gentlemen have left their box. It took you an eternity to decide whether you wished to proffer them a polite look. Really, Lizzy, you are acting rather strangely, my dear. You are not quite yourself."

"If *those* gentlemen are not drawing your attention any longer, ladies, perhaps you would allow *this* gentleman to escort you to the foyer for a few moments before the second act begins," offered Mr. Gardiner, which only caused his wife to laugh affectionately, take his arm, and squeeze it tenderly.

Elizabeth delayed in following them, casting another look toward Miss Darcy; there still were no gentlemen in the box. Her glance caught Lady Cassandra's notice once more, and Elizabeth felt her face flush as though she had been caught doing something improper. She turned her head, embarrassed, and quickened her steps to catch up to her relatives.

No more than a minute passed before Elizabeth had the answer to what would happen during the first intermission. Her party had barely entered the foyer when they were abruptly stopped by the surprising appearance of Mr. Darcy and Colonel Fitzwilliam.

Elizabeth was so startled she did not have time to feel embarrassed; her unwavering gaze met Mr. Darcy's eyes for a few moments. Without a doubt, he looked pleased at their unexpected meeting though he remained a little behind the colonel and considerably more silent.

Colonel Fitzwilliam did not lose a moment in his joyful greeting of their party, and before Elizabeth could fully recover, Mr. Gardiner had already been introduced to both gentlemen.

"It is a pleasant surprise to meet all of you here this evening," declared Darcy with the same warm politeness. He then lowered his head a little as though attempting to address her directly. "I had the impression I saw Miss Bennet earlier, but given the fact that only a few moments remained before the play started, I could not be certain. I am pleased to see I was not wrong."

"Yes, we were very late," explained the colonel with an openness that greatly amused both Mr. and Mrs. Gardiner, "and I am afraid it was entirely my fault. We arrived only a few moments before the play began."

"I am sure there was a good reason for your delay, Colonel," offered Mrs. Gardiner.

"I know how easily a man's demanding business can interfere with one's fixed engagements. Certainly, Mr. Gardiner finds it so."

"I thank you madam, but unfortunately, I cannot claim such a worthy excuse. I simply forgot we were to attend the theatre this evening, but I could not refuse the invitation; Darcy would not have it, though I must admit I am wondering at the wisdom of this. Who would willingly spend an exceedingly warm evening crowded among hundreds of little-known acquaintances now that the season has ended? Must be the reason Covent Garden is closed during the summer; any reasonable man —"

He caught himself and stopped, the smile frozen on his suddenly deeply chagrined face while his eyes looked in panic from the Gardiners to Elizabeth. "Oh, please, I sincerely beg you excuse me. I truly meant no offense. Of course a good play — a good performance — is to be enjoyed anytime in any season."

Mrs. Gardiner smiled kindly. "Sir, no need to worry; we took no offense."

To the colonel's utter relief, Mr. Gardiner added, "Indeed no offense is taken, sir. I totally understand your meaning and find I share your feelings. Given the opportunity, I would gladly prefer a quiet evening at home in the cool solitude of my study; however, this is a sacrifice I gladly make for my wife and my dear niece as this play is a particular favourite of theirs."

"I easily understand your desire to gratify the ladies' wishes, sir; our own presence this evening is due to the insistence of my cousin Georgiana and Lady Cassandra. What gentleman would not sacrifice his comforts to please a beautiful lady?"

Mr. Gardiner laughed and hurried to approve the colonel while Mrs. Gardiner smiled, trying to catch her niece's eyes to share their amusement — with no success. The mere mention of her ladyship's name caused Elizabeth to startle, and instinctively, she cast a quick glance towards Darcy who returned her insistent gaze. Blushing, she quickly averted her eyes.

"Mr. Darcy, is Miss Darcy enjoying her time tonight? Has the performance been to her liking thus far?"

"Yes, Mrs. Gardiner, she likes it very much, thank you. I must say she was very happy to notice your presence and has expressed her hopes that she would be able to speak with you this evening. She did not join us presently because she finds herself uncomfortable among the crush of the crowd."

"Well," the colonel intervened, "perhaps Georgiana *could* have been persuaded to join us; however, we left the box in quite a hurry. We did not want to lose the opportunity to greet you properly."

Mrs. Gardiner smiled again and insistently looked at her niece, whose face turned crimson; neither of them failed to understand the reason for the gentlemen's *hurry* to greet them. Mrs. Gardiner could only suspect which of the two gentlemen was more eager to meet her niece. For a moment, it even crossed her mind that *both* of them shared an eager interest in that regard; however, she dismissed it instantly, hoping it were not true.

In an attempt to hide her uneasiness, Elizabeth finally gathered her wits sufficiently to speak. "I did have the pleasure of seeing Miss Darcy a few minutes ago; in fact, we greeted each other from afar."

"Is that so? I am glad to hear it. Indeed, I —" Darcy paused briefly, as he looked from Mrs. Gardiner to Elizabeth. He seemed to search for the proper words until he finally voiced an invitation that Elizabeth never would have expected to hear. "Mr. and Mrs. Gardiner, Miss Bennet, if we are not intruding on your plans, I...we would be very happy to have your company this evening. My box is quite spacious, and I would be only too happy if you would do me the honour of joining our party for the rest of the performance."

Their surprise was complete, and for a few moments, none of them knew how to answer. Mr. and Mrs. Gardiner exchanged wondering glances, trying to discern Elizabeth's opinion — as it was clear she was the main object of the invitation — but she insisted on keeping her eyes averted as she bit her lower lip in a barely perceptible gesture. She was nervous; her aunt was certain of that, but what was the cause of her unease? Mrs. Gardiner could not tell for certain, yet neither could she imagine any serious reason for Elizabeth to be displeased with it except for the modesty and shyness inherent in accepting attention from a man of Mr. Darcy's consequence.

After a moment of reflection, Mrs. Gardiner decided it was unwise to lose such an opportunity of improving their acquaintance with the Darcys.

"Mr. Darcy, we would be honoured and delighted to join you; however, we do not wish to intrude on your private family party."

"It is no intrusion at all, I assure you. My sister will be as pleased as I am to see you again, and I am certain you will find Lady Cassandra's company equally pleasing."

"Mr. Darcy, perhaps Lady Cassandra will not be pleased with unexpected additions to your group." Elizabeth did not realise she was speaking until the words were out of her mouth, at which moment she panicked, desperately attempting to discern how her words sounded and affected the others.

"You must not concern yourself, Miss Bennet," Darcy continued with warm persuasion in his voice. I am certain Lady Cassandra will be pleased to make your acquaintance and highly appreciate your company, as will we all."

The warmth of his response did little to settle her unease — in fact, quite the contrary. The compliment, as well as his insistence, again took her by surprise, but this time she dared to lift her eyes to meet his. Whatever relationship might exist between Mr. Darcy and Lady Cassandra, it could not be doubted that he wished for her company. He remained equally as attentive toward her as he was two days before — even more so. However, the motives for his attentions — so openly displayed in front of her relatives and his — she could not resolve, nor did she make the attempt; the circumstances did not allow for such reflections.

The second act of the performance was about to start, and the pressure of time forced a reply to the invitation. Mr. Gardiner accepted on behalf of himself and the ladies, a fact that drew a jovial "Excellent!" from the colonel.

Darcy chose a more restrained but no less eloquent manner of expressing his satisfaction. He offered his arm to Elizabeth — only a second earlier than the colonel did. Elizabeth accepted it with obvious restraint, barely daring to touch the sleeve of his coat with her gloved hand.

Elizabeth began to wonder and worry about Lady Cassandra's reception, not only toward herself but her relatives as well. Of course, she did not expect open rudeness — not when their presence was at the invitation of Mr. Darcy — but how would her ladyship receive her relatives from Cheapside and her appearance on Mr. Darcy's arm?

The moment they faced each other, Elizabeth's eyes were instantly drawn toward Lady Cassandra's intense, inquiring stare. She witnessed the surprise on the lady's face and the unmistakable change in her countenance when the introductions were made. Elizabeth was grateful for the advantage of having a little time to prepare for their encounter.

Miss Darcy seemed to waver between the pleasure of seeing the ladies again and shyness at her new acquaintance with Mr. Gardiner. However, the gentleman — whose manners were easy and pleasant — managed to obtain the hint of a smile, a couple of monosyllabic answers, and a deep blush from her in less than a minute.

To Elizabeth's surprise, the introduction to Lady Cassandra was not at all unpleasant. Her Ladyship's manner resembled that of the colonel or Mr. Bingley. She openly smiled at the Gardiners, declared she was informed by Miss Darcy of their previous encounter, and was indeed pleased to have at last made their acquaintance.

Finally, Lady Cassandra turned to Elizabeth — who seemed content to remain silent — and their eyes met once more.

"So, Miss Bennet, we meet again; at least this time, we have the advantage of being properly introduced."

"Indeed, your ladyship; it is a pleasure to have made your acquaintance."

Any further conversation was interrupted as they all hurried to take their places for the second part of the performance. Miss Darcy was seated on Lady Cassandra's right, and on her left was the colonel. However, he gladly offered his seat to Elizabeth, preferring to move closer to Mr. Gardiner in the hope of garnering some conversation during the rest of the evening.

This change pleased Miss Darcy exceedingly, and she expressed her joy to Elizabeth more than once in the minutes that followed. The girl's friendly manners made Elizabeth's opinion grow warmer, and she tried to answer with equal gentleness. She liked Miss Darcy more than any other young lady she had met in Town. If not for the awkward situation with her brother —

"Miss Bennet, is everything well?"

She startled and turned to her younger companion, meeting her preoccupied gaze. "Yes, thank you, Miss Darcy; everything is wonderful." She smiled, said something neutral, and then turned the topic to the play. Whispering to each other, they spoke for a few moments before the performance drew their attention to the stage.

Yet, Elizabeth's attention was *not* entirely concentrated on the stage — quite the contrary.

Mr. Darcy had politely helped Elizabeth take her place prior to making sure that the Gardiners were made comfortable; only when everything seemed to meet his approval did he finally resume his place on the left side of the box near Lady Cassandra. That was precisely the point toward which Elizabeth's furtive glances and most of her attention were drawn.

From time to time, Miss Darcy would address her with a question, and in order to answer her, Elizabeth leaned to her left. Each of these times, her gaze travelled a little further toward the end of the box. She could *sense* more than *see* the slight moves and whispered conversation on the other side of Miss Darcy; once, her eyes met Darcy's for a brief moment.

Though she promised herself to pay attention to the stage, Elizabeth could not resist the temptation to examine Lady Cassandra's reactions during their brief encounter and try to understand her relationship with the Darcys.

She had to admit the lady's manners were more pleasant than she had expected considering her ladyship's situation in life. In fact, Lady Cassandra was ten times more pleasant than Miss Bingley and Mrs. Hurst, who were undoubtedly greatly beneath her in consequence, social standing and manners. It suddenly crossed Elizabeth's mind, *I wonder if Lady Cassandra is acquainted with the Bingleys,* and a large smile spread over her face as she pictured Miss Bingley attempting to compete with the lady.

Her smile turned to a frown when she noticed Mr. Darcy leaning to his right toward her, disturbing both Lady Cassandra and Miss Darcy. "Miss Bennet, I happen to have an extra pair of opera glasses, and I thought they might be useful to you."

Elizabeth took the glasses from him. Her heart started beating regularly again only after a few moments; she felt so unsure of herself that she did not dare to turn or even attempt a gesture of thanking him, nor did she dare to actually use the opera glasses. She simply held them absentmindedly.

When she regained some composure, she became alarmed, wondering what the others — especially Lady Cassandra — would think of his gesture. Undoubtedly, Miss Darcy did not seem in the least surprised; she continued talking to Elizabeth in a low voice of how considerate her brother always was. Elizabeth could do nothing but nod in agreement, hoping she did not look as embarrassed as she felt.

Finally, after several seemingly long minutes, Elizabeth decided at least to express her thanks to Mr. Darcy by actually using the glasses while desperately trying to understand what was happening on the stage. All she could think was, *Thank heavens I know this play by heart!*

Time passed tortuously slowly for Elizabeth; yet, when the second part of the play was ended, she discovered the new intermission brought her more unease than relief.

The ladies were talking of the actors' performances and the play while Mr. Gardiner and Colonel Fitzwilliam immediately rose from their seats, declaring their intention of taking a stroll in the halls. None of the ladies accepted the invitation to join them; Mr. Darcy seemed to hesitate a moment and then exited the box with the other gentlemen.

Their departure made Miss Darcy more animated, and she daringly initiated a lively conversation with Mrs. Gardiner and Elizabeth.

"Mrs. Gardiner, I am so pleased you and Miss Bennet are here with us."

"Thank you, Miss Darcy."

Her gaze moved from the younger lady to Lady Cassandra, who answered with a smile, "We are enjoying your company very much, Mrs. Gardiner, I assure you. As for Miss Bennet, I confess I have long desired to meet her! From what I have heard of her so far, she apparently has the happy ability to charm everyone around her."

Elizabeth's cheeks coloured instantly as her eyes met Lady Cassandra's amused ones. The expression on the lady's face proved she was partially speaking in jest. Elizabeth could easily notice the hidden irony in her apparently friendly tone; she also noticed that there was no hint of malice in the lady's tone. It was more…a challenge?

Elizabeth held that green, insistent gaze for a moment and then allowed a large smile to accompany the gentle mockery in her answer. "Lady Cassandra, I cannot possibly imagine what your ladyship could have heard that brought you to such a conclusion. Unfortunately, it is further from the truth than I should like to admit."

"Ah…then perhaps I might be deceived."

"I am afraid so, your ladyship."

"But that is not very likely; my authority was too good, and I do trust *it* implicitly."

Their eyes remained locked in a challenge until Lady Cassandra spoke again, causing a new wave of redness to overspread Elizabeth's cheeks. "Or perhaps my *source* was blinded by a partiality to you, and the report has been favourably exaggerated."

Elizabeth did not have the time — or the words — to answer or understand fully the implication of the statement before Mr. Darcy unexpectedly returned, and that topic of conversation was suddenly dropped.

The gentleman was received with open and welcoming smiles by both Miss Darcy and Lady Cassandra. He seemed well humoured and, to Elizabeth's chagrin, inquired as to the subject of their conversation.

"Well, Brother, mostly Miss Bennet and Lady Cassandra talked, and we listened." Miss Darcy seemed equally as good-humoured as her brother.

"Ah…I hope I did not interrupt you." His eyes travelled from one mentioned lady to the other.

"Well, actually you did, Darcy. But I dare say the interruption was not completely unpleasant, was it, Miss Bennet?"

Elizabeth wished she possessed the ability to hide her embarrassment as she felt her cheeks flushing full red again. "No, indeed it was not. And I dare say, sir that being the owner of this box offers you the unique privilege of interrupting any conversation that might take place within it."

He laughed openly in a way Elizabeth had never heard before. "Thank you, Miss Bennet. I shall remain forever indebted to you for reminding me of this privilege."

"You know, Darcy"—Lady Cassandra spoke again with a familiarity that left no doubt regarding the intimacy of their relationship—"Miss Bennet and I had met before you introduced us."

"Really? That is truly a surprise! And may I dare ask when this happened?" His wondering gaze was upon Elizabeth again, and a sudden lump in her throat forbade her reply.

Colonel Fitzwilliam and Mr. Gardiner returned, but their presence did not stop Lady Cassandra from continuing to relate the events.

"It happened in the lobby before the three of you arrived while I was speaking with the Crawfords. Apparently something drew Miss Bennet's attention on her way inside the theatre, and I noticed her insistent stare; I confess I was intrigued and was wondering who she was. I even asked the Crawfords about her. But now that I am thinking of it, I should have *known* it was Miss Bennet."

Her tone grew more amused as her lips twisted into a large smile, mixing the jest with seriousness so Elizabeth could only hope she was not annoyed by her breech of etiquette when she had *stared* at her. She was prepared to apologise while wondering at the meaning of the statement, *"I should have known it was Miss Bennet."* Were her appearance and manner of dress viewed so poorly among the other ladies, or was her ladyship only trying to offend her as Miss Bingley used to do?

"Oh, come now, Lady Cassandra!" said the colonel. "How could you have known it was Miss Bennet? You have never met her before. I know Miss Bennet quite well, and still I did not notice her the other day in the Park until Darcy drew my attention to her."

The colonel's eyebrow rose with incredulity, and her ladyship turned to him, fixing him with her eyes for a moment. "Colonel — let us have a more private conversation about *your* attention and perceptiveness, shall we? I do not want to spoil our guests' good opinion of you."

"I am entirely at your disposal any time, milady! Still, I cannot abandon my inquiry about how *your* perceptiveness could help you identify an unknown lady in a room full of ladies."

Only one more moment did Lady Cassandra hold the colonel's gaze before turning and noticing the same curiosity in the others' faces. She smiled with confidence and addressed Elizabeth directly. "Miss Bennet, I would gladly answer if you would favour me with an answer of your own."

"I shall try, your ladyship."

"Miss Bennet, what exactly concerned you, causing you to turn your head and stare at me in the lobby?"

Georgiana gasped softly, shocked by the impropriety of such a direct question, and Mr. Darcy's brow furrowed deeply in obvious disapproval of this incivility.

Curiously, however, Elizabeth did not feel at all offended. Suddenly, daringly and well humoured, she returned her ladyship's confident smile. "Nothing gave me cause for *concern,* Lady Cassandra — quite the contrary. Your ladyship looked stunningly beautiful; I simply stopped to admire you. I apologise if I caused you any discomfort."

Her unexpectedly honest answer and her eyes sparkling with amusement clearly disconcerted Lady Cassandra, and her ladyship's expression, as well as her smile, changed and warmed in an instant. "Thank you, Miss Bennet," was her only reply.

"Now, it is your ladyship's turn to answer my question," said the colonel. "I hope you will keep your promise."

"I *always* keep my promises, Colonel! As for my answer — come now, it is very simple, and I feel really ashamed for not guessing from the beginning. Just look at Miss Bennet!"

Elizabeth's cheeks started burning in embarrassment again as she felt six pairs of eyes fixed on her, filled with curiosity.

Lady Cassandra continued, pleased with the interest she aroused in her audience. "As I am sure you are already aware, Colonel, Miss Bennet has a very specific and rare quality; she has an unpretentious elegance, a natural beauty and an intelligence that is apparent in the expression of her eyes. So being beautiful, unpretentious and intelligent — it was obvious she could not be one of the young heiresses from Town!"

None of them succeeded in holding their choking gasps and chuckles, drawing the attention of everyone in their vicinity. Darcy attempted to shake his head in censure, but the mirth he felt was clear. The corners of his mouth tightened noticeably and a smile formed upon his lips. "Lady Cassandra, though I tend to agree with your characterisation of Miss Bennet, I would suggest you postpone the rest of your *reasoning* until we are in a more private situation."

Elizabeth was too mortified to share everyone's amusement; to be complimented in such a way by Lady Cassandra and then hear Mr. Darcy loudly declaring his agreement with that flattering characterisation seemed impossible to believe and highly embarrassing.

The performance began, and Elizabeth cupped her face with her palm in an attempt to cool the heat of her cheeks.

What an evening!

THE NEXT — AND FINAL — INTERMISSION passed with considerably less excitement than did the previous two. The members of the party by now were reasonably well acquainted, and a convivial conversation developed among them.

For Elizabeth, however, the situation grew more difficult to bear as her heart became heavier with each passing moment — not because she did not enjoy being with the Darcys and their companions but because she enjoyed them more than she ever thought possible.

Mr. Darcy continued to be attentive to her, and Miss Darcy was nothing but warm and friendly. As for Lady Cassandra — Elizabeth could not assess with certainty the lady's opinion of her, nor did she have reason to complain. The lady was gracious to the Gardiners and seemed to have an amazing influence over Mr. and Miss Darcy as well as the colonel. *She* was the one who seemed to charm the people around her.

While observing her in silent contemplation, Elizabeth noticed Lady Cassandra was not as young as she had initially presumed; her age was likely only a year or two younger than was Mr. Darcy's. She addressed both siblings in the same manner as the colonel: as someone from within the family. It was true Mr. Darcy was constantly using the polite "Lady Cassandra" when addressing her; however, their exchanges proved clearly that they were closely acquainted with each other.

Absorbed in her thoughts, Elizabeth interjected little into the conversation. She welcomed the beginning of the last act of the play, and while pretending she was fully concentrating on the performance on stage, she heartily wished the eventful evening would finally end.

THEY REMAINED AMONG THE LAST to leave as their conversations continued almost a quarter of an hour past the end of the performance. The farewells took place in the front of the theatre while waiting for their carriages, and Mr. Darcy brought up another topic just before they were to depart.

"Mrs. Gardiner, Mr. Gardiner, I was wondering… Have you — or Miss Bennet — any fixed engagements for tomorrow?"

"I will be out for business, Mr. Darcy, but as far as I know, my wife and niece will be at home."

"My sister and I were considering calling on you tomorrow afternoon if that is convenient." His eyes were fixed on Elizabeth as though awaiting some response from her, but the acceptance came from Mrs. Gardiner, who expressed her delight in having them as guests the following day.

As if awakened from a deep sleep, Elizabeth gathered herself and remembered the basic rules of polite behaviour. "It would be a pleasure to see you again tomorrow, Miss Darcy, Mr. Darcy. I look forward to it."

As the carriage departed, Elizabeth blamed her lack of courage for not looking at Lady Cassandra during the last exchange. She now dreaded knowing how much the lady approved or disapproved of the impending visit.

Supper at Gracechurch Street was an animated affair that evening. Mr. and Mrs. Gardiner seemed to have interest in nothing more than sharing impressions about the unexpected party that they had the good fortune to join.

The colonel's manners were much appreciated, and Miss Darcy was declared a beautiful and graceful young lady. As for her brother, he was deemed "perfectly well-behaved, polite, and unassuming," by Mr. Gardiner. Privately, he wondered about Elizabeth's previous and decidedly unfavourable opinion of him.

"There *is* something a little stately in Mr. Darcy, to be sure," replied her aunt, "but it is confined to his air, and is not unbecoming. He is not as voluble as the colonel, but he is very pleasant nevertheless."

Mr. Gardiner nodded. "I could not have been more surprised by his behaviour to us. It was more than civil; he was very attentive. To invite us into his box and be so amiable on such a trifling acquaintance was amazing and very gracious. There was no necessity for such attention, to be sure; in fact, I would fully comprehend if he did not seek our company at all the entire evening. We are not closely acquainted with him or his social circle, and neither is Elizabeth."

"But my dear — what do you think of Lady Cassandra?" asked Mrs. Gardiner; and for the rest of the evening, she was the main subject of conversation between her uncle and aunt. It was also a major interest for Elizabeth, but she preferred to analyze it in the seclusion of her bedchamber.

Alone, Elizabeth spent the next hours listening to the sounds of a warm summer night through her open window. Her thoughts were divided between the day that had just passed and the one that was about to start.

It was almost dawn when Elizabeth finally fell asleep. Countless recollections of the evening were still spinning in her head. Meanwhile, the icy hole in the pit of her stomach grew deeper; its coldness had her shivering.

Before sleep finally took her, Elizabeth became certain of two things: first, she liked Lady Cassandra very much, and second, the lady was a perfect match for Mr. Darcy.

"Darcy, I have to say that Miss Bennet was not exactly what I expected," said Lady Cassandra as soon as their carriage began to move.

"Oh, I think Miss Bennet looked lovely tonight." Miss Darcy avidly entered into the conversation. "I truly like her."

Darcy chose to remain silent for the moment, only staring inquiringly at Lady Cassandra who was sitting opposite.

"I do not disagree, my dear Georgie. In fact, I found her quite beautiful, though perhaps not a classic beauty. I noticed something very open and natural in her appearance that I truly liked. Even the first time I noticed her in the hall before knowing she was *your* Miss Bennet" —she nodded toward Darcy — "I was quite impressed by the lively expression in her eyes. And yes, you were right in that respect — beautiful eyes, I will grant her that."

"Cassandra, Miss Bennet is not *our* or anybody's property, so please refrain from speaking in jest about her. And secondly, I am only curious…if you so approve of her, why did you say she was not what you expected?"

"Oh, come now, Darcy. You are so sensitive! I meant no offense. As for what I did *not* like…well…I barely saw anything of the wit and cleverness of which you spoke so highly. I can hardly believe she was the one expressing such decided opinions in front of Lady Catherine. I would rather believe she needed protection, or your frightening aunt would have devoured her completely!"

"Cassandra!" Darcy's tone expressed the deepest disapproval, while Georgiana laughed openly. "Could you humour me just once by speaking without offending anybody?"

"I shall try — but only to humour you, especially when the subject is Lady Catherine. Now, to resume: Miss Bennet's behaviour was everything proper, but in truth, I barely heard her speak at all. She seemed a little more animated only when she talked to Georgiana and the colonel. And I have to say, Georgie, that both you and your cousin seem quite taken with her."

"I confess I do like Miss Bennet very much, Cassandra. And I am sorry you did not completely approve of her."

"Oh, but I do, dearest, believe me, and I am certain that my opinion of her will improve upon closer acquaintance. It is just that —" She paused and stared intensely at Darcy, holding his gaze. "I never would have guessed that *she* was the lady you told me about, Darcy — that is all."

He sustained her stare a bit longer. "Miss Bennet always got along quite well with my cousin's easy manner from the first moment they met, but that is hardly surprising. David excels at everything I lack to be at ease in pleasant company. As for Georgiana…"

He stretched to catch his sister's gloved hand gently. "My dear, I have to say I am quite pleased to see how friendly you have become in such a short time with both Mrs. Gardiner and Miss Bennet. As for your comment"—he turned to Cassandra—"I have to admit that you are right. Miss Bennet's manners were more restrained than usual, and considering that she seemed comfortable with Georgiana and the colonel and even with you, I have to draw the conclusion that it was *my* presence that made her uneasy. It seems I have a habit of making people around me uncomfortable."

"Oh, that is not true, Brother." Miss Darcy seemed appalled that he would say such a thing about himself. "I saw nothing strange in Miss Bennet's behaviour toward you. She seemed to enjoy your company as much as did Mr. and Mrs. Gardiner."

"I truly enjoyed the Gardiners' company," admitted Lady Cassandra.

However, Mr. Darcy seemed to lose interest in any subject and preferred to admire the view through the carriage window until the they reached Lady Cassandra's house. Only then, did he move to help her exit the carriage and then accompany her to the front door.

They made their goodbyes, and as he hurried to return to the carriage where his sister was waiting, Lady Cassandra's voice delayed him and made him return.

"Darcy...about Miss Bennet's being uncomfortable in your company —"

"Yes?"

"You might be right about her reasons, but then again — you might be completely wrong *once more.*"

Before he had time to comprehend her words, she smiled mischievously and entered the house, leaving him to stare at the closed door.

Chapter 3

"Well, my dear, apparently it was *not* Lady Cassandra whom we met last night," said Mr. Gardiner good-humouredly after entering the salon to greet his wife and niece.

Mr. Gardiner had spent the morning settling business and then visiting his club. He had agreed to be home sometime after noon, prior to the time Mr. and Miss Darcy were to call. Eager to share his news and latest source of amusement with the ladies, he arrived well before he was due.

"What do you mean, husband? Not Lady Cassandra? Then who was she?"

"Well, apparently a kinder, friendlier copy of her." He sat upon his favourite chair after he poured himself a glass of his best brandy, carefully watching the effect his words had upon both ladies.

Elizabeth scrutinised her uncle closely while Mrs. Gardiner's eyes narrowed. "Mr. Gardiner, are you trying to vex us with your secretive attitude? It is far too early for games of this kind."

"Well, Mrs. Gardiner, I suggest you use a more persuasive tone, or I shall not reveal what I discovered this very morning, both at my office and the club. On second thought, perhaps it would be better to keep it secret; I am ashamed to admit how much gossip has reached my ears in such a short time. Most of it came from a group of the most honourable gentlemen in Town. In fact, I almost felt as if I had been listening to Mrs. Long." He hid a satisfied smile behind his glass while his wife sighed in exasperation. He was in high spirits, induced largely because the business that had kept him in Town seemed to be coming to a favourable conclusion. There was other news to be shared with his impatient companions, and he enjoyed himself, toying with their curiosity a bit longer.

"Uncle, do not try our patience too long! That is cruel, you know."

Elizabeth had rested very little the previous night. She awoke in the morning with her eyes red and slightly swollen, and she had spent the next hours preparing both her appearance and her composure for the Darcys' call. She found herself walking by the window and casting stolen glances outside. When a carriage stopped in front of the house and she heard the main door opening, she instantly rose from her seat, putting her needlework aside. Yet, her anxiety was hardly gratified when she discovered that it was only her uncle arriving. Then he seemed determined to test her patience and curiosity with a series of strange statements.

"Very well, ladies! You need not be so harsh with me. It seems that the honour of spending the evening in Mr. Darcy's box did not go unnoticed. At least five persons — either clients or partners — mentioned it to me and asked me about it. Mr. Thornewill, a client of ten years, visited me today accompanied by his wife! That has never happened before, and I was quite shocked. Yet, I soon discovered that the reason for this astonishing visit was their curiosity for more details about our night at the theatre and our illustrious company."

"Indeed? How strange... I realise the Darcys are well known in Town, but I never thought they could provoke such interest. They are not royalty, after all." Mrs. Gardiner could not hide her displeasure at the idea of gossips having their way with the son and daughter of Lady Anne Darcy.

"No, they are not royalty. It may interest you to know it was not the Darcys who were the centre of everyone's interest, but Lady Cassandra. It appears that Mrs. Thornewill's brother, Lord Gordon, is the closest relative of Lady Cassandra. Better said, his wife is a cousin of Lady Cassandra's late mother. Mrs. Thornewill did not waste any time relating to me that Lady Cassandra completely disobeyed Lord Gordon's advice and left England four years ago precisely because of an enormous scandal relating to him. According to Mrs. Thornewill, Lady Cassandra's behaviour kept London society entertained for many seasons as she publicly refused to accept the hand of the most eligible bachelor of the season."

"Oh, come now, Mr. Gardiner! I have been married to you for thirteen years and have never known you to be such a gossip." Mrs. Gardiner shook her head in displeasure and cast an exasperated glance at Elizabeth. However, Elizabeth's curiosity defeated her propriety and common sense.

"*I* am not a gossip, my dear. Well... yes I am, but only with you. I scarcely spoke more than a word to Mrs. Thornewill. I only tried to disagree when she harshly criticised Lady Cassandra's manners and character, but I had not the slightest chance to finish even a sentence. When I finally managed to say how delighted we had been with her ladyship's kind politeness, she told me I had most likely not met the *real* Lady Cassandra who was presumably the worst type of shrew.

"Oh please... This is entirely unacceptable! No matter how many earls Mrs. Thornewill might have as brothers, she has no right to talk in that fashion to you, a complete stranger. I hope there is nothing more you want to tell us about the subject."

"Well, actually there is — as I received the whole of Lady Cassandra's biography in less than ten minutes. But I do not want to upset you, my dear, so I shall stop here."

"Oh please, Uncle, do not stop!" Elizabeth's voice sounded pleading and oddly serious in a conversation that should have been interpreted as humorous. Mr. Gardiner decided to indulge her inquiry but not before some gentle teasing about her newly discovered tendency to gossip. He even went so far as to remark upon her resemblance to Mrs. Bennet and Mrs. Long.

"Very well then, let me tell you what I have found out. Both of Lady Cassandra's parents belonged to well-known, titled families. Her mother, Lady Lavinia Russell, passed away ten years ago and her father, Lord George John Russell, three years later. She was left with a splendid inheritance, including a large estate in the North which, Mrs. Thornewill assured me, had been terribly neglected." At this, Mr. Gardiner smiled ironically, and his wife only rolled her eyes and sighed in exasperation.

"She has no other close relatives except those of Lord Gordon's wife with whom she was not on friendly terms," continued Mr. Gardiner. "Apparently, Lady Cassandra's parents had been old and very close friends with Lady Anne and the late Mr. Darcy; after her father's death, she spent much of her time at Pemberley rather than relying upon the protection of her own relatives. Mrs. Thornewill seemed quite put out by this situation, which she believes was highly improper."

"So, is there more? You have told me enough to fill an entire novel already. I imagine Mrs. Thornewill spent all her morning in your company."

"Yes, there is more! And you will be surprised to find that Mrs. Thornewill told me the entire story in less than an hour."

"Please continue, Uncle, if there is more for us to hear."

"Well, it was precisely after the late Mr. Darcy's death that Lord Gordon decided it was time for the family to intervene — on Lady Cassandra's behalf, of course — and to convince her to settle down and have her own family. According to Mrs. Thornewill, she was already in great danger of remaining a spinster as she was already two and twenty."

Both Elizabeth and Mrs. Gardiner gasped at that statement, much to Mr. Gardiner's amusement. He continued, pleased to see how intrigued his wife and niece were; at least all that wasted time — as Mrs. Thornewill toyed with his nerves and patience for an hour — ultimately had been worthwhile.

"However, Lady Cassandra would have none of their interference. She had refused the most advantageous marriage arrangement, and she refused it publicly at a ball after having a very noticeable fight with Lord Gordon. Everyone in Town was appalled by her outrageous behaviour; Mrs. Thornewill was certain of that. A couple of days later, she left Town and then the country without a word to anyone. It appears that her return now is as much a shock as was her leaving four years ago. Again, she informed no one of her plans, nor did she meet with her relatives though they learned she has been in Town for nearly a month."

"I am sure she informed Mr. and Miss Darcy of her plans to return," said Elizabeth, trying to understand what she had been told.

Mrs. Gardiner attempted to deflect the topic of conversation. "Yes, she most surely did. As for Mrs. Thornewill and Lord Gordon, I think I have heard enough about them. Would you not agree?"

"Did she tell you the identity of the *most eligible* gentleman?"

"No she did not, Lizzy, and I surely did not consider asking. I was afraid she would not end her story before noon, so I did everything I could not to engage her further. However, if you are still curious, I believe I can arrange a private meeting for you with the lady."

Mr. Gardiner's amusement grew, but Elizabeth remained lost in her thoughts. It was clear to her that the gentleman who was meant to marry Lady Cassandra could *not* have been Mr. Darcy. The first question that bothered her was why Lady Cassandra, if they were on such familiar terms, did not marry Mr. Darcy? Could he have been the reason for her refusal to marry the other gentleman and for leaving the country? But why would she go so far away? Even if her relatives were somehow opposed to a marriage with Darcy, she was of age and did not need their approval. And what was the reason behind her sudden return? She and Mr. Darcy seemed quite intimate, but he had made *her,* Elizabeth, an offer of marriage only two months earlier — so there could be no understanding between them. Yet, Lady Cassandra had returned a month after Hunsford, and somehow, Elizabeth was certain she was not unaware of Mr. Darcy's proposal. Was *this* the precise reason for her return? Did the notion that he could marry *another* woman compel her back to London?

Her head was spinning, and she was unconsciously playing with her needlework as she struggled to understand this latest quandary. When the servant announced Mr. and Miss Darcy, she startled so violently that she dropped her needle and sampler on the floor.

Mr. and Mrs. Gardiner hurried to greet their guests, and a few moments later, Elizabeth found herself curtsying to the Darcys.

Miss Darcy took a place on the settee near Elizabeth while Mr. Darcy chose to sit across the room, close to Mr. Gardiner. His gaze rested upon Elizabeth, and she turned her eyes to meet his for only a moment. Nevertheless, she continued to feel his eyes upon her as she spoke with Miss Darcy and expressed delight in seeing her again.

Tea and refreshments were ordered, and a few moments passed in relative silence with only polite exchanges and smiles as each of them tried to become accustomed to one another's company. Even Mr. and Mrs. Gardiner, usually easy in any group and exceedingly pleased with the Darcys' visit, seemed at a loss for the proper words to begin an easy conversation.

"Mrs. Gardiner, Mr. Gardiner, you have a very comfortable home." Mr. Darcy was the first to speak, his warm and friendly voice drawing Elizabeth's eyes toward him again.

Certainly, the Gardiner's house could not be compared to Mr. Darcy's, yet Mrs.

Gardiner took tremendous pride in her home, and Mr. Darcy's compliment gave her great pleasure.

Elizabeth was grateful to him once again for his attentiveness toward her relatives, and she allowed her gratitude to shine in the smile that brightened her face. When their eyes met again, he seemed surprised at first, but then his face instantly lightened and he returned her smile.

Mrs. Gardiner thanked both Mr. and Miss Darcy — who had joined her brother in expressing her delight with the house — and thus the conversation began tentatively but soon grew more animated.

Elizabeth struggled not to look at Mr. Darcy too often but with little success.

Miss Darcy's shyness and Mr. Darcy's reticence soon vanished. Mr. Darcy was not as jovial as the colonel was and likely never would be, but he was polite, even friendly, or at least he was trying to be. He obviously was taking the *trouble of practicing* more, as she had advised him earlier at Rosings. A smile twisted her lips while their conversation came to her mind again. *"I certainly have not the talent which some people possess of conversing easily with those I have never seen before..."*

Deeply immersed in her memories, Elizabeth attempted to recompose herself when the servants entered with refreshments. Only then did she notice that her eyes had unconsciously been fixed again in Mr. Darcy's direction and that he was staring back at her with a puzzled expression on his face. *I have made such a fool of myself,* was the only thing she could think of before taking the cup of tea with trembling hands.

"Miss Darcy, would you like some more tea?" Still not completely restored, Elizabeth realised that Miss Darcy was holding an empty cup in her hand and looking between them without daring to join the conversation.

"Yes please, thank you," answered the young lady with a tentative smile. Elizabeth rose from her seat and then turned to her brother. "Mr. Darcy, may I offer you some tea, as well, or some coffee?"

"Or perhaps you could join me in the library for a glass of wine, sir?" offered Mr. Gardiner. "That is... if you are not in a hurry. I would not want to detain you from other appointments."

"Not at all, sir. Fortunately, we have nothing scheduled until later this evening. I would be delighted to see your library, and yes, a glass of wine would be splendid."

"Excellent!"

Once the door closed behind the gentlemen, the conversation among the ladies continued in a more animated manner.

"Miss Darcy, your visit is a pleasure as well as an honour for us. I imagine how busy you must be and how many engagements you must have."

"Oh... not so many engagements. We wanted to come yesterday, but we had prior plans with Cassandra that occupied us the entire morning. My brother said we would not have time to visit you for more than half an hour; we did not want to call in haste, so we preferred to wait another day."

"Is Lady Cassandra a relative of yours?" Elizabeth knew she had no right to question her guest, but she could not restrain her curiosity, especially when Miss Darcy seemed inclined to pursue that particular topic.

"No, she is not a relative, but she has been a friend of ours for many years. For as long as I can remember, Cassandra has been a part of our lives. I love her as dearly as I would a sister, and I hope she will never leave again."

"Lady Cassandra seems to be a wonderful person," offered Mrs. Gardiner. "It was a pleasure for us to have made her acquaintance last evening."

"Yes, she is wonderful; both William and I are very happy to have her here, and I can assure you that she was very pleased to meet you, too. She confessed that she enjoyed your company very much."

"I am happy to hear that. Are you planning to remain in town long?"

"No, Mrs. Gardiner. We plan to leave town for Pemberley in a fortnight. My brother has invited Lady Cassandra as well as Mr. Bingley and his family to join us. You are familiar with the Bingleys?"

"No, we are not," answered Mrs. Gardiner. "By the time we arrived in Hertfordshire, Mr. Bingley and his family had left Netherfield."

"Mr. Bingley is a friend of my brother. He is very amiable and kind."

"Yes, he is," agreed Elizabeth, though her thoughts about the "amiable and kind" gentleman who so hurriedly abandoned his happiness and Jane's were not entirely cordial.

The gentlemen's entrance and their animated voices interrupted their conversation. Elizabeth's eyes were instantly drawn toward Mr. Darcy, and she saw him looking as good humoured as was Mr. Gardiner, that small smile never leaving his face.

"We decided not to be separated from your charming company for too long, ladies. I hope we are not intruding," said Mr. Gardiner.

"No, not at all. We were talking about leaving London in the near future, and Miss Darcy was just telling us that your family planned to depart for Pemberley very soon."

"Indeed we are, Mrs. Gardiner, and it is quite a coincidence that Mr. Gardiner and I were discussing the same subject. In fact, I asked him if you intended to visit Lambton during your tour."

"We have not planned our travelling agenda in detail as it largely depends on my husband's business. But I would like to see Lambton again as I have not been in the area for quite some time," answered Mrs. Gardiner.

"As I mentioned to Mr. Gardiner, if you will be in the area, I hope you will inform us of your presence. It would be a pleasure to have you all as our guests at Pemberley. Mr. Gardiner and I just discovered that we share a passion for fishing."

Elizabeth's astonishment was great, and she looked at Darcy in disbelief. Had he just invited the Gardiners to Pemberley? This could not be; she must have misunderstood him. His words *"…relations, whose condition in life is so decidedly beneath my own…"* instantly resounded in her memory.

Yet, his invitation was clear, and no misunderstanding could be applied to it. But what could be the reason for such extraordinary civility? This time it was not Miss Darcy who initiated the overture; rather, his will and desire prompted an insistent request for their presence at Pemberley and for Mr. Gardiner's company while fishing.

"Well, sir, if we are in the area and will not be intruding upon your privacy, of course, it would be an honour for us to visit you at Pemberley," answered Mrs. Gardiner with no little emotion.

"Excellent! Then it is settled — if you happen to be in the area, I mean."

Elizabeth dared a quick glance at Mr. Darcy and once more was surprised to see the expression of delight upon his face as he smiled at her. She was too overwhelmed by emotion to say more than a few polite words, consumed by both the excitement and the dread of actually being invited to Pemberley and shocked to see Mr. and Miss Darcy excited at the prospect.

The conversation continued for another quarter hour until the guests prepared to leave. As they made their goodbyes, Miss Darcy invited both Elizabeth and Mrs. Gardiner to join her for tea on one of the following days, and her invitation was accepted without hesitation. Throughout their visit that afternoon, Elizabeth was able to ascertain that both Darcys seemed to be taking an interest in her. While she dared not admit the reason for their kindness, she was pleased to notice it. Gone was most of the awkwardness that had gripped her whenever she was in their company.

Her aunt and uncle showed the guests out. Before they reached their carriage, Mr. Darcy bowed to the ladies with perfect politeness, his eyes never leaving Elizabeth's, and then joined his sister in the carriage. Miss Darcy waved her delicate hand at Elizabeth as the horses moved off, and she responded with a wave of her own — but her gesture was meant for *both* Miss Darcy and her brother.

ELIZABETH SPENT THE REST OF the time before dinner in her room, lost in contemplation of everything that had occurred.

The nature of Lady Cassandra's connections to the Darcys was clearer, yet this did not put her mind completely at ease. At first, when remembering Miss Darcy's words, she impetuously assumed that Lady Cassandra had returned to ensure she became Georgiana's *true sister*. This seemed to be the most logical conclusion, moreover, as the attachment between the Darcy siblings and the Lady was obvious and openly declared. With their considerable fortunes and their situations in life, theirs would have been one of the most advantageous matches of the year.

Although her mind searched for the logic, her intuition — nay, her heart — knew this could not be the case. No matter how she had tried to convince herself that Mr. Darcy's attentions meant nothing but politeness, after this last call, she was forced to reconsider her judgment. He was polite, to be sure; he was also kind, friendly and considerate. Everything she had reproached him about that day in Kent was no longer visible in his manner. However, there was something more. His eyes, his small gestures, and his smiles were more eloquent than any words he might have uttered. Nevertheless, could she really trust her intuition in reading his eyes and his smiles? She had grossly misjudged him before when she was certain he had looked at her only to find fault and wrongly assumed the slight smiles meant nothing but disdain. How could she be certain she was correct now? How could she allow herself to be deceived by vain hopes? *Hopes? Hopes of what? Surely, I cannot expect him to renew his addresses, can I? Oh, but do I wish he would?*

Then Lady Cassandra appeared in her thoughts again. Yes, she would have certainly been the perfect match for Mr. Darcy. However, her closeness to him seemed…different than Elizabeth would have expected. She could not say in what way it was different; she just felt it was. On the other hand, her ladyship's attitude toward her was not in the slightest bit offensive, not even when she appeared in the box upon Mr. Darcy's arm; quite the contrary — she had declared Elizabeth to be beautiful and smart. That could mean either that Lady Cassandra was not affected by Mr. Darcy's attentions toward Elizabeth or that Lady Cassandra was so certain of Mr. Darcy's affection and devotion that nothing could shake her faith in their relationship.

Closing her eyes, Elizabeth leaned on the bedpost as her head spun and her temples ached with sharp pain. When she managed to calm herself a little, the recollection of everything that transpired between them in the last few days offered her a measure of relief. Since meeting in the park, Mr. Darcy surely did not behave in her eyes as a man attached — or who was soon to be attached — to another woman. It was clear in the way he talked to her in his home, the way he touched her fingers when he handed her into the carriage, the way he looked at her, his attentions toward her relatives, and the invitation to Pemberley. Her presence could not be easy and pleasing for him unless he —

Unless he is still fond of me.

The mere thought made her shiver, and she wrapped her arms around herself. More than an hour passed wherein she questioned her own feelings and wondered whether she would really wish for him ever to renew his proposals — presuming, of course, that it were possible.

The next morning another surprise interrupted Elizabeth's newfound tranquillity. Mrs. Gardiner received a note from Lady Cassandra with the most astonishing content. Her ladyship personally invited the Gardiners along with their niece to a private ball she was hosting in a week's time.

A heated and prolonged debate followed the receipt of the invitation, Mrs. Gardiner and Elizabeth both wondering about the lady's reason for wishing to introduce them — new acquaintances for her — into the intimate circle of her friends at such a private event.

In such refined company, their modest presence would surely look strange. However, the tone of the note that accompanied the formal invitation was warm, even friendly, in Mrs. Gardiner's estimation. It read, *"It will be only a private ball with no more than 40 guests, and a few of them are close friends of mine and old acquaintances of yours."* It was a clear indication that the Darcys and the colonel would be present, too.

Laughing, Mr. Gardiner remembered Lady Cassandra's remark about the "young heiresses of the *ton*." Ultimately, a note of acceptance and gratitude was sent back to Lady Cassandra. Half an hour later, Mrs. Gardiner — together with her niece — toured all the shops she knew in search of the perfect gowns for them to wear to this special event.

"CHARLES! CHARLES!! CHARLES!!!" THE EXCITED voice of his sister grew more strident, and he perceived it as sharply as a knife slicing into his head.

Charles Bingley was not feeling well at all. In fact, he had not felt himself since the previous November when he left Netherfield Hall. He had spent the entire Season in town, and his sisters had dragged him to every event to which they could secure an invitation, but nothing managed to draw his attention; nothing could distract him from the remembrance of Jane Bennet. He spent nights and days thinking of her, and though his suffering diminished not a whit, he came to the conclusion that she had every reason not to return his affection. After all, she was the most wonderful woman he had ever known, and he, Charles Bingley, was only a man like so many bachelors of his age. Truly, he had nothing to recommend him except his five thousand a year, and even in this regard, there were others in far better circumstances and more worthy of the affections of the angelic Miss Bennet. He had resigned himself to the loss of her and pledged to continue loving her forever even if he did one day become the husband of another. Never did he believe he would be able to find her equal.

Suddenly, there was silence again, and he hoped his sister had ceased searching for him. However, when the door to his study opened abruptly, causing him nearly to topple off his chair, he realised his wishes for peace were in vain.

"Charles, look what I just received!" cried Caroline as Bingley struggled to resume his place in the chair.

"Caroline, for heaven's sake! What happened? It looks like nothing more than an ordinary letter to me —"

"No, Charles, this is not a mere letter! It is a letter from my friend Annabella, who has informed me that Mr. Darcy has been spotted about Town in the company of Lady Cassandra, who has just returned after being abroad. And now Lady Cassandra is hosting a private ball, and we are *not* invited! Who is Lady Cassandra, and what, pray, is she doing with Mr. Darcy?"

To Bingley, Caroline's pique sounded like bells clashing inharmoniously. Desiring nothing so much as to be rid of her, he rose and walked to the door.

"Caroline, I cannot follow you and have no desire to try. I will only tell you this: I do not know who Lady Cassandra is. I have never met her and only heard the Darcys speak of her a few times."

"You heard them speak of her? And why did you not inform me? We should have returned sooner. I think we should return to Town in a couple of days to prepare for our departure to Pemberley."

Before exiting, Charles looked at his sister as though she spoke a foreign language. He shook his head in misapprehension. "Caroline, as I said, you have lost me. Why should I have told you about Lady Cassandra? And why should we return so soon? You may do as you please, but I surely do not intend to chase Darcy and this lady about London. Be pleased that Darcy invited us to Pemberley at all, or we would have remained in Town for the summer after you insisted that I give up Netherfield. As for Lady Cassandra, I failed to mention that she will be at Pemberley as well, so let us hope we will have the opportunity of seeing much of her there."

"You failed to mention? Hope? I do not hope for that at all, Charles. The only hope I entertain is to see dear Georgiana and of course Mr. Darcy! As for this lady — Charles! Charles! Where are you going?"

Charles Bingley was already outside, asking for his horse to be saddled. He wanted desperately to be alone with his thoughts once more.

THREE DAYS AFTER THE DARCYS' visit, Elizabeth and her aunt received an invitation to tea from Miss Darcy for that afternoon or, if they were already engaged, any other day they might find convenient.

Mrs. Gardiner had a few fixed engagements. Moreover, as Mr. Gardiner's business had finally been concluded, they were busy making plans for their tour a few days after the ball. However, she advised her niece to accept the invitation for herself if she wished, so a couple of hours later, Mrs. Gardiner escorted her niece to the Darcys' townhouse before continuing on her way.

Various feelings arose in Elizabeth as she stood before the main door. Miss Darcy had not mentioned her brother, so Elizabeth could not presume he would be present. She did not know whether she desired or dreaded seeing him again, but she had decided to enjoy the company of Miss Darcy without allowing any dark thoughts to mar her time there.

As soon as she entered the house, a servant showed her to the music room, where she was told Miss Darcy was awaiting her. As she approached the room, she heard music; reports of Miss Darcy's expertise on the pianoforte were not exaggerated.

The moment Elizabeth appeared in the doorway, Miss Darcy hurried from her place at the instrument, an open smile brightening her face. "I am so happy to see you again, Elizabeth!"

The couple of hours Elizabeth spent with Georgiana were a continuous source of enjoyment and revelation. First, she discovered that, like her brother, Miss Darcy improved on closer acquaintance. Once she was able to put her shyness aside, she proved to be a lively companion with a sweet disposition who was inclined to find amusement in many things. Her talent at the pianoforte amazed Elizabeth because it was more than a simple consequence of practicing diligently. Both Miss Bingley and Mrs. Hurst were proficient at the piano, but they could not compare to Georgiana.

Secondly, Elizabeth was surprised to find that Miss Darcy knew many of the details surrounding her brother's stays in Hertfordshire and Kent. While she evidenced no awareness of Mr. Darcy's proposal, she appeared to know about Mr. Collins, her *confrontations* with Lady Catherine and even her discussions with Miss Bingley and Mrs. Hurst. Mr. Darcy obviously had talked *a great deal* about her — and Elizabeth's heart seemed to beat irregularly at this new proof of his interest in her.

In time, she grew more at ease in Georgiana's company and was beginning to feel as if she had known her all her life; even the prospect of seeing Mr. Darcy again caused her no more distress.

They were playing and singing together at the pianoforte and did not notice the door open, revealing Mr. Darcy and Lady Cassandra.

Darcy had been out the entire morning and had tried to finish his business as quickly as he could; Georgiana had told him of Elizabeth's visit, and he hurried home, forgetting a previous engagement with Lady Cassandra. When he arrived to discover her waiting for him in front of his house, he was subjected to a round of merciless teasing before he was able to enter. He was indeed desirous of seeing Elizabeth again and did nothing to conceal it.

The call at Gracechurch Street had given his spirit a boost. He could not deny the obvious: Miss Bennet was not as opposed to him as he previously imagined. She seemed uncomfortable in his presence, and her manners were more restrained than before, but that was understandable considering their history.

He still could not credit his good fortune in meeting Elizabeth again; he was given a chance to show her he was not mean-spirited or resentful about the past. With the small signs he perceived during his call, he was determined to do all in his power to obtain her forgiveness and lessen her ill opinion of him; she must see that he was attending to her reproofs.

Of course, he could not be certain of the accuracy of his judgment. After all, he had failed miserably before to recognise her feelings, as well as those of Jane Bennet and Bingley. His presumptions had caused nothing but suffering to those around him; this time, he promised himself not to act in haste. He would show her he had taken her words to heart and changed because of her and for her. He would not conceal his feelings behind challenging talks and silent stares across the room. He would show her — and everyone else — his preference for her, but he would do it with as much decorum as possible, careful not to embarrass her or place her in an indelicate situation.

He heard the sound of music and followed it, stopping in the doorway. Darcy watched as Elizabeth played a duet with his sister, laughing and at perfect ease — so beautiful and natural in her enjoyment. He wished nothing more than for her to appear as contented in his presence.

However, just as he feared, the moment she noticed him, the laughter died on her lips, and she hurriedly rose from her chair. Her cheeks turned crimson, and she tried to avoid his eyes, causing his doubt to rise again. Clearly, it was his presence that made Elizabeth uncomfortable. *Yet in her uncle's home, she seemed so different. Perhaps that was the reason*, he thought while advancing toward them. *Perhaps she feels more comfortable among her relatives than in my home.*

He approached and bowed to her, expressing his delight in seeing her again. Then he took a seat quite far from them, allowing her the opportunity to regain her composure while talking to Cassandra.

He intended to become involved at some point, when Lady Cassandra insisted Elizabeth play and sing. He noticed her reticence; he did not want her to feel obliged to comply with anyone's wishes while in his house. Yet, she agreed in the end and began to play. He was certain the sound of her voice was the most beautiful he had heard in some time. To lessen her embarrassment, he struggled to direct his eyes away from her. However, in the end, her beauty was simply too much for him to withstand, so he permitted himself to gaze upon her and hoped he was not the reason for her high colour and embarrassment.

"Miss Bennet, you play very well indeed. It is a pleasure to listen to you," said Lady Cassandra as soon as Elizabeth ended her song.

Elizabeth knew her cheeks were already burning under the penetrating stare of Mr. Darcy — she even lifted her eyes a few times and met his — yet the compliment took her by surprise, and she was certain it was responsible for her blushing even more. "Thank you, Lady Cassandra; you are too kind. However, I know only too well that I am not very good; I am neither as proficient nor as talented as Georgiana." She did not fail to notice Mr. Darcy's surprise at the familiarity of her address, but he did not seem displeased at all.

"I agree you are not as proficient or talented as Georgie, but then again, few people are. However, your interpretation was quite enjoyable — a true pleasure to hear."

"Indeed," Mr. Darcy finally spoke up, "to hear you playing and singing has always been a pleasure, Miss Bennet."

"Thank you, sir."

"So, did you ladies have a pleasant time?" asked Lady Cassandra, as Elizabeth managed to breathe deeply in an attempt to calm her emotions.

"Yes, we did; Elizabeth is the most delightful company."

"Yes, so she seems. Miss Bennet, how is your time spent in London when you are not going to the theatre or visiting Darcy's home?" asked the lady with a tone that confused Elizabeth and made her wonder about the meaning of her words. "Do you miss your family?"

Elizabeth hesitated a moment before answering. "Yes, I do, very much. Though I am very fond of my entire family, I must confess I mostly miss my father and my eldest sister, Jane."

"Yes…Miss Jane Bennet. Darcy told me about her." Elizabeth's face paled and unconsciously turned to him. Had he told *everything* to Lady Cassandra?

"From what I have heard, she is remarkably beautiful," she continued.

"Yes, she is, thank you. But aside from her beauty, she is a most kind and gentle lady and has the sweetest disposition. She is much like Georgiana in many respects." Miss Darcy blushed, taken aback by the compliment.

To Elizabeth's shock, it was Mr. Darcy who spoke further. "Georgiana, I did not know Miss Bennet's true character well enough to see the similarities while I was in Hertfordshire, but now that Miss Elizabeth mentions it, I am sure she must be right. She is far more perceptive than I am. While I fancy myself a good judge of character, I have learned I am by no means always correct in my initial impressions."

Elizabeth's eyes — wide in surprise after his declaration — fixed on his, and for a few moments, they stared wordlessly at each other. Upon his countenance was the deepest regret, which he took no pain to hide.

"I am also told that you have three other sisters besides Miss Bennet. Are they all as beautiful as your eldest?"

"Well, they are my sisters, and I love them, so I am by no means objective. But I dare say they are all pretty and pleasant in their own ways."

"I can hardly imagine how that must be — with so many sisters of different ages around you."

"For me, it is truly wonderful, although I have to confess it is a little tiresome at times."

"I can well imagine. Do all your sisters play the pianoforte as well as you?"

"My other sisters do not play at all, except for one. Mary, the sister next to me in age, also plays and sings."

"Well, I have to confess I do not play either. I never had the patience to learn. Mrs. Ashburton, my governess, suffered greatly because of this; she had always considered it her personal failure. But, of course, the fault was entirely mine." She laughed, and Mr. Darcy asked about Mrs. Ashburton's health. Lady Cassandra answered that she was well before returning her attention to Elizabeth.

"How many governesses did you have, Miss Bennet? Surely, one would not be enough for all of you."

"We never had governesses." Elizabeth almost laughed aloud at the similarity of these questions to the ones Lady Catherine had asked her the first time they met.

"What, five daughters and no governess?" was Lady Cassandra's surprised reaction, and Elizabeth could contain her laughter no longer. Embarrassed by her outburst, she covered her mouth with her hand and then started to apologise.

Lady Cassandra's brow rose in wonder at her. "Did something happen, Miss Bennet? Did I say something amusing?"

"No, your ladyship, please forgive me. It is just that —"

"Oh come now, it is very rude to laugh like that without sharing the reason with us."

"Lady Cassandra, I dare say that insisting any further to discover what Miss Bennet does not want to share with us would be equally as rude," Darcy intervened soundly.

His interference, though in her favour, did not make Elizabeth any easier. In fact, it had quite the opposite effect. Lady Cassandra appeared offended, but her expression changed in a moment. As the tension was caused by her bizarre reaction, Elizabeth decided to put an end to it as soon as possible, even if it meant the risk of giving more offence to her hosts.

"I beg you will forgive me. My behaviour has been rude indeed. I was amused by the fact that your ladyship's questions were similar to those of Lady Catherine last March."

The effect of her words was exactly as she feared. Mr. and Miss Darcy frowned, and Lady Cassandra remained speechless for a few moments before shaking her head and exclaiming, "Heaven forbid! Is that true? Oh dear, you absolutely must forget this instant that I ever asked you for such details. The same questions as Lady Catherine? That is not to be borne; it is the worst thing I have ever done!" The expression of distress on her face seemed so earnest that Georgiana began to laugh, quickly joined by the lady herself.

Shortly after this exchange, Elizabeth declared her intention of leaving. Her call had lasted more than two hours, which was considerably longer than propriety dictated. Mr. Darcy rose to ask for the carriage, but Lady Cassandra stopped him.

"Miss Bennet, if you can bear my company a little longer, I would be delighted to take you in my carriage."

Elizabeth looked at her in utter shock, noting that the Darcys were as surprised as she was.

"I thank you, your ladyship, but I would not want to trouble you. My uncle lives in Gracechurch Street and —"

"Oh, I know where Gracechurch Street is, Miss Bennet, and I feel quite in the mood for a longer ride before returning home."

Elizabeth cast a short glance toward the Darcys, and she noticed Mr. Darcy's eyes searching her face closely; she likely looked disconcerted, and he had noticed. She could refuse, and he would surely offer her his carriage, but why all these ridiculous hesitations? Surely, Lady Cassandra presented no danger to her. She struggled to change her expression, careful not to cause another awkward moment.

"Thank you, Lady Cassandra. Of course I accept your kind offer."

"Excellent! Let us go then, and during the ride, we may talk about the ball. What colour gown will you wear?"

They went toward the carriage, closely accompanied by the Darcys. Lady Cassandra entered first, helped by the gentleman. She reminded them she was expecting them later for dinner.

Georgiana took a warm leave of Elizabeth, embracing her, while Mr. Darcy bowed politely and took her hand to help her into the carriage, again holding it longer than necessary. She blushed, as she knew the other two ladies must have noticed his gesture, but she found the courage to smile tentatively as she thanked him.

"I hope to see you again soon, Miss Bennet," he said as he closed the carriage door.

Elizabeth continued to look through the window until the house and the Darcys were out of sight; only then did her eyes turn to her companion.

One glance was enough for her to understand that Lady Cassandra had no intention whatsoever of talking about the ball.

Chapter 4

E lizabeth bore Lady Cassandra's scrutiny a few moments rather uncomfortably. She was about to break the annoying silence when her ladyship finally spoke.

"Miss Bennet, I have been told you are a bright woman. You are also sincere, as I have observed myself. As it is likely we shall see each other quite often in the future, I think we should clarify a few things. May I speak plainly?"

"Of course! I very much prefer openness and sincerity. However, I must confess that your ladyship's tone is a little frightening."

"I surely hope not. I dare say you are not easily frightened; not even being alone in the room with an *angry gentleman* would seem to deter you."

Elizabeth frowned. The confirmation that Lady Cassandra was aware of the dreadful circumstances of Darcy's proposal made her tremble with mortification and rage toward him for not keeping private such a delicate affair.

"It appears that your ladyship has already heard many things about me."

As though she had guessed the nature of Elizabeth's thoughts, Lady Cassandra continued. "Do not be too upset with Darcy. Under normal circumstances, he never would have told me about that unfortunate event. However, he was not quite himself by the time I returned, and Georgiana was even more affected by his state, so you may understand that I could find no peace until I discovered the reason behind his distress."

"Under normal circumstances… he was not quite himself…" The words echoed in her head so clearly that she could barely hear or understand anything else. Had he been so deeply moved by her refusal that his mood had affected even his sister? Suddenly, the carriage became too small, and she felt she could not breathe.

"I must tell you that I have known the Darcys for twenty years now; they are my only remaining family. No other people are closer to my heart."

"I see. I am sorry to have caused anyone such distress, especially Miss Darcy. She surely does not deserve to suffer."

"No, she does not, and neither does Darcy. Do you also regret making *him* suffer?

53

Or perhaps you have come to regret your refusal now that you know exactly *what* you have refused?"

"Lady Cassandra, I do not mean to be rude, but I am not comfortable having this conversation with you. It is too painful to share with anyone."

"Very well then; I shall not pursue the subject further. I will only add that Georgiana is oblivious to all that happened. Everything she has been told about you is favourable, mainly from Darcy and partially from the colonel."

Elizabeth had no answer. What else was there to say?

"Moreover," continued Lady Cassandra, "Georgiana does not know that you are aware of what occurred at Ramsgate. As you know, it was a private matter, and so it should remain."

"I understand, and I beg you to rest assured that their secret will be perfectly safe with me."

"I have no doubt of that. If Darcy decided to tell you, it is certain he had complete trust in you. Ironic, is it not, for a man to trust so completely the woman who has just refused his marriage proposal and accused him of atrocious behaviour?"

Elizabeth again became livid as the accusation cut to her very soul, and her ladyship's rudeness became difficult to bear. She had no time to answer before Lady Cassandra continued. "You must be a remarkable woman, Miss Bennet, to have earned such attention from a man like Darcy."

"Lady Cassandra, I will confess that I have regretted my lack of understanding and the unfair accusations I heaped upon Mr. Darcy. I did blame myself for speaking with such vehemence about a subject that was not my personal concern and for allowing myself to be so easily deceived by Mr. Wickham. Though I know I had every reason to reject Mr. Darcy's proposal at the time — and I *did* know perfectly well *what* and *whom* I was refusing — I cannot help but feel sorry for all the distress I caused both Mr. and Miss Darcy…especially now, when I have come to know them better."

"So you are still certain you were right to refuse Darcy? Is that what you are telling me? Are you not asking yourself whether you have made the greatest mistake of your life?"

Elizabeth's rage surpassed her patience; she took a deep breath and glanced out the window to gauge their location, hoping they reached her destination quickly.

"I presume that you are not as *pleased* with your refusal now."

Lady Cassandra's voice held sharp irony, and Elizabeth finally erupted. "May I presume that your ladyship is *not displeased* with my refusal?"

She noticed with no little satisfaction that her words had the desired effect; Lady Cassandra's expression changed instantly, and she frowned.

"You think I am *pleased* that you refused Darcy?" Her voice was calm but determined, demanding a response. When no answer came, she continued. "Then you are not wrong, Miss Bennet; I am quite happy. If not for your refusal, I likely would not have returned so soon."

"I see." Elizabeth started to play with her reticule. Surely, her distress was obvious. She hated the idea of looking weak and pitiful before this formidable creature.

"Miss Bennet, rest assured: the secret of everything that occurred between you and Darcy will be perfectly safe with me. Also, I had no intention of being rude or upsetting you; I only wanted to clarify a few things for the benefit of everyone involved. Georgiana seems to feel friendship for you, and I cannot allow her to suffer again." Lady Cassandra's voice lost its sharpness and became gentle and soft as she spoke of Miss Darcy. "Georgiana has developed a strong, genuine friendship for you after only a few days. Undoubtedly, she has been influenced by her brother's generous praise. I have never seen her as animated with anyone outside the immediate family, and Darcy does not appear at all concerned. In fact, he seems to encourage the growing intimacy of your acquaintance. The power you have over the Darcys is quite amazing!"

Several emotions overwhelmed Elizabeth completely; each of Lady Cassandra's words felt like a knife piercing her thoughts. Her ladyship had done nothing more than voice aloud the same thoughts that had preoccupied Elizabeth since she first met Georgiana.

"Does your ladyship believe that my presence is harmful to Miss Darcy? Would your ladyship prefer that I spend less time in her company? I am asking because I believe your concerns are in Miss Darcy's best interest."

"I am not the one to make decisions in this matter; Darcy and the colonel are her guardians, and they seem to consider your friendship beneficial for her. I only hope you are the honest and sincere person we believe you to be and that you will not overlook the sincerity of her friendship."

"Lady Cassandra, I know your opinion about me is not favourable. I also know you would prefer not to be in my company —"

"No indeed, Miss Bennet, quite the contrary. Trust me; if I did not desire your company, you would be fully aware of that by now."

"Thank you. Your ladyship is very kind. And speaking of kindness, please allow me to thank you for inviting us to the ball. My aunt and uncle have been delighted by the opportunity —"

"And are *you* not delighted? You know, there will be a few handsome young gentlemen among the guests, so I dare say you will amuse yourself as well." Lady Cassandra was talking to her as though they were long-time friends with nothing but perfect understanding between them, and the lady continued to run on about the ball until they reached the Gardiner's house.

As a matter of courtesy, Elizabeth invited her companion in for a cup of tea. She was surprised, however, when Lady Cassandra agreed most readily to join her. In turn, Mrs. Gardiner was shocked to receive the unexpected visit of such an illustrious guest.

In Mrs. Gardiner's presence, Lady Cassandra's manners softened and warmed. She became nothing but kindness, complimented Mrs. Gardiner on her home, and even asked after Mr. Gardiner. More than half an hour passed before their guest took her leave, expressing her hope to see them again at the ball, which would occur in three days' time.

Thus, three days later — as the maid was helping her prepare for the ball — Elizabeth still could comprehend neither the truth of Lady Cassandra's character nor her intentions with regard to the Darcys.

CAROLINE BINGLEY HAD RARELY BEEN so displeased. She had returned to Town three days earlier and discovered alarming details about Lady Cassandra. Her anger — and panic — grew with each new report about the Darcys being seen in the company of the illustrious lady. Moreover, though she had sent around her card announcing her arrival in Grosvenor Street, she had received no invitation nor had either of the Darcys visited her.

Charles, absentminded and oblivious to the situation, admitted he had met Mr. Darcy briefly but refused to offer any details except that their departure for Pemberley had not changed.

The most alarming news was the private ball Lady Cassandra would be hosting to which they had not been invited. Mrs. Hurst managed to calm her younger sister, insisting it was likely that only the closest friends and relatives of her ladyship had been included in her guest list.

Yet, Caroline sensed that something horrible was about to happen, something that would destroy her future plans. None of Miss Bingley's acquaintances had been invited to the ball, so she held no hope for the consolation of a detailed report the following day. Consequently, she could only wait and hope something would occur to put an end to her distress. However, the day of the ball arrived and found Caroline shrouded in the deepest misery. She was certain it was the most horrible day of her life and the situation could not possibly get any worse.

THE DRIVE FROM GRACECHURCH STREET to Lady Cassandra's home seemed to Elizabeth longer than a trip from London to Longbourn. She had always loved balls; however, this particular ball caused her to feel uncomfortable and distressed.

Until that moment, Elizabeth had always felt at ease among people and never allowed herself to be intimidated, no matter the illustrious company in which she might find herself. Suddenly, the thought that she would be viewed as a last-minute addition to the elegant ball was overwhelming. That Mr. Darcy would also be present only added to her bewilderment.

The gowns Mrs. Gardiner procured for both of them were exquisite. While examining her hair and dress in the mirror, she knew she had never looked better. Nevertheless, with great effort did she finally admit to herself that the true cause of her distress was not what *she* thought about her appearance but what Mr. Darcy's opinion might be.

Lady Cassandra's house was everything Elizabeth had expected in terms of beauty and greatness. It spoke eloquently of its mistress's wealth and situation in life — as Mr. Darcy's home revealed the same about him. Elizabeth busied herself with an examination of the home; at the same time, she perceived the inquisitive gaze of several guests examining her.

Elizabeth's worries about their reception vanished as Lady Cassandra greeted them with obvious pleasure and warm politeness the first moment they entered. The friendly and joyful presence of Colonel Fitzwilliam was a blessing to Elizabeth, and she smiled openly at him as he hurried toward them and offered to accompany her into the ballroom. Mr. Darcy, however, was nowhere to be seen, and Elizabeth did not dare inquire after him.

"Miss Bennet, I shall take this opportunity to ask for the first set if you are not otherwise engaged."

"I am not engaged, Colonel," she answered, and then she leaned toward him slightly, whispering, "In fact sir, I am quite grateful for your invitation. I do not know anyone else in the room; therefore, I am quite sure my dance card will remain empty until the end of the evening."

"Oh, I should not be so certain about that, Miss Bennet. I dare say that more than one gentleman cast admiring glances in our direction as we entered, and I doubt the admiration was meant for me. I think I was wise to secure myself a set at the beginning of the evening." She could not help laughing again, feeling much of her uneasiness dissipating.

A moment later, Mr. Gardiner asked after Mr. Darcy; the colonel explained that he had already arrived but some urgent business regarding Lady Cassandra's estate needed his attention. "He is in the study, but I anticipate he will appear soon. He asked after you a few times, and I promised I would send a servant to inform him when you arrived."

Elizabeth's cheeks coloured, and her heart skipped a beat. *He asked to be informed when we arrived?* His interest was difficult to believe but flattering, and she was torn between excitement and distress.

Colonel Fitzwilliam remained in their company and introduced them to some of the guests. To Elizabeth's surprise, less than half an hour later, she found herself engaged for another three sets. Colonel Fitzwilliam immediately began to tease her about her popularity, but Elizabeth was certain that her "success" was due in large part to the other guests' curiosity about her and her relatives rather than an indication of her charm.

Why is he so late? Of course, once Mr. Darcy made his appearance, she could not expect the same friendly manners he had shown during their private meetings. But would he at least speak to her or ask for a dance?

Her thoughts were interrupted as a gentleman stopped near them, bowing politely to her as he also greeted the colonel.

"Colonel Fitzwilliam! It is a pleasure to see you again. I hope I am not intruding." As he spoke, his eyes never left Elizabeth's face, and she blushed at his insistent stare.

"Lord Markham, what a surprise! I did not expect to see *you* here." The colonel's voice was cold and stern; however, the gentleman seemed to take no offence.

"Well, apparently Lady Cassandra forgot to invite me as I was out of town, but my cousins asked me to escort them, and I could not refuse the request of two lovely ladies."

"I see. Well then, do not allow us to detain you from your escort duties. I am sure your cousins are missing you." Elizabeth startled at this open rudeness and gazed in surprise at the colonel. He was frowning, and he made no attempt to hide his displeasure.

The other gentleman, however, laughed shortly but did not leave, his eyes fixed intently on Elizabeth. "I am sure they will do very well without me for a while. Would you do me the honour of introducing me to the loveliest lady in the room, Colonel?"

"I would surely do so if you tell me of whom you are speaking," answered the colonel blankly, and Elizabeth did not know whether to chuckle or feel offended.

"Colonel, I am pleased to see your sense of humour is unaltered; however, I cannot believe you missed my meaning. I had the pleasure of seeing Miss Bennet last week at the theatre, and since then, I have wished for a formal introduction." Lord Markham bowed to her.

Though intrigued by the exchange, Elizabeth trusted that the colonel would not treat another gentleman rudely without good reason. She used all her civility to answer as politely as she could, but it was not an easy task. The viscount's manners, pleasant features and warm voice suddenly struck her as being similar to those of Mr. Wickham.

Lord Markham remained in their company for a few minutes, showing no restraint in expressing his admiration for her. His stare and his compliments made Elizabeth slightly uncomfortable; she was relieved when the viscount suddenly excused himself and left, but not before repeating to Elizabeth his pleasure at the prospect of dancing with her later.

Immediately following his departure, Elizabeth's eyes turned to the colonel, who displayed a preoccupied gaze. "Miss Bennet, I must beg your forgiveness. I acted most improperly in your presence. However, Lord Markham has often tested my patience in the past. "

"Yes, I imagined you were not the best of friends." Elizabeth forced a smile.

"Yes — not the best of friends, indeed. In fact, I dare say there are few people in London who are less friendly than we are."

"Sir, I hope his presence will not ruin your disposition for tonight. I was counting on you to help me rid myself of my anxiety and distress."

"Have no worry, Miss Bennet! Lord Markham is not capable of ruining anything for me and certainly not tonight. I intend to enjoy myself as much as possible. However, I am sorry I could not think of a way to avoid introducing him to you. Now you will have to dance with him."

"Colonel, you make him sound quite frightening. There was no way you could have avoided such an insistent demand for an introduction. But he seemed a pleasant sort of gentlemen, and I hope he is not unskilful when we dance. I think I can manage to bear him for half an hour."

"Yes, he seemed pleasant. As for dancing, I think he is not completely unskilful. I most assuredly have never danced with him."

"You never danced with whom, Colonel?" Lady Cassandra's voice startled Elizabeth; she had not noticed her ladyship approaching them and, apparently, neither had the colonel.

"We were talking about Lord Markham. Unfortunately, he managed to gain access to your ball by way of his cousins."

"Ah, yes. His impertinence is unlimited, but I hope you will not allow him to disturb you in any way. What on earth did he have to say?"

"He demanded an introduction to Miss Bennet and asked her for a set."

"I see. Well, Miss Bennet, at least he is not a poor dancer. And speaking of dancing, I hope Darcy will appear soon as the music is about to start, and I surely would not want to be without a partner for the first set."

I should have known they were engaged for the first set, thought Elizabeth with bitterness, but a moment later, she censured her childish reaction. The Gardiners joined them, expressing their admiration for the house and the exquisite arrangement of the ballroom. Lady Cassandra smiled and whispered to them that the credit should go to her companion who was the "author from the shadow" of all the preparations. "I am very pleased I invited you," her ladyship addressed the Gardiners, "though I have to confess my reasons are mostly selfish! Except for the colonel, Darcy and probably another ten people who truly came out of consideration for me and my family, yours are the only friendly faces in the room."

The conversation flowed easily until Mr. Darcy appeared in the ballroom. At first, Elizabeth did not see him enter, but her eyes were drawn toward his direction, and she stopped breathing for a moment. He was staring at her as he had so many times before — the same stare she noticed the night of the Netherfield ball. *Now* she knew the true meaning of his stare, and cold shivers gripped her.

Darcy remained near the entrance, watching Elizabeth. There she was — in the middle of their little group — talking to the colonel and her relatives, smiling, and looking perfectly at ease in a room filled with strangers, most of whom were staring at her. She was so beautiful in her pale yellow dress, with no other jewels accept her small garnet cross — which of course he could not see from a distance but knew was there nonetheless. A few flowers adorned her hair, and those two rebellious locks, which were always dancing on her neck, were ever present.

The moment their eyes met, her smile faded, yet her gaze remained locked with his across the room. She did not smile openly at him as she did at his cousin, nor did she appear at perfect ease when he started walking toward her; however, he was certain she was *not displeased* to see him.

He approached the group and greeted them, pleased to see the Gardiners again and even more pleased to see *her* again. Elizabeth's smile was tentative and her eyes seemed strangely shy when they met his. Still, the way her lips whispered, "Mr. Darcy…" as she curtseyed to him was incredibly charming and highly disturbing, and he could not take his eyes from her.

Yes, she is wearing the garnet cross, he thought as his eyes moved from her face to the creamy skin of her neck.

"I apologise, but the appointment lasted longer than I anticipated," he said, finally averting his gaze from Elizabeth. Nevertheless, in mere moments, he returned his attention to her.

"Miss Bennet, if you are not otherwise engaged would you do me the honour of dancing the second set with me?"

"I am afraid I am already engaged for the second set, sir… and for the third and forth." The expression of disappointment upon his face was so obvious that she could not retain a smile.

"Oh — it seems I am indeed very late. Then perhaps the next set that is available?"

"I would be delighted sir. That would be the fifth set, I think."

"Excellent," he answered, and his countenance lightened in an instant.

As the music started, the couples took their places on the dance floor. Elizabeth and the colonel were situated immediately behind Darcy and Lady Cassandra, and she was furious with herself for the raging emotions she could not control. She knew for certain that the dance would involve a change in places, and she would come to face him. She found herself nervously counting the steps until that moment would occur. When it happened and Darcy's hand joined hers, she was startled as she felt countless chills from his touch travelling wildly along her arm. After a few more steps, the colonel's hand once again held hers, and then the steps brought her near Darcy as their hands joined once more. At that moment, no doubt remained for Elizabeth: the sensation of his touch was different — shockingly, delightfully different.

Half an hour passed with a tumult of reactions in Elizabeth; she enjoyed her time with the colonel — who was an excellent dancer — however, her attention was often focused on the couple next to them. Lady Cassandra looked more beautiful than she had seen her before, and her moves were graceful and elegant. While they danced, she talked to Darcy constantly, and Elizabeth easily could see they seemed pleased with each other's company. That was hardly a new revelation for her;

however, she could not keep her eyes away from them and blushed in embarrassment when, more than once, her partner was forced to repeat a question. A few times, her gaze locked with Darcy's, and he offered her a barely visible smile.

The end of the dance reunited Elizabeth with her uncle and aunt. Mr. Darcy accompanied Lady Cassandra around the room a few minutes and then, to Elizabeth's surprise, joined their little group and remained with them, engaged in a lively conversation with her uncle. At one point, he moved near her and, while they were talking about the journey they were to begin the next day, addressed her. "Mr. Bingley and his sisters returned to town three days ago."

"Oh. Mr. Bingley is well, I hope?"

"Yes, he is well — though a little out of spirits. In fact, he has been quite out of spirits since last November, and apparently, his mood has not improved. He obviously regrets giving up Netherfield. I look forward to discussing this further when we meet at Pemberley."

No, there could be no misunderstanding. Mr. Darcy was telling her not just that Bingley was as affected as Jane by their separation but also that he intended to talk to him about the matter. Was it possible? Could Mr. Bingley be tempted to return to Netherfield? *To Jane?* And was Mr. Darcy truly determined to encourage him? The expression on his face, however, was a clear indication of his true meaning. "Thank you," she whispered, just before the music began again.

Elizabeth's partner came to claim her hand; she turned her head a little and saw Darcy following her with his eyes. She blushed again, unaccustomed joy overwhelming her heart.

For the second set, Lady Cassandra stood up with the colonel, yet Darcy remained in a corner, talking to her relatives. Elizabeth barely knew her partner's name and understood little of what he was saying. Her thoughts turned repeatedly to Darcy and the new revelation he had shared with her concerning Mr. Bingley — and how it would affect her sister Jane.

Throughout the next hour and a half, Elizabeth and Darcy rarely met. She danced every set; he, on the other hand, danced only once and, during the dance, seemed caught up in a deep conversation. She felt his gaze upon her from across the room many times and allowed her eyes to meet his, wishing she could talk to him or be in his close proximity again.

When Lord Markham came to claim his set, Elizabeth was in the midst of deep reflection and never noticed his approach.

"Miss Bennet, I have been waiting for this moment the entire evening."

She smiled grimly when he took her hand, squeezing it slightly. She released her fingers from his and forced a polite expression. "I hope you will not be disappointed, my lord. I am afraid the reality will not meet your expectations."

"I am sure the reality will exceed my every expectation, Miss Bennet."

She had been informed by Mrs. Gardiner — who seemed to possess interesting information about almost everybody in the room — that Lord Markham was the heir of one of the most illustrious families in the realm. He was undoubtedly handsome; however, Mr. Gardiner was clearly displeased with the gentleman's impetuous manner of seeking an introduction to Elizabeth and remembered the viscount was known at his club to be an unwise and wild young man who was not to be trusted by any young lady interested in maintaining her good reputation. Elizabeth laughed and assured her Uncle she was in no danger of trusting Lord Markham at all.

The dance began, and Elizabeth discovered that Lord Markham was a perfect dancer and pleasant company. However, he made no attempt to conceal his curiosity about her; he inquired about her family and their connection to Lady Cassandra. Elizabeth tried to answer his questions politely but evasively, declaring they were pleased to have her ladyship's friendship. He pressed her further, asking if she knew anything of Lady Cassandra's plans now she had returned to town. Archly, Elizabeth offered to request that her ladyship inform him later about her intentions, and for a time, her derision caused him to put an end to inquiries regarding Lady Cassandra.

If Elizabeth believed she would have occasion to meet with Lord Markham again, she would have attempted more earnestly to restrain the conversation. However, knowing perfectly well she would be unlikely to meet him again, she allowed herself to enjoy the dance and laugh silently at his open admiration of her. *Mr. Collins would truly envy Lord Markham's ability to compose little compliments to delight the ladies,* she thought gleefully. Her eyes met Mr. Darcy's gaze that instant — he was still not dancing — and he seemed serious and…worried. *Surely, he does not consider Lord Markham a rival. Could he be jealous?*

She smiled at Darcy and held his eyes until she realised her dance partner had noticed the direction of her gaze and was looking at her with great curiosity. He might have intended to say something, but fortunately, the dance ended, and he had no choice than to lead her back to her relatives. To Elizabeth's surprise, the viscount asked to be allowed to call on her the next day. Mr. Gardiner informed him it would be impossible as they were leaving London the next morning. Lord Markham inquired about the length of their absence from town and seemed highly displeased to hear that Elizabeth would likely return directly to her father's estate and not soon visit London again following their journey. Darcy approached at that moment, and Lord Markham finally left them after asking her for the favour of a second set. Elizabeth found no valid reason to refuse him, so she thanked him politely and accepted the invitation.

Although Mr. Darcy offered no opinion, she could not mistake his displeasure. She was afforded little time to consider it fully as the music was due to begin again shortly.

Elizabeth felt herself trembling and blushed, furious at her reaction. This was *his* dance. Mr. Darcy's hand silently claimed hers, and she did not leave him waiting long. His fingers gently caught hers, and not even their gloves could protect her from his burning touch. The air in the room was suffocating, yet she shivered under the wave of coldness that enveloped her body. They started to dance, but she could barely hear the music; she was staring at him, yet she could read nothing in his eyes, which merely returned her stare nonchalantly.

"Miss Bennet — we should have at least some conversation, I think. What is your opinion of the ball? It has been very satisfying so far, would you not agree?"

Her cheeks coloured as she remembered her rudeness on the evening of the Netherfield ball. She cringed now imagining what he must have thought of her impertinence on that evening.

"It is *your* turn to say something now, Miss Bennet — *I* talked about the dance, and *you* ought to make some kind of remark on the size of the room or the number of couples," he continued levelly. A peal of laughter escaped her lips; he smiled, looking very pleased at her reaction.

"This is the moment when I should apologise for my outrageous behaviour on that night, Mr. Darcy," she said, holding his gaze.

"No indeed, Miss Bennet. This, I believe, is the moment when you should say something that will amaze the whole room."

She laughed again at his unexpected teasing. "Very well, sir. There is no need to say more. I admit I merit your subtle censure and I *insist* on apologizing. My manners and my entire attitude during our dance at the Netherfield ball were unforgivable. Actually, I am amazed you would ask me to dance with you ever again."

"Miss Bennet, let us not discuss our behaviour on that night. I confess that dancing with you was quite enjoyable, despite our disagreement. The rest of the evening I recall with little pleasure. Please forgive me for referring to it."

He sounded serious, and his expression was remorseful. Without considering her gesture, her fingers squeezed his when their hands met again and remained entwined until the dance forced them to part.

"Your attempt to mock me was very good indeed, sir, as was your teasing. You have improved considerably in this aspect; it is obvious you have given yourself the trouble of practicing more." Her cheeks were burning in self-mortification as she heard herself *flirting* with him, yet the expression of delight on his face was reward enough for her archness.

Darcy felt a wild urge to kiss her right there — to silence those teasing lips with a mouth that burned with desire for her. He longed to make her sparkling eyes hide behind her lashes as his passion overwhelmed her. His gaze remained fixed on her face while his steps moved him closer to her and around her, his arm brushing hers. He noticed her blushing under his stare, a wave of redness covering not only her cheeks but also her neck and delicious ear lobes, yet she daringly kept her eyes on his. Her smile now belonged only to him, and he hoped this time he was not misjudging her regard for him.

From the time he entered the room, he had barely done anything but watch her. He knew he was acting ridiculously; anyone with a modicum of perception could easily guess the nature of his interest in her. He even knew his behaviour could place her in an embarrassing situation, but he was no longer capable of controlling himself, especially as he knew this was the last time he would see her for a while. In the past fortnight, her presence had become such a constant in his life that the mere thought of her disappearing again was unbearably painful.

"I think we really *must* have some conversation, sir. We have been silent for too long."

He startled and forced his eyes to be drawn away from her lips as he answered. "You are perfectly right, Miss Bennet. Since books are not your favourite subject to discuss while you are dancing, let us talk…ah…about travelling, for instance."

"A wonderful topic indeed sir," she agreed. "I am certain you have much more to say than I do, and I would be delighted to hear your thoughts on the subject."

The topic seemed to inspire great interest in both of them, for they did not cease their conversation, not even when the music stopped. Elizabeth felt her cheeks burning with pleasure as his entire discourse seemed to have one goal: to calculate the day she would arrive in Derbyshire.

Darcy held her hand while escorting her to the Gardiners, and again, he remained with them. Elizabeth was slowly recovering her emotions after their dance; she was unsure whether she was content to have him remain with her or would rather he leave her while she restored herself fully.

Colonel Fitzwilliam joined them and delighted them with his general good humour, declaring he was starved. A moment later, Lady Cassandra approached their group wearing an expression of utter delight upon her face.

"Lady Cassandra, am I wrong if I presume you are not inviting us to supper? Your expression is a bit frightening," declared Darcy, and her ladyship arched her brow at him.

"Darcy, how can you say I am frightening? Do I look frightening, Mr. Gardiner?"

"No indeed, Lady Cassandra; you look beautiful and charming," he declared. She responded by casting a satisfied glance at Darcy, who in turn rolled his eyes.

"However, Darcy, you are right in one respect: I do have a surprise for you all before supper! In fact I am curious as to whether my guests will *appreciate* my surprise," she said, smiling mischievously while Darcy cast an intriguing glance at both Elizabeth and her relatives that said: *You see that I was right about being frightened!*

However, nothing prepared them for what came next. The music started again, and it took only a few moments for everyone in the room to recognise the notes of the infamous waltz!

Rumours and agitation spread throughout the room, and Lady Cassandra threw them a satisfied look, perfectly matched with the expression of delight in her eyes. "So Darcy, Colonel, which of you will help me to execute my surprise? I know both of you are proficient at this dance."

"Lady Cassandra, as you know, I am *not* proficient at all. Of course, if you insist, I will dance with you, but I am not fond of surprises of this sort that will only provoke more gossip."

"Oh come now, Darcy," said the colonel. "You are much too serious and preoccupied with society's opinion. Let us enjoy the delight of the waltz, Lady Cassandra."

Elizabeth's eyes followed them, mesmerised by the spell of their harmonious moves and the enchanting music. So absorbed was she in her admiration that it took her some moments to notice the Gardiners had joined Lady Cassandra and the colonel on the dance floor.

"Mr. and Mrs. Gardiner are quite proficient, too," whispered Darcy, and she only nodded.

She had heard of the waltz previously, but she had never seen anyone dance it. The proximity of the couples, the intimacy the music inspired, and the romantic manner in which each couple entwined their hands all led Elizabeth to delight in the experience of simply watching the dance unfold. Slowly, other couples courageously joined the two couples in the dancing area, and while not as skilled as the first dancers, more and more couples followed their example. Elizabeth watched the dancing in awe. Unconsciously she whispered, "Beautiful," almost oblivious to the presence of Darcy until he lowered his head to speak to her.

"Yes, it does look beautiful indeed, though perhaps not quite proper."

She startled and blushed, not daring to meet his eyes. "I am sorry. I must look silly, lost in my reverie, but this is the first time I have actually seen this dance, and I am afraid it has an enchanting effect on me." She tried to sound light and amused to hide her embarrassment, but any attempt failed a moment later when he spoke again.

"Miss Bennet, would you be tempted to… I mean would you like to try to dance? I did learn the steps some time ago, and I would be delighted to show them to you."

She stood speechless, looking at him as though he spoke another language. "Are you inviting me to waltz, sir?" *You just refused Lady Cassandra!* was the thought that raced through her head. The mere idea of his embracing her, her hand clasped in his was enough to send her mind reeling. If she agreed, she feared she would not be able to breathe, let alone follow what appeared to be the complex set of steps required of the dance.

"Yes… that is if you are tempted to. Many find the dance offensive and never would consider trying it." He appeared to be deeply embarrassed, but there was something else in his expression that she could not comprehend.

However, she thought, *he could not possibly be more embarrassed than I am. I am so tempted to accept, even if by doing so I shall make a fool of myself. After all, he knows I do not know how to dance the waltz, but still he insisted. What would happen if I agreed?"*

"Sir, I cannot accept, and you surely must not insist. It would be the most embarrassing moment for both of us. We just danced together a few minutes ago, so let us —"

"You are perfectly right, Miss Bennet. Please forgive me." Darcy was deeply mortified. Immediately after inviting her to join in the waltz, he knew he was making a mistake but he could not fight his desire to hold her in his arms. Once again, he had selfishly considered only his desires and had shown no respect for hers. Surely, she would not welcome becoming a spectacle before a room full of strangers. The very idea now seemed ridiculous!

What was he to do? He had gained a moment of privacy with her and managed to ruin it. Should he depart and leave her alone to enjoy the view before making a complete fool of himself?

"Mr. Darcy, are you well, sir?"

"Yes, perfectly well, Miss Bennet."

"I was telling you, sir, that we just danced, and I dare say we made a reasonably good impression. So, as much as I would be *tempted to accept* your offer, I would suggest we not jeopardise your reputation with my clumsiness. Lady Cassandra would never forgive me for ruining her waltz."

Her tentative smile showed that she was not completely at ease, and she was obviously trying to lighten the tension he had created, but her eyes were laughing at him.

"A very wise decision, Miss Bennet," he agreed, regaining his spirit.

They spent the next few minutes silently admiring the dancers; when the music stopped, he offered his arm and accompanied her to the dining room.

Elizabeth had another surprise when she discovered that they were placed close to Lady Cassandra at the table. At her ladyship's right was Mr. Darcy, and next to him Mrs. Gardiner; she, Elizabeth, was most happily situated between her uncle and Colonel Fitzwilliam, facing her aunt.

During supper, Elizabeth allowed herself a few minutes to reflect on the evening. She was having a better time than she had expected; her aunt and uncle seemed to enjoy themselves even more than she and looked perfectly easy, content to ignore the sharp looks and whispers from some of the guests. She knew her relatives to be fashionable people, accustomed to London society, but their boldness in joining Lady Cassandra and her partner for the waltz surprised Elizabeth. However, her ladyship was exceedingly pleased they had joined her and Colonel Fitzwilliam — of that, there was no doubt.

Colonel Fitzwilliam was as agreeable and friendly during dinner as he was the entire evening. Elizabeth found herself laughing a few times at his exchanges with Lady Cassandra. Mr. Darcy, on the other hand, was considerably more serious; his gaze travelled along the table more than once, carefully watching all the guests. Sometimes she met his look, and sometimes she only felt it burning her face, yet each time her reaction to him was equally strong.

Her doubts concerning the nature of Mr. Darcy and Lady Cassandra's relationship remained. At one point Elizabeth heard some whispered speculations about a possible engagement to be announced between the two of them, and for a moment, she was afraid the rumours might prove to be correct. However, she put aside that worry quite soon; Mr. Darcy's attentions toward her — repeated and openly displayed — were the strongest proof that his interest, affection and honour were *not* engaged elsewhere. About Lady Cassandra's interest and affection, she could not be certain; however, her ladyship by no means showed any kind of jealousy nor did she try to keep Mr. Darcy's attentions to herself. *Except that she placed him at her right,* she thought, and then instantly scolded herself for her silent doubts.

The most intriguing character for Elizabeth was Lord Markham, who was seated quite close to them — probably because that seat was planned for someone else. Mr. Darcy and the colonel seemed to share the same ill opinion of the viscount. Their dislike was so obvious that they avoided him in their conversations and made no attempt to answer his direct questions. Elizabeth was certain that the reasons for their negative opinion must be quite serious; however, the viscount did not seem affected by their disregard of him in the slightest. From time to time, he cast quick glances at Lady Cassandra, but her ladyship patently ignored him the entire evening.

Elizabeth could not ignore him as Lord Markham continued to extend his courtesy toward her. She tried to remain polite, yet she became more restrained with her smiles; she was afraid he might take her mere politeness as a sign of encouragement. She shuddered to think of the talent she seemed to possess to attract persons whom she wished to avoid.

The second part of the evening was equally as pleasant. Elizabeth was engaged for every set and once more danced with Lord Markham — to whom she made a marked effort to behave politely but distantly — and with the colonel, with whom she experienced nothing but delight.

However, with every hour that passed, Elizabeth grew more distressed, enjoying her time less and less. All she could think of was their imminent departure and her separation from *certain acquaintances* she truly did not wish to leave. A few times, she was certain Darcy could understand her thoughts and — daring presumption! — experience the same feelings.

Immediately after supper, he had asked her if she was engaged for the last set. Fortunately, she was not, and he immediately secured it for himself. For the remainder of the ball, he availed himself of every opportunity to be near her. In fact, he spoke very little with anyone else except Lady Cassandra and the colonel — who teased him about his sudden low spirits and constant gaze that rarely left her.

When the last set was announced, he gravely and silently claimed her hand, holding it tightly. They barely talked at all for the entire half hour — yet Elizabeth felt no need for words. Everything that could be said between them had been said.

Although she was not completely free of doubt, the intensity of his gaze, the light brushing of his fingers against hers, the bittersweet look of sadness mixed with contentment, the tentative smile that appeared on his lips from time to time — all boded well for their expected meeting at Pemberley. All of this left her with many hopes — hopes for her sister, hopes for herself, and hopes for the future.

Chapter 5

Darcy remained, stunned, in the middle of Pemberley's library as he watched an enraged Charles Bingley charge from the room and slam the door.

Yes, he had anticipated his younger friend would be angry; however, the meeting proceeded differently than Darcy had expected.

In the first minutes, Bingley had borne his confession with calmness; in fact, he seemed not to accept that Darcy had been wrong in his estimation of Miss Bennet's feelings and could not understand why Darcy was apologizing for his interference at all.

However, when Darcy told him that Miss Bennet had been in London for three months and even called at his home, Bingley turned completely white, and he seemed not to breathe for several minutes. In utter rage, he demanded to be told how Darcy became aware of Jane Bennet's visit, and his violent words were spewed out at his friend as well as his sisters.

"I cannot bear to breathe the same air as you any longer," he said at the end of his outburst. "I shall remove myself from this house as soon as my belongings are ready. As for my sisters, you may keep them for a while, as it appears you share an intimate similarity of mind."

The master of Pemberley remained stunned; neither his mind nor his body were able to react.

LADY CASSANDRA HAD LOVED THE grounds of Pemberley all her life and, since returning there a week ago, had spent at least a couple of hours each day riding and enjoying the beauty of the grounds. Usually she rode in the company of Darcy, Georgiana or both, accompanied by Charles Bingley who was also an excellent rider.

That morning, however, she was alone since Georgiana felt tired and Darcy mentioned that he and Bingley were to have a private talk.

"Oh, *the talk*... Good luck," she wished him, confident that he would need it.

With the gentle breeze of a July day playing in her hair, Lady Cassandra would allow no dark thoughts to mar her enjoyment. Her attention was drawn toward a rider galloping over the fields so wildly that she frowned and turned her head after him. With utter surprise, she thought she recognised Charles Bingley, but she could not be certain, so she turned her horse to follow. When, after more than ten minutes, she decided to stop her animal to spare him from exhaustion, she found Bingley sitting upon the grass, his horse's reins tied to a tree.

"Mr. Bingley, what on earth is the matter?" she asked, dismounting.

"Lady Cassandra!" He looked shocked to see her, leaped to his feet and, after a moment, turned his back to her in an attempt to hide his face; however, a glance was sufficient for her to notice his red eyes.

Has he been crying? she wondered as she moved closer. "Mr. Bingley, I can see you are upset, sir. I presume it is your discussion with Darcy that has brought you to such a state."

He turned to her, his eyes and mouth open in shock. "How can your ladyship possibly know about what Darcy and I spoke? Does *everyone* in the country know except me?" he shouted.

Lady Cassandra fixed him with her stare, her brow arching questioningly. "Sir, I can understand your anger, but are you certain that yelling at me will heal your hurt feelings?"

The gentleman's sense of propriety won over his anger, and he averted his eyes in embarrassment. "I beg your forgiveness; I completely forgot myself. I would rather leave before my rudeness appals you further." He moved toward his exhausted horse.

"No need to apologize, sir, and please have no worry about my being appalled. I am not quite that sensitive. I want to ask you to indulge me and remain a few minutes. Both your horse and mine need rest, and we could have a little conversation."

His first reaction was to continue walking toward his mount, but after a brief look at the animal, he turned to his companion. "How is it possible that your ladyship knows — about my conversation with Darcy, I mean?"

She smiled. "Darcy mentioned it to me this morning."

"Mentioned what — that he would have a nice chat before breakfast with witless Charles Bingley? To offer him more wise advice? Such a pity I did not take it as easily as I used to! Perhaps I should apologise for ruining his breakfast. However, he might be pleased, as I intend to leave Pemberley this very moment and never cross paths with him again."

"Mr. Bingley, I cannot believe Darcy treated you with such carelessness and lack of consideration. Did he offend you in any way?"

"Oh, no, he was everything polite and proper — as he always is. He apologised, in fact. He apologised for ruining my happiness, your ladyship! But, as he did it with much consideration, I should be grateful to him!"

Lady Cassandra watched in silence, allowing him to express his rage. He was still turned with his back to her when she suddenly exclaimed, "Mr. Bingley, what on earth has happened to your hair? It is all red at the back, and I have to say it is very unbecoming to you."

He stared at her in complete misapprehension. "I beg your pardon? I cannot understand your ladyship's meaning; my hair is certainly not red!"

"Are you sure, sir? Because it certainly looks red to me."

"I am positive! I did look in the mirror this morning. Since then I have had no time to alter the colour of my hair. I think your ladyship is trying to mock me in order to distract me."

"So you accept completely that your hair cannot be red, Mr. Bingley. What if Darcy had told you the same thing? Would you have contradicted him with the same arguments and determination that you have with me, or would you simply have accepted his word without question?"

His face instantly turned white again, and his eyes remained fixed on her inquiring ones. Her eyebrow rose in expectation as he tried with great effort to knit his thoughts together.

"That is hardly the same thing, your ladyship."

"I agree; it is hardly the same thing, yet I dare say my question has a valid point."

"Yes, it has," he admitted with sadness. "I have been such a fool. I never for one moment questioned Darcy's word. I did not trust my sisters' opinion, but when Darcy told me he did not think Miss Bennet returned my affection — that she would only accept my attentions to satisfy her mother's wishes — how could I have doubted him? I have always trusted Darcy, and he has never disappointed me. I know he always considered my well-being and my best interests. To discover that he deceived me on purpose — that he lied to me!"

"Mr. Bingley, you do have reason to be angry with Darcy, though I think he was honest in his estimation of Miss Bennet's feelings at the time. He truly believed her to be indifferent to you, and now it appears he was wrong. But you cannot lay the entire fault upon him! He was not always close to you and Miss Bennet; he was not privy to your private conversations and certainly did not catch all those little signs that help a gentleman recognise a lady's preference! If you had contradicted Darcy, perhaps he would have recognised his error."

"But *I* was not certain of Miss Bennet's affection either, my lady! I admired her so much and thought her so perfect. I knew she could aspire to a better match. I was not certain at all."

"I see." Lady Cassandra watched him as he became less agitated and more depressed. "Mr. Bingley, if you want to leave Pemberley and put an end to your friendship with Darcy, of course we will all respect your decision. However, I would advise you to consider whether *this* is the best solution to the situation. I know his interference gave you much grief and great suffering —"

"Lady Cassandra, do you not understand?" She startled at his abrupt outburst. "This is not about *me*! I do not blame Darcy for being wrong in his presumptions while he was in Hertfordshire, but when Miss Bennet came to London to call at my house… If it is true that he was wrong — if Miss Bennet *did* return my feelings — how she must have suffered when I left without a word! And how hurt she must have felt when she received no sign from me after her visit! I cannot blame Darcy for *my* pain during all these months! But I *do* blame him for all the grief *Miss Bennet* had to endure, and I do not think I will ever forgive him for that!"

His voice was trembling; Lady Cassandra was certain he was close to crying — and she smiled. Better hope for a favourable resolution there had never been!

"Mr. Bingley, your affection for Miss Bennet is impressive; I will make sure to point that out to her the first time I meet her."

His eyes opened in shock. "Lady Cassandra, *when* will you meet Miss Bennet?"

"I am not certain yet, Mr. Bingley! It depends on your plans. What do you intend to do in the future, sir? Or let me ask you this: what is it precisely that you want to *accomplish* in the future?"

"I do not understand. I am not certain at this point. I do not think there is much I can do. I am certain that any feeling Miss Bennet might have had for me is now gone. Surely she must despise me; I doubt she could look at me without disdain." He looked simultaneously confused and grieved, and Lady Cassandra could not help smiling in sympathy.

"Mr. Bingley, you should refrain from drawing such *absolute* conclusions about Miss Bennet's feelings. You did misjudge them completely when you were near her; surely you cannot presume you are correct when you are so far away!"

He could detect the half mockery in her tone, and he also sensed that her ladyship was actually scolding him. Yet he did not feel offended; in fact, he felt better than he had in a long time. For the first time, somebody — and not just anybody, but Lady Cassandra whom he did not dare to even address directly until that day — was talking to him about Miss Bennet.

"Your ladyship is correct. I should not attempt to presume anything about Miss Bennet; I am the worst judge of ladies' feelings."

"Well, not *the* worst but one of the worst," she laughed. "So, did you consider returning to Netherfield?"

"Yes I did. But if Miss Bennet has finally put aside any feelings for me, my return would only upset and pain her. I cannot be so inconsiderate."

"Very well, sir. Being considerate of Miss Bennet's feelings in making your decision is proof of your character. I agree that your return might have unpleasant consequences if Miss Bennet's feelings have suffered a drastic change in the last months; however, if the lady still holds some regard for you, she might still entertain hope, and there is still time for you to assure her happiness — and yours — would you not agree? Of course, there is always the risk of being wrong and the lady refusing your courtship. You might even be more hurt than you already are."

Bingley's countenance instantly lightened in utter happiness. "Yes, yes, of course I agree. Oh, please believe me, your ladyship, I am not in the slightest worried about being hurt. Miss Bennet deserves any risk or effort on my part. Then I should return to Netherfield, do you think?"

"Mr. Bingley, is Netherfield prepared to receive you immediately?"

"No, it is not, but I do not really care; I can accommodate myself quite easily. If only Miss Bennet would not be displeased to see me again."

"Well — there is one way to discover that for certain. Miss Elizabeth Bennet and her relatives are expected to arrive in the neighbourhood in a week's time. You might suggest to Miss Elizabeth that you intend to return to Netherfield and see what she thinks of the matter. Miss Elizabeth is an opinionated young lady and quite fond of her sister. I am sure she would have no restraint in letting you know whether that decision might harm her sister."

"Oh, such a wonderful idea! Miss Elizabeth and I were already friends. I could talk to her. She will let me know her opinion; I am sure of it." He started pacing again, and then he suddenly frowned. "But, I cannot remain at Pemberley another week. Darcy would not allow it. I offended him badly, and I said I would leave the house this very morning."

Lady Cassandra moved closer and patted his arm familiarly. "Oh, I am sure Darcy would welcome your staying, Mr. Bingley, as I am sure Darcy values your friendship more than you think. Perhaps another talk with him would do for you both — a real, honest talk with no anger or guilt from either of you. You may still be upset with him for a time, and you may not forgive him for his deception, but I dare say that, as you deserve another chance to win Miss Bennet's heart, your friendship with Darcy deserves another chance as well. Go and clarify; settle things between you as two proper gentlemen should. Will you do that for me, Mr. Bingley?"

"Lady Cassandra, I cannot express my gratitude for all the help your ladyship has offered me today. I will be grateful to you my entire life —"

"There is no need for that, Mr. Bingley. I have done nothing really. However, we should return now as the others most likely have finished their breakfast — not to mention that we have been alone for an extended time, and if anyone saw us, I would be compromised, and you would be forced to marry me. Your chance to win Miss Bennet would disappear forever!"

She mounted and galloped across the field, laughing heartily at the image of an anguished Bingley, terrified at the revelation that he might be bound to her life.

"STEVENS, THE GREEN ONE, PLEASE!" demanded Darcy as his servant hurried to bring him the coat.

Darcy looked in the mirror to check his appearance and then walked down the main stairs of Pemberley, nervous but light hearted and full of happy anticipation. Finally, she was there!

The past week had been as deeply gratifying for Darcy as it had been annoying. After their disastrous talk, Bingley had returned an hour and a half later and asked for another meeting. More than two hours passed in serious, animated conversation. Bingley apologised for his offensive words, and Darcy warmly accepted them and offered his own apologies. It was then settled that Bingley would not leave Pemberley for the moment, but he asked many questions and demanded clarification. It was not difficult for Darcy to notice that his friend seemed more self-confident and determined than ever before, especially when he informed Darcy that he intended to re-open Netherfield as soon as possible.

Since that day, the situation improved between Darcy and Bingley; besides the qualities Darcy had always admired in his friend's character, more positive aspects of the younger gentleman slowly revealed themselves. He was uncertain whether Bingley had changed or he — Darcy — had finally become perceptive enough to appreciate his friend.

However, together with Bingley's change, other events transpired, not all of them pleasant for Darcy. On one hand, Lady Cassandra became unexpectedly friendly with Bingley, a fact that Darcy considered astonishing since his friend had exchanged few words with the lady during the first part of their visit. On the other hand — and more disturbing to Darcy's peace of mind — Bingley's sisters grew more tiresome, and their persistent insinuations about the Bennet family became more impertinent. If Bingley previously had borne his sisters' mean remarks about the Bennets and their demanding attitude toward him in silence, lately most of their conversations ended in conflict, which annoyed Darcy, distressed Georgiana, and irked Lady Cassandra.

Caroline Bingley's attentions to Darcy were equally tiresome, and Lady Cassandra found a strange satisfaction and amusement in irritating Caroline and increasing her jealousy. *This intolerable situation must end soon or I shall be forced to take measures,* thought Darcy.

But now that he finally would see Elizabeth again and enjoy the Gardiners' company, he hoped conditions might improve.

"Are you ready yet, brother?" Miss Darcy touched his arm to bring him back from his reverie.

"Yes, I was waiting for you. The carriage is prepared."

"I am so happy I will see Elizabeth again! I have missed her so much."

No more than I. He smiled to himself and nodded in approval to his sister.

ELIZABETH COULD NOT BELIEVE SHE was finally there; she had thought of, dreamed about, and dreaded this day since they left London.

Their tour had lasted three weeks, and she enjoyed every day of it. However, her thoughts mostly had been directed to a place in Derbyshire. Restless days and sleepless nights were filled with wonderings and fears about a certain gentleman. The most important question remained without an answer: was this love? What was the overwhelming, frightening feeling that brought her torment and joy — the feeling that trapped her heart and mind, and gave her no peace? How could she be certain? And if it were love, what would be its fate?

As the carriage progressed into Lambton and Mrs. Gardiner shared fond memories with her husband, Elizabeth could not help inspecting the surroundings, hoping to catch a glimpse of something related to the Darcys. Secretly, she had wished that her uncle would accept the invitation to stay at Pemberley. The mere possibility of spending the night in Mr. Darcy's house made her heart race and her cheeks redden.

They were enjoying a cup of tea in their rooms at the inn when a servant announced Mr. and Miss Darcy. Elizabeth was so surprised that she could not gather herself to rise when the guests entered. *How did he know we were here? Did he specifically inquire about our arrival?* The possibility instantly filled her heart with joy.

She managed to recover only when Miss Darcy, with a radiant smile, greeted them warmly and then approached her and took her hands. "Elizabeth, I am so happy to see you!"

Elizabeth embraced the young lady; her gaze, however, travelled over his sister's shoulder to meet Mr. Darcy's dark, penetrating stare.

He moved closer and bowed politely to her. "Miss Bennet, welcome to Derbyshire!" His voice was warm and soft, as warm as the small smile barely noticeable on his lips.

"Thank you, sir," she answered, as her knees suddenly seemed unsteady.

Again, Miss Darcy sat close to Elizabeth while her brother took a place near Mr. Gardiner. For more than half an hour, they shared impressions of their tour. As was usual in Mr. Darcy's presence, Elizabeth felt uneasy and contributed little to the conversation. However, the gentleman himself asked her direct opinion a few times, and she had to answer him and meet his gaze; she was furious with herself for feeling embarrassed and behaving childishly.

"Do you have any news of your family, Miss Bennet? They are all in good health, I hope."

"Yes, they are all in excellent health, sir, thank you."

"I am glad to hear it. Mrs. Gardiner, have you met your friends yet?"

"No, sir. We announced our arrival and expect some calls later today, but you are the only guests we have had the pleasure to receive thus far."

"I see. Mr. Gardiner, did you decide how long you will remain in Derbyshire?"

"Yes we did, Mr. Darcy. Most likely a fortnight."

"I hope we shall meet again often during that time," continued Mr. Darcy. "Mr. Gardiner, everything is prepared for our fishing party, and Mr. Bingley also wishes to join us."

"I confess I have been looking forward to it since we left London, sir, and I am prepared to take the best advantage of your kind offer."

"Elizabeth, I would like so much for you to stay at Pemberley; we even have rooms prepared for you in case you decide to accept my brother's invitation."

"Miss Darcy, I am sorry we had to refuse your kind offer," Mrs. Gardiner interjected. "Please believe me, it would be a great honour, but circumstances do not allow us to reside at Pemberley and also spend time with my relatives and friends as I would wish."

"Oh, Mrs. Gardiner, I beg you do not presume that I was questioning your decision. I was only… Oh, please forgive me." The young girl became pale and could not speak any further.

"Georgiana, please do not distress yourself; in truth, it is we who are delighted and truly honoured by your attentions and your invitation," said Elizabeth with warmth and affection.

"Mrs. Gardiner, Mr. Gardiner, Miss Bennet, may I speak openly?" asked Mr. Darcy unexpectedly, his voice somewhat agitated.

He allowed his eyes to rest upon Elizabeth before speaking further. "Both my sister and I are very pleased to see you again, and I have to confess we would have been delighted to have you stay at Pemberley while you remain in Derbyshire. However, I do understand your reason for not accepting, and if in your place, I would make the same decision."

"Thank you, sir." Mrs. Gardiner smiled comfortingly.

"Even more," the gentleman continued, "I am sure you must be anxious to meet your family and old friends and spend as much time as possible with them; that is why I want to extend a permanent and informal invitation to you. Whenever you do not have any other fixed engagements, we would be delighted to have you at Pemberley."

"Thank you, Mr. Darcy," answered Mr. Gardiner. "We are not only honoured but deeply touched by your kindness, sir. Of course, we gratefully accept."

"Besides," said Mrs. Gardiner, "I am sure Mr. Gardiner will infinitely prefer fishing early in the morning to anything else. As for Elizabeth, as she is not acquainted with any of my friends, surely she will not spend as much time in their company as I will."

"So you see, you will have to take care of me and entertain me," said Elizabeth in a low voice to Miss Darcy, who finally forced a smile.

"Speaking of entertaining," continued Mrs. Gardiner, "How are your other guests at Pemberley? Is Lady Cassandra in attendance?"

The question, skilfully addressed to both Mr. and Miss Darcy, turned them more voluble. After the assurance that everybody in the party was in perfect health, Miss Darcy hurried to inform the ladies that Lady Cassandra was desirous to meet them again, while Mr. Darcy told Elizabeth that Mr. Bingley was also happy to be renewing their acquaintance.

"Thank you, sir, I am also anxious to meet Lady Cassandra and Mr. Bingley again… oh, and of course Miss Bingley and Mr. and Mrs. Hurst," answered Elizabeth. He smiled, and she returned it. In truth, she was not that anxious to meet Mr.

Bingley's sisters again, but apparently that was the price she had to pay to enjoy her time in Derbyshire.

"Do you have any plans for dinner today?" inquired Mr. Darcy.

"We have hardly had time to make any plans as we have just arrived," Mrs. Gardiner spoke cheerily.

"Of course…" The gentleman looked embarrassed by his own question, and Elizabeth smiled.

"Then, if you are not too tired after your journey, may we have the pleasure of your company later for dinner?"

"We would be delighted, sir," answered Mr. Gardiner with no hesitation, making Elizabeth's heart race wildly. She was not comfortable — that was impossible — but she was flattered, pleased, and hopeful from all the attention, which, she finally dared to admit, was directed mostly at her.

Their guests only remained a brief time, and the moment they took their leave, Elizabeth began preparing to dress for dinner with an eagerness that made her aunt tease her mercilessly.

As the carriage ambled along, Mr. and Mrs. Gardiner talked animatedly about the beauty of the grounds, but Elizabeth bore every moment that brought her closer to Pemberley with great perturbation. She saw and admired every remarkable spot and point of view; but her spirits were in a high flutter, and she found her hands trembling slightly in her lap.

The carriage entered the large park and drove for some time through a beautiful wood stretching over a wide extent. They gradually ascended for half a mile, and then found themselves at the top of a considerable eminence, where the wood ceased, and the eye was instantly caught by Pemberley House, situated on the opposite side of a valley. It was a large, handsome, stone building, standing well on rising ground and backed by a ridge of high, woody hills.

Elizabeth forgot to breathe, and her heart nearly stopped, as she could not take her eyes from the sight before her. She had never seen a place for which nature had done more or where natural beauty had been so little counteracted by an awkward taste. Pemberley looked strong, handsome, and impressive in its natural grandeur. *Much the same as its master,* she thought.

The master of Pemberley was awaiting them in front of the main entrance, together with Mr. Bingley. Darcy greeted them warmly and helped the ladies remove from the carriage. He offered Elizabeth his arm, even before Mr. Bingley had time to bow to her with unconcealed joy.

Mr. Darcy performed the introductions, and to the Gardiners, Mr. Bingley was as amiable and friendly as Elizabeth expected. However, she had the impression, though she could not say exactly why, that Mr. Bingley had changed since she met him last.

Mr. and Mrs. Gardiner had long wished to meet Mr. Bingley, and the gentleman was exactly as they expected him to be. Also, their suspicions of Mr. Darcy and their niece were suspicions no longer; the gentleman was overflowing with admiration, and Elizabeth's reaction in his company spoke clearly of her own feelings.

Only when she actually had to greet Lady Cassandra and Georgiana did Elizabeth notice she was still holding — quite tightly — onto Mr. Darcy's arm. She blushed with embarrassment and withdrew her hand as she answered her ladyship's polite questions.

With the other guests, however, things went differently. Mr. Hurst barely acknowledged their presence with a slight nod of his head; Mrs. Hurst managed to behave politely though her coldness could not go unnoticed. Miss Bingley's entire attitude — from her dry tone to her stiff countenance — left no doubt of her dislike toward the arrival of the newcomers, and her lack of civility, though not loudly expressed, was evident nonetheless.

A neutral conversation began about Pemberley, the neighbourhood, Lambton, Derbyshire in general, and the work of many generations who made Pemberley such a grand estate.

"Mrs. Gardiner, as I understand it, you lived near here. Have you visited Pemberley previously?" asked Miss Bingley unexpectedly.

"No, Miss Bingley, I have not. I had the honour of meeting Lady Anne many years ago, but have seen Pemberley only from afar."

"Yes, I imagined as much. From what I heard, Lady Anne was very selective in choosing her guests," answered Miss Bingley triumphantly with a meaningful glance at her sister.

The offense in her voice was so obvious that Elizabeth felt her cheeks turning red with anger.

"Yes, you are correct, Miss Bingley," Lady Cassandra interjected. "Lady Anne had exquisite taste in selecting her guests; unfortunately, it seems that Darcy has not maintained the same habit. *As for Mrs. Gardiner*, I am certain Lady Anne would have been quite delighted to see her today. Indeed, she is one of the most pleasant ladies I know, and her home is a pleasure to visit."

"Thank you, Lady Cassandra. You are too kind," answered Mrs. Gardiner.

"Oh, but Miss Bingley has had the opportunity of forming an opinion of her own! I understand she visited my aunt several months ago. Am I mistaken?" Elizabeth knew she should not intensify the moment, but she could not help herself.

Miss Bingley blinked a few times and then looked with worry at her sister, apparently unable to formulate an immediate answer.

"Oh really? So would you not agree with me, Miss Bingley?" Lady Cassandra's voice was all politeness.

"To be honest, that visit was quite short, and I paid little attention to my surroundings. I barely remember anything." Miss Bingley seemed to have recovered, and her impertinence had not diminished in the slightest.

"Then perhaps a longer visit or a second one was required, Caroline," said Mr. Bingley with a sharp tone and an unflinching glare at his sister.

"Mr. and Mrs. Gardiner, Miss Bennet, would you like a short tour of the house until dinner is ready? I would be happy to accompany you." Mr. Darcy's intervention was sudden but welcome. Besides being genuinely interested in seeing as much of Pemberley as possible, Elizabeth was also anxious to take a short break from Miss Bingley's company.

"Georgiana, you may go, too, if you like. I will remain here with Mr. Bingley and his relatives." Lady Cassandra settled things with a determination that admitted no opposition, and Elizabeth noticed that Mr. Darcy thanked his friend with a small smile of gratitude.

Mr. Darcy offered his arm to Elizabeth, and she took it with confidence.

The tour was brief as they visited only the rooms opened for guests, but it gave them immense pleasure.

At one point, an enormous window displayed the beauty of the landscape around the house, and Elizabeth unconsciously released Mr. Darcy's arm and walked near the window to admire the prospect. The hill, crowned with wood from which they had descended and receiving increased abruptness from the distance, was a beautiful object. Every disposition of the ground was good, and she looked on the whole scene — the river, the trees scattered on its banks, and the winding of the valley as far as she could trace it — with delight, a deep sigh of admiration escaping her lips.

"It is beautiful, is it not?" She heard the master's soft whisper just behind her as he gazed over her shoulder, admiring the same sight. She could feel the heat of his body close to her and his breath warming the nape of her neck. She only nodded without turning to him; in a moment, his hand gently touched her arm. "We should go and catch the others; I think Georgiana already directed them to the music room."

Indeed, her relatives and Miss Darcy were in the music room where the young lady was showing them the piano her brother had just presented to her for her sixteenth birthday. It was at that moment that Mrs. Reynolds entered to announce that dinner was ready.

"Miss Bennet, have you decided about your schedule tomorrow?" asked Mr. Darcy in a low voice as they returned to the dining room.

"Yes, we have, sir. My uncle will come to Pemberley to join you for fishing in the morning, and then my aunt and I will come to meet Miss Darcy around noon. Afterwards, my aunt and uncle will return to Lambton as they have a few calls to pay."

"And will you return with them?" His voice became deeper as his head slightly lowered to her.

"It depends on Miss Darcy. If she wants me to remain, I may stay until late afternoon." She felt herself blushing and did not dare to meet his eyes.

"I am sure she will want you to stay as long as possible, as will I." She stopped breathing; yes — he had said it, aloud and quite clearly.

Elizabeth was certain her cheeks were crimson when they entered the dining room, and she felt all eyes on her. Yet again, she cared little for the others' opinions. Only *one* opinion mattered to her — *his* opinion — and it was clearly in her favour.

The dinner was a mostly pleasant affair until Lady Cassandra, in the middle of a casual conversation, unexpectedly addressed Elizabeth.

"Miss Bennet, I was talking to Mr. Bingley about Hertfordshire a few days ago, and he mentioned to me he would like to return there but was uncertain whether that would be wise of him. Is it not so, Mr. Bingley?"

"Yes — we were talking of that very subject! Indeed, I have considered returning to Netherfield if... I mean, I was wondering whether I should."

Elizabeth, incredulous, gaped at him, and then her gaze moved to Lady Cassandra, who had initiated the conversation.

"So, Miss Bennet, as you are obviously the one in possession of the most pertinent information — what would you advise Mr. Bingley? Should he return, do you think?"

Elizabeth's head was spinning as she was still afraid to hope or presume too much. She breathed deeply, looking once more at Lady Cassandra, who was watching her with an unreadable expression on her face, and then to Mr. Bingley, whose eagerness was apparent. Well, he had asked for her opinion, so she would give it to him — straight and honest.

"Mr. Bingley, I think your return to Netherfield would be welcomed by all your neighbours *if your intentions are clear* and you plan to remain longer than a few months. However, if you intend to return for a brief time, then perhaps it would be better for the estate to be left in the care of a gentleman who would give it the required care and attention."

She knew she had said too much; it was not proper to give such a direct answer. However, to her utter relief, Mr. Bingley's face lightened instantly. "Thank you, Miss Bennet. I shall write to my steward to prepare the house for my return as soon as may be. And this time I intend to remain *as long as necessary.*"

"Well, well. I have always admired a determined gentleman." Lady Cassandra laughed, and Elizabeth joined her. Then Elizabeth lowered her head imperceptibly toward her ladyship and whispered a barely audible, *"Thank you."* Her ladyship nodded slightly then changed the topic instantly, asking Elizabeth what she liked most of all the places she had seen during her tour.

The rest of the evening passed in pleasant conversation. Miss Darcy and Elizabeth planned a ride in the carriage through the grounds, and Lady Cassandra mentioned that she might join them at some point on horseback. Mr. Bingley's sisters would never consider such a way of amusing themselves, and nobody tried to change their opinion.

An hour later, the guests took their leave. Mr. Darcy offered his arm to Elizabeth, and they walked at a slow pace a little behind the others through the impressive halls. The sky was dark, and Pemberley's yard was lit by numerous torches; a brisk breeze cooled the warm air of the July night and played with a lock of hair on her neck. Elizabeth shuddered as she breathed deeply and closed her eyes to enjoy the moment.

"Miss Bennet, are you cold?"

"No, I am not cold at all, sir. I am just happy," she answered impetuously. She felt him growing steadily tense, and he stopped. Mortified, she stopped as well, as did her breath. Her eyes remained fixed somewhere in front of them where her relatives were chatting animatedly. He was silent.

Trembling, Elizabeth felt his hand taking hers from his arm and lifting it briefly to his lips. She was not certain whether his lips actually touched her gloved fingers or she merely dreamt it. However, of two things she was absolutely certain: his hand remained upon hers until they reached the others, and his touch was still burning her hours later in her small room at the inn.

Chapter 6

Darcy followed the carriage with a yearning gaze long after it disappeared from view. The night became cold. *He* felt cold when she was gone.

Now that she had been there and left, he became more certain than ever of his need for her presence. Fortunately, he finally had reason to hope: she told him she was happy to be at Pemberley — perhaps happy to be with him, too. Indeed, she looked delighted, especially when she spent time in front of the window simply admiring the grounds.

When he entered the drawing room, the first thing that crossed his mind was to find an excuse and retire to his apartment. He wanted simply to lie in his bed and think of Elizabeth. He wondered where Georgiana planned to take Elizabeth for their walk; his sister had been quite secretive as she confessed she wanted to spend some *undisturbed* time with Elizabeth, and he knew well which the possible disturbances were.

"How very ill Eliza Bennet looked this morning, Mr. Darcy," cried Miss Bingley the moment he poured himself a glass of wine and took a seat.

Speaking of disturbances, he thought, unconsciously rolling his eyes.

Miss Bingley continued impassively: "I never in my life saw anyone so much altered as she is since the winter. She has grown so brown and coarse! Louisa and I were agreeing that we should not have known her again."

However little Darcy liked her ridiculous statement, he remained calm, content with coolly replying that he perceived no other alteration than her being rather tanned — no miraculous consequence of travelling in the summer.

"I think Miss Bennet has looked quite well every time I have met her," Lady Cassandra interjected. "She is indeed one of those ladies whose natural charm needs little adjustment to be very agreeable. I can understand why both Darcy and Georgiana seem to approve of her so much."

"Oh, Mr. Darcy did not approve so of Miss Bennet in the past, as I well remember. He shared his opinion of her long ago when we were at Netherfield," said Miss Bingley, looking at the named gentleman. She saw him somewhat nettled, and she

82

considered she had all the success she expected. Darcy remained resolutely silent, however, and she continued: "I remember, when we first knew her in Hertfordshire, how amazed we all were to find that she was a reputed beauty, and I particularly recollect your saying one night, Mr. Darcy, after they had been dining at Netherfield, *'She a beauty! I should as soon call her mother a wit.'* But afterwards she seemed to improve on you, and I believe you thought her rather pretty at one time."

"Yes," replied Darcy, who could contain himself no longer, "but that was only when I first knew Miss Elizabeth; for it is many months since I have considered her one of the handsomest women of my acquaintance."

Miss Bingley blinked repeatedly as she could not believe the gentleman's words. Allowing no misunderstanding, he continued. "It is also many months since I understood how wrong I was in hastily judging not only Miss Elizabeth but many other things during our stay in Hertfordshire. I will make sure never to repeat such a grave mistake again."

His last words were spoken in a severe tone that admitted no reply, while his gaze, which lay upon Miss Bingley for a moment, showed no warmth or cordiality. Miss Bingley remained strangely silent for the rest of the evening. His response gave no one any pain but herself — pain, rage and the strongest desire of never seeing Miss Bennet again, even at the risk of having Mr. Darcy married to Lady Cassandra. After all, being defeated by her ladyship was considerably less humiliating than being defeated by Eliza Bennet.

IT WAS A LITTLE BEFORE noon that Elizabeth and Mrs. Gardiner descended in front of Pemberley. A strange sensation of peaceful bliss brought a smile to Elizabeth's face as she admired the beauties around her.

A servant showed them in to where the other ladies were expecting them. Half an hour was spent in pleasant conversation — mostly between Lady Cassandra and Mrs. Gardiner. Miss Darcy whispered to Elizabeth a couple of times about how anxious she was to spend the afternoon together. It was not difficult for Elizabeth to notice that Miss Bingley and Mrs. Hurst were even less friendly than the previous day, and they seemed unpleasantly impressed by the obvious closeness between her and Georgiana.

Less than half an hour later, Mr. and Mrs. Gardiner departed as they were expected to make a few calls. Mr. Darcy promised to take care of Elizabeth's being sent under proper escort to the inn later that day; he expressed his hopes of their all being reunited at Pemberley in the evening.

Elizabeth knew little about how Miss Darcy intended to spend their day together or who else would attend them; so, when her hostess invited her on a long walk around the grounds, she accepted with pleasure. She only hoped neither Miss Bingley nor Mrs. Hurst would be tempted to join them.

Miss Bingley clearly expressed her disapproval at the mere idea of walking a great distance rather than taking a phaeton, especially considering the sky was cloudy and there was the possibility of rain. Mr. Bingley quickly contradicted his sister, insisting the beauties of Pemberley were better enjoyed on foot, and he expressed his hope that the young ladies would have a wonderful time. His sisters, however, seemed to ignore what little he said.

"Dear Georgiana, you should be careful how far you go. As for Miss Bennet, she is well known to be an excellent walker, despite the weather. I remember how surprised we were when she appeared one morning at Netherfield after walking three miles on a muddy road. I have always wondered how she managed to walk so far with all that mud on her shoes and petticoat. Mr. Darcy, you remember that, I am sure."

Elizabeth blushed lightly at the obvious offense. She cast a quick glance at the others, noticing Mrs. Hurst's satisfied smirk and Lady Cassandra's frown of displeasure. Miss Darcy's face was crimson; Mr. Darcy's countenance darkened.

"Indeed, Miss Bingley. I vividly remember how impressed I was with Miss Bennet's courage and concern for her sister's well being."

"Perhaps," insisted Miss Bingley, with a sharp voice and a meaningful look to Mrs. Hurst, "but you also agreed you would not want to see Miss Darcy in such a state."

Caroline Bingley's attempt to show Elizabeth in an unfavourable light began to irritate her; before saying anything, though, she looked again at Mr. Darcy. His face, vaguely pale, made it clear to her that Miss Bingley's recollections were likely true.

Trying to put aside any doubts, the gentleman answered soundly, "You are correct, Miss Bingley. I did unwisely declare that I would not want to see Georgiana in such a state. However, what I did *not* declare at that time was that I would wish for Georgiana to have a sister who cared for her as much as Miss Elizabeth cared for Miss Bennet."

Elizabeth felt all the blood drain from her face. Did he realise what he was saying in front of all these people? She dared look at him only a moment; his slightly embarrassed expression and the uncertainty in his eyes proved to her that he knew very well the meaning of his words. She became dizzy.

"Miss Bennet, so — how did you come to walk three miles with your shoes and petticoat full of mud?" asked Lady Cassandra, and then she suddenly turned to Miss Bingley, adding, "By the by, Miss Bingley, as I told you last night, your perception amazes me again. I never look at a lady's shoes or petticoats, no matter the situation. I must be more attentive in the future."

Elizabeth could barely contain a chuckle as she struggled to regain her composure and answer her ladyship coherently.

"My sister Jane, who was visiting Miss Bingley and Mrs. Hurst, was caught in the rain and fell ill; she sent me a note saying she needed my presence, and since I am not much of a horsewoman and our carriage was not available at the moment, I had no other option."

"I see. I have to agree with Darcy; that seems very courageous and caring of you. I am sure the goodness of your reason can excuse the poor state of your gown. And I dare say you would walk three miles for Georgiana, too, if necessary." Her words shocked Elizabeth as they were an obvious extension of the idea of Georgiana having a sister. While she desperately sought a proper answer, Lady Cassandra rose from her seat.

"Now, if you will excuse me, I should go and prepare myself for riding. Darcy, please do not leave without me. I shall be ready in half an hour."

She walked to the door, but after only a few steps, Miss Bingley's voice stopped her.

"Lady Cassandra, do you plan to go riding with Mr. Darcy?"

"Yes, I do. Why do you ask, Miss Bingley?"

"I...but I thought — I remember Mr. Darcy mentioning it would be a full hour of riding."

"And? What is your point?" Lady Cassandra was growing impatient; it was obvious that she was close to the edge of her tolerance.

"I was only wondering whether it would be wise for you to ride such a long way alone with Mr. Darcy. I mean people could talk and..."

Lady Cassandra cast a quick glance at Darcy and then at Elizabeth and Georgiana before she turned to Miss Bingley, smiling with apparent warmth.

"Miss Bingley, I thank you for your considerate care, but I am an excellent rider. As for the impropriety of riding alone with Darcy, what harm can there be? In the worst case scenario, he would have to marry me, which is not at all an unpleasant prospect, would you not agree?"

She lrft the room without further delay while Miss Bingley stared at the door, so pale that Elizabeth was certain she might faint. Obviously sharing the same impression, Mr. Bingley offered his sister a glass of water or wine, but she, again, did not hear him.

MISS DARCY SEEMED HAPPIER THAN Elizabeth had ever seen her. A servant brought them a basket with some cold refreshment and a rolled blanket, so Elizabeth understood her friend had also planned a little picnic. Miss Darcy's exuberance was contagious, and Elizabeth made every effort to match her delight.

"I see you are ready to leave." Mr. Darcy's voice startled Elizabeth, and she forced a weak smile, trying to regain her composure.

"Yes, we are, brother," replied Georgiana.

"I also see you are prepared for a picnic. May I inquire where you plan to go?"

Miss Darcy hesitated a moment, and her expression changed vaguely as she looked soundly at her brother. "I was planning to take Elizabeth to Sunny Grove. I hope you approve."

Mr. Darcy's expression changed in an instant. The siblings silently looked at one another intently, and Elizabeth began to worry that a simple walk could affect them so.

Then the gentleman's face lit up, and a smile spread over it, warming his features. "I do approve; I think it is an excellent idea. In fact, as I have not visited that area in a great while, would you allow me to accompany you until Lady Cassandra is ready for our ride?"

"Oh, brother, that would be wonderful! Thank you!" She had regained all her enthusiasm while her beautiful eyes brightened with happiness. Then she remembered her manners and turned to Elizabeth. "Elizabeth, forgive me for not asking you. I hope you do not mind."

Elizabeth did not mind at all — quite the opposite. To hide her nervousness, she tried to reply in jest with a light tone. "Dear Georgiana, how could I mind that the master of the house offers to carry our baskets? And even if I did mind, how could I dare admit it while I am on his grounds?"

Georgiana laughed, and Elizabeth glanced at the gentleman to see how her teasing affected him. He was smiling — not an open smile but a barely noticeable one — as his eyes fixed on hers; however, he said nothing, only took the basket and the blanket and motioned for them to precede him.

They walked less than ten minutes before they reached a lake, quite large and seemingly deep as well. Miss Darcy took Elizabeth's arm and directed her toward a footbridge.

"We have to pass over here. My father ordered this bridge built a long time ago, and it is quite safe; if we make a detour around the lake, it would be at least an hour-long walk."

Elizabeth returned Georgiana's smile as she following the young lady across the narrow bridge. "Well, if you say it is quite safe, how could I contradict you?"

They reached the other side and waited for Mr. Darcy to join them. The footbridge seemed to be violently swaying under the gentleman's weight, and Elizabeth frowned. Miss Darcy laughed while whispering to her, "Do not worry. Even if the bridge should break and William should fall in the water, nothing bad would happen; he is an excellent swimmer."

Elizabeth nodded in mortification as her thoughts suddenly formed an image of Mr. Darcy swimming in the lake. In order to hide her crimson cheeks, she averted her eyes from the gentleman and asked her friend how long it would be before they reached their destination?

"Only ten more minutes. Are you tired?"

"No, not at all — quite the contrary."

They walked at a slower pace through a small wood on a high hill; it was a pleasant day — not too warm as the sky was slightly clouded and a cool breeze was gently blowing. From time to time, Elizabeth stopped and turned to appreciate the view of Pemberley House before continuing to walk; then she would again turn to look at the valley and the beautiful home. Her companions only smiled at each other.

Suddenly, Elizabeth froze. In the middle of the wood, some of the trees formed a perfect square the size of a spacious ballroom; their fronds and the grass were glowing, highlighted by the warm rays of sunshine. She gasped, breathless, and moved to the middle of the square, spinning around as if to catch every spot of light; finally, after some moments of silent bliss, she turned to her companions: "Sunny Grove."

"Yes, this is the place," answered Miss Darcy, emotion hardly allowing her to speak.

"Beautiful. Perfect," whispered Elizabeth as she lifted her eyes to the sky. In that solitary place, the sun seemed determined to appear from behind the clouds and shine upon the grove.

"I am pleased you enjoy the place, Miss Bennet," said Mr. Darcy after he put the basket down and arranged the blanket. She turned to him and smiled with delight.

"How could I not enjoy it, sir? Was there ever anyone who did not enjoy all this beauty?"

He seemed suddenly uneasy, averted his eyes from her a moment, and then turned to her again. "I could not say. We do love this place very much, and so did my parents. As for others... We have never brought anyone here; it is a private place, meant for the family alone."

Elizabeth felt her strength leave her as her knees seemed unable to bear her weight. Was he upset that Georgiana had brought her here to invade the privacy of their special place? The siblings' eyes were still fixed on each other, and she hoped she was correct in assuming he was not displeased. As if guessing her thoughts, he spoke again, his voice warm and gentle.

"I am pleased that my sister decided to come here, and I hope you will have a wonderful time together. I am sorry I cannot remain in your company longer. However, I am sure we will have another opportunity quite soon."

Before Elizabeth could regain her composure, he took his leave; her eyes followed him until he disappeared from view. Her attention returned to the present when Miss Darcy's voice invited her to sit and asked if she would like some refreshments.

For a few minutes, they talked of their surroundings and the weather, trying tentatively to establish a subject of conversation agreeable to both.

"Georgiana, thank you for your kindness and your trust in bringing me to this place that is so special to you."

"You are very welcome. I knew you would like it as much as we do." She paused a moment, searching for words, obviously struggling to say something more. "But Elizabeth, I have to confess I have a selfish reason for bringing you here, too. I needed your strength and encouragement to supply my lack of courage, as I have not dared to come here alone." She turned her head, but a moment was enough for Elizabeth to notice tears shining in her friend's eyes.

"Georgiana, what is the matter? Why are you upset?"

"Oh, it is nothing… Please forgive me for disturbing you. I promised you a lovely day, and I intend to keep my promise." She forced a smile, wiping her eyes with her hands. Elizabeth took her hand.

"My dear, I cannot imagine a more pleasant manner in which to spend this day than to talk to you about anything you want."

"Thank you. You are the kindest person I have ever met."

"No, I am not," laughed Elizabeth. "Quite the contrary. I am only fortunate to have gained your good opinion, so you are very partial to me."

Miss Darcy laughed, too, and then looked around them for a few moments in silent contemplation. "My brother tells me my parents used to take us here often. I cannot remember because I was only three when my mother passed away. When I was seven, William brought me here again, and I recognised this place as being very dear to me."

"How lovely!"

"Yes… Since that day, we would come here at least once a week, no matter the season. This place is as sunny in winter, spring or autumn as in summer."

"I can imagine how wonderful it must be when it is snowing."

"Yes, it is wonderful." The girl smiled with delight, but then she frowned again. "My father refused to join us…until the summer when he was very ill and demanded that William bring him here. The doctors decidedly opposed it, but my brother obeyed his request; my father refused to leave here for an entire day. He asked me to stay with him, and he spoke to me about my mother for hours." She paused as the tears flowed over her cheeks, and Elizabeth wiped them gently away with her handkerchief. "A week later my father died…" She struggled against her emotions with no success. Elizabeth moved closer and embraced her, caressing her hair.

"Please forgive me, Elizabeth," whispered Georgiana when she finally stopped crying.

"My dear, please do not apologise. There is nothing to forgive."

"Yes there is! There are many things for which I have to apologise. If you only knew how silly I acted and how badly I betrayed my brother's confidence, you would not be so kind to me. It was my behaviour that forced William not to come to this place last year, and he likely would not come now if not for you."

Elizabeth blushed again while she tried to smile and caressed her friend's hand. "Oh, I think you are too harsh on yourself and give me much more credit than I deserve."

"No, I am not. I know the truth of what I am saying. I almost ruined myself and my family name last year with my inconsiderate behaviour. I grieved and disappointed my brother. I do not deserve his forgiveness." Elizabeth's worry turned into distress as she could easily guess the reason for the girl's disturbance and desperately wondered how to react. Should she confess that she knew about Ramsgate? Would that be a betrayal of Mr. Darcy's confidence in her?

"Georgiana, from what I have witnessed every time I was in your company, I am convinced beyond any doubt that your brother has nothing but the deepest affection and love for you."

"Yes, he is the kindest and best brother anyone could hope for, but if you had seen him last summer — his pain, his sadness. It breaks my heart when I remember. I have suffered so much more for him than for myself. Then we were separated for a few months, and he started writing to me several times a week as he did when I was at school. I was so happy! When we met again last December, I could easily see he was not yet well. He always looked preoccupied — distracted — but he seemed to enjoy my company. We used to talk and walk through the park; sometimes we would read together. I played the instrument for him every evening, but then…"

Elizabeth struggled to find a way of stopping the confession, as the grief obviously was too much for Georgiana to bear. However, before Elizabeth could say a word, the girl resumed her tale. "Then I remained alone to spend Easter with my relatives — the Fitzwilliams — and my brother left for Rosings as is his habit every year. When he returned… Oh, Elizabeth, if you had seen him then!" The tears that threatened were flowing freely down Georgiana's face; Elizabeth's eyes were filling, too, as she fought in vain to comfort her friend and hide her own torment.

"For a whole week he barely spoke to anyone. I did not dare confront him, but I begged him a thousand times to tell me how I could help him. Of course, I could not possibly help him in any way as clearly his pain was caused by my behaviour."

"That cannot be, Georgiana! You said you were not even with Mr. Darcy during that time!"

"Yes, but the consequences of my actions remained! I almost eloped with a man who cared nothing for me and wanted only to take advantage of my silliness — and of course my dowry — to take revenge on William. Something must have reminded him of it while he was in Kent, which brought him to that state. If you knew, Elizabeth… He barely left his room, and when he did, he secluded himself in the library; he never joined me for either breakfast or dinner. In fact, I think he barely ate anything; he only drank and demanded silence and solitude."

Elizabeth gasped and covered her mouth with her hand, and Georgiana, startled, then added in a great hurry, "Oh, please do not presume William became so drunken as to lose his mind. He is not that kind of man! But he was drinking excessively and rarely ate anything, and he hardly ever slept! I could hear him walking through the house in the middle of the night and could not bring myself to sleep either. I knew not what to do. I asked my cousin David's help, but for some reason, William refused to talk to him either. So I wrote to Cassandra. She was my last hope."

Georgiana paused again and breathed deeply a few times without looking at Elizabeth. She kept her eyes fixed on a tree in front of them and continued her tale. "Cassandra was in Paris but returned immediately. She arrived in the middle of the night; we talked for more than an hour. I remember crying the whole time. Then she suddenly left me and dashed into William's room. I followed her to his study but did not dare to go further. I could hear their voices. They talked calmly at first; then they fought. I could hear Cassandra yelling at him and then his angry voice. They argued for such a long time, and then everything was quiet, and I could barely hear them speaking. It was almost dawn when Cassandra came out, and she looked so distressed, so sad. She said I did the best thing in writing her. She was so kind, so loving to me. She remained with us that night and the following week. The next day, William slept until nearly dinnertime. Can you imagine? Cassandra sent a tray of food to his room, but he did not eat much. So she sent the tray back to him and threatened that she would have the servants tie him up, and she would force-feed him with her own hands." Georgiana started to laugh — a nervous, liberating laugh — but Elizabeth had no strength to join in her amusement.

"Can you imagine, Elizabeth? William tied up and Cassandra feeding him? The next day she demanded he join us for dinner or else she would move the dinner table into his room and we would all eat there with him — so he finally came down to join us."

She laughed again, this time turning her eyes to Elizabeth, and gasped at seeing her white face.

"Oh, my dear Elizabeth, I am so sorry! Please forgive me! I have been so selfish to take advantage of your friendship and burden you so! I have certainly ruined your day completely."

Elizabeth could bear it no longer. "Georgiana, please stop and allow me to speak now. I am afraid you will not be so willing to call me your friend when I finish."

The young girl frowned, staring inquiringly and incredulously at her. "Georgiana, all this time you have tormented and blamed yourself for no reason. It was *I* who brought so much distress to Mr. Darcy, though I never could have imagined something would happen as you just described. I could not have imagined our *dispute* would affect him so much."

"You? I do not understand, Elizabeth. How can that be? My brother has spoken so highly of you since the beginning of your acquaintance. He never mentioned any disagreement between you."

"Oh, but there have been many disagreements between us. In fact, Mr. Darcy and I misunderstood each other completely for months. We came to realise that when we met again in Kent. Did your brother not mention to you that we met last April in Kent?"

"Yes, he wrote me from Rosings and informed me you were visiting your cousin and his wife."

"So it was. Then one day Mr. Darcy and I had a grave quarrel, and though I remain convinced that my decision at the time was correct, I now deeply regret it, mostly because of my own faults and shortcomings. We both said things that never should have been said. Only the next day did I come to understand how wrong my opinion had been and how unfair I had been in my judgement. Even worse, I foolishly trusted another man's lies about your brother, which I had angrily thrown in his face during our argument. What do you think of me now?"

A lump in her throat made her voice tremble. She felt Georgiana gently squeezing her hands; only then did she notice that her hands were trembling, too. "Elizabeth, I cannot understand. You said you were correct in your decision. *What* decision? And how did you come to quarrel so violently with my brother? Were you alone?"

"Georgiana, please do not be upset with me, but I cannot offer you more details, at least not at the moment."

"I see…" The girl's tone was different and so was the glare she fixed upon Elizabeth. "But if your quarrel was the reason for my brother's distress, how was it possible that he kept you in such high esteem? After he somehow regained his old spirit, he used to mention your name quite a lot, but he never spoke one unkind word about you. When we met that day in the park, I am certain he was pleased to see you. Even more so, he has encouraged me to become your friend. He certainly would not have done that if he did not think highly of you. How can that be?"

"I really do not know, Georgiana. I confess I was certain that, were Mr. Darcy and I ever to meet again, he would avoid me as his worst enemy. I never dared to imagine he would be so kind and friendly toward me, especially after what transpired between us in Kent."

"I see…" Georgiana rose from the blanket and started to pace the grove. Elizabeth followed with her eyes, suddenly feeling cold; she shivered and wrapped her arms around herself.

Finally, the girl returned to the blanket, sat down again, and then asked in a tone that demanded straight answers, "Elizabeth, can you at least tell me who the man was you trusted against my brother?"

She hesitated only a moment. "Mr. Wickham."

Georgiana immediately turned pale but did not seem surprised. "I suspected as much. My brother told me he was in Hertfordshire, and I guessed it could not have been a coincidence. Maligning William's name seems very much like Mr. Wickham. He is also the man I told you about, but I am certain you already knew that."

"I did. Mr. Darcy trusted me with this revelation when we were in Kent."

"Why did you not tell me? Why did you allow me to speak as if it were a secret just revealed?"

"Because I felt you needed to free yourself of this burden. Then, during your confession, I could not find the proper moment or the proper way to tell you what I already knew."

"I see…" she repeated, a stern expression on her face. Miss Darcy seemed sadly to have aged several years in a few minutes. "Elizabeth, you said you cannot tell me much about your disagreement with my brother, but I confess that, after everything you told me, I have strong suspicions about the nature of your quarrel. May I ask you another question? I know it is highly improper, and you may feel free not to answer; I would not mind."

"Of course, please ask me. I would not mind either."

"What is your opinion of my brother now?"

Elizabeth needed a few moments before she felt comfortable enough to answer. "I think he is among the best men I have ever known."

Miss Darcy smiled meaningfully. "Well, that is what *I* would say about my brother. I was wondering if you could say something more."

A deafening thunderclap startled them and made them both scream. Only then did they notice the dark clouds that had covered the sky and the wind that started to blow furiously.

Suddenly, a cold darkness and fierce rain fell all around them. Georgiana shouted something, but another clap of thunder muffled her voice. Instantly, Elizabeth grabbed the blanket and took Georgiana's hand, forcing her to move under a bushy tree. Elizabeth pulled the girl close to her, trying to find a poor shelter under the soaked blanket, watching with horror as the rain violently turned to hail. The sky was streaked with flashes while the sound of hail and thunder made Georgiana tremble. "Elizabeth, what can we do?" she cried, her voice barely audible.

Elizabeth knew not what to answer; the tree offered them some protection against the hail, but not for long. Branches began to fall, breaking around them, and Elizabeth lifted her eyes, desperately trying to see something — to discover a new place or a new shelter — with no success.

She was certain her senses betrayed her a few moments later when the silhouettes of two horses moved through the curtain of rain and Mr. Darcy's voice called to them.

Less than a moment later, Mr. Darcy dismounted together with Lady Cassandra and moved toward them.

"We must leave immediately," cried Lady Cassandra.

"We have to go on horseback around the lake," added Mr. Darcy, and Elizabeth struggled to understand his meaning.

With little patience, Lady Cassandra grabbed Georgiana's hand. "Pull your dress up, and let us go, now!"

Elizabeth watched as Georgiana lifted her dress and mounted straight, as a man, with Lady Cassandra behind her in the same manner. A moment later, their horse disappeared from sight, and Elizabeth turned her eyes, frightened and mortified, to the gentleman. Surely, he could not ask her to do the same. He suddenly unsaddled the horse, keeping only the bridle. Then he leaned toward Elizabeth and spoke in her ear so she could hear him.

"Now we can go, too. Miss Bennet; we must hurry." She looked at him wide-eyed and tried to explain she could not possibly ride in such weather on an unsaddled horse.

"We must leave now," he repeated, as another thunderclap made the animal nervous and restless.

She remembered little of the next moments. She was only aware of being lifted and placed on the back of the horse, both legs dangling over one side, with Darcy's body close behind her. She felt she was sliding down and unable to stop her fall, but his right hand embraced and supported her back while his left hand rested on her thighs around her waist, pulling her forcefully and protectively against him as he grabbed the reins.

His hands seemed to burn her though the thin, soaked fabric, and she felt herself quivering. Lightning and thunder frightened the horse; he bucked and then ran wildly; she cried and her hands entwined desperately around Darcy's waist, her legs pressed against his inner thighs. He somehow managed to calm the animal, which continued to run steadily. The rain was whipping Elizabeth's face, but she was too scared and overwhelmed by the novelty of her sensations to feel the cold. Suddenly, he removed her hands from him, opened his large gray coat and pulled Elizabeth closer as her arms found their own way back around his waist. Then he gathered the side of his coat together to protect her from the rain as much as possible. Without thinking, she allowed her head to rest on his chest. She sensed him breathing deeply, and then his hands tightened their grip around her, almost crushing her against him.

Instantly the storm around them lost significance and vanished from her mind. Elizabeth was no longer frightened or cold; she felt safer and warmer than ever before.

Chapter 7

Elizabeth could not be certain how long they rode through the rain. All she knew and all she wished was that the peaceful happiness around her would never end. Yet end it did; the horses stopped, and she was pulled away from him — from the warmth and security of his arms — and down from the horse. She heard Mrs. Reynolds give quick orders as two maids accompanied her upstairs in a great hurry.

In a few minutes, she was inside a room, and before she could recover completely, she was undressed and in a tub of hot water; one of the maids handed her a cup of tea. Elizabeth inquired after Miss Darcy and Lady Cassandra. On being told they were both very well, she sighed in relief.

As she slid deeper into the tub, her thoughts went to Georgiana. The recollection of their conversation was still vivid; her regretful torment over the effects of her refusal on both Darcys was matched only by her worry over Georgiana's present state. She wondered how the girl would behave now that she knew the truth. Would she still consider her a friend? Just before the storm, they had been affable enough, yet Elizabeth knew that her young friend might reconsider their talk in the days that followed, and she might change her opinion completely. However, not for a moment did she regret having confessed the truth; it was unbearable that Georgiana had suffered and blamed herself unjustly all those months.

The maid invited her out of the bath. A friendly fire warmed the room, and though she was no longer cold, she climbed into bed, pulling the covers around her.

She heard a knock at the door, and there was barely time to issue an invitation before Lady Cassandra barged into the room, followed closely by another maid.

"Miss Bennet, I hope you are well."

"Yes, your ladyship, I am very well, thank you. I was told that Georgiana is well, too?"

"Yes she is; I just saw her. She inquired after you, but we convinced her to have hot tea and remain in bed for another hour, as should you. Darcy decided to delay dinner so both of you could rest a little if you feel inclined to join us."

"Mr. Darcy has been most considerate, but I will not be able to join you for dinner; my…my clothes are unwearable, and I do not have others."

"Yes, I thought as much. In fact, I would have found it quite strange if you had dresses to change into here at Pemberley, especially in this room, which is part of the family wing." She laughed, obviously amused by the idea, while Elizabeth's cheeks coloured. "That is precisely why I take the liberty of offering to lend you some of my nightgowns and dresses, so you may choose an appropriate one for tonight."

Elizabeth could not hide her surprise at this unexpected civility as the maid placed three dresses on the bed. For a moment, she considered refusing but instantly realised the absurdity of such behaviour.

"Thank you, your ladyship; that is very kind and considerate of you. I will accept with pleasure, though I have to confess it is difficult to decide. All three are beautiful."

"Yes, they are, but I would suggest the pale pink one. I believe it would fit you quite well."

Elizabeth was not sure whether she should be amused or offended by her ladyship's attitude; she wisely decided to incline toward amusement.

She turned to the aforementioned gown as the maid spread it over the bed so she could better admire it. To Elizabeth, the dresses would have been more fitting for a ball; however, to avoid a new debate, she accepted it with as much politeness as gratitude.

Her ladyship looked pleased. "I shall leave you now so you may prepare yourself. My maid will help you with your hair. 'Til later, Miss Bennet," she said, not even waiting for a reply.

Elizabeth sighed and rolled her eyes, shaking her head in mock exasperation. She felt treated like a child in a manner that blended her mother's style with that of Lady Catherine. The combination sounded so diverting that she began to laugh, wondering what Lady Cassandra would say if she voiced the thought aloud.

In less than half an hour, Elizabeth was dressed and her hair masterfully arranged. Though she knew that dinner would be served later, Elizabeth had no patience for remaining within her room. The rain was still striking wildly on her windows, and she moved closer to look outside.

The sound of the storm brought to her mind the memories — embarrassing and impossible to reveal — of her ride with Mr. Darcy. Now that the danger was past and she did not need his protective care any longer, his gestures, his mere closeness, and his strong body near hers aroused different feelings: feelings she had never experienced before, feelings similar to that quivering sensation she had experienced when he touched her hand — yet more compelling and frightening. His hands had pressed against her back, around her waist, and against her legs to prevent her from falling from the bareback horse, his wet shirt unable to diminish the warmth of his body, his thighs trapping her in their grasp —

The sudden opening of the door startled her as Lady Cassandra entered impetuously and then stopped and searched her face. "Miss Bennet, are you well? You look a little flushed; I hope you are not feverish."

"No, no — I am well, thank you. I was only deep in thought and did not hear your ladyship entering —"

"Oh, I am sorry. I did knock, you know."

"I am certain you did, Lady Cassandra. Please forgive me for my lack of attention. I am ready to go downstairs, but I was wondering about Georgiana. Is she still in her room, do you know?"

"Yes, she is still in bed. I am afraid she will catch a cold, and we tried to convince her to stay in her room, but she seemed determined to join us for dinner. Perhaps you will be more successful in changing her mind."

"I shall try, but I am inclined to believe that Miss Darcy can be very determined when she chooses." Elizabeth was not at all certain how much Miss Darcy would welcome her interference.

With no little surprise, Elizabeth discovered that Miss Darcy's apartment was only two doors from her room in "the family wing" she remembered as she felt her cheeks burning again.

Miss Darcy was already awake and dressed. At Elizabeth's entrance, she dismissed the servant and invited her in. After a moment of awkward silence, Miss Darcy moved closer to Elizabeth and took her hand daringly, though her trembling voice betrayed her distress. "Elizabeth, thank you."

"Why do you thank me, Georgiana? I have done nothing except take advantage of your servants and Lady Cassandra's new dress."

"I remember perfectly well how you took care of me, Elizabeth, how you tried to protect me from the hail...and all that after I had been so impolite to you. I spoke harshly, and yet you answered me kindly —"

"Georgiana, there is nothing for which you need thank me. I beg you; let us not talk of it ever again. As for your being impolite to me, let me assure you that I treasure every moment we spend together. I am happy and relieved that we talked — that you trusted me enough to have such a conversation."

Miss Darcy attempted to answer, but Elizabeth tightened the grip on her hands and shook her head. "Dearest, your hands are warm; you seem to have a little fever. Should you not stay in bed tonight?"

"You and Cassandra are plotting against me, I am certain of it. But I assure you I feel very well indeed, and I want to join you downstairs. I promise I will drink at least two more cups of Mrs. Reynolds' miraculous tea — just in case. Is that acceptable?" After a few more minutes of negotiation, Miss Darcy won, but only after she promised that, as soon as she felt tired, she would retire with no thought of her duties as hostess.

"WELL, I WOULD NOT BE surprised if dear Georgiana had caught a cold. I tried to warn you earlier today, but of course nobody listened. Eliza Bennet is well accustomed to walking, and of course, she gave no consideration to Georgiana's delicate constitution. She dragged her through the storm, exposing her to danger —"

Mr. Bingley tried to make his sister see reason. "Oh come now, Caroline, that is absurd! Surely, Miss Bennet did not drag Miss Darcy through the storm! From what she told us this morning, it was Miss Darcy who fixed their plans. How could either of them know a storm would come?"

They had gathered in the parlour — both Bingley siblings and Mr. Hurst — for more than an hour, waiting for their hosts to join them, when a servant had informed them about the extraordinary escapade of Miss Darcy and Miss Bennet.

"Of course it was Eliza's fault; I have not the smallest doubt. I have been an intimate friend of dear Georgiana for many years and never have ventured out through the woods with her in the middle of a rainstorm. So it must be Eliza Bennet's doing."

"In fact, Mr. Bingley is correct. Miss Bennet did not drag anyone anywhere. Quite the contrary," Lady Cassandra interrupted; she had entered unnoticed and now was walking impetuously through the parlour, her appearance as perfect and impressive as ever. "In fact, it was *I* who 'dragged' Georgiana out of the storm, and Darcy was the one who 'dragged' Miss Bennet. I wonder how they managed it all that way, completely soaked, riding together bareback on Darcy's horse. It must have been a daunting task for both of them," she concluded, taking a seat on the couch and asking Mr. Bingley for a glass of wine.

As Lady Cassandra enjoyed her wine, Miss Bingley was still not recovered enough to voice a reply. For some minutes, she could only swallow convulsively and stare at her ladyship.

"Lady Cassandra, I am afraid I do not understand; how is it possible that Mr. Darcy rode together with Miss Bennet? This cannot be borne! I have never heard of anything more improper in my life!" she finally cried.

"Well, I do agree that it was highly improper, but we had no choice at that moment. And poor Darcy is placed in a most difficult position: he must decide which situation was more improper — riding alone with me for more than an hour, or riding in the rain on the same horse with Miss Bennet. Now he will have to *choose* which of us he must marry."

It was precisely at that moment that Elizabeth entered the room, and the first thing she noticed was Miss Bingley's crimson face, gaping mouth, and heaving chest as she desperately attempted to breathe. She was tempted to ask what was wrong, but Miss Bingley's irate look changed her mind.

A few minutes later, the Darcys joined them. Miss Darcy greeted everyone with politeness; Mr. Darcy acted the same as ever, paying equal attention to all his guests. However, every time their eyes met briefly, Elizabeth had the distinct feeling that she could see a trace of redness on his cheeks. As for herself, she was unable to look in Mr. Darcy's direction without remembering the sensation of being in his arms, and she was certain that she never had blushed as much as she did in that half hour before dinner was served.

During the meal, things settled a bit for Elizabeth. Mr. Darcy asked her opinion more than once; they talked of literature and the theatre — mostly between themselves with a few contributions from Lady Cassandra and Miss Darcy — then he praised her taste in books and openly invited her to borrow anything from his library. Elizabeth blushed and thanked him, allowing her eyes to meet his while she assured him she would take advantage of such a generous invitation.

She was abruptly brought back from her pleasant reverie by Miss Bingley's harsh voice. "Miss Bennet, are the militia still in Meryton?"

She attempted to redirect her thoughts from Mr. Darcy before answering. "No they are not. They left for Brighton for the summer."

"It must be a great loss for your family," Miss Bingley continued.

"We are doing the best we can, Miss Bingley, but thank you for your kind concern. I dare say we shall all survive."

"Oh, but there was one gentleman in the regiment whose absence I am sure will be greatly regretted."

"I am not certain to whom you are referring, Miss Bingley."

"I am sure you do, Miss Bennet. Mr. Wickham was a great favourite in the neighbourhood from what I heard, and more than one lady found his presence highly agreeable."

Miss Bingley's tone and insistent stare tried to force a confession. Elizabeth was tempted to answer her accordingly as she turned toward Miss Darcy — intending to roll her eyes in exasperation — but frowned when she saw the young girl's pallor and trembling hands. Instantly Elizabeth forgot any offense or rage she might have felt and turned to Mr. Bingley, smiling charmingly at him. "Mr. Bingley, *you*, sir, are one of those whose presence has been greatly missed in the neighbourhood, I must confess. The ball you hosted was one of the most wonderful we had the pleasure to attend. Everybody regretted that you left so unexpectedly."

Her statement had the desired effect: all eyes and attention turned to Mr. Bingley, and Miss Bingley was silenced immediately. While Mr. Bingley, with some discomfort, expressed his regrets at leaving and promised to host another ball as soon as he was settled back at Netherfield, Elizabeth stretched her hand to hold Georgiana's. Without drawing attention toward them, she gently asked her younger friend if she were feeling well; the girl's silent nod did not convince Elizabeth at all, more so as she could feel Miss Darcy's hand was burning. She cast a quick glance to the master of the house and saw his worried and tender gaze enfolding them both. Slowly, Miss Darcy recovered from her distress, but soon after dinner, she asked Elizabeth if she would mind being left alone with the other guests.

"Not at all; do not worry, Georgiana. If you want to retire, please do so."

"Yes, I would like that, but I do not want to leave you. After all, you are my guest, and I do not want to leave you unprotected."

The girl tried to smile, and Elizabeth joined her. "Oh, I shall be fine; I have been in the same company at Netherfield, and I managed to escape unscathed." She laughed.

"Well, my brother will protect you this time; you may count on that," Miss Darcy said meaningfully, and Elizabeth did not know how to answer.

They exited the room together after Miss Darcy said a quick good night. Elizabeth saw that both Darcy and Lady Cassandra were aware of the reason for Miss Darcy's poor mood, and her ladyship's expression was not to be trifled with.

Elizabeth waited while the maid prepared Miss Darcy for the night. She was worried not only because of the feverish state of the girl but also because of her obvious distress, which continued unabated.

"Elizabeth," Miss Darcy suddenly spoke with a trembling voice, "I was wondering how Miss Bingley knew — about Mr. Wickham, that is. I doubt William told her, but then who did? I know Miss Bingley would not do anything intentionally to harm me, but I am afraid she may have talked to others. How many people are aware of the... *incident* at Ramsgate."

"Georgiana, you misunderstood Miss Bingley. She knew nothing about you or Ramsgate, and she meant no reference to you when she mentioned Mr. Wickham's name. *I* am the one she tried to make uncomfortable as I considered that gentleman a trusted friend at the beginning of our acquaintance. She only wanted to make me look bad in front of —"

"She tried to make you look bad in front of William? I never knew her to be so mean! Elizabeth, I am so sorry! I think she is jealous, you know."

Elizabeth blushed and chose not to answer; she changed the topic again. "I think you should try to sleep now, miss. As you said, I am indeed your guest, and I expect you to entertain me properly tomorrow morning, so you will need all your strength." She decidedly insisted upon the matter until Georgiana finally declared herself defeated and obeyed.

When Elizabeth returned to the others, they were gathered in the music room, but nobody was playing. She presumed Miss Bingley had performed already, and she hoped nobody would insist on her doing so. She was in no mood for entertaining.

Mr. Darcy and Lady Cassandra hurried to meet her, asking about Georgiana. She could assure them that Miss Darcy seemed quite well when she left her, but still Mr. Darcy looked worried.

"I will send a servant to Lambton to inform your uncle and aunt that you are well, Miss Bennet; I will also fetch the doctor, just in case."

Elizabeth did not think Miss Darcy would need a doctor, but she offered no opinion on the matter; after all, prudence was a good thing when health was involved.

She only thanked Mr. Darcy for his consideration.

"Will you return to Lambton too, Miss Bennet? If the rain stops, I mean," Miss Bingley intervened.

"No, Miss Bennet will certainly not return this evening," answered Mr. Darcy sharply, and his interlocutor was instantly silenced.

Another few minutes passed while they enjoyed their drinks. Lady Cassandra broke the silence with a strangely friendly voice.

"So, Miss Bingley, you find Mr. Wickham's presence agreeable? I would not have guessed that; I was certain your interest lay in another direction."

"I beg your pardon?" Miss Bingley startled, almost dropping her glass. "I most certainly did not. How did your ladyship get such an idea?"

Elizabeth looked at Mr. Darcy and saw his glare, impossible to misread, which asked Lady Cassandra to cease the upsetting joke immediately. However, her ladyship turned her head toward Miss Bingley, ignoring him.

"Oh, but you just confessed it; there is no need to deny it now. After all, we are among friends here; you must not feel embarrassed."

"Lady Cassandra, I assure you, you misunderstood me. I was not talking about *me*! I barely know Mr. Wickham at all."

"Barely know him and yet you feel inclined to him so quickly? Strange, but not singular; it has happened to many other young ladies before."

"No, no!!! Nothing can be further from the truth! I had always known Mr. Wickham to be an unworthy gentleman, and I knew of the poor opinion Mr. Darcy had of him. How could I have been inclined toward a steward's son anyway? It was not I but *other ladies* in Hertfordshire who found Mr. Wickham's company agreeable. My sister and brother can testify to that!"

Shifting between mortification and amusement, Elizabeth saw both Mrs. Hurst and Mr. Bingley nod in agreement, but Lady Cassandra seemed to ignore them completely. "Oh, you are only trying to play at modesty, Miss Bingley, I am sure. You mentioned to me that you barely knew any ladies in Hertfordshire and had no close acquaintance among the inhabitants, so how could you have known their preferences?"

Unable to form a reply to such an open censure or find a valid argument to justify her behaviour, Miss Bingley stared in helpless silence at her ladyship, squeezing her glass with both hands.

Elizabeth admitted to herself that she greatly enjoyed the way Lady Cassandra was torturing Miss Bingley. However, she felt she could not remain silent any longer; the notion that Mr. Darcy knew the truth, as well as her own conscience, made her determined to speak.

"Lady Cassandra, Miss Bingley is correct; the general opinion about Mr. Wickham was quite favourable in Meryton from the first day he arrived. As someone very wise once told me, Mr. Wickham was blessed with such happy manners as may ensure his making friends, though it is less certain he may be equally capable of retaining them."

Though she did not dare look at Darcy, she felt his stare.

"I confess I was one of those who considered Mr. Wickham a friend, and I was inclined to think highly of him. However, for a couple of months now I have understood that I was completely wrong in my initial estimation. I assure you, Miss Bingley, I consider Mr. Wickham's departure more a relief than a loss, and my opinion is not singular in Meryton."

She ended her little speech in a relative hurry, afraid that emotion and embarrassment would transfigure her voice. The public admittance of her own folly and the memory of how badly she had maligned Mr. Darcy's reputation and defended Mr. Wickham in front of all Meryton — and in front of Mr. Darcy himself — threw her into a pit of shame and mortification, and she was unable to keep her countenance.

"Ah, Miss Bingley, now I understand why you seem not to be fond of Miss Bennet. It is about an old rivalry between two ladies for a gentleman's attentions." Lady Cassandra's reply stunned the others in the party. Elizabeth stared at her, eyes wide in disbelief at such impropriety, and Miss Bingley became livid, her mouth trying in vain to attempt an answer. Lady Cassandra continued with a smile that proved her delight with the reaction she provoked. "I am talking about Mr. Wickham, of course."

Elizabeth dared to look at Mr. Darcy's scowling expression; their eyes met for a moment, and she thought his countenance softened a little. He rose and moved to where the ladies were sitting; when he spoke, his voice was neither kind nor amused, and his tone admitted no contradiction.

"There has been more than enough talk of Mr. Wickham in this house for at least a year, so I will have no more of it. I do not find the subject amusing nor even tolerable, so let us move forward, shall we? Mrs. Hurst, would you indulge us with some music, please?"

Mrs. Hurst was surprised to be addressed directly; she took her place at the pianoforte with some urgency and began performing.

Elizabeth startled when she heard Lady Cassandra whisper to her. "Miss Bennet, I am sorry if I upset you by insisting on the subject of Mr. Wickham, but I simply cannot control my temper with Miss Bingley. She knew she should not broach that subject in this house, yet she did not care — not to mention her rudeness to you."

Elizabeth looked at her ladyship for a long moment. "Lady Cassandra, you did not upset me; there is no need for apologies. In fact, I confess I was quite amused by your little revenge against Miss Bingley."

"I am happy to hear it. I had the impression that you looked distressed at one point, but it appears I was wrong."

"No, your ladyship was not wrong — I was and still am distressed, but not for me. I am afraid that neither of us acted much better than Miss Bingley, and we offended our host as much as she did."

Lady Cassandra's eyebrow rose in displeasure at such a censuring statement. "I am afraid I do not follow you, Miss Bennet."

"I apologise for speaking so freely, Lady Cassandra — but that is my opinion. Though Miss Bingley showed no consideration for Mr. Darcy and brought up the subject of Mr. Wickham just to attack me, your ladyship did the same with Miss Bingley without any regard for Mr. Darcy's feelings; I then followed you into the conversation until Mr. Darcy was forced to scold us openly. I truly do not know how I can ever apologise to him."

"There is no need to apologise, Miss Bennet." Darcy's voice near her shoulder surprised Elizabeth so utterly that her arm brushed against his when she turned around. She felt her cheeks burning — as much from the embarrassment of her earlier behaviour as from being overheard or from his unexpected closeness — and, when her eyes met his from such a short distance, any reply was lost. Their gazes held, both of them ignoring the presence of Lady Cassandra; his countenance was soft and light, and his eyes showed nothing but warmth.

"Well, apparently *you* will not have to apologise," said Lady Cassandra, a mischievous smile on her lips as she left them and moved toward the couch, but neither of them heard her.

"Mr. Darcy, I would like to —"

"Miss Bennet, I —"

"Oh, forgive me, please continue —"

"No, no, please, I am sorry for interrupting you. Pray go on."

"I wanted to tell you, sir, how sorry I am for the entire incident earlier."

"Miss Bennet, this time I *must* interrupt you. As I said, no apologies are necessary, even more so as you were not at fault. Quite the contrary, I want to thank you for your kindness toward Georgiana, she —"

"Mr. Darcy, now *I* absolutely must interrupt *you*! And to tell you the truth, I am surprised at how rude both of us have become lately, continually interrupting each other." She smiled, and her lips twisted teasingly; his face lit completely, and his eyes moved slowly lower to her mouth, and for a moment, she felt his gaze drying her lips. She struggled to continue, despite the sudden lump in her throat. "I would suggest finding a subject that will allow us to finish the conversation in a more proper manner."

"You are correct, of course, Miss Bennet," he whispered, leaning toward her so she could hear him. She shivered again. "I trust you, Miss Bennet, to find a topic to your liking, and I will try to be a diligent partner in the conversation. In the meantime, would you like to sit down and enjoy Mrs. Hurst's performance?"

They sat together a little apart from the others, apparently listening with great attention, yet neither aware of anything in the room except the other. Miss Bingley's angry glares in their direction remained completely unnoticed. From time to time, Elizabeth's eyes moved toward Lady Cassandra; she could not tell for sure whether

her ladyship was displeased or approving of their obvious intimacy — yet she refused to give the question much consideration. Their host was her only interest.

As soon as Mrs. Hurst finished at the instrument, Mr. Hurst proposed playing cards; his wife indulged him as did Mr. Bingley and Lady Cassandra. Darcy declared that he and Miss Bennet were in the middle of an interesting conversation, and he would rather not stop. Miss Bingley also refused to play, walking around the room, attempting to move closer to where Darcy and Elizabeth were sitting and to overhear their tête-à-tête.

In truth, Elizabeth and Mr. Darcy talked about everything and nothing in particular. She rejoiced in the pleasure of being the recipient of his particular attention in the middle of a room filled with his friends. His preference for her could no longer be doubted by anyone — not even herself. With crimson cheeks and a racing heart, she listened to him talk about many small, yet private, things: his library, which was his favourite place in the house, his parents' and Georgiana's favourite rooms, and the room that was offered to her. He asked her if she would rather move to a guest apartment, which was more spacious and offered her all the accommodations; she hurried to answer — too passionately in her own estimation — that she was more than pleased with the current arrangements. He then took the opportunity to tell her that, despite the danger she and Georgiana had to face, he was happy the storm kept her at Pemberley for the night. At this, she knew not what to answer; she only allowed her eyes — captured by his — to speak for her.

Mr. Darcy enjoyed his relatively private time with Elizabeth. He could not believe his good fortune as she obviously accepted his attentions with pleasure and did not leave his side for more than an hour. She seemed interested in everything he said, her eyes barely moving from his, blushing charmingly from time to time, smiling at him — only at him — as he had wished and dreamed so many times in the past. Her behaviour toward him was everything and more than he had dared to hope a few days before, and for a moment, a wild idea crossed his mind: he should take the opportunity to propose to her that very evening! But the next instant his reason took control over his impetuosity. He would court her properly; he would show her and everyone else his feelings for her; he would be patient. He would consider only her feelings and desires this time. As for his, he knew them only too well. His second proposal would not come until he could be certain that this was what she wished and anticipated.

While deep in his own thoughts, he noticed her wondering glance searching his face. He recovered quickly and asked her if she wanted something to drink. Elizabeth accepted; Lady Cassandra asked for one too, and he indulged her. Then Miss Bingley asked for the same favour, and he complied again. After that, he took two glasses and moved back near Elizabeth, indifferently and quite impolitely returning his attentions only to her.

Elizabeth was tired — more tired than usual for that hour — yet she refused to consider that the evening might come to an end. She felt happier than ever and grew increasingly certain of her feelings for Mr. Darcy. Though she knew it was unwise and dangerously presumptuous, her imagination — filled with hopes and desires — made her believe that his feelings for her were as strong as they were two months earlier and that he was not far from declaring himself again. Of course, her sensible voice advised her to remain rational, yet her heart spoke considerably louder and with more determination — so it was to her heart that Elizabeth listened.

DESPITE ELIZABETH'S WISHES, THE EVENING did come to an end. Before retiring for the night, Lady Cassandra insisted on checking Georgiana once more; Miss Bingley hurried to do the same, but Darcy politely thanked Miss Bingley for her concern and offered to advise her if any significant event occurred regarding Miss Darcy. Miss Bingley seemed content with this proof of appreciation; however, before leaving the salon, she asked Elizabeth what room was offered to her. The explanation that Elizabeth resided in the family wing made Miss Bingley livid with shock and anger.

As they climbed the stairs to the family apartments, Lady Cassandra asked, "Darcy, are you angry with me for my earlier exhibition with Miss Bingley?"

"Yes, I am, but let us not discuss the matter now; we should not expose Miss Bennet to our private quarrels," he replied, offering Elizabeth his arm.

"Oh come now — do not be so serious."

"I must be. I would rather see you more preoccupied by my wishes than by your own amusement at Miss Bingley's expense. Not to mention that Miss Bingley is my guest too, and despite her behaviour, I would not have you answer her in the same manner again. Please indulge me."

"Very well, then, I shall do as you please," she answered with mocking obedience. Then, to Elizabeth's mortification, she added. "As for Miss Bingley and your other guests, you did not seem too preoccupied with any of them in the last couple of hours as far as I noticed."

Elizabeth was certain her face was burning. How could Lady Cassandra say such things with no restraint? To her even greater shock, Mr. Darcy laughed while answering. "Yes, I cannot deny that. I have to confess I had the most wonderful conversation with Miss Bennet tonight; I only hope I did not bore her completely. My conversational skills are not what they should be." Elizabeth *sensed* him smiling, and she finally lifted her eyes; he was indeed smiling, an intimate, meaningful, even daring smile.

"Well, though I am by no means as perceptive as Miss Bingley, I wager that Miss Bennet has no complaints about your conversational skills. Am I correct, Miss Bennet?"

It was Elizabeth's turn to laugh, sighing deeply; there was nothing to do with Lady Cassandra except take her as she was. "You are absolutely correct, your ladyship.

Mr. Darcy's abilities at making pleasant conversation continue to improve."

"It must be the result of following Lady Catherine's advice; one can become truly proficient only by practicing constantly," said Lady Cassandra.

Elizabeth felt relieved when they all reached Miss Darcy's room as she was afraid of where their conversation might have tended. A servant was watching Miss Darcy; she informed them that the young lady had been a little feverish, but she was well and slept restfully for the last couple of hours.

They walked on until they reached Elizabeth's door; there, Mr. Darcy took her hand once more and lifted it to his lips while bowing to her.

"Thank you, Miss Bennet," he whispered, and she felt her knees unable to support her. She hoped she answered a *"good night"* both to him and Lady Cassandra; then dashing from her closed door, she only stopped when she reached the bed and threw herself onto the soft, silky sheets.

It was well past midnight when Elizabeth was startled in her sleep by a deafening thunderclap and the sound of rain pelting the window. She looked around, disconcerted for a moment, until she remembered where she was. She felt cold and covered herself in the bed sheets. Looking at the fireplace, she saw the flames were strong, yet she could not feel their warmth. She was shivering badly, and her own arms wrapped around herself did not help. She needed *his* arms. She needed and wished for *him* — his closeness, his warmth, his comforting embrace, his tender, caring voice, his arms crushing her against his chest — and then she would not be cold any longer. She closed her eyes, ashamed of her desires but not wanting to abandon them. She knew how improper her thoughts were, but if she could not truly have *him* close to her, at least she could keep him near in her mind. She remembered his voice whispering in her ear, and the trace of his kiss on the back of her hand was still alive on her skin.

Her lips become dry, so dry that she could not move them. She was thirsty; she had been thirsty the entire night. She rose from the bed, still shivering, and went to pour herself another cup of water, but there was none left. She pulled the robe around herself and left the room; she needed to find some water or at least a servant to ask for assistance. She walked as silently as she could along the long hall without noticing the shadow in front of her; a short scream escaped her parched lips when she bumped into a tall, dark form.

"Miss Bennet, what is the matter?"

Darcy's voice startled her but equally comforted her; yet, only a moment later, her embarrassment prevented her speaking. He was clearly dressed for bed, wearing a robe over his nightclothes, and her eyes moved from his face to his uncovered neck and then lowered to the ground.

"I . . . I was trying to find some water; I finished what was in the pitcher and felt really thirsty. I am sorry to have disturbed you."

"No, no, you did not disturb me. I went to ask about Georgiana once more before going to sleep. You should not have left the room but rung for a servant. You seem very cold."

He was right; she was shivering and had hoped he would not notice. Yet he did, and he encircled her shoulders with his right arm as he took both of her hands in his left. She shivered even more at the feeling of his fingers caressing hers in an attempt to warm them.

"Miss Bennet, you must return to bed this instant. I will send you a servant immediately. Your hands are frozen." She did not answer, allowing him to support her. She felt quite tired — hardly able to walk.

He opened the door to her bedchamber and walked inside, his arms protectively around her. Elizabeth knew she should not allow him inside; there was nothing more improper. But how could she refuse what she had wished for earlier — the warmth of his closeness?

She felt herself gently deposited on the bed; he was frowning, and she wondered why he was displeased. Maybe she had disturbed him after all. He arranged her pillow and then wrapped her in the covers. She blushed, averting her eyes from him; she had never imagined how it would be for a man to perform such gestures for her. Every move drew him closer to her until she could feel his breath against her skin.

"Miss Bennet, you have a fever; that is obvious. How on earth did I not notice it earlier?" His distress was clear, and she tried to answer that she was well, but he would not hear of it. "I will send for a servant this instant. In the meantime, I will bring you some water." He left and returned quickly with a glass full of water. He handed the glass to her; her fingers were trembling, and he covered them with his as she drank. Afterwards, he leaned her against the pillows once more, and in a moment, he was gone.

She did not have time to thank him nor did she notice how much time passed before a maid entered her room with tea, fresh water and medicines. Just before sleep took her, she asked the servant about the time: it was past midnight.

Elizabeth woke some time later, feeling much better. She pleaded with the girl to go to sleep herself, but the maid refused. After much negotiation, the girl agreed to retire after she was certain everything was fine with Miss Bennet and her fever was gone for good.

IT WAS DAWN, AND THE rain had stopped when a slight movement in the room awakened her. She did not open her eyes, but she wondered why the maid had not retired as she promised. Freezing, she felt somebody sitting next to her on the bed, taking her hand gently then placing a soft, light kiss on her forehead. She did not move nor even breathe; she knew it was *him,* and she did not dare guess why he was in her room again and what he would do next. For an instant, the realisation of what would happen if somebody found him there struck her, but she put the thought aside as quickly as it arose. His fingers were still holding her hand, and all her blood seemed to race to that precise point on her skin. She felt his gaze travelling over her face, and then she felt him lowering over her again, his fingers tenderly playing with a lock of her hair. She could not pretend she was asleep any longer; she wanted to see him. She opened her eyes, and before he had time to recover from the shock of being discovered, she smiled at him, their fingers still tightly together.

"Mr. Darcy, why are you not sleeping, sir? It is almost morning."

In the light of the fire, she saw him frown, his face turning pale; he looked mortified, and it was a moment before he could speak, desperately attempting to remove his hand from hers and rise from the bed.

"Miss Bennet, please forgive me. I should not be here... It is only that... I checked on Georgiana, and I could not rest until I was certain that you were well, too. I thought the maid was still here, and I wanted to ask her... and when nobody answered my knock, I could not restrain myself from entering. Please forgive me... I have no excuse for my scandalous behaviour."

Her heart melted, and she wished for nothing more than to caress his handsome face and tell him how happy she felt that he — the most proper of men — had broken the rules of strict propriety because of her and could not sleep until he was certain she was well. She did not dare do so but she did dare something else: to choose honesty instead of the demands of decorum. She was not offended by his care; she was grateful to have him there, and she intended to show him that. She also wanted him to stay a moment longer. The harm had been done anyway. What would another moment cost?

"I asked the maid to retire earlier. She had been most dutiful, and I was feeling very well indeed, so there was no need to keep her awake." She struggled to explain as she gathered all her courage to continue. "Sir, there is nothing to forgive; I know there is no excuse for your being in my room at this hour, as *I* have no excuse for allowing you to stay. However, I want to thank you for your care and concern. I am feeling very well indeed," she repeated, then added teasingly, "And I certainly hope *you* will finally get some rest, too. It would not do to for you to become ill from lack of sleep."

An expression of heartfelt delight lit his face and softened it; Elizabeth was certain he was more handsome than ever. She was no longer cold, yet she quivered when she felt his fingers returning to caress hers.

"Thank you, Miss Bennet," he whispered. "As for my becoming ill, there is no need to worry; I am better than I have been in the last many years."

"As am I," she whispered, her eyes gazing steadfastly into his.

"I shall leave you now," he said after a long moment. "However, Miss Bennet, I hope tomorrow we will have the opportunity to talk again... and if the weather will allow us, there are some places I would like to show you — together with Georgiana, of course."

She dared to presume she knew what he wanted to tell her and did not have the confidence to do it. How could she make him understand he had nothing to fear? Was she not eloquent enough in showing her feelings? After all, she had admitted him to her room in the middle of the night with not a single word of censure. Was that not proof enough?

"Mr. Darcy, I will look forward to *anything* you would like to show me...or tell me." She blushed, mortified by her desperate audacity in encouraging him. Her reward was immediate as the light smile on his lips told her he understood her meaning.

"Thank you, Miss Bennet. I also look forward to tomorrow." He lifted her fingers to his lips and touched them briefly, while his eyes caressed her with breathtaking tenderness. He rose from her side, and with a slow pace and a last look, he finally left.

She sighed, and then she placed her lips on her own fingers, on the same spot that had touched his lips. The gesture made her want more, and until she fell asleep again, she wondered about the feeling of his lips upon hers.

DARCY CLOSED THE DOOR TO Elizabeth's room with great care, peering down the hallway to see whether anyone was around. It was empty and silent as was the entire house.

However, in a dark corner of the hall, hidden from Darcy's vigilance, a pair of inquiring eyes watched in shock as Mr. Darcy exited the room that was occupied by Miss Elizabeth Bennet.

Chapter 8

Walking along the hallway to his room, Darcy felt happy and grateful for his good fortune and so light hearted that he was certain he could fly. He laughed at the foolish thought, instantly imagining how he would look actually flying and what the servants would say.

There could be no misunderstanding or doubt left now: her feelings had changed since April, and she wanted him to see that. She had showed him and told him as much. The first moment she opened her eyes and saw him there in her room on her bed in a scandalous, shocking situation, he was alarmed to a degree he had never been before. He was concerned he might have shocked or offended her so badly that her good opinion would be forever lost. He expected her to scold him, throw him out of her room and then leave his house at the first opportunity. In fact, most women in a similar situation would have demanded an immediate marriage to compensate for their ruined reputation, but Elizabeth would not have done that, and a forced marriage was not what he desired in any way.

However, all his fears were put aside when Elizabeth, eyes sparkling with surprise, smiled at him; he felt, undoubtedly, her hand squeezing his, so he could not leave. Even now, he could feel her soft fingers warming his with the most delicious sensation he had ever experienced.

No, not the most; the most delicious, shockingly, scandalously pleasant feeling he experienced had been when he held her in his arms on the horse, sensing every part of her body crushed against him in a fervent, amorous embrace. He had known other women — intimately — but he had never held a woman so tightly to him, so tightly to his heart, nor had he ever experienced such blissful happiness from a woman's closeness. The moment they had arrived at Pemberley and she was taken from his arms, both his body and his heart felt torn in half, longing for her to complete him again. And his desire had been fulfilled — though only to a small degree — during dinner and afterwards when they had spent the entire time together.

Then, in her bedchamber, the way she spoke to him — the way she teased him — and then told him she was anxious for anything he wanted to show her or tell her.

No, there could be no doubt; she wanted him to talk to her and he would — the very next day. He planned not to demand an answer but to declare himself and ask permission to court her properly until she was prepared to accept him. Yes, this time he was certain she would accept his love and, eventually, his hand in marriage.

He entered his room, wanting nothing more than to lie in bed and sleep as long as he could, which would not be long considering the appointment he had for the morning. He startled in shock when the door of his bedchamber opened and a wet and unsightly Colonel Fitzwilliam barged in.

"David, what on earth happened? What are you doing here at this hour? Come in, sit by the fire and let me pour you a glass of brandy; you look very ill." He instantly filled two glasses — his only half full, the colonel's to the top — but as he turned to hand it to his cousin, he met the colonel's glowering countenance. There was a chill in his tone that Darcy had never heard in all the years they had known each other.

"I was on my way to Pemberley earlier today when I was caught in the storm and forced to seek shelter. One of your tenants hosted me in his home until the rain stopped, which was only an hour ago, and I hurried to ride here as fast as I could. Now I realise I made a mistake. I never should have come without announcing my visit."

"Nonsense, David, you know this is your home, too; you may come and go whenever you please. Let me call Stevens to prepare you a bath."

"No need to bother; I talked to Stevens when I entered — and with one of the maids, too. She was kind enough to offer me a cup of tea, which she mentioned, was prepared for Miss Bennet who is here and not feeling well." As he spoke, his voice mixed sharpness with mockery, and his icy eyes narrowed as he watched Darcy.

"Yes, Miss Bennet and Georgiana had a picnic today and were caught in the rain, but fortunately, Cassandra and I arrived in time to bring them home safely. Now they are both unwell and a bit feverish, but we hope it is nothing serious," explained Darcy, puzzled by his cousin's strange attitude.

"Yes, I heard about your heroic rescue. The maid as well as Stevens were very impressed and related it to me with great enthusiasm. Yet I cannot help wondering why saving Miss Bennet from the rain gives you the right to place her in a room close to your apartment and visit her in the middle of the night." By now, his voice was steely cold, and his eyes were full of rage.

Darcy froze for a moment, unable to formulate an answer and considering what he should say. He decided to trust his cousin and confide in him as his best friend; yes, he needed to talk to someone about his impropriety and its happy result: the discovery of Miss Bennet's true feelings for him.

"How dare you, Darcy?" cried the colonel before he could say a word. "What has happened to you? Have you lost your senses? To have both Lady Cassandra and Miss Bennet under your roof and act like the worst of scoundrels — trifling with them both only a few steps from Georgiana's apartment. You must be completely mad, and I will not allow you to go on with this!"

Darcy instantly turned white, staring at his cousin as at a complete stranger who spoke an incomprehensible language. He put his glass down and then walked slowly to the nearest armchair and sat down.

The colonel was a bit more clearheaded than his cousin. "I shall send a note to the Gardiners first thing in the morning to come and retrieve their niece; she cannot remain here a moment longer. Even if you have no consideration for her, I have. As for Lady Cassandra, you clearly have no affection for her, but you at least should have a little respect if you indeed intend to marry her."

Struggling to control his own rage, Darcy finally lifted his eyes to his cousin's face, red with anger. He breathed deeply and managed to calm himself before answering coldly, "I would be tempted to kill anyone else if they had said such things to me, but with you I am too grieved and pained to even be angry. I never would have guessed this is your opinion of me after you have been like a brother and best friend all my life. Thank you for this enlightening disclosure. And now please be so kind as to leave my room — and feel free to do what you think is necessary. As for Mr. and Mrs. Gardiner, I have already sent them a note and am expecting them as soon as the weather permits them to travel, so there is no need to trouble yourself."

The colonel remained still, eyes and mouth opened in disbelief. "Darcy, now I am certain you are completely mad! That is all the answer I can expect from you? Have you nothing more to tell me?"

"Indeed, that is all I have to say to you."

"But Darcy…"

"Cousin, please leave. My anger will soon defeat my control, and I do not want a scandal in the house at this hour. We shall talk at some point — another time when I am able to face you again."

The colonel threw his glass in the fire and quit the room with the same expression of rage on his face. Yet, after only a few minutes, while Darcy still had not recovered from the shock of their conversation, the colonel returned, poured another glass of brandy and fell into an armchair. Darcy did not even lift his eyes to look at him.

"Darcy, kill me if you wish to, but for God's sake, talk to me! What should I believe? I arrived an hour ago, I was told you were not yet asleep and came to talk to you — and I saw you exiting Miss Bennet's room at four in the morning. What else am I to believe?"

"Yes indeed, what else could you think except that I took advantage of her poor condition to dishonour Miss Bennet while she is my sister's guest and lies feverish in a room next to Georgiana. That is something any gentleman would do and I more than anyone."

The colonel started pacing the room nervously, swallowing all the brandy violently and then pouring himself another glass.

"Very well, very well, I admit that maybe I was wrong. I was in too great a hurry to accuse you, but you must understand that I was tired and cold, and I was so shocked when I saw you. You know I have always admired Miss Bennet and considered her a friend; and Lady Cassandra is... Well, I assume you had a valid reason to be in Miss Bennet's room, but still it was unacceptable. What if somebody else had seen you? The scandal would have ruined Miss Bennet's reputation forever. Did you consider that?"

Immediately, Darcy's affection for his cousin and his worries for Miss Bennet's reputation defeated his anger and the offense he took at the colonel's words. No matter how unfair and outrageous his accusations had been, he knew the colonel was right, and anyone in his place would have shared the same opinion. He rose, poured more brandy for himself, and finally turned toward his accuser.

"Yes, I did consider it, but unfortunately, I unwisely chose to ignore my misgivings. I checked on both Georgiana and Miss Bennet before retiring to my room because I was worried for them both. And when I entered Miss Bennet's room, I was under the impression the maid was still about, so my intention was only to inquire after her. It is equally true, however, that when I discovered Miss Bennet was alone, I still entered. I know what scandal my behaviour might have aroused, but I cannot regret it, because I was fortunate enough to have everything resolved to my satisfaction."

"Oh, indeed? Well, at the risk of sounding even more offensive, did you consider Miss Bennet's satisfaction as well? What if she discovered your little escapade?"

"In fact, she did discover me. She awoke while I was there —"

"Did she? Then how can you say all is well? I know Miss Bennet to be an honourable young lady, and I imagine she was outraged to see you."

"Yes, she is everything you said and so much more. But, no, she was not angry at all. I have reason to believe she was pleased, so much so that tomorrow I intend to talk with her privately, and if the result is the one I am hoping for, I shall speak to her uncle and then write to Mr. Bennet as well."

The colonel's shock grew alarmingly until he was forced to fall into his chair once more; another glass of brandy was gulped instantly, and he felt so dizzy he could hardly keep his eyes open. "What private talk, Darcy? What result? You cannot possibly intend to propose to Miss Bennet!"

"Why on earth not? I can and I surely will do precisely that."

"But... but what about Cassandra?"

"Cassandra? Why are you involving her in this conversation?"

"Why? Because you are about to marry her. Everybody knows that!"

"Oh, come now; that is ludicrous. How can you say such a thing? I love Cassandra dearly; next to you, she has been the dearest and closest friend I have ever had. I would do anything for her. But marry her? Are *you* out of your senses? Where did you get such an idea?"

"Where? From you and her of course! Since Lady Cassandra returned, you have been together constantly; you and Georgiana have declared how happy you are to have her company. And she kept talking about marrying you! I imagined she was mostly talking in jest, but you never did anything to contradict her."

"Oh come now, David. Cassandra and I have behaved that way since we were children."

"Well, you are not children anymore, Darcy. And it is not only my opinion; the whole of London is waiting for the announcement —"

"Aaaah, yes… well, *'the whole of London'* has speculated about the event since the first season we were out, so that is nothing new. Nobody can seriously consider it after all this time."

"Well, my mother said it is only a silly rumour, and she laughed at it. So, you will not marry Lady Cassandra?"

"Certainly not!"

The colonel started pacing the room again in even greater agitation. Darcy, tired and under the warm influence of the brandy, demanded rest. "Cousin, now that we hopefully have cleared all misunderstandings, is there anything else that cannot wait until morning? If not, I should like to sleep a few hours at least."

"What? Oh… no, no there is nothing urgent, nothing at all. I shall leave now. I am sure my bath is ready."

"Very well. We shall talk again at breakfast."

"Breakfast? A late one if you please," he added as he exited the room.

His cousin's apparent preoccupation puzzled Darcy, but his fatigue was even greater, so he allowed himself to enjoy his comfortable bed. So many extraordinary events had occurred that day, and he could hardly believe them. Closing his eyes, he rejoiced in the happy memories that began when Elizabeth arrived at Pemberley. *"Elizabeth,"* he whispered, and her very name caressed his heart like a tender touch.

Now that things were calm and clear, he could smile at the absurdity of the incident with the colonel and even take pity on his cousin for his misapprehension. What pain and disappointment he must have suffered, imagining all those horrible things regarding him and Miss Bennet. *Surely, it must have been the effects of his exhaustion, or else he never would presume I am to marry Cassandra.* He laughed. Since they were quite young, their families had discussed the possibility, and later, in the first years of their youth and after their first Season in Town, the speculation was on everyone's lips. Both he and Cassandra had laughed about it endlessly.

Of course, there had been that dreadful moment when their marriage was needed and would have helped Cassandra — and he had been more than willing to do it; yet even then, Cassandra had rejected him, and it was many months before he understood the reason for her decided refusal. After all, most marriages were arranged, and those spouses certainly did not share the affection and friendship he and Cassandra possessed. At that moment when their parents had passed away and they were all alone — he, Cassandra and Georgiana — the prospect of a lifetime together was the best thing he could imagine.

However, after he met Elizabeth and his heart succumbed helplessly to her, he understood what a man should feel for the woman with whom he wished to spend his entire life. The fact that most gentlemen did not possess strong feelings for their spouses was no longer of any importance to him. And now, when he finally had reason to hope that Elizabeth was returning his ardent love, he managed to comprehend fully the wisdom of Cassandra's refusal of an arranged marriage. What a tragedy it would have been for him to meet his true love after he had pledged himself to another! Once more, he discovered a further reason to feel indebted and grateful to Cassandra — *even if she sometimes pushes me past the limit of my patience as she did last night with Caroline Bingley. What a torture!*

Cassandra had always enjoyed putting proper manners aside, and their behaviour toward each other had seemed difficult to accept or understand by the people around them, especially members of the *ton*. Had they been family — true brother and sister — the liberty with which she always addressed him and teased him in public would have been hardly acceptable. But there was nothing to be done with her manners, not after her parents as well as his had always allowed her those little breaks in decorum. Their close acquaintances and friends had become accustomed to their friendship, and Darcy was certain that, despite the colonel's assertion, no one could misread their familiarity as an indication of romantic involvement.

Of course, to a complete stranger, their closeness could be bewildering, but that rumour about his marrying Cassandra was ridiculous considering that he also had been in the close company of Elizabeth and openly shown his preference for her. Even the first time they all met at the theatre and later at the ball, surely it was clear that his behaviour toward Elizabeth was different than his friendly familiarity with Cassandra, and his intentions toward her surely were clear enough. How could anyone confuse that? It was also true, he admitted on closer introspection, that Elizabeth's manner was more proper and restrained then Cassandra's, but still —

Suddenly, Elizabeth's beautiful face filled his thoughts, and he let himself be spoiled by those delightful memories, but a moment later, he almost jumped from his bed. *Elizabeth!*

Elizabeth was surely one of those who had witnessed his familiarity toward Cassandra without being aware of the nature of their connection. How was it possible for him not to have considered that until now?

He tried to ward off the sudden headache that seized him, while images of his previous encounters with Elizabeth in London flew into his mind: that first day in the park, her visit to his home, the night at the theatre, his visit to the Gardiners, and then the ball. He remembered how puzzled and troubled he had been by the unsteadiness in Elizabeth's manners and attitude toward him. Moment by moment and memory by memory, it became clear to him that the changes in her behaviour were due not to *his* presence — as he had presumed then — but to Cassandra's presence. *What a horrible situation for Elizabeth! What must she have thought of me — paying attention to her and, at the same time, being so familiar, so intimate with Cassandra! How could I have been such a fool? And that day she and Cassandra left my house together… God knows what Cassandra said to her!*

He paced the room and stopped at the window; it was almost light outside. He struggled to remain calm and use good judgement. It was likely, due to her admirable intelligence and perception, that Elizabeth had already understood his intentions; so much was obvious. Had she any doubt about the honour behind his attentions, she surely would not have behaved warmly toward him, nor would she have allowed him in her room, let alone held his hand. *How have I been so fortunate to gain the affection of such an admirable lady despite my folly and my thoughtless actions?* he wondered, smiling to himself with pride and joy.

Now, there was nothing for him to do except prove himself worthy of her and remove every obstacle from the path of her serenity and happiness. *"Elizabeth,"* he whispered again, while allowing sleep finally to conquer him. It was already daylight.

DARCY SLEPT NO MORE THAN a couple of hours, but he felt rested and remarkably alive when his servant entered the room quietly.

"Good morning, Stevens. Would you bring me a cup of coffee, please? Or even two?"

"Certainly, sir. I have already taken the liberty of bringing you the coffee."

"Thank you; you are truly a mind reader." Darcy answered with a familiarity that surprised the servant. Stevens was certain he had not seen his master possess such an easy disposition since he took over full responsibility for the estate five years before.

"Stevens, would you please inquire after my sister and Miss Bennet? Has the doctor arrived yet?"

"I already did that, sir. Mrs. Reynolds informed me that both Miss Darcy and Miss Bennet slept quite well and are not yet awake. Apparently, the fever is gone, and she said she doubted the doctor would be needed, but she sent the carriage for him regardless."

"Excellent! Excellent," Darcy declared, his mood brightening even more.

"The colonel is still asleep, sir," continued Stevens.

"Ah, yes, I imagined as much. Please take care that he is not disturbed; he needs as much sleep as possible. These last months with his regiment have been trying for him, I am afraid." The servant did not answer; discussing the colonel's condition was again an extraordinarily uncommon event for his master, so he wisely chose not to comment.

An hour later, Darcy was informed that the doctor had arrived and was examining both Miss Bennet and Miss Darcy.

The doctor departed with a most satisfactory report, and Darcy went to talk to his sister. His surprise was great when he found Elizabeth there as well, both of them chatting amiably. At his appearance, they stopped, and he could see that Elizabeth was nervous; yet, the mirth in her eyes and her becoming blushes showed she was pleased to see him.

"Good morning, ladies. What a pleasure to see you so well."

"Good morning, Brother; please do come in. Elizabeth and I were just discussing the weather. I truly hope the rain will be gone for some time."

"Miss Bennet — I hope you rested well?"

The trace of a blush over her beautiful face was the only indication of her slight embarrassment. "Yes, I did, sir. I did not sleep much, but I feel well and rested. I hope you are well."

"I am. Thank you." Despite their apparently neutral conversation, Georgiana did not fail to notice there was something more behind their polite inquiries, but as long as they both seemed pleased, she was as well.

"Do you have any plans for today, Brother?"

"Unfortunately I do, at least for the morning. I intend to check whether the storm may have affected the land or the tenants."

"Can you not send someone else?"

"No, I cannot, though I confess I would rather spend the day at home." He could not help looking at Elizabeth, but she shyly kept her eyes averted; however, her cheeks and throat down to her neckline coloured visibly. "Yesterday I only managed to check on Mr. Eaglewood and had to return immediately because of the rain."

"Oh, I forgot to ask you — how was Mr. Eaglewood?" asked Georgiana.

"Worse than we hoped and better then we feared," he answered and then turned to Elizabeth to explain to her. "Mr. Eaglewood was the oldest tenant of Lord Russell, Lady Cassandra's father, and he resides exactly at the border between his estate and Pemberley. Both my father and Lord Russell shared a high opinion of Mr. Eaglewood. Lady Cassandra and I have known him most of our lives and have grown very fond of him. Lord Russell even recommended and supported Mr. Eaglewood's son at school. The young Mr. Eaglewood is now a respected army doctor."

"Oh, yes," Miss Darcy intervened with much enthusiasm. "Cassandra and I met them while we were in London, and we agreed that Mr. Eaglewood's wife is a lovely lady; they have three beautiful children."

Mr. Darcy smiled and continued. "Unfortunately, the old Mr. Eaglewood has been alone since his wife passed away two years ago, and he has been quite ill lately. But he is stubborn and refused to live with his son. Instead, he pretended he was strong enough to keep his own home. That is why Lady Cassandra accompanied me yesterday. She intended to convince him either to move in with his son or accept my offer of moving into a smaller house closer to Pemberley, so we can help him as needed. And she succeeded, as always. He will move in a few days, and she has hired two maids and two male servants to stay with him."

"That is wonderful of Lady Cassandra — and of you too, sir — to have such concern for the gentleman."

"Well…yes, perhaps…but I confess we had a selfish motive, too: Cassandra said Mr. Eaglewood is one of the last of the remaining living proofs of our past and our childhoods — and she is right, of course."

"Mr. Eaglewood also seems to be a bond between your lands," Elizabeth whispered, forcing a smile. "I was not aware that Lady Cassandra's estate was so close to Pemberley,"

"Yes, it is. I am sorry that I did not mention it earlier," he said, his eyes never leaving hers. "In fact, I must apologise that I neglected to be more specific about many things regarding Lady Cassandra."

The barely noticeable blink of her eyes, together with a slight change of her expression, were proof enough for Darcy that he had been right in his suspicions: she was still affected by his relationship with Cassandra.

Before she could reply, he added, "Lady Cassandra's estate is in our immediate vicinity. Our fathers had grown up as friends since their childhood, as have Georgiana and I with Cassandra." He paused a moment to allow her time to understand his meaning completely. "I know that for many people it might appear strange, but Cassandra is like a sister to us; I truly behave no differently toward her than toward Georgiana."

Despise her struggle to remain calm, Elizabeth released a deep sigh of relief; Darcy smiled at her.

"I love Cassandra so much; I have always been happy when she was near me," added Georgiana. "She has always been my dearest friend.

"Lady Cassandra seems a wonderful lady," offered Elizabeth, lightheartedly.

"Yes, she is wonderful, Elizabeth, and I am glad you like her, because I really hope she will stay with us even after you —" Georgiana's enthusiasm paled instantly, and she turned white as she heard her own words and understood their audacity.

Though she was not certain exactly what Georgiana meant, Elizabeth guessed — and she blushed in mortification. Darcy, obviously a little disconcerted himself, smiled at both of them and tried to put things in order before they all grew more embarrassed.

"We indeed hope that Cassandra will remain with us for as long as possible as a part of our family, no matter what changes might occur in the future. That is, of course, if she does not find a worthy gentleman to win her heart and make her a wonderful husband."

He then changed the subject, inquiring whether their plans for the day were fixed and whether they were including the other ladies in the house. Elizabeth fought to regain her spirits, though her mind kept wondering whether Mr. Darcy truly meant somehow to ask her consent regarding Lady Cassandra's presence in their family after… Or perhaps he meant nothing of the kind, and she simply read too much into his words.

Mr. Darcy offered to accompany both ladies down to breakfast. "Miss Bennet, I received a note from Mr. and Mrs. Gardiner; they are quite well and informed me they will join us later, around noon. I hope they will remain for dinner," Darcy said as they walked along the hallway.

"Thank you for telling me, sir. My aunt sent me a note too, as well as some clothes." She blushed, remembering the previous day and the poor state of her soaked clothes — as soaked as his. She thought she could feel a slight tightening of his arm as she was holding it and dared to presume he was thinking of the same thing.

"I have other news to share," he said a few moments later. "Colonel Fitzwilliam arrived during the night. It is likely that we will see him very soon." The colonel's presence was a most pleasant prospect for both Elizabeth and Georgiana, and they enthusiastically expressed their enjoyment.

However, when they entered the room, everyone was gathered except the colonel. They broke their fast without him, as Darcy suspected his cousin was in greater need of sleep than food for the present.

Breakfast was a pleasant affair for many in the party. Elizabeth felt more light-hearted than she had been since Hunsford as all her doubts — about *her* feelings, *his* feelings and the intriguing Lady Cassandra — had vanished. She did not fail to understand that, somehow, Mr. Darcy had finally understood her uncertainties regarding him and Lady Cassandra, and he took the first opportunity to clear up any misapprehension. In the meantime, she felt nervous at the thought that Mr. Darcy might solicit a private talk with her as soon as he returned from his riding inspection of the estate.

Mr. Darcy specifically insisted upon the fact that he was anxious to leave as soon as possible so he might return quickly. Though Elizabeth was not looking at him as he spoke, she could feel his gaze upon her, and she knew his words were meant mostly for her. She blushed with happiness and no little distress. Would he truly propose again that very day? And if he did, how would he ask her? How should she answer so that he would be certain of her feelings and forget her angry and deeply offensive replies from that day at the parsonage?

The colonel eventually appeared when they had almost finished breakfast — with dark circles under his eyes and an obvious need for coffee; his entrance was met with enthusiastic greetings, but to everyone's surprise, the colonel seemed more restrained than ever before. He chose to sit near Elizabeth and across from Lady Cassandra, and he ate in silence. Lady Cassandra asked him a few direct questions despite his obvious lack of volubility, but she did not succeed in obtaining more than a few short, though polite, replies.

The party separated again after breakfast. Mr. Bingley and the colonel decided to accompany the master of the house on his excursion, and Miss Darcy invited all the ladies to join her in the music room. However, Miss Bingley and Mrs. Hurst declined, insisting they would rather retire to their apartments, while Lady Cassandra insisted she wanted to go for a short ride.

Therefore, it remained for only Elizabeth and Georgiana to move to the music room, both equally pleased to be left to themselves as they still had much to share with each other. They sat at the instrument, but they talked rather than played. They did not even notice when Mr. Darcy opened the door and moved toward them, closely followed by Colonel Fitzwilliam.

"William, Cousin, I thought you already left," cried Miss Darcy

"We will in a few minutes, but we wanted to say good-bye first," declared Mr. Darcy, looking more at Elizabeth than his sister. Miss Darcy exchanged a few meaningful glances with the colonel, who was busy studying both Darcy and Miss Bennet with great attention.

"Good-bye, Mr. Darcy, Colonel. Please ride safely, and I hope we shall meet again soon."

"Thank you, Miss Bennet, we will," Darcy answered. But before he departed, he took a few steps forward until he was close to Elizabeth, and only then did he add, "Miss Bennet, if I am not asking too much, I was wondering if you could allow me a few minutes later today. There is something of great urgency about which I would speak to you."

His tone was so serious that Miss Darcy startled and looked with worry at both her brother and Elizabeth. However, their eyes were fixed on each other, oblivious to the others in the room, and the expression on her brother's face — as well as on Elizabeth's, who agreed with obvious embarrassment — was a clear indication that, no matter how urgent the matter was, it was certainly nothing to worry about.

To Elizabeth's surprise, not an hour later a servant announced to Miss Darcy that the Gardiners had arrived.

The greeting was warm and friendly, and Miss Darcy seemed to have lost all her timidity and shyness with the Gardiners. She apologised that her brother and the other gentlemen were not present to give a proper welcome to Mr. Gardiner but was certain all would return soon.

"Oh, it is we who should apologise, Miss Darcy," Mrs. Gardiner offered. "We had informed Mr. Darcy we would arrive much later — after noon — but the sky was clouded again, and we were afraid of another storm, so we hurriedly changed our plans to arrive sooner."

"I am pleased that you have come earlier, Mrs. Gardiner. As you well know, I always enjoy your company very much."

While the guests were offered drinks and refreshments, Miss Darcy asked Mr. Gardiner if he would rather visit her brother's library, as it was obvious their chat was of little interest to him; the gentleman accepted with no hesitation. In fact, he declared he would enjoy the company of a book until Mr. Darcy returned. A servant was fetched to show him the way, and just before he left the room, Mr. Gardiner turned to his niece. "Elizabeth dear, I almost forgot: These letters arrived early this morning for you."

"Two letters? I wonder who they might be from," she asked and then smiled. "They are both from Jane — none from Papa. Well, I expected as much. Oh, on the first of them the direction was written remarkably ill. How strange, Jane is always so careful with her letters."

Miss Darcy smiled understandingly. "Elizabeth, would you rather go in the salon and read your letters privately? I am sure you are anxious to receive news from home after such a long time."

"Oh, thank you! I would like that very much if you do not mind."

"Of course not. Mrs. Gardiner and I shall entertain ourselves for awhile."

"Indeed we shall," agreed Mrs. Gardiner.

As ELIZABETH READ HER LETTERS, a breathtaking pain cut her heart, and her mind refused to believe the words written in great disorder on the sheet of paper.

After a beginning containing an account of all their little parties and engagements, the latter half, which was dated a day later, had been written in evident agitation and gave more important and shocking intelligence, hard to believe and even harder to accept. Lydia had eloped with Mr. Wickham? When she first read that, she was certain it was a mistake, and she returned to read it again, holding the paper with trembling hands. She instantly seized the other letter and tore it open with the utmost impatience. It had been written a day after the conclusion of the first, and Elizabeth's shock was now complete, as complete as the ruin of them all.

Lydia *had* run off with Mr. Wickham! And no, he will never marry her as Jane suggested, nor will they go to Scotland; he will abandon her in misery and disgrace. Jane had asked for their immediate return! Yes — they must return with no delay! But how much could Mr. Gardiner — or anybody — help them?

"Oh! Where, where is my uncle?" cried Elizabeth, darting from her seat, the letter still in her hands; she stopped, desperately trying to remember in what chamber she was and where her uncle was, but as she reached the door, she almost collided with Lady Cassandra.

Her pale face and impetuous manner made her ladyship stare at her in wonder; Elizabeth, in whose mind every idea was superseded by Lydia's situation, hastily exclaimed, "I beg your pardon, your ladyship, but I must find Mr. Gardiner this moment; I have not an instant to lose."

"Good God! What is the matter, Miss Bennet? What has happened? Are you hurt? And where is Mr. Gardiner? Is he here at Pemberley?"

"Yes, he is in the library. I must find him…" she could not hold her tears as she tried to move past Lady Cassandra.

"Miss Bennet, I shall go and fetch Mr. and Mrs. Gardiner. I shall call for a servant too; you need help!"

"No, no, please!" Elizabeth's voice was not only tearful but frightened, too. "Please do not call a servant or my aunt; she is with Georgiana, and I do not want Georgiana to know. I only want to talk to my uncle…"

"Very well then," Lady Cassandra agreed, but she grabbed Elizabeth's arm and placed her in an armchair. "I shall call Mr. Gardiner in a moment, but please stay here."

Elizabeth felt too weak to fight; she remained sitting, her hands trembling in her lap as she ceased fighting her tears. A moment later, Mr. Gardiner arrived, his countenance transfigured by worry. "Elizabeth my dear, what on earth happened?"

She spoke with great difficulty as the lump in her throat and the pain gripping her chest left her breathless. "Lydia…she has left all her friends in Brighton and she… She has thrown herself into the arms of Mr. Wickham… "The words died on her lips, and she handed the letter to her uncle, who read it fervently. When he finished, he was as pale as she was.

"We must leave at once; we have not a moment to delay."

"Mr. Gardiner…" Lady Cassandra's voice startled them both; until that moment, they had forgotten her presence in the room. "I would suggest remaining a little longer until Darcy returns. In this delicate matter, you will need all the help you can find, and nobody knows Wickham better than Darcy."

The gentleman hesitated a moment, and then he seemed to agree. "Your ladyship is correct; we will certainly need the help of somebody who is acquainted with Wickham's habits, but time is a very important matter, too. Do you happen to know whether Mr. Darcy will delay long? I am afraid the storm will begin, and we will be kept here."

"No, please, we cannot wait," cried Elizabeth, trembling even harder. "We must leave immediately, and we cannot allow Mr. Darcy's interference in this; it is a very private and delicate matter for the family alone. We cannot expose it to anybody else!" Her extraordinary agitation distressed Mr. Gardiner even more than the news. In one and twenty years, he had never seen his niece in such a disastrous state. He seemed inclined to listen to Lady Cassandra's reasonable advice, yet he could understand Elizabeth's desire not to expose the shameful event publicly. For the first time in a long while, he could not choose the best course of action.

"Mr. Gardiner, please be so kind as to allow me a moment with Miss Bennet. In the meantime, you may want to inform Mrs. Gardiner —"

"Uncle, please…my aunt is with Georgiana, and I do not want her to be told anything; nobody must be told anything," she insisted, determination mixed with a pleading cry.

Mr. Gardiner nodded in agreement. Suddenly he felt the urge to speak with his wife and seek her support.

As soon as he left the room, Lady Cassandra turned to Elizabeth. "Miss Bennet,

I think there is something you should know before you leave — something that might alter your decision."

Elizabeth did not answer, nor did she look at her ladyship; she doubted anything else might interest her at such a moment.

"Miss Bennet, I must insist that you delay your departure until Darcy returns. He might be of the greatest help to you, and I am certain he would be more than happy to assist you and your family in anything you need."

Tears were flowing freely down Elizabeth's cheeks, and she shook her head in denial, her hands trembling so violently that she had to clasp them together. "Lady Cassandra, please... I have to leave before Mr. Darcy returns. He said... he asked to talk to me privately today... That cannot happen now... I must leave immediately."

"A private talk? Then I truly do not understand your stubbornness. I assure you Darcy is not the kind of man to allow any incident — not even one as grave as this one — to affect his decision. If he asked for a private conference, you may be certain he will not break his word."

Elizabeth's sobs meant she could not talk for a few long minutes, and Lady Cassandra only looked at her in puzzlement and concern.

"Lady Cassandra, can you not see that this is precisely the reason I have to leave as soon as possible? I know Mr. Darcy will do what is right though he has not made any promise to me. But I know he will, and I cannot bear to see the look on his face when he hears such dreadful news. I cannot bear to see him forced to keep his word — a word he did not even give me — with the price of ruining his and his sister's name and peace of mind... I cannot allow that to happen. If I leave now, there is still time to prevent everything before it is started between us, and by the time the scandal becomes public, Mr. Darcy will surely understand my reason. It is much easier to lose something you never truly had."

"Miss Bennet, forgive my boldness, but I must say your entire reasoning is incorrect. I doubt very much that Darcy will accept the news of your sudden departure calmly. Please do not presume how he will react. Of course, your sister's elopement will raise a scandal, especially if they do not marry soon, but this is not the first or the last situation of its kind. It has happened to more illustrious families, and every time, people gossiped for awhile and soon put everything behind them."

"Can you not understand, your ladyship? It is not only about elopement; it is so much more than that! If my sister had eloped with any other man, I might agree with you. Even more, perhaps I would have been selfish enough to put my desires and my happiness above anything else. In such a situation, I would have been pleased to have Mr. Darcy keep his word, and I may have even asked for his help. But considering it is Mr. Wickham, how can I put Mr. Darcy and Georgiana in such a horrible situation? Only yesterday, they could not stand even to hear Mr. Wickham's name. How can I torture them by forcing them to be part of this disgraceful calamity? I cannot do that to them, not after all they have gone through in the last months.

They will not suffer again because of me; I will not allow that, no matter the price I have to pay."

Suddenly, her countenance froze and her eyes fixed on her ladyship. "Lady Cassandra, you must help me with this. You must promise you will not tell anybody the reason for our departure."

"Miss Bennet, you are not being reasonable. You surely know that such a thing cannot be kept secret; besides, Mr. Bingley is settled to return to Netherfield in a short while. Surely you cannot forbid him to do that —"

"No…no…Mr. Bingley…the situation is different in his case. This scandal would not affect him as much; he will not be harmed as much as Mr. Darcy and Georgiana…and when he returns — well, we shall see… But you must promise not to tell anyone for now."

Her eyes had lost all their brightness, and the lady could feel the burden of her grief; it was not the time for an argument, so Lady Cassandra decided to do anything to calm her. "Very well, Miss Bennet, I promise I shall keep the secret as long as possible."

"Thank you, your ladyship."

Lady Cassandra remained silent for a moment while her eyes searched Elizabeth's with the greatest care. She then put her arm around her shoulders and gently pulled her close until Elizabeth began crying on her shoulder, continually whispering, *"Thank you."* The Gardiners and Georgiana found them thus a few moments later.

"Elizabeth, what has happened? Mr. Gardiner said no one died — thank God — and no one has fallen ill but that some events require your immediate return home."

"Yes…yes, my uncle is right. We must leave immediately."

"Oh, I am so sorry! Mr. Gardiner told me it was an urgent family matter. Is there nothing I can do to help you? Can you not stay a little longer until William returns?"

"No, we cannot delay; please understand me, Georgiana. It is very likely that the rain will begin any moment, and we need to leave as soon as possible and travel as fast as we can."

The sadness and disappointment brought tears to Miss Darcy's eyes, and she did not fight to hold them back.

"Very well then, if you need to go, so be it, but please, write me to inform us as soon as you can. I shall not find rest until I have news from you, nor shall William either."

"I…I shall try…if the situation will allow me…but…" Her tears stopped her from speaking further.

"Oh, Elizabeth, something very bad has happened; you are suffering so much, yet you will not allow me to help you and do not want to wait a little longer until my brother returns. Did we do something to offend you? Are you upset with us? Is that why you want to leave so quickly?"

"Oh no, no, dearest, please do not say that…" She took the girl's hands and held them tightly while looking deeply into her eyes. "My dearest friend, please believe me that these last days here at Pemberley have been the happiest in my life. I will treasure their memories as long as I live, and my affection for you will ever remain unchanged, please remember that."

"Elizabeth, we must leave now," interrupted Mr. Gardiner, and she obeyed. When she rose to move to the door, Georgiana was still holding her hands tightly. She embraced her quickly; then she ran and did not stop until she was in the carriage. She could bear it no longer; her heart was broken, and she knew parts of it would remain at Pemberley. Her heart would never be the same.

The Gardiners joined her shortly, and they were about to leave when Lady Cassandra detained them. "Mr. and Mrs. Gardiner, Miss. Bennet, I want all of you to promise me something."

"What could that be, Lady Cassandra?" asked Mr. Gardiner

"This searching will be a daunting task, and you may need support in matters you cannot even imagine now. I want you to promise me you will not hesitate to ask my help in anything. You know my location in London; send word there, and my servants will direct it to me as soon as possible."

"Thank you, your ladyship, your kindness is —" Mrs. Gardiner tried to express her gratitude.

"Oh please, enough of this nonsense! This is no time for politeness. I hope you find Mr. Wickham in time." She paused and looked at them all before adding, "I shall not take a serious good-bye of you, because I dare say we shall meet again soon. Have a safe journey."

The carriage left a moment later, and almost instantly, the rain began; Pemberley remained behind with Elizabeth's weeping heart.

IT WAS RAINING AGAIN, AND Colonel Fitzwilliam and Bingley spent the entire return to Pemberley complaining about the weather and even cursing from time to time. By the time they reached the house, they were soaked and hungry and wanted nothing but the comfort of their rooms.

For Darcy, the rain meant only beautiful memories; nothing could ruin his spirit. He hardly noticed he was wet and cold; and if he was indeed, the mere thought of seeing Elizabeth again and talking to her — confessing himself to her — was enough to warm him.

Darcy was tempted to go in search of her the moment he entered the house, but at the last moment, he came to his senses as he realised the poor state of his clothes. He hurried to his room and was grateful when Stevens efficiently informed him that a bath was already prepared. In less than half an hour, with the servant's silent help, he was properly attired and prepared to meet Elizabeth — to meet his happiness.

"Stevens, do you happen to know whether Mr. and Mrs. Gardiner have arrived? I hope the bad weather will not keep them at the inn the entire day."

"Mr. and Mrs. Gardiner? They were here but they left, sir, together with Miss Bennet."

"They left?" Darcy's shock changed his countenance instantly. "In this weather? But why?"

"I do not know, sir. I believe Miss Darcy might know more," the servant answered, and Darcy dashed through the doorway, almost knocking him down.

He barely knocked and did not wait for an answer before entering Georgiana's room. At first, he did not even see her until he heard her barely audible sobs coming from an armchair near the window.

He moved closer and knelt near her; it took a great effort to make her take her hands from her red, swollen eyes. When he took her hands gently, she could barely whisper, and he could hardly fathom the meaning of her cruel words. "William, she is gone... Elizabeth is gone."

SEVEN HOURS HAD PASSED AND his mind still did not understand what his heart refused to accept. Georgiana was performing for him with great difficulty; he knew she was expending this great effort only in a desperate attempt to comfort him. He needed no comfort as he needed no company, no food, and no rest; he needed Elizabeth — more than he had needed anything else in his adult life, but Elizabeth was gone. How was that possible?

Since the moment he had heard the news, he had asked everybody what happened: Lady Cassandra who apparently had witnessed everything, Georgiana who was not coherent as she herself was confused and pained, Mrs. Reynolds, Stevens, and the other servants. Despite the bad weather, he sent Stevens to the inn to ask for more details, but the only clarification was the fact that they had left within half an hour of returning to the inn.

Cassandra had been the only one who could offer him the reason — a reason that seemed insufficient to him and gave little palliation to his torment. Something happened back in Hertfordshire but apparently nothing tragic. Yet, Elizabeth hurried to leave because she was afraid the rain might delay them.

Delay them from what? What was so important that she cared so little about him as to leave without a word through his sister? Even more impossible to bear was that she had told Georgiana she would remember her and love her for the rest of her life. Was that a last farewell? Had she taken this opportunity to run — to run away from him and from their private talk? Was the mere idea of a second proposal so dreadful to her? Had he completely misunderstood her signs, behaviour, and desires again as he had in April?

He attempted an apology before swiftly leaving the room, away from Pemberley, out through the rainy night, walking with no direction and no stars in the sky to light his footsteps. He needed neither stars nor light. He only needed to know what happened to Elizabeth and to his long-desired happiness. His steps took him farther and farther away until he could barely see the contour of Pemberley House; only then did he stop, alone in the night with his thoughts — and her memory.

Many hours later, when he returned to the house tired and soaked through from walking in the rain, his boots and greatcoat caked with mud, he felt like dancing with joy and hope: he had discovered the answer!

No, this time he had not misunderstood her; this time he would not allow despair to cloud his mind. Her every word, every gesture, every look, every blush, and every moment they had spent together since that day in Hyde Park were testimony to her changed feelings and desires — and especially last night. She could not have run from *him*! He must follow her!

He entered his room, and while he summoned Stevens and started throwing his soaked clothes carelessly on the floor, he hurriedly poured a glass of brandy to warm himself. But he startled and dropped the glass when he heard Lady Cassandra's irritated voice from near the fire.

"Oh, for heaven's sake, Darcy, are you trying to kill me with worry? This situation cannot continue any longer. We must talk!"

Chapter 9

"Sometimes I wonder how I can restrain myself from strangling Wickham," Darcy shouted as he paced angrily in Lady Cassandra's parlour.

"Well, perhaps you should not restrain yourself so much," answered Lady Cassandra; her mocking tone drew Darcy's reproachful look. He was in no mood for jokes.

"I warned you he would take advantage of you," Colonel Fitzwilliam spoke up from his chair. "The moment he saw you, he guessed you had an interest in this affair, and he speculated on it as much as he could."

Darcy answered with no more than a tired gesture of his hand. "You know too well that Wickham is my responsibility, and the present situation is my mistake."

The colonel attempted to contradict him, but Lady Cassandra interrupted first. "Of course it is your mistake, Darcy! You have always been too kind to Wickham; you always allowed him to take advantage of your generosity. When he approached Georgiana last summer, you should have taken drastic measures against him."

"Cassandra, I am sorry, but I have to contradict you; I doubt any measures would teach Wickham to be an honourable man," said the colonel.

"Well, perhaps neither of you is considering the *proper measures*," she answered, and the colonel stared at her, not daring to inquire about what such 'measures' might be.

Darcy, however, seemed oblivious to their conversation. A week had passed since Elizabeth and the Gardiners had left Pemberley and six days since he arrived in London in search of the runaway pair.

That terrible night in his room at Pemberley, he and Cassandra had talked for more than two hours; she finally revealed everything to him, and only in the end did she mention that Elizabeth insisted on her keeping the secret from Darcy. Though he knew he should feel ashamed of both Cassandra and himself for ignoring Elizabeth's desire and that he should suffer for Elizabeth's pain and torment, Darcy selfishly felt nothing but utter happiness. Elizabeth had left not because she wanted to be away from him but because of the deepest consideration for him and Georgiana!

He, who had always taken great pride in his self-control, impulsively considered saddling his horse that moment to follow her, let her know that his peace of mind meant nothing without her, and assure her he would do everything in his power to settle things. He would not allow Wickham to darken the brightness of his future with Elizabeth.

Eventually, Cassandra convinced him to leave for London the next morning. The other guests — who had been informed that urgent business called Darcy to town immediately — left Pemberley a few days later. Among the others in the party, only two were told about the misfortune that befell the Bennets: the colonel — because both Darcy and Cassandra agreed that he would be useful in their search — and Bingley — because Darcy did not want to hide anything from him regarding Miss Bennet.

It was not difficult for Darcy to discover Wickham's hiding place; one trip to Mrs. Younge's house was enough for him to understand she was well-informed about the man's location. Another visit and the proper sum severed her loyalty with her old friend. A day later, Darcy was climbing the stairs of a sordid inn where Wickham was hiding with Miss Lydia. He refused to marry the girl unless his demands were accepted — nothing less than 10,000 pounds. Darcy gladly would have given him that sum if he had the smallest hope the money would help Wickham put aside his old habits and become an honourable gentleman, but that would never happen — not with Wickham. *Perhaps Cassandra was correct; perhaps harsh, drastic measures were required against the man.*

He was also angry that the youngest Bennet sister would not even consider a return to her relatives' home or any other place. She wanted only to remain with her "dear Wickham" until they were married, which would surely happen someday. There was nothing to be done except make them marry as soon as possible.

"Darcy, have you informed the Gardiners that you discovered their niece?"

"No, not yet; I plan to do so tomorrow. I did call on Mr. Gardiner as soon as I ended my meeting with Wickham, but I was told Mr. Gardiner was out with his brother-in-law, Mr. Bennet. The servant, who remembered me, informed me that Mr. Bennet is to depart tomorrow morning for Hertfordshire, which is the best turn of events. I would much rather talk to Mr. Gardiner alone as I would not want Mr. Bennet to be aware of my interference in any way."

"But, Cousin, why on earth do you not want to talk to Mr. Bennet, as well?" asked the colonel. "He has the first interest in this as it is about his daughter and the honour of his family."

"I do not want Mr. Bennet to know about my involvement — nor Elizabeth. I want you to promise me this will remain a secret matter among the three of us; nobody must know any details. I will tell Mr. Gardiner and perhaps Bingley as much as I consider necessary."

"Oh, for heaven's sake, Darcy," cried Lady Cassandra, rolling her eyes in exasperation. This is quite ridiculous. Elizabeth made me promise I would not tell you about the elopement, and now you want me to promise I will not tell her about your involvement in resolving the elopement. Quite ridiculous!"

"Cassandra, it is not ridiculous at all! And it is your duty as a friend to respect my wish in this; you should understand better than anyone that I do not want Elizabeth's gratitude! I do not want her to feel she owes me anything or is obliged to repay me."

"Oh, let it be as you want," she relented, and the colonel smiled. "But truly, Darcy, if you still believe *'gratitude'* is the word for Miss Bennet's feelings, you are an utter fool!"

Then she turned to the colonel — who was laughing openly — and added: "Can you possibly believe this clueless man is the same one who gave Bingley advice on matters of the heart? Of course, I will not share my opinion about Bingley and his wisdom in asking advice, particularly from Darcy. Oh well, I had best go and see whether dinner is ready. In the meantime, Colonel, perhaps you can change his opinion about Miss Elizabeth."

However, neither the colonel nor Lady Cassandra succeeded in changing any of Darcy's opinions. He remained firm in his decision to deal with Wickham in his own manner and in his desire to keep everything secret from the Bennet family.

The gentlemen left immediately after dinner. An hour later, after struggling to find the best solution for everyone involved, Lady Cassandra wrote two short notes and sent her servant to deliver them immediately.

"COLONEL, THANK YOU FOR COMING so early. May I offer you something to eat — a coffee or some tea?" Lady Cassandra hurried to meet the gentleman and invited him into the drawing room.

"Good morning, Lady Cassandra. I just had a quick breakfast, but some coffee would be lovely. And in the meantime, allow me to ask about this secrecy at such an early hour. Did anything happen since last evening?"

"Sir, I dare ask for your assistance in a private matter of some importance; forgive me for disturbing you, but there are few people I trust."

"I am glad you consider me worthy of your trust; however I am still intrigued."

"I can understand that, sir. Allow me to inform you briefly, as it is most likely that —"

She was interrupted by a servant's entrance, informing her that a Mr. Wickham had just arrived to see her. She asked the visitor to be shown in as she cast a quick glance at the colonel; his countenance wore a frown, and the reproach in his eyes was easy to read. He was deeply displeased — that was obvious.

Equally obvious was the shock displayed on the visitor's face the moment he saw not only Lady Cassandra but also Colonel Fitzwilliam in the middle of the drawing room.

"Lady Cassandra, what a wonderful surprise to see you after all these years! I cannot tell you how flattered I was last evening when I received your invitation for a private meeting."

"Mr. Wickham, before going any further with this conversation, please do me the favour of not playing the *charming cad* with me. Surely you remember I never liked you — not even when we were children."

"Well then, if not tender affection for me, your invitation must be an attempt to support your friend Darcy. Perhaps your ladyship knows how to negotiate better than he, or perhaps you have more to offer? Let us hear what you have to say."

The colonel jumped from his seat instantly, and only Lady Cassandra's grip on his arm stopped him from whipping the man's impertinent smile from his face. He remained at Lady Cassandra's side as she addressed Wickham with a steely voice.

"Mr. Wickham — we have been talking only a few minutes, and you have already made two major mistakes: you have behaved most impertinently, and you have presumed I invited you to negotiate. You should remember I am not one to negotiate or to allow any impertinence without retribution."

"Regarding your accusation of being impertinent — your ladyship has known me all your life, so you cannot be surprised. As for negotiating — Darcy and I spent three hours last evening trying to reach an understanding about a situation that seemed to be of the highest interest to both of us. Now, I cannot help wondering about the nature of Darcy's interest … or yours. Surely Darcy was not a friend of the Bennets while he resided in Hertfordshire."

"Mr. Wickham, let us clarify one thing: I know that you just ran away a few days ago with a young girl of sixteen named Lydia Bennet. Your lack of honour is no surprise to me, and I did not invite you here today to discuss that; as for Lydia Bennet's honour, it is not my main concern. In fact, allow me to tell you that I care nothing at all about her — you may do with her as you please."

"I am sure the Bennets would not agree with you —"

"I am sure they would not, but their opinion is of little importance to me either. In any case, I think it would be much better for that girl *not* to marry you! After all, she is not the first — and certainly will not be the last — young girl to run off with a rascal."

"Your ladyship is very outspoken, as always. I wonder if Darcy was informed of this meeting —"

"You are making another mistake, Mr. Wickham, by presuming I am in any way interested in Darcy's opinion of this matter. In fact — he cannot have much to say; if he had dealt with you *properly* last summer, you would not be in a position to take advantage of any innocent young lady ever again."

Wickham's brows furrowed, and he struggled to regain his composure. "Lady Cassandra, may I ask again why your ladyship fetched me here this morning? I should be home, waiting for Darcy to come and discuss the remaining details of

130

this important matter."

"Oh, but *this* is a very important matter as well, Mr. Wickham. I asked you here today to tell you that I am seriously displeased with you. And you might remember that, when I am displeased with something, I simply *remove* the object of my displeasure."

"Your ladyship should be more specific. As I said, I am mystified about this entire situation."

"You are not mystified; you simply do not understand that you are in a difficult position."

"Lady Cassandra, I am not here to be insulted. If your ladyship is displeased, as you said —"

"Indeed, that is not enough insult for you! And I am more than displeased. I was angry and disgusted when you approached Darcy like a beggar, pretending you wanted to study law. If I had been in Darcy's position, I would have known better how to answer such a shameful attempt at deception! Yet he complied, hoping there might still be a chance for you to change for the better. So how did you repay his generosity? You took advantage of Georgiana without the smallest consideration for all the pain you caused her! For heaven's sake — she was a child with whom you grew up! You held her in your arms when she was an infant! You watched her learn to walk and speak! What kind of human being are you?"

Anger took control of her senses, and the turmoil made her face livid. Colonel Fitzwilliam was watching the heated exchange, his curiosity replete with worry. Wickham was pale and immobile in the middle of the room, staring at Lady Cassandra and blinking repeatedly. He tried to answer but could not.

"I...I never hurt Georgiana... I barely kissed her hand a few times —"

"I know that, Wickham; that is why you are here now, healthy and free to talk to me. You did not physically abuse her in any way, but you still hurt her as well as Darcy. In fact, for the last ten years you have done nothing but hurt the Darcys and anybody else who was foolish enough to trust you. Hurting them meant you hurt me as well — and I will tolerate that no longer. "

She paused again, allowing Wickham little time to comprehend her words.

"Lady Cassandra, I did not even meet the Darcys in the last year. It was Darcy who interfered in my business this time, so perhaps he is the one with whom you should have this talk."

"You are a liar, too — and a very poor one; in fact, you are quite poor in every way."

"Lady Cassandra, these offences —"

"These offences are what, Mr. Wickham? Are you surprised that I am not treating you as politely as Darcy did? You should become accustomed to that, because I am not Darcy! Darcy is an honourable gentleman who does only what is proper. I am just a spoiled, rich woman who cares about nothing but her own wishes and her own happiness. I am also quite resentful and possess a fearful temper; you should know that by now. I do not admit contradiction and never forgive those who have defied me. As I said — if something bothers me, I simply pay people to get it out of my way. And you, Wickham, are just *something* in my way!"

Pale and wordless, his jaw tightly clenched, and a vein pulsated wildly at his temple. Wickham looked at Lady Cassandra for a moment; her sharp, cold gaze held his defeated one.

"What do you want me to do, Lady Cassandra? Do you want me to accept Darcy's offer?" he asked eventually, averting his gaze from her.

"You may do whatever you please, Mr. Wickham; my only wish is to be happy and content, and I cannot be so unless my friends Darcy and Georgiana are also happy and content. Last night after he met with you, Darcy was extremely discontented, and I am sure his poor mood affected Georgiana as well. I do not know that his state of mind had anything to do with you, and I will not speculate about it. I only hope he will be *more happy* this evening. Now, if you have nothing important to tell me, please excuse me. I wish to return to my usual concerns."

NOT UNTIL WICKHAM LEFT THE room, his shoulders slumped and his eyes studying his shoes, did Lady Cassandra seem to lose her strength. She moved tentatively, as her knees appeared unable to support her. The colonel hurried to help her and almost took her in his arms as he helped her to the nearest sofa. He then filled a glass with wine, brought it to her, and sat beside her. She took the glass with trembling hands and raised it to her lips. "Thank you," she whispered, attempting a smile.

"Colonel Fitzwilliam, please forgive the spectacle you had to witness," she said a few minutes later. "I cannot imagine what you must think of me now."

He looked at her in earnest as he took her hand and pressed it to his lips.

"I know that you are not simply a rich, spoiled woman, and I know there are many things that matter to you beyond your own wishes and pleasures. I know you are kind and generous, and many people have had the benefit of your caring heart. I cannot even imagine how hard it must have been for you to act as you did in front of Wickham. However, I dare say your performance was quite convincing. Poor bastard — he was really frightened that you might actually pay somebody to take his miserable life." He smiled, trying to lighten the tension and make her smile; however, her countenance remained sombre.

"I am not at all as good as you believe me to be. I have hated Wickham since I was very young. He took advantage of one of my maids, and she almost died giving birth. She survived, but the child was born dead. I shall never forget that dead baby's little face and his mother's despair when she had to bury her son. Since that moment, I never forgave Wickham; my father allowed me to take care of the maid, but Wickham was never punished. My father said these things happened all the time with young gentlemen and servant girls. Sadly, now I know this is true, but back then I was deeply upset with my father and with the late Mr. Darcy. And when Darcy told

132

me how Wickham attempted to elope with Georgiana, I really wished he were dead! I am sorry to say it, but that is the truth."

"Lady Cassandra, I understand you perfectly, as I have had exactly the same feelings about him, but please do not allow that scoundrel to upset you so. He does not deserve such attention."

"You are very wise, Colonel. I must follow your advice, sir! I shall think of Wickham no more — but God, I am truly sorry for that girl. I hoped my intervention would help Darcy reach an understanding with Wickham today, but on the other hand, I feel I need to do something more — perhaps visiting Mrs. Gardiner and offering to help Miss Lydia in some way. I could send her to the country with a companion, and we could pretend she is visiting a distant relative — anything to save her from marrying that scoundrel!"

"Lady Cassandra, I applaud your generosity, but remember, Darcy already attempted to take Miss Lydia away, and she refused him soundly. She seemed determined to marry Wickham, so I doubt there is much we can do. We must be patient, and we surely must not interfere further without Darcy's knowledge. He will be angry in any case that you met Wickham and exposed yourself so much. He could have hurt you!"

"No indeed, Colonel — not as long as you were here to protect me," she said sweetly.

"Hmm...your confidence flatters me, but I am sure Darcy will not be impressed by it; we will try to find something else to keep his rage under control." He laughed, and she did the same; neither of them seemed to notice he was still holding her hand.

"Colonel," Lady Cassandra continued in an earnest voice, "I truly want to thank you for assisting me and supporting me in this though I did not inform you of my intentions. I know you disapprove my actions, so your support is even more appreciated. As for Darcy, if he discovers our little scheme, I will insist you knew nothing, and the entire fault was mine."

"Lady Cassandra, I shall pretend you did not say that," he answered good-humouredly. "What will you think of me if I allow a lady to shoulder the blame? In any case, I hope this situation will end soon; Darcy seems very taken aback, and Georgiana is not much better — not to mention Bingley, who keeps asking when we will return to Hertfordshire with him."

"But...Colonel, you know it is very possible that, once he returns to Hertfordshire, Darcy will propose to Miss Bennet again."

"Well, I surely hope so; to tell you the truth, I grow tired of this uncertain and dramatic situation."

His joyous voice and light countenance contradicted the seriousness of his words.

"You do? I was under the impression that you —"

"Pray continue, Lady Cassandra. What about me?"

"I thought you might have an interest in Miss Bennet yourself. I could not help noticing you seemed to admire her very much."

He looked at her, an incredulous expression on his face. "I do admire Miss Bennet, but not for a moment has she been the centre of my interest or my attention. I…umm…had hoped…well, that is I have hoped that your ladyship — who is so very perceptive — would have noticed long ago where my admiration lies."

It was her turn to look at him with wonder and no little concern. "Colonel, I must ask what you mean, as I am certainly not as perceptive as you might believe."

They were still sitting on the same couch, only a few inches between them. Suddenly, that distance seemed too confining for him; he rose and took a few steps away from her.

"Lady Cassandra, I know this is not the best moment for such a conversation, and I will not insist any further for now. I am more than willing to wait as long as necessary for your answer. However, since the subject has been raised, I cannot go further without asking your permission to…court you…as I do not dare ask for more at the present time."

Her perfect brows furrowed, and her cheeks turned crimson. She hurried to her feet and stood still in front of him, shaking her head in disapproval.

"Colonel Fitzwilliam, please do not do that to me. I beg you, let us finish our conversation this instant and forget that you asked me that question."

His countenance darkened, and for a moment, he forgot to breathe. "Lady Cassandra, I am afraid I do not understand your meaning. Forgive me, but I cannot accept that reply without insisting you tell me why I am to receive such an immediate, sound rejection? Was it not a quarter of an hour since you let me know you have a positive opinion of me?"

"I do, I do, and that is precisely why I ask you not to go further with this…" For a moment she covered her face with her hands and then, trying to regain some composure, moved a step closer. "Colonel Fitzwilliam, we have been dear friends all my life. I will not deny that I value your friendship, and I esteem you. I also understand that, in your situation, you must marry a woman with a fortune; please believe me, if I had any intention of entering into an arranged marriage, I would accept your offer with gratitude. But such is not the case. I do not intend to marry *at all,* and surely, I would not accept an arrangement of this kind. You must have known that…" She tried to touch his arm with her hand, but he took a step back. His eyes narrowed as they found hers.

"Indeed, Lady Cassandra, your words do not betray any kind of consideration you might have for me. May I wonder why, with so little patience, your ladyship hurried to presume that my reason was a mercenary one? And why, if your ladyship had such a good opinion of me as you just declared, did you not spend a single moment considering that, perhaps, it was not an *arranged* marriage I had in mind?"

"Colonel, please, let us speak with calmness —"

He was raising his voice and he could not control his anger — no, not anger, but utter disappointment. He had asked some questions, but he could not wait for her answer. Her reply had been eloquent from the first moment.

"No, I believe talk is unnecessary. In fact, I must beg your forgiveness for placing you in such a delicate situation. Your ladyship was correct; we should put this matter behind us and never mention it again. Now please excuse me —" He turned almost violently and hurried to the door with no further word; no more than a moment passed before she reached him and grabbed his arm with strength and determination.

"Colonel Fitzwilliam, you cannot possibly leave now! Please allow me a few more minutes. We are both very tired and still affected by the meeting with Wickham; obviously this entire situation is a misunderstanding."

He stopped; her hand seemed to burn his arm through the fabric of his coat. "There is no misunderstanding. Unfortunately, there is nothing to clarify. My feelings are quite clear — at least to me — and if I did not speak sooner, it was because I did not want to interfere —"

"But we have known each other for twenty years! All this time you have treated me with the care due a younger sister. I have never noticed any other kind of attention —" She paused and looked deeply into his eyes for a moment. "Countless times when I was in your company, I saw you among many charming young ladies; in fact, you were a great favourite of *all* the young ladies! I am sure I correctly interpreted the difference between your behaviour toward them and toward me."

His gaze remained fixed on hers, and his countenance changed instantly; yet, he found no answer.

"As for my presumption that your interest is in an advantageous marriage arrangement, not for a moment did I intend to offend you. It was you who mentioned so many times in the past that, as the second son of an earl, you needed to be very careful whom you married. When I said I have no wish to enter into such an arrangement, I did not mean to sound offensive — I only gave you my opinion on a matter that is quite common and sometimes even agreeable to many people."

She knew her words — at least partially — had the desired effect on him. Comprehension appeared clearly on his face, and it was soon followed by an expression of utter distress. He averted his eyes from her for some time in an attempt to search for the proper words.

"Lady Cassandra — again you are right, and I was wrong, completely wrong. Aside from choosing the most unfortunate moment to declare my feelings, it is true that nothing in my past behaviour could testify to the seriousness of my intentions. I also must beg your forgiveness for my ungentlemanly behaviour these past few minutes; my temper betrayed me."

She attempted a smile to show her acceptance of the truce, but the smile vanished a moment later when he continued. "I shall only speak of this as long as is necessary to gain your trust in my affection — and for you to come to regard it not as a brother's affection! I shall renew my professions and my addresses only when I am certain you welcome them."

"Colonel, please, you misunderstood me, sir! I did not mean to encourage you in this nor did I intend to toy with your feelings. Sir, let me be quite clear: I have no intention of marrying you or anyone else — either now or in the future. I cannot promise that my intentions will ever change, so please do not waste your time with something you will never accomplish."

His disappointment was so openly displayed that her heart melted; yet she knew there was nothing to do for it. He moved slowly toward the door, and she was certain she would never see him the same way as before nor would their friendship ever be the same. After a few steps, he stopped and looked straight into her eyes, his gaze losing its usual joy and easiness.

"Lady Cassandra, may I ask you a highly improper question?"

"Please do, sir." Her voice was barely audible.

"Is there another gentleman who owns your heart — a gentleman whom you would want to marry but you cannot for some reason? Is that why you are not allowing me any chance at all?"

She paused for a long moment and then averted her eyes as she replied. "Sir, there is no other gentleman I would wish to marry, nor is my heart engaged in the way you presume. Please allow me the benefit of your kindness and ask me no further questions." She kept her eyes averted, as she did not trust her emotions well enough to remain calm and look at him again.

"I see… Of course I will not insist further. You must have long desired my absence, so I will go now." Another pause and he turned to her again. "Lady Cassandra, will you allow me to be in your company again, or would you rather not see me for a while?"

"Sir, I have never wanted your absence. As I said, there are few people in the world whom I value as much as I do you. That will never change."

"Thank you." He stepped outside her view and pulled the door behind him.

Later that day, Darcy arrived to take Lady Cassandra to call at Gracechurch Street, and he was shocked to see his dear friend pale, not the smallest smile on her lips and her eyes devoid of expression; it was as if all her blood and liveliness were drained from her.

Neither that day nor in the days that followed could Darcy convince Cassandra to confess to him the reason for her unusual sadness. For the first time in twenty years, she refused to open her heart to him, and all he could do was be near her and watch over her.

He knew it would soon be his turn to help her as she had helped him a few months earlier.

A MONTH HAD PASSED SINCE Elizabeth left Pemberley, yet it seemed like a lifetime.

That day, with the rain mirroring her own tears, Pemberley and her heart had retreated in the distance behind their speeding carriage; she was certain she would not be able to endure the pain that was piercing her soul.

Yet, the moment she had reached the door of her home at Longbourn, she understood there was no room for grief in a family so deranged.

With their father absent and their mother requiring constant attendance, Elizabeth immediately took the greatest share of the burden on herself and occupied every minute of her day with the mundane chores of the house, allowing Jane to soothe Mrs. Bennet's nerves.

She never felt the weariness; in fact, it was helpful to think of nothing and, thus, suppress the pain buried deep in her heart. Nor did she require food or sleep. In fact, she avoided sleep as sleep meant dreams, and her dreams — all of her dreams — were the same. No, not the same — of great variety — but all had one person at their centre.

Some of her dreams pained her, some made her wake up crying, and some made her ashamed of her lack of fortitude and her wantonness. Mr. Darcy, of course, was the focus: his deep, tender voice, the look in his eyes — either tender and light or darkened by a feeling Elizabeth could not name but only guess — his fingers entwined with hers, his soft lips touching her hand or her forehead.

To her utter distress, there were times when she dreamed more than that. There were nights when, in her restless sleep, she had imagined his kiss, his caress, his whispers covering her with passion and tenderness and leaving her breathless and crying for more; and each of those times in her dreams, she desired with all her heart to answer him with the same passion, yet each time she could not. Instead, she felt unable to move, to speak, or to reveal to him her true feelings and desires; and each time he eventually vanished into the darkness, and she awoke with a wildly racing heart and a body soaked in clammy perspiration. No, she did not need sleep; it was her worst enemy, leaving her mind and soul more exhausted than before she retired.

After a week of searching and acquiring no other news than that the fugitives had yet to been found, a letter came from Mr. Gardiner that Mr. Bennet would return home. Elizabeth knew any hope was lost, and later that night in their room, she and Jane both cried for Lydia — and for other causes neither of them dared share with the other.

However, to their utter surprise a few days later, another letter from Mr. Gardiner arrived, stating that Lydia and Wickham had been found; a week later, they were married. A glimmer of hope rose in Jane's spirit; as for Mrs. Bennet, she was in raptures.

Not possessing Jane's genuine heart, Elizabeth was not so easily persuaded by the unexpectedly happy conclusion. She wondered continually what had happened; by what method and with what expense did Mr. Gardiner convince Wickham to marry Lydia? She dared to talk only with her father about that delicate matter and was shocked when Mr. Bennet confessed he suspected a sum of 10,000 pounds. Surely, that was more than her uncle could afford and, undoubtedly, more than Mr. Bennet would ever be able to repay.

If only Lydia had a chance at happiness or at least of having a comfortable life! Yet, the hope was small; Elizabeth was convinced of that a few days later.

Noisy and thoughtless as ever, the newly married Wickhams arrived at Longbourn before departing for the North where Mr. Wickham was expected very soon to take a new commission.

Mrs. Bennet and perchance Kitty were the only ones pleased with their visit. Mr. Bennet's reception was cold; Elizabeth and Jane, though pleased to see their sister well and unharmed, could not hide their disapproval of Lydia's untamed, unabashed, and fearless behaviour.

Wickham was no less distressing than his bride; his manners were as pleasing as before, and his smile was charming as he claimed their relationship. Elizabeth was disgusted, and even Miss Bennet was appalled.

During dinner, Wickham, who happened to sit near Elizabeth, began inquiring after his acquaintance in the neighbourhood with good-humoured ease, which she felt unable to equal in reply. After dinner while they were all gathered in the drawing room, her new brother-in-law approached Elizabeth, who tried to retire to a corner as far from the others as possible.

"I am afraid I interrupt your solitude, my dear sister," said he.

"You certainly do," she replied, forcing a smile to conceal her displeasure, "but it does not follow that the interruption must be unwelcome."

"I should be sorry indeed if it were. We were always good friends, and now we are better."

"True; now we are family. Things have changed unexpectedly and very quickly indeed."

"Things have changed," he repeated, looking at her with interest. "I found from our uncle and aunt that you have actually seen Pemberley."

"Yes, I have had that pleasure."

"I confess I was surprised to hear that you and Mr. and Mrs. Gardiner grew quite close to Darcy. I know how much you have always disliked him."

"Mr. Wickham, if I remember correctly, I mentioned to you when we last met that my opinion of Mr. Darcy had changed completely after I had come to know him better, and being more in his company in the last weeks only helped me to understand why so many people admire and appreciate his character. As for Mr. Gardiner, I cannot speak for him, but I dare say he seemed to value his acquaintance with Mr. Darcy and Colonel Fitzwilliam a great deal."

Elizabeth hoped she had silenced him, but he soon afterwards continued.

"Yes, I remember our conversation just before we left Meryton. However, it appeared that Darcy had improved even more on closer acquaintance, had he not?"

Elizabeth's patience reached the edge of her tolerance. "Sir, may I dare ask how Mr. Darcy's character came into your conversation with my uncle? I should think you had more urgent business to discuss," Her raised eyebrow clearly expressed her opinion about that "urgent business." But he remained as calm as before.

"Oh, but I had the opportunity actually to witness the relationship between Darcy and Mr. Gardiner. Did you not know that we met at your uncle's home a few times?"

Elizabeth's heart nearly stopped; of what was the man talking?

"Mr. Darcy? Mr. Darcy was in Town — in my uncle's home?" She realised her surprise and interest betrayed her, but she could not contain herself, and indeed her brother-in-law did not miss her reaction.

"Yes, he was, and he seemed quite familiar with the surroundings, so I assumed it was not his first visit there. And he was not alone but in the company of Lady Cassandra. You did meet Lady Cassandra, did you not?"

Elizabeth's head was spinning with countless questions, fears and hopes, and several moments passed before she could breathe properly again. The notion that he had been in London and met Wickham was impossible to believe and even more so to understand. What was he doing there — and with Lady Cassandra? It could not be a simple coincidence, yet it was also unbelievable that either Mr. Darcy or her ladyship would have willingly met Lydia or Wickham. But if it were true, that meant he knew what happened to Lydia; he knew and, even more so, agreed to meet with Wickham — more than once. *No, that cannot be… I surely misunderstood.* How was it possible? Had Lady Cassandra betrayed her confidence?

"Dear sister, I hope I have not upset you with this news," he said, a pleased grin on his face.

"No indeed, sir, why should I be upset? Surely it is my uncle's privilege to receive any guests he pleases into his own home." She struggled to maintain her calm, yet she desperately searched for a reason to retire to her room. She needed to think, and she needed to write her aunt immediately! Mrs. Gardiner was the only one who could clarify things for her.

"Lady Cassandra did not seem as friendly as Darcy was to your relatives, to tell the truth. In fact, I dare say she highly disapproved of Darcy's closeness to the Gardiners. And even more so — as we are now brother and sister — I must warn you she confessed to me she cared not at all about Lydia or any of your family."

"Sir, I am truly surprised that Lady Cassandra would confess such a thing to you in my uncle's house in the presence of my relatives."

He appeared clearly disconcerted and averted his eyes instantly; his countenance changed. "It was not in Mr. Gardiner's house … we met one day, and it was then that we spoke."

"I see… You met Lady Cassandra privately? That is also astonishing as I know from an impeccable source that Lady Cassandra does not care much for you either, sir." Before he found words to reply, she continued.

"It appears that your time in London was rather eventful. In a short time, you met my uncle and aunt, Mr. Darcy and also Lady Cassandra more than once while you managed to arrange your marriage to my sister and obtain a new commission. You have all my admiration for such efficiency, sir — as I said, quite astonishing!"

As she spoke, her words seemed to clarify the answers to some of her tormenting questions. Everything sounded so logical and clear that she was afraid to dare believe it. Everything was connected; she could now see that clearly. But how tightly things were connected and to whom she had no courage even to presume. She needed certainties not wild guesses, and she knew to whom to apply.

"If you will be so kind as to excuse me now, sir, I have to join my sisters and spend a little time with them. Lydia will leave tomorrow, and I have hardly spoken to her at all."

The rest of the evening, Elizabeth could do nothing but consider the extraordinary information she had discovered. That night, she wrote a long letter to her aunt, asking for all the details of Mr. Darcy's presence and his meetings with Mr. Wickham. The letter was sent the next morning, and Elizabeth began to count the hours until Mrs. Gardiner's reply might arrive.

A WEEK AFTER THE WICKHAMS left, Mrs. Philips barged into the house, her impatient voice resounding in every corner. Netherfield was re-opened, and Mr. Bingley was expected back, together with a large party of friends.

From that time, Jane began to blossom. She would not admit that her changed state had anything to do with the long-expected return of a certain neighbour, but her beauty and the light in her eyes spoke more than her words. Jane was happy and hopeful and so was Elizabeth —not for herself but for her sister. If Mr. Bingley had decided to return, then Jane must be the reason for his decision. At least *she* would be happy.

Mr. Bingley's party finally arrived, and the news reached Longbourn just before dinner; Mrs. Bennet's agitation was unbearable, and dinner turned into a noisy argument. Mr. Bennet strongly resisted his wife's demand that he visit Mr. Bingley first thing the next morning. His refusal made Mrs. Bennet more impatient, and her nerves overwhelmed her appetite while she insisted — with no success — that Jane and Elizabeth support her demand.

As she did so many times before during those weeks, Elizabeth resisted sleep that night. She wondered continually about the identity of the other members of the Netherfield party, and she dared not allow hope to envelop her heart. Even if *he* had come with the others, surely his intentions toward her had utterly changed. No matter how strong his feelings for her at Pemberley, they could never overcome a sentiment as natural as abhorrence for a relationship with Wickham! Every kind of pride must revolt at the connection. No, there was no hope that her mind could admit.

The next morning, Elizabeth woke with the sun after several hours of restless sleep. She needed fresh air to breathe and solitude for her memories.

As she left the house, her steps took her along old and well-known paths until her home was far behind and the beautiful prospect of Netherfield appeared before her. She stared at the big house until her eyes hurt, though she knew it was not possible actually to *see* anyone. Upset with her own foolishness, she turned and walked back as quickly as she could.

She closed her eyes as the wind caressed her face and took off her bonnet, allowing the breeze to play in her hair. Her soul was still heavy, and her heart still a prisoner of her grief — but at least she could breathe. And she could dream in the daylight, a dream so real that she could feel his presence behind her; she was still convinced she was dreaming when she heard his voice softly calling her name.

"Miss Bennet... I have been walking in the grove some time in the hope of meeting you."

Chapter 10

Three weeks had passed since Colonel Fitzwilliam left her home following his astonishing proposal, and Lady Cassandra could scarcely believe it happened. Colonel Fitzwilliam — to have such deep feelings toward her and actually propose to her?

Not for a moment did she doubt his words; not for a moment did she presume he only pretended to possess tender feelings for her to induce her into matrimony. She knew him to be a deeply honourable man, and she trusted him enough to be certain he would never try to deceive her. He would never declare a love he did not possess. But to love her? After all those years? After a lifetime of friendship? How could that be?

The more she thought about it, the more her turmoil increased and the more she fought the undeniable evidence; her heart was not stone even if she wished it to be. Or at least it had not hardened in front of the younger Fitzwilliam son.

Yes, it was a lifetime of friendship, but not the kind of friendship she and Darcy had shared.

She had not met David Fitzwilliam as much or as often as she had met Darcy nor had she spent more than a couple of months of each year on the same estate. However, when they met and were in each other's company, he had always been the one who knew how to treat her and make her stubbornness as a spoiled girl disappear instantly. Even when she was very young, no one — not her governess, her parents whom she loved deeply, the Darcys whom she cared for as much as her parents, or even her best friend, the young Fitzwilliam Darcy — succeeded in their attempts to temper her, control her, or scold her without opposition in the manner David Fitzwilliam could do. He was the only one she listened to without argument when she was a child; he seemed always to know what she should be allowed to do without putting herself in danger or feeling restricted. And she had always accepted his advice.

Lady Cassandra smiled again at the remembrance of her childhood. *Oh dear, my poor, beloved mama — what she had to go through with me.* She shook her head in a tender scolding against her past behaviour and went to the wall where the miniatures of her parents smiled at her. She caressed the pictures with trembling fingers as she wiped her tears. Even now, all these years later, she still could not think of her parents without being overwhelmed by emotion.

She had been a difficult child — she knew that — and all because her parents and their friends the Darcys were overly kind and indulgent with her. Fathers did not involve themselves in their small children's education, especially the girls; her father and the late Mr. Darcy were no exception. If they were preoccupied with anyone's education, their interest seemed to be the young Fitzwilliam. Now she understood that, in all likelihood, both fathers shared the hope that she and Darcy would some-day marry, and he would take the responsibility of both estates. She often felt ne-glected and a bit envious of her dear friend for all the attention he received.

However, she really could not complain about a lack of attention from either par-ent. Her father had two weaknesses — his wife and his daughter — and Cassandra learned that fact early and took every advantage a child could gain from it.

Sometimes, her parents did not allow her to do things that could prove danger-ous for a little girl; on the other hand, they never forced her to do anything she did not wish to do. She had grown free and unrestrained by anything except a good, healthy education based on fair principles, applied with the generosity she inherited from both her parents. Some people might have called her a wild girl, and Lady Catherine de Bourgh did so — many times.

When Cassandra was seven, her parents offered her a beautiful horse instead of her old pony but did not allow her to ride with her much older friends — young Darcy and the Fitzwilliam siblings. She had cried, feeling disappointed and certain everybody was unfair to her, and she refused a meal that day.

A couple of days later, Lord Russell presented her a compromise: she could ride with the boys only if she remained close to David Fitzwilliam, who was seven years older than she and kindly offered to supervise her. She immediately argued that she was an excellent rider and did not need supervision, but David, with his happy dis-position and ready smile, assured her they trusted her riding abilities, but they did not trust the horse well enough and wanted to be certain the animal would behave. That seemed a reasonable explanation, and she accepted it happily.

From that moment, Cassandra concluded that David Fitzwilliam was — next to her friend Darcy — the nicest and the wisest young man in the whole of England, and she retained that opinion until she turned seventeen and things changed for her.

From the age of eleven, she rarely saw David Fitzwilliam who, like Darcy, had been sent away to school. She saw him once when Lady Anne passed away and twice in the next few years. He joined the army, and she heard little about him; Darcy mentioned him from time to time in the regular letters he sent her.

She met David Fitzwilliam again the year she turned seventeen; her mother had arranged a sumptuous ball for her coming out.

Lady Lavinia was much more excited about the event than Cassandra herself and certainly more pleased with it. Cassandra did not wish to have a ball; she did not truly wish to be "out" either. She was content to spend time with her family and the Darcys, riding through the fields and playing with Georgiana. Who needed to be "out"? Not she, that was certain!

However, her mother wanted the ball, so she did everything she could to appear pleased with it. In truth, however, she felt bothered and nervous about the ball. She did not know many people among the guests and did not feel comfortable in the midst of so many strangers.

When David Fitzwilliam had approached her, she had been startled with surprise and relief. He looked utterly different in his uniform, different than she had last seen him and different from the other gentlemen in the room.

He stayed with her and Darcy for quite some time, asked her about everything that happened during the past years, and declared more than once that he would certainly not have recognised her if they had met by chance, and that she had grown into a beautiful young lady.

She remembered how she had blushed at every word and was shocked by her own reaction. She knew she behaved childishly, and she was afraid she had made a fool of herself. As for David, he had acted as always: friendly, open, and kindly. He was not flirting with her, no indeed; even she — with her lack of experience in the matter — could tell that. He simply stated his opinion of her, about how she looked and about the entire event.

And then, with his friendly voice and open smile, he had asked her for the favour of the first set. For the first time in her life, Cassandra had felt her stomach turn into an icy hole and her heart race wildly. Furious with herself and fighting to understand what was happening to her, she had managed to formulate a reasonable acceptance.

The dance — the whole evening — had been lovely; David, together with Darcy, offered her his full attention, being discreetly around her all the time. She had felt better than ever and, as the hours had passed, had begun to realise that what she was feeling in David's presence was different from anything she had experienced before. Her gaze followed him around the room, and when their eyes met, he smiled at her. From time to time, he had sneaked near her and whispered something, making her laugh and blush. He had asked her for yet another set, and during supper, he talked to everybody around him but had turned to look at her more than once and even winked at her in a barely noticeable gesture. Yes, at her coming out ball, Lady Cassandra's innocent heart had been touched for the first time.

The next morning, after barely sleeping from excitement, she allowed herself countless speculations. She admitted that David had turned into a handsome and charming gentleman and that she enjoyed his company exceedingly. She also had been certain he was not indifferent to her, either. And she remembered that, as the second son of an earl, he must be careful in his choice of a wife. What better choice than herself, the heiress of a great fortune from a noble, titled family? That indeed should have been a marriage to the advantage of both.

However, her dreams shattered painfully the next day when she saw David at the theatre in the intimate company of a young countess who was a recent widow.

He was staying in the countess's box, which was quite near her family's, and he behaved as he had at the ball: he came to greet them, complimented Cassandra for the ball and whispered to her that everyone in Town was talking of her, and all the eligible bachelors were vying for her attention. He added that he was as proud of her as he would be of his own sister. Then he returned to the countess with whom he had indeed been flirting, and there was no doubt about the intimate nature of their relationship.

That night and for many nights that followed, Cassandra had wet her pillow with the bitter tears of her dashed, first romantic hopes. For a few months, she avoided seeing David Fitzwilliam as much as she could; then, finally, her mind and senses overcame her disappointed heart, and she understood that her sudden and strange change of feeling could not force his to change as well.

He had remained the same as he ever was — her dependable, trusted friend — and he would no more consider a marriage arrangement with her than she would want a marriage with Darcy. It was a fact she learned to accept, forcing herself not to allow it to affect their friendship.

Later that year when her mother passed away, David Fitzwilliam had come for the funeral, and his warm, gentle embrace gave her nothing but comfort and a sense of safety. He was there to take care of her, protect her if need be, and offer her support and friendship.

His help was much needed not long after that when Lady Cassandra's soul — and the wonderful world of her childhood — disappeared forever with the death of Lord Russell. From that moment, she remained alone in the world. She had cried for days, allowing no one around her except Darcy and David Fitzwilliam, who spent more than two weeks at Pemberley, precisely to be close to her; he told her as much. Darcy and David — her closest friends in the world.

And now, after all these years, David comes to profess his love for her and to ask her to marry him! Now, when she had put all her past feelings for him aside before they managed to blossom — now, after all that had happened in the last four years; now, when she could not possibly marry him. Her world broke into thousands of small pieces again, and so did her heart!

Thank heavens she had left London — and him — behind. She was in Hertfordshire now and looking from the window of her room as Darcy rode along the hill, his horse moving at a quick pace. She smiled; she knew where he was going.

No — IT WAS NOT A dream! He moved slowly toward Elizabeth as she moved toward him, her eyes captured by his, her steps tentative, her face pale, and her dry lips slightly opened. She heard his soft, tender voice — the voice to which she had become accustomed while she was at Pemberley — but her mind could barely understand the meaning of his words. He said something about walking out to meet her. Should she answer? And what was she to answer? He came closer and closer; she was already aware of his scent and the warmth of his nearness, and he kept moving forward — so she stopped.

"Mr. Darcy..." did she truly say the words? She was not sure, as she did not hear them. He moved a step closer.

"Sir, I did not know... I did not expect to see you here at this hour."

"I am sorry; I did not mean to disturb you."

"No, no... you did not disturb me... it was just..." *It was just that I was thinking of you, and you just appeared. Could it be my thoughts that brought you here?* The unsaid words made her cheeks redden; suddenly, her knees seemed unable to support her.

"Miss Bennet, are you unwell?" Without waiting for her answer, he instantly placed his hands on her upper arms to support her. The gesture only made her dizzier.

"I am well, thank you." She did not dare to lift her head, as he was so close that she could feel his breath. She suddenly remembered her manners and, with her head still down, almost leaning against his chest, tried to proceed politely. "Have you travelled safely to Hertfordshire, sir?"

"Yes, we travelled uneventfully, thank you. We arrived yesterday, late in the afternoon." His hands were still resting on her arms.

"Yes, I have heard that... I mean, I have heard that Mr. Bingley was expected to return but... I did not suppose you would join him. Is Georgiana still at Pemberley, sir? I hope she is well."

"No, she is here as are Lady Cassandra and Mr. and Mrs. Hurst. Only Miss Bingley remains in Town."

"You brought Georgiana, too?" she cried, her surprise making her forget the proper tone.

"Yes, I did." They were so close to each other that their heads were almost touching. "Miss Bennet, are you displeased with our presence here?"

His voice was no stronger than hers was, and its slight tremble of uncertainty drove her finally to look at him. Did he think she was displeased to see him?

"I am not at all displeased, sir, only... I did not believe it possible that you would return to the neighbourhood after —" She stopped and blushed in embarrassment, angry with herself for perhaps saying too much. She was still not certain about his involvement in the unhappy situation that ended with Lydia's wedding. "My sister Lydia married Mr. Wickham last week."

Darcy's countenance changed a little. "I am aware of that. I met Wickham and Miss Lydia in Town a few times while I visited Mr. and Mrs. Gardiner."

His eyes were still fixed on her face, and she noticed a trace of worry in them. Daringly, she continued.

"Yes, I heard as much, and I cannot tell you how surprised I was. I imagined there was a very important matter that brought you to town so unexpectedly. When I left, you were at Pemberley among your friends."

"It is true, you *left me* at Pemberley," he answered, the emotion in his voice impossible to hide. Suddenly realizing what he said, he withdrew his hands and took a few steps away from her.

Elizabeth remained still, only her eyes following his agitated pacing. After a few minutes, she could no longer continue to witness his turmoil. "I am sorry I left Pemberley so suddenly, sir. I know it was our duty as guests to leave you a note at least, but I thought it was better for us to depart as soon as possible. Please do not blame my aunt or my uncle; it was my decision and my insistence to do so; I am the only one to blame."

He turned to her and met her eyes again. "You are not to blame for anything, Miss Bennet; please forgive my improper words. I only admired you for your decision even more…when I understood it properly."

His confession took her utterly by surprise, and she was speechless for a moment; her fingers felt cold, and they trembled.

"Sir, please allow me to thank you for your undeserved kindness to my poor sister. My gratitude cannot be expressed in proper words. Without your help we would never —"

He frowned and averted his eyes. "Miss Bennet, I shall not deny my assistance in discovering Wickham, but my help meant nothing compared to your uncle's efforts. Please let us not talk of that further, else we should talk first of my earlier fault in not exposing Wickham publicly. If he was able to elope with a young girl such as Miss Lydia, I must share the blame."

"This is not true, sir! How could you —" she cried, but he took both of her hands in his.

"Miss Bennet…" His voice sounded deep and soft, while she felt his eyes piercing her soul; her fingers were trapped in his, and she dared not move them, hoping he could not sense her trembling. Her lips went dry again.

"Miss Bennet, if you want to express some kind of gratitude, you may do so by never speaking of Wickham again. I dare say he has already tormented both of us far too frequently."

Flustered by the memory of everything that happened between them because of Wickham and her own folly, she only nodded in agreement. "Very well, sir. That will be an easy way to express my gratitude, indeed."

"Then everything is settled," he replied, returning her smile.

No, she cried to herself, *nothing is settled.* There were countless things she wanted to ask him, but she did not dare; she had to respect his wish; she owed him as much.

Darcy continued without releasing her hands. "I am pleased to be here; that is all that matters now. We have no fixed plans for how long we will remain in

Hertfordshire, but if everything is well and our presence is welcomed, I dare say we will stay for quite some time."

That lump in her throat again! And that shiver — Could he feel her shivering? "I hope you will enjoy your stay, sir. We…we are delighted to have *you all* here. I cannot wait to see Georgiana and Lady Cassandra again."

A trace of distress shadowed his countenance for a moment, and she did not miss it. Suddenly, she became uneasy again and inquired of him with much concern, "Sir, is anything wrong with Georgiana or Lady Cassandra?"

"No, there is nothing wrong, but they have been a little distressed lately. I am sure they will recover during their stay at Netherfield. And I thank you for your concern."

"Will I see them both later — during your call, I mean?"

"I am not sure; I hope so. If not, I am sure there will be plenty of opportunity for you to meet again soon." Again, his voice sounded unsettled, and she knew something was not well.

"Miss Bennet, it is time for me to return. Bingley insisted we have an early breakfast and be prepared to pay calls as soon as propriety allows. He seemed eager to visit his neighbours again."

She withdrew her hands, embarrassed that she did notice how late it was.

"Oh, I have to leave, too. You are right; it is quite late."

"Please, allow me to accompany you on your way back."

"But…do you not have to return to Netherfield? Please do not bother yourself; I will be quite safe; this is one of my favourite paths, and I walk here daily."

"I know it is your favourite path, Miss Bennet. I remembered when you talked it last year. Still, it would be my pleasure to have your company a little longer."

She found nothing to say and accepted his offered arm; they walking in silence until Longbourn appeared before them.

"Sir, thank you for your company. I shall look forward to seeing you later."

"Then I shall ask Bingley to be ready as soon as possible." For some moments, as neither seemed willing to depart first, they remained in front of each other, smiling tentatively yet wholeheartedly, their eyes silently speaking what their words did not dare.

She seemed to recover first, curtseyed, moved a few steps, and then quickly turned back until she was only a few inches from him. "Mr. Darcy, I am very happy to see you in Hertfordshire again."

The expression of delight on his face melted her heart, and with a sensation of deep happiness, she departed again, almost running from him. She did not know that, had she stayed a moment longer, she would have received the first real kiss of her life.

MISS BINGLEY HAD HER FIRST good moment in recent months: an invitation for tea with her old acquaintance, Lady Sophia, an exceedingly rich heiress of three and twenty. What a wonderful surprise the invitation was, considering Lady Sophia had rarely invited her in the past!

Of course, she refused to accompany Charles to Netherfield; that could wait another week or so, but Lady Sophia's invitation could not be refused under any circumstances.

It was unbearably warm, and Miss Bingley blamed the carriage, the driver, the roads and the sun for her discomfort. Oh, what a pity they had to leave Pemberley! Pemberley was everything she ever wanted; it was ideal for both summer and winter. Pemberley was simply perfect.

That Eliza Bennet — it was all her fault; Miss Bingley was certain of that. As soon as *she* left, Mr. Darcy left too, and they were practically forced to leave Pemberley and return to London in the middle of summer. What horrible distress! Then they all went to Hertfordshire — close to all the Bennets! It was unacceptable, especially after the youngest Bennet girl eloped so scandalously with that officer. Yes, they married, but she knew what that meant — oh, those reckless, thoughtless, tiresome Bennets!

Finally, the carriage stopped, and she descended in front of Lady Sophia's home — an imposing, wealthy structure, speaking clearly of its mistress's situation in life — such a home as she, Caroline Bingley, deserved and craved.

The servant opened the main door, and Caroline was shown into the drawing room where Lady Sophia and other guests were gathered. At her entrance, she had the impression that they all paused in their conversation and many pairs of eyes turned to her.

The hostess hurried to greet her, and she was pleased to be so welcomed; a moment later, her satisfaction grew, and she congratulated herself for accepting the invitation when she was introduced to the most charming gentleman she had seen of late — Lord Markham.

MR. BINGLEY, MR. DARCY AND Lady Cassandra left Longbourn after a long and satisfactory visit.

Mrs. Bennet reminded Mr. Bingley many times that he still owed her a dinner from last autumn. Only Mr. Darcy's mention that his sister was at Netherfield — resting after the journey and waiting for them to join her at dinner — stopped Mrs. Bennet's insistence.

However, Lady Cassandra, who — shockingly for Elizabeth — managed to get along well with both Mr. and Mrs. Bennet, assured the mistress of the house that she, for one, was most eager to accept a dinner invitation at Longbourn, as were the gentlemen. From that moment, Lady Cassandra became the object of Mrs. Bennet's unrestrained admiration and the recipient of her complete attention, especially once she was certain the lady had no interest in Mr. Bingley.

Jane Bennet was more beautiful but less talkative then ever during the visit. She and Mr. Bingley barely took their eyes from each other, and every time the gentleman spoke to her directly or smiled at her, she nearly fainted. She managed to answer Lady Cassandra's polite and friendly questions reasonably enough. However, she was grateful that her sister took care of her ladyship, allowing her to fully enjoy Mr. Bingley's presence — Mr. Bingley, whom she had been certain she would never see again and the one who still possessed her heart and her thoughts; Mr. Bingley, who said he had no intention of leaving Netherfield again soon.

Elizabeth was both happy and embarrassed to meet Mr. Darcy again. Only minutes after their arrival, Mr. Darcy approached Elizabeth, who was sitting on a sofa near the window. She immediately asked about Georgiana, whose absence surprised her.

"Georgiana is fine," he answered after a brief hesitation. "She is at Netherfield, resting after the long trip. She seemed a little tired."

"I was hoping she would join you today; I confess I dearly missed her."

"Thank you. I am sure my sister has missed your company as well."

Then why did she not come with you? she wondered to herself.

"Mr. Darcy, I cannot help inquiring further if everything is well with Georgiana. You seemed…Something seemed to worry you when you talked about her."

"Miss Bennet, your discernment amazes me again. I am not certain whether I should be happy or concerned that you know my disposition so well as to see behind my words."

"I cannot answer to that, sir. It is for you only to decide whether there are reasons for concern regarding me and my discernment." Her lips narrowed in a smile. He smiled back.

"I shall try to be in your company as much as possible in order to clarify this aspect of your character, Miss Bennet." Elizabeth was upset at being able to do nothing but blush again at his words.

Before she could form a coherent sentence, he continued in a more serious tone. "As for Georgiana, I am grateful for your concern, and I can assure you my sister is in excellent health. However, there is indeed something concerning her about which I would like to speak with you. Could we talk more privately — tomorrow morning, perhaps, should we happen to meet again on your morning walk?"

She was certain her cheeks coloured so highly that they were burning.

"I…that would be lovely, sir. I look forward to…I mean, if we should happen to meet again tomorrow. It is my habit to walk early every morning before breakfast."

"An early morning walk before breakfast is beneficial to one's health, I am sure. Perhaps I should try it as well, rather than riding."

"Riding might be desirable, as well. Fortunately, the paths between Longbourn and Netherfield are appropriate for both riding and walking."

"And for private talks, I hope," he added with a deep voice that made her shiver.

Private talks? she wondered, barely controlling her emotions. *Could he mean "that" private talk? Or did he simply intend to talk about whatever bothers Georgiana? Oh, I am so foolish!*

"Miss Bennet…?" his voice startled her and she managed to gather her wits enough to reply.

"Yes indeed, sir, for private talks, too." She knew her answer was an agreement — but to what?

Mrs. Bennet's high voice drew their attention toward the others in the room. Darcy whispered a thank you for her time and then moved toward Mr. Bennet and took a chair close to him; a few minutes later, they were engaged in a serious, and apparently pleasant, conversation.

Not for a moment did Mr. Darcy become as exuberant as Mr. Bingley, but his behaviour was pleasant and almost friendly, unlike his brooding aloofness in the autumn. However, just as last year, he spent most of his time staring at Elizabeth with intense, dark eyes that made her shiver and kept her cheeks crimson; this time, however, she understood the meaning of his gaze. Their eyes met quite often across the room. When he spoke to her father, she knew his affability was meant for her; when he congratulated her mother on her youngest daughter's marriage, Elizabeth blushed in mortification but was grateful for his generosity toward her mother. *He is everything a man should be,* she concluded as she watched every gesture, every movement — and every handsome feature.

They would meet again the next morning, and she wondered how she would be able to endure the hours of waiting.

Mrs. Bennet gave her eldest daughters several causes for mortification during the visit, but Lady Cassandra appeared relaxed, entertained, and not at all bothered by her hostess's lack of propriety. When the call ended and the guests departed with the promise that they would return the next day, everyone agreed it was the most pleasant visit they had had in many years. Jane and Elizabeth, completely absorbed in their personal happiness, hardly heard a word of the praise their mother bestowed upon the gentlemen and the beautiful, elegant Lady Cassandra.

"So Darcy, what do you think?" They were in the Netherfield library, enjoying a glass of wine before dinner.

"About what, Bingley?"

"About Miss Bennet, of course! Is she not the most beautiful angel? Oh, if she could forgive me, if she could still think well of me and accept my attentions… What do you think, Darcy?"

"Bingley, I am sure you have no reason to worry; Miss Bennet seemed pleased to see you, though her pleasure was not as exuberantly displayed as Mrs. Bennet's. As for her feelings toward you, the coming days will soon clarify everything for you."

"Whose feelings?" Lady Cassandra entered the room impetuously.

"Miss Bennet's feelings. Bingley asked my opinion, and I told him the next few days would offer him all the certainties he needs."

Lady Cassandra looked at them and rolled her eyes in utter exasperation.

"Excuse me, but is Miss Bennet the young lady we just met at Longbourn?"

"Yes, of course she is," answered Bingley, puzzled.

"The beautiful one with blond hair and blue eyes — am I correct?"

"Yes, your ladyship."

"The one who looked at you, Mr. Bingley, as if you were some sort of idol? The one who almost swooned when you spoke to her and appeared to forget how to breathe when you were smiling at her? *That* was Jane Bennet? *That* was the lady whom you exceedingly perceptive and intelligent gentlemen believed to be indifferent last year and about whom you are still uncertain, Mr. Bingley? *She* was the one you were talking about?"

Lady Cassandra's tone grew more sarcastic, matching her sharp gaze that moved from Darcy to Bingley. Before any of them could answer properly, she turned and exited the room as she whispered loudly enough to be heard, "What utter fools…"

A surprised Bingley and a furious Darcy tried to protest Cassandra's insult, but they were thwarted as the door closed behind her. Later that evening, Bingley easily accepted that he was a complete fool and worse, but he understood precisely what he must do the next day.

Chapter 11

A couple of *"utter fools"* Lady Cassandra had called him and Bingley, and Darcy knew she was absolutely correct. In fact, he was an even bigger fool than Bingley, as Bingley's major mistake had been to trust Darcy's friendship and judgment in a matter that could have ruined his chance of happiness. As for Darcy — he had more faults and, in many ways, had been a greater fool. However, he seemed to be a fortunate fool, as things were definitely moving in the desired direction.

Bingley would undoubtedly propose to Miss Bennet the next morning; he was decided! As for Darcy, he would meet Elizabeth in the grove first thing in the morning — alone. The mere thought made him shiver with anticipation and anxiety as never before in his life. He felt and behaved like a schoolboy — that was certain — and it did not bother him in the slightest.

In truth, he had never possessed much restraint or self-control in her presence — or in her absence. Both her nearness and his own vivid memories had inspired the most delicious dreams as well as the worst nightmares during those months spent at Netherfield last year.

He saw her eyes — always sparkling with wit and laughing at him even when they argued — her lips — softly narrowed into an ironic smile or half-parted as she laughed openly with her sister or a friend — and her neck —creamy skin framed by dark, curled hair. He also saw the garnet cross that rested innocently at her neckline, her voice, her brightness, her natural and pleasant — though not always proper — manners, and her kindness and care for others. She, with all her being, seemed to fulfil perfectly his every wish and aspiration in a woman, yet he had denied the evidence for months and changed a possibility for happiness into a lasting misery.

During those days she stayed at Netherfield to care for her sister, his turmoil had been complete. All of their shared meals, the long hours spent together in the evening, their challenging conversations — what bittersweet torture! He forced himself barely to speak to her and avoided any opportunity to meet her more than he was obliged, otherwise he was afraid he would simply take her in his arms and run away with her to some secluded place where nobody would find them. He could show her just how little he was a man without fault, indeed!

One day they had even spent half an hour together in the library without speaking to each other — just reading. That is to say, *she* was probably reading. As for himself, he had spent the entire time staring at her, secretly caressing her with his greedy, shameless eyes: her face, her ears, her neckline and lower to the edge of her dress and then along her arms. His lips had ached with desire to touch everything his eyes admired.

In the privacy of his room, a glass of wine in hand, Darcy laughed — and even blushed slightly — at those highly improper thoughts. Yet it was perfectly true; he imagined how it would be to finish their arguments by crushing her lips in a kiss right there in the middle of the room, or grabbing her in his arms in the midst of a shocked audience and taking her upstairs to his rooms. It was a frequent daydream and happened for the first time at Lucas Lodge when Sir William encouraged them to dance and she refused him. At that moment, he desperately wished to cover her lips with his hungry mouth until she fell breathless into his arms. Of course, he laughed to himself, she likely would have slapped him, and Mr. Bennet would have hunted him down all over Hertfordshire; yet, merely imagining her scent and the feel of her against him had been delicious. Dreams of that kind had repeated themselves countless times during the hours spent together at Netherfield and then every night for long, endless months.

Yes, this had been his major fault: he desired her more than he ever imagined he could desire a woman, and his need for her had been so powerful that it had frightened him. Therefore, he convinced himself that the sensation meant nothing more than the normal attraction toward any beautiful, exceptional lady and that his lustful wishes and needs would disappear once he was away from her. What an *utter fool*, as Cassandra had said! Of course, he had been as wrong about her as he had been about Bingley. She had not disappeared from his thoughts for a moment. Instead, her image, her voice, her beautiful laughing eyes, and her witty conversation made the other ladies in Town shrink to insignificance and monotony. Indeed, no other woman, no matter how beautiful, made him feel close to what he felt for her.

When he met her again in Kent, he had been the ultimate fool: he had proposed to her as no gentleman should ever propose to a lady. Of course, she had refused him as he deserved, and those dreadful moments he again wished to take her in his arms — not with desire but all the love he possessed for her — and let his caresses speak the intensity of his feelings. However, it was quite obvious she desired none of it, so he had left and, from that moment on, had dreamt of her less because he slept very little. For many weeks, night and day blended together and he forced his mind to think of nothing, or of anything but her. When this proved an impossible task, he abandoned it and spent his time remembering every word, gesture, smile, and movement. Though his days and nights had been filled with her, they had been as empty as hope frozen in time. Her memory was there, yet she was gone forever, and he fought desperately to regain his life — a hopeless fight.

Since the day he miraculously met her in Hyde Park, a breeze of liveliness swept over him, and his dreams began again, as different as his feelings for her were different. From that moment on, even in his dreams, he never simply grabbed her in his arms or covered her lips with violent, passionate kisses; instead, he dreamt not of fulfilling *his* desires or wishes, but *hers*. He used to imagine that she desired to be kissed, embraced and caressed by him, that she wished to be taken away by him and carried far from everyone and everything she knew. At Pemberley, his dreams seemed finally to come to life!

And tomorrow…he would do nothing but what he could be certain she desired.

When Darcy finally fell asleep, Elizabeth's fingers combed through his hair, caressed his forehead, moved slowly along the line of his jaw, and then returned to brush against his lips. The sensation was so real and powerful that he sighed, and his sleep deepened into blissful contentment.

ALONE IN HER ROOM, LONG after dinner , Elizabeth wondered when Mr. Bingley would finally propose to Jane and how on earth she would be able to bear her sister's enthusiasm until the long-desired wedding. Not for a moment had Elizabeth imagined that her dear, sweet, Jane would became a tiresome burden for her — yet that was what had occurred since the moment the guests left Longbourn. She opened the window widely to allow the August night's breezes to enter her room. Not only that, but the open window made her feel she was somehow closer to a certain apartment in the guest wing at Netherfield. They would meet tomorrow morning; for the first time in more than a month, Elizabeth was able to sleep soundly but was afraid to do so, wary that she would not wake up early. However, her fatigue defeated her determination, and she fell into a deep, restful sleep.

She woke as dawn appeared, but to no avail; it was raining — a wild summer rain that made any morning walk impossible. She went to the window, furious and helpless, looking over the fields as though she might see something, but the raindrops hit her face and mixed with tears of disappointment and frustration. When she finally withdrew her head and returned to bed, her hair and nightgown were soaked, and her hopes for the day were completely ruined. She could do nothing but wait.

AS THUNDER AND LIGHTNING INVADED Darcy's suite, he abruptly woke, unable to control his anger at the sight of rain. Rain? How was that possible? Precisely that morning? Could his plans be delayed again?

After a few moments of pacing around the room, he tried to regain his composure. Surely, he could not be angry at the weather; that was absurd. He could not command the rain to stop falling just so he could meet Elizabeth in the grove, but he allowed himself to be furious and frustrated. He had put all his hopes into their meeting, if only for the pleasure of talking to her unrestrained, maybe holding her hand for a few moments and nothing more, but he was forced to wait; there was nothing else to do.

A couple of hours later, the rain seemed to lose its power, and the sun moved shyly from behind the clouds. Darcy suddenly became more animated, inquiring about his friend's intention of calling at Longbourn and his mode of transportation — whether he intended to go on horseback or take the carriage. Bingley had no time to answer before Lady Cassandra entered the room asking for a few private moments.

"Sir, since the weather seems to have improved, I would like to ask your permission to invite Miss Bennet and Miss Elizabeth to join me for tea here at Netherfield later today."

"Your ladyship has my permission to do anything she pleases."

"Thank you, sir," she answered with a friendly smile.

"However," he whispered to her in secret, "I am not certain that will be possible today. You know, I planned to call at Longbourn later, as we promised, and I wanted to speak privately to Miss Bennet."

"Yes, I am aware of that," she whispered. "But Longbourn, though very charming, is quite crowded, would you not agree? Netherfield seems more appropriate for private talks."

Bingley looked at her with an expression of deep gratitude, and Lady Cassandra burst out laughing. "I shall write Miss Bennet a note; I am sure Mrs. Bennet will forgive you for breaking your promise to call again today."

"CHARLES, THERE IS SOMETHING I would like to discuss with you," demanded Mrs. Hurst half an hour later. "I understand you intend to visit Longbourn today, and I thought perhaps I should join you."

"Yes, perhaps… But then again, perhaps not. I know how daunting a task it has always been for you to be in the Bennets' company, and I would not want to expose you to such agony."

"That is not true. I have always loved dearest Jane; she is such a sweet person. If not for her poor connections and disastrous family —"

"Precisely; I would not have you bear her disastrous family until it is absolutely necessary." Bingley moved toward the window to join Darcy in his preoccupation with the weather.

"Charles, what do you mean? What will be absolutely necessary? I do not understand you! I demand an explanation," she cried, her voice rising higher.

"The rain has stopped," Darcy announced soundly. "I need some fresh air." Before Bingley was able to inquire, the door closed behind him.

Shortly after, Mrs. Hurst left the library to conceal her frustration in the solitude of her room, hastening to write a letter to her sister in London to ask her help against their stubborn brother.

However, she had little hope that Caroline would join them in the next few days. She had just received an express letter the night before; it contained the detailed description of a party hosted by Lady Sophia where Caroline had enjoyed a wonderful time and had met Lord Markham, a wealthy and handsome viscount who appeared to be interested in her. Furthermore, Caroline had mentioned she was invited to the opera the next evening and then to a private ball where only Lady Sophia's closest friends would join them.

Indeed, Mrs. Hurst could not count on her younger sister's support. If only she would manage to secure the viscount and compensate for Charles's infatuation with the insignificant Jane Bennet.

THE CLOUDS HAD VANISHED BY the time Elizabeth reached the grove, and with each step, her heart raced more wildly. Her common sense told her she was behaving childishly; she should not expect that Mr. Darcy would be there so many hours after their arranged appointment.

Yet, again, her heart won over her reason, and her hope became utter happiness when she saw Darcy descend from his horse and slowly walk toward her.

Their eyes met long before he finally stopped a few inches from her.

"Mr. Darcy…what a wonderful surprise…" Her voice sounded barely audible even to herself.

"Miss Bennet — I did not expect to see you here at this hour."

She struggled to smile back, desperately trying to think of something — anything — to say, but all she could do was remain still, staring into his eyes and wondering what would be the use of mere words.

"No, that is not true," he continued as he moved a step closer. *If he comes any nearer,* she thought, *there will be no space left between us.*

"Miss Bennet, I *did* expect to see you here. In fact, I came here with the express hope of seeing you. I know I had no right to expect such a thing, I am aware of that, but somehow… I came here as soon as the rain stopped, hoping to meet you," he repeated, his dark gaze burrowing into her soul.

"I came here hoping to see you, too," she whispered, wondering if he heard her. Indeed, he had heard her; the immediate change of his countenance and his fingers daringly taking her hands proved that. Her own fingers instantly entwined with his as had happened their last night at Pemberley. He smiled, showing her that he remembered.

"I was so angry with the rain this morning," he continued while lifting their joined hands to his chest. I was tempted to come through the rain."

"So was I," she replied; her nervousness made her knees weak. He was so close that his scent intoxicated her. "But I restrained myself, as I could easily imagine the picture I would present to you after walking in the rain all the way up here," she laughed, forcing herself to breathe normally.

"I remember that picture," he answered, his voice low, his head leaning to whisper in her ear. "I remember the picture of you in the rain, and I can testify it was most wonderful."

A wave of cold chills shook her body; he felt her quiver and withdrew a few inches to look at her, still not releasing her hands. Unconsciously, she moved a step forward to maintain their closeness. His hands suddenly released hers and, with tender care, his arms encircled her. She was ensnared close to his chest, crushed against his heart.

With a will of their own, her arms shyly slid around his waist and, though she knew it was the silliest thing she had ever done and was embarrassed that she was making a fool of herself, Elizabeth began to cry silently — not from sorrow, yet countless tears spilled from her eyes and rolled down her cheeks. How was it possible for her eyes to cry while her heart was dancing with delight?

She thought she could not be happier but proved herself wrong when she felt his lips placing light kisses over her forehead just below her bonnet. He noticed her frown and stopped, afraid she was displeased with his gestures. And yes, she should have been displeased and should have separated from him instantly; that was what a proper lady would do. Instead, she withdrew her hands from around him and untied her bonnet, threw it at her feet, and embraced his waist again, placing her head against his chest and waited — afraid and eager — anticipating his touch.

He did nothing, but his voice whispered her name, calling her "Elizabeth" with such tenderness, that it left her breathless. How was it possible that her name sounded so differently coming from him?

She lifted her eyes to him; his head was already lowered toward her, and their faces almost touched — so when his lips brushed against hers, she was not even surprised. She had no time really to feel their first kiss before he withdrew and his eyes searched hers with worry and hope.

"Elizabeth…were you crying?"

"Yes," she admitted, yet her voice sounded light and lively and her eyes were laughing at him.

His thumbs gently wiped her tears away, and his lips followed them, tenderly touching her closed eyes and then travelling slowly down her face. When he reached the corner of her mouth, he stopped once more and looked at her soundly.

"My beautiful, crying lady, we cannot go further without talking first. You have owed me a private conversation since the day you left Pemberley."

Her eyes saddened instantly as the smile vanished from her face. Her lips were trembling as she spoke. "That day…I was certain I would never see you again. While I waited for you to return, I received Jane's letters…and after reading them, I was certain everything was lost forever."

His fingers were caressing her hair and his lips came to rest on the top of her head. This time she released those past pent-up tears from the remembrance of the last time they were together at Pemberley. He remained still, holding her silently until she calmed herself, and then he slowly moved with her in his arms, to an old stump she had sat on the previous day. He took his coat off, placed it down, and then sat and embraced her again.

"That day, when I returned home and was told you had left, I have never felt so lost or in such despair. I was certain you had run away to avoid me — to avoid another proposal from me. I was convinced all my hopes and wishes had been in vain, that I had somehow grossly misunderstood your feelings once more, that you never wanted to accept me."

He paused, trying to regain some composure; she remained silent, waiting for him to continue.

"I looked for you in Lambton, I sent my men to inquire after you. Nobody could discover anything about your sudden departure. It was a stormy day, like today. I could not bear to see anybody, to listen to anybody, so I left. I left Pemberley and walked through the storm for hours. And I must confess to you that…I cried."

He stopped, and her heart almost stopped once more, pained and grieved by his past suffering as well as her own.

"Several hours passed before I finally forced my mind to remember you — your smiles, your gestures and your fingers entwined with mine that night in your room, and I began to realise that you did not deceive me or run away from me. It began to dawn on me that something grave must have happened to take you away from Pemberley and from me. I had faith in you; I trusted in you and everything you told me or wordlessly showed me. But perhaps *you* had little faith in *me*? You must have known after that night in your room that I intended to propose to you the next day. Yet, you presumed I would not keep my word because of Wickham. Did you really imagine that, for fear of a scandal, I would throw away so easily my only chance for happiness?"

Elizabeth withdrew from his embrace and looked at him. His handsome face, so tender, so light a few minutes before, had darkened into a frown, and his eyes avoided hers. She took her gloves off and, with her hands bare — shy and trembling — she touched his face and turned him gently to her.

"Mr. Darcy, you *did* misunderstand my feelings and my actions after all. Could you not see, sir, that I left that day, not because I *doubted* you, but precisely because I *trusted* you implicitly? Yes, I confess I hoped you would propose to me that day, and I knew that you would not alter your intentions because of the scandal! That was the reason I had to leave! Can you not understand? It was not a mere elopement; it was *Wickham*, whose name you cannot bear to hear spoken in your presence, and whose name simply mentioned upsets Georgiana excessively. How could I allow you to propose under those circumstances? How could I have asked for your help, involving you and Georgiana in such a scandal? It was not only about preserving your good name, but about your peace of mind, your happiness and your future. So I had to leave without concern for my own broken heart. And I had to leave before your return, or I never would have been able to leave at all."

He did not answer; only his bare palms, mirroring hers, cupped her cheeks, and they remained so for what seemed like an eternity, simply drowning in each other's eyes.

"Elizabeth," he finally whispered, "my peace of mind does not exist without you — I learned that long ago — and neither my happiness nor my future matter to me if I cannot share them with you. You must promise you will never leave me again, and I promise nothing will stop me from renewing my addresses to you again — or from convincing you to accept me."

Her laugh, nervous, still incredulous and hopeful, was mixed with tears that threatened to overwhelm her again.

His head leaned closer to hers, and his lips rested upon her ear, whispering, "I love you, Elizabeth Bennet. I love you as I never believed it possible for a man to love a woman. *Now*, only now do I truly know what *ardent love* means. Only now do I fully understand what a treasure my life with you can be and what it would mean to lose you. So *now* I am asking you again —"

Her fingers pressed his lips, forcing him to silence while her lips tentatively moved to his ear, brushing against it as she continued, "And *now*, Mr. Darcy, I have come to know and to *love* you so dearly that I will happily cry for you and laugh for you anytime you want, as long as we are together. *Now*, sir, I do not even need to hear the question as my answer is long prepared. And I am sure you do not need to *hear* my answer —"

"I *do* need to hear your answer," he interrupted as his lips started to travel along the line of her jaw. "I do need to hear your answer, my dearest, loveliest Elizabeth."

"Then you shall have it, sir," she replied as she murmured her acceptance against his hungry mouth. And she proved to be right; he did not need to hear the answer — at least not completely. A moment later, his lips captured hers and did not release them until he professed to her the depth and the ardour of his love.

Not that she had any doubts remaining!

Chapter 12

The carriage stopped, and Mr. Bingley hurried to meet his guests. As he handed Jane Bennet out, her shining, blue eyes bewitched him so that he completely forgot the other Miss Bennet inside.

It was fortunate that Elizabeth greeted him aloud and drew his attention back to his duties. He ushered them both inside, delighted to see Jane's continuous blush and pleased to notice that only Lady Cassandra was in the drawing room to meet them.

Elizabeth, however, could not hide her disappointment at not seeing Darcy. As if guessing her thoughts, Lady Cassandra smiled at her as she welcomed them warmly.

"Darcy is still in his room preparing himself. He returned from an early ride less than an hour ago. I believe he did not notice it was time for your visit. Mr. and Mrs. Hurst are in their apartments, and Georgiana is resting, I believe."

"Yes, I really could not understand why Darcy went to ride in such weather; the roads must be horrible after that rain," said Mr. Bingley as he invited them to take their places.

Nervous but happy with the kind attention Mr. Bingley bestowed upon her and flattered by Lady Cassandra's praises about her beauty, Jane intervened sweetly, willing to support the conversation.

"Oh, I can understand Mr. Darcy's fondness for riding. Lizzy possesses the same love for the outdoors — in fact, she had just returned from a walk shortly before we left Longbourn."

Elizabeth's mortification turned her face and neck crimson; Mr. Bingley and Jane were too engaged in staring at each other to notice anyone else. Lady Cassandra's wondering glaze rested upon Elizabeth a moment, and she struggled unsuccessfully to hide the enormous smile that tugged at her lips.

"Lady Cassandra, do you think Miss Darcy would agree to see me for a few minutes?" asked Elizabeth as she regained some composure.

"Yes, I believe she would. In fact, I would suggest we go and ask her directly. Miss Bennet, would you mind if we left you in the company of Mr. Bingley for a short while?"

"Oh no, your ladyship. I know my sister has long wanted to see Miss Darcy. I would not mind at all." Jane's cheeks coloured at her obvious and improper enthusiasm. To remain alone with Mr. Bingley with no chaperone was unthinkable, yet it appeared the only possible alternative for the moment. She blushed and cast her eyes to the floor. Lady Cassandra smiled again.

"Thank you, Miss Bennet. You are very kind. Mr. Bingley, I trust you will take excellent care of Miss Bennet while we are gone."

"Indeed, your ladyship, with pleasure." Bingley hurried to assure her though no one in the room really doubted it. Jane's face seemed on fire.

"MISS BENNET, THERE IS SOMETHING we should talk about before visiting Georgiana," said Lady Cassandra immediately after they exited the room.

"Of course, your ladyship; is anything the matter?"

"Well, not quite, but…Georgiana is upset with you and claims no desire to meet with you. In fact, she is also upset with Darcy and me as well, but I imagine that is little comfort to you." She looked at Elizabeth for a sign of surprise, but none appeared.

"Lady Cassandra, thank you for telling me. I feel deeply sorry for Georgiana's distress. If she does not want to see me, I shall respect her decision; however, I would still like to talk with her this one time. Then I will not disturb her any further if that is her wish."

"I am glad to hear it; you are being a caring and devoted friend to Georgiana. But are you not curious to know why Georgiana is upset with us all?"

Elizabeth glanced at her quickly and then averted her eyes, searching for the proper answer that would help her conceal the truth without lying.

"Walking out of doors is not only healthy but also surprisingly enlightening at times," continued Lady Cassandra.

Elizabeth startled and then met her eyes. There was no need to deny the evidence — surely not with Lady Cassandra. "Your ladyship is correct again," she admitted with a tentative smile.

"Very well, Miss Bennet, I shall not insist on further details…for the moment. Here is Georgiana's room; I shall leave you to talk privately."

"Thank you." Before Lady Cassandra turned to leave, Elizabeth touched her arm gently. Lady Cassandra, surprised, stopped and waited.

"Lady Cassandra, I thank you for *everything* you have done for me and my family."

"Oh, stop this nonsense. There is nothing for which you need thank me."

"Yes, there is. How can I express my gratitude for your incomparable generosity in visiting my aunt during the dreadful time of my sister's elopement? As for myself, I —"

"Miss Bennet, this will be the last time we have this kind of conversation, so I will tell you as clearly as I can that there is indeed nothing for which to thank me." She paused a moment, looking straight at Elizabeth. "I do like you, you know. I liked you the first moment I saw you on the stairs at the theatre without even knowing who you were."

"I will admit I am a little surprised to hear it; at the beginning of our acquaintance, I was not at all certain that your ladyship harboured any kind feelings toward me."

Lady Cassandra laughed. "It is refreshing that you are not in the slightest intimidated by my forward manners, Miss Bennet. Yes, you are correct; my behaviour toward you was not as proper or as kind as it should have been when I discovered your identity. I confess that, when Darcy told me of your previous dealings, I was equally intrigued and angry with you for your unfair treatment of him. The daughter of a country gentleman with four more sisters and a small dowry who could refuse Darcy — such behaviour is not often seen. And a woman who could misjudge Darcy so completely was a mere simpleton to me. So you can imagine how I felt when we were introduced to each other."

"Yes, I can imagine, and I remember your ladyship did not struggle much to conceal her opinions."

"No, I did not hide my feelings at all — quite the contrary; you are perfectly right, Miss Bennet. But in that we are alike, are we not? Neither of us made any effort to conceal our opinions."

"No, perhaps we did not," answered Elizabeth, slightly blushing. "I, too, expressed my opinion with rude frankness on some occasions, and unfortunately, I soon discovered how wrong I was."

"I see — so you mean I was rude and wrong in what I said, as well."

"I spoke of myself," replied Elizabeth, trying to hide a smile.

"And well you should, because I was not wrong in the slightest, Miss Bennet! That evening at the theatre, it was not difficult for me to notice your opinion of Darcy had changed. I have also come to understand that you were jealous of me that night. Am I wrong?"

The abruptness of this unacceptably rude question startled Elizabeth, and her first impulse was to answer accordingly; no one had the right to address her in such a manner. Yet, a moment later, she abandoned that thought; indeed, perhaps it was time for them to have an ultimate, clear understanding.

"No, your ladyship is not wrong. You are correct in your understanding."

"Thank you for your honest reply; I will end my speech shortly. My last doubts vanished the day I found you and Georgiana playing at the pianoforte during your second meeting. I watched your face as you were talking to her. Many times in the past, I have seen other women insinuate themselves into Darcy's life and use Georgiana's acquaintance to do so. You looked nothing of the kind."

"Yet, that day when we left in your carriage, I was under the impression you rather disapproved of my newly formed friendship with Georgiana."

"I see you are still bothered by our conversation in the carriage that day."

"Not truly bothered, Lady Cassandra, rather — intrigued. I was not accustomed to being addressed so directly, and I did not expect your ladyship to do it, that is all."

"Yet, you did not object overmuch; in fact, you were kind enough to answer most of my questions."

"Yes, I did, because I felt your ladyship was mainly considering Georgiana's well-being, which was more important than my hurt feelings, especially as I felt... guilty and responsible for the pain and suffering I had caused Georgiana." The last words were spoken in a slightly trembling voice.

"You are a remarkable young lady, Miss Bennet; I have known that for quite some time, and you continue to prove me right. My good opinion about you, begun in London, was further improved at Pemberley, and it was not long before I wished for an understanding between you and Darcy. I am certain your presence would be good for them both, as well as for Pemberley."

Elizabeth's emotions left her little to say, so she silently waited for Lady Cassandra to continue.

"And then, during those moments that followed the revelation of your sister's elopement, I will not conceal that I was profoundly impressed with your character, Miss Bennet — and I am rarely impressed. I know you refused Darcy last spring, despite his situation in life, because his manners were disastrous and your feelings for him were not of a tender kind. But to leave, to run from him after you had actually seen Pemberley and all his properties, after you were certain of the nature of his feelings and yours, to throw away your greatest chance of happiness, the chance of making a love match with such a wealthy man — it was astonishing. And to know you had done so to protect Darcy and Georgiana, without considering your own well-being and interest was unfathomable. You have gained my deepest respect, Miss Bennet."

"Your ladyship is too kind; I do not deserve such praise."

"Of course you do, but let us not argue about which praises are more deserved, shall we?"

Elizabeth laughed — more from uneasiness than amusement — and struggled to regain her spirit as she answered teasingly, "You are correct again, your ladyship; there is no reason for us to argue at all. Let us just affirm that we are both worthy of praise, shall we?"

Lady Cassandra burst out in peals of laughter and nodded. "As for the Gardiners, I was not being kind to them, Miss Bennet — quite the contrary; I sought out their company for selfish reasons. I am simply delighted to be around them, as I truly like them and have come to appreciate them more with each new encounter. There are few people whom I like as well as your uncle and aunt. And now you had better go and talk to Georgiana so you will be able to join us all downstairs."

"Thank you. I shall do so at once. Would you be so kind as to inform my sister I shall return shortly?"

"Of course — when I return to the drawing room. However, it might take me quite a while as Netherfield is still new to me, and I could easily get lost. But I am sure Mr. Bingley will act as the most perfect host in the interim," she said, a mischievous smile overspreading her lips.

Elizabeth could not believe that her ladyship was devising a scheme worthy of Mrs. Bennet. Then she laughed. "A little delay could do no harm, Lady Cassandra. I shall see you later then."

"Oh, Miss Bennet... Should I say anything to Darcy in case I see him? Or would you rather tell him personally?"

Elizabeth's face coloured anew. She turned her head impetuously and daringly answered, looking straight at her companion: "There is no need to say anything to Mr. Darcy; I have already told him *everything* I wanted to. As for the rest, it can wait until we meet."

Lady Cassandra remained motionless in the middle of the room, staring at the closed door.

ELIZABETH KNOCKED TENTATIVELY AT THE door; Georgiana's soft voice invited her in. When she did so, the younger girl's surprise could not be misinterpreted.

Elizabeth advanced a step further, summoning a smile to dissipate the obvious tension in the room.

"Georgiana, welcome to Hertfordshire! I am so happy to see you again. I have missed you."

"Miss Bennet... I am pleased to see you, too." Her voice showed anything but genuine pleasure.

"I hope you are well. Mr. Darcy and Lady Cassandra told me of your fatigue from the journey."

"I am quite well; thank you for your concern. You are well, too, I hope?"

Elizabeth remained equally disconcerted and saddened by her cold attitude. She was pained by this unexpected rejection, especially as they were soon to be sisters.

"Georgiana, I have missed you so," Elizabeth repeated, her voice even more soft.

"Miss Bennet, may I offer you some sweets or some tea? Or have they already been offered? Have you been at Netherfield long?" Her tone was proud and distant; Elizabeth had never seen her so before.

"We just arrived a few minutes ago, and I have come to see you directly. But no, I do not need sweets or tea; I should like my friend Georgiana back, if possible."

The girl turned instantly, and their eyes met: dark eyes moist with warmth and hope, and blue ones casting cold barbs and displaying profound sorrow.

"I am quite at a loss to understand your meaning, Miss Bennet; to which friend do you refer? The one who trusted you implicitly and confessed to you her darkest fears, opening her heart to you though she had barely known you a month? Or the one you purposely deceived when you left Pemberley, despite the fact she had begged you to tell her the truth?"

The harshness of the girl's words and her bitter tone made Elizabeth pale; she stared at her young friend, their eyes again in a painful, silent confrontation for several, unbearable moments.

"You had better leave now, Miss Bennet; I am feeling unwell. Thank you for visiting me," the girl said, struggling to defeat the tears that invaded her eyes and made her voice tremble.

"I know you are upset, and I know I deserve your censure, but I have never deceived you, Georgiana. If I caused you pain when I left unexpectedly, I beg your forgiveness. But you must believe that everything I did was to protect you." Her voice was overwhelmed by emotion, and Elizabeth did nothing to conceal it.

"To protect me? How did you imagine you were protecting me, Elizabeth? Keeping me ignorant and hoping I never would discover the truth? Can you imagine my shock when I accidentally found out about your sister's wedding in my uncle's dining room, where apparently everybody else was aware of it? Can you imagine how I felt when I understood that this was the reason for your sudden departure and that you deceived me?"

As her tone grew angrier and her face lost its colour, tears rolled down her cheeks. Elizabeth could not resist moving closer and taking her hand. Georgiana withdrew it furiously.

"Georgiana, I cannot tell you how sorry I am. I never imagined you would discover the truth in such a manner. That day at Pemberley... I did not say anything precisely because I knew how insupportable the subject would be for you. I was ashamed, distressed and deeply worried for my family — and for you, as well. I was certain that leaving Pemberley as soon as possible was the best thing for me to do in order that you not be exposed to the situation. I would have done the same for my own sister. I care deeply for you, Georgiana."

"I know you care for me, Elizabeth; I never doubted that, but you never trusted me enough to tell me the truth and allow me to decide what was best for me to do. You said we were friends, but you did not consider me so. I know I am younger than you, but I had hoped we could trust each other."

"Your age has nothing to do with this situation — I would have done the same if you were ten years older than me. I do trust you and cherish our friendship. How can I convince you?"

"You told Cassandra, though I believed you two were not on such friendly terms as we were. And she told William, but she kept me in the dark and concealed the truth from me even when we went to London. Did you ask Cassandra and my brother to keep the secret from me? Or did they simply treat me like a child, too, as always?"

"I did ask — demanded — from Lady Cassandra that she keep the secret from you and from Wil — from Mr. Darcy, too. I would not have said a word to Lady

Cassandra if she had not happened upon me when I read the letters that revealed the dreadful event."

"But my brother knew. I am sure of it!" she replied, looking doubtfully at Elizabeth. "He went to London the very next day, and I am certain he went in search of your sister."

Elizabeth's cheeks coloured highly from mortification. She smiled bitterly to herself as she warmly squeezed Georgiana's hand.

"Georgiana, Mr. Darcy was not informed by my wish. In fact, I had tried diligently to keep this matter from him as well as from you. I had hoped to keep you both unaware of the scandal and disgrace in which my family was involved. But Mr. Darcy somehow figured everything out for himself...and perhaps he had also spoken to Lady Cassandra. I do not know all the facts myself! I did not know he was involved in the search for my sister, and the notion that he attended their wedding was astonishing to me — almost as astonishing as it was to see Mr. Darcy return to Hertfordshire!"

"I do not understand! I thought you were the one who informed him! How could you have been astonished to see my brother again? I was certain you had an understanding."

Elizabeth turned pale and then crimson in the next instant. She looked at her companion for a moment before averting her eyes.

"My dear friend, let us move to the sofa, and I will tell you everything — shall we?"

Half an hour later when Mr. Darcy entered his sister's room, his gaze instantly enveloped both ladies as he searched their expressions with alarm. The warm smile on Elizabeth's face and Georgiana's tearful eyes melted his heart and put aside any concern about a possible argument between them.

"Miss Elizabeth, how delightful to see you again! Please forgive me for not being able to receive you properly when you arrived. I hope I did not interrupt your conversation —"

"No interruption at all, Brother. Elizabeth was kind enough to share the latest news with me."

"I am pleased to see you, too, sir," whispered Elizabeth.

"Are you well, I hope? And your family?"

"Yes, I am very well, thank you."

"I am glad to hear it."

Their neutral dialogue would have been considered merely a proper and polite greeting if not for their intense glances at each other and Elizabeth's constant blushing. Georgiana was slightly embarrassed as she felt like an ignored intruder in their intimacy; then she smiled, finally lighthearted for the first time in weeks.

"Would you please excuse me for a moment? I would like to prepare myself and then will join you downstairs. I would like to greet Miss Bennet."

"Yes, by all means," answered Darcy, only half hearing what she said. She seemed very well and reconciled with Elizabeth, and that was all that mattered to him.

The moment Georgiana exited the door toward her dressing room, Darcy stepped closer to Elizabeth, his eyes never leaving hers. He did not touch her, nor attempt to take her hand; only his eyes captured hers. Her lips became drier as her hands ached from the longing of being held. Slowly, his gaze left hers and travelled along her face, toward her half open mouth then back to her cheeks and returned to meet her eyes again, so tenderly that his intense stare felt like a caress.

"I presume you and Georgiana solved all the differences between you," he said in a low voice.

She swallowed hard and licked her lips so she could speak. "Yes, we did."

"I am happy to hear it, and I am happy to see you again, Elizabeth."

She had no time to tell him how happy she herself was as Miss Darcy returned to the room and froze in the doorway. She apologised and attempted to exit again, but Elizabeth regained her composure immediately.

"Georgiana, do not leave please! This is your room, my dear, is it not?"

"Yes it is, but... I thought you were talking, and I did not want to interrupt you."

"You were not interrupting us, my dear. In fact, there is something I wanted to share with you — something nobody else knows at the moment. I wanted you to be the first to hear it."

Elizabeth looked at Darcy and smiled at him — a smile that left little doubt for Georgiana.

"Sir, I think that, before going further with this, before even speaking to my father, we should ask for Georgiana's opinion on the matter."

"Oh, Elizabeth, you are engaged," cried the girl the next instant, and in a gesture that shocked her brother, she threw herself at Elizabeth, embracing her so forcefully that they almost toppled over.

"Well, I dare say her opinion is not completely unfavourable." Darcy barely checked his laughter while his heart danced with joy at his sister's hearty approval.

"I am so happy, Brother." Georgiana hurried to embrace him, too.

"I am very happy, too, dearest."

"When did you propose? May I ask that? Is it true that nobody else knows yet — not even Miss Bennet? And you did not speak to Mr. Bennet yet?"

"Dearest, let us all sit a moment and talk calmly," he suggested, and the ladies followed him to the sofa. Elizabeth seated herself between the siblings, one of her hands held by Georgiana; Darcy took the other.

"I proposed to Miss Elizabeth earlier today, and it is true: no one else has been informed yet. I plan to speak to Mr. Bennet later today."

"Oh, Elizabeth, thank you for telling me first!"

"Georgiana, my dear, I am so happy to see your enthusiastic approval, but you must take into consideration a painful fact: Mr. Wickham will be a part of my family. It is possible that his name will be mentioned often by my mother and sisters, and you may even meet him again someday. Will you be able to endure that?"

"I hope that day will not be soon; I have no desire to see him or hear of him again. But that will not change how happy I am to have you as my sister."

"Georgiana —" Darcy attempted, but she stopped him.

"Oh, let us not be talking about such unpleasant subjects now. I could not care less about George Wickham. Instead, you had better tell me — have you fixed the wedding day? And did you inform Cassandra? She will be very angry if you keep her ignorant. Where will you marry?"

Her exuberance, though a little forced, left little choice for Darcy and Elizabeth, and after a short glance, they decided to indulge her.

"No, my dear, we have not decided anything yet! And I beg you, speak a little lower or everybody will find out long before I am able to speak to Mr. Bennet."

"Forgive me," she whispered, covering her mouth with her palm, and then she continued. "But you will marry soon, I hope?"

Darcy laughed and squeezed Elizabeth's hand, unable to tell his young sister how eager he was for a short engagement; they chatted a few more minutes until finally they all decided it was time to join the others downstairs.

At first, they stopped at the door in wonder and surprise, hearing the bustle inside the drawing room. It was not difficult to distinguish Bingley's joyful voice accompanied by that of Lady Cassandra.

They entered, and it took Bingley less than a moment before he ran to Elizabeth and then to Georgiana and Darcy, demanding their congratulations. On the sofa, a blushing and highly embarrassed Jane Bennet hardly dared to look at them. A few paces further on a settee, Mrs. Hurst's countenance was dark and bitter; Mr. Hurst was enjoying a glass of wine. Lady Cassandra was standing in the middle of the room, clearly enjoying herself.

In that din, it was an unquestionable success for Darcy to be able to calm Bingley and properly introduce his sister to Miss Jane Bennet. Georgiana offered her congratulations, and Jane graciously accepted them; finally, a calmer and more intelligible conversation commenced.

"As soon as Mr. Bennet gives us his blessing, I think we should plan an engagement ball," said Mr. Bingley enthusiastically. "Of course, if you will agree to it, Miss Bennet," he added, looking at Jane.

"An excellent idea, sir," Lady Cassandra agreed.

"That would be lovely, sir," replied Jane Bennet, still incredulous that everything had happened in such a short time.

The conversation continued with everyone's involvement, and even Mrs. Hurst was forced to show an interest in her brother's engagement and future plans.

The visitors finally prepared to leave, and naturally, Mr. Bingley accompanied them, as did Darcy — much to Elizabeth's delight.

The Bennet sisters received a warm farewell from Lady Cassandra and Miss Darcy. Mrs. Hurst was all politeness, expressing her pleasure with the happy news. However, as soon as the guests left, she excused herself as not feeling well and retired to her room. In a great hurry, she wrote a long, furious letter to her oblivious sister in London, insisting that she return to Netherfield immediately.

"ELIZABETH, WHEN SHALL WE SHARE our news with your family?" Darcy asked as he helped her descend from the carriage in front of Longbourn's main door.

"Oh, let my sister and Mr. Bingley have the joy of this evening, please! Let this be their day; they have waited so long, and my sister is so happy that I cannot do anything to disturb her state of bliss."

"I have waited for this day, too, Elizabeth. I am not a patient man, you know. I have no desire to wait any longer; I want to have the right to court you, enjoy your company, and be certain I have your father's blessing. I still cannot believe you have accepted me," he replied passionately.

Elizabeth moved a little closer so their arms brushed against each other as they walked.

"I am not asking you to wait long…only a little more…because you see," she blushed slightly in mortification as she admitted, "when my mother hears of our understanding, she will give little attention to Mr. Bingley and direct all her interest to you, I am certain of it. So perhaps I am a selfish being, and I am asking to keep our engagement secret for a little longer not only for my sister's peace of mind but for my own, as well."

"You are a wise lady, Elizabeth — a very wise lady indeed," he replied after a few moments of meditation. They had reached the entrance to Longbourn.

"I am considering asking for a private meeting with Mr. Bennet as soon as possible — perhaps tomorrow morning — as I do not wish to distress him overmuch for one evening, and after that I will allow you the complete liberty to decide when you want to publicly announce our engagement. Would that be acceptable, Elizabeth?"

"And you are a wise man, sir," she responded, teasing him tenderly as they both entered the house.

The evening passed in much agitation and considerable torment for Mrs. Bennet and everyone else in the house. Mr. Bingley's interview with Mr. Bennet was quite short and completely satisfactory for both gentlemen. Immediately thereafter, the wonderful news was announced to Mrs. Bennet, and for a moment, she seemed to faint in happy distress. Fortunately, she soon recovered, and her loudly expressed satisfaction overwhelmed Mr. Bingley, who was embraced frequently, warmly and maternally.

Miss Jane Bennet was glowing in complete happiness; every time she passed near Elizabeth, she whispered how fortunate she felt and wondered how she would ever be able to bear so much felicity. Elizabeth smiled at her in loving understanding. Her own felicity was difficult to bear.

The ladies retired to prepare for dinner, and of course, the gentlemen were asked to join the family — an invitation they accepted gladly.

The guests were seated at the table on each side of Mr. Bennet, and — to Darcy's delight — Elizabeth took the place next to him. The evening passed unmarked by anything extraordinary except Mrs. Bennet's exuberance, which increased when Mr. Bingley announced plans for a ball within two weeks' time. From that moment, she spoke of little else except the beautiful bride Jane would be and the perfect wife she would make.

To his utter shock and complete delight, while he was speaking to Mr. Bennet, Darcy felt Elizabeth move slightly closer to him. Without thinking, he stretched his leg to the right and touched hers. He felt her tense for a moment, but then she relaxed and even joined the gentlemen's conversation. She never withdrew her leg from his during the entire dinner.

Furthermore, as nobody seemed to pay much attention to them, their fingers brushed against each other more than once while they ate — as if by mistake — and Darcy's eyes were captured by Elizabeth's lips, wet from the sweet, red wine. *Not as sweet and as red as her mouth,* he said to himself, and the desire of actually tasting her lips again become intensely painful.

"Do you know at what time you will call tomorrow, sir?" whispered Elizabeth when her father was conversing with Mr. Bingley.

"As soon as it is proper for a call," he answered with the same low voice. "But perhaps we should talk more about that tomorrow morning," he added, and she looked at him inquiringly. Then she blushed as she understood his meaning.

"Very well, sir."

She could not say much as she was afraid she would betray her emotions. In a deep part of her heart, there was still a shadow of fear and doubt that her felicity would last. She was still incredulous that everything that occurred that day had truly happened: that he finally proposed and she accepted, that Georgiana shared their happiness, and that Jane and Bingley were engaged. Could such perfect bliss be real and everlasting?

Yet, it must be true — if for nothing else than the proof of his strong leg pressing intimately against hers — and she shamelessly and wantonly enjoyed the novel sensations that rose inside her from the touch of his body. And his lips — which now took small sips of wine from his glass — his lips so demanding yet so tender, capturing her mouth, exploring it…

She became dizzy; countless chills made her shiver as she burned inside. She rushed to take her glass and almost dropped it; his hand reached to catch the goblet, covering her hand with his own.

"Miss Bennet, are you well?"

"Yes...yes, Mr. Darcy, I am quite well, thank you." She felt his stare fixing her profile, but he said nothing more, for which she was grateful. She drank a little wine and then asked for cold water and swallowed it quickly. When she dared to look at him from the corner of her eye, she saw a hidden smile twisting his lips.

"Is there a reason for your amusement, sir?" she inquired, trying to sound light and teasing.

"Oh, of course there is, Lizzy," Mrs. Bennet interrupted from the other side of the table. "You are so distracted this evening that you almost dropped the glass. It would be very nice indeed to spill the wine over Mr. Darcy now that he seems to be more amiable."

Elizabeth found nothing to say at such a statement and returned her attention to her plate. If her mother only knew how *amiable* Mr. Darcy truly was!

By the end of the evening, despite some other embarrassing moments, Darcy and Elizabeth had become masterfully skilled at fully enjoying each other's closeness and stealing moments of sweet privacy in a room full of people.

The acknowledged lovers talked and laughed; the unacknowledged were silent — but they needed no words to express their feelings. They knew as much as they felt how happy they were, and everything that was left unsaid between them would be most eloquently expressed the next morning when they would again meet in the grove. As much as Darcy was eager to speak to Mr. Bennet and ask for his consent, he was even more eager to hear and feel the daughter's consent again — many times over.

Chapter 13

Never had a night been so long for Elizabeth nor had she wished for the dawn with more eagerness. She barely slept, and yet she felt rested; she stared out the open window, looking at the stars and allowing the summer night breeze to caress her face. It was late August and autumn was near — almost a year since she had met him. *How early should I go? Surely, I cannot presume him to be there at dawn. He cannot be as silly as I am to remain awake the entire night.*

After an hour, Elizabeth's patience evaded her. She observed the clock; it was four in the morning. She hurriedly dressed herself, put in two hairpins to keep her locks straight and then covered them with her bonnet. She walked carefully through the trees; she was alone — only herself and her thoughts.

Her heart nearly stopped when she heard steps moving closer and the sound of a horse; she remained still, not certain whether she should hide or simply return to the house as Longbourn was still in view. She had no time to do either, as the man appeared before her, and she gasped in surprise.

In two quick steps he was in front of her, his hands cupping her face as their eyes met.

"Elizabeth, what are you doing here at this hour?"

Her heart raced wildly, and she struggled to breathe normally again. She barely managed to speak.

"I could ask you the same question, sir… William…"

He did not answer; in utter silence, his fingers tentatively explored her face from her cheeks up to her eyes, her temples, her forehead, and then lowered again to trace the line of her jaw, brushing against her throat before returning toward her cheeks as his thumbs, as gently as a breeze, caressed her lips. His eyes followed his fingers and remained fixed on her mouth. Instinctively, her hands encircled his waist searching for support.

"It is not safe for you to be here at this hour, Elizabeth. It is almost the middle of the night."

"I could not sleep; it is safe now that you are here." She tried to smile. "But why are you here, sir? This is not where we were supposed to meet."

His dark gaze and gentle thumbs were still caressing her mouth, now half-open as she spoke.

"I could not sleep either. I just wanted to look at your house and to wait for you..."

His head lowered toward hers, and she stopped breathing, waiting to feel the delicious touch of his kiss. His lips tenderly pressed over each of her eyes then he pulled her to his chest and held her tightly.

"Come." He put one arm around her shoulders and, with the other, took the horse's reins.

Within a quarter hour, they reached the grove where they had met previously. Darcy bound his horse to a tree and then pulled a packet from behind his saddle. She looked at him in wonder and then started to laugh when he undid the packet and a blanket appeared.

Skilfully, he laid the blanket under a tree; Elizabeth laughed even harder. "It appears, sir, that you are well prepared."

He smiled, obviously satisfied with her reaction. "Shall we?" he invited her to sit.

He sat near her, his back against the tree. She blushed and was grateful it was still dark so he could not see her flushed cheeks. He was close, and they were both sitting on the blanket upon the grass, shockingly and improperly intimate. She expected any moment he would take her in his arms; but he only took her hands in his and pulled them to his lips.

"I cannot believe you are here with me, Elizabeth. I am still afraid something will happen... or that I will say or do something to make you leave again."

"I shall never leave you again. There is nothing possible you could do or say to make me leave."

"I have said so many inconsiderate things in the past, Elizabeth, that —

She would listen to him no longer or bear the painful need of feeling his kisses. Her hand daringly touched his face as her lips pressed against his mouth, silencing him. He was surprised and remained still for a moment, and she dared not move her lips at all, only pressed them against his. Then his left arm encircled her shoulder, while his right hand slid along her cheek and her ear, entering her silky hair. The hairpins fell out immediately, and her locks covered his fingers.

His mouth remained passive only for an instant, and then it trapped her lips, tentatively, gently at first, and then tenderly but daringly, as though possessed by a thirst only she could quench. She gasped and froze momentarily when she felt his tongue tasting and caressing her lips and then slipping inside, taking possession of her mouth. As if in a dream, she felt his fingers untying her bonnet and pushing it aside, finding their way into her hair while their bodies moved together lower and lower until they were both reclined upon the blanket, never ceasing their passionate kisses. Elizabeth did not realise what was happening except that his body moved closer, and his scent made her dizzy; she could barely breathe, but it was all right; she did not want her lips to be free from his nor did she want him to withdraw from her. His mouth left hers for a moment and his lips traced countless small kisses over her face before returning to her mouth again. Then they lowered to the line of her jaw and caressed her throat softly; she moaned as her hands held him tighter. He covered her moans with another kiss, and she was grateful; she already missed his lips! His fingers brushed her arm then slipped around her waist and travelled upward along her ribs until his hand reached and rested upon the place where her heart was beating. She gasped loudly and stiffened.

In a moment Darcy stopped, and only then did they both realise he was almost covering her with his weight. His first reaction was a deep worry that he had gone dangerously too far, taking advantage of her confusion. He might have gone even further. He instantly realised his hand was cupping her breast and withdrew it instantly, leaning away from her to free her body. He tried to regain his normal breathing enough to be able to beg for her forgiveness and, while doing that, dared to meet her eyes. Her face was flushed, and she was breathing with difficulty. Her lips were swollen, red and moist from his kisses while her hair, in great disorder, was spread around her and a few locks were resting on the soft, creamy skin of her neck. Her eyes were darker than usual and sparkling with a passion he had never seen in them before.

"Elizabeth... please forgive me if I frightened you. I know what I did was highly improper and —"

"You did not frighten me. I *was* a little frightened, but not by what *you* did, rather by what I did and what I felt. Never before —"

Darcy smiled at her, and his fingers again caressed her face; he lowered his head and placed a soft kiss on her swollen lips. He rose to sit and pulled her with him, quite unceremoniously. She laughed as she almost fell. He embraced her tenderly, his back against the tree, holding her against his chest. His arm encircled her shoulders again, and his right hand took both her hands in his.

She relaxed and calmed herself, her passion replaced by comfort and safety. "Elizabeth, I know I should apologise for kissing you so, but I cannot say I am sorry for doing it. I do not regret it — not for a moment. I have longed for, dreamed of and desired for so long to kiss you, to hold you. But I do regret that my eagerness perhaps made me too intense in my expression. I would not have you be afraid of me, Elizabeth. I shall never do anything that you would not wish for; I hope you know that."

"I do know that, William, and I thank you for not apologising, because I *felt* you did not regret it... any more than I did. I was the one who kissed you first," she admitted, her embarrassment obvious.

"Yes you did, but I doubt you expected my response to be so... unrestrained." He smiled.

"Well, perhaps you are not as restrained as you used to consider yourself to be." She laughed back.

"No, I am not — certainly not when I am with you. Do you remember an evening at Lucas Lodge when you refused to dance with me?"

She was a little surprised at the sudden change of topic. "Yes, I do, sir."

"That evening while we talked, I felt such an urge to kiss you right there in the middle of the room! I could hardly restrain myself from removing the teasing, satisfied smile from your lips."

Her hand caressed his face, and he placed a small kiss inside her palm.

"I was such a ridiculous, pompous fool all those weeks. I tried so hard to repress my feelings for you. During the ball at Netherfield, your beauty and liveliness bewitched me; I wanted nothing more than to be near you. Instead, I resigned myself to staying apart, following you with my eyes. I saw you looking around for Wickham. You *were* searching for Wickham then, were you not?"

She nodded with regret and mortification.

"Then I saw you dancing with Collins and... I felt jealous — jealous of Wickham, jealous even of Collins for being able to dance with you, to hold your hand —"

She wanted him to stop recalling such painful memories — painful and ridiculous because they were the result of their follies and their mistaken pride and prejudice. Nevertheless, he still had more to say.

"Then I asked you to dance — and it was the most painful torture. I felt you were so perfectly suited to me. I knew we were well matched in our dance, yet we argued bitterly the entire time. And instead of talking to you and attempting to correct your wrong impression of me, I chose to run — taking Bingley with me. Now I know that, in doing so, I broke Bingley's heart and Miss Bennet's, too. But no heart was as painfully ripped apart as mine. Until that day, I had never been forced to separate from the woman I loved. In truth I had never loved anyone until I met you, my Elizabeth."

She felt warm tears burning and did not struggle to stop them. Her fingers began to unbutton his coat — shyly, awkwardly. He looked at her, mesmerised and incredulous.

Finally, her hand slide inside his waistcoat, and for a moment, she tensed at the feeling of his warmth smouldering through the thin fabric of the shirt. She felt briefly disconcerted, but her hand explored further and came to rest over his heart.

"From now on, I shall take excellent care of your heart, William," she said, lowering her head and placing a soft kiss upon the same spot. Both her hand and her lips were covering his heart.

He said nothing, but embraced her while her warm, steady breath seared him through the thin fabric. It was not just pleasure, passion, or desire... but pure and complete love.

"Look, William," she suddenly cried after they had lain together in utter bliss for a time. "The sun is rising. What a perfectly beautiful sight to behold." She rose to admire the magnificent view, and he joined her. From behind, he embraced her, she ensconced within his arms. She leaned her head against his shoulder while her free hair tantalised his neck. "You are the perfect beauty," he whispered, as his lips remained to tease her earlobe.

"Oh, do be serious! Is it not beautiful? I am so happy I have seen the sunrise with you."

"I *am* serious, my love," he answered, and his words gave her shivers. "But do you realise that having seen the sunrise together means we have spent the night together?"

"Indeed, it does mean that," she replied blushing. She suddenly turned in his arms so she could face him. Their bodies were crushed against each other as her hands found their way around his neck.

"Elizabeth…" he whispered hoarsely and lifted her off the ground to gently deposit her on the blanket again. "We should leave soon. Someone might appear…"

"Yes, we should…very soon," she admitted.

She knew he would kiss her again, and she desperately wished for him to do so. Under the assault of his hungry lips, she leaned on her back again, pulling him with her. His kisses were different in a million ways, yet so perfectly and equally delightful. Small, tender kisses, gentle and light, tantalisingly spread over her face, her throat, even down to her shoulders, and then daringly to the neckline of her dress — hungry, long and possessive kisses that devoured her mouth and left her breathless, throwing her into a storm of sensations.

With gentle, warm caresses, his hands explored her arms, her neck, her shoulders, her face — every spot of uncovered skin — and again his right hand encircled her waist for a moment and then moved upward. Elizabeth stopped breathing. Even in that tumult of feelings, she knew what was next; when his fingers brushed lightly against her breast, she moaned, and her back arched instinctively. He slowed his kisses and allowed her to breathe as his fingers continued gently to caress the soft roundness through the thin fabric and then moved slowly toward the other. His touch was so light that she could not say if it was real or only imagined, and it soon turned into a sweet torture — a torture she did not want to end but to turn into something more.

"My love…we really should be going now," Darcy said, drawing her shockingly back to reality. "And I think I should accompany you home and speak to your father without delay."

Darcy helped Elizabeth restore her hair and arrange her bonnet — not an easy task as, each time his fingers touched her hair, a new storm of kisses followed. Finally, they began walking together in silence, their fingers entwined, as Darcy's horse followed obediently.

"Elizabeth," he said the moment Longbourn came into view. "As soon as Mr. Bennet grants me his consent, I would like you to think about setting a date for our wedding."

She looked at him, surprisingly astonished and confused. "A date? I do not know.

I thought we would consider it together. How could I possibly decide it alone?"

"Well, we could consider it together, but I am not sure you would approve the date I have in mind."

"You already have a date in mind, sir? What date is that?" she asked incredulously.

"Tomorrow," he answered, and she burst out laughing. At her demand of being serious, he replied with perfect soundness. "I am serious, Elizabeth. If it were for my desire only, we would marry as soon as I procure a special license, which might take a few days. But, I shall allow you complete liberty to make the decision for us."

Elizabeth stared at him, uncertain whether he was serious or speaking in jest, but she had no time to reply. In front of Longbourn's main door, Mr. Bennet was looking at them with an impenetrable expression upon his face.

"Mr. Bennet, good morning, sir." Darcy bowed properly to the master of the house.

"Papa! Good morning. Mr. Darcy and I have just met and he was kind enough to accompany me home." Elizabeth explained, wondering about her father's countenance.

"Indeed? It was very kind of him — and such a happy coincidence that you two happened to meet."

"As a matter of fact, it was not quite a coincidence, sir; it was my intention to call on you this morning and ask for a private conference, so I was on my way toward Longbourn —"

"A private conference? With me? Well, then this is an even greater coincidence, as I have long desired to speak privately with you, as well."

"A happy coincidence, indeed, sir. I am at your disposal whenever you wish."

"Then let this be the moment for it, Mr. Darcy. If you would be willing to indulge me, let us retire to my library just now." With a strange look toward his daughter, he turned his back and directed Darcy, who brushed his fingers over Elizabeth's arm in a reassuring gesture, to his favourite room.

"Would you care for something to drink, Mr. Darcy," asked Mr. Bennet as soon as the door closed.

"No thank you, sir; it is early yet."

"It is early indeed; we have not even had breakfast, and I suspect neither have you."

"You are correct, sir; I have not."

"And you decided to visit me at such an early hour? You must have a very important reason to do so," Mr. Bennet said, mockery obvious in his voice. "My sister and brother Gardiner have spoken very highly of you and seem to value your character as well as your perfect manners, sir. I confess I have not been in your company enough to form my own opinion on the subject."

Darcy's countenance changed in a moment. Mr. Bennet's words, attitude and tone were meant to offend him; he was aware of that. Yet, he was Elizabeth's beloved father, and Darcy wanted his consent and, possibly, his blessing more than anything else at that moment. With prudence, he decided to guide the conversation toward the goal he wished to achieve.

"I apologise, sir. I realise the hour is highly improper for a visit and in truth —"

"Oh come now, sir, you must not apologise for that! There are many other improper things you have done lately if we are to speak the truth!"

"I am afraid I do not understand your meaning, sir."

"Mr. Darcy, the matter is of too much importance for me to afford being considerate of your feelings. In truth, the offence I might give you means nothing compared to my daughter's felicity."

At that point, Darcy lost his patience. "If you are referring to your second daughter, Miss Elizabeth, I assure you, sir, that her felicity is more important to me than my own feelings."

"Truly? Such nice words, sir. But I wonder how it is possible that private meetings on secluded paths early in the morning and ruining her reputation could help my daughter's felicity."

Darcy's face darkened instantly, and his self-control deserted him. He was not to be spoken to in that manner — not even by Elizabeth's father — yet he had little time to respond.

"I am not as inattentive to the behaviour of those around me as some might believe, Mr. Darcy. Last autumn, while my family found great amusement in retelling how you called Elizabeth barely 'tolerable' and refused to dance with her, it did not take me long to notice things were not quite so." Darcy paled and, as rarely in his life, had no apt words in reply.

"I noticed you during the Netherfield ball, sir. I can still remember how shocked I was to see you staring at my daughter the entire night, following her every movement with your eyes and then asking her to dance. I searched your expression during that dance, and it was not the expression of a man who finds a lady only *tolerable*."

Darcy froze in the middle of the room as Mr. Bennet continued: "But your look was not the look of a gentleman who admires and wants to enter into an honourable arrangement with the lady either, Mr. Darcy. In fact, I also noticed that very night the disapproval — I might say the disgust — in your expression as you looked at us, the other members of Elizabeth's family —"

"Mr. Bennet, if you would allow me to explain, sir..." Darcy's face was white and immovable while his wounded pride fought against remorse for his past behaviour.

"Oh, but please do, sir; please do contradict me. Did you not have a certain interest in my daughter in the autumn? And does that interest have anything to do with a marriage proposal? I admit that I should have said something at that moment, but I did not. I was rather amused by your sudden change of opinion, as I knew how much my Lizzy disliked you and how much delight she found in laughing at your pride and haughtiness."

Mr. Bennet paused long enough to pour a glass of wine and gulped it instantly.

"But now, things seem to be frighteningly different, Mr. Darcy! I know my daughter met you in London and spent some time at your property in Derbyshire. What happened to her I can hardly say, but I see that somehow you managed to change her opinion. Even more, her behaviour is shockingly altered, and she had no scruples in meeting you privately or sharing all manner of improper attention with you at dinner in front of her family. So, since you are in my library now and others seem to consider you an honourable gentleman, I expect you to tell me how far you intend to take this dishonourable behaviour toward my daughter. Are you only searching for something diverting while you await your friend's wedding, sir? "

Darcy stared at his host; Mr. Bennet proved to be a different gentleman in every respect than Darcy believed him to be. The fact that he managed to recognise all the feelings Darcy had struggled to conceal astonished him exceedingly, and truly, there was little for him to say in his defence.

Therefore, forcing himself not to allow his hard feelings to affect his voice, Darcy looked straight at his accuser and said, "Mr. Bennet, yesterday I made an offer of marriage to Miss Elizabeth, and she did me the great honour of accepting me. I am here today to ask for your consent and your blessing."

A few, awkward moments passed as the two gentlemen stared searchingly at each other. Mr. Bennet's countenance changed again, this time to a most distracted one. He seemed unable to remain standing and stretched his hand for a chair. Darcy hurried to assist him. Once Mr. Bennet was seated, his gaze returned incredulously to Darcy.

"You made an offer of marriage to Lizzy?"

"I did, sir."

"And she accepted you?"

"She did."

"How can that be? I was certain that she had a true revulsion toward you." Darcy cringed at that but tried to keep his countenance. "And you, sir, how could you have made her an offer? I was certain that you had no desire of joining our family. Why did you allow me to continue my offensive speech, sir? Did you find great amusement in my distress, Mr. Darcy?" Mr. Bennet's tone was sad and bitter, while his manner seemed to bear equal reproach toward himself as toward Darcy. The latter filled a glass of water and handled it to his host.

At that moment, the door opened, and Elizabeth entered the library. She needed no more than an instant to notice things were not going as well as they should. Without waiting for any invitation, she stepped forward daringly, her eyes meeting those of Darcy. She could see that neither gentleman looked well.

"Papa…is something wrong?" She approached her father who met her with half a smile.

"I do not know, girl; you tell me. Is something wrong? Mr. Darcy applied to me with the most astonishing request. Do you know to what I am referring?"

"I do, Papa."

"I see… Mr. Darcy, I should like to speak to my daughter privately for a few minutes."

Darcy hesitated only a moment. "Of course, sir. I shall wait outside."

"Mr. Darcy, please do not leave. Papa, if you want to talk about Mr. Darcy's request, there is nothing I shall say that he cannot hear."

Her father's sadness grew more pronounced. "Lizzy, can you not oblige your father?"

"I can and I will, Papa, in anything else. But if you have something to ask about this subject, I would like for Mr. Darcy to witness it."

"Well, my child, in this case there is nothing to inquire about, after all. You seem already to have decided upon the matter, so my opinion is of little importance. Mr. Darcy," he said, turning to face the gentleman, "have no concern that I will refuse my consent. If my daughter is decided to have you, I will not oppose her."

"Papa…" Elizabeth took a chair and sat near her father. Mr. Bennet did not appear pleased with the gesture. "I can see you are upset. Please believe me; this is hurting me deeply. Your opinion does matter to me."

"Yes, my opinion matters to you… in any case except this, is it not so?"

"But, Papa… is there any reason for your unfavourable opinion of my marriage to Mr. Darcy?"

"Not exactly, my child. No other reason except the fact that I have always known you to be decidedly against him, and my fear is that you might now accept him for all the wrong reasons."

"Papa…" She leaned toward him so she could whisper. Darcy moved to a far corner.

"My child, I know your disposition, and I cannot understand what has come upon you now. You might have been impressed with his fortune while you were in Derbyshire, and perhaps you became more sensible to the advantages of such a union now that your sister is soon to be married. But I know you will never be happy if you are not able to respect your husband."

The distance did not prevent Darcy from hearing what was said. The frustration of being unable to assist in the conversation without interfering made him pace the room nervously. It would have been better for him to be outside the library. More than anything, he was distressed at the thought that Elizabeth's father had such a poor opinion of him, and he had no opportunity to clear the misunderstandings.

"Papa, believe me when I say that I am not marrying Mr. Darcy for any wrong reasons, and neither his situation in life nor his possessions have anything to do with my decision. He is the best man I have ever known… and I truly love him." She took her father's hands and held them lovingly.

Mr. Bennet's eyes were moist with tears. His heart ached for his favourite daughter, and it was caught by an icy fear that she — and he — were making a mistake that would bring her nothing but misery, despite the wealth with which she would be surrounded. Yet how could he refuse her and pain her?

"My dearest Lizzy, if this is the case, I have nothing to do but trust your judgment." He leaned, kissed her forehead, and then caressed her hair. "I hope you know what you are doing, my child."

"Mr. Darcy," he called for the gentleman who seemed exiled in the corner. Darcy turned and stepped toward them slowly.

"Sir, I will not pretend that my heart is at ease or that my doubts about this union have vanished. However, I have little choice. My daughter is decided in your favour, and I have to trust my brother and sister Gardiner who hold you in the highest esteem. I hope they are not wrong. And, as you will be my daughter's husband, I hope you will be able to overcome the offences I directed toward you earlier today."

Darcy could see Mr. Bennet's suffering was intense, and it was easy to understand the concern he felt for his daughter's well-being.

"I certainly cannot remember any offences, sir. We had a long conversation in which you expressed some concerns regarding Miss Elizabeth, and let me assure you that she is my chief concern, as well. Making her happy is the most important thing to me, sir, and I dare say in time I will convince you of that."

"We shall see. And now you may go if you wish. Lizzy, please tell your mother to send me a tray in here. I have no disposition to breakfast in company."

In a dismissive gesture, he rose from his seat and moved to the window with his back to them. Elizabeth and Darcy exchanged a quick glance, but as she took his arm and directed him toward the door, Darcy stopped.

"In fact, if I am not asking too much, I should rather remain with you a little longer, Mr. Bennet. There are still some things I should like to discuss with you, and I am not particularly disposed toward breakfast, either."

Mr. Bennet turned to him instantly. "You want to talk to me more? Now?"

"Yes, sir. It is a matter of some urgency, and I dare say we should clarify it without delay."

Mr. Bennet shrugged with an intriguing gesture of invitation. Elizabeth looked at Darcy somewhat worriedly as she left the room, but he smiled reassuringly.

"Mr. Bennet, I wanted to speak to you because there are still many unsettled things between us, and any misunderstanding would affect Miss Elizabeth greatly. I cannot allow that."

"I doubt any more clarification is possible for one day, but if you have anything to say, I will listen." He took his seat and looked at Darcy inquiringly. That was a gaze Darcy finally recognised.

He felt more uncomfortable than ever before, and the notion of humbling himself threw him into extreme torment, but it was the price he had to pay for Elizabeth's peace of mind.

"Mr. Bennet, I am not a man to speak openly of my private affairs and even less of my feelings. But now it cannot be avoided. Not everything you said before, sir, regarding my opinion of Miss Elizabeth last fall…was wrong."

The effect of his words upon Mr. Bennet was obvious, yet that only increased his uneasiness.

"You were also correct in assuming that I had no intention of making an offer of marriage to Miss Elizabeth at that time. For many years I have considered it my duty to choose a lady of the same situation in life as my own to became the mistress of my estate, and your family's situation was…different." He looked at Mr. Bennet but could not read much in his face.

"However, in one respect you have been utterly wrong: never, not for a second were my intentions toward Miss Elizabeth anything but honourable! I assure you, sir, that more than anything I was bewitched by the liveliness of her mind, her wit and her uncommon understanding. I knew her behaviour was beyond reproach, and I could not have dared to think otherwise. Anything dishonourable regarding Miss Elizabeth was far from my mind at that time or at any time. Since I was not considering making her an offer, I was certain that my admiration would remain without an object as soon as I left Hertfordshire and that I would never see her again."

Mr. Bennet listened with equal attention and astonishment. Seeing a man so private, so restrained making such a declaration involving his most secret thoughts was difficult to fathom.

"I must have been too rushed in judging you in this regard, Mr. Darcy. However, since we have reached this point, I cannot help but wonder how it happened that your opinion about marriage and the necessary wealth of your future wife changed so dramatically?"

"Well, it happened one day last April when I was properly humbled and shown how insufficient were all my pretensions to please a woman worthy of being pleased."

Mr. Bennet's quizzical look made Darcy smile bitterly as the memory of those moments and the mortifications of sharing them with his future father-in-law caused greater distress.

"It was the day I presented myself to Miss Elizabeth and asked her to accept my offer of marriage. I came to her without a doubt of my reception, and her answer was a most painful yet well-deserved punishment."

Mr. Bennet's shock made him abruptly stand as he frowned, staring at his visitor in utter disbelief. "You made Lizzy an offer last April? But last April she was in Kent."

"You are correct, sir; I was visiting my aunt at Rosings Park."

"And she refused you?"

"She did, sir, and she was correct to do so."

"And…you asked her again?"

"I did, sir, but not before I was certain I would succeed in improving her opinion of me. You see, sir, I unexpectedly met Miss Elizabeth and Mrs. Gardiner in London in June and…"

For more than half an hour Darcy revealed their entire history to a deeply shocked and utterly astonished Mr. Bennet. When he reached the part of the narrative concerning Lydia's elopement, he tried nonchalantly to pass over those moments, but Mr. Bennet did not allow him to escape so easily. At that point, Darcy refused to debate the subject further, abruptly continuing with the reasons he returned to Hertfordshire. Mr. Bennet's eyebrows remained arched in wonder.

"So you see, sir," concluded Darcy, "I am certain, after all these months and our particular history, that Miss Elizabeth did not accept my second proposal for the wrong reasons."

Mr. Bennet remained speechless for a time. The man in front of him was someone he was just beginning to know and understand, someone who surely deserved more consideration than he, the father of the bride, had given him so far. He realised he owed Mr. Darcy an apology. In fact, he was fairly certain he owed Mr. Darcy far more than he would ever be able to repay.

"Mr. Darcy, I thank you for your generosity in confessing all these things to me. I imagine how difficult it must have been for you, and I know you did it to put my worries aside. Your effort is not unappreciated, sir."

"If I have managed to clarify your misunderstandings and make it easier for us to collaborate for Elizabeth's peace and happiness, then that is all the reward I need, sir."

"Then you may consider yourself rewarded. I have no misunderstandings left, sir, and feel I need to apologise again for my harsh words."

Darcy insisted there was no reason to apologise, and Mr. Bennet ceased to offer them any longer; instead, he said Mr. Gardiner expressed great admiration for Pemberley's library and for its streams and lakes, and that became the next subject of conversation. Of course, Darcy assured him there would be no need for formal invitations and he would be more than welcome there at any time.

When Elizabeth returned, bringing a tray of food for them, she could sense things had changed. The expression on both gentlemen's faces softened when she entered, and she smiled at them — the two men who were dearest to her heart.

"Lizzy, have you informed your mother about your engagement?" asked Mr. Bennet. "Considering the silence in the house, I should guess not."

"No, I have not," Elizabeth answered as she served them tea and coffee. Darcy hurried to help her with the cups. Mr. Bennet smiled with satisfaction.

"In fact, Papa, I was thinking — considering Jane and Mr. Bingley's engagement — that we should keep ours secret a few more days. I mean, now that you have given us your consent."

"Ah, I see," smiled Mr. Bennet. "So you want to keep your intended away from your mother's enthusiasm a little longer; now that I have given you my consent, you could feel engaged without sharing it with the others for some time. Hmm, Lizzy, that is not fair of you — to let only poor Jane and Mr. Bingley be the recipients of your mother's loudly expressed satisfaction."

Elizabeth blushed, and Darcy smiled to hide his embarrassment.

"Well then, let it be as you wish. Considering I gave Mr. Bingley not the least bit of the hard time I gave poor Mr. Darcy when he applied for my consent, it is only just that he suffer a little more in other areas. You may announce your engagement whenever you please. Just try to do it when I am not in the same room with your mama and preferably not during dinner. Promise me this, will you? And let me know when you decide what date to have your wedding, Lizzy, so I am in attendance to play my part in accompanying you to the altar."

He continued to tease them a bit longer until they finished eating and having their coffee. An hour later, when Mr. Bingley arrived to invite them to Netherfield for dinner, the discussion in the library remained animated.

CAROLINE BINGLEY HAD JUST AWOKEN when she received her sister's letter, sent by express. She read it a few times, threw it on her bed and rang for her maid. So, stupid Charles let himself get trapped by that Jane Bennet. What a fool! And now Louisa demanded that she quickly return to Netherfield. Why on earth did Louisa need her? Surely, there was nothing to do about the engagement once it was made public. She did not want to leave London! What was there for her to do in Hertfordshire? To bear the impertinence of Lady Cassandra? To be annoyed by that insupportable chit, Eliza Bennet?

How could she abandon the select and most elegant company of Lady Sophia? And, most of all, how could she leave the presence of Lord Markham, the most charming gentleman she could ever imagine? Mr. Darcy was nothing in comparison — not in wealth, charm or politeness. Lord Markham was everything Caroline ever dreamed of in a gentleman and in a suitor. He was ever so kind to her, always seeking her company, pretending to be interested in her relatives, in Netherfield, even in Darcy, Lady Cassandra and those boring Bennets.

To Caroline's utter satisfaction, neither Lord Markham nor Lady Sophia seemed to hold Lady Cassandra in high esteem — and why would they? The woman was pure impertinence with an abominable sense of independence.

Thinking of this fresh news, Caroline noticed that she was not as bothered by it as she thought she would be. So Charles will marry Jane Bennet…that was it! Her only concern was the reaction of her new friends and especially of Lord Markham. Would the unfortunate alliance diminish her chances of happiness? If that were the case, she would never forgive Charles for ruining her brilliant future. *Lady Markham — how lovely that sounds, indeed!*

She hurried to prepare herself. Once more, she was invited to tea at Lady Sophia's — the third time in a week — and Lord Markham would be there, too. She would handle the situation to her advantage; yes she would. She was a very clever woman; everybody said so. *The future Lady Markham!*

LADY CASSANDRA REMAINED IN A corner of the drawing room, looking around attentively. Dinner was over, and the gentlemen separated from the ladies for less than a quarter of an hour.

Earlier that day, when he returned from Longbourn, Darcy shared with her the news of his engagement with such enthusiasm that she could not help laughing at him. He looked like a schoolboy, she told him, and he did not protest. He only insisted that their engagement remain a secret as only Mr. Bennet and Georgiana had been informed. *Secret indeed.* She smiled to herself. It was enough to look at both Darcy and Elizabeth to see they were betraying their arrangement with every fibre of their being: every gesture, every word, and every stolen glance. However, she promised to keep their secret.

Her eyes were drawn toward Elizabeth and Jane Bennet — such an astonishing difference between them. Not such a classic beauty as her sister, Elizabeth Bennet looked more beautiful in a lively, joyful, vivid way. They were both happy, that was obvious, but while Jane Bennet was smiling toward her intended, Elizabeth Bennet was laughing with her eyes and her whole being — she was laughing at her betrothed and at life itself. Her happiness was palpable, as was the bond between her and Darcy. Their connection was evident in many particulars: the way they searched for each other's eyes, the way she blushed every time their gazes met, and the way Darcy stared lovingly at her No, they certainly could not keep their engagement secret for long!

Lady Cassandra turned her attention toward Charles Bingley. He talked of nothing but their engagement and the ball about which he had asked her opinion to complete the list of guests.

The ball that David Fitzwilliam will also attend — no doubt about that. Lady Cassandra had thought about it innumerable times that day since she had seen his name at the top of the list. Although she hated herself for it, she had to admit she was anxious and desirous to see him again. She felt helpless and defeated — again.

Chapter 14

Netherfield and Longbourn were two houses in chaotic disorder. With each day that brought the ball closer, agitation grew and brought Darcy to the edge of his tolerance — and beyond it.

Repeatedly he marvelled — with enormous gratitude — at Elizabeth's wisdom in keeping their engagement secret a little longer. However, his state did not go unnoticed, so Elizabeth, Lady Cassandra, Mr. Bennet, and even his own sister found great enjoyment in teasing him.

The families spent a good deal of time together. The Longbourn inhabitants were invited to dine at Netherfield, or Darcy, Bingley, Lady Cassandra, and Georgiana had dinner at Longbourn.

Georgiana's reaction toward the Bennets had been a revelation to Darcy. They were introduced to her the same day Mr. Bennet gave his consent, and she was clearly overwhelmed by Mrs. Bennet and Miss Catherine's loud exuberance. However, in the three days that passed since then, Georgiana became increasingly comfortable with them and seemed to enjoy and even seek their company. She appeared at ease with both Miss Catherine and Miss Mary and found something to talk about with each of them. She also appeared to bear Mrs. Bennet's attention quite well. Mr. Bennet complimented Darcy more than once on his sister's impeccable manners and then teased him saying that the girl had taken all the sweetness in the family and left the aloofness to Darcy.

Lady Cassandra also appeared to have a wonderful time in the midst of the commotion. She was the only one who managed to temper Mrs. Bennet, and she also spent time in conversation with Mr. Bennet; the gentleman declared to Darcy, "Since you have stolen all Lizzy's attention for yourself, thank God you brought Lady Cassandra so I have somebody with sense to talk to."

Yes, Mr. Bennet was right; he had indeed stolen all of Elizabeth's attention. Four days had passed since he had asked for her hand, and they had been four days of complete and utter bliss, despite the annoying agitation around him. He knew he was selfish and should have been happy for Bingley — and he was — but he wanted nothing but peace and tranquillity in which to enjoy every moment in Elizabeth's company. Yes, he was selfish. He was so selfish that he was increasingly tempted to elope with her to Gretna Green and return two days later satisfyingly married. *Perfect plan,* he thought, leaning against the chair's back with his eyes closed.

Of course, eloping was not an option; upon their return, Mr. Bennet, Georgiana and Cassandra in all likelihood would kill him. But the idea was sorely tempting!

"You seem pleased with yourself, sir!" His recollections were happily disturbed by the sound of a well-known voice, and his gaze rested with utter delight on Elizabeth's smiling eyes.

"Have I interrupted you? You seem to be covered by a mountain of letters." Elizabeth appeared in the doorway and moved toward him. He reached his hand to her and she took it gently as they sat together on the sofa. Their fingers entwined together, caressing one another.

"No indeed, I have done little but think of you." His free hand caressed a lock of hair near her ear.

"You are a most considerate betrothed, sir. You always say the most pleasant things to flatter me."

"I only speak the truth, Elizabeth." His head lowered, and she was not surprised to feel his lips on hers. The kiss started gently, both of them attentive to any noise that might indicate an intrusion, but after a few moments, everything but their closeness seemed to vanish around them. When his tongue, soft, warm and daring, slid between her lips, she gasped with more delight than surprise as her mouth opened to admit him. One of her hands encircled his neck and the other his waist as she leaned against him. His hands travelled along her arms, down to her spine and up to her nape in a torturous exploration. His touch was a pleasant, unbearable torment, assaulting all rational thought, which kept reminding her that her entire family was around and anyone might discover their shockingly improper interlude. A moment later, he stopped and withdrew his lips enough to stare into her eyes. She tried to swallow and regain her breathing; his breath was no calmer then hers. "Elizabeth?"

"Yes?" Their voices sounded so strange that they both chuckled, struggling to regain their calm.

"Would you like some water?"

She withdrew her head a few inches to look at him in disbelief. His countenance seemed quite disturbed as he forced himself to smile.

"Yes. Thank you." She returned his smile.

He came back with two glasses of water, handed one to her, and then sat beside her again. "So — you abandoned the others? You needed exceptional skills to escape from them, I imagine."

"Not at all," she laughed. "Nobody noticed my leaving; they are all too busy with...something."

"You came to see me?" he asked.

"No," she teased him, "I simply lost myself in the house and entered the library by mistake."

"I see," he answered, a mischievous smile on his lips. "As you did last year on your first day at Netherfield when you happened upon me in the billiard room?"

"Yes, quite the same," she answered with laughing eyes at the remembrance of those days.

"I have missed you, Elizabeth," Before she had time to reply, he hurried to his feet. "Could you wait for me here a few minutes? I will speak to my man; I want to be sure we will have a little privacy." She only nodded in surprise, wondering how his servant would assure their privacy. However, she did not worry about that. She trusted him to do the right thing, as always.

Elizabeth rose, began pacing the room and then stopped in front of the window. Recollections of the days she had spent at Netherfield the previous autumn were vivid, and once more, she frowned at the notion that she could have misapprehended him so profoundly. Now that she had the chance to know him better — to appreciate his character and enjoy his love — she suffered to think how easily she could have lost her chance of happiness forever. Now she was certain she never would have been able to love another man the way she loved him, to give herself completely and to be eager to share everything.

She did not notice Darcy's return and startled, feeling his warm breath on her nape.

"Elizabeth, is everything well?"

"Yes... I was just thinking of you..."

"Any particular thoughts?" He encircled her with his arms, and she leaned back against him.

"I was thinking about last year. Do you remember the day we spent an entire half an hour in the library and you did not speak a word to me?"

"Of course I remember. I remember every moment I spent in your company, Elizabeth. And yes, that occasion is quite fresh in my memory — for I did nothing but stare at you."

"You did? I was certain you purposely ignored me completely. Your only interest seemed to be your book."

"Well, it appears I was quite proficient in deceiving you about the nature of my interest. Such a fool I have been..."

He held her tighter, and she entwined her hands with his; they remained that way for a long time, and she only murmured, "*We* have been a couple of fools..."

"So," she changed the topic, not allowing such emotions to change their disposition, "may I be of some help with all these letters? You looked quite overwhelmed."

He smiled and brought her hand to his lips. "You are right; I am a little overwhelmed. I have many things unsolved from the past few months and others remained unsettled when I unexpectedly left Derbyshire a month ago."

The tone of his voice was carefree, but instantly he felt her tensing in his embrace and silently condemned himself for his unfortunate statement. She turned to face him, and her hands slowly lifted to cup his face.

"I am sorry that I caused you so many problems…"

"Lizzy… I am sorry to have mentioned those events again. I would not have you apologising for the past ever again. You most promise me that —"

"You called me Lizzy." Her voice was soft as she looked at him with wide eyes.

Yes, I did… Lizzy," he whispered again, and she leaned forward to steal her name gently from his mouth with her lips.

"William, I do have a question… and I would be grateful if you would tell me the truth."

He nodded in agreement, and she continued, obviously embarrassed. "I have wondered about your involvement in the arrangement that ended with Lydia's marriage. Mr. Wickham had many debts, I am certain. I also know he would not have married Lydia without compensation; he is no fool when it comes to his own benefit. But suddenly everything was solved: his financial situation improved miraculously, and he was offered a new assignment. Are you the one who paid for all this?"

He looked at her for a few moments, and the change in his countenance was obvious. Then he averted his eyes and answered briefly: "Yes."

"Yes?" Her breathing stopped at the confirmation of her suspicions. "So you… you left your home and your friends to search for Lydia… then you had to convince him… to offer him money to marry her. Dear God, what a shame…"

"Elizabeth, look at me please." She did not obey, so he lifted her pale, tearful face toward him.

"My love, you asked me a question, and my answer only pained you. That is precisely why I did not want you to be told about —"

"It was not fair for you to bear so many expenses, so much distress, so much trouble…"

"No, it was not fair to have so much trouble because of Wickham, but that must not be your concern. I cannot blame your sister for what happened; she was but a silly, young girl ensnared by a scoundrel with nice manners. Unfortunately, she will have to pay for her imprudence as she must share her life with him."

"I have been as silly as Lydia. I also let myself be fooled by Mr. Wickham. I gave him complete credit and believed everything he said. And by doing so, I have treated you unfairly and given you so much pain. I was a complete fool." Her voice was barely audible, and her eyes would not meet his.

He cupped her cheeks with both his palms and forced her to meet his eyes.

"My love," he smiled with an unexpectedly light voice while his thumbs caressed her, "indeed you have been a fool to believe him, and I was furious when I heard you defending him, so furious that I was tempted to kiss you until I left you breathless and unable to speak again. But then again, I wanted to kiss you breathless so many times that I am not sure it was because of Wickham."

She mixed her tears with peals of laughter, and he gently kissed her eyes while he held her in his arms. "You, sir, are excellent at teasing me, and your sense of humour is quite exquisite,"

"Well, Miss Bennet, being so much in your and Mr. Bennet's company, I have no other choice than to become proficient at teasing — or hide in a dark corner."

She laughed and raised her head to him. "No need to hide, sir! Now I think I should leave you. I have disappeared for quite some time, and besides, you must take proper care of your business."

Elizabeth rose from the sofa, and he followed her, holding her hand. She cast a quick glance toward the desk where an envelope, obviously from Lord Matlock, seemed to demand his attention.

"William, have you informed your other relatives of our engagement?"

"No, I have not — yet — since you did not tell me when you want to make it public. I shall, as soon as possible — and most likely, I should go to London to talk to my uncle and aunt personally. As for Lady Catherine — I would rather write her, as I am in no disposition to travel to Kent."

She looked at him with much preoccupation. "You just said you have much unsolved business waiting. Would a trip to London be helpful? Perhaps sharing the news with Lord Matlock?"

"It would be very helpful, indeed, but not possible. I have no intention of going to London and being apart from you." He kissed her fingers tenderly.

She frowned slightly as she squeezed his hand. "William, I would not want to be away from you a single moment either, but... if you do not take care of your business now, you will have to at some point, will you not? You are not the kind of gentleman to neglect his duty."

"Yes, I suppose I will have to eventually; I will manage to handle it somehow."

"I was thinking that I would rather be parted from you for a few days now than after we are married. I am so occupied with ball preparations that we barely have time to spend together these days, and you are not at all happy in the middle of all this turmoil. After we are married, things will —"

He stared at her, eyes wide open. "Elizabeth, have you decided on the date for our wedding?"

"No, not decided yet. But I have watched you carefully these last days and have noticed how... little enjoyment you find in all the preparations and arrangements and my mother's enthusiasm, so I was wondering... since my mother is preparing a wedding with so much care, why should we not take advantage of it? We could marry the same day as Jane and Mr. Bingley if you would not mind."

His face darkened instantly, and his displeasure was obvious; she turned pale and wished she could withdraw her words. "If that is not agreeable to you, we can choose any other date you wish."

"Elizabeth, of course it is not agreeable to me!" he burst out. "Bingley's wedding will be in two months' time! When I suggested we should marry in three days, I was hoping you would suggest something around a month — in the worst case."

Darcy's reaction made Elizabeth laugh in complete relief; light-hearted, she impulsively rose on her toes and silenced him with a long kiss. Though her lips were daringly *wanton* in their ministrations, he did not seem eager to prolong their passionate moment. Quite determined, he looked at her soundly.

"I am being very serious! Less than an hour ago, I was thinking that poor Bingley had to wait two months to be married. You cannot do that to me!" He was truly upset, and Elizabeth could not withhold her peals of laughter.

"Sir, where is the calm, restrained, aloof gentleman I met last autumn — the one with a 'superior mind' who always kept himself 'under good regulation'? Surely, you cannot expect to have a hasty wedding without being at the centre of a scandal! Besides, if we are to marry sooner, we should tell my mother today so she can begin the arrangements." She raised her eyebrow at him in mocking challenge, and he cast her an annoyed look.

"I do not think it is fair of you to repeat my words in order to defeat my opposition, soon-to-be Mrs. Darcy. This is not the proper attitude I expect from my wife."

"Indeed, sir? Then perhaps you should consider searching for another wife."

"Or perhaps I should speak to your mother about your disrespectful attitude toward me."

For Darcy it was a joy to see her "arguing" with him; for Elizabeth, it was heart melting to see that Darcy was willing to expose himself to her teasing.

"Or," he continued, moving closer to her and lowering his head to whisper in her ear, "I could try to make you *wish* to be married as soon as possible."

Though he did not even touch her, Elizabeth shivered, and a sudden lump in the throat made her answer difficult. She struggled to continue her previous reasoning. "So…that is why I was thinking you could go to London now to settle all your business…and to inform your family…and we could announce our engagement immediately after the ball. We could talk to Jane and Mr. Bingley earlier to ask their opinion about a double wedding and —"

"Very well, Miss Bennet," he said, his fingers pressing her mouth to stop her from speaking. "I shall not oppose your suggestion. We shall have a double wedding if your father and Bingley agree."

"Thank you, sir," she answered with maidenly blushes. From outside the library, the faint din of voices and steps could be heard, yet that did not prevent Darcy from kissing her once more — this time daringly and passionately, oblivious to the possible consequences of their imprudent behaviour.

It was no wonder that neither of them heard the door opening, or noticed Lady Cassandra and Georgiana entering the library.

"Well, Caroline Bingley is here in case you are interested," her ladyship said.

Darcy and Elizabeth startled, quickly withdrawing their hands from each other. Elizabeth's cheeks turned crimson, while Darcy could hardly hide his mortification at being caught in such a situation.

Recovering his composure, Darcy — not at all interested in Miss Bingley's arrival — took the opportunity to share the latest news with the ladies: the presumptive date of their wedding and his departure to town for a few days.

"So, you two are trying to steal from Mrs. Bennet the pleasure of organising a second wedding now that she is becoming a true proficient," laughed Lady Cassandra. "She will never forgive you; I hope you know that."

They started planning the events of the next days; the more he talked about it, the more Darcy was grateful to Elizabeth for suggesting this trip to London. It was indeed the perfect time to have everything settled so he would be able to spend all the time before and after their wedding worrying about nothing except her delightful company. He planned to return the day before the ball, and asked Elizabeth's opinion about that. To his surprise, she lost more of her spirit with each passing minute, and her countenance became troubled.

"Elizabeth, is something wrong?" he asked. She shook her head in a silent, unconvincing 'no'. As she saw the others' worried looks upon her, she forced a smile and answered with no little embarrassment. "It is nothing, really; I am behaving childishly. It is just…you will be gone for more than a week." Darcy took Elizabeth's hand and kissed it, despite the presence of the others.

"Oh, come now, Miss Bennet," Lady Cassandra intervened. "I promise we will use this time most efficiently! I have planned a surprise for the ball and cannot wait to share it with you!"

It was obvious she was attempting to raise their spirits, and Elizabeth took the opportunity to change the subject by asking more about the ball. Neither of them discussed Caroline Bingley's return. It was their last concern.

ELIZABETH TALKED TO JANE, AND Darcy to Bingley later that day — and the result was similar. The suggestion of sharing the same wedding day was pure bliss to Jane and a matter of deep pride for Charles Bingley whose affection toward his friend was matched only by his respect. However, it was more difficult for Bingley to understand why they would want to keep their engagement secret for the moment since Mr. Bennet had given his blessing.

The burden of such a secret was difficult for Bingley to bear, and that was fully proved that evening at Longbourn. All of them were invited for dinner. Countless meaningful glances exchanged between Jane and Bingley and his many stares at his future sister, Elizabeth, made both Lady Cassandra and Mr. Bennet smile at each other in mutual understanding of the torture poor Bingley was enduring.

Mr. Bennet received the news of the wedding date with complete approval; he could easily see the wisdom in having a double wedding instead of two separate ceremonies. However, he did not miss the opportunity to tease Darcy about Mrs. Bennet's disappointment in not being allowed to plan another wedding.

The news of Mr. Darcy's departure for London affected Mrs. Bennet very little as she was still not on friendly terms with "that aloof, silent gentleman." In fact, she wondered many times how he could be brother to "that sweet girl" and a friend of the "spectacular Lady Cassandra."

Dinner was not a pleasant affair for Elizabeth despite the fact that she was seated next to Darcy. She was furious with herself for suggesting he leave for London and, though she knew she was acting unreasonably, could not combat the chill that gripped her heart. She felt alone, lost and — for some unknown reason — frightened. She retired to a corner after dinner while the gentlemen were in the library and her mother and the other ladies were chatting joyfully.

Mr. Bingley returned, and Elizabeth looked eagerly for Darcy, yet he did not appear. Instead, Hill came to fetch her to the library where it was announced that her father was waiting for her. She headed for the library, fearing that something had happened, but instead of her father, she found Darcy alone.

He hurried to take her hands and raised them to his lips. "I have done the most shocking thing! I have asked your father to allow us a few moments alone!" he said with a mischievous smile.

"You did? And he accepted?"

"As you see...but only a few minutes," he added, embracing her tightly. "My love, why are you so sad? Something has happened to you since we talked earlier today."

"No, no, nothing happened; please believe me. I cannot explain what came over me. I have no real reason...it is just..." She met his worried gaze and felt his fingers caressing hers — a gentle and mostly unsuccessful attempt to comfort her. Suddenly, she realised how much her silly reactions distressed him and that it would not do to let him leave in such a disturbed state of mind. She smiled at him and encircled his waist, leaning her head against his chest.

"William, there is nothing wrong, trust me. I am only sad that I will not see you for so many days, but after all, a week is not such a long time. Please take care of your business and return when you finish it, and then I will not allow you to leave for a very long time."

"If you want me to stay, I will. There is nothing so urgent that cannot wait."

"No, no, there is no need for that! Besides," she said, blushing at the impropriety of her words, "the more I become accustomed to your...closeness, the more I dread being away from you. So you had better go now before I cause the ruin of Pemberley."

He almost carried her to the sofa and sat her down without freeing her from his embrace. His fingers moved along every inch of her face, and she closed her eyes to imprint his touch on her mind for the time he would be gone. Tenderly, his lips followed his fingers, placing countless light kisses along her beloved face; there was no passion, no eagerness in his kiss — only infinite love and care.

After some time, she lost all control and tearfully trapped his head in her hands. Her mouth captured his and she kissed him wildly until they both remained breathless. There also was no passion in her kiss — only infinite love and despair.

CHARLES BINGLEY WAS READY FOR bed after a difficult day. So he would be married the same day as his friend! What joy! And the ball — where on earth did all those names come from? Who were those people?

"Charles, thank God you finally returned! I need to speak to you immediately!" The appearance of his sister, Caroline, shocked him, and he desperately pulled the sheet around him.

"Caroline, for heaven's sake, I am in my night clothes! What on earth are you doing here?"

"I need to speak to you immediately — right now — as there is a situation that requires your attention tomorrow morning! You must invite Lord Markham to Netherfield for the ball. I am sure he intends to propose to me very soon! And yes, I know it is not proper for you to invite him as you are not acquainted, but he said he would not mind! Can you imagine that? He said he would love a country ball, especially as his family is visiting a relative only twenty miles from here — I forget the name of the estate. So you will write him today and invite him. In fact, no — your writing is horrible — I will write him in your name, and you will only sign it. What do you say to that?"

He followed her tirade with a shocked expression, barely able to comprehend. He nodded stupidly and wondered briefly who Lord Markham was. Caroline's suitor? A viscount? Can this be true or just another of Caroline's fantasies? He soon came to understand that he would have no peace if he did not invite the man, and frankly, what would one more matter among so many.

"Of course, Caroline, this is your home, too. You may invite whomever you choose, my dear. Just write your letters and let me sign them."

For the first time in ten years, Caroline kissed her brother's cheeks before she ran out of his room.

AFTER DARCY LEFT FOR LONDON, Elizabeth was certain she would not be able to put aside her fears until she saw him again. Fortunately, his daily letter — sent by express to Mr. Bennet — worked like magic and soothed her, and she even managed to sleep during the night

She spent most of the time with Jane, Lady Cassandra and Georgiana. Mr. Bingley's sisters avoided their company as much as possible and seemed to give little consideration to the engagement or the ball. Only Miss Bingley mentioned a few times "a special guest who certainly would be a great surprise to Lady Cassandra," but Elizabeth paid little attention to her.

About a week before the ball, Colonel Fitzwilliam arrived at Netherfield, and his presence animated everyone. To their previous friendship, Elizabeth could add the joy of knowing they would soon be family, and she was even more pleased to find that Darcy had already informed him of their engagement. Georgiana was delighted to have a temporary replacement for her brother, and Bingley kept saying, "Man, I am so happy to have you here!"

At Longbourn, the colonel became a quick favourite of Mrs. Bennet — "such a charming, handsome gentleman!" — and an acceptable replacement for Darcy to Mr. Bennet.

The third day after his arrival, Lady Cassandra woke early to ride. She was angry with herself for her foolish thoughts. The colonel was everything he had been in the past: kind, charming, pleasant, and attentive to everybody. With her, his manners were impeccable; he was neither indifferent nor insistent. His behaviour was friendly and gentlemanlike — and she hated that! There was no sign of the passion he declared previously — no special attention to her, nothing — but, she did not hate him for that. She hated herself for wanting something else! She needed to ride, to free her mind — and her heart — of everything.

She entered the stables lost in thought and, inattentive, almost fell into the colonel's arms.

"Lady Cassandra! Are you all right?"

"Yes, yes… Please forgive my lack of attention, Colonel."

"There is nothing to forgive. Are you… Do you intend to ride? Would you…" He paused a moment, looking at her in earnest. "Would you allow me the pleasure of your company?"

She hesitated a few moments. "Yes, I would be delighted." And in truth, she was delighted.

For more than an hour, they rode through the fields and groves and along hidden paths at a slow pace or a gallop, side by side. They spoke little — mostly about the scenery — and from time to time they cast brief glances at each other. As time passed, she grew easier in his company, and shortly, happy memories of their past together became more powerful than any present distress.

The following days, the couple met and rode together again. Starting the next morning, they not only rode in silence but also raced for some time and then slowed their pace, spending the time in long conversations recalling earlier times. To her surprise, the colonel remembered things she never knew: about herself as a small child, her parents, and her disobedient behaviour. He seemed as pleased to talk as she was to listen, and neither noticed the time pass; they were both late for breakfast and drew the Bingley sisters' reproachful looks. Yet, neither of them noticed.

LADY CASSANDRA RETURNED FROM A long walk together with the colonel, Georgiana and Elizabeth. They were all tired, hungry and in excellent spirits. Elizabeth was happy to have the opportunity of speaking of Darcy and learning about his childhood — and what stories she had heard! Lady Cassandra and the colonel seemed to take the opportunity of Darcy's absence to make fun of him — his seriousness, his propriety, and his first love, the sixteen-year-old daughter of an earl; he was five and wanted to marry her. Georgiana hurried to defend her brother against those stories, but she could do little as all of them had happened before she was born. Elizabeth did not give much credit to the colonel's stories, but the mere mention of Darcy's name gave her joy — so she accepted them with serenity.

On reaching the main entrance of Netherfield, they noticed a large carriage and, a few steps further, a small gathering of people. The identity of the newcomer remained uncertain until they were closer and could not avoid him. Caroline Bingley, elaborately dressed and full of loudly expressed enthusiasm, approached them with superior satisfaction as she performed the introductions.

"Lady Cassandra, Colonel Fitzwilliam, Georgiana — I think you are acquainted with Lord Markham! He is our special guest and will remain at Netherfield until after the ball."

Lord Markham followed Miss Bingley, a most enchanting smile spread over his face, acknowledging their party politely.

Georgiana greeted him properly while Elizabeth remained a little behind, amused by Miss Bingley's bad manners in ignoring her.

Lady Cassandra turned slightly pale, and her eyes narrowed with obvious anger; the colonel breathed deeply, wondering how long he would be able to sustain his manners.

However, to Miss Bingley's utter shock and complete disappointment, Lord Markham stepped forward to Elizabeth and bowed to her. "Miss Bennet, what a delightful surprise to see you again!"

IN THEIR CARRIAGE RIDE BACK to Longbourn, accompanied only by Jane, Elizabeth could not but recollect and analyse the reactions of her friends toward the viscount. She had seen that reaction before — during the ball hosted by Lady Cassandra — but had overlooked it quickly as Lord Markham was not in her sphere of interest. Yet, now their responses were repeated and apparently with greater intensity.

The last hour she spent at Netherfield, Lord Markham behaved more than properly. He was quite amiable, congratulated both Charles and Jane on their betrothal, and praised Netherfield and the entire county. Elizabeth was certain she would have nothing with which to reproach him if not for the hostile attitude of the colonel and Lady Cassandra. To herself, Lord Markham seemed especially cordial — to Miss Bingley's furious displeasure.

Except for Mr. Bingley, the atmosphere at Netherfield was neither easy nor light, so Elizabeth was pleased they were not invited for dinner that evening. She had had enough of Netherfield for a while.

LADY CASSANDRA WAS SO ANGRY that she remained outside to take a stroll around the house in order to calm herself. The nerve of that bastard Markham! What was he doing there? And that stupid Caroline Bingley, almost jumping on him! What was in her head? Was that the man she suggested was her suitor? He could not care less for her — that was obvious. Oh, just wait until Darcy returned and saw him. *That might result in a scandal*, she thought, instantly searching for a way of calming Darcy enough to bear the viscount's presence until after the ball. *What an idiot!* she thought, so preoccupied that she nearly bumped into the very idiot who appeared in her way.

"Lady Cassandra, what a pleasant surprise!"

"The pleasure is all yours, sir," she answered, attempting to move past him.

"Lady Cassandra, please... only a moment."

"What do you want to tell me in a moment, Markham?"

"I know we are not friends, but I was hoping we could be civil while we are both guests here."

"I assure you I will be quite civil, Markham; I was civil when you sneaked into my ball without invitation, was I not? But now I cannot help wondering what you are doing here. Do not offend me by suggesting it is a mere coincidence."

"But it was a coincidence, I assure you. I would have attended this ball in any case."

"Is that so? Are you suddenly so fond of Hertfordshire?"

"I am! My family is visiting my aunt only twenty miles from here, and since Miss Bingley and I have become friends lately, I was happy to receive the invitation."

"Really? You and Miss Bingley are friends? What kind of friends? Come now, Markham. I know you too well; you could not have serious designs on Caroline Bingley. Admit it!"

"Indeed, there is nothing to admit. As I said, my only request is that we be polite to one another. I would not want to hear all manner of rumours about me —"

"Oh, now I see. You are afraid I would betray your true nature —"

"Lady Cassandra, you would not dare —"

"What would Lady Cassandra not dare, Markham?" The colonel's voice fell as thunder upon them.

"Colonel Fitzwilliam!"

"Markham, what the hell are you doing in Hertfordshire? What business do you have here? And what the hell are you doing alone with Lady Cassandra?"

"Colonel, I will not be spoken to in such a manner. I am a guest in this house as you are, and —"

"Markham, I could not care less about you, so spare me. I will tell you this only once: if you dare to bother Lady Cassandra or Georgiana even with a breath, I will break your face, guest or no guest. So be careful to stay away from me." Without another word, he offered his arm to Lady Cassandra; she took it instantly, and they departed together. Around the corner, she stopped and leaned against the side of the house. Her countenance was pale, and her hands were trembling.

"Cassandra, are you unwell? Did he do something to you?"

She shook her head almost violently as she put her hand on his arm. "No, do not worry. Please calm yourself. We do not need a scandal here — not now, just before the engagement ball."

"I shall speak to Bingley about throwing him out."

"You cannot do that, Colonel. As he said, he is a guest as we are and did nothing against us, not the slightest gesture. In fact, we were the ones who offended him just now. Perhaps he is telling the truth. Perhaps he is only an acquaintance of Caroline, and his presence here is a mere coincidence."

"Yes, indeed…and perhaps it will snow tomorrow," he said with angry mockery.

"Colonel, trust me. I will be fine. I give you my word he has neither done nor said anything improper; it is just that, seeing him, recollections assailed me, and some of them are difficult to bear, but that is my fault, not his. He had no direct involvement either in my past or my present distress."

He took her hand gently. "Perhaps you should not join us for dinner; you should rest. You do not look well at all."

"Oh, I will surely not hide because of Markham, be certain of that. Of course I will be ready for dinner soon."

"Very well, but I demand a seat next to you."

"Oh come now…" She was tempted to laugh at his protective attitude but suddenly changed her tone. "Colonel, you do not have to do that —"

"To do what?" he asked, with a puzzled expression.

"To become involved in an argument with Markham or with anybody to protect me. It is not your duty to… We are not —" She stopped, not knowing how to continue.

"Cassandra," he said, using her given name for the second time. "I must tell you something though you might become angry with me; yet, I cannot be other than completely honest with you."

She nodded, and he continued firmly. "For me, nothing has changed since that day in London. Neither my affection, nor my wishes, nor my desires are different or less powerful. I will not insist upon, nor will I force a courtship upon you. However, despite the fact that the nature of my feelings for you has grown so different lately, my care and my concern for you are the same as ever. Anyone who dares harm you — or Georgiana — in any way will have to confront me. That will never change — not even if you decide to marry another man."

"You are very kind," she whispered. "Thank you."

"Very well then — it is settled! Do not try to tell me it is not my duty to protect you, because it is!"

She rolled her eyes and then took his arm again, and they walked to the house together. "Oh dear…and I thought of how I would calm down Darcy when he sees Markham! Now I see you are an equally big problem!" She sketched a smile, attempting to laugh.

"Ah, yes…Darcy! Now that will be an interesting meeting — one I would not want to miss!"

They finally entered the hall and separated in front of the main stair. Before she started climbing it, she turned to him and, looking straight in his eyes, smiled at him, this time openly and brightly.

"Thank you, David!"

Then she left in a great hurry while the colonel remained still, following her with his eyes. She had not called him "David" in almost ten years.

ELIZABETH BECAME TIRED — QUITE TIRED and bored — with all the agitation. She and Jane were again at Netherfield having dinner, but for her those visits were not as pleasant as they used to be. In fact, now that dinner was over, she retired to a corner, looking absently around her. The gentlemen chose not to separate from the ladies; Miss Bingley was preoccupied with Lord Markham, and Mrs. Hurst kept them company; Lady Cassandra and the colonel, together with Jane and Mr. Bingley, formed another group, talking animatedly. Georgiana had retired a little earlier as she was bothered by a slight headache — and Elizabeth could understand only too well!

Since Caroline's return — with her usual impertinence and continuous, concealed offences — and with Lord Markham's presence in the house, Elizabeth lost all her interest in Netherfield. *Well, not quite all my interest,* she corrected her own musings, smiling to herself. She used to sneak into the library and the billiard room, and meander around the gardens — every place that Darcy's image was palpable. The library was her favourite room, and she spent as much time as she could there in peaceful solitude. If she closed her eyes, she could vividly sense his touch, his kisses, and even his scent.

Only two more days until I see him again and less than six weeks until we are married.

Suddenly, in that crowded, noisy room, the longing for him became difficult to bear, and she cast a quick glance around, looking for an opportunity to get out of the house for a few minutes. She did not even see Lord Markham approaching; she noticed his presence only when, with the most charming smile, he bowed politely to her.

"Miss Bennet, I hope I am not disturbing your solitary reverie?"

200

Chapter 15

"Miss Bennet, I hope I am not disturbing your solitary reverie!"

"No indeed, sir. Besides, solitude is hardly the proper word in such animated company."

He seemed pleased with her reply and cast a quick glance around. "Yes, Netherfield is very animated these days. I confess I was surprised to see Lady Cassandra and Miss Darcy here."

"Mr. Darcy is a friend of Mr. Bingley and has been a guest at Netherfield previously. So it does not appear surprising to me that Mr. Bingley invited Miss Darcy and Lady Cassandra."

"Yes, you are correct of course. I was only wondering about their presence while Darcy is in Town. That appears surprising to me. Do you happen to know how long Darcy will be away?"

"I am afraid I cannot offer you a satisfactory answer," she said, searching his expression with great interest. "But perhaps Lady Cassandra or Colonel Fitzwilliam could enlighten you."

"Neither they nor Darcy is exactly my friend, so I doubt they would willingly offer me any information at all. But then again, since you seem to be a close acquaintance, I imagine you know our past dealings."

"You are giving me too much credit, sir. I know nothing about your past dealings with either the lady or the gentlemen, and in truth, I do not feel comfortable speaking on this subject. It is not my custom to invade others' privacy."

"Then you are not aware that Lady Cassandra was supposed to marry my brother?"

Elizabeth looked at him in utter surprise — not only from the revelation but from his impropriety in persisting with a matter about which she had just suggested she was uncomfortable.

"No, I am not, sir. And as I said, I would rather not discuss it. I am sure Lady Cassandra herself will tell me anything she would like me to know. As for the rest, I do not require additional details from other sources." Although her voice was rather harsh, Lord Markham did not appear disturbed.

"Oh, but Miss Bennet, you should consider that people like Lady Cassandra are not always inclined to share their affairs with others, especially those whose consequence in life is beneath them. In fact, I cannot help wondering how she came to be on such friendly terms with Bingley and accept the invitation to Netherfield for such an extended period of time."

The nerve of this man! "Pray tell me, Lord Markham, what do you mean by, *'people like Lady Cassandra'*? You, sir, as the son of an earl, are certainly one of the people like Lady Cassandra, and you seem more than willing to share your affairs with me — not to mention that you accepted the invitation to Netherfield as well and are not even on friendly terms with the master of the house. Then again, being an intimate friend of Miss Bingley, your reason is quite understandable."

She threw him a sharp glance, her eyebrow rising inquiringly. She knew she was being impertinent, and if he felt offended, all the better. Perhaps he would leave her and return to Miss Bingley, who was speaking animatedly in another corner of the room, apparently oblivious to their conversation.

A strange, disconcerting smile twisted his lips. "Miss Bennet, you are an astonishing woman! Your wit is a perfect match to your beauty, and it is as much a pleasure to watch you as to talk to you!"

"Thank you, sir. You are too kind," she replied, equally amused and annoyed.

"I am only being honest, Miss Bennet. I am sure you did not fail to notice my admiration for you when we met in town. Since that moment, I have been wishing to see you again, and the opportunity fortunately arose when I received the invitation to Netherfield. In fact, you are the main reason for my presence here!"

The shock of his words left her speechless, and for a few moments, she looked at him in disbelief.

"I thank you, sir," she said wearily, "but let us not forget you are here at the particular invitation of Miss Bingley! Now if you would excuse me, I should like to speak to my sister."

"Miss Bennet —" She turned toward him, but to Elizabeth's relief, Miss Bingley seemed at length to remember her interests and walked in their direction with great determination. Elizabeth smiled at her briefly with cold politeness and then moved past her. She joined her sister's group and tried listening to their conversation about the ball, but her concentration was deeply disturbed.

A few minutes later as Bingley spoke with the colonel, Lady Cassandra approached Elizabeth and whispered, "Miss Bennet, what is the matter? I saw you talking to Markham, and you seem unwell!"

Elizabeth blushed in embarrassment and then looked around her, afraid someone else might hear her. "There is nothing really, your ladyship; no need to distress yourself."

"Miss Bennet! Everything that involves Markham *means* distress, so please indulge me!"

Not even at the beginning of their acquaintance had Lady Cassandra spoken with such a demanding tone; she became conscious of her rudeness and added in a low voice, "Miss Bennet, please accept my apologies. I had no right to address you in such a manner! But my curiosity has good cause: Markham is not to be trusted, and for somebody unaware of his true character, he can be dangerous."

"Lady Cassandra, there is no need to apologise. I understand you meant well. Please be assured I have no intention of trusting Lord Markham. You are right; I was distressed because of him. But really — he is more ridiculous than dangerous."

Lady Cassandra looked at her quizzically, and Elizabeth smiled, mortified. "Oh well — if you like, I will tell you. In fact, I would rather have somebody to tell because it is quite entertaining."

"Then please, do tell me." Lady Cassandra's voice held no trace of amusement.

"Well, it appears Lord Markham was rather enchanted by my *charms* when we met in London, and he came here mostly to see me! Can you imagine anything more ridiculous? And he confessed it to me here! Poor Miss Bingley! Though, on the other hand, the situation could be dangerous. I am sure Miss Bingley would kill me if she discovered the truth!" She anticipated her companion's laughter.

Lady Cassandra's frown persisted. "Miss Bennet, did he say anything else?"

"No, he did not! In fact, he had no time, as I walked away from him."

"Very well; you must promise me that, if he bothers you again, you will tell the colonel."

"Oh, come now. Your ladyship must not worry; I am able to take care of myself. After all, I did handle Mr. Collins remarkably well. Nothing can be worse."

ANOTHER HOUR PASSED, AND JANE showed no inclination to leave. In the meantime, Elizabeth managed to regain her spirits and was more indulgent of her sister's delay. It appeared that Jane could not bear to depart from her betrothed, and Elizabeth understood completely.

Miss Bingley exhibited little civility, continually indicating to the Longbourn guests that they should leave. She mentioned loudly and often that she felt quite tired and was tempted to retire, but she would not leave as long as Lord Markham remained in the salon.

Lord Markham, on the other hand, spent most of his time enjoying Mr. Bingley's brandy. He tried several times to talk to Elizabeth but with little success. Elizabeth remained close to Lady Cassandra and her sister — not because she had taken Lady Cassandra's warning seriously but because she did not want to provoke a scandal. Miss Bingley would surely have become furious if she suspected anyone were interfering between herself and her "suitor."

When Lady Cassandra rejoined Jane and Bingley in their conversation, Elizabeth took the opportunity to slip out of the house into the fresh, cool, late September air. It had rained the previous night, and the ground was muddy. She laughed to herself, remembering her appearance at Netherfield the previous autumn after walking three miles as well as Darcy's surprise. Unconsciously, her steps took her to the precise place where she met him after climbing over a stile and landing in a mud puddle. Now she could see clearly — with the eyes of her mind — the expression on his face the moment they faced each other. *Poor William, how I shocked him,* she thought, missing him painfully.

The night was starless, and Elizabeth could barely see where she was walking. She turned to admire the sight of Netherfield and decided to return to the house as the night chill was making her shiver.

She recoiled, however, her heart pounding, when she noticed the shadow of a man mere inches away.

"Miss Bennet, forgive me for startling you —"

"Lord Markham! Indeed, you startled me, sir. Excuse me; I must return to the house this instant."

"Miss Bennet, please, just a moment… I noticed you have avoided me the entire evening, and I cannot bear the thought that you will not speak to me! Have I upset you in any way?"

She hesitated for a moment and then decided to behave normally; after all, he was an educated man of the world, and he could understand reason. The situation had become ridiculous beyond belief.

"Lord Markham, I am not upset with you; I have no reason to be. But you must understand my surprise, sir, when I heard your earlier statement. You are in my soon-to-be brother's house; he trusts you and treats you with respect. You must know everybody suspects you have an interest in Miss Bingley, and unless you utterly and publicly contradict that, you are expected to behave accordingly."

"So, if I declare I have absolutely no design on Miss Bingley, you would accept my attentions?"

"I said nothing of the kind. Sir, we met only once a couple of months ago. I do not think you can have any serious design on me, either. Let us put the matter aside this instant."

"You must allow me to tell you everything I have to say before leaving. I am not the kind of man to be dismissed; I promise if you would let me prove my true feelings, you would not remain indifferent to my attentions." He stepped closer and attempted to take her hand, but she pulled it away violently.

"Lord Markham, I will allow you nothing! I tried to be polite and show you some consideration, but you do not deserve it. Any feelings you might have are not my concern — not now or in the future."

"Elizabeth, I shall not accept such a reply! I am not accustomed to being refused and certainly not in such a manner! No other woman, ever —"

She turned her back on him and grimaced when he seized her arm painfully.

"Lord Markham, unhand me immediately!"

He moved in front of her, his free hand trapping her other arm; he was so close that she could feel his breath, reeking of alcohol. She grew angry and, full of rage, tried to free herself.

"You are a brute, Lord Markham, and I shall have you pay for that! Everyone will find out the kind of man you are, and you will be out of the house this very evening! Let me go this instant!"

"Elizabeth, I care nothing about the others! Have me thrown out of the house if you want, but I will still think of no one but you! Since the night I danced with you, I have thought of no one but you! You — and that bastard Darcy, never leaving your side! It is he, is it not? He is the reason you are refusing me in such a manner! What did he propose to you? A house in town? An allowance? Can you not see that all he offers I can give ten times over? I will take better care of you, Elizabeth. I cannot let you make such a mistake. I cannot let you choose Darcy over me!"

So surprised was Elizabeth by the attack and so shocked that a man of his consequence could behave like a savage that, in the first moments, she barely reacted. She hardly listened to him; his words reached her ears but she thought of nothing except freeing herself from him. She felt no fear — only rage against him and fury at her own lack of strength. She struggled with little success; his grasp became more powerful, and she tried violently to pull away.

Elizabeth heard him saying he did not want to hurt her; he only wanted to prove to her how much he desired her. As all her efforts at resistance failed, her anger turned to fear and then panic. She realised such wild behaviour would not listen to reason. She was his prisoner with little chance of escaping. In horror and desperation, she saw his face moving toward her in an obvious attempt to kiss her, and she felt sick; she turned her head to avoid his mouth and cried with disgust when she felt cold lips touch her cheek. The hand that trapped her arm moved to her shoulder and pulled down the neckline of her dress; as she fought, the move ripped apart the thin fabric.

Cringing at his touch, she pushed him away with all her remaining strength and a determination borne of desperation. She was free — for a moment. The forced separation threw her backward, and her shoes slipped in the mud; she fell, desperately attempting to grab the fence with one hand. The last image she saw was the moon peeking from behind the clouds. A sharp pain shattered her head and threw her into a hole of cold darkness.

Someone was calling her name, but she could not answer. She could not even move, nor did she want to. She only sensed the alcohol-drenched smell and vicious hands touching her skin — and she could do nothing but pray the earth would swallow her completely. And then she knew nothing else...

An eternity later — or was it just a moment — only the darkness and the coldness remained and a voice — another voice — calling, crying out her name.

THERE WERE MANY PEOPLE AROUND her; Elizabeth could hear them. She was no longer on the ground but on a soft bed with a pillow beneath her head; the pain at the nape of her neck made it difficult to move her head. She did not wish to talk to or see anybody — nor did she wish to open her eyes or even to think. She did not want to think of anything. She did not want to feel anything.

Memories invaded her mind, and her body shivered in disgust as she remembered the violence of his touch. He had tried to kiss her. Had he only tried? She knew at some point he was lying on her, his weight and smell still vivid recollections in her mind. But had he —?

"Oh God, no!" she cried. "No, please no!" Unconsciously, she began to struggle against him until she felt her hands trapped — and then she fought even harder.

Moments later, Elizabeth managed to recognise her sister's voice calling her name. Her movements calmed, and she tried to breathe steadily again. Then, with great effort, she slowly opened her eyes. Yes, Jane was there, as well as Lady Cassandra and her maid. They were holding her hands, and she looked at each of them briefly and then closed her eyes again. She did not want to see anyone.

"Lizzy, please open your eyes, dearest," cried Jane with a tearful voice, but Elizabeth did not obey.

She heard Lady Cassandra saying something, but she did not care enough to try to understand her words. A door opened, closed again, and then silence. Were they all gone? No, they were not; she could feel Jane caressing her hand. She violently pulled her hand from her sister's grasp, turned her face against the pillow, and started to cry. She wanted neither Jane's comfort nor her pity.

"Elizabeth, look at me!" Lady Cassandra's voice was compelling, and Elizabeth's sobs stopped instantly. Strangely, the first thing she noticed was that she had called her *"Elizabeth."*

Elizabeth did not answer or open her eyes. The darkness was easier to bear. As long as it was dark, there was still a chance that everything had been a nightmare.

She felt Lady Cassandra sit on the bed beside her, trying to make her face them. She resisted — even fought her — and her ladyship abandoned the attempt but remained near her.

"Elizabeth, I know you are frightened and hurt, but you must talk to us." No reply.

"Please, Lizzy," added Jane, "staying like that will do no good! We sent for the doctor; he will be here soon. And we called Papa, too."

"No," she screamed, "I do not need the doctor; there is nothing a doctor can do for me! And why Papa? He cannot see me like this! What about Mr. Bingley? And the others?"

"Elizabeth, calm yourself," said Lady Cassandra softly, touching her hair. Elizabeth startled and pushed her hand away.

"Very well then; as you wish. I shall leave you alone with your sister; perhaps you will talk to her. And I asked the servant to prepare a bath for you and to bring you

206

some tea —"

"Yes, leave." Elizabeth spoke in a voice she herself could not recognise. "And take Jane with you. I do not want to talk to her! I do not want to talk to anyone. I do not want to bathe. I do not want tea! I just want to die," she added, barely audible, and turned her face against the pillow again.

"Oh come now," replied Lady Cassandra. "Stop this nonsense immediately! I know what you think and how hurt you must feel, but you are a smart woman and —"

"Do not tell me to stop," cried Elizabeth, rising from the pillow. "You have no right to tell me what to do! How dare you say you know how I feel and what I think? How can you know that?"

Jane startled, looking at her sister in shock and then at Lady Cassandra, desperately trying to find a way to counter such a harsh argument. She knew her ladyship would be offended, and in truth, she had every reason to be so. However, Lady Cassandra's reply was nothing but kindness.

"You may yell at me as much as you wish, Elizabeth. Be upset with me, fight with me if it makes you feel better. And you are right; I have no reason to tell you what to do. However, you are wrong when you presume I do not know how you feel. I remember vividly a time when I wanted only to die. But you, my dear, have no reason to feel that way. Everything is well now."

Elizabeth stared at her, her eyes wide open, breathing deeply as the air was not enough.

"Everything is well? How can you say that? Everything is lost! That man — that man…" She could not continue as she was close to tears. She covered her eyes, and Jane hurried to embrace her warmly.

"I can see you do not desire my presence, so I shall leave you now, Elizabeth. Miss Bennet, please call me if you need anything. I shall be in the library with the gentlemen."

She left, carefully closing the door behind her. Elizabeth breathed in relief and shut her eyes again.

"Jane, how did I get here?" she asked a few moments later.

Her sister took her hand and caressed it gently while answering. "Lady Cassandra and the colonel found you. It appears that her ladyship followed Lord Markham as he left the house. She was the one who discovered you, and then the colonel appeared, and they told us."

Elizabeth looked at her sister briefly and then turned her head in the opposite direction. "You should have taken me home directly, Jane. I am among strangers here; how can I bear the looks of Miss Bingley and Mrs. Hurst? They will be so happy to see us thrown into a new scandal. I have ruined everything for you — with only three days before your engagement ball."

"Lizzy dearest, how can you say that? You have done nothing wrong; it was not your fault!" As Elizabeth shook her head in disapproval, Jane continued with a determination that defeated her emotions. "As for a scandal, you must not worry. Lady Cassandra has been so wonderful. Oh Lizzy, you have been too harsh with her. She talked to Charles privately; she called him into the library and then came and told us that Lord Markham had retreated to his rooms and you were not feeling well, so Charles invited us to stay the night. I was surprised at first, and I asked about you; Lady Cassandra accompanied me to you. You were already in this room — apparently the colonel brought you here — so you see… neither Caroline nor Mr. Hurst and Louisa truly know what happened."

"Where is *he*?" she asked, afraid to pronounce his loathsome name.

"Lord Markham? He is locked in a guest room in the north wing. His man is with him, and two of Charles's people are watching the door so he cannot leave. So you need not worry about him. He will never harm you again. You see dearest? Everything is settled."

Elizabeth listened to her sister, both tearful, holding their hands in comfort. As always, Jane was inclined to believe everything was well, but such a scandal could not be kept secret; she knew that. The servants would talk, and by the next day, they would be the subject of gossip in the entire county. Their good name would be lost forever, especially after what happened to Lydia a month earlier.

If only Mr. Bingley would not break his engagement with Jane. As for her own engagement, there was nothing left. The mere thought of William returning and facing her like this… She began crying so violently that she frightened Jane, who desperately attempted to calm her. When she had no tears left, she finally spoke with perfect composure. "Jane, I want to take a bath. I need to clean myself."

"My Lizzy has been hurt?" Mr. Bennet stared blankly at the two young men gathered in the library. "Who the hell is this man, and what does he hold against my daughter? She has done nothing to him!"

The colonel proceeded to explain to him what had happened, assuring him that Lady Cassandra had intervened in time and Miss Elizabeth was now well and resting. The elder gentleman instantly swallowed a second glass of wine while pacing the room, his agitation growing every moment.

"Where is he now? I will kill him," Mr. Bennet finally burst out, throwing the glass in the fireplace. Bingley and the colonel looked at him in shock.

"Mr. Bennet, please do not give me more trouble, sir," said Lady Cassandra, entering the room unannounced. "I barely managed to calm down the colonel and Bingley here — as both shared the same intentions regarding Markham. I hoped I would be able to count on your support to settle things before scandal could arise. Your daughters do not need that with only a month before their weddings."

"I beg your pardon?" he cried. A moment later, Mr. Bennet frowned seeing the bruises on her face and neck. "What on earth happened? Did he hurt you too? And you want to keep us from killing him?"

"Mr. Bennet, I am well. There is no need to worry about me. As for killing Markham — if you want to do so, by all means please do! I will surely not stop you — quite the contrary! But you are not the sort of man simply to murder him — we both know that — nor is the colonel or Bingley. As for your calling him out, that would be madness you must admit. And the scandal would be worse."

"Lady Cassandra, I do appreciate your concern, and I understand you are doing everything for the benefit of my daughters. But the scandal will erupt; we cannot avoid that. The servants, my daughter's state and yours, the sudden absence of Markham — these things cannot be hidden. And to all that, just consider what will happen when Darcy finds out. I doubt you will be able to appease him. He would not hesitate a moment to do what is right, and I will surely support his decision."

"I agree," said the colonel and Bingley in unison.

"Oh, you do?" cried Lady Cassandra, her voice so enraged that all three gentlemen looked at her in shock. "Indeed, what a lovely, honourable thing! Let Darcy call Markham out and risk his life. Of course, he might be killed — along with Elizabeth and Georgiana's chances of happiness — but at least we will all be satisfied to know he has done what any man of honour would do!"

"Lady Cassandra, you are too hasty and too emotional," said the colonel, stepping toward her. "Darcy can defeat Markham any time with any weapon and on any ground, I assure you —"

"Really? You can assure me? What a relief! Can you assure me that Markham will fight with respect for the rules? And, even if Darcy kills him, what then? Duelling is illegal; we all know that."

"Oh, come now... You cannot possibly suggest letting Markham leave unpunished. Most likely, Darcy will not kill him — only give him a proper punishment and make sure he will never approach Miss Bennet again. But let us not speak more of that. This is men's business, and there is little for you to do. We had better discuss something else and try to solve what can be solved."

"You are mistaken, Colonel. I know only too well how these things are done, and that is why I will not allow anything of the kind to happen. As for things that can be resolved, I have already found a solution to everything. There is a simple way to avoid any scandal falling upon the Bennet family and prevent Darcy from risking his life in a fight with Markham."

Three pairs of eyes stared at her inquiringly in utter disbelief. "There is no such way, Lady Cassandra," replied the colonel and the others nodded in agreement.

"I beg to differ. There is a way — a perfect way! Markham's father — the earl — is visiting a relative; he resides less than twenty miles from here. I have already sent him an express telling him that his son attacked me, and I have asked him to come immediately to remove him."

"You did what?" cried all three gentlemen.

"Cassandra, that was a foolish thing to do," said the colonel, barely hiding his anger.

"Indeed, you should not have done that, Lady Cassandra," Mr. Bennet spoke severely. "Besides, I cannot allow you to take this matter upon yourself; I shall not protect my daughters by exposing you nor save their reputation by ruining yours. I am sure Lizzy will agree with me."

"Mr. Bennet, perhaps your daughter will agree with you," she answered, her eyes daringly confronting them. "But it is already done, and it is done for the best — and it is indeed the wisest solution. My reputation means little to me, and as I have no family left, no one will be affected. Furthermore, Mr. Bennet, you do not know that I have a history with the Markhams; any gossip would harm their name more than mine. They will be most careful about the rumours. I know how to deal with the earl and his unworthy son. If the earl takes Markham from here soon enough, Darcy will have time to calm himself and think properly before making any decisions. I will speak to Elizabeth about that, and I am sure she will see my reasons and eventually accept them."

"I doubt that very much," replied Mr. Bennet. "Elizabeth will not allow you to take such a burden upon yourself. And even if we accept your version, Markham himself could easily contradict you — not to mention the fact that the servants will talk, and rumours and gossip will spread in no time."

"You should trust me more, Mr. Bennet," she answered with a bitter smile. "I have already informed my maid that *I* was the one attacked by Markham and that Miss Elizabeth came to my rescue and was injured in the process; I am sure she has already shared this news with the other servants as I did not ask her to be discreet about it. By tomorrow night, it is likely all of Meryton will be informed of my version of the incident. As for Markham, he was too inebriated to know what he was doing, so nobody will take his word seriously, at least not in this county."

Three men watched her, eyes and mouths gaping, as if they could barely understand her words.

"You intend to lie and expect us to support you in concealing the truth," the colonel concluded.

"No, I do not expect you to do anything. The truth? What truth, Colonel? What was it you saw exactly when you arrived?"

He hesitated only a moment. "I saw you fighting with Markham."

"Precisely. That is the only thing you can testify about on your word of honour, but I doubt anyone will actually inquire about or even doubt my word. What reason would a woman like me, with wealth and position, have to lie about such a scandal? Am I not right?"

"I do not know what to say," whispered Mr. Bennet, looking from one to the other. "We should talk to Lizzy and see what she thinks and then wait for Darcy's arrival. Has Darcy been informed?"

"Yes, I sent him a note," answered Bingley.

"You sent him a note? When did you do that?" asked Lady Cassandra, obviously surprised and highly displeased. "And what did you write in the note?"

"Immediately after... *the incident.* I thought he should know. I wrote him that Lord Markham attempted to attack Elizabeth," Bingley whispered in front of Lady Cassandra's open censure.

"That was a stupid thing to do, Bingley," she said coldly. "We must hurry. I will go and talk to Elizabeth immediately," she added while exiting the door.

Three gentlemen remained motionless in the middle of the room — gazing at Lady Cassandra as she left — each of them helplessly and unsuccessfully contemplating what was best to be done.

Lady Cassandra entered Elizabeth's room and found only her sister. She cast a quick glance around before looking inquiringly to the obviously distressed elder Miss Bennet.

"Lizzy is still in the bath," Jane whispered, her eyes tearful. "She has been there since you left; the water must be quite cold by now. I tried to talk to her, but she said she still was not clean enough. She... she kept cleaning herself. She behaves so strangely that I do not know what to do."

"I shall go and talk to her if you agree." Jane nodded silently, her eyes full of gratitude and hope.

Elizabeth was sitting in the bathtub, her hair down and wet, lying on her back. She did not even turn her head when Lady Cassandra entered. "Jane, I am not ready yet," she said, continuing to rub her hands against her body in an obvious gesture of washing herself.

"Yes, you are ready," Lady Cassandra stated, and Elizabeth startled. Her ladyship moved forward, taking a robe from the chair. "You are ready and will get out this instant, Elizabeth. You are cold."

"No, I am not," Elizabeth answered with the obstinacy of a child. "And I am not yet ready. I am so dirty. I feel all that mud on me, and..." The tears burst out, rolling down her cheeks, and she wiped them off furiously and continued to wash her neck and face.

Lady Cassandra kneeled near the tub and took Elizabeth's hands, stopping their violent movements and forcing Elizabeth to look at her.

"You must get out of the water, and then we must talk. You must trust me; all will be well!"

Elizabeth continued to cry silently, her eyes — pained and vacant, utterly devoid of their usual liveliness — stared at Lady Cassandra.

"You are calling me *Elizabeth,*" she said softly.

"I am? Yes, I suppose I am," her ladyship admitted, slightly uneasy. "I apologise."

"No, there is no need. I have long wanted you to address me by my given name, but you never did."

"I do not know why I did not call you by your given name sooner, but for heaven's sake, let us not have this conversation now. Come; let me help you out of the tub."

As Elizabeth still did not move, Lady Cassandra took her arms firmly. "Elizabeth, I will give you one more minute; then, if you do not remove yourself, I will call the servants to pull you out of that bathtub. I am not joking; you know that to be true."

"You have no right to order me like that," Elizabeth replied, wrapping her arms around herself.

"If I am worried about a friend, I care little about rights or wrongs; I do everything I consider proper. So — shall I call the servants? Or perhaps your father, who is downstairs?"

Elizabeth flinched violently; then, after only a few moments of hesitation, she reached her hand to take the robe and wrapped herself in it as she stepped out of the tub. She almost lost her balance and was about to fall when Lady Cassandra hurried to support her.

A few minutes later, Elizabeth sat in the middle of the bed, propped up with pillows. Her colourless face and her eyes stared toward a blank point somewhere on the opposite wall. Neither Lady Cassandra nor Jane spoke, patiently waiting and exchanging quick glances with each other.

"Elizabeth..." whispered Jane after an interval of unbearable silence.

"I feel nothing," Elizabeth said, her voice hardly audible. "Not even shame — only dirty and angry. I thought... I thought there would be *pain...and blood...* But there was nothing..."

Jane gasped and turned pale, whispering, "Oh, Lizzy..."

Lady Cassandra stared at her wonderingly, searching for the meaning of her words.

"Oh, my dear!" she burst out. "You think *that*? You believe that Markham took advantage of you?"

Elizabeth's shocked expression confirmed that she was indeed correct in her assumption. "My dear, what you are afraid of did not happen! There is nothing for you to *feel* because nothing *happened*! Elizabeth, I cannot say how sorry I am that you had to go through that nightmare, but fortunately, he was stopped in time. *It* did not happen," her ladyship insisted, watching Elizabeth carefully.

Elizabeth stopped breathing, her eyes searching Lady Cassandra incredulously as her heart pounded with desperate hope. "Lady Cassandra, what do you mean? I can remember that something happened. He touched me and he tried to kiss me...and then I fell, and I felt him upon me and —"

"My dear, please calm yourself. I left the house a few moments after Markham, but unfortunately, it took me some time to find you. I saw you fighting with him. Less than a minute later, I was there."

"But..." Elizabeth's face regained some of its colour; she released herself from Jane's embrace and moved out of the bed. She felt dizzy as she stood and leaned slightly, almost falling.

"Lady Cassandra, how can you be certain? Where is my dress? I know my dress was ripped off —"

"I am certain; trust me, my dear." Lady Cassandra looked at Elizabeth's confused, pained expression and then at Jane, who seemed as tormented as was her sister. "Oh, dear! How can I explain this? It requires some amount of time to ... *accomplish* that activity, much more than it took me to reach you. Besides, he was *fully dressed* ... if you understand my meaning."

Lady Cassandra hoped her assurance would calm Elizabeth to some degree — and apparently, she succeeded. To her utter surprise, Elizabeth's eyes remained fixed upon her, inquiringly, still obviously distrustful, and then suddenly Elizabeth started laughing, loudly, nervously, covering her face with her palms. Then her peals of laughter turned into painful sobs that shattered her entire body.

They allowed her time to cry — a relieving, liberating cry — and Jane's tears joined those of her sister. Lady Cassandra tried to keep her composure as she watched the two sisters.

Suddenly, Elizabeth's sobs stopped, and she turned toward Lady Cassandra. "You saved me," she said. Then, as if seeing her for the first time that evening, she touched her ladyship's cheek.

"And you have been hurt because of me. Your face is bruised —"

"Oh, that? He was stronger then I imagined when I tried to take him off you, but do not worry; it is just a scratch. You should see his face. The colonel actually broke it!" she added with forced laughter.

"You have been hurt because of me. You exposed yourself because of me, risking your own safety," Elizabeth continued with no little emotion.

"No, Elizabeth, that is not true. *You* have been hurt because of me. I should have taken better care of you. I should have warned you more seriously about Markham."

Elizabeth shook her head in disapproval. "You had done everything to indicate the danger, but I did not take your warning seriously. I should have been more prudent. My impertinence exposed my family to scandal again — and only three days before your engagement ball, Jane. I am so sorry!"

"Lizzy, how can you apologise? You have done nothing wrong; it was not your fault. I certainly do not care about the ball and neither does Mr. Bingley, I assure you!"

"Mr. Bingley?! Jane, does he know what has happened? What did he say? Oh, of course he knows, I am in his house after all ... I cannot think rationally, I only —"

"Elizabeth, let us talk calmly for a few minutes, shall we?" Lady Cassandra resumed her place on the bed near Elizabeth. "There is no scandal at all. Only the colonel, your father and Mr. Bingley are aware of what happened. The colonel followed me when I exited the house and made a timely and fortunate appearance while I was fighting with Markham. He silenced Markham, but we needed Mr. Bingley's assistance, so we informed him and your sister. There is something I need to talk to you about immediately so we can settle this thing for good. I really hope you will use your good judgment and your sense to support me in this."

"What about William?" she whispered.

Lady Cassandra hesitated only a moment. "Well, Bingley informed him — and I am afraid he did not accomplish that task in the best way possible. In truth, Darcy is precisely the reason I want to talk to you about this if you feel strong enough to bear a difficult conversation."

"Of course, Lady Cassandra," Elizabeth answered, her eyes still downcast. "I can tolerate anything if it is about William. But do you think he will come? And if he does… I do not think I will be able to bear the expression on his face. What if he —?"

"Elizabeth!" Lady Cassandra cried, with a severe voice. "Please listen to me — Darcy will come sooner than you think, and the only one who can put this horrible incident behind us is you! Now, here is what I have done and how I need your help… And, by the way, from now on — no more of this *Lady Cassandra*, if you please! I can predict we will have a long and difficult argument this evening, and it will be much more comfortable to call each other by our given names when fighting."

DARCY HAD COMPELLED HIS MOUNT to a gallop since the first moment he touched the saddle, and his only coherent thought was that he was moving too slowly — unbearably, painfully slowly. The servant needed three hours to reach his house with the express from Bingley, and Darcy needed a quarter of an hour after he read it to be ready and on his horse, rushing to Netherfield — rushing to her.

First, he was certain Bingley had somehow mixed things up in a deplorable manner. He said Elizabeth had been attacked by Markham — but that was the most ridiculous thing ever; how could Markham be in Hertfordshire? Of course, he could not ask the servant for details, so all he could do was leave within a few minutes to discover the truth for himself. The only thing that mattered and the only thing he prayed for while careening through fields in the middle of the night was the hope that he would arrive in time but fearing the worst.

As he hurtled wildly, his mind was vividly invaded by Elizabeth's pained eyes, her fears, her sadness and the desperation in her kiss when they parted, and he hated himself for leaving her. She was afraid of something that evening, and he was so insensible that he dismissed her fears lightly. He was not there when she needed him; he was not there to protect her. He hated himself as much as he loved her. The night was dark with no moon or stars — nobody to witness his tears of anger and helpless despair.

THEY TALKED FOR A LONG time, neither of them willing to accept the other's justification. Lady Cassandra tried to impose her version on a stunned Elizabeth, who instantly rejected the idea of allowing her ladyship to take the blame upon herself.

Jane was unable to intervene, as she could not decide whose side she should take. She could see the wisdom in Lady Cassandra's plan, and she could understand her sister's reason for not accepting her ladyship's generous offer. For the first time in her life, Jane Bennet hated a man with all her heart — the man who had done so much harm to her beloved sister.

"Elizabeth, you must trust me; everything will be much easier this way, and besides, you have few choices. What do you propose to do — tell everyone that I lied and that, in fact, Markham attacked *you*? You can easily imagine what kind of speculation and gossip that revelation would raise; and the damage would affect both your family and me. What would be the use of it?"

Elizabeth hesitated a moment, long enough for Lady Cassandra to feel she had gained the advantage. "Moreover, there is something you have not been told: almost the same thing happened to me four years ago. The earl's eldest son forced me into a compromising situation during a ball, and we were caught; afterwards, they insisted I marry him, and when I refused, they spread all kinds of rumours about me. Back then the scandal did affect me," she admitted with a light tone, trying to prove those memories affected her no longer. However, her pale face and the expression of distress did not go unnoticed by either sister.

"The earl has another son?"

"He had… That son passed away two years ago."

"That was the reason you left town?" The improper question escaped Elizabeth's lips.

"Yes, partially… I was very young then, and since I had spent all my life away from London, I was not accustomed to such shameless schemes. I confess that, when I first met young Lord Markham, I enjoyed his company very much. Then he became quite insistent in his courtship, and I withdrew to the point where I did not accept his calls. And then, at the first ball where we happened to be together, he pretended he wanted to talk to me and apologise. We were on a balcony, and there were people around us, but he felt no remorse in kissing me right there. You can imagine what followed."

Jane gasped in shock while Elizabeth looked at her incredulously. "And did not William or the colonel do anything? I mean —"

"The colonel was not in town at that time and Darcy… His father had just passed away the year before, and he had all many responsibilities on his shoulders, including Georgiana, Pemberley and, partially, my estate. I could not allow him to confront a scoundrel like Markham, so I told Darcy that I willingly allowed him to kiss me, but I did not want to marry him, as he was not the honourable man I thought him to be. Darcy accepted my explanation; furthermore, he suggested that we should marry to put all the gossip aside."

Elizabeth could not help blushing as her heart ached at the mere idea of Darcy proposing to another woman — no matter the circumstances. A moment later, she regained her calm enough to continue.

"So you lied — twice — on Markham's behalf," she said in a lower voice.

"Not on his behalf, I assure you. If I could, I would have —" Lady Cassandra stopped instantly and hurried toward the window, the expression of grief so powerful that it darkened her face.

Elizabeth moved to her, gently touching her shoulder in a comforting gesture. She was highly distressed by what Lady Cassandra had revealed to them and even more so by what she suspected remained *untold*; obviously there was more to the story, which affected Lady Cassandra more deeply than she was willing to admit.

A tentative knock on the door interrupted their argument, and Lady Cassandra's maid entered.

"Your ladyship asked to be informed as soon as the earl arrived."

All three ladies startled and cast quick glances at each other. Lady Cassandra thanked her maid, dismissed her, and then quickly arranged her appearance in the mirror.

"I shall go downstairs," she said and, without allowing for any opposition, left the room.

NETHERFIELD LIBRARY HAD NEVER BEEN heated by so much tension; Bingley thought it was ready to erupt any moment. Here they were: his future father-in-law, pale and angry; the colonel, who seemed a storm ready to demolish everything in his way; and the earl with his son, both wearing self-confident expressions and appraising their surroundings with great disdain and no little anger.

"My son has been treated in the worst possible manner, and somebody will pay for it. His face has been injured, he has been beaten, and he has been locked away in a room —"

"Your son has not been beaten, Lord Markham," the colonel interrupted and stepped toward them. Instantly, the younger Markham took a step backward. "If he had been beaten, he would look much worse, I assure you."

"This is scandalous, Colonel. I will not accept —"

"You will not accept what, Lord Markham?" The men turned to the door in utter surprise to face Lady Cassandra, her green eyes flashing fearlessly at the two Markhams. "What will you not accept — the fact that you have raised two sons who have proved to be the most unworthy of men?"

"Lady Cassandra, I will not admit —"

"You are in no position to admit anything, sir! I have done you a great favour by informing you of the incident so you can remove your spoiled brat from this vicinity while you still have time."

"You have no right to insult me and my sons! My eldest son, may God rest him in peace, had nothing but the most honourable intentions toward you, and you refused him with no consideration."

"Let us not talk about your elder son, Lord Markham. You should better pray as much as you can that God will forgive him for everything he did in this world and finally allow him to rest in peace…some day." Her voice was so full of emotion that she could not control her words.

"How dare you talk about my son in such a manner? You are nothing but —"

"Lord Markham!" Mr. Bennet's voice — powerful and admitting no contradiction — silenced the entire room for a moment. "I am not familiar with the proper etiquette for your social class, but if you dare say another word against Lady Cassandra, I shall ask my future son-in-law to have you both thrown out of his house this instant. You should have enough shame to leave with no further arguments; that is the least you can do."

"Mr. Bennet, I understand your protective attitude, but you do not know all the facts," replied Lord Markham with an unexpectedly calm tone. "And you do not know that Lady Cassandra is trying to deceive you all; my son just told me he did not attack her, as she pretended, but he tried to talk to your daughter, Miss Elizabeth, when an accident occurred that caused this entire misunderstanding."

"Lord Markham, I know everything I have to know; I am afraid you are the one who has been deceived — by your own son. What happened tonight between your son and a *certain lady* was by no means an accident, of that I can assure you. As Lady Cassandra suggested, you had best remove your son from this house before somebody gives him the punishment he deserves."

"Mr. Bennet, you must listen to me," the younger Markham intervened. "I did not attack Lady Cassandra; she was not even there. I was speaking with Miss Bennet when she accidentally fell. I…I tried to help her recover, but Lady Cassandra arrived, and things were grossly misinterpreted. But I am ready to pay for my mistake by agreeing to marry your daughter. I know she has not much dowry, and I am aware she is not what my family expected for a wife, but I am sure my father will not oppose the union. That will settle everything most conveniently."

"But she is engaged to Darcy," cried Bingley.

"She is engaged to Darcy?" repeated both Markhams, visibly stunned by that revelation.

Lady Cassandra and the colonel had no time to intervene before Mr. Bennet continued.

"So you agree to marry my daughter. How kind of you! Are you out of your senses, young man? Viscount or no viscount, can you really believe that my daughter would agree to marry you? Or that I would give you my consent?"

Suddenly, the young Markham's attitude turned more daring, and he replied with an impertinence that made Mr. Bennet red with anger. "Well, it is not a matter of consent after all, Mr. Bennet. Like it or not, after word of this incident reaches your neighbours, your daughter will have little choice but to accept me. Your youngest daughter has just eloped scandalously with George Wickham, am I right? The rumours of your second daughter's improper behaviour in being alone in the dark with a man would ruin your family forever; we all know that."

None of them noticed the library door open or the entrance of Elizabeth into the room until she was halfway toward them. Bingley was the first who hurried to offer her his arm.

"Elizabeth, you should have remained in bed," said Lady Cassandra, moving to her side. In the full light, Elizabeth seemed even more pale and weak than she had appeared earlier in the bedchamber.

"Good, you are here!" said the younger Markham with no trace of distress in his voice. "You are an honourable woman, Elizabeth, and I am sure you will not lie. Tell them the truth; tell them I did not attack Lady Cassandra as she pretended. Tell them you were with me in the garden earlier."

Before entering the library, Elizabeth had dreaded the idea of seeing him again; but with the protection of the others nearby, her fears proved unjustified. She felt nothing but rage toward the man who almost ruined her life. She stepped closer to him, never averting her eyes from his.

"Do not dare call me *'Elizabeth'* ever again, sir," she said icily. "And do not ever expect me to contradict Lady Cassandra, whatever she might have said; she has my full trust and support."

"Miss Bennet," the earl intervened politely, "My son said everything was an accident; he said he only tried to talk to you. He even offered to marry you. You must see he is an honourable man."

"An accident, sir? My dress was ripped and my head wounded so badly that I lay unconscious for a time. Lady Cassandra's face is bruised; anybody can see that. How can all that be an accident, sir? And I would rather die this instant than marry your *honourable* son!"

"It was her fault that she interfered," said Markham, pointing to her ladyship with anger. "But I see that you feel daring and protected by your connection with her, Elizabeth! You imagine you may offend me and refuse my generous offer with impertinence! You feel certain of your future because of your engagement to Darcy. But you must know he will not want you after what happened between the two of us. You will beg me to marry you when ruin falls upon you all," he continued, his voice becoming louder and more furious with every word.

Elizabeth took a few more steps to cover the distance between them, and then she swiftly lifted her hand and slapped him with all the power of her released fears, suffering and anger.

"I warned you not to call me 'Elizabeth' again!"

He staggered, losing his balance from the surprise and strength of her gesture, and then immediately grabbed her hand forcefully. Instantly, the colonel and Bingley stepped forward to protect Elizabeth, but a voice from the door turned

Markham to stone.

"If you dare to *breathe* in her direction, I shall rip you apart, Markham."

Darcy's appearance was a shock to everyone. Tormented, his clothes in disarray, his hair unruly and his face grimy after a frantic ride from London, his countenance held an expression of untamed rage. Markham withdrew his hand from Elizabeth and slithered closer to his father; Lady Cassandra and the colonel glanced at each other, silently sharing their worry over what might ensue; Mr. Bennet and Bingley simply sighed in relief.

Elizabeth turned her gaze to him, trembling with emotion, fearful of what she would see in his eyes, and afraid her knees would support her no longer.

Darcy walked toward her, suddenly oblivious to everyone else in the room. Until a few moments ago he had been petrified by the fear of what had happened to her; then, when he saw her in the middle of the room slapping Markham and the villain grabbing her hand, Darcy knew he needed little incentive to kill the man instantly.

But now, all he saw, all that mattered to him, more important than his own life was Elizabeth — pale, tearful, barely standing — looking at him with the same eyes that had tormented him every moment since he left the week before. He strode quickly to her and, heedless of those in the room, took her in his arms. Their eyes met for only a moment, but they said all that was needed. She encircled his neck with tentative arms and pressed her head against his shoulder.

He cast a short, meaningful glance toward Mr. Bennet, and then without the slightest concern for the others, Darcy left the room, bearing a sweet and precious burden in his arms.

Chapter 16

Darcy had never before felt such extreme relief and intense grief at the same time. To see Elizabeth pale and sorrowful and be unable to help was an unbearable torture; yet, he felt grateful that, at least, she did not seem as harmed as he had feared. He entered the room and gently settled her on the bed. Her hands remained entwined around his neck, so he sat beside her, his face close to hers. His fingers caressed her hair, removing a rebellious lock from her forehead. Tears began to roll over her cheeks.

"Elizabeth, how are you feeling?" His voice was even gentler than his tender touch, yet she could do little but cry.

"I am well... Now that you are here, I am well. I was afraid you would not come... after what happened. I would have understood if you had been upset with me and changed your mind —"

"How can you think that? How can you believe anything would change my mind about you? Do you not know how much I love you?"

"I..." She seemed startled at his intensity, and instantly his voice softened; his eyes, moist with emotion, caressed her face with an adoring gaze as he continued.

"Do you not know that nothing could keep me from you? As soon as I received Bingley's express, I did not spare a moment." He paused, looking at her with utter sadness. "Yet, I am so very late. Will you ever forgive me for not being here to protect you when you needed me? If I had known —"

"Please, do not blame yourself. If there is anyone to blame, it is me." Her tears continued to fall.

"You? How could you be blamed?"

"Yes, me! I was so careless... I did not pay enough attention to Cassandra's warning. I never imagined a man could act in such a way; I still cannot believe it."

Darcy felt lost in his weakness, watching her distress as he struggled to control his anger. He would have done anything to take her pain upon himself, but there was nothing to be done.

"Please do not cry, my love," he said hesitantly, uncertain how to comfort her. "I am here to take care of you now. Nothing is important except you and your health. Has the doctor visited you?"

Elizabeth fought to stop crying, more affected by his obvious grief than by her own distress. "No...not yet, but I do not need a doctor. I am quite well now that you are here."

"But...you have been injured," he whispered averting his eyes from her, unable to control his emotions. "The doctor must see you."

"Oh, I only hurt my head when I fell, which is why I am feeling a little dizzy, but I will be fine."

"But...are you in pain?" he continued warily, his voice barely audible, his eyes not meeting hers.

Elizabeth stared at him in confusion for a moment, and then her hands moved to cup his face as she turned his head to look at her. He must be thinking as she did after the attack — that Markham had compromised her — yet he came back to her and declared his love for her without hesitation. Her heart melted with joy and gratitude as her fingers tenderly caressed his handsome, weary face.

"My love, I am in no pain. I have been injured in no other way than my head. Cassandra saved me before anything worse occurred."

Darcy's expression betrayed all the feelings that wrestled within him, and Elizabeth found the strength to reassure him quietly once more. "I am not injured, and I am in no pain."

"So you are well?" he inquired further, afraid to trust this new revelation.

"I am well. Nothing happened," she assured him and then suddenly turned pale as she continued, her voice trembling with distress, barely able to reveal her painful secret. "No, that is not entirely true. Something did happen. He tried to kiss me, but I fought him...but I think he still kissed my face. And...he touched me...and...I am so sorry, William. I cannot remember clearly, as I fell and knew little afterward. But Cassandra said he had no time to do anything. I..."

"Elizabeth..." Heartbroken by her painful distress, yet enveloped by incredible relief and gratitude, Darcy seemed at a loss for words and unable fully to comprehend the meaning of her revelation. Could it be true? Could his worst fear be unfounded? Was it possible she was unharmed? Then why was she still so tormented, so grieved? Had she been wounded in some other way? She said the bastard had kissed her. Darcy would not hesitate to kill him for that, but it was little compared to what he had imagined a few minutes earlier. Still shocked, he struggled to understand and find a way of dissipating her misery but could do nothing except hold her tightly.

They lay on the bed, embracing, Darcy caressing her hair and placing light kisses on the top of her head. She cuddled to his chest for a few moments, and then she moved slightly and lifted her face to him in a shy attempt to meet his lips. Instead of the expected sensation of his mouth on hers, he only smiled tenderly, moving a lock of hair from her forehead and pressing his lips upon it. Elizabeth felt a sudden chill and remained still in his arms, not daring to attempt any further intimacy.

"I understand you," she whispered after a few moments.

Darcy withdrew a few inches and stared at her in misapprehension. "Understand me?"

"I can understand why you do not wish to kiss me... after that man..."

He looked at her — eyes wide open. Elizabeth shivered; he seemed upset. How could he not be? No honourable gentleman would accept his betrothed's being touched by another man.

"Elizabeth, what on earth are you talking about?" He cupped her face forcing her to look at him. "Oh, my dear, despite everything that occurred this evening, you truly make me laugh." Indeed, he did laugh, and tears rolled down her cheeks as she did not comprehend his sudden amusement.

He smiled while gently kissing her tears away. "My dearest, I want nothing but to kiss you; have no doubt about that. Nothing will ever diminish my desire... except perhaps the thought that your father is downstairs and could intrude on us at any time."

She burst out in nervous peals of laughter, and he continued to kiss her cheeks as he spoke. "I have spent too much time fighting to regain your father's good opinion to risk being shot by him; however, let us hope he will not make an appearance for a few more minutes."

She laughed again, and her lips brushed against his face in countless, small kisses. "I thought you would be upset. I was so upset, so angry with myself for allowing that... I have always imagined you would be the only man to touch me, kiss me..."

"And so it is, my love; so it will be! What happened this evening was nothing but an unfortunate accident you will soon forget. These are the kisses... and these are the touches you will remember..." Leaning her against the pillow, Darcy covered her face with soft kisses, his lips travelling along her jaw and then down to her throat, followed by his gentle fingers that brushed lightly against her skin as though trying to wipe away her painful memories.

Darcy broke the embrace gently; his hands were still caressing her hair. Their faces almost touching, he smiled with a last short kiss on her chin.

"Elizabeth, this will not do. You must rest, and I must go."

"No, indeed... I do not need rest. I do not want you to leave."

"As much as I would like to stay with you, my love, that cannot happen, not with your father in the house. And I am so dirty from the road and likely smell horrible."

"You smell beautiful," she replied, and they laughed, staring at each other adoringly. The torment and pain seemed to dissipate, and there was nothing in the room but them and their bond of love.

Though Darcy had insisted he should leave, he remained with Elizabeth, holding her in his arms and caressing her hair. Finally, closely cuddled against his chest, with her hands around his waist and his fingers caressing her hair, Elizabeth fell asleep. From time to time, his heart heavy with worry, he heard her sighing in her dreams; he placed a soft kiss on her cheek, and he heard her whispering, "You do smell beautiful." He laughed softly, wondering how it was possible to love her as much as he did.

Suddenly a cold sense of panic — the panic of losing her or seeing her hurt in any way — overwhelmed him. His worry for her safety had vanished, indeed, and he felt fortunate and grateful that Elizabeth was unharmed. But now his rage took control, and he could barely restrain himself at the thought of Markham. While Elizabeth was sleeping in his arms, Darcy's distress grew again as he was still unable to understand how everything occurred. What was Markham doing there, and how did he come to attempt to force himself upon Elizabeth?

Thank God she is well and healthy, was his primary thought. However, aloud, without considering his words, he whispered coldly, "I shall kill Markham!"

"MR. BENNET, I HAVE TO say I am shocked to see that you allowed Darcy to leave with your daughter in such a disgraceful manner," the earl said with no little disdain.

"I am afraid I do not understand your meaning, sir," said Mr. Bennet, his voice suddenly regaining his usual sharp irony. "Are you, by any chance, teaching me about proper behaviour, Lord Markham?"

"I surely am," the earl stated.

"Well, you are truly diverting; I wonder if all earls are as amusing as you are," Mr. Bennet replied.

"How dare you, sir?" the earl burst out in anger. "I have not been so offended in my entire life!"

"Offended?" Bingley intervened, impromptu. "Lord Markham, your son insinuated himself upon my sister and pretended to have a serious interest in her; he convinced her to procure him an invitation to Netherfield, and when he came here, he harmed Lady Cassandra and my soon-to-be sister! He deceived us all and acted like the worst of savages — and *you* are offended? You are fortunate I would not want such a man in my family or I would force him to do his duty regarding my sister since her reputation surely has been affected by his behaviour!"

"I never claimed to have any intentions regarding your sister; it was all in her imagination!" The younger Markham seemed to lose control, his face coloured highly, and his eyes assumed a strange expression. "The only woman I truly want is Elizabeth! Mr. Bennet, you must —"

Four pairs of eyes stared incredulously at Markham, and Bingley finally put aside his anger and simply shrugged to the others. "He is out of his mind! I will call the servants to show them out of the house."

"No need to disturb yourself, young man! We shall leave this disgraceful house immediately!"

Hesitating for a moment to follow his father, the younger Markham stepped near the colonel and Cassandra and whispered in a low voice, "This will not end here!" and then hurried to the door.

The colonel moved toward him, but Lady Cassandra grabbed his arm.

"Please, let them leave. Bingley is right; he is out of his mind. Let us put all this behind us."

The colonel seemed unwilling to listen to her, but a moment later, he met her pleading eyes and nodded in agreement. "Very well…it will be as you wish…for now."

WHEN HE WAS CERTAIN ELIZABETH was breathing steadily and there was no danger of waking her, Darcy gently freed himself from her embrace and cautiously left the room.

He went downstairs, his rage increasing as each step brought him closer to the library. The moment he entered, his mood became darker as he saw his friends talking, apparently calmly.

"Darcy! How is Elizabeth?" Mr. Bennet and Cassandra asked him almost at the same time.

"Elizabeth is well enough now. But *you* seem very well indeed — all of you! If I did not know better, I would never suspect the gravity of the situation mere hours ago."

Before any of them found the proper words to reply to his statement, Darcy continued, talking mostly to Cassandra and his cousin. "What on earth was Markham doing in this house? And how is it possible he was alone with Elizabeth?"

His voice was so reproachful that Bingley hung his head guiltily while answering, "It was my mistake, Darcy. I never knew who Markham was. Apparently, he and Caroline had become quite friendly during the last few weeks, and she asked me to invite him to Netherfield for the ball. We thought…I thought he was courting Caroline. I am very sorry."

"Markham courting Caroline? Upon my word, Bingley, sometimes you are so naïve." Bingley only blinked a few times but remained silent. "But why did you not throw him out of the house when you found out who he really was? He is not a man to be allowed near any respectable lady!"

"Darcy, there is no need to blame Bingley! He knew nothing. We did not tell him anything about Markham," the colonel interrupted, but Darcy's rage turned on him.

"You told him nothing?! How could that be? Of what were you thinking?"

"He wanted to talk to Bingley, but I would not allow it," Lady Cassandra replied. "After all, Markham appeared to be nothing more than Miss Bingley's guest, and I thought we had no reason to worry. We never guessed he might have an interest in Elizabeth until tonight, and I warned her —"

"No reason to worry? Cassandra, are you out of your mind? But of course, as always you presumed your opinion to be the only correct one, and you cannot be wrong. Your presumptions put Elizabeth in such danger —"

"Darcy, you forget yourself!" shouted the colonel with equal anger. "How dare you address Cassandra in such a manner? She was the one who saved Miss Bennet, and she did so with no concern for her own safety. Have you asked how badly Cassandra was injured? Or has your anger blinded you to all reason?"

"Colonel, calm yourself... Darcy is upset, and he has reason to be so. It was my fault indeed —"

"No, it was not your fault — not at all," the colonel replied soundly.

Darcy continued, his tone slightly lower as he made an apparent effort to regulate his response. "Markham should not have been allowed to remain here, and you two were aware of that!"

"You are correct," admitted the colonel. "I should have been more careful. I am to blame! My only excuse is that I did not remember that Markham and Miss Bennet had ever met each other, and I kept my attention upon him only regarding Cassandra and Georgiana. I am very sorry."

"Come now, son," Mr. Bennet said warmly, taking Darcy by the arm and directing him to a chair. "Take a seat and let us talk calmly. There is no need to fight amongst ourselves."

"I shall take care of Markham myself," Darcy whispered.

"Markham is gone, together with his father," Lady Cassandra said with the same low voice. "I dare say you will not meet again anytime soon."

"Gone? Where?" Darcy cried, instantly rising from his seat.

"I do not know and really do not wish to know."

"But *I* wish to know! I shall go after him directly!"

"He has been gone for more than an hour. There is no way you could find him now, and besides, you had better take a bath and get some rest. Elizabeth will need you tomorrow morning. Running through the countryside after Markham surely will not give her much comfort."

Darcy cast a furious look toward her. He attempted to continue on his way, but the colonel grabbed his arm. "Darcy, she is right. Let it be... for the moment."

"Are you out of your mind? You want me to stay here and put everything aside? You expect me to forget what he has done and let him live in peace?" His countenance darkened with each word, and he paced the room like a caged beast.

Suddenly, he hurried toward the door without giving them another look. The colonel fought to stop him, but Darcy pushed him aside.

"Darcy," said the colonel in a low voice. "Cassandra is correct. Miss Bennet will surely need you. She will ask after you first thing tomorrow. She does not deserve more distress and fear, would you not agree? Besides, there will be a ball in two days' time."

"You are out of your senses if you believe I am in any disposition for a ball," Darcy replied, struggling to contain his anger. "The ball? Is that what you are thinking of?"

His tone was offensive, yet the colonel would not allow another argument to develop. "Oh, you should think of the ball, too, Darcy. That would help you to calm a little and think reasonably — and to find a more appropriate time to finish this business to your satisfaction."

Tired and too exhausted to balance his own angry stubbornness with his cousin's insistence, Darcy forced his mind to grasp the colonel's words and judge their wisdom. Seemingly defeated and with a silent nod to David, he finally returned to the library. "Please forgive my wild behaviour," he whispered as he fell into a chair.

Darcy's gaze remained fixed on the fireplace, and none of the others disturbed him for a time. Eventually, Mr. Bennet decided to leave for home to calm his undoubtedly nervous wife, and he asked for the carriage. Darcy barely heard the elder gentleman when he took his leave, nor did he move when the door closed behind him.

Silence and apparent peace finally enveloped Netherfield. It was almost dawn.

NOT EVEN A HOT BATH and another glass of wine were able to calm Darcy. He was still restless; not a single moment passed without blaming himself for the attack on Elizabeth and for his unfair behaviour toward Cassandra. The need to do something — to be of assistance or to punish the man who had caused so much pain — was unbearable. The only palliation to his distress was the knowledge that Elizabeth was well.

The desire of seeing her turned his steps toward her room. He entered as silently as he could; inside, sitting on Elizabeth's bed, he found Cassandra. She turned her head to him with a warm, friendly smile. He wanted to smile back but simply could not. He felt too guilty and ashamed of himself.

"She is sleeping. She seems well and calm," she said.

"I hope she is well. I shall stay with her a little longer," he whispered back.

"She will be happy to have you here She was more affected by your possible reaction than by anything else."

"Cassandra, I… Please forgive me for acting so rudely, so unfairly to you. I was principally angry with myself and allowed my anger to fall upon you. But I cannot tell you how grateful I am for everything you have done for Elizabeth. If not for you —"

"I know, I know. Do not worry so. You are not very pleasant when you are angry," she replied, her smile growing on her lips. "You never have been, even as a child."

"Yes, I know." He finally smiled back. "I am difficult to bear. I was extraordinarily fortunate to be accepted by Elizabeth."

"Indeed you were, my friend," she replied, her voice wearing an unexpected trace of sadness. "Be careful not to waste your chance at happiness. More than anything, keep yourself healthy and safe, close to Elizabeth. I am sure that is what she wishes."

"Cassandra, I can imagine how difficult this evening's events must have been for you. And you were hurt, too," he said with much affection, gently touching the bruises on her cheek.

"Do not worry about me. Good night — as much as there remains of it."

Darcy's gaze followed Cassandra for a few moments, deep in thought. Until the morning light entered through the heavy curtains, he stayed by Elizabeth, watching her, caressing her hair with infinite care not to awaken her, his heart filled with gratitude and love. He would not waste his chance at happiness — of that, he was certain!

CASSANDRA DID NOT GO TO her room. She did not want to dream, as she knew her dreams would haunt and terrify her after such a night. She was tired of nightmares and did not want to be alone in the coldness of her bed.

Unconsciously, her steps directed her to the library; the room still held the tension of their earlier arguments. The nerve of those Markhams! The young one was out of his mind, obviously, but his father? Had he lost his common sense, too?

She entered and poured herself a glass of wine. She was thirsty; the Markhams made her thirsty as Mr. Bennet said. Cassandra smiled, remembering the gentleman — she had really come to admire and even feel affection for Mr. Bennet. And that very evening, when he so decidedly had refused the earl's offer for Elizabeth… The earl likely had never been mocked that way.

Yes, she truly liked Mr. Bennet, as did Darcy. He and Mr. Bennet seemed quite close. Darcy was fortunate — he was correct — in being accepted by Elizabeth. She would be perfect for him and for Georgiana too, and there would likely be plenty of little Darcys at Pemberley. She smiled with tender affection at that thought, then sadness and emptiness cut sharply at her heart; there would be no room for her in their felicity. She would only disturb them. She had always brought pain and disorder to the people around her. That was why she was alone — and always would be.

She gulped her wine with a greedy swallow and then filled the glass again. She found a place on the settee near the fireplace, but the fire had already died. Only then, staring at the ashes, did she notice how cold the room was. That chill was negligible, however; her soul and her life were much colder. Everything was frozen around her — frozen and empty.

She felt herself lifted by strong arms, and she was startled, fighting against the intruder. As soon as she regained her senses, even before opening her eyes, she knew it was David; their eyes met, and the tenderness in his gaze seemed the perfect nourishment for the emptiness in her soul. *He* seemed the perfect solution to her loneliness. Her hands encircled his neck and her head rested against his shoulder.

"I shall help you to your room; you look exhausted." She only nodded in agreement.

What was happening was not right; she knew that. It was not right for David to carry her up the stairs to her room in the secluded guest wing. It was not right, but it *felt* so right! She knew she should end this instantly, yet she was too tired, too powerless, and too afraid of remaining alone again to do what she ought. His warmth through the thin fabric of his shirt, his arms holding her tightly, his breath, a little vein pulsing wildly in his neck, the sensation of being so close to him, to actually hearing his heart beating — she could not let these things go so soon. She needed him just a little longer; she *wanted* him a little longer.

They reached the door of her room, and he stopped, but she did not move; so, after a momentary hesitation, he entered and stepped forward, tentatively, until he reached her bed. He put her down then, and as her hands remained locked around his neck, for a moment their faces almost touched; the room was dark and silent, so silent they could hear the fire. Her hands pulled him closer, and her lips brushed against his. They both startled and withdrew instantly, and then their lips met again, first tentatively but gradually more daring, more passionate, more demanding. Neither of them could think or breathe, and neither could stop.

David found the strength to put a few inches between them before finally speaking, his eyes fixed on hers. "Cassandra, this is not right… I should leave you now. You are exhausted; you ought to sleep… I *have* to leave, I *must*," he whispered with a determination that struggled to defeat his desire.

Without thinking and against every reason, even against her will, she whispered back. "Please, do not leave… Please, stay with me…"

He frowned as their eyes met. "Cassandra… I am afraid to ask and dare not presume what you mean. What do you want?"

"I want you to stay… I do not want to be alone," she repeated, her eyes more pleading than her voice.

"I want to stay, more than I ever wanted anything in my life. But… are you certain? I cannot bear the thought that you are asking me to stay only because you feel lonely or that you will wake tomorrow believing you made a mistake and that I took advantage of you in a weak moment."

"I know my wishes, David… and I will still know them tomorrow morning."

He lowered his body upon hers. "Cassandra, tell me… Why do you want me to stay? Please tell me…"

She looked at him so intently that he was certain her eyes became tearful. She seemed unable to find the answer; finally, her barely audible voice broke the silence. "I… David, there is no other man in the world whom I would ask to be here with me… That is all I can tell you."

"And that is all I need to hear," he replied.

For long, torturous moments he made no gesture — only stared at her silently, intently with a mixed expression of wonder and desire; his face displayed the torment of such a storm of feelings that Cassandra could hardly bear it. She tried to move, to touch him, to make him do something — but he half leaned upon her, and his weight kept her prisoner.

"David," she whispered, her hands gingerly touching his face. Suddenly her moves turned shy and uncertain, and her voice was trembling.

"Cassandra, if only I could tell you how much I love you... I cannot believe that —"

"David, please, please do not speak... please..." Her voice sounded so painfully pleading that for a moment he was certain she was crying. But he had no time to look at her eyes as she pulled him toward her, and her lips pressed against his. He still had so many things to tell her — but they could all wait! If she wanted no words, so be it. The only thing that truly mattered to him was that she finally accepted him, despite everything she had said before. She would finally be his.

Her lips were softer and sweeter than he could ever imagine. He was kissing her, tasting her, savouring her flavour impatiently as his hunger grew, and her skin was the only food he needed. His mouth desperately wanted more of her, *all* of her, but for the time being, it simply could not leave her beautiful face. Countless kisses covered her cheeks, her eyes, her earlobes, until his greedy lips returned passionately, possessively to capture hers again and again.

He could feel her fingers entwined in his hair and her mouth allowing, returning, and seeking his kisses; but beyond that, his senses were hardly aware of anything except her warmth, her scent, the movement of her body beneath his, and her soft moans. She was finally his.

Yes, every fibre of his body, his boiling blood, an urge he could not control, a passion whose violence frightened even himself — everything was desperately screaming to make her truly his that very moment, to bind her to him forever before she could change her mind and before anything could interfere to stop him.

Strangely, the storm of feelings brought him back from the abyss of his desires, and his heart ached with worry for her — for *her* feelings and desires.

David suddenly stopped and withdrew from Cassandra, his gaze searching her face. Her head was resting against the pillow, her eyes closed, her lips red and swollen, her chest rising rhythmically as she obviously struggled to breathe. In shock, he saw her nightgown ripped apart — the result of his violent explorations — and her creamy, smooth skin was exposed to his avid scrutiny. His right palm was still rounded upon her left breast and he could feel her heart racing wildly.

Gently, with infinite care, his lips brushed against her eyelashes; her green eyes met his, and what he saw there cut his soul like a knife. There was sadness — a deep, powerful sadness that he thought he could understand.

"My love, I am so sorry! Please forgive me. I did not mean to frighten you. I know I have behaved like a savage. I had better stop; I do not want to hurt you —"

"No, no," she interrupted him, forcing a smile. "You did not frighten me." Her voice trembled and her eyes locked with his as she spoke with no little difficulty. "You must not worry for me. It is not the *first time*..." Her eyelashes fluttered as she waited for his reply.

"It is the first time for *us* together. That is all that matters," he answered, returning her smile.

Their lips found their way to another kiss — a caring, patient kiss; tender caresses replaced their initial urges; the hunger of possession turned into the certainty of lovemaking.

Gently, he removed the remaining fabric of her nightgown and then his own attire; slowly his mouth left hers and travelled down on a wonderful discovery of her beauty. The perfect roundness of her breasts made his fingers and his lips rest upon them, to caress them in a maddening play that made them both moan and their bodies quiver. She whispered his name, and he looked up at her for a moment only to see her face flushed with passion. The next moment, his mouth followed his hands as he continued to explore her burning skin: her belly, her ribs, her arms entwined around his neck, her hips, and then down to her legs. Each of his touches made her shiver and turned his desire into a wilder urge that he refused to satisfy with the urgency he felt.

It was not the mere submission to his lust, the desire of reaching the moment of absolute pleasure that he was looking for. It was much more than that. It was the simple, absolute need of having her *all* in every sense for as long as possible — to discover every part of her body, which might help him discover her soul, and to learn how to make her his and assure her happiness.

His hand slid between her closed thighs, and he heard her crying softly. He lifted his head to look at her and covered her face with light kisses, never taking his eyes from her, while his hand moved up slowly until it reached the hidden spot of her desire. She cried again, and he leaned to capture her lips and her cries as his fingers began a dance against her burning flesh, gentle at first and then more daring. Her body shuddered violently, and her legs parted in complete abandon.

A small cry and her body suddenly tensing caused him to stop; his brow knit in worry as he saw her obviously pained expression. She smiled, tearfully, at his reaction and, in a gesture of reassurance and further invitation, pulled his head toward her and kissed him gently as her legs encircled his waist. Struggling to maintain his control, his senses alive, he allowed his body to slide deeper inside her. She moaned against his mouth, but his long-denied desire forbade him to stop again.

Their bodies began a dance of passion in the most perfect harmony — a dance in which he was the absolute leader and she wanted only to follow his lead, a dance he would not allow to end for a very long time. His thrusts alternated between slow, gentle tenderness and wild, unleashed passion as his lips and hands, restless and tireless, never ceased their hungry exploration of her skin.

With unconcealed satisfaction, he watched her shudder with waves of pleasure, her lips crying his name again and again — but his passion seemed inexhaustible, unable to reach completion. His lips lowered to her ear, and despite the vow of silence he had made earlier, he whispered countless times, "I love you," his words barely audible between broken kisses. After some time, she captured his mouth in another kiss, and for a moment, he wondered if she did it only to silence him. An instant later, the sweetness of her kiss made any concern vanish.

As daylight appeared shyly through the windows, their exhausted bodies demanded their final reward. For some minutes, neither moved nor said a single word.

He gently rolled from atop her as his arms embraced her gently. She turned her back to him as she did not want to face him, but she remained close, her arms covering his. Their bare bodies still seemed to seek the warmth of each other while her long hair caressed his face and chest.

His happiness was greater than he had ever experienced — not only because of the dreamlike, blissful passion they had shared but also because she seemed to allow him to remain with her in her bed despite the fact that morning had come and they were in danger of being discovered. He could not be wrong in his judgment. Her wishes had wholly changed since he had proposed to her.

He was exhausted — the most wonderful lethargy he had ever experienced — and her delicate presence in his arms made him want to prolong their intimacy, so he allowed sleep to envelop him, holding her as near to him as he could. He was not certain whether his lips actually whispered, "I love you," in her ear before his eyes blissfully closed.

DAVID AWOKE WITH AN ODD perception of coldness; in fact, he felt he was freezing. He needed a moment to remember everything that happened, and only then did he realise Cassandra was no longer there. He rose and saw her in the armchair near the fireplace, wrapped in a robe, her knees lifted to her chin, the long hair falling to her shoulders almost hiding her face. He covered himself with the sheet and walked toward her. He took her hand and lifted it to his lips, smiling at her. "I already missed you," he said. The smile she returned to him bore nothing but sadness.

"David, we must talk…"

"Yes, I know." He felt lighthearted and wanted only to hold her in his arms again. "Cassandra, is there anybody whom I will have to ask for your hand? Except Darcy, of course, who will have the shock of his life, poor man," he laughed, sitting near her, his arms encircling her shoulders. She disengaged herself and rose from her seat.

"David, there is nobody you will have to ask for my hand, because there will be no marriage; nothing has changed since we last talked."

Instantly all the blood drained from his face, and he turned livid; a sudden lump in his throat barely allowed him to speak or even breathe.

"Of course, everything has changed; you know that! Surely you knew that last night when you asked me to remain in your room."

Cassandra struggled to fight back her tears without much success; she wished nothing but to be able to take upon herself his obvious pain, the grief that was darkening his handsome face, his most profound disappointment, everything that saddened him so deeply.

"David, please forgive me... I understand how angry you are, and I am sorry if I gave you the wrong impression —"

"The wrong impression?" He was almost yelling, unable to control himself. "You asked me to stay with you, Cassandra! You almost begged me to make love to you! And I know you enjoyed it as much as I did; you cannot deny that!" Her face became pale, and she turned her back to him.

"You are right; I was the one asking you to stay! It was unwise and selfish of me to ask you that; it was a mistake, but it will not change anything," she repeated as her words angered him further.

"No, no, no! You cannot say that; you are not allowed to say that! We talked about this last night! You promised me you knew your wishes and would know them this morning, too. How dare you tell me now that it was a mistake? Are you trying to make a fool of me? Do you delight in mocking me, Lady Cassandra?" His voice was harsh — even rude and offensive — and for a moment she was tempted to release her own anger and answer him in the same manner. Then his grieved countenance, the nervous pacing around the room as he looked so vulnerable covered only in the sheet, and the pain she had provoked in him broke her heart, and she could do nothing but bear the burden of his reproaches. Tearfully, she moved near him and gently touched his arm as she tried to make him look at her.

"David, you have done everything in your power to respect my wishes; you are beyond reproach. Everything that happened was my own will and at my insistence. And last night, that moment, I wanted nothing but to be with you. I do not regret anything except the fact that I have caused you pain now." She paused a moment, her cheeks flushed but her eyes facing him boldly. "And you were right in another way too. What I felt last night was much more than enjoyment. I never thought that... I..." She hid her face and fought to sweep her tears away before continuing. "But that cannot change what I told you a few weeks ago. I cannot marry you; I shall not marry you."

"Oh, what a relief to know I was right," he replied sarcastically. "And what a relief to know you enjoyed our time together so much. So perhaps... may I dare to hope that, though you have no intention of ever marrying me, you might ask for my *services* again some time? And if a child should happen, what harm can that be, as long as your ladyship has her enjoyment?"

Her small hand slapped him so violently that his head snapped back. His eyes challenged her, but she could hardly keep her countenance enough to speak; she was trembling, and she stretched her hand to reach for a chair. He made no attempt to support her.

"I truly hope you are feeling better now, madam. If you wish to slap me again, please do so. I shall not stop you nor shall I apologise for what I said. You are right; you are selfish and inconsiderate, and I wonder why I am punished to love you. Because no matter how much you ask me to remain silent or try to keep my words unsaid, I do love you, madam. I love you as I never thought it possible to love a woman. Until this day, I never believed the notion of being heartbroken to be true, but now I have experienced it most precisely. You managed to make me feel grieved and ridiculous at the same time. Congratulations, madam. I hope you rejoice in your success."

At that, he grabbed his clothes and exited the chamber. Sometime later, in the solitude of his room, Colonel Fitzwilliam, though at the advanced age of thirty-three, actually cried. He had not cried since he was an infant. Now he was crying with anger at her and at himself — and also with hatred.

He hated her with his whole being! She had been — was — cold hearted, selfish and insensible. How could he not see that earlier? But how *could* he see that when he was so blind? Even now, when he closed his eyes, he could feel her warmth in his arms, smell her scent, and taste her flavour; he could hear her sweet moans of unmistakable pleasure.

He had had many women in his bed over the years; he enjoyed ladies' company, and they enjoyed his. He had always been certain he knew what a woman wanted and needed to take her pleasure. And he always needed little to find his own pleasure in the company of a beautiful woman.

Why had everything been so utterly different this time? Yes, he loved Cassandra; he had known that for quite some time. In fact, he had known it almost since her return to town last spring. From the moment he saw her, he lost interest in other women, even a harmless flirtation. For months in his mind, there had been nobody but Cassandra, but he dared not admit it until he was certain there was no understanding between her and Darcy. Then he proposed to her, and she refused him. Since that day, her presence and image in his mind became even more powerful; she was always with him.

And now…she seemed to have offered herself to him, but she deceived him so grossly. Why was everything so different with her? Why did he kiss her more than all the other women in his life together? He had touched, caressed and known every single part of her body, and her skin had burned and shivered under his touch. He still remembered the way she embraced him, the way she kissed him, the way her eyes looked at him. "Oh, what do I care about that?" he yelled to himself, causing his servant to enter and ask if he could be of any help. The colonel almost threw the man out of the room; he wanted to see nobody. The only thing he cared about was the answer to his question: How could a man hate and love a woman so completely at the same time?

"BE GONE," he said harshly when the servant entered his room again half an hour later.

"I beg your forgiveness, sir; there is somebody to see you urgently."

"Damn and blast! I do not want to see anybody; can you not understand a simple request?"

"The poor man is not at fault. I asked him to let me in." Cassandra's voice disturbed the silence, and he jumped from his seat, prepared to throw her out together with the servant, but the moment he saw her face, he frowned and remained still in the middle of the room. Cassandra's eyes were swollen and red, and her ghostly pallor made her look illusory. He did not know what to say or do. It was at that precise moment that he realised his love would never diminish, no matter how much he hated her.

"What is your ladyship doing here? Someone might see you in my room, and you would be utterly compromised."

His voice did not lose its sharpness, but this time his rudeness pained and affected him more than her. She only smiled bitterly and took a seat without waiting for his invitation.

"David, I know you are very angry with me. Do not worry; I shall leave soon... As soon as Darcy and Elizabeth are married, I shall leave England. They will be a wonderful family together, and Elizabeth will be perfect for both Darcy and Georgiana. They will not need me anymore."

He made no reply, though he wanted to shout, *I need you.*

"I realise you will probably never want to see me again, and that is the best and wisest thing to do, but I cannot bear the thought of hurting you so deeply, to see you suffering so much without knowing why. I never imagined your feelings were that powerful or that my refusal would affect you so."

"You did not know? But did I not speak to you of my feelings? Or perhaps you considered me a cad who liked to play at words of love to make an advantageous marriage arrangement?"

"David, please..." Her voice was barely audible. "Let us not argue more, I beg of you. I have no strength left, and I still have to do the most difficult thing I have ever done."

Her eyes become tearful again, and this time he hated himself. What on earth was happening to him that he behaved like a lunatic and made her cry?

"David, what I shall tell you now is something I have never told anyone. Darcy is aware of every detail as he partially witnessed the events, but I never really talked to him about it. You are the single soul who will share this burden with me, and if you want, you may stop me now before I begin."

"I will gladly share any burden with you," he answered before he knew what he was saying.

"No, do not say that! Please do not say that! You do not know what you are saying."

"Cassandra —"

"Please do not interrupt me, or I shall never be able to finish the story. Let me speak before I change my mind."

David nodded and took a few steps, taking a seat in the nearest chair. She sat on the settee — only a few inches apart, yet the gulf between them seemed immense.

"You know, of course, that I left town four years ago after the scandal with the Markhams. You were not in Town then, so you do not know the kind of rumours that were spread. They implied Markham wanted to do his honourable duty by marrying me, but I refused him My refusal of such an extraordinary match could only be attributed to the wantonness of my character.

"Of course, not everybody was on Markham's side — quite the contrary. The respectable families in Town were well aware of the Markham heir's reputation. Lady Fitzwilliam herself was kind and tried to comfort and support me. However, the damage was especially bad as it fell upon Darcy too — and by association upon Georgiana. You know that Darcy had the crazy idea we should marry to put the scandal to rest, but I knew that was not possible. Darcy deserved a true marriage to give him a chance of happiness and an heir for Pemberley. So I left London… I left England, with only the company of Mrs. Simmons, my companion."

"I never knew how bad things became. Mother sent me a few words, but —"

"Oh, do not distress yourself; there is nothing you could have done. When I left, my plans were to visit Italy and who knows what else. My only thought was to put as much distance between England and me as possible. Of course, Darcy knew every detail of my plans, step by step, or else he would not have allowed me to leave."

She smiled bitterly, a small, barely visible smile. He only nodded silently.

"On my first night aboard ship, I walked out on the bridge-deck and stayed there for more than an hour, watching the water and sky. I loved the sea the first moment I saw it. A little after midnight, a gentleman approached me — a man with the most serene blue eyes I have ever seen. He said I should have dressed in warmer clothes if I wanted to spend the night outside. Then he offered me his coat, and I could never explain how we came to spend the night talking. It had never happened to me before; by dawn we knew everything about each other. Thomas — his name was Thomas — was a doctor in His Majesty's army. He had retired because he had been wounded in the chest, and he was travelling to Italy to visit relatives. His father had been in trade, but his parents had passed away when he was very young. He was an orphan with not much family left — as was I."

She stopped and looked at David; his countenance had darkened, and his face was paler than before. "I am sorry if I hurt you, but you must know the entire truth. I fell in love with that man with all my heart. Thomas taught me the meaning of utter felicity; in three days we were married."

The shock on David's face made Cassandra stop again, but he did not ask for further details.

"We spent the next three months visiting Italy, and each moment we spent together made me feel we were perfect for each other. After two months, I discovered I was with child. How could happiness be more perfect, more complete?" Her voice trembled and she went to pour a glass of water. David helped her, but her fingers could not hold the glass; she took a small gulp from the glass in his hand.

"We were in Rome and used to take long strolls through the town before retiring for the night. We both loved walking and riding, but he could not ride for the time being. One evening, during our walk, there was a noisy group behind us. At some point, they passed near us; they were a large gathering, including ladies and gentlemen. With no little annoyance, I recognised the elder Markham son among them. They all seemed euphoric, and Markham looked at my husband and me and then bowed politely. But I did not miss the impertinent smile on his face.

"He said, *'Lady Cassandra, what an unexpected, wonderful surprise to meet you here!'*

"I should have ignored him and turned the other way. Instead, selfish, impudent, and inconsiderate for nothing but my wounded pride, I answered, *'Unexpected, but by no means wonderful, Lord Markham.'* *'Oh, your words wound me,'* he answered. *'I have longed to see you, and my wishes have come true. You must admit we are meant to be together.'*

"Of course, at that, Thomas interfered and demanded explanations. Markham laughed and suggested he join them for a man-to-man talk. His impertinent expression and the looks he gave his companions suddenly alerted me, and I became agitated and frightened. I turned around, asking Thomas that we leave, as I was not feeling well. At first, he insisted on having a discussion with Markham, but I kept insisting we leave, and he finally relented. Markham and his friends started to laugh, calling after him to return if he wanted to know more about me. I could feel how angry he was, but he said nothing until we reached our home — and there he allowed his rage to come forth.

"He acted almost wildly, as I had never seen him before — not at me directly, but reproaching me for not allowing him to clarify things. He demanded I tell him who Markham was, and I related everything with complete honesty, trying to prove to him that Markham did not deserve his attention. He grew even angrier and demanded that I stay inside while he returned to settle things. I was petrified. I begged him to put the matter aside. I actually crawled and clung to him; he was looking at me as if I were out of my mind. He asked me to be rational and listen to him, as nothing would happen. But I did not. I do not know why; I could never explain to myself why I was so terrified. Seeing me in such a state, he seemed to overcome his own rage. He tried to calm me; he put me to bed and held me in his arms, talking to me, until well after midnight. He…we made love and all the time I did nothing but ask him, beg him, force him to promise me he would not leave me that night or ever, that he would never go to seek Markham again. Finally, I fell asleep."

The tension in the room was so intense that it became unbearable even for David; he kept staring at her as she was speaking, but she seemed a completely different person than the Cassandra he knew. He wanted to move closer to her in support and comfort as, obviously, the emotions were overwhelming, but he did not dare.

"During the night I awoke, frightened by a nightmare… I can still remember the sensation. I felt trapped in a cage of ice, everything dark around me, and I began to fall into an abyss, unable to stop. I woke up sweating, crying. But the nightmare was just beginning. The more frightening, life-draining nightmare started then and would end more than one year later. I looked for Thomas, but he was not there. Instead of his warm presence, I found a note on my pillow. He said there was something he had to do — his honour and love for me demanded it — and he would return soon. Nothing else…but I knew he had broken his promise to me. I knew where he had gone."

She started pacing the room with growing anxiety, her voice trembling. "He did not return — not that night nor the next. I sent my servants to search amongst his acquaintances in all the places he might have frequented. I hired more men to form search parties and retrace his movements around the town and beyond. They found him two days later in a secluded grove outside Rome. He had been shot…twice…in the back."

She was not crying, her eyes fixed on the fireplace, and she was clasping her fists together so tightly that the fingers were livid. David felt helpless, dying of sadness and of wishing to protect and comfort her, yet he knew it was not the moment for him to interfere. There she was, alone with her memories, alone with *his* memory. There was no place for anyone else. The colonel remained alone — and lonely.

"I do not know what happened the next few days; Mrs. Simmons must have taken care of the funeral because I cannot remember much. I only remember staying near his coffin and staring at him. I did not even cry…not for a moment. The next weeks I did not leave my room. I spent all my time hating him. I hated him with all my strength because he made me lose everything — after he had given me the whole world. He had put his stupid pride above my wishes and happiness. His child was inside me, and I hated him even more for what he had done to that innocent life. I only wanted my thoughts to stop forever, as I could not bear them any longer. Then… one morning I woke, and I felt warm…too warm. The only thing I knew was that the doctor had been fetched — not for the first time, so it was of little importance. Then more time passed, and Mrs. Simmons told me my child was also gone. The doctor said my child had died because I did not eat or sleep for all that time. Can you understand that? What kind of mother was I? What kind of *woman* am I?"

Unconsciously, the colonel shivered. His eyes were fixed on her beautiful — now transfigured — face in an expression of the deepest sorrow. There she was — in front of him — revealing to him a part of her soul that was kept in the darkest, most secret place until that moment. She then started to cry, and her body knelt on the floor. "That moment I understood: it was not my husband's fault, but mine. It was I who provoked everything. Had I not confronted Lord Markham that evening, had I pretended I did not see him, none of it would have happened. I killed my husband, and I killed my child."

He knelt by her on the rug, his arms around her shoulders; she fought to push him away. "Cassandra, do not reject me, please. It is not the man trying to comfort you now, but your friend."

His emotion barely allowed him to speak; she remained still in his arms for a few moments, then her head fell on his shoulder and despair burst from her chest in the most heartbreaking weeping. He had never before experienced such pain as he felt while holding her in his arms unable to do anything to share her grief. If only he could take her burden upon himself.

After some minutes, her sobs stopped. She withdrew from him and resumed her place on the sofa. He rose with her but did not sit near her, allowing her the separation she wanted.

"The doctor told me I might not be able to have children again, and at that moment, I gave it little consideration. I no longer wanted to live...so what would I care whether I could have children again? And then one day Darcy arrived. Later I found out that three weeks had passed since my husband died — only three weeks, and I was certain it was a lifetime." She stopped and looked at David, smiling painfully. "I recovered because of Darcy; he was such a tiresome burden and such a wonderful, annoying brother! He stayed with me more than a month. He tried to discover what happened but found no real clues; we had no proof that Thomas ever met Lord Markham. He and his friends had left Rome some time earlier, and Darcy could not find them; I was so happy for that, as I was afraid something would happen to him too. A year later, I left Italy and spent another two-and-a-half years travelling — that is all. That is my life."

"The elder Markham son died two years ago," said the colonel. "There were rumours that his death was a horrible one and he had lost his mind near the end."

"Yes, I have been told that, but I cared little about it. His death was no comfort to me."

"How is it nobody knew — about your marriage, I mean...?"

"Who would care to know? My life is of little interest to anyone except Darcy and Georgiana...and you; I shall not deny that, which is why I decided to tell you everything. I hope now you can understand my reasons for refusing your proposal. I shall never open my heart again; my heart is stone, and so it will remain."

Suddenly, he rose to his feet. She followed him with her still tearful eyes.

"Cassandra, I am deeply grateful to you for sharing this story with me and for being so considerate of my feelings. I cannot tell you how angry I am with myself for my unfair reaction earlier in your room. I did not —"

"No, no, please do not blame yourself. How could you have known? I hope we will be able to forget everything and be friends again someday."

He continued, pacing the room in torment. "You talked about your fault and your husband's fault, but I can see neither. All I can see is the unfortunate story of a most worthy and honourable gentleman who, in an attempt to protect the honour of the woman he loved, was defeated by a cowardly rogue. He did nothing any man of honour would not have done."

"I shall not have this conversation with you, Colonel," she said coldly as she prepared to leave the room. "I can well imagine you see no fault in a man breaking the promise he made to his wife to satisfy the demands of honour; I am sure you would have done the same. You declared as much last evening in the library when we talked about Markham. You would have been very pleased to see Darcy confront him and expose his life only because the rule of honour demands it!"

"A gentleman must defend his honour and the honour of those for whom he cares; that is how things are, Cassandra, whether you like it or not. I will always protect you and Georgiana; you must know that. I will always do what is right for you, and so will Darcy with Miss Bennet. How is it possible you do not see the justice in such a gesture — you, of all people, who jeopardised your own reputation to save Miss Bennet's?"

She looked disconcerted for a moment. "That is utterly different; it cannot be compared."

"It is absolutely the same; you bear no fault in what happened to your husband — you must see that — or in losing your child. But I am afraid you do not *permit* yourself to see the truth. You have become so accustomed to living with this burden — with this profound suffering — that it has become a part of you, and you cannot imagine your life without it. You cannot bear the idea of forgiving yourself and trying to be happy again."

"How dare you speak to me in such a manner? You, who never knew what love was, who never cared for any woman more than a couple of nights? How dare you tell me what the truth is!"

"I love you. I have not known love before, but I do now so very painfully," he whispered, and she ceased her angry tirade and turned to him in shock. "I shall be your friend if that is your desire, or I shall leave if you prefer, but I shall always love you."

He stopped talking, and she seemed to stop breathing. Her beautiful green eyes appeared as lifeless as her pale face. In the silence of the room, he was certain he could hear their hearts beating as he waited for her reply.

An answer did not come — at least not the one David longed to hear. Cassandra's trembling voice, so soft he could barely perceive it, whispered as her tentative steps directed her toward the door.

"You may do as you please, sir, and I shall do what I must."

Chapter 17

Elizabeth awoke with the painful sensation that her head was too heavy to be lifted. She moaned and leaned back against the pillow, momentarily disoriented. Then, gradually, the memories of past events overwhelmed her. The light of a sunny day was warming the room, as was the fire — burning steadily — yet she shivered.

Georgiana's sweet face, clouded with worry, appeared in the doorway.

"Oh, Elizabeth, I just discovered you are still at Netherfield. What happened? I am so sorry I did not come until now! But last evening you seemed fine. I never imagined… And William returned in the middle of the night. I know something must have happened, but nobody told me anything."

Georgiana's voice was trembling, her face colourless, and Elizabeth took her hands, struggling for the appropriate words to offer in response.

"Georgiana, there is no need to distress yourself so, dearest. Everything is well now. Please try to calm yourself, and I promise I will tell you everything."

For the next half hour, nothing remained untold, not even Lady Cassandra's scheme of pretending *she* had been the victim of Lord Markham's attack.

Georgiana's state became worse in the face of such an extraordinary revelation — the notion that a *gentleman*, the son of an earl for that matter, could behave in such an outrageous manner. The sudden revelation that a lady cannot be completely safe, even in the home of a close friend, made her spirits desperately low.

Elizabeth explained in every detail the extraordinary gesture Lady Cassandra had made.

"Yes, Cassandra *is* wonderful, is she not?" whispered Georgiana.

"Indeed she is; even more, she is generous and courageous. I have never met anyone like her."

"You are *both* wonderful; I am so fortunate that I will have you both with me from now on."

A few minutes later, Jane — pale with dark circles around her eyes, a sign she had slept little — joined them. The elder Miss Bennet's distress and worry were obvious, and Elizabeth's sombre expression returned.

At Elizabeth's insistence, clearly embarrassed by Georgiana's presence yet incapable of dissimulation, Jane said with a faint voice, "Lizzy, if you are feeling better, we should take our leave. Miss Bingley is quite upset with us."

CHARLES BINGLEY PUSHED HIS CHAIR away and stepped toward his sister who was still sitting at the breakfast table. His face was red with anger, and his eyes narrowed in fury as he looked at Caroline.

"The betrayal of your unworthy friend Lord Markham seems to have affected your senses and reasoning, Caroline, so I will try very hard to forget the grave offense you have just given my intended. But that is the last time you will speak to her in such a way. I shall not accept your rudeness any longer. And do not forget that, in less than a month, Jane will be the mistress of this house, and *she* will decide if you are allowed to live in our home."

"*I* should be angry with *you*, Charles, not otherwise! I went to bed last night knowing Lord Markham was well and contented. I woke this morning to find he is gone! Instead, I found Jane and Eliza Bennet, who apparently had spent the night here! What reason could possibly induce Lord Markham to leave so suddenly in the middle of the night?"

"That is something you will have to ask the man himself when you meet him again, which I hope will happen in fifty years!" He was furious and could hardly rein in his impulse to blurt out the truth.

"Charles, how can you be so cruel as to say such a thing? You are simply jealous at the prospect of my marrying into such a fine family, so different from that of your future relatives. I am sure that was the reason he left: he was offended by the improper company in which he found himself! What was that scheme with the Bennet sisters remaining overnight? Jane has trapped you already, so maybe Eliza had hoped to accomplish something similar with Lord Markham."

Lady Cassandra's cold, impersonal voice brought all eyes to her as she entered the room. "Miss Bingley, you should not harbour any hopes of ever connecting yourself to Markham as you wish. Mr. Bingley had the honour not to tell you the truth, but *I* have no such scruples, so you can cease accusing the Miss Bennets of nonexistent deeds." Bingley watched her in shock, suddenly forgetting his previous anger toward his sister; her ladyship looked shockingly different. Her face was pale, and bruises — now turned blue — were visible on her right cheek; her eyes — black circles around them, red and swollen as though she had been crying — seemed lifeless.

Though Caroline's face coloured highly with anger against such a statement, she could not gather her senses enough to reply as she would have wished.

"Lady Cassandra, are you well?" Bingley hurried to offer her his arm.

"I am perfectly well, sir. Please do not disturb yourself. I am just tired, as I scarcely slept."

She sat and then continued, turning to Miss Bingley. "These bruises you see on my face, Miss Bingley, are proof of Lord Markham's ungentlemanlike behaviour. You should be pleased by his departure and grateful if he appears nowhere near you in the future."

Caroline's eyes opened in shock at such a statement. "Lady Cassandra, surely you cannot imply —"

"I imply nothing; I am *telling* you frankly. You should accept that Lord Markham came here not to court you but for mischievous reasons of his own. He took advantage of your credulity."

"That cannot be," Caroline cried out, her cheeks suddenly pale, her eyes narrowed in anger.

"It is true." Bingley's tone was softened as he was clearly affected by his sister's distress. "He is not a man of honour, Caroline. He behaved like a savage and injured not only Lady Cassandra but also Miss Elizabeth. That is why she had to remain overnight; she was simply not well enough to return home. Markham told me he never had any intention of connecting himself with you; he declared as much in the presence of his father and other witnesses."

"That cannot be…" Caroline's voice grew lower, as her countenance wrinkled and darkened.

After many minutes during which she seemed unaware of the others in the room and oblivious to her brother and sister's worried inquiries, Caroline Bingley crept from the room. Charles Bingley felt a cold emptiness in the pit of his stomach. He had never seen Caroline in such a state before.

LATER THAT AFTERNOON, ELIZABETH AND Jane departed Netherfield for Longbourn, accompanied by Mr. Darcy and Mr. Bingley on horseback, and Georgiana sharing the carriage with them.

The colonel behaved strangely all day, only leaving his room for a long ride, and then avoided all company. As for Lady Cassandra, Darcy was as worried as he could be; she looked far worse than the previous evening and refused to provide any explanation. She insisted she was well, only not desirous of company. She also declared she would be her usual self for the ball and demanded he allow her to rest without further disturbance.

Riding on Elizabeth's side of the carriage, Darcy was far from light-hearted, although he was pleased to see Elizabeth so well recovered, at least physically. Earlier that day he had insisted on her not attending the ball if she felt poorly, but she had replied — with a mischievous, delicious smile — that she was well enough to dance more than one set with him. She looked well, no doubt, though from time to time, her face clouded in concern and her eyes lost the liveliness of their usual sparkle.

At times, Elizabeth's gaze rested on his face, and he hurried to meet her eyes and smile comfortingly. He was trying to deceive her — in fact, to keep the truth from her — he knew that and felt equally disturbed and guilty for the decision he had made. Nonetheless, there was no other option; she could not be forced to bear further distress — not for the world.

The party reached Longbourn shortly and barely entered the house when Mrs. Bennet hurried toward them, crying so loudly that Darcy was certain she could be heard in Meryton.

"Oh Lizzy, my child, you finally came home! Let me see how badly you have been injured."

"Mama, do not distress yourself. I am quite well; I am not injured at all!"

"Oh my child, you must be, I am sure, but you are trying to keep everything from me as your father did. You two always find pleasure in vexing me! I had to be told by the servants how brave you have been! Oh, you saved Lady Cassandra from that horrible man, Lord something! Who cares if he is a viscount? Nobody really cares about him! Such a horrible man!"

Her state became more and more agitated, and Elizabeth was pale with mortification.

"Mama, please, I truly did nothing. Please let us forget about this —"

"Nothing? How can you say that? You saved poor Lady Cassandra! Oh, I knew you could not have been so wild in your childhood for nothing! You are so brave; you always liked to climb trees and run across fields!"

"Mama!" cried Jane. But Mrs. Bennet took Elizabeth's arm while directing everyone to the drawing room.

"Oh, that poor, beautiful Lady Cassandra. Such a lovely, elegant lady! So pleasant and sophisticated — she always complimented my food and my dishes when she came to dinner. I like her very much — better than any other lady I have ever met! And everybody in town shares the same opinion! The poor dear — and that horrible man! My sister Philips and I are quite sure he attacked her to force her to marry him! As if she would ever have him! He is the most unworthy of men, I am sure of that, and not at all good looking! Hill's niece works at Netherfield, and she declared that the man was quite ill favoured indeed! The nerve of him!"

"Mrs. Bennet, *your* nerves will not last much longer if you remain so excited," Mr. Bennet intervened, but his wife still had more to say.

"Mr. Darcy, you should call him out and teach him a lesson; you are taller than that man, I was told, and have a much better constitution!" she continued to Elizabeth's utter shock.

"Mama! How can you say such a thing?" Elizabeth's voice matched the scowl on her face as she looked from an imperturbable Darcy to a pale Georgiana.

"What? Am I not right, Mr. Darcy?"

"You are perfectly right, Mrs. Bennet."

"See? See Lizzy? Mr. Darcy agrees with me!"

Elizabeth was heartily grateful to her father when he interrupted his wife quite unceremoniously and invited both gentlemen to the library to have a drink before dinner. She seized the opportunity, with a brief glance directed at Darcy, took Jane and Georgiana by their hands and hurried to their rooms to prepare for dinner.

Downstairs, Mrs. Bennet's nerves discovered another reason for even greater distress: Mr. Bingley and Mr. Darcy were to remain for dinner, and she was not properly prepared for such an event! Oh, and the Gardiners were expected to arrive any minute — and tomorrow was the ball! She would gladly faint and ask for her smelling salts if she did not have so many things to take care of! And nobody around to help her!

"Hill! Mary! Kitty! Where are you all? Come here this instant!"

MR. AND MRS. GARDINER FINALLY arrived at Longbourn, and the reunion was pleasant; the entire evening was generally a relaxing and enjoyable time for everyone.

At some point after dinner, Hill discreetly fetched Elizabeth and directed her to the library, where her father was expecting her. She obeyed with no little surprise, but her surprise turned to shock when she saw Darcy waiting for her in the hall. He took her hand and directed her not to the library but into a small adjoining room. He closed the door behind them.

"William, what on earth are you doing?" She was half-amused, half-worried about his strange behaviour in the proximity of her family.

"Do not distress yourself. I have your father's permission to talk to you a few minutes."

She instantly turned pale. "William, what has happened?"

He held her hand tightly as they sat together on a small settee, facing each other.

"Please do not worry, Elizabeth. Nothing has happened, but there is something of importance I wish to talk about with you, and I do not think we will have another chance for privacy before the ball."

She looked at him intensely. "Something *did* happen..."

"My love, are you still willing to announce our engagement tomorrow night and to share a double wedding with Bingley and Miss Bennet?"

"Why should I not be? I mean...if you are..." She stopped, a little disconcerted, not knowing what he intended.

"Very well then; that is how it will be. Your father seemed quite excited about making the announcement. I dare say he finds great amusement in anticipating reactions to the news." He laughed shortly, and she joined him.

"But, William, I am sure that is not what you wanted to talk to me about so privately — though I do not mind spending a few minutes alone with you," she said sweetly.

He lifted her hand to kiss it and then leaned forward, his lips brushing lightly against hers. "Something *will* happen...immediately after the ball. I have to return to London as I left some unfinished business that needs my attention immediately.

After that, I promise I will not leave you again before the wedding."

Elizabeth instantly turned pale, and any trace of a smile vanished from her face. Some time passed in complete silence, only their eyes searching the other's with intense interest and worry.

Finally, she breathed again and whispered, "Then you should go. If you say you need to go, I trust you completely. Last night you returned unexpectedly, so of course you had no time to conclude your affairs."

Her voice sounded weak but determined, and her eyes, moist with tears, never wavered from his.

"I..." Darcy tried to speak, yet his voice seemed more affected than hers. "There is old business and some new, as well. I just spoke with Mr. Bennet and informed him about its nature."

"I see... and will you tell me more about the nature of this business? Is it related to me?"

"It is," he answered after a brief hesitation. "But I would rather tell you everything upon my return."

"Can you not trust me now?"

"Elizabeth..." His voice was beseeching her, as were his dark eyes.

She felt ungrateful and ashamed. He had ridden wildly from London to be with her. He showed the depth of his love when he believed her to be utterly compromised. He shared his private affairs with her father. He had already offered her much more than any other gentleman would have. How could she dare demand more from him? However, her suspicions were painfully and unbearably strong, so she needed to ask — she needed to know.

"Early this morning, Mr. Bingley sent a servant to inquire after the Markhams. He discovered they departed during the night in the direction of their own estate. Has... has your business something to do with that part of the country? Please tell me you will not leave London." She searched his face thoroughly while speaking and did not miss the trace of a shadow on his countenance.

His eyes met hers, and she could easily read the turmoil inside him. His voice came as another proof, but it was his words that calmed her; she was certain he would not deliberately deceive her. "My business will keep me in London; I shall not travel to that part of the country. Please let us not talk more on this subject for now; I promise I will tell you all you want to know when I come back."

Her heart was still heavy, and she felt somehow betrayed that he did not trust her enough to share his affairs with her. After all, she would soon be his wife. Yet, her senses forbade her to go further. He did promise he would tell her everything, and he did talk about those affairs with another gentleman he trusted — her own father. She could hardly ask for more. She had to trust him.

"William, I shall not insist further; go, my love. I shall wait for you here, but please finish *all* your business, as I have no intention of letting you leave me again soon. I intend to keep you prisoner, sir."

Neither her voice nor expression showed utter relief, but she undoubtedly gave him the opportunity of doing as he wished. She was proving to him that she respected his will and trusted his decisions. The first thought that came to Darcy's mind was simply to thank her, but he had little time to do it, as her lips, soft and sweet, tantalised his and then captured them daringly.

There was only love and tenderness expressed in their kiss. Their lips did not part for a long time, as there was a stronger need for each other than the simple need for breathing. They separated only when a short knock on the door and Mr. Bennet's voice forced them to do so.

SHE LOOKED BREATHTAKINGLY BEAUTIFUL! DAVID stood in the main hall of Netherfield unable to move, looking at Lady Cassandra as she walked down the stairs with Georgiana. Everything was glowing around her, yet her face — still wearing the bruises despite her maid's obvious effort to conceal them — was pale and inexpressive, almost lifeless.

Their eyes met only for a brief moment. He bowed to her, and she tried to force a small gesture of polite courtesy that barely succeeded. Georgiana hurried to her cousin and took his arm.

"David, are you well? I did not see you the entire day."

"I am sorry dearest; I am simply in no mood for company lately, but I am well."

"Indeed, you look quite handsome."

He laughed nervously. "Thank you, my dear. You are too kind. However, you truly are beautiful. I am sure all the gentlemen in the room will fight for a dance with you."

Georgiana blushed violently. "Oh, you delight in teasing me so! You know too well that I will not dance — I am not out yet. And in truth, I have not the slightest inclination to dance, even if I could."

He kissed her hand with affection and then smiled and winked at her. "Well, well, and I was tempted to ask you for the first set. Now I shall have to wait for another ball. If you will excuse me, I think the Bennets are here, and I want to greet them."

He departed with only another short glance at Cassandra. Georgiana's puzzlement grew until it became distressing: something strange was happening. She had never seen Cassandra and David be in each other's company and not talk to each other at all.

In another corner of the room, Bingley was looking around with eyes and mouth open in bewilderment: Who were all these people? They had been arriving since morning, and Bingley barely remembered ever having met some of them before. At least five families invited by Caroline and Louisa were completely unknown to him. As for his sisters, he had been equally shocked to see Caroline's disposition utterly changed from the previous day. She was neither angry nor rude anymore. Was it possible for her to become so reasonable overnight? Bingley could only hope for such a miracle.

Several of his guests — Lady Something and her cousins — were just walking down the stairs, attended by a most accommodating Caroline. He politely bowed to them and expressed his hope that they were comfortably installed at Netherfield. They said they were very pleased with their rooms.

He had no time to reply as Jane Bennet and her family entered at that moment. He hurried to her and instantly forgot about the other guests.

Mrs. Bennet's attention was all bestowed on Jane and Mr. Bingley, and she took great trouble in following them around the main ballroom. The majority of those in attendance were families from Meryton, and toward them Mrs. Bennet directed her enthusiasm. Her pleasure in talking about Jane's engagement knew no restraint. Her daughter — and implicitly she — was the beneficiary of this ball; it was an engagement gift from her betrothed, Mr. Bingley — together with some jewels, naturally.

Darcy was happy to be mostly ignored by Mrs. Bennet. He simply could not take his eyes off Elizabeth from the moment she arrived. She seemed serene and calm, and her eyes were sparkling with joy as she spoke to her sisters. Her beautiful face was wearing an open, bright smile, and it actually shone when her eyes met his; yes, she was happy to see him — no doubt about that. This was the night their engagement would be publicly announced, so he did not think twice before offering Elizabeth his arm and walking with her into the ballroom. If Mrs. Bennet was too closely engaged with Bingley and Jane to observe them, their obvious intimacy did not go unnoticed by other guests. Only a few minutes later, Miss Bingley's friends from Town showed great curiosity in asking her about the woman on Mr. Darcy's arm. The gentlemen were rather surprised to witness Mr. Darcy's clear interest in a young woman of no consequence, but they were more inclined to understand his preference than not. Miss Elizabeth Bennet looked a very pleasant young lady, and the lively expression of her eyes was quite diverting.

The Gardiners joined Elizabeth as Darcy and Georgiana hurried to bring them all together with Lady Cassandra. The reunion with the Gardiners was mutually delightful, and Cassandra's spirits improved slightly while talking to them. However, she was far from her usual self — Elizabeth could see that. And then, there was the colonel! Though he had always been friendly with the Gardiners, he seemed purposely to avoid them after only a short greeting. He loitered in another corner of the room, staring at them from time to time but never approaching.

Only a few minutes later, Mrs. Bennet approached their group and took complete control of the conversation. She noticed the colonel watching from afar and called to him with no hesitation. The gentleman looked around slightly embarrassed — as were Darcy and Elizabeth who shared a quick glance at each other — and then had no alternative but to walk toward their animated party.

Lady Cassandra took a few steps backward until she had nearly retreated into a corner.

Elizabeth could not miss the opportunity; though her ladyship's gaze was by no means inviting, she followed Lady Cassandra and tried to keep her voice low while addressing her.

"Cassandra, please forgive me for intruding, but I cannot go any further without asking you what has happened? You look truly ill since yesterday."

Cassandra laughed nervously. "Why, thank you for the compliment, Miss Elizabeth. Not even Miss Bingley has been so blunt in expressing her disapproval of my countenance."

Elizabeth, however, was in no disposition for teasing chat. "You know what I mean. You are as beautiful as ever. But you look truly ill; you seem troubled and distressed — and sad." Cassandra was tempted to refuse to answer, but Elizabeth's worried countenance altered her decision.

Yet, it was Elizabeth who continued to speak. "I have heard the rumours since I returned home yesterday. I know all of Meryton is gossiping about the way I saved you during the attack, and I cannot allow the deception to continue. For that lie to be spread around and affect you —"

"Elizabeth, please listen to me carefully. There is indeed something that has been bothering me. It is also true that I would rather not see anyone and be away from here; I am in no disposition for a gathering and attended this ball only because I did not want to disappoint the others. However, my disposition has nothing to do with the rumours being spread — in fact, this gossip is exactly what I had hoped for, remember?"

"I see…" Elizabeth replied, obviously not convinced by her statement.

"I will not talk to you about this, and I am asking you not to inquire further on the subject. Please do not feel offended by my honesty; it is simply a matter too private to be shared."

Elizabeth nodded silently, her disappointment obvious. She did not expect such a direct, cold rejection; she believed their acquaintance had become closer, but apparently, she was wrong.

"There is nothing that you or anybody else can do for me, Elizabeth. I shall be fine again in time. And please believe me that your genuine concern is not unappreciated. I do value your friendship."

Elizabeth was certain she had never met anyone whose face was such a total expression of utter sadness. "Cassandra, I only wish I could do something to help you…"

"Oh, but you can," she said with a forced smile. "You can demand that Darcy dance every dance and at least one with Miss Bingley and one with Miss Cardington."

Elizabeth looked at her in puzzlement, and Cassandra laughed.

"Did something happen, ladies? May I be of some service to you?" Darcy's voice took Elizabeth by surprise as she did not notice his approach. He looked with equal worry from Elizabeth to Cassandra; the former smiled at him reassuringly while the latter laughed again.

"Well, Darcy, Elizabeth and I were just saying that you absolutely must change the poor impression you made last year — so you will have to dance every set."

"Well, my dear friend, I am exceedingly pleased to see you take such a delight in laughing at me."

"Thank you, Darcy. You are such a sweet, kind boy — as Mrs. Reynolds would say!"

Elizabeth burst out in peals of laughter and immediately covered her mouth with her gloved hand. Darcy's amusement was openly displayed in an immense smile.

"And," Lady Cassandra continued, "did you notice your old friend Miss Cardington?"

He cast a quick glance at Elizabeth, trying to find a proper explanation; he had no time to reply as Cassandra addressed Elizabeth.

"Miss Cardington is one of Darcy's greatest admirers — even more so than Miss Bingley. In fact, I can safely say that she and her mother have chased Darcy for almost five years now —"

"Cassandra, that is not a jesting matter. I have done nothing to encourage their behaviour; I have never called at the Cardingtons, and if I remember correctly, I danced with Miss Cardington on one occasion a few years ago at a ball in my aunt's home, but I never spoke privately with her — not for one moment."

"Oh, come now, Darcy, it was only a joke! Elizabeth is not jealous that there were other young ladies competing for your attentions, I am sure of that!"

"Oh, but I am jealous," replied Elizabeth. "And I will surely not approve if you should dance more than one set with Miss Cardington this evening."

Cassandra laughed once more, and Darcy was certain she had winked at Elizabeth.

"Are you both mocking me now, ladies? I certainly have not the slightest intention of dancing with Miss Cardington at all, not even half a set! In fact, I plan to dance with no one except Elizabeth." He paused briefly and continued, "Oh well, maybe with you, too, Cassandra, and with Miss Jane…and…oh for heaven's sake, how many sets are in a ball? And how many sets am I allowed to dance with you, Elizabeth?"

This time both his companions laughed so openly — despite their efforts to keep their voices down — that Mrs. Gardiner and Georgiana turned to them and approached their little group. In a corner of the room, the colonel was talking to Mr. Gardiner and Mr. Bennet and cast brief, repeated glances in their direction.

As the music began, Mr. Bingley took his place with his betrothed. It was universally acknowledged among the guests that Jane Bennet was extraordinarily beautiful. Never had Mrs. Bennet been so pleased in her life, and there was not a single person near her who did not hear of it.

Elizabeth and Darcy talked very little during the first set. They spent the entire half an hour with eyes only for each other. Their hands touched and squeezed tenderly, and their fingers entwined briefly each time the steps brought them together. Darcy's eyes left Elizabeth's only to allow his adoring glance to travel along her face, to rest some long moments upon her crimson lips and then to move down to the creamy skin of her neck and return to meet her loving gaze. Shocked by his own thoughts in a room full of strange people, all he could think of was the taste of her soft lips and the sensation of her arms embracing him.

Never had a set of two dances passed so quickly for Darcy, and never before had he regretted the end of a dance. He accompanied Elizabeth to her relatives while she congratulated him for his elegant dancing skills. She was teasing him, and he adored her.

In the next set, Elizabeth stood up with Mr. Bingley and Darcy with Cassandra.

For the third set, Elizabeth's partner was the colonel, and during that half an hour, her feeling that something had occurred between the gentleman and Lady Cassandra became a certainty. It was not something the colonel said but more the lack of his usual liveliness and his reticence in mentioning her ladyship's name.

Cassandra exited the house as soon as she could. She needed fresh air; she felt she could no longer breathe properly. She departed quickly, hoping no one would see her as she could benefit from the solitude. She simply could not bear the noise, the crowd, the eyes staring at her, and the rumours. Moreover, she could not bear trying to keep her attention away from him.

In truth, nobody followed her, and she sat on a stone bench for quite a while. She forcefully wiped away a tear from her eye, breathed deeply and walked back toward the ballroom. She hoped that she would be able to retire to her room shortly.

The colonel's sudden appearance startled her, and for some time, all she could do was stare at him. He bowed to her, while people around them cast quick glances at the strange pair frozen in the middle of the doorway.

"Lady Cassandra..."

"Colonel..."

"Would you allow me to escort you inside?"

"I..." He had already offered his arm, and the hall was crowded, so she could do little else than accept it. She took his arm tentatively.

They walked toward the ballroom, but he quickly directed her down the left hall toward the library. She barely had time to react; when she did, her disapproval was obvious.

"Colonel, what on earth are you doing? I have to go to the ballroom this instant."

"Please forgive me; I will only delay you for a moment. Cassandra, are you well?"

"I am well enough, thank you for asking, sir. Let us return to the others."

"You are quite pale —"

"Colonel, please..." Her voice was severe and cold, and she pulled her hand from his arm. "As I already said, there is no need to worry about me. It is a ball, you know; you had better go and dance. I have noticed you barely danced at all, and I am sure there are many ladies who would enjoy your company." She prepared to leave, turning her back to him, when he violently grabbed her hand and forced her to face him.

"I beg your pardon? Did you just suggest that I go and dance?" Their eyes met in a furious challenge as he continued, struggling to keep his voice down.

"So this is your opinion of me? I am a heartless cad who has put everything aside, and I am now ready to enjoy other women's company. Did you take any pains to consider my situation in the slightest? Certainly not! Excuse me for detaining you so long, your ladyship. I shall leave you now."

"David, please…" She seemed not to breathe at all. Her voice was trembling, and this time she took hold of his arm.

"Forgive me for offending you; it was not my intention. I just… I know I have been cruel to you. I do not know what has possessed me. I did consider your situation; believe me. That is why I do not know what to do; I do not know whether I should stay until the wedding or leave now. I cannot cope with this much longer."

She could not fight the tears that were now rolling over her cheeks. She covered her face with her gloved hands and turned to hide from his glare. Desperately, she ran from him and entered the first room she found — the library. In a moment, he was behind her, and though she fought to push him away, he embraced her tightly until she finally abandoned herself to his arms.

"Cassandra, there is no need for you to leave. *I* shall leave tomorrow morning after the ball." She tensed and lifted her eyes to him.

"I still hope that someday you will change your mind and heart about me. I cannot give up this dream nor can I give up on you. No, do not say anything. I expect no answer for now. Let us return to the ballroom, shall we?"

David took her arm and escorted her back into the ballroom. No one noticed their entrance; the general attention was turned toward the musicians, who started to play the first notes of the most infamous of dances.

ELIZABETH HAD SPENT MANY MINUTES searching the room for Lady Cassandra. She had walked around the room, greeting friends and old acquaintances and smiling politely to the new ones, but Cassandra was nowhere to be found. She intended to continue her search outside the ballroom when she heard Miss Bingley calling her name.

"Eliza, how lovely of you to come to speak to us!"

"Miss Bingley!"

"Miss Cardington, allow me to introduce to you Miss Eliza Bennet, Jane's sister. Eliza, this is my friend, Miss Cardington."

"One chaser — two chasers," was Elizabeth's first thought, and she barely suppressed a laugh.

"Miss Eliza Bennet, I have heard so much about you!"

"And I about you," replied Elizabeth, instantly casting a quick, amused glance toward Darcy.

"You must be very happy with your sister's engagement, Miss Eliza," said Miss Cardington.

"I am indeed. Mr. Bingley is a most worthy gentleman, and their affection is mutual. She will be very happy and deserves to be so."

"Mr. Bingley is quite wealthy, too," Miss Cardington added with a meaningful smile.

"Yes, he is, and my sister's good fortune is even greater. A worthy, wealthy gentleman — is that not what all of us are looking for?"

Elizabeth was certain both Miss Cardington and Miss Bingley were disconcerted by her rather impertinent answer, but she continued to smile genuinely.

"Are you looking for someone, Miss Eliza? You seem very preoccupied scrutinising the room," said Miss Bingley.

"Yes, in fact I was looking for Lady Cassandra. Have you seen her, by any chance?"

"No indeed. However, I have to confess I did not look for her at all. But does Mr. Darcy not know about her? I am sure you could ask him, considering you danced the first set with him."

Miss Cardington's insinuating voice, instead of disturbing Elizabeth, only amused her all the more. At that moment, she saw Lady Cassandra entering the room with the colonel, and she breathed in relief. She then turned her full attention to the two ladies in front of her.

"I imagine you are a close acquaintance of both Mr. Darcy and Lady Cassandra since you know so much about them."

"I am, indeed. Mr. Darcy and I have been very close acquaintances."

"How fortunate," was all Elizabeth could say.

"Yes, quite. And because of our closeness, I have to say I was very surprised to see him dancing almost every set. I know he dislikes this kind of diversion."

"He is a wonderful dancer, though." Elizabeth could not hide her smile as she replied.

"Yes, he is. I have had the pleasure of dancing with him in the past. However, I am sure he only tries to be polite to his friend. Mr. Darcy cannot find any pleasure in dancing at a country ball."

"Indeed, Mr. Darcy is all politeness," said Elizabeth. From the corner of her eye, she noticed Darcy walking toward them slowly. She returned her attention to her companions and could see the expression of utter shock and disgust on their faces a moment later when the music started, and the sound of a waltz invaded the room.

"Waltz? That cannot be!" cried Miss Bingley, turning to her friend to gain her support. "Surely Charles has lost his mind completely to admit such an outrageous thing."

To complete the disaster, Charles Bingley seemed to have lost his mind, indeed, as he smiled in utter happiness as he took his betrothed's hand, inviting her onto the floor. Raising both whispers of admiration and complete disapproval, they began to dance gracefully, and Mr. and Mrs. Gardiner joined them almost instantly. Then, shortly, Elizabeth could see the colonel leaning toward Cassandra and apparently whispering an invitation to her, as after a brief hesitation, she allowed him to escort her toward the other pairs.

The expression of shock on Miss Bingley and Miss Cardington's faces was something to remember.

"I never would have imagined something like that, Caroline!" cried Miss Cardington. "If I knew, I must say I would not have accepted the invitation. I surely cannot be associated with such a scandalous event."

"Please believe me. I am as shocked as you are. This is the most —"

"Mr. Darcy, what think you of that?" asked Miss Cardington the very moment Darcy was close enough to them. She even moved closer to him and attempted to take his arm but he linked his hands behind his back, taking a step back to post a greater distance between them.

"Think of what, Miss Cardington?" His eyes rested on Elizabeth, and they were met by hers. He could see how amused she was.

"About that! About the waltz! How can you tolerate such a thing?"

"Indeed Miss Cardington, this is Mr. Bingley's house and his ball, and we are all his guests. It is not for me or anyone else to tolerate anything. We can only retreat to our rooms if we are displeased with the progress of the evening."

His voice was polite, even friendly, but decided. Miss Cardington's mouth and eyes opened widely, and she stared at him, hoping she had not heard properly.

"Mr. Darcy!" At Elizabeth's voice, three pairs of eyes turned toward her, but she was only interested in his. "I certainly hope you do not intend to retire now, sir."

"Surely not, Miss Elizabeth," he replied, moving toward her, completely ignoring the others.

"I am glad to hear it! And…would you do me the great pleasure of dancing with me?"

She could see that he was surprised and found great delight in his reaction. She had waited for this since the moment she had learned to waltz. She briefly wondered whether Miss Cardington and Miss Bingley were still about or had merely fainted — but only for a moment as she cared little about them.

"Miss Elizabeth, I wish for nothing more at this time than to dance with you." He offered her his arm, and a moment later they were tightly embraced in the flying rhythm of the waltz.

Elizabeth moved awkwardly at first, her feet seemingly refusing to listen to her as they had during their rehearsals. Darcy whispered to her, his voice burning her skin from such a close embrace.

"Allow me to direct you. There is no need to worry about the dance steps; the music will conduct you — and so will I."

She blushed violently and nodded in agreement. Her eyes were locked on his; one of his hands was holding hers and his other arm encircled her waist; her head was spinning with happiness, and gradually the sound of the music enveloped her as she forgot her anxiety about the order of the steps. As Darcy said, he was directing her.

"This is the most extraordinary surprise," he said when he saw her more relaxed.

"It was all Cassandra's idea, of course."

"Of course." He laughed. "And Bingley and Miss Bennet approved of it?"

"Without hesitation. I was surprised to see Jane so willing to shock the entire neighbourhood." Her eyes sparkled with delight. "Cassandra was our teacher, and Georgiana played for us!"

"I see... there was an entire conspiracy meant to surprise me." He smiled. "I am very impressed, I must say."

"Unfortunately, I have not been a very apt pupil. My dancing skills are in great need of improvement. I am sorry I embarrassed you." Her cheeks were crimson, and she was slightly uneasy.

"Embarrassed me? My dearest, you could not be further from the truth. I would tell you what I truly feel this very moment, but I am afraid *I* would embarrass *you* with such declarations."

She blushed even more — her neck burning as much as her cheeks — and averted her eyes from him to cast a quick glance around the room.

"Besides, you are a very good dancer; Sir William Lucas himself has declared it so, remember?" She nodded and smiled at the memory of that dance — that fight — when Sir William interrupted them to express his admiration and to congratulate them for their superior dancing.

"However, it is true your steps are not perfect yet, but as my aunt said last spring, you will never waltz truly well if you do not practice more." She laughed and closed her eyes a moment, allowing the music to spoil her.

"On the other hand, you, sir, are truly proficient. Should I suppose you have practiced very diligently? And if so, may I wonder when and with whom?"

Her eyebrow rose and her lips twisted in reproach. Yet, he could see she was truly curious.

"You may ask, and I will answer you some day. However, we were talking about the improvement of *your* dancing skills. Would you allow me to tell you what I have in mind?"

"Please do, sir." Elizabeth began to feel warmer — partially from the effort required of the dance but also from his closeness. The way he talked to her was more distracting than his hands embracing her.

"I think what you need are some private lessons, and I am more than willing to be your teacher. We will be able to practice as much as you like once we are married.

While in town these next days, I will take the opportunity to order a music box — a most special one — which will play the waltz for us so we can dance any time we wish."

She laughed with utter delight and did not dare allow her mind to imagine how their dance would be once they were married. She forced a light-hearted reply.

"Oh, there is no need for a music box. Georgiana can play for us; she plays the waltz masterfully."

Darcy looked at her with such an intense gaze that she forgot to breathe.

"Elizabeth, if you think a private lesson would include the presence of my sister, you do not know the meaning of the word *privacy*. However, I will be more than willing to teach you that as well."

Elizabeth had no reply, for she was preoccupied with the attempt to remain upright as her knees grew weak and she fought to hide a most pleasant embarrassment. She changed the topic suddenly.

"When will you leave tomorrow?"

"I plan to leave early in the morning, immediately after the ball. David will accompany me." He seemed tense and averted his eyes from hers.

"Will you not be too tired?"

"No indeed. I will go on horseback as I want to arrive in London as soon as possible and return immediately after I conclude my business."

They were still waltzing, and the dance floor became more animated and crowded. Several other pairs joined the first couples, and the murmurs of disapproval diminished considerably.

"I... Will you be leaving on the main path to London?"

"Most likely, yes. Why do you ask?" He seemed truly puzzled.

"I...I might take a walk in the morning and thought perhaps I would see you briefly before your departure."

"The ball will finish at dawn... You should be home and asleep. It is cold, and you will be tired."

"If you will not be too cold or tired to ride twenty miles to London, I will certainly not be too cold or tired to see you for a few minutes."

Her eyes showed equal determination and entreaty, and he could do nothing but agree with her, grateful for her affection and devotion.

"Very well then. Within an hour's time of your arrival back at Longbourn, I will wait for you in the wildish corner of your garden. That way we will have some privacy, and you still will be close to the house and able to return safely inside. But I will stay only a few minutes."

"That is a most perfect plan, sir," she replied with a daring smile that expressed her contentment. "And, sir, I do know the meaning of the word privacy," she added as the last notes of the waltz directed their steps around the floor.

SHE WOULD FAINT; SHE WAS certain of it. She would faint, and thank heavens she was sitting on a chair so she would not fall to the floor. And Hill was not there with her smelling salts. As for her sister Gardiner, there could be little support from her as she seemed also to have lost her mind; otherwise, why would she dance the waltz?

How could she not faint? How could she bear such a flagrant breach of propriety at her daughter's engagement ball? Waltzing in Hertfordshire! Who would believe it? What would people say?

Suddenly she cared not in the slightest about other people and very little about Jane and her Mr. Bingley.

Was it possible? Could her wishes and hopes be exceeded in such a way? Lizzy and Mr. Darcy? Mr. Darcy with his ten thousand a year? Yes, she would faint; Mrs. Bennet was certain of that, but there was no room for misunderstanding — not after the way they looked at each other as they danced, not after he had asked her for the first set, and not after all the times they disappeared to walk alone. They stayed close to each other when he dined at Longbourn, and she had a close friendship with Miss Darcy. It was all so obvious! And she had been so silly to see nothing — nothing at all! She had neglected Mr. Darcy and paid all her attention to Mr. Bingley. Oh, she had been such a fool! Would Mr. Darcy ever forgive her? She must do everything in her power to accomplish that.

The music has stopped? Oh, so much the better. Her nerves could not stand that waltz much longer. What was Mr. Bennet doing there? It was suppertime, and he seemed determined to make a speech. *What on earth has come over the man? An announcement?* She rose from her chair, struggling to listen to her husband while trying to find a way to reach Lizzy and Mr. Darcy. Mr. Bennet was just talking about them. What was he saying? Oh yes, he said Lizzy and Mr. Darcy were engaged to be married. Oh well…she would still go and talk to them.

Mr. Darcy and Lizzy engaged to be married?! Was that what her husband had just said?!

Mrs. Bennet fainted — and Hill was not there with her smelling salts.

Chapter 18

Elizabeth listened for a time until she heard the door of her mother's room close and Hill's heavy steps move down the stairs. *If they would only go to bed and fall asleep quickly!* Darcy had promised to come no more than an hour after they left Netherfield. She would not consider allowing him to leave for London before she saw him again as planned. She could not control the sensation of utter happiness that enveloped her and made her feel as though she were still dancing — or flying. It was the first night of her "official" engagement.

She threw herself on the bed and laughed heartily, remembering the facial expressions on the people in attendance the moment her father made the announcement. Never before had Elizabeth witnessed eyes and mouths widened into such perfect "O's" as those of Miss Cardington and Miss Bingley. She knew she should feel sorrow for their hurt feelings, but she was certain neither lady held any genuine regard or affection for Mr. Darcy.

With a mixture of embarrassment and amusement, Elizabeth remembered her mother's swoon and the reaction of everyone who witnessed it. Together with Jane, Elizabeth had actually run toward their mother and escorted the servants who carried an unconscious Mrs. Bennet to the nearest private room. When their mother recovered a few minutes later, her cries of utter happiness and her loudly expressed admiration and gratitude for Mr. Darcy — such a tall, handsome gentleman — turned Elizabeth's worry into mortification; she was deeply grateful that such effusions were heard only by herself.

Taking advantage of the privacy of the room, Elizabeth had answered a few questions and tried to calm not only her mother's nerves but also her desire to leave immediately and find Mr. Darcy. To Elizabeth's relief, Mrs. Gardiner arrived a moment later and sent her niece to reunite with her intended while she offered to remain and care for her sister Bennet. When they had at length rejoined the others, Mrs. Bennet was somewhat calmer and her behaviour astonishingly proper. She did offer her congratulations and expressed her approval to Mr. Darcy, but she did so in such a quiet, discreet way that nobody could have found any fault in her manners.

Mr. Darcy was more than gentlemanlike in his elegant bow to her; no one in the ballroom actually heard what the gentleman and his future mother-in-law spoke of, but it was clear to everyone that it was an amiable conversation.

The rest of the night had passed as expected: a cold reception of the news from Mr. Bingley's relatives and much curiosity and speculation whispered around the room from the inhabitants of Meryton. The latter could not decide whether they should envy the Bennets for their fortune or pity Elizabeth for having to spend the rest of her life with such a severe, aloof gentleman as Mr. Darcy. There was also the early retreat from the ball of Miss Cardington; a sudden headache forced her to prefer the solitude of her bedchamber to the din of the supper room.

Eventually, Mrs. Hurst remembered her duties and addressed Elizabeth with brief words of congratulation, but Miss Bingley was too engrossed in comforting her headachy friend to meet Elizabeth face-to-face. Jane had suffered and been ashamed of the cold attitude of her future sisters toward her beloved Lizzy, and Mr. Bingley could not have been more angry with his relatives' lack of propriety. As for Elizabeth, as long as she was able to be with Mr. Darcy, enjoy his company during supper, and stand up with him for another set afterward, she was able to bear the disdain of Miss Bingley and her ilk remarkably well.

By the end of the ball, the Meryton population in attendance shared the opinion that Mr. Darcy was not quite so disagreeable — especially when he smiled — and perhaps Elizabeth Bennet would not be wholly miserable married to him. In any case, it was universally admitted that Mrs. Bennet had every reason to be satisfied with her elder daughters' success in securing good husbands. Lady Lucas was nothing compared to her.

Elizabeth opened the door silently and slipped out; the coldness surrounded her instantly, and she shivered, wrapping the pelisse around her and struggling to see *anything* through the darkness. The next moment she gasped in fright as two strong arms imprisoned her, giving her no chance to escape. In an instant, her senses and her heart told her she had no reason to fear. She knew it was Darcy long before her eyes discerned his beloved face, and his low, gentle voice apologised for alarming her.

He directed her toward the garden, holding her tightly in his embrace.

"You are freezing... You must return to the house immediately."

"I will certainly do no such thing, sir — at least, not immediately."

"Then let us sit and I will keep you warm." Before she had time to inquire *where* precisely to sit, he was already on the cold ground, wet from the autumn frost, and drawing her down with him. To her astonishment, Elizabeth found herself sitting in his lap, crushed to his chest, while his left arm encircled her back. He unbuttoned his coat and enclosed them both, nestling her even closer to him.

"You will ruin your clothes completely," she said, still not recovered from being in such an intimate embrace. She felt her cheeks burning as she struggled to do something with her hands, their faces so close that she could almost feel his mouth. The sensation of their bodies so intimately touching, the warmth of his thighs beneath her, their faces at the same level, and his lips lowering to touch hers made her quiver. His free hand found its way to meet hers and directed them to encircle his waist, and then his fingers moved up to brush along the line of her jaw and stopped to tantalise her earlobe as his palm cupped her cheek.

"I daresay my income affords me the ability to procure as many new clothes as needed," he replied teasingly as their lips met.

Only that moment did Elizabeth realise how she missed being alone with him and longed for his kisses, his closeness, his taste. She knew he desired her in equal measure, and she had positive proof when his kisses became more demanding and his lips more hungry. His hand travelled down, caressing her neck, her shoulder, her waist, until she felt his fingers stroking her thigh. She tensed and he stopped, their mouths separated by the space of a breath. After a moment of hesitation, she resumed the kiss, and her hands encircled his neck, resting at his nape. When his fingers began to move again — his caresses more determined, more daring, more breathtaking — she abandoned herself to the exquisite pleasure he was giving her. She was wearing her nightgown, robe and pelisse, but all those garments were insufficient to protect her skin from his burning touch.

She completely lost track of time, but apparently, he did not. His assault on her mouth changed from fierce to gentle and became small kisses exploring her face. She could not suppress her regret when his caresses ceased.

"Elizabeth, I must leave now," he said, and her heart sank.

"I know. Will you not stay just a few more minutes?"

"Of course I will," he replied. "I could not possibly separate from you so abruptly after having you so close." She knew that he was forcing himself to smile and make light of the situation.

Elizabeth nestled her head on the warm spot between his neck and shoulder, and cuddled close to his chest. She felt his fingers playing in her hair, and thought she would swoon.

"We shall be married in a month," she said, wondering what possessed her to say that.

He laughed. "Indeed — a month can be a very long time."

She felt her cheeks flushing. "Oh, I did not mean that."

"Then what did you mean?"

"I…" She considered her answer for a few moments; indeed, what did she mean?

"I would be happy to know you wish this month were shorter — that you share my impatience to be married."

She breathed deeply and cupped his face with her palms so she could see his eyes in the darkness. "Then you may be happy, sir," she said as she placed a soft kiss on the corner of his mouth.

"And you must leave now as you have a long journey to London and must return as soon as possible. I have your word for that, sir."

"Indeed you have. You may rest assured, Miss Bennet, that I have not the slightest intention of delaying a moment longer than necessary."

They rose; without hesitation, she threw her arms around his waist and crushed herself against him. His arms embraced her so forcefully that neither of them could breathe. His lips rested upon the top of her head, and then he lifted her face to place soft kisses upon each of her eyes.

"When I return, I shall ask Mrs. Bennet's help to secure as much time with you as possible," he said, hoping to hide the emotions that made his voice tremble. "Private, unchaperoned time."

Tearfully, she fought the lump in her throat that hindered her words.

"You must know my mother would refuse you nothing."

"Yes, I do know that; in fact, I depend upon it. And now you must leave, Elizabeth. Please return to the house. I will stay here until you have closed the door behind you; I want to see you safely inside."

"As you wish." She was unable to argue with him and unwilling to burden him further with tears she could no longer control. "Will you send me a note when you arrive?"

"Of course I will." He lifted her hands and placed a kiss in each of her palms. She turned to leave, but he held her a moment longer.

"Elizabeth? I want to tell you how ardently I love and admire you —"

"I do know that you love me. But I must confess I am not entirely certain what *'ardently'* implies. I have always had some difficulty understanding the true meaning of that expression."

He laughed back in delight, recollecting their flirtatious conversation during the waltz.

"I shall be more than happy to teach you the complexity of its meaning... as soon as I return."

"I depend upon that, sir."

A quick brush of her lips upon his, their faces touching one last time, briefly, and she was gone; his mouth remained dry and thirsty for her sweet flavour while his cheeks were wet with her tears.

DARCY HAD BEEN ON HIS way to London for several hours, but Elizabeth still could not sleep. She tried to keep her eyes closed beneath the warm bedcovers — hoping sleep would come — but the cosy warmth only reminded her of his embrace and her worry about his journey.

She grew angry with herself for being weak and not inquiring more persistently about his business in Town. She was frightened about a particular possibility and struggled to force it from her mind.

However, Darcy said he would not go after Markham, and she trusted his word.

No, in truth he did not say he would not go after Markham. He said his business was in London, and he would not travel in that part of the country where Markham was. That should be reassuring, yet she felt heavyhearted and troubled. At least he was not alone; the colonel was with him.

She wondered when they would arrive and how long it would take an express to reach Longbourn with a message from him. She wanted proof that he was well and safe, and then she could bear the separation as long as necessary.

It was full daylight by now, but the house remained silent; the entire family was sleeping soundly after their lively evening. The room suddenly seemed too small for her torment; she needed fresh air. She needed the openness of the outdoors and a stroll along the paths they had walked together.

She dressed properly for a long walk and left the house.

AFTER A PROTRACTED AMBLE IN the brisk air of the autumn morning, Elizabeth almost lost her balance on the muddy grass when she heard Lady Cassandra's insistent voice calling her name.

"Elizabeth, what on earth are you doing? Are you walking in your sleep, or are you daydreaming?" She dismounted and approached Elizabeth who greeted her with a smile of embarrassment.

"Good morning, Cassandra. No, I am definitely not sleeping; in fact, I did not sleep at all after the ball. Hopefully, this walk will calm me, and I will be able to find rest later."

"No wonder you are distressed after such an animated night as the centre of attention."

Elizabeth laughed. "I have had enough attention to last a few years at least! What about you? What are you doing here at such an early hour?"

"I needed a long ride to calm my nerves before meeting the Netherfield inhabitants for breakfast. I can only imagine Louisa and Caroline's faces, not to mention Miss Cardington's. And it is entirely your fault, you know." Her eyebrow rose in mocking reproach.

"I am sorry to cause such a difficult situation for you," Elizabeth replied in the same manner.

"So, are you walking alone, or are you expecting company?" Cassandra asked slyly.

Elizabeth blushed but did not avert her eyes from her companion. "This time I am walking alone," she answered daringly. "In fact, this is my favourite path. I used to walk along it almost every day."

"You must learn to ride. You could not walk around Pemberley."

"Oh, I do know how to ride, but I am not fond of horses. And speaking of that, I should warn you not to ride on this path; it is quite abrupt, and there are many trees and bushes. Your horse might slip at any time!"

"Do not worry about me; I have ridden on far worse paths. And you should be fond of horses; they are wonderful creatures! You will love them if you become better acquainted with them."

"Well then, perhaps, once at Pemberley, you will help me choose a nice, gentle mare, and I will improve my riding skills."

"I am not sure that will be possible. I am not sure when I will be at Pemberley in the future. You and Darcy and Georgiana will be a family now and will not need any intrusion on your time together."

"Cassandra…"

"Besides," she continued, ignoring Elizabeth's interruption, "once you are at Pemberley, I doubt Darcy will allow anyone except himself to help you choose anything! I fact, I wonder if he will allow anyone to see you or talk to you at all; I daresay he will lock you in your chambers for some time." She laughed. Elizabeth's face was crimson with mortification, her countenance a blend of embarrassment and boldness as she spoke in a teasing voice.

"Cassandra, when Mr. Darcy unlocks my chambers and finally allows me to see other people, I hope with all my heart that those people will be you and Georgiana. If you presume that I would consider your presence at Pemberley an intrusion, you could not be farther from the truth. I do cherish your friendship, and I depend upon your help to learn my duties as Mrs. Darcy."

Cassandra's face darkened, and her tone became grave. "Elizabeth, not for a moment did I presume you would not want me at Pemberley; do not distress yourself. But for some time I have been considering leaving the country again once you and Darcy are married. There are some circumstances that have led me to believe my departure would be the best solution for everyone involved."

"The same circumstances that have made you so sad and tormented lately?"

"Yes…the same circumstances I previously told you I did not want to talk about; do you remember?"

"I do remember," replied Elizabeth, purposely ignoring the implied reproach. "I will not force your confidence, nor will I insist on discovering a secret you do not want to share, but I will insist on finding a way to offer you help or at least comfort. And I most assuredly will not calmly rejoice in my own felicity while you exile yourself away from your closest friends and your home. And I doubt very much that William would allow you simply to leave, no matter how preoccupied he might be in keeping me locked in my apartments!"

Her speech became increasingly animated, and her voice showed determination that would brook no opposition. For the first time in their acquaintance, it was Elizabeth who demanded Cassandra's obedience — and without argument. Cassandra remained silent and lowered her eyes.

"Upon my word, you are *truly* irritating, Elizabeth, do you know that?" she finally said.

"No more than yourself, your ladyship."

"Very well, we shall talk about this again soon. However, we shall also talk about your riding skills. You cannot expect to ride bareback on the same horse with Darcy forever, no matter how much you *enjoy* it." Cassandra's triumphant voice and mischievous smile took a small revenge upon her friend.

Elizabeth's cheeks coloured, and her embarrassment was obvious at the recollection of their ride in the rain. However, it was Elizabeth who had the last word in their debate. Her voice was witty as her eyes sparkled with boldness and amusement.

"Well, I am not sure you are correct, your ladyship. As the future mistress of Pemberley, I am quite certain I *will* be allowed to ride in any manner I wish, as *often* as I wish, and to share *anything* with my husband — including a bare-backed horse."

Cassandra remained still, her eyes wide in surprise as if she were still trying to understand the reply. Elizabeth burst out in peals of laughter, and Cassandra looked at her in mocking disapproval.

"I have no reply to such a statement. I had best be leaving now, as it seems my wit cannot surpass yours this morning; you are simply in too lively a mood for me. I will go and have a most unpleasant morning with Miss Bingley, Mrs. Hurst and Miss Cardington; that is all I can hope for."

"I would be happy to invite you to have breakfast with us. I cannot bear to know that Miss Bingley and Mrs. Hurst will ruin your appetite."

"Oh, that sounds tempting indeed, but I cannot abandon Georgiana and especially poor Darcy; they would never forgive me."

"But Cassandra… is William not gone? I imagined he must have reached Town by now; he left quite early."

"Darcy is gone? Where?"

"Where?! To London!"

"To London? What on earth is he doing in London again? And why did he not tell me?"

"He had some unfinished business; he did not have time to complete everything when he returned in haste. It is something about settlements and other things. He mostly spoke to my father about it. I imagine he did not find the time to mention it to you. But do not worry; he will return in a few days."

"What a coward! I am sure he simply tried to get away from Miss Bingley and Miss Cardington after they found you were engaged to be married! Otherwise I cannot understand why he left in such a hurry."

"Oh, do not be so harsh on him!" Elizabeth smiled, struggling not to allow her own concerns to overwhelm her again. "I suggested he wait and rest a day or two, but he seemed determined to leave today. I imagine he wanted to take advantage of the colonel's company as they travelled together. However, I am quite sure he did not run from any lady. He is a brave and honourable gentleman and can handle Miss Bingley quite skilfully."

Elizabeth expected Cassandra would laugh and was prepared to join her, but to her utter shock, Cassandra's countenance darkened instantly, and Elizabeth was sure her friend forgot to breathe. The reins were trembling in her hands, and her eyes blinked nervously as she tried — with little success — to mount her horse. She seemed unable to control her movements, as though she were a beginner riding for the first time.

"Cassandra, what is the matter? Wait, you cannot ride in such a state —"

"Elizabeth, I must go. I have not a moment to lose. I must return to Netherfield this instant."

"Cassandra, wait! I will accompany you to Netherfield. Let us walk together. You cannot —"

However, Cassandra did not listen or turn toward Elizabeth as she rode away.

Elizabeth felt her knees become too weak to remain upright, and she found support against a tree. Cassandra's reaction frightened her beyond description, and many minutes passed before she dared contemplate what had caused it. Eventually, she understood it was the mention of the colonel's name that had affected Cassandra so powerfully.

Later that afternoon, Mr. Bennet received a letter from London with a note for Elizabeth inside it. Elizabeth took the envelope and ran to her chamber; as she opened it, she burst into tears of sheer happiness. They had arrived safely, and she could not wish or pray for more.

But there was more: almost two pages speaking of his love and longing for her. After reading it several times, Elizabeth finally lay down on her bed, exhausted, holding the paper tightly to her heart — and fell asleep.

HER HORSE WAS HURTLING THROUGH the trees and then sliding down a hill, but Cassandra pushed him further. All she did, all she tried, all she fought for was to no avail. They did only what they wanted with no consideration for her or Elizabeth; they cared for nothing except their stupid rules.

Elizabeth had said that Darcy was an honourable man — that he was no coward. She had spoken in jest, but her words brought to Cassandra's mind the most painful recollection: her fight with David the morning after they spent the night together. His words resounded as if he were speaking to her that moment. *"A gentleman must defend his honour and the honour of those for whom he cares; that is how things are, Cassandra, whether you like it or not. I will always protect you and Georgiana; you must know that. I will always do what is right for you, and so will Darcy for Miss Elizabeth."*

That was where Darcy had gone; Cassandra was certain of it.

He had gone to defend Elizabeth's honour and did not confess the reason for his journey. It proved that he presumed Elizabeth would not agree. He must have known she would not allow him to leave, so he had lied.

What rule of honour compels a man to lie to the person he loves and wants to protect? What sorts of rules were governing the life and behaviour of these brainless men? It was the same nightmare happening again, and she could do nothing to prevent it!

Or maybe she could. Was it possible that Darcy would fight Markham that very day? Probably not — that kind of arrangement needed preparation. If only she could speedily reach Netherfield and leave for London without delay. Maybe there was still time.

She became annoyed and impatient with the trees that prevented her riding as fast as she wished. Fortunately, she had almost reached the open field where nothing would delay her. Netherfield was in sight.

MRS. BENNET COULD NOT DECIDE whether she was utterly happy or deeply distressed. What was this madness of having a double wedding?

It must have been Lizzy's wild idea; that girl always delighted in vexing her poor mother! How could she even consider forcing Mr. Darcy — whose worth was ten thousand a year — to share his wedding day with Mr. Bingley whose income was only five thousand a year? Ten thousand a year — and probably more! And he wanted to marry Lizzy!

As Mr. Darcy's presence for dinner was not to be expected, Mrs. Bennet lost interest in choosing the dishes for the courses, so she spent the day talking with Mrs. Gardiner and Jane. Lizzy did not join them as she was still sleeping, and Mrs. Bennet heartily approved; Lizzy must look as rested and beautiful as possible when Mr. Darcy returned.

It was almost dinnertime when a servant announced the arrival of Mr. Bingley. Normally, Mrs. Bennet would have hurried to greet her future son-in-law, but this time she was too deep in conversation with Lizzy — who had recently joined them — about Mr. Darcy's favourite dish.

Jane invited him to sit, but the gentleman rejected any polite conversation.

"I am afraid the reason for this visit is not a pleasant one, and remaining for dinner is completely out of the question. I only stopped by to ask if by any chance you have seen Lady Cassandra today. I —"

"I met Cassandra earlier today," answered Elizabeth, moving closer to him. "Why do you ask, Mr. Bingley? Did anything happen? Is Cassandra well?"

"I am afraid I cannot answer you, Miss Elizabeth, as I have not seen her at all since the ball. I was only told she went riding early this morning, and she has not been seen since. Her horse returned to the stables some hours ago, but Lady Cassandra is nowhere to be found."

Chapter 19

"You did not see her today at all? Has no one been worried about her missing before now? It is almost dinnertime!" Elizabeth's voice was so reproachful that Bingley averted his eyes, embarrassed.

"I...we...you are correct of course, Miss Elizabeth, but after the ball, everyone spent most of the day in their rooms. Only recently did Lady Cassandra's maid approach me to ask if I knew where her mistress might be as she left the house quite early. She said her ladyship was wearing riding clothes and could not possibly remain dressed so for the entire day. We initiated a search of Netherfield, and the stable boy told me about her horse."

Mr. Gardiner offered his support in their quest.

"Oh, brother — of course you must go! Oh, poor Lady Cassandra — she is so pleasant and so elegant. Oh, I hope nothing has happened to her! Mr. Bingley, why did the stable boy not speak sooner? I am quite vexed with your staff, I must say! He really must be scolded for this negligence —"

"Mrs. Bennet, let us try to calm ourselves, shall we?" Mr. Bennet said, though his own voice was neither calm nor tranquil.

"How can I be calm? Last night I discovered my second daughter was engaged to be married and nobody told me beforehand! Now Lady Cassandra is missing! Oh, my poor nerves! And you Lizzy — why are you dressed for travelling? Where on earth are you going?"

"With Mr. Bingley and my uncle! I know where I last met Cassandra and can easily find the way she must have taken on her ride back to Netherfield."

She sounded so determined that not even Mrs. Bennet attempted to change her mind. Mr. Bennet and Jane whispered a "Take care, Lizzy."

They walked for more than fifteen minutes, none of them speaking. Mr. Bingley tried to share some suggestions with Mr. Gardiner, as Elizabeth was unwilling to participate in their conversation. She could think of nothing except Cassandra's expression the moment they separated, and she could not stop reproaching herself for being inconsiderate and selfish. She had returned to Longbourn and found all the comfort she needed in Darcy's letter. She failed to send a servant to inquire after Cassandra to be sure she had reached Netherfield safely, and now Cassandra was missing! Cassandra — who was a most excellent rider as well as a good walker! She was unlikely to fall from a horse, and even if she did, she would have walked back to Netherfield — that is, if she were well enough to walk at all.

A sudden din of voices interrupted Elizabeth's thoughts; two of Netherfield's servants appeared before them and ran toward their master.

"Lady Cassandra has been found, sir," they cried with great agitation.

"She has been found? Show me to her immediately," said Elizabeth.

"I will go and fetch the doctor. I think I will be more useful that way," said Mr. Gardiner.

"Good, sir. I will try to find a way to get Lady Cassandra to Netherfield. I shall see you later then."

They reached the place where several servants from Netherfield were waiting, gathered around Lady Cassandra's inert form. Elizabeth sobbed and knelt near Cassandra, touching her face, desperately trying to see whether she was still breathing. Her cheeks were pale, her hair splotched with grass and mud. She seemed lifeless; however, to Elizabeth's relief, the worst had not happened. Tearfully, Elizabeth took Cassandra's hand and caressed it; it was ice-cold. She called her name, but as expected, no answer came — not the slightest move. Hopeless, Elizabeth raised her eyes to search for help from Mr. Bingley, but he was busy giving orders to his servants, who obeyed instantly. Two of them rode in great haste toward Netherfield while Mr. Bingley removed his coat, knelt near Elizabeth, and covered Lady Cassandra.

"She is frozen. She must have been lying here for hours," he whispered.

"We must take her to Netherfield without delay."

"Yes, but I do not know how to do it. We cannot possibly put her on horseback. I sent my men to bring some blankets, and we will put her on them as if she were on a bed. I saw a doctor do that once a few years ago."

"That is a good idea, sir — the best idea possible, I think."

"In the meantime, we should try to keep her warm." He moved to the other side of Cassandra and took her hand. He was startled at how cold she felt. Exchanging a quick glance with Elizabeth, he understood they were both of one mind: if not from her injuries, Cassandra might well freeze to death.

The servants returned with a carriage. Mr. Bingley arranged a blanket on the ground and, with infinite care, nudged Cassandra's inert body upon it inch by inch, moving her as gently as possible. Finally, four servants took each corner of the blanket and lifted it, placing it carefully on the carriage floor. Again, Mr. Bingley took upon himself the task of driving the carriage as Elizabeth sat in the back, her eyes on Cassandra's still form at her feet.

The ride to Netherfield was blessedly brief. Cassandra was removed and transported toward her room. The doctor had yet to arrive.

Georgiana was so pale and trembling that she could not speak; her desperate question was unspoken, but Elizabeth understood.

"She is alive; I must go to her now. Will you come with me, Georgiana?" The girl's grip on her hand was so forceful that no other confirmation was needed. Hands joined, they hurried to Cassandra's room, precisely as the men who had carried her were returning, Mr. Bingley with them.

"Lady Cassandra's maid is with her; I will send the female servants to assist her, but I instructed she not be moved until the doctor arrives."

"I will help Janey," Elizabeth interrupted. "So I think two more maids will be sufficient."

"I... I do not know what else I can do. I shall send a note to Mr. Bennet to inform him. Is there anything else I should do?" He received no reply as Elizabeth and Georgiana had already entered Cassandra's room.

THE DOCTOR HAD BEEN WITH Lady Cassandra for an hour while all the others were gathered in the dining room.

Jane had accepted with gratitude the invitation of Mr. Bingley that she and Elizabeth remain at Netherfield for as long as they wished. Blushing, she noticed the looks of exasperation exchanged between Mr. Bingley's sisters and their obvious displeasure at the prospect of so many bothersome guests. Mrs. Gardiner knew she could be of little help except in offering comfort to her nieces and perhaps Miss Darcy; as Longbourn was close enough for daily visits, the Gardiners declined Mr. Bingley's kind invitation but remained for the conclusion of the doctor's examination.

In the library, Mr. Bingley joined Mr. Hurst, Mr. Gardiner and Mr. Bennet, all of them partaking of more than one glass of brandy while waiting for the result of the doctor's lengthy examination.

Elizabeth barely heard a word. She was sitting by Georgiana, and the still trembling girl held her hand tightly as tears rolled silently down her cheeks.

"I wonder why the doctor is taking so long," asked Mrs. Hurst.

"I believe he is examining Lady Cassandra carefully as any good doctor should," Mrs. Gardiner replied, forcing herself to sound light-hearted as she smiled reassuringly at Georgiana.

"Is he... is he a good doctor?" Georgiana finally replied.

"Oh, he is as good as any country doctor can be," Miss Bingley replied. "Surely you cannot expect him to be an expert, as his only patients have been the inhabitants of Meryton."

"He is a good doctor, Georgiana; have no fear," whispered Elizabeth. "We must have faith, dearest. I am sure all will be well."

"But what if... Elizabeth, what if...? Oh, has William been informed? He must be told what has happened; he must be here to help Cassandra when she needs him. He would know which doctor is best for her..." She could scarcely continue as tears overwhelmed her.

Caroline's voice made the young girl startle. "Georgiana, my dear, you really should not distress yourself so. I know Lady Cassandra is your friend, but really — her present injuries are the result of her own reckless and stubborn conduct. A lady should never ride with the men — having no care for etiquette or propriety — nor should she dash wildly across the fields. In truth, as my friend Miss Cardington has said many times, Lady Cassandra has much to learn of manners and language in order to display the requisite decorum. Perhaps this hard lesson will be useful after all."

Elizabeth's furious eyes narrowed, and she took a deep breath before she attempted to speak normally. She had no time, however, for a reply as the door opened and Janey, Lady Cassandra's maid, entered shyly.

"What is it that you want, girl? Why are you disturbing us?" asked Miss Bingley, angrily.

The servant turned pale and stepped back to leave but gained courage from Elizabeth's inquiring glance and walked toward her.

"Excuse me, Miss Elizabeth, you asked me to inform you when the doctor finished his examination. You said you would help me to..."

"I certainly will, Janey! Did the doctor say anything?" Elizabeth and Janey had nearly reached the door, followed closely by Georgiana, when Miss Bingley's voice stopped them.

"Oh, come now, Miss Eliza, this is too much! You cannot possibly share the duties of Lady Cassandra's maid; we do have enough servants at Netherfield to take care of an injured guest. Besides, I really think you should moderate your behaviour toward Lady Cassandra; you will be Mrs. Darcy soon, will you not? There is no need to attempt to impress either Georgiana or Mr. Darcy any longer; you have accomplished your goal."

Elizabeth released her hand from Georgiana's and turned on her heels. In a few steps she was inches from Caroline's chair. She looked down at her, her voice perfectly calm and composed.

"Miss Bingley, since we first met, you have treated me rudely and disrespectfully beyond the bounds of acceptable manners. For my sister's sake and the goodness of her heart, I willed myself to overlook that you purposely interfered between Mr. Bingley and Jane and then deceived him about my sister's presence in town last winter. I also gave no consideration to your disdainful behaviour toward me once you acknowledged my engagement to Mr. Darcy, because I imagined you were merely jealous and resentful. But to offend a woman — a guest in your brother's home who lies hurt and unconscious with no chance of defending herself — this is too much even for you. Have you no feelings of remorse or compassion?"

Caroline Bingley glared at Elizabeth in utter shock, her face red with rage.

"How dare you, Eliza Bennet?" Miss Bingley found a strident voice and, rising from her seat, stepped closer to Elizabeth. "How dare you speak to me in such a manner? Who do you think you are? You shall leave this house immediately; your presence here is no longer acceptable. Leave now!" she screeched at the exact moment the gentlemen appeared in the doorway.

Jane and Georgiana, livid, lost for words, were unable to react to such a violent confrontation; their eyes remained fixed on the combatants.

Disturbed and attracted by the din, all three gentlemen entered the room. Mr. Bingley was about to inquire into the cause of the quarrel when Elizabeth addressed Caroline again.

"Who am I? I am the soon-to-be sister of the master of this house, and I insist upon being treated properly. If Mr. Bingley wishes me to leave, I will obey without objection, but I will no longer allow any offense against my family, my friends or me. Now if you will excuse me, I must attend to Lady Cassandra; she may need me."

Mr. Bingley and Jane looked at each other instantly, silently searching each other's faces. Mr. Bennet tried to hide a small smile behind his glass of brandy; Mr. Hurst emptied his own glass while Mr. and Mrs. Gardiner and Mrs. Hurst were obviously embarrassed by Caroline's unseemly behaviour.

"Charles, did you hear that? Did you see the scandalous manner in which Eliza Bennet treated me in my own house?" cried Miss Bingley.

"Caroline, keep your voice down. I really do not have time for your nonsense. I am quite concerned about Lady Cassandra, and I surely do not need more distress."

"I am not causing any distress. Eliza's shocking language is the cause of all this. She has been the cause of all my distress these last several days," she continued, barely able to breathe from agitation.

"Lizzy was only —" Jane tried to intervene, but Caroline interrupted her.

"Eliza cannot remain here! There is no room for both of us at Netherfield. If Eliza Bennet is allowed to remain in this house, I shall leave! I cannot endure being under the same roof with her!"

"Caroline, perhaps all these events have been too much for you; you have had to bear so much unexpected news and so many disappointments that perhaps you need some rest and serenity to recover yourself. If you desire to leave, I shall not try to stop you, but neither Miss Elizabeth nor Jane will leave until Lady Cassandra is fully recovered. So you may either stay here with us and soften your manner toward our guests or feel free to prepare your belongings for a journey to wherever you wish to go. Now, please excuse me; I need a generous glass of wine before seeing the doctor."

"My examination is complete, Miss Lizzy; however, I am afraid I have nothing much to tell you —"

"Not much, sir? But you surely have *something* to tell us! How is Cassandra? What should we do to help her? Will she get well? Surely you will prescribe some medicine for her present state!"

"Lady Cassandra's left ankle was hurt — twisted — when she fell from the horse; perhaps her legs became entangled in the stirrups, but she does not appear to have any broken bones. I cleaned her wounds and bandaged the ankle tightly. She should not move it for at least three weeks. Her left shoulder also seems badly hurt, but I dare say it will heal well in time —"

"But that is wonderful news, doctor! Why did you say you had nothing to tell us? You practically told us everything we needed to know —"

"Not at all, I am afraid, though I would wish to. My examination, though lengthy, was far from satisfactory, as Lady Cassandra never awoke, moved, or made a sound. We cannot know whether there are other injuries I cannot discover or whether she feels any pain. I discovered a few wounds on her head. Also, she spent so many hours on the ground that she has likely developed a severe chill, and I will certainly prescribe you some medicine; laudanum would help her. Some tea would help, too, but I cannot see how she can drink it. In any case, I would strongly advise you to seek a second opinion regarding her ladyship's state. I shall confess that — fortunately — in our small town, I am rarely confronted with such a situation. I only remember the old gardener — Johns — being thrown from his horse ten years ago. I do not know if you have any recollection of him."

Elizabeth shivered and paled. She did indeed recollect old Mr. Johns — a kind, gentle man who had died two weeks after the accident. She tried to swallow the sudden lump in her throat.

"Elizabeth, what happened to Mr. Johns?" inquired Georgiana weakly.

Elizabeth cast a quick glance toward the girl and then to the doctor. "Sir, please be so kind as to instruct Janey in detail about anything we must do for the present; in the meantime, if you would be so kind, please join us in the library in a few minutes. Mr. Darcy will be informed instantly, and he will surely fetch his personal physician. You are correct, sir; we should seek another opinion — not because we do not trust you but precisely because you advised us to do so."

Elizabeth's voice sounded so cold and impersonal in its determination that both Georgiana and the maid looked at her in surprise. Elizabeth seemed to have lost any warmth, feeling, or emotion; she even avoided looking at the bed where Cassandra was lying. Only her pallid features and the slight tremor in her voice betrayed her anguish.

Elizabeth exited the room, and Georgiana followed. "Elizabeth, our doctor is Cassandra's doctor, too. He is the best surgeon... Elizabeth, please, wait for me..." Though she received no answer, Georgiana could not fail to notice Elizabeth's violent gesture as she wiped the tears from her eyes.

"We have no time to lose, Georgiana," she said as they entered the room where the family, including Miss Bingley, was still gathered. Elizabeth related everything she had heard from the doctor, and nobody interrupted her until she concluded.

"We must inform Mr. Darcy immediately."

"I shall take care of that," said Mr. Bingley, rising from his seat.

"Just a moment, sir." Mr. Bennet drew all eyes toward him. "I…I would like to write to Mr. Darcy myself if you would allow me."

"Of course, sir," accepted Mr. Bingley, not without surprise.

"Papa, we must send the note without delay," Elizabeth insisted, and her father nodded in agreement. "He must return immediately and bring his surgeon with him."

"I shall send a servant as soon as I return home, which will be in a few minutes. We will not bother Mr. Bingley any longer. We will be home if you need us, Lizzy. And tomorrow morning we will call again," Mr. Bennet said as he prepared to leave, accompanied by the Gardiners.

"Mr. Bennet," Georgiana spoke up, "Mrs. Spencer must be informed, too. She has been Cassandra's companion for years."

"Miss Darcy, can you give me Lady Cassandra's direction and perhaps the doctor's, as well?"

"Of course, Mr. Bennet, but William knows them —"

"Yes, I imagine," Mr. Bennet replied, avoiding his daughter's glance. "I was thinking that maybe…just in case…"

"Very well, sir, I shall write them down this instant," Georgiana said.

THE SMALL CARRIAGE MOVED AT a slow pace toward Longbourn. It was a cold, bleak autumn night, yet it was not as bleak as the spirits of its passengers.

"I cannot believe this is happening," said Mrs. Gardiner. "Last night at this hour we were in the midst of a delightful ball, and now… How could this happen? I keep praying that the Lord will have mercy and all will turn out well in the end."

"We must have faith," agreed Mr. Gardiner. "Lady Cassandra will be well taken care of, especially when Darcy brings his doctor. I am sure —"

"I cannot inform Darcy…at least not tonight." Mr. Bennet's companions looked at him in shock.

"What on earth are you saying, brother?" cried Mrs. Gardiner. "This is no time to jest."

"Thank you for informing me; I *am* aware of the gravity of the situation," Mr. Bennet replied coldly. "I am surely not jesting, but —"

"But? You are surely not acting properly either," said Mr. Gardiner. "*I* will write to Mr. Darcy and will take care of sending the servant as soon as we get home.

"You cannot do that. We cannot inform Mr. Darcy until we are certain he has successfully concluded the duel with Markham." The gentleman seemed almost relieved at his slipped confession.

"What?" cried Mr. and Mrs. Gardiner so loudly that the driver stopped the carriage to inquire whether something was wrong.

"You must keep this in the strictest confidence," Mr. Bennet continued as soon as they were moving again. "I had promised not to tell a soul, but the situation is so complicated that I need to consult with someone."

"You are out of your senses," Mrs. Gardiner concluded while her husband urged Mr. Bennet to reveal the entire truth.

"The day before the ball...after that night when...well, Darcy went to talk to Markham. I do not know whether you are aware of it, but the Markhams were visiting a family only ten miles from Netherfield. Darcy went to speak to him secretly. The talk did not go well, and Darcy had no other option but to call him out. I think they will fight tomorrow morning at dawn on a field near London. Only the colonel was informed as he will be Darcy's second."

"You are out of your senses," Mrs. Gardiner repeated. "You, Mr. Darcy, and the colonel — three gentlemen without sense or reason!"

"This is madness," Mr. Gardiner agreed. "Duels are not legal; you know that! Mr. Darcy is jeopardising his life, now, before his wedding!"

"The colonel assured me Mr. Darcy is superior to Markham in every respect, and he can defeat him any time with any weapon." Mr. Bennet sounded like a child attempting to justify misbehaviour.

"Oh, the colonel assured you; then we can sleep in peace." Mrs. Gardiner's mocking tone was such as neither of the gentlemen had heard before. "Is Lizzy aware of this? I dare say not."

"No, Lizzy knows nothing, and you must swear your secrecy, and Madeline, do not look at me with such reproach. I do know how dangerous the situation is. Darcy confessed everything to me precisely because I am Lizzy's father, and he felt responsible for her because they are now officially engaged. If anything should happen to him, he asked my consent to have an arrangement settled on Elizabeth in case he...in case the duel should not end as we hope."

He took a deep breath before continuing, obviously affected. "Of course I tried to change his mind...at first...but I could not heartily say I disagreed with him. He attempted to speak reasonably with the Markhams. He gave me his word that, if Markham admitted his fault and said that it all had been a drunken man's wild behaviour, Darcy would put everything aside, but Markham insisted he wanted Elizabeth, would finally have her, and would gladly fight Darcy for her. Brother, if you could have heard him that night — he seemed out of his senses. Kept telling me he wanted to marry Lizzy. Can you imagine? Lizzy will never be safe if Darcy does not teach him a hard lesson. And what if Darcy hurts Markham? Maybe he will — I pray God he will — but what then? The earl could hold that against Darcy. What would he do — expose his name and his reputation to censure? How would that help Lizzy?" he concluded, exhausted.

"Let us not think so far ahead," Mr. Gardiner intervened. "The situation is difficult, indeed, but let us find a way to handle it for everyone's benefit."

"I see no way out," said Mr. Bennet. "If I inform Mr. Darcy this evening, the news might affect him so that he would not be in a proper state of mind for the duel. If we wait until he sends me notice after the duel, it might be too late for Lady Cassandra. What should I do? I managed to get the doctor's direction from Miss Darcy. I thought I could fetch the doctor, but how can I convince him to come to Hertfordshire and attend her ladyship without involving Mr. Darcy?"

A few long moments of silence followed; Longbourn was before them when Mr. Gardiner spoke again, trying to meet his wife's eyes in the darkness.

"I shall go to London personally; I shall leave as soon as I change my attire. I will be there in a couple of hours. I will first talk to Lady Cassandra's companion; I was introduced to her at the private ball. I am certain she will want to come to Netherfield immediately. She will help me fetch the doctor. I will send them here as soon as possible; in the meantime, I will seek out Mr. Darcy, and hopefully, we shall all return tomorrow night."

Mrs. Gardiner and Mr. Bennet listened without a word; the carriage stopped in front of Longbourn, and they all exited. "I shall help you prepare yourself," his wife said briefly.

Mr. Bennet sighed. "Thank you, brother. I shall always be grateful to you."

In Cassandra's room there was silence — profound, frightening silence.

Janey and Georgiana refused to leave the room at all, so the former had fallen asleep in a chair and the latter was resting near the bed, her head close to Cassandra's, holding her hand.

Elizabeth sat in an armchair on the other side of the bed. She had abandoned any struggle or pretence of composure — any mask she had tried to wear during the day. She allowed the tears to flow as painful, vivid recollections brought her back to the day when she had first seen Cassandra at the theatre.

How much their relationship had changed in such a short time! That day at Netherfield — the first day of her engagement — they finally had talked openly and clarified everything between them. Cassandra's compliments and praise were dear to Elizabeth as she was certain they were honestly expressed. Cassandra was not a woman to practice disguise of any sort. *Very much like William,* Elizabeth thought, tearfully.

Looking at Cassandra's form beneath the sheets, Elizabeth could scarcely bear the pain she felt. She had enjoyed her growing friendship with Cassandra and known for some time that she truly cared for her, but only then in that dark, silent room did Elizabeth truly *feel* she had come to consider Cassandra more than a friend. She could not grieve for her own sisters more than she grieved for Cassandra at that moment as she wondered how long she would be with them.

What happened to that lively, fearless woman? What unbearable burden had thrown her to the ground? What cruel secret had drained her of life, spirit, and wit and left her tormented these last weeks? How was it possible that a woman who had ridden wildly through a dreadful storm at Pemberley to save her and Georgiana could simply fall from her horse?

The more Elizabeth pondered it, the more certain she was that the explanation for Cassandra's transformation was the colonel. Something happened between them when the he appeared in the neighbourhood — maybe even sooner as Cassandra's low spirits had been apparent since she first come to Hertfordshire. But what was it?

As she began to think with more clarity, Elizabeth realised that Cassandra's behaviour was not unfamiliar to her. She had seen such turmoil before in her sister Jane after Mr. Bingley left unexpectedly last winter.

Could that have happened to Cassandra, too? Not very likely — she and the colonel seemed perfectly suited to each other, and there was no apparent reason for them to be apart if their desire was to be together. But what if it were not mutual affection but the unshared inclination of only one of them? Was it possible that Cassandra had tender feelings toward the colonel that were unrequited? Could that be the reason for her desperation?

But no — the colonel did not seem to reject her at all — quite the contrary! Of course, Elizabeth could not be entirely certain of her perceptions regarding either friend, since every time she had been in their company, Elizabeth's thoughts and attention were directed solely at Darcy. Yet, she could be fairly certain the colonel did not behave like a gentleman rejecting a lady.

"Elizabeth, come quickly! Cassandra has moved! She squeezed my hand, and she is saying something!"

Georgiana's cries so startled Elizabeth that for a moment she could not move; an instant later, she leaned as closely as she could toward Cassandra's face to understand the words she struggled to whisper. Elizabeth's eyes met Georgiana's and they shared both the relief of seeing Cassandra's first moves and the surprise of hearing her repeating, more than once, a single word: *"David."*

It was dark, so very dark that Cassandra could see nothing, not even herself. And cold… freezing… She wanted to wrap her arms around herself for warmth, but they would not move. She was trembling from cold as well as fear. She was alone; she was lost. The hole in which she was trapped was so deep there was no possible escape alone. She was too small — too powerless. She tried to run, but her feet would not obey, and where could she run? There was no hope left. She was lost. She could scream, praying someone would help her, but if they came after her, they would punish her for being disobedient. They always told her a little girl should not ride like that… yet, any punishment was better than the darkness that surrounded her. She had never been afraid of darkness, so why was she so frightened now? And why was her voice so weak? She must cry louder, louder. If she could only cry loud enough so he could hear her… he would surely come and save her… David… David…

A DAY AND NIGHT OF torment and fears had passed — a time spent in prayers and dim hopes.

Early in the morning before breakfast, Mrs. Spencer and Lady Cassandra's personal doctor arrived at Netherfield. Though she was relieved to have the second doctor's assistance and Mrs. Spencer's presence, Elizabeth was deeply concerned that Darcy had not accompanied them. Mrs. Spencer mentioned briefly that Mr. Darcy had some last-minute business and most likely would return later. How could that be? What kind of business could possibly keep him in London when his lifelong friend, as dear to him as a sister, was in grave danger of losing her life?

Even worse for Elizabeth's peace of mind was the revelation that Mr. Gardiner himself had travelled to Town to carry the news of the accident and had remained there to return with Mr. Darcy. She desperately struggled to find a reasonable explanation for such a strange event, but she was exhausted, and her mind refused to provide the answers to so many questions. There was nothing to do but wait — and spend time at Cassandra's side, together with Georgiana and Mrs. Spencer.

Unfortunately, Cassandra did not awaken, and her state showed little improvement. As the doctor predicted, she had developed a high fever, and they watched helplessly as her body shivered almost continuously despite the laudanum and their united efforts at cooling her hands, cheeks, and forehead. Yet, it was encouraging that Cassandra did move and speak although she remained unconscious. In truth, her movement was a result of the high fever, and the words she muttered were unintelligible. Nevertheless, it was better than they had feared the previous evening.

Elizabeth remained in the room, lost in her thoughts, watching as her friend struggled and whispered the same name: *"David."* Elizabeth could no longer bear it; if Darcy brought the colonel with him when he returned, she would have an honest, forthright talk with the colonel.

"Miss Bennet, if you do not get some rest this instant, I will ask Mr. Bingley to see that the servants tie you to your bed," said Mrs. Spencer, entering the room. "You ate nothing at all! This is not to be borne, and I will surely not accept it! I will not have you ill; I cannot bear to have two ladies suffering." Her decided voice admitted no resistance, and Elizabeth could only smile back at her.

"You must not fear, Mrs. Spencer, I will not become ill. I simply cannot eat anything. As for sleep, it is out of the question for now."

"Out of the question? Young lady, do you know to whom you are talking? I have asked that a bath and some food be prepared for you in your room, and then you will go and sleep for at least a couple of hours. Only then, if you wish, may you come and take my place while I sleep a little. I will send Georgiana to rest too, and I will not allow any of you to disobey my order. Do I make myself clear?"

Her severity was half in jest, yet she was not joking. Even more, Elizabeth could see the reason and wisdom in Mrs. Spencer's demands. And in truth, she dearly longed for a warm bath.

"Very well, Mrs. Spencer. I can see I stand no chance of winning this argument."

"Indeed you do not. So let us not fight in vain."

AFTER HALF AN HOUR SPENT in the tub, surrounded by hot water and immersed in her thoughts, Elizabeth felt significantly better; her spirits rose as her body relaxed, and she was certain she would need no sleep at all — only a few moments of rest on the bed. All would be well; her hopes were stronger than at any time in the last few days. And Darcy would return soon; she could sense that. If he were only there, half of her worries would vanish, and the other half would be easier to bear.

She allowed her thoughts to fly to him and her memories to recollect the comfort and safety she felt in his arms. Her mind was still full of him as her exhausted body claimed its long-needed rest. His face was the last thing she "saw" before she fell asleep, and she smiled in her dreams, her heart melting from love and longing.

A few hours later when she opened her eyes, struggling to awaken and understand where she was, Darcy's face was the first thing she saw. She certainly was still dreaming, and she closed her eyes, desiring the image to linger. But his lips gently pressed upon her eyelashes to open them, as his fingers caressed her hair; his scent, more powerful than any essence, and the tenderness of his touch proved to her — again — that no mere dream was as wonderful as the reality of his presence.

He was finally there — and all would be well!

Chapter 20

"You are here," she whispered as her arms encircled his neck.

"I am here... And I will not leave again — not without you."

Her smile quickly turned to a worried frown. "Cassandra..."

"Yes, I know. I returned as soon as it was possible."

"But you are late. Mrs. Spencer arrived much earlier. Why are you so late? And the colonel? Has he returned with you?"

"My cousin is here as well. I left him speaking to Bingley. He was shocked when we learned about the accident and pressed Bingley for more details. In truth, we were both shocked and out of our minds with worry during our return journey — David, it seemed, more so than I. Mr. Gardiner could hardly speak reasonably with us —"

"But why were you so late?"

"I will explain everything when you are more rested — maybe tomorrow. You do not need more to worry you now. Mrs. Spencer told me you spent all your time nursing Cassandra and hardly rested at all these last few days. There are two doctors taking care of her now, and you must think of yourself. You need to sleep until morning. I am sorry to have been so selfish in my desire to see you that I woke you."

She attempted to protest, but he gently pushed her down against the pillows and wrapped her in the bedclothes; his lips pressed against her forehead as his fingers caressed her hair.

"Mr. Darcy, I am surprised and displeased to see how little consideration you give to your promises," she said teasingly when he rose from her bed, obviously preparing to return to his room.

He looked puzzled, and she continued, a smile lightening her weary face.

"You promised you would not leave again without me, yet you are leaving just now."

Darcy returned to sit and lifted her hand to place a soft kiss on her palm. "My love, it is quite unfair of you to tease me so. You know I am reluctant to leave you, but I cannot possibly remain in your room with a house full of people wandering the halls. If someone should see me..."

Elizabeth's smile suddenly vanished and her face became solemn.

"William, these last days have been unbearable. Do you seriously imagine I would care about propriety now? Do you believe I could possibly sleep after seeing you for such a brief time?"

Her voice trembled as she spoke, and her eyes became watery though she was obviously fighting her brimming tears. His heart melted from sorrow for her distress, and he became angry with himself.

"Forgive me, Elizabeth; you are right! Blast propriety!" The next moment he was lying by her in a close embrace.

She recovered from the surprise of his impromptu reaction and carefully covered them both with the sheet. She nestled to his chest, chuckling.

"'Blast'? Sir, I am shocked at your use of such an unseemly expression."

Equally impromptu, he rolled her on her back so that she was lying against the pillows and his body was above hers, their faces almost touching.

"Miss Bennet, you just invited me into your bed! I could hardly say you are the proper person to criticise my language. Now, I would strongly suggest you desist teasing me and try to sleep — or you will be in great danger of having me not only speaking outrageously but acting likewise."

"I would never be in any danger from you," she said seriously, as her fingers entwined in his hair.

His adoring gaze and warm smile made her body quiver. She saw his face lower toward her own and closed her eyes, anticipating the feel of his lips on hers — but the contact was brief. He withdrew only the distance of a searing breath when he spoke. "Elizabeth, we cannot…"

She daringly tightened her arms around his neck and imprisoned him in her grasp. She had no thought for their improper intimacy as she whispered against his lips, "I only want you to kiss me…for a brief time. I have missed your kisses exceedingly."

Darcy had no thought of refusing her. All sense of propriety or concern about being caught in a scandalous situation vanished in a moment as her eager mouth met his. Only a desperate need for air forced them to separate. He rolled onto his back, taking her with him as she nestled against his chest, her breathing laboured. Her cheek rested upon his wildly beating heart, and her legs playfully entwined with his.

"We should really sleep now," she said, holding him tightly. "I will sleep only an hour or two. I have to check on Cassandra; she might need me."

Darcy did not contradict her or try to convince her she needed to rest more than an hour; she looked exhausted, and he was certain she would not wake soon. He was proved right, as her voice grew weaker and her breath more regular; a few minutes later, she was soundly asleep.

He continued to stroke her hair, overwhelmed by the love he felt for her, ashamed and agitated by the temptation of her warm body next to his.

Darcy also suffered deeply for Cassandra; the moment he heard about her accident was as painful as when he had heard about his parents' deaths. He would do anything to see Cassandra healthy again. He would give up all his possessions for her recovery. He would gladly take her pain upon himself.

Then how was it possible that in these moments — with his dear friend lying unconscious a few rooms away in danger of losing her life, with Elizabeth exhausted precisely because she spent hours taking care of his friend, with his own sister tormented by the distress and fear of losing Cassandra — the only thing Darcy could *think* of was Elizabeth's soft breasts crushing his chest and burning his skin through the thin barriers of his shirt and her nightgown. How could he possibly sleep? Even if the shame and guilt of the preposterous direction of his thoughts and wishes were not present, his hungry desire for Elizabeth would surely keep him awake — painfully awake. No doubt remained in Darcy's mind: he was undeniably the most ungentlemanlike, inconsiderate, egocentric man who ever lived!

ELIZABETH AWOKE COLD AND LONELY; when she managed to remember her whereabouts, she understood that Darcy had left.

For a moment, she thought she might have imagined his presence, but the pillow still carried his scent, and her body still sensed his warmth. She closed her eyes and burrowed beneath the sheets a few moments, rejoicing in the remembrance of his embrace and dreaming of a future when sleeping in his arms would no longer be a stolen pleasure.

It was already dawn, and though she still felt tired and the softness of the bed was tempting, she rose and began to dress herself, eager to see Cassandra and praying for good news. The house was silent; she met no one on her way to Cassandra's chambers, but when she entered, it became clear her hopes for a favourable result were in vain. Mrs. Spencer was resting in an armchair, half-asleep and holding Cassandra's hand.

Mrs. Spencer smiled affectionately when her gaze met Elizabeth's and nodded to her to take a seat near her.

"Did you sleep well, my dear?"

"Yes, I did," Elizabeth answered, blushing. *Quite well indeed,* she thought. "Has there been any change?"

"No, nothing. Do not distress yourself."

Their chat was interrupted by Cassandra's movement and incoherent whispers. Both of them hurried to her and called her name, but the only reaction was another long silence.

"She has her shoulder bandaged," Elizabeth said.

"Yes. The doctor examined her again more closely. He suspected she had some broken ribs. Oh, dear, my poor girl. She suffered so much…" Mrs. Spencer could not fight back her tears and hid her face in her handkerchief, crying in desperation.

She whispered, wiping the tears from her eyes. "I did not help much, in fact I only watched from afar. I could not bear to look too closely. Thank God the colonel was here to help the doctor."

"The colonel was here?" Elizabeth asked, and Mrs. Spencer startled with obvious discomfort.

"Yes…he…he just happened to inquire after Cassandra. Dr. Barrington said he could use the colonel's help. Dr. Barrington has been their families' doctor for a lifetime; did you know that?"

"Yes, yes, I was told that," Elizabeth replied, unable to let the conversation shift to another subject. "Mrs. Spencer, I know it is highly improper of me to raise such a subject, but I hope you will understand that I am only concerned for Cassandra's well-being. Last night, when she first recovered, she spoke only one word; she only called the colonel's name. I was wondering if that happened again while you were with her."

The lady nodded in agreement, and Elizabeth continued. "It is obviously a matter that distressed her greatly. I was wondering if you know *anything* that might help relieve her distress."

Their embarrassment was mutual and neither found the words to dissipate the tension in the room. They looked at each other for a time, and Elizabeth was certain that Mrs. Spencer was trying to assess how much she should trust her.

"Miss Bennet, your devotion and affection for *my girl* has not passed unnoticed or unappreciated. I am deeply grateful to you and would not want to sound disrespectful when I say that I do not know anything I could share with you."

"I understand," Elizabeth replied uncomfortably.

"However, I will confess to you — and I trust your secrecy implicitly — that I allowed the colonel to stay with her after the doctor left. He practically begged me, and I had no heart to refuse him. I know I should not have done that. Cassandra was certainly in no condition to have a man in her room, and I know she will be furious that someone has seen her in such a state, covered in bandages, her nightgown damp from fever. I was tempted to refuse the colonel despite his obvious pain and torment. But then she called his name, and he heard her and hurried to the bed. He took her hand and started to talk, and she seemed to calm. Then he moistened her lips with a little tea, and she actually licked it. She fell asleep while he remained kneeling by her bed, holding her hand and whispering to her. What should I have done? How could I refuse him when his presence seemed so beneficial for my dear girl? I retired to a corner and left them alone. Miss Bennet, I do not know what is happening, but if something or someone might help my girl's recovery, as God is my witness, I will not refuse it! She might be angry with me when she recovers, but I would give my life to see her well and sound — and angry with me!"

Mrs. Spencer turned pale as she spoke, and she appeared unable to stand. Elizabeth hurried to take her arm and directed her to a chair.

"Mrs. Spencer, I know it is not my part to decide, but I heartily agree with you! I do not believe the colonel's presence would harm Cassandra. I have the highest opinion of the colonel," Elizabeth was interrupted by Darcy's unexpected entrance.

He greeted them warmly, his eyes falling tenderly on Elizabeth. Mrs. Spencer smiled to herself.

Darcy's worry for his friend made him grimace in grief that there was no improvement and her fever had little diminished. He stayed near her, held her hand briefly, and then touched her forehead, startled at how hot it was. He rose nervously, and then asked where the doctor was and why drastic measures had not been taken. In his agitation, he declared he must fetch other physicians from Town, as neither Dr. Barrington nor Mr. Jones had seemed to discover a remedy.

"Mr. Darcy, please calm yourself, sir," Mrs. Spencer said gently. "I understand your worry, but I am sure the doctors have done everything that could be done. Please let me inform you about the result of their latest examinations. Besides," she added with a slight hesitation, "Cassandra did speak a few words — though not quite coherently. The mere fact that she is not completely unconscious should be a good sign, should it not?"

Darcy barely heard Mrs. Spencer and only tried to control his temper in order not to distress Elizabeth further. His resolution increased a few moments later when Georgiana joined them, her blue eyes ringed by dark circles, her face pale, and the lack of sleep aging her appearance. Once she entered the chamber, Georgiana sat near Cassandra and held her hand; she could not fight back her tears, nor did she make the attempt.

When Cassandra broke the silence and whispered a few words, they all gathered around, but none of their entreaties brought Cassandra to consciousness. If the ladies were sad and desperate, Darcy felt generally helpless, watching Cassandra struggle with the fever — as though trapped in a cage from which he was unable to free her. He would prefer to leave the room than suffer being powerless to help, but how could he desert the ladies when they might need him? On the other hand, was it proper for him to be in Cassandra's room? Likely not! Then why did nobody tell him that? Yes, perhaps he should leave for now.

"Mr. Darcy, if you have some business to attend to, please do so, sir. We will call you if we need anything," said Mrs. Spencer.

He nodded silently in agreement and, slightly uncomfortable and with a last look at Elizabeth, moved to the door. Then he turned unexpectedly to them.

"Ladies, what did Cassandra whisper? I cannot be certain, but I thought I heard her calling a name — something like '*David*'."

Mrs. Spencer and Elizabeth exchanged a quick glance and then looked at Georgiana who nodded in agreement.

"Yes, she called '*David*' more than once — I heard her," Georgiana explained with excitement.

"But *David?*" Darcy sounded puzzled as he looked from one lady to the other. "Who might this be? I do not know *any* David except my cousin."

Georgiana looked quizzically at his misunderstanding while Elizabeth exchanged another quick glance with Mrs. Spencer. The elder lady could not help rolling her eyes at such naiveté.

"But brother, she is calling our cousin! It is so obvious."

"Why on earth would she call David? It is true that she was fond of him when she was younger, but why would she call only his name? Well, after all, it matters little if her health improves. I would not —"

A moment later, his face turned pale at the sudden revelation.

"No, that cannot be! He would not trifle with her! Not with Cassandra." Before any of the ladies could stop him, he exited the chamber, slamming the door behind him.

It took Elizabeth a few moments to recover, and while silently wishing for advice from Mrs. Spencer, she hurried to follow her betrothed and intervene before he instigated an unnecessary argument.

IN THE BACK GARDEN OF Netherfield, away from curious eyes, a shocked, incredulous Darcy stared at a troubled David Fitzwilliam who had just finished an extraordinary revelation.

When he left Cassandra's chamber, Darcy was so full of rage that he could not think properly; all he had in mind was that his cousin — who had always found great enjoyment in female company — behaved improperly toward Cassandra, a situation that had seriously affected her and continued to trouble her even in her precarious state. He had searched for David, but he was not to be found in either his apartment or the library; not even Bingley knew his whereabouts. Finally, Darcy discovered his cousin taking a solitary stroll around the house and hurried to him, demanding explanations and reparations.

However, the instant he saw the colonel's grievous expression and the sorrow in his eyes, Darcy's anger vanished.

Still, he demanded an explanation, and he got one. It appeared that David had been waiting for his cousin to inquire so he could unleash his agonising secret.

"Now you know everything, Darcy. Forgive me; I know you are angry with me. I know I should not tell you these things. But I cannot bear it alone any longer when she might… I desperately needed to speak to you, but I did not dare approach you. I have never felt like this before."

He looked devastated, and Darcy wished to comfort him, but how does one gentleman comfort another?

"So, she refused to marry you, but she agreed to…*you know*…"

"No, she did not *agree*. I mean, it was not I who suggested it. I never would have dared to…not with Cassandra."

"So, what do you plan to do now?"

"I am at a loss as to what I ought to do. After she told me about her husband, I was half desperate, half relieved. I understood I could not possibly compete with his memory or with her desire to punish herself for something that was not even her fault. On the other hand, the situation was not completely hopeless, as I was content to know her heart is not otherwise engaged. I even told her I do not intend to abandon my hopes. I only planned to depart for a time to allow her to regain some peace and serenity."

"She must have a tender regard for you or else she never would have... *you know*. She is not that sort of woman."

"I know what sort of woman she is, Darcy! That is precisely why I was so angered by her rejection. I was certain she had affection for me. I *felt* she had loving affection for me," he said passionately, and Darcy averted his eyes. They should not be discussing this and certainly not about a friend who was like a sister to him.

"What do you plan to do now?"

"What is there to do? The only thing that matters to me now is Cassandra's health. I do not care about her marrying me or about my wishes. I pray only to see her recovered; I will ask nothing more. However, I must stay with her. I know it is highly improper, but you cannot refuse me!"

"I have no right to refuse you anything. God knows my concept of proper behaviour and decorum has changed dramatically since last autumn. The only one who might keep you away is Mrs. Spencer. Elizabeth and Georgiana also might consider your presence in Cassandra's chamber to be strange. You will have to inform them of *some* of the particulars of your recent history with Cassandra."

"Mrs. Spencer was wonderfully sympathetic. She allowed me to stay with Cassandra last night. But you are correct. I must tell them something... and Bingley, too, as he is the master of the house. The servants will likely gossip about my being in Cassandra's chamber, and I will need Bingley's support in this."

"I agree. So will you tell? Surely you will not lie to them — nor can you tell the entire truth."

"I will confess my feelings for her and that I proposed but she refused me; it should be enough."

"Very well; now let us return to the house; I am in great need of a brandy before breakfast." The colonel agreed with him immediately.

That day at a late breakfast, Elizabeth was relieved to see that, despite the fact she did not find the gentlemen in time to prevent their argument, they seemed to be on friendly terms. They had obviously talked and, during the meal, remained more silent then ever; they often exchanged glances of unknown meaning. Elizabeth was curious but content simply to wait to be informed of the details. She was certain that, if it were something to be shared, Darcy would tell her.

Miss Bingley was still in the house; for reasons of her own, she did not leave as she had declared a few days earlier. She granted the guests a superior coldness and completely ignored their presence. Only Georgiana was offered a few polite words; however, Miss Bingley's admiration of Miss Darcy seemed to diminish with every day of Mr. Darcy's engagement to Eliza Bennet.

THE NEXT THREE DAYS PASSED with increasing fear and turmoil for Cassandra's friends.

Despite the doctors' continuous efforts and the ladies' care, Cassandra's state did not improve. She continued feverish, her body burning and shaken by tremors; all the medicines, though seeming to give her momentarily palliation, were not enough to cure her.

The colonel confessed part of his story to Elizabeth, Georgiana and Mrs. Spencer; furthermore, he blamed himself for insisting too vehemently in his proposal of marriage, which had disturbed her greatly. If neither Elizabeth nor Mrs. Spencer believed her refusal to be the reason Cassandra feverishly called the colonel's name, it was to their credit that they did not pursue the matter.

Georgiana, however, became animated about it. She was convinced — and told David as much — that beyond any doubt Cassandra did share his affection and, when she was recovered, would declare her true feelings for him. No matter how much the colonel tried to temper her joyful prophecy, she remained steadfast in her conviction; it was obvious to everyone that the only person to whom Cassandra reacted was the colonel.

The nights were the most difficult time, as her fever seemed to increase dangerously after midnight, and though not conscious, she became agitated, her violent movements jeopardising the healing process. In those moments, nothing helped her but the colonel's soothing presence. He spent hours sitting near her bed, whispering to her in a gentle voice and caressing her hand until she seemed to calm and eventually sleep.

When they needed to give her medicine, David was the one to hold her, and though nobody knew what he was whispering to her, his words allowed her to co-operate with the doctors.

In truth, the colonel was never alone with her; there were also Elizabeth, Mrs. Spencer, and Georgiana or at least one of them; and Janey, Cassandra's maid, never left her mistress's side for more than a few minutes. The doctors, Mrs. Spencer, Darcy and Bingley — as master of the house — accepted the arrangement without hesitation in consideration of Cassandra's recovery above the demands of decorum. Georgiana was simply happy to see the colonel with Cassandra and could see nothing improper in it.

Elizabeth barely slept for the next three days and nights, and she spent little private time with Darcy. Their only moments of peace were spent in short strolls around the garden, arm in arm.

Their wedding day was less than four weeks away, but for both of them it seemed impossibly distant. Although neither of them actually dared to speak of it, both were terrified at the idea that Cassandra might leave them forever in the coming days. Their own desire for happiness seemed frightfully selfish compared to such a dreadful possibility, and they could not think of their own felicity when shadowed by their friend's loss.

The doctor had confessed to them that the more time passed without any improvement, the more reason he had for concern. At Darcy's insistence, the doctor informed them of the permanent damage of a high fever that lasted too long, and Elizabeth hardly left Cassandra's room from that moment on. She did everything in her power to make Cassandra react: she read to her, spoke to her, asked Mrs. Spencer and Georgiana to speak — loudly — of Cassandra's youth; she even asked Mr. Bingley to bring the small instrument from Cassandra's dressing room for Georgiana to play.

Elizabeth's obvious exhaustion, paleness, and visible loss of weight increased Darcy's concern. He tried to defeat Elizabeth's stubbornness with little success. It appeared that the doctor, Mrs. Spencer, Mrs. Gardiner and Georgiana supported her decision and offered their unconditional assistance.

On the fifth day after the accident, Elizabeth was resting in an armchair after dinner a short distance from Mrs. Spencer. She felt weary and powerless and briefly considered that she had not slept an entire night since the dreadful evening of Markham's attack. She could not believe that only a week had passed. It seemed a lifetime.

Cassandra had just received her medicine; apparently, her fever was down as she seemed to sleep peacefully. Elizabeth allowed her eyes to close for a few minutes, but she was instantly startled by the sound of her name spoken softly.

At first, she thought she was dreaming, but the whisper repeated, and she turned toward the bed to see Cassandra's hand moving and her weak voice addressing her clearly.

"Elizabeth…" Elizabeth hurried to her and took her hand, tears rolling down her cheeks.

"Dearest Cassandra, I am here… Oh my dear, it is so good to hear you speaking to me —"

Her voice was interrupted by a cry of pain, as the lady attempted to move. "Oh Lord, my head hurts."

"Please lie still! You have been badly injured, but you will be fine! I am going to fetch the doctor."

Elizabeth moved toward the door, but Cassandra's insistent call brought her back.

"Elizabeth, how is Darcy? How did the duel end?"

"William? He is well — very well — only quite worried about you. Of what duel are you speaking? There was no duel," Elizabeth replied, puzzled, certain that her friend was delirious.

"Oh, thank the Lord! So he did not fight Markham after all. I was so frightened that he would be killed. I tried to go to Town after them, but then I cannot remember what happened… Oh God, my head aches," she said as she tried to bring her left hand to her forehead but cried again in pain.

Elizabeth was unable to move from shock, her lips and hands trembling, struggling to understand Cassandra's words, and praying that she was merely feverish and confused.

"Mr. Darcy is well, and so is our colonel." Mrs. Spencer affectionately caressed Cassandra's hair.

"David is here?" she asked weakly, her eyelashes closing slowly. "I knew he would come…" Her voice was barely audible as her breathing steadied, and she quickly fell asleep.

"Elizabeth, dearest, please send for the doctor." Mrs. Spencer repeated herself before Elizabeth, deep in thought, heard and answered the request.

Elizabeth sent Janey to fetch the doctor as she moved to the dressing room and leaned against the wall, her knees weak. Her mind, tormented by fatigue and the distress of the last week, was loath to admit that what she had just heard was true, yet it was too obvious to be denied. Of course, there had been a duel!

So that was the mystery behind Darcy's sudden departure! He went to fight Markham!

Her heart raced wildly as she struggled to breathe. But how was that possible? Cassandra said something about Town, but Markham was not in London — or was he?

She remembered — vividly — the moment she told Cassandra about Darcy's trip and the shock on Cassandra's face. That, undoubtedly, was the moment Cassandra realized the truth.

How was it possible that she, Elizabeth, had been so stupid not to guess the simple fact that Cassandra understood instantly? How could she have been so blind?

All of Darcy's twisted words, his refusal to confess to her the reason for his hasty decision to leave again — he deliberately put himself in danger and concealed it from her! Thank the Lord he returned safely, but what if…? And what happened to Markham? Had he been killed? If so, what would the earl do? The duel was illegal; any child knew that. How could Darcy have exposed himself so only a few weeks before their wedding?

And, of course, the colonel was part of his plan — and her father, as well! Now everything was clear as crystal: her own father and uncle were part of the outrageous plot. They conspired together!

She felt exhausted, disappointed, and betrayed by the men she cared for most, frightened by what could have happened, and could no longer fight the tears that rolled down her cheeks. Increasingly, however, her turmoil of emotions grew into anger.

They had showed no consideration for her opinion, her wishes, or her worries! Of course, not — she was only a woman after all! Why should she expect the men to treat her as one of them and ask for her advice? What could a mere woman have to say about the importance of fighting for one's honour?

Well, this *woman does have something to say, and you will hear it all, gentlemen,* she whispered to herself as she wiped furiously at her tears and stormed from the room, slamming the door behind her.

She hurried down the stairs to the library, where she knew the gentlemen were gathered after dinner, and paused to catch her breath before entering.

"Elizabeth, what a surprise," said Darcy warmly as she burst through the door without knocking. They were all there with the exception of Mr. Hurst who had likely retired early.

"Miss Bennet, please come and sit down." Bingley spoke politely but was somewhat disconcerted at her unceremonious entrance. "How is Lady Cassandra?"

"I have wonderful news. She is awake and spoke to me clearly; I have great hopes that she will recover." Elizabeth then took a seat, avoiding Darcy's eyes.

The gentlemen became excited and asked countless questions, but she tempered them, saying the doctor had just started his examination and would certainly come with fresh news shortly. Her tone was cold and impersonal, and the gentlemen could not fail to notice it.

"Elizabeth, you seem unwell. May I offer you something?" asked Darcy.

"No, thank you," she replied, still avoiding his eyes. "My only plea is that, while we are waiting for the doctor, I be allowed to join your little club."

"I do not understand your meaning. Of what club are you speaking?"

"Really? Then allow me to enlighten you, sir. I refer to the exclusive club of honourable gentlemen, whose primary objectives are the arrangement of duels and the derision of naïve ladies like me!"

This time her eyes did meet his, and Darcy frowned as he tried in vain to formulate an answer. Silence fell upon the library.

"Elizabeth, let us discuss this calmly. It is a private matter, and we should not speak of it publicly."

"A private matter, Mr. Darcy? How is it, then, that the colonel, my father and my own uncle — perhaps even Mr. Bingley — were aware of this *private matter* while *I alone* was kept in ignorance?"

"Elizabeth, you do not understand. Your father and uncle are blameless, and Bingley knew nothing until our return. I alone am at fault. I simply had no other choice than to conceal it from you. You have already suffered so dreadfully that I could not torment you further by revealing my intentions."

"Of course you are at fault, sir! You did not want to torment me? And may I ask, should something have happened to you, how your secrecy would have spared my suffering? And what occurred with Markham? Has he been... Is he still alive?"

"He is alive," the colonel interceded. "He only got what he deserved, and hopefully, he will be more attentive to proper behaviour in the future."

Smiling charmingly at Elizabeth, he continued, "Miss Bennet, I am more than willing to share the blame with Darcy as I knew of his intentions from the beginning and understood them."

"Oh, really, sir? Why does that not surprise me? Am I wrong to presume that you not only understood but supported him as well?" Elizabeth's voice was sharp and as cold as ice.

"I confess I did! I even offered to fight Markham on his behalf, but he, of course, refused, and I accepted his decision. It was his duty and his wish to fight for your honour."

Elizabeth rose from her seat and stepped closer to him, her eyes crackling with unleashed fury.

"Dear colonel, my honour is here with me — safe and sound — and was never affected by a drunken rake who barely knew what he was about. My only riposte to Lord Markham's action would have been to ignore him utterly for the rest of his sorry life. But of course, what do I know? I am only a nonsensical woman and cannot possibly understand the rules of honour among gentlemen!"

"Elizabeth, my child, I understand your anger, but you must control your words; you should not address your betrothed and the colonel in this impertinent manner." Mr. Bennet's tone was as severe as a father scolding a disobedient daughter, but the effect was not the one he anticipated.

Elizabeth turned to her father, and for the first time in his life, he failed to see the usually affectionate countenance that was meant only for him.

"Oh, I do apologise, Father! I shall certainly tell Mama of your displeasure. She will surely understand why you purposely agreed to put Mr. Darcy in danger of losing his life."

Mr. Bennet's mouth gaped open as he stared at his furious daughter.

"I will spare you the displeasure of seeing or hearing me any longer, gentlemen. If you would excuse me." Suddenly her strength evaded her, and she desperately fought back tears, which again were imminent. She had to leave immediately; she had to be alone with her pain and her anger.

Gently but firmly, Darcy grasped her arm. "Elizabeth, please..." he whispered.

"Mr. Darcy, please have the wisdom to distance yourself from me at the moment. I would not trust myself to behave like a lady."

Their eyes met in silent confrontation, ignoring the others in the room.

"Elizabeth, we *must* talk." His voice was more a plea than a request.

"Talk, Mr. Darcy? But we did talk, sir! Even more, you held me in your arms, kissed me, and lied to me! What could we possibly have to talk about?"

Elizabeth's reply exploded as thunder in the room. The other gentlemen desperately examined their empty glasses with unusual interest.

Darcy frowned, staring at his future father-in-law, unable to reply. Fortunately, Mr. Bennet was too affected by his daughter's reaction and too sympathetic toward Darcy's distress to inquire further.

THE DOCTOR'S REPORT DID NOT raise Elizabeth's spirits.

Dr. Barrington insisted he would watch his patient —sleeping deeply from the medicine — the entire night for any change, so Elizabeth took the opportunity to retire to her room and try to rest. Her body felt so heavy that she could barely walk, but her spirit was even heavier.

However, sleep would not come to bring her release. She startled as she heard the door open softly but calmed immediately when she recognised Darcy's steps. He had come, but she did not want to see or speak to him. She closed her eyes, pretending to sleep.

He moved closer and sat on the bed; she sensed his gaze caressing her face. Then his fingers brushed a lock of hair from her forehead and his lips touched her cheeks briefly. She felt the need to cry, but she remained still.

When he left, the room — and her heart — remained empty. She was glad he had gone. She was too angry to see him now. She hated him for putting himself in danger, for jeopardising their future happiness, and for not trusting her. She hated him with all her heart — she hated him with all her love!

Sleep eventually took pity and enveloped her.

ELIZABETH DID NOT SLEEP LONG. The room suddenly became cold, and she knew someone had entered.

She opened her eyes and saw Markham, an evil grin on his face and a pistol in his hand pointed at Darcy's chest. Elizabeth screamed and tried to stop him, but she was trapped, seemingly tied to the bed. The next moment, the thundering sound of a gunshot shattered the room, and she knew Markham had shot him.

Suddenly, she could move, and she threw herself on the floor near Darcy's fallen body. A warm, red spot was spreading across his shirt over his heart; she touched it and felt his blood on her fingers. She screamed again and cupped his face, crying his name, but the only reply was her name whispered by his pale lips. He died in her arms, and she never had time to tell him how much she loved him.

ELIZABETH AWOKE, TREMBLING WITH FEAR, and the pain in her chest left her breathless.

She looked around and saw herself in the bed — the room silent — with no one around. It had been only a nightmare her mind kept telling her, but she could not stop trembling; the recollection was so vivid — Darcy's body on the floor, Markham's smirk, the sensation of Darcy's cold face on her fingers.

The window was open; that was the reason she was so cold. She closed it, put more wood on the fire, wrapped herself in a robe and settled herself on the settee near the fireplace.

It had been a nightmare, obviously, she kept repeating that to herself, demanding her mind to see reason. Yet her heart was grieved and unable to beat regularly. Was it merely a nightmare? Was he truly safe? No, she would not be content unless she convinced herself of his safety. She pulled her robe together, tied it to cover herself and exited the room. She had to be sure.

There was only one place he could be — a place she never would have dared enter. Looking around tentatively to be sure she was not seen, Elizabeth opened the door and crept in silently.

No servant was within; she stepped forward and, with infinite care, entered his bedchamber.

Oh, he sleeps quite soundly, she thought, half relieved to see him so peaceful, half irritated that he was sleeping when she could not!

She took two more steps and was now close to the bed. His hair was tousled, and his face, relaxed in sleep, seemed even more handsome. His chest was moving steadily with his breath; his neck was exposed above his nightshirt, and she blushed at the sight of it. Yes, all had been a nightmare.

"My love, what are you doing here?" His voice sounded not only tender but also obviously pleased and relieved to see her. If he was convinced she had forgiven him, he was mistaken!

"I came to…see you. I had a nightmare and wanted to be sure that…" She blushed as she spoke, her words a poor excuse even to her own ears.

"Elizabeth, please, let me explain to you…please…"

She looked straight into his eyes. "You lied to me, William."

"I only kept the truth from you to protect you."

"You did not trust me enough."

"I did not trust you would understand and allow me to go."

"Certainly not!"

"Yet, I had to do what I thought was my duty."

"I cannot accept that. I cannot bear the thought that you will continue to put yourself in danger and conceal it from me."

"It will not happen again; but can you not understand that I had to protect you?"

"Protect me? You wanted to protect me! Then you should have stayed with me, and nothing would have happened. What did you accomplish by fighting Markham?"

"I taught him a lesson. I warned him never to bother you again."

She rolled her eyes, not knowing whether she should slap him or laugh at him. "How badly was he injured? What if his father raises a scandal against you?"

"I shot him in his right arm — painful but not life-threatening. However, he will not be able to handle a weapon for some time. The earl will keep his history private — no need to worry. I could have killed Markham but chose not to. The earl knew that and was grateful; he promised to take Markham on a long trip to the continent; they will likely be away for a couple of years."

"I see..." Her voice softened, and he did not fail to notice. He placed a light kiss in her palm, and then kissed each of her fingers. She shivered.

"I can never forgive you for what you did," she said, and he frowned.

"I will struggle all my life for your forgiveness if you will still agree to marry me. I cannot bear the thought that you might leave me. I would gladly give my life for you, Elizabeth."

She sighed furiously, and her eyes — only a few inches away — glared into his.

"I do not want you to give your life for me, you stupid man! I want you to take care of your life and share it with me for many, long years."

"My dearest, loveliest Elizabeth..." he whispered adoringly, his arms embracing her as his lips brushed her face with countless kisses.

She was still angry with him, but she could not resist his kiss. She was so cold that, when he pulled her close to him in bed, she only moaned in contentment. His caresses, even sweeter than she remembered, warmed her; when she quivered again, it was not from cold.

She was breathless from his weight crushing her; she felt her gown pulled up to her thighs and his legs entwining with hers as he lay on top of her. She was a little frightened to be trapped beneath him; however, it was not fear but a lack of air that made her stop him.

"William, please stop," she whispered, but for a moment, he seemed not to hear her. She repeated her plea, and he obeyed instantly, breaking the kiss and looking at her closely.

"Elizabeth, I am so sorry. I forgot myself." He looked devastatingly handsome as he gazed at her, begging forgiveness for his impulsive desire.

"Do not apologise, sir," she smiled, struggling for air. "It is just that...you are too heavy to bear," she said, blushing.

"Oh, please forgive me. I did not think that it might be uncomfortable for you. I have lost myself," he repeated and hurried to move away from her, but she trapped him with her arms.

"It is not at all uncomfortable, sir," she replied, forcing a smile to conceal her mortification. "I was just wondering whether you could...do something...not to be so heavy," she concluded.

He moved a little, and she felt easier. His warmth was still there — he was still lying upon her — but his weight had become bearable.

"I am so sorry, my love," he said, his eyes fixed on hers.

"Oh, you were not that heavy," she replied teasingly.

"Not for that." He smiled back at her, yet he was obviously affected.

"Well, that other subject will not be so easy to resolve, sir. I still do not forgive you; I am just happy to see you unharmed and to know Cassandra is better, and I am rejoicing in all this good news after such torment. But I still want more details about the duel," she said severely.

"I will tell you everything you want to know."

"And I will have some very clear demands if we are to be married."

"Will I be allowed to negotiate them, madam?"

"Not much, I am afraid. Furthermore, I still intend to punish you for your actions," she smiled mischievously, and he seemed finally to relax.

"Do you have any specific punishment in mind?"

"No, I am too tired to think, but I will give it proper consideration once I am more rested."

"I will wait patiently and accept my sentence."

By that time, his lips were already touching hers, softly brushing them without completing the kiss.

"Elizabeth, though you might not know it, you are already punishing me."

"How is that, sir?" she inquired, but the last words went unheard as his mouth finally captured hers. She enjoyed the kiss much more than any answer and did not complain.

Now that their bodies were not quite pressing against each other, there was room left for his insatiable hands to explore and caress with tender passion. She vividly remembered the sensation of his touch, yet when his fingers brushed over her breasts and cupped them with gentle possessiveness, she shuddered and cried against his mouth.

When the need for air made him break the kiss and his lips rested upon her temple, she managed to whisper as she impulsively pressed her lips against his ear, "How do I punish you, sir?"

Darcy lifted his head so he could look deeply into her eyes. "You are not aware of it, my love, but your generosity in allowing me to hold you, to kiss you, to caress you without joining as man and wife is a painful torture — a sweet one to be sure, but truly painful."

"I see…" She knew she should feel ashamed of having this conversation, of being with him in such a scandalous position, of enjoying his attentions so wantonly. "I did not intend to punish you this way. If you wish it, I would not oppose… putting an end to your torture."

Darcy's look was incredulous, but if he doubted the meaning of her words, the passion sparkling in her eyes and the acceptance and invitation in her gaze were eloquent proof of her intentions.

"I have desired nothing more in my life, nor have I been more tempted," he whispered. And if I considered my wishes alone, I would not hesitate for a moment, but I am thinking of you."

"Of me? But I would not mind. I trust you, and we are to be married in less than a month."

"Oh, that is not what I am worried about," he replied and his dark gaze made her tremble; she felt thirsty and licked her suddenly dry lips.

"You see, my love, our joining as husband and wife should not be rushed through fear of being heard or interrupted by a curious servant. When you become my wife, it will be a day of joy with no worries, no concerns, no people around to interfere, and no asinine mistakes on my part to distress you. Only you and me, and the perfect solitude of our chambers."

She looked disconcerted, and he was delighted to see her disappointed.

"Trust me, my love. I cannot explain in more detail, but you will better understand what I mean now after *that* has actually happened."

Elizabeth tried to smile "Mr. Darcy, you are presumptuous to ask me to trust you upon your word this evening. You have much to do to regain my trust — in every respect."

"As I said earlier, I will spend the rest of my life striving for your forgiveness and your trust."

"I am glad to hear it, sir. And Mr. Darcy, when you left for London in such a hurry, I missed telling you something of great importance."

He stared at her with concern. She smiled and her thumb brushed against his mouth as she replied. "I missed telling you how much I love you, sir."

Later that night, Darcy carried her back to her room and secured her promise that she would try to sleep until late in the morning. She agreed but did not forget to mention she was still upset with him. He smiled and asked for her forgiveness — again — kissed her hand ceremoniously and bowed politely before leaving the room.

A few minutes later, Elizabeth was sound asleep. As for Darcy, dawn found him in his chamber, gazing out of the window, thankful for the greatest fortune of his life: Elizabeth.

Chapter 21

Elizabeth's heart was still melting as her mind vividly recollected those sweet, forbidden moments she spent in the warmth of Darcy's arms: the exquisite sensation of sharing a bed — though not quite *sharing* it — of their bodies lying together, his breathtaking kisses and caresses that made her head spin as she felt her cheeks burn from pleasure and embarrassment.

A few minutes later, when Elizabeth opened the door to Cassandra's chamber, she managed to appear calm — but only for a moment. In the next instant, she actually cried with happiness; her ladyship was awake though still lying against the pillows; she wore a new gown, her hair was dressed by a diligent Janey, and she was watched carefully by a tearful Mrs. Spencer.

Cassandra's gaze met Elizabeth's, and she forced a smile. Elizabeth hurried to the bed, taking Cassandra's hand gently; the maid retired politely.

"You look beautiful, Cassandra. Oh, I am so happy to see you like this!"

Cassandra laughed, but even that slight exertion pained her, and the smile turned into a grin; she struggled to conceal a deep moan as she replied, "*You* look beautiful, Elizabeth. *I* look like a woman who has broken half of her bones. Poor Janey worked so hard to give me a normal appearance."

"You look beautiful," Elizabeth repeated. Cassandra took her hand gently.

"Elizabeth, I was told everything you did for me — your care, your sleepless nights, and your devotion. I do not know how I can possibly find the words to thank you — to show my gratitude —"

"Then do not! As you told me some time ago, let this be the last time we speak of gratitude and thanks."

A moment later, Georgiana entered, almost throwing herself on the bed to embrace her friend.

Cassandra moaned again in obvious pain, but did nothing to push the girl away — quite the contrary.

"Cassandra, how are you feeling?"

"I feel perfectly well, dearest."

"You are not *perfectly* well, but you do look so much improved! Oh, I missed your smile."

"And I missed you; I am sorry for giving you such a hard time, dearest."

"Do not be sorry. I am just happy to see you improving. William, David and Mr. Bingley are downstairs; they will be here in a moment. They were so happy when the doctor told us —"

"David is here?" Cassandra inquired abruptly, with obvious disbelief.

"Cassandra, you know the colonel is here. I told you as much last evening," said Elizabeth, but the patient stared at her without understanding.

"I did *not* know he was here."

"Of course he is here!" continued Georgiana enthusiastically. "He has been here all the time. If you could see his devotion! He rarely left your side while you were unconscious."

Georgiana's eyes were bright with emotion and tears as she tried to describe the proofs of David's affection. Cassandra turned quite pale, her eyes narrowed in anger.

"You allowed David to stay in my room while I was unconscious? How dare you do that?" Cassandra's reproach was directed to Mrs. Spencer, but Elizabeth and Georgiana startled under the severity of her words.

"Has my illness been such an entertaining spectacle? Did you invite the whole of Meryton?"

"Cassandra, why are you speaking so? I do not understand…" Georgiana's voice trembled, and her eyes opened wider with shock.

"What is so difficult to understand, Georgiana? How is it possible that strange men were allowed into my room while I was ill? Do I not have a reason to be upset?"

"Please calm yourself, my child." Mrs. Spencer tried unsuccessfully to temper her.

"I am not your child, Mrs. Spencer! I am your mistress, and you should treat me accordingly."

Elizabeth and Georgiana looked at each other, embarrassed. Mrs. Spencer's only reaction was a slight, reproachful move of her head. In the throes of their argument, none of the ladies noticed the three gentlemen staring at them from the doorway.

Georgiana, still trying to make Cassandra see reason, continued, "Cassandra, there were no strange men in your room. Only William and David. But you called for David —"

"Georgiana, I was unconscious! How could I call for anybody? I may have mumbled a name in my delirium, but that does not mean you should allow into my room any man with that name."

"Cassandra, do not speak to Georgiana in such a way. If anyone is at fault, it would be me," said the colonel soundly, stepping inside.

Cassandra looked at him, helpless, weak and trapped lying there in the bed under his intense gaze. Unable to reply, she turned her head in an attempt to dismiss them.

"David is not 'any man'," continued Georgiana with an unusual determination. You *did* call for him, and I know why you did so. David told us everything that happened between you…"

Cassandra tried to move, but a sharp pain sapped her strength.

"Indeed, that was a very good strategy, Colonel, and very gentlemanlike. Exactly what did you intend to accomplish by informing everyone that we shared a bed?"

The room grew silent — not a breath could be heard, perhaps because everyone had ceased breathing. Cassandra and David were still glaring at each other, their eyes locked in a silent battle.

Mrs. Spencer took a few steps and, with perfect calm, addressed Cassandra. "In fact, the colonel told us that he had proposed to you and was refused. He took the blame upon himself for your calling his name while you were unconscious. He explained that he had been too insistent in his address and likely had distressed you too much."

Cassandra's eyes blinked repeatedly as her teeth bit her lower lip; a small drop of blood appeared, but she seemed not to notice. She continued to gaze at David until, with a long, last look, he apologised and quit the room. Darcy hesitated a moment, looking from Elizabeth to his sister and finally to Cassandra, and then he followed his cousin with Bingley on his heels.

When the last of the gentlemen quitted the room, Cassandra's weak cry broke the silence.

Elizabeth resumed her seat on the bed close to Cassandra. She did not know exactly what had happened but, from Cassandra's reaction, felt it was much more than a forsaken proposal. And, despite Cassandra's harsh, ungenerous words toward the colonel, Elizabeth could easily see Cassandra was suffering at least as much as the rejected gentleman. Something painful was separating the two, and this was not the proper time to press for answers. Still, Elizabeth could not refrain from resolutely pursuing the painful subject.

"Cassandra, you did call for the colonel, and he came more than willingly. He has been so grieved — his suffering so genuine. He wanted nothing more than to help you. It is not that you were delirious. You did not cry out random names — only his. He was never alone with you; one of us was always here. You calmed when he spoke to you; you slept peacefully while he was here; you took your medicine only when he gave it to you. I know you can understand our reasons, but if not, I still cannot repent that we allowed him in the room. We were so worried that we would lose you; we would have done anything to help you. And the colonel did help you recover. Can you not see? You were in great danger of dying —"

"You should have let me die; it would have been better for everyone," she replied weakly. Cassandra turned her head to the side, her beautiful face so transformed by grief that Elizabeth trembled. She could sense that Cassandra was in earnest. How could Elizabeth possibly respond to such an assertion?

"How dare you?" Georgiana's cry of anger and desperation came from nowhere.

"How dare you say such a thing when we spent the last days and nights praying for you? Do you know that Elizabeth has not slept at all since your accident? Nor has Mrs. Spencer or Janey! And now instead of thanking them, you are yelling at them and pretending it would have been better for everyone if you were dead? What gives you the right to say so?"

Neither Elizabeth nor Mrs. Spencer could intervene to interrupt Georgiana's outburst.

Cassandra's cheeks turned from pale to crimson, and she stretched her hand toward Georgiana. The girl stepped away to increase the gulf between them. "Georgiana, you do not understand —"

"Oh, but I do understand perfectly! I understand that you are upset with David when you should be grateful for his affection and devotion. He did not hesitate to open his heart to us, to confess his feelings and his failure in securing your hand in order to be allowed to watch over you. He did not care for decorum or for exposing himself to ridicule; his only concern was your well-being. Instead, for some strange reason, you purposely deny what is so obvious to all of us: your own affection for him. It is like…like you are afraid to admit it, like you fight against your own heart. Are you afraid, Cassandra? Is that why you behave so selfishly, so inconsiderately toward your friends? You were never afraid of anything!"

The girl's face was flustered from her emotional speech, but she continued in a trembling voice, tears flowing in earnest. "For years you and William were my only family; I could not love a sister more than I love you, and I admired you even more than I loved you! And now…now you wish you died just because you cannot admit your own feelings for David?! This is not the Cassandra I have known! This is not *my* generous, brave Cassandra! I pray to the Lord that you are not yet fully recovered and that tomorrow everything will be different and you will be yourself again."

Georgiana promptly left the room, wiping her tears furiously. Elizabeth's calling after her was unanswered, so she followed the girl with a final brief glance toward Cassandra, whose face was crumpled in shock.

As soon as they were alone, Cassandra managed to whisper a plea, as a child begging for a favour. "Mrs. Spencer, would you excuse me, please? I would like to rest now… I am not feeling well…"

The elder lady smiled lovingly and, with a slight move of her head expressing her gentle reproach — a gesture well known to Cassandra since she was a girl — arranged the bed sheets around her.

"Try to rest, my child. Everything will be fine; you will see."

Cassandra turned her face to the fire and allowed the tears to come with no attempt to hide them. Nevertheless, Mrs. Spencer knew when she was crying, laughing or simply being unfair to those around her. After all, Cassandra had been "her girl" for years.

FOR THE SECOND TIME IN the last few days, Darcy was speechless in front of his cousin. Bingley had respected their privacy and remained in the drawing room with Jane and Mrs. Hurst, unsuccessfully attempting to appear calm as he answered their questions about Lady Cassandra's improvement.

Darcy poured a glass of brandy for his cousin. "David, I truly do not know what to say. I feel I need to apologise for Cassandra's reaction —"

"That is ridiculous, Darcy. You have nothing to do with this. Besides, there is no need to feel pity or embarrassment for me; I am quite fine. I am more worried — and deeply ashamed — for what Miss Bennet and Georgiana might believe of me. I am afraid they might believe I took advantage of Cassandra to...you know."

"It was a shock for them, there is no doubt about that, and I really do not know how we could clarify things. This is not something I can openly discuss with them, especially with Georgiana."

"Of course, you cannot discuss the matter with your intended or with your sister; I would not expect that of you. You have been more indulgent than one could hope. I must apologise for placing you in such a delicate position."

"David, you know Cassandra is as dear to me as a sister. If I knew about...that delicate situation before it actually happened, I would have done everything to prevent it as long as you two did not have an understanding of any kind. However, it did happen, and I trust you did not take advantage of Cassandra in any way. So there is little for me to do except be indulgent and accept your current disagreement, hoping for a happy outcome."

"I do appreciate your concern. However, my friend, you may say I am being presumptuous, and I might sound stupid, but I am more hopeful than I have ever been in the last few months."

Darcy's surprise made the colonel laugh while emptying his glass.

"I never expected Cassandra to waken and a minute later accept my hand. I am a reasonable man and know her too well. But now I know her feelings — better than she does. She called for *me*, not her late husband, not you or Georgiana, not even her parents — only me. Am I mistaken in assuming so much? Perhaps, but I will continue to do so until I am proved wrong. Yet, I will not persist in my pursuit; I decided that even before her accident. As soon as she is completely recovered and out of any danger, I will allow her time to explore her own heart and find the answers she still seeks. I am in no hurry; I can wait. Now I know that only her mind forbade her from being happy again. Her heart has betrayed her reason, and I was there to witness it. She does care deeply for me, Darcy. I can wait."

David Fitzwilliam was not asking for advice nor did he seek approval; he was only stating his feelings and his decision, and no answers were required. Darcy — remembering how his previous advice almost ruined Bingley's life — did not dream of offering even one piece of wisdom. His cousin knew better in matters of the heart; that had been a universally acknowledged truth their entire lives.

THE ONE MOST AFFECTED BY the recent revelation was Mr. Bingley. As the master of the house, burdened by his responsibilities and torn between his loyalty for Cassandra and his friendship with the colonel, he could not decide whose side he should take. Moreover, he struggled to understand when they did *that thing* Lady Cassandra talked about. Thank God Caroline was not there! And thank God dear Jane did not know the particulars of the affair, or she would have been excessively distressed herself! It was indeed a most trying time for Charles Bingley.

The Gardiners called, together with Mr. Bennet, and they were invited to stay for dinner. Elizabeth embraced her father, and a truce was settled between them. Mr. Bennet did not lose the opportunity to inquire whether she remained determined to betray him to Mrs. Bennet and was pleased to hear his daughter laugh and assure him she would forgive him just this once. Furthermore, Mr. Bennet declared that the stress he had been through during the last several days greatly affected his health, and he would need some days of complete solitude, preferably in Pemberley's library! Mr. Darcy seemed disconcerted for a moment, and then hastily assured his soon-to-be father-in-law that he would be most welcome in any of their houses whenever he pleased. Mr. Bennet was content.

The colonel was not his usually jovial self, nor did he appear to be in exceptionally low spirits. He spoke little, mostly with the Gardiners and Mr. Bennet, some with Georgiana and a few words with Elizabeth. After all that happened, Elizabeth felt more concern for him than anger, so she concluded that a smile and support would be more helpful than acrimony. Any punishment he might deserve for being arrogant and selfish in the matter of the duel, he would surely receive — in double measure — from Cassandra.

The gentlemen's separation after dinner was as brief as possible, and Darcy wasted not a moment in securing a seat near Elizabeth when he returned.

"You seem very quiet tonight, Miss Elizabeth," he said politely.

Her eyebrow rose as her lips narrowed in a smile.

"I depend on you, sir, to find an interesting subject of conversation so I will be quiet no longer."

"You seem preoccupied," he whispered, his voice turning serious.

"Oh, do not worry; 'tis nothing. I was merely thinking of Cassandra and Georgiana. The poor dear looked exhausted, and I insisted she should retire soon. The colonel, however, seems...well enough; he appears to bear the situation quite calmly," she said. Her hidden reproach did not go unnoticed.

"Elizabeth, please do not judge David from his appearance. His affection is sincere, and his feelings are as strong and honest as are his intentions. Unfortunately, the circumstances are uncommon."

Darcy was obviously struggling to imply more than he was saying, and Elizabeth, though curious and somewhat annoyed by his secrecy, made no further inquiries.

"You must be correct as you know your cousin much better than I, and I am certain you would never allow him to hurt Cassandra. I do hope she is feeling better."

"The doctor said she was. She merely requires rest, as do you and Georgiana! You both should retire early; I am sure your aunt will understand. Miss Jane and Mrs. Hurst can keep her company."

"Yes, I will; however, I intend to visit Cassandra before going to bed," she said, casting a quick glance at him. The memory of her previous night's visit in his room and the mere mention of the word "bed" brought a fierce blush to her cheeks. She averted her eyes from his, mortified and furious with herself for such a reaction.

"I am sure Cassandra will be pleased to see you. Mr. Gardiner and Mr. Bennet intend to stay longer, and I will join them; so I suppose I will retire quite late as we have business to discuss — real business," Darcy said, after a moment of hesitation.

She finally raised her eyes to his and struggled to smile as she replied teasingly, "Oh, I sincerely hope you are not planning another duel so soon."

He returned her smile and, hoping no one would notice his gesture, brushed his fingers against her hand. "You find great enjoyment in teasing me quite cruelly, Miss Elizabeth Bennet."

"I confess I do, sir."

They continued in the same manner, smiling and teasing one another on a variety of subjects; yet, their intense looks were speaking of what mattered most and words dared not express. There would be no chance for them to meet privately that evening. Their mutual regret was easily read in each other's eyes, even more so as they were unlikely to have other intimate moments until their wedding. With Cassandra's improving condition, Elizabeth and Jane planned to return to Longbourn the next day.

Perhaps it was best; their nightly interludes had become increasingly perilous for their reputations — in every possible respect.

Mrs. Gardiner insisted that Elizabeth and Georgiana retire for the night very early, and they eventually obeyed.

In a room full of people, Darcy said a polite "good night," bowing to Elizabeth, without even touching her hand. His tender gaze lingered only a few moments upon her face, but Elizabeth could feel his eyes burning her cheeks and lips. Flustered and mortified, she hurried from the room.

She needed to rest — immediately — before she made a complete and irremediable fool of herself.

An hour later, prepared for sleep and dressed in her nightgown with her hair about her shoulders, Elizabeth entered Cassandra's chamber. Mrs. Spencer was seated in an armchair close to the bed. Cassandra seemed asleep, but the moment Elizabeth entered, she called her name.

"Elizabeth, how nice of you to come and see me."

"I do not want to disturb you. I only wished to see that you are well."

"I am well, thank you. You are too kind to worry for me so much, kinder than I deserve…" Before Elizabeth could contradict her, she continued shyly, "Elizabeth, how is Georgiana? Is she still upset?"

"She is upset, indeed; but it will pass soon, I am certain of that."

"Are *you* upset with me, too, Elizabeth? I thought you might not come to visit me again, after…" Cassandra's voice sounded weak and hesitant, as if dreading the answer.

"I am not upset; I am only concerned for you. How could you think I would not come to see you?"

"I wonder what you must think of me…of my scandalous behaviour. I dare not ask how your opinion of me has changed."

"Cassandra, my opinion has changed but not in the way you think."

Elizabeth set near her and held her hand. "I have come to like you more with every day spent in your company, which is why I understood Georgiana's anger when you said you would have rather died. That was cruel, unfair and so untrue! But I also understood your pain. I did not forget that, less than a fortnight ago on a horrible night, I said the same thing, and you were there to comfort me."

"I know I have been unfair. I hurt Georgiana so much! And David…it is true that he proposed to me and I refused him and then…it was not his fault, but mine! It was I who invited him to my bedchamber! But you must believe me, Elizabeth. I am not a wanton woman; I am not in the habit of —"

"Cassandra, please stop! There is no need to distress yourself or explain anything to me —"

"But I want to explain it to you! I do want you to understand, and then I beg you to help Georgiana to understand, too. I would never dare speak to her directly about such a scandalous subject; I simply cannot. Will you allow me to burden you with a dreadful story, a story I kept the deepest secret for more than four years? I know I am horribly selfish in exposing you to such a confession, but I cannot bear it alone any longer. I need a friend to help me carry it, to understand my fears and my nightmares. Because Georgiana was correct: I am so frightened, Elizabeth — so very frightened!"

Elizabeth forgot to breathe at such an extraordinary outburst.

"Cassandra, I will listen to anything you want to share with me. Just let me know in what way I can possibly help you, and I will not hesitate to do it."

An hour passed with only the sound of Cassandra's quiet voice, weary and drained of emotion, as her eyes, weak from tears, stared persistently at Elizabeth. When she completed her story, Elizabeth had to remember to breathe again. She looked at Cassandra with wide eyes, afraid to believe what she had just heard and helpless in the face of her friend's grief.

"I do not know what to say," she whispered, after a long silence.

"I do not need an answer — only understanding," Cassandra replied. "I hope you understand why I have not the courage to allow myself to suffer again."

"Is William familiar with this story?"

"Yes. He and Mrs. Spencer are the only ones who met my husband and participated in the tragic events that followed."

"And the colonel?"

"I told David the day after...you know. I invited him to my room — did I tell you that? I behaved so scandalously, so selfishly! I had already refused him a month ago in London and then, when I felt lonely and frightened, I asked him to keep me company. Afterwards, he insisted we should marry, and I persisted in refusing him, so he became angry. He seemed so affected, so hurt...and I could not bear for him to believe I was only toying with him, that I was a shameless woman...so I told him."

Elizabeth began pacing the room; she walked to the window, returned to Cassandra's bed, and then stopped to stare through the window again. Finally, she resumed her place.

"Cassandra, I would not presume to advise you in any way — I do not consider myself wise enough to do so. I just...your story is astonishing — *you* are astonishing for enduring so much grief, so much pain all these years and still remaining such a spirited, lively woman."

Cassandra laughed nervously. "Yes, it is a wonder I did not lose my sanity."

"Cassandra, mock your pain if you like, but I am sure you understand my meaning. Will you allow me to speak openly — to dare ask you a question?"

"Yes, by all means. Please ask me anything; there is nothing I would conceal from you. I truly do not have other secrets, which is quite fortunate, is it not?"

Cassandra continued to speak in jest about herself, but Elizabeth did not join her.

"I understand now why you were so affected by the duel, and why you were so angry with William and the colonel. In truth, I am growing angrier myself! But you seemed to be confident in the colonel's affection, and your words betrayed your own feelings for him. From what you have said, he cannot be blamed for what happened in the past. So why would you reject him?"

"Why reject him? But Elizabeth, I thought you understood! How can you ask such a question?"

Cassandra seemed shocked and incredulous that Elizabeth was unable to see her reasoning, yet Elizabeth, who managed to regain some of her usual spirit, did not allow herself to be intimidated.

"Yes, why? I beg your forgiveness if I upset you, but I see no motive. I imagine the memory of your husband is vivid, but he is not here and will never be again. It is not as if you were betraying him."

Cassandra startled and paled but did not reply.

Elizabeth gently took Cassandra's hand and caressed her hair as she often did with her little cousins. "Cassandra, I would not dare pretend to understand your pain and despair in losing the man you loved. But I sense that you are not afraid of suffering; it is being *happy* again that frightens you."

Elizabeth's dark eyes sparkling with determination and affectionate support met Cassandra's green ones: fearful, empty and almost lifeless. Then, a whisper broke the silence of the chamber.

"Elizabeth, I do not even know if what I feel for David is real affection. He is so different from Thomas, and what I feel for David is so different from what I felt for Thomas."

"Cassandra, I am no expert in this. I have never fancied myself in love with any other man except William, but I imagine it is not possible to experience the same kind of affection for two different people. I mean, even with my own sisters... I do love all of them, I care for them deeply but in different ways. And look at Jane and myself; I am certain she loves Mr. Bingley very much, but she behaves so differently from me. Of course, she is more proper!"

Cassandra laughed — a small, tearful laugh — and Elizabeth joined her.

"Yes, I suppose you are correct."

"Then what is it? Do you doubt the nature of the colonel's interest in you or yours for him? Do you think you might only be interested in... each other's temporary company?" Elizabeth asked daringly, mortified that she had the courage to address such a question.

Cassandra was obviously surprised and slightly embarrassed, but she did not avoid the question.

"Elizabeth Bennet, you are a bright young woman, despite your lack of experience," she replied, attempting a teasing smile. "I confess I did suspect that of David — at least in the beginning as I knew his disposition for flirting. I also accused him of a mercenary interest when I refused him."

"I watched the colonel for almost a week, nursing you and suffering for you, and though I am still very angry with him for his involvement in the duel, I can testify to the depth of his affection for you."

"Oh, I do believe you, Elizabeth. I no longer doubt his feelings —"

"But what about your feelings — your interest in David? I might upset you again, but I saw you with him while you were unconscious, and I can testify to your feelings as well."

"I... Except for my husband, I never... It was only David who... I will not deny I enjoy his presence, his closeness, and I am sure you understand my meaning. But how could I marry him when we argue all the time? I am glad to see him, and I confess I did miss him when he was away. And I do think of him often, but I also disagree with him in so many ways! And he is so stubborn, so inconsiderate sometimes — as happened when he supported Darcy's decision about the duel! How could I marry such a man? We would both be miserable. He deserves a more docile woman, a woman without a past like mine, a woman who will never compare him to another man. Do you not agree?"

Elizabeth smiled and squeezed Cassandra's hand. "In this I do have some advice as I have vast experience in fighting the man I love and will shortly marry! In truth, I am in the position of marrying the *last man in the world* I thought I would ever marry! Can you believe that?"

They laughed again, a liberating laugh that seemed to bring them back to life.

"Cassandra, as for what kind of woman the colonel deserves — well, you already said you two argue all the time, so you would likely argue in this, too. He seems to be convinced you are the woman he desires. Fortunately, there is time to give everything proper consideration. We may speak of this again soon when your health is completely restored. You have had enough torment for the first day of your recovery and must not distress yourself further, nor must you make a decision this moment. I doubt the colonel will return tomorrow morning with a renewal of his proposal."

"I doubt he will ever renew his proposal, especial after my outburst earlier this morning."

"Oh, I said that, too, a few months ago and was proved utterly wrong." Elizabeth smiled.

"Things were different with you and Darcy."

"Indeed they were, and I admit your situation is more difficult. However, as long as there is a chance of happiness, I am certain you will not let it vanish forever."

"But, Elizabeth…am I allowed to think of happiness when Thomas and our child are dead?"

Suddenly, Elizabeth felt her hand trembling. How could she answer such a question?

"Cassandra, I think… I think you should cherish the memory of your husband and child forever, but since God offered you the gift of love a second time, I believe you are not allowed to waste it."

ELIZABETH WALKED THROUGH THE MAIN hall to her room, barely conscious of her own steps. Everything she had imagined, everything she had speculated in the last weeks was nothing compared to this extraordinary revelation. And the fact that Cassandra had actually asked for her advice, guidance and support was a responsibility almost too heavy to bear.

She stopped to rest against the wall before reaching her door and almost screamed when she noticed a shadow approaching and felt two strong hands imprisoning her shoulders.

"Elizabeth, what are you doing here? What happened? You look very ill!" Darcy's voice reverberated strongly in her ears, and she was certain the entire house had heard him, but she did not care. She encircled his waist and nestled herself to his chest, her head leaning against his heart.

He lifted her in his arms, carried her inside her chamber, and gently placed her on the bed. "Elizabeth, what is the matter, my love?"

"Nothing is the matter," she replied, raising her eyes to meet his. "Now that I see you, everything is fine. It is just that I spoke to Cassandra. She told me the entire story... I am so grieved for her."

"I know, my dearest," he whispered and leaned by her side to embrace her. She cuddled in the comfort of his arms and closed her eyes, melting in the warmth of his embrace.

"And I am so angry with you," she continued in a severe tone, though she remained in his embrace.

Elizabeth, forgive me for keeping the secret from you, but I simply could not speak of something so intimate, so painful and so very personal for Cassandra. It was not my secret to share —"

"I do understand that you could not betray Cassandra's confidence! I would never expect you to dare reveal such a tale without Cassandra's consent. That is not why I am angry."

"Then it must be Cassandra's confession...that she and David... It is true that David told me about the incident, but I could not find a way to discuss it with you."

"Oh, you must be the least perceptive man in the world! Or perhaps all men are alike, but I did not know until now." She looked even angrier and Darcy was at a loss to understand why.

"Then why are you so displeased with me? I do not know myself guilty of any other charge."

"Why?! You knew what kind of people the Markhams were! You knew the eldest had no scruple to murder Cassandra's husband in the most dishonourable manner, and the younger was likely there to witness it! And you exposed yourself to such danger, risking your life for a stupid confrontation."

"So *that* is the reason. Elizabeth, trust me; I was in no danger! I was not alone; David and other witnesses were present. David would shoot Markham instantly if he attempted anything."

"Oh, what a relief, and what a consolation it would be for me to know Markham was dead were he to hurt you! Are all men so unreasonable, or is this just a trait on the Fitzwilliam side of your family?"

She seemed sincerely angry, and Darcy struggled not to laugh. He simply could not understand her worry or her furious delayed reaction. After all, everything ended well, did it not? Elizabeth, usually possessed of a strong understanding, was simply being unreasonable. She could not understand what duty and honour require from a man! But then again — it was expected for a woman not to understand! That was why such things were always a gentleman's business.

He replied with an open smile, caressing the long hair entwined about her shoulders. "It is a Fitzwilliam family trait...but other men are even worse, so you must be content with having me."

He expected her to laugh, but she narrowed her eyes in obvious exasperation, laid herself against the pillows once more, and turned her back to him in an attempt to dismiss him.

For some time only Elizabeth's steady breath could be heard in the room, and Darcy was certain she was finally sleeping. *"My dearest, loveliest Elizabeth,"* he whispered and, with a last kiss on her temple, attempted to rise and return to his room.

Elizabeth's soft voice startled him, and to his surprise, she turned toward him and their eyes met.

"William, if anything should ever happen to you…I will never be able to love anyone else ever again. My heart is so full of you that there would never be room for anyone else."

He frowned, unable to take his eyes from her, unable to speak, unable to breathe. He knelt near her bed and took her hand, gently taking it to his lips.

"Nothing will happen to me, as long as it is in my power."

"Will you promise me that? Will you promise you will protect not only me, but yourself as well?"

"I promise."

Elizabeth moved to the edge of the bed to reach his face and cupped it, and then her own lips met his in a gentle, lingering kiss. There was no passion in it, only tenderness, love and a promise for their future life — and their future happiness.

ELIZABETH WAS AT LAST IN the soft comfort of her own chamber at Longbourn. She felt as though she had been absent for a year, when only ten days had passed since Cassandra's accident.

She had departed Netherfield with a warm farewell from both Cassandra and Georgiana. Elizabeth was pleased to discover that Cassandra had gained enough strength and courage to speak to Georgiana personally and explain everything to her. The details and extent of their conversation remained their secret, and Elizabeth did not attempt to inquire further. What mattered to Elizabeth was that Georgiana — despite her shock at discovering Cassandra's past — appeared to be as loving as ever toward Cassandra and inclined to accept her decisions.

Mr. Darcy and Mr. Bingley accompanied them to Longbourn. Elizabeth felt equal parts pride and gratitude for her betrothed's skill in talking to Mrs. Bennet and accepting her effusions of motherly love and deep admiration for everything Darcy said or did. Elizabeth's eyes kept turning to Darcy, seeking his own — which were constantly cast toward her. When they met at the coffee table or sat near each other, their fingers brushed briefly as their smiles spoke wordlessly to each other. They were scarcely aware of Mr. Bennet's amusement, Mrs. Bennet's inquiries about the season in London, or Kitty and Mary's shy attempts to enter the conversation.

"Lizzy why are you so flushed?" asked Mrs. Bennet with obvious concern, and Elizabeth felt her face and neck burn even more. "You must take care of yourself, child. It would not do for you to fall ill before your wedding!" Then she suddenly stopped and turned to her soon-to-be son-in-law.

"Mr. Darcy, you must not worry; Elizabeth has a strong constitution. I am sure she is not ill at all. It is just that she is very careless; she is always walking out among the fields. Oh, no, I did not mean to say careless! She is a very good girl, and I am sure you will be pleased with her. I will talk to her; you must not worry."

Mrs. Bennet grew more distressed and agitated; Darcy tried to hide a smile as he answered politely. "Mrs. Bennet, *'pleased'* is a word that does not do justice to Miss Elizabeth. I confess I am indeed honoured that she agreed to be my wife."

"Oh, Mr. Darcy, you are a true gentleman! I cannot tell you how happy I am that you decided to marry Lizzy, though you did not want to dance with her in the beginning! And thank God she accepted you, as she was very angry with you, and she had already refused poor Mr. Collins —"

She stopped again, struck by her own words, covering her open mouth with her hands and looking desperately for her husband's support. Mr. Bennet did nothing but smile, watching each of them with mocking interest. He was pleased to see his future son-in-law hiding a grin rather than being offended. Clearly, Darcy had undergone a vast improvement in temper since last autumn. Elizabeth, however, seemed in low spirits, and Mr. Bennet wondered with even greater amusement whether his daughter had exchanged her usual playfulness for her betrothed's formerly bad humour.

After a long moment, Mrs. Bennet moved to pour herself another cup of tea, and Mr. Bennet took pity on all involved in the silly conversation, inviting the gentlemen to the library for a drink.

A MOMENT AFTER THE GENTLEMEN's departure, Elizabeth claimed a sudden headache and expressed her wish for some fresh air. Before Mrs. Bennet could stop her, she grabbed her pelisse and bonnet, and escaped to the rear garden, greedily inhaling the cold breeze of the autumn evening.

She gazed at the stars for a while, breathing deeply to calm herself. As much as she loved her mother, Elizabeth could not think without anger of her complete lack of decorum and constant insensitive and improper remarks; her behaviour continued to be as distressing as it was at the Netherfield Ball almost a year earlier.

Fortunately, both Mr. Bingley and especially Mr. Darcy had improved significantly in their humour and tolerance. Elizabeth thought with tender gratitude of her betrothed's civility in handling Mrs. Bennet and ignoring all the liberties in her long and unrestrained praise of her favourite son-in-law!

"May I share this beautiful evening with you?" Darcy's soft voice startled Elizabeth, and she turned to meet his adoring gaze caressing her face. He stepped closer and took her hand.

"Are you trying to hide in the night? You should know by now there is no escape from me."

"And you should know by now that I have no intention of escaping you, Mr. Darcy," she replied with a sweet smile. Darcy was certain that no star ever shimmered as brightly as her eyes. "How did you know I was here?"

"I saw you from the library window and asked your father's permission to join you."

"Gazing from windows is one of your more interesting habits, sir." She smiled teasingly and took his arm as she started to walk along the lane.

"So you are pleased with at least one of my habits?" he teased her back.

"I am sure I will be pleased with many of your habits once I become accustomed to them, sir."

"I hope so. But I would be more than willing to change those habits of which you do not approve." He was speaking in jest, but she could sense the promise behind his words. His palm covered her hand and their fingers entwined; she leaned against him, their bodies touching as they walked.

"This evening was quite difficult to bear, was it not?" she inquired shyly a few minutes later.

"What do you mean by *difficult*? Did anything happen?"

"No, nothing happened... I mean... I know my mother can be very insistent sometimes. I imagine how tiresome it must be for you, all those —"

"Please believe me when I say there is nothing 'tiresome' for me about anyone in your family although I *am* a little bothered at constantly being compared to Mr. Collins. Are there many similarities between us?"

Elizabeth frowned for a moment; then she began to laugh loudly.

"No sir, not so many — except the fact that both of you are closely acquainted with Lady Catherine de Bourgh."

Heedless that, despite the darkness, they were in full view of the house, she rose onto her toes and kissed him passionately. Darcy seemed to resist for a moment, then he surrendered with equal fervour.

After a time, determined to maintain a modicum of control, he gently broke the embrace.

"We should return; it has turned quite cold."

"I rather enjoy the freshness of the cold air...especially if you are here to keep me warm."

"Still, we should return, and you should prepare to retire shortly. You have had such a difficult time lately that I wonder whether you slept one entire night through in the last fortnight."

"I am exhausted," she admitted. "But you are wrong — I did sleep a few nights, quite soundly and restfully; you must remember that," she added blushing, with a quick playful glance.

"I do remember, but it was not enough. You must promise me you will try to rest as much as you can; in the meantime, I will call on you every day but will retire early."

"I shall rest as much as possible. However, I am not sure if I will succeed as I have been quite spoiled of late and discovered I sleep much better when I am being held," she answered boldly. "So, if I am unable to keep my promise, I am sure I shall recover all the sleep I have lost after we marry."

Elizabeth could hardly believe she was flirting with him so shamelessly.

"Miss Bennet," he replied as he opened the door for her, "I strongly advise you not to depend upon that too much. I will do everything in my power to hold you in my arms every night — but I cannot guarantee anything regarding *sleep*. That is why I must insist and advise you to be perfectly rested *before* our wedding."

When they entered the drawing room, Elizabeth was still flustered, and her hands were trembling; she was the one who had started the teasing and flirting, but she could not believe he replied in such a manner, mere feet from her family. Of course, nobody heard them, but still…

A few minutes passed, and everyone in the room was enjoying animated conversation — except Elizabeth. She knew she must look a sight with her reddened cheeks, staring at her hands and casting repeated glances at Darcy who was speaking with her father — but what else could she do? How could she possibly carry on an intelligent conversation when all she could think of was the picture of them, intimately embraced in an enormous bed, his strong arms holding her tightly — and not sleeping at all?!

As soon as the Miss Bennets together with Darcy and Bingley left, Netherfield's inhabitants parted. Miss Bingley retired to her room with only a cold excuse to Georgiana and the colonel, and Mrs. Hurst followed her.

"They do not seem very pleased to have us here," Georgiana whispered. "Now that William is engaged, Miss Bingley does not seem as friendly as she used to be." The colonel laughed.

"I am pleased to see you are not affected by their incivility, dearest. You have changed," he said affectionately.

"If I have, I certainly hope you are not displeased with the change."

"No indeed — quite the contrary. I am happy to see you so much more confident and daring."

"I do feel I am somehow changed. I think it is the benefit of Elizabeth's presence — and Cassandra's."

"Just be careful to behave in the presence of Lady Catherine. She might not approve of these changes."

"Oh dear, did any of you announce the news of William's engagement to Lady Catherine?"

"Not exactly. Darcy only informed my parents when we were in London."

"I see. Were they displeased with the news?"

"Well, I will not deny that my parents were surprised and not entirely happy with the news. You must know by now that they had some expectations for Darcy's choice of wife — as for mine."

"Yes, I do know. I hope and pray my Aunt will come to like Elizabeth very soon."

"I am sure she will; Miss Elizabeth is the perfect choice for Darcy, and my mother will see that."

"I know Aunt is very fond of Cassandra," Georgiana said meaningfully.

"Dearest, let us focus on Darcy's betrothed, shall we?"

"I spoke to Cassandra early this morning, David. She told me everything."

He blinked in obvious surprise, and to Georgiana's shock, she saw him blushing for the first time in her memory. "I am sorry — I truly am. But at least now you are able to understand things better."

"I do. I understand why she refused you, but I also understand that she needs you."

"It is for her to decide what she needs and desires. Let us not insist upon this subject, dearest," the colonel concluded gently but decidedly.

Georgiana averted her eyes and whispered, "She might be with child after...*you know.*"

The colonel stared at her in shock and then hurried to pour himself a glass of wine. "Georgiana, I will not have such a conversation with my little cousin! Let us change the topic, shall we?"

"Of course."

They remained in the music room for another hour, Georgiana at the pianoforte and the colonel turning pages for her; however, the tension of their unfinished conversation endured.

It was late afternoon when they were interrupted by Mrs. Spencer's entrance; she approached and handed the colonel a folded sheet of paper, which he took with a puzzled expression.

A quick look at the page was enough to startle him and make him move toward the window, leaving an intrigued Georgiana staring at him from the instrument.

Twice he read the short note — less than half a page long — and then finally met Georgiana's eyes.

"It is a note from Cassandra. She wishes to speak to me."

"I will remain here to practice a little more. Please tell Cassandra I shall see her later."

With hesitant fingers, Georgiana searched through the music sheets but was unable to find anything to her liking. When the door closed behind the colonel, she put all the music down and remained still, lost in her thoughts, unable to decide what she should do next.

DAVID HAD BARELY KNOCKED WHEN the door opened and Mrs. Spencer invited him in.

"David," said Cassandra with a gentle, pleading voice, "thank you for coming."

"I...you said you wished to speak to me. Are you well?"

"I am perfectly well, thank you. Please take a seat close to me. I cannot see you from here." Her voice was so soft that David hesitated before obliging her. Something must be wrong, he thought.

"Are you sure you are feeling well? You do look much better."

"Indeed, I am much better. I only wish to apologise for my unfair and cruel outburst yesterday and to thank you for your care and devotion. Allow me to express my gratitude for —"

"Cassandra, please stop this. No gratitude is needed. I accept your apologies, though most of your reproaches were deserved; I should not have stayed in your room without your consent."

"You were here only to help me."

"No, I was here for a selfish reason; I could not bear from afar the worry and uncertainty of knowing you were unconscious. That is the truth, and I deserve your anger. I should have respected your privacy."

"I thank you nevertheless. And you are right," she admitted, "I would be uncomfortable with anyone seeing me in such a state. I can only imagine how horrible I must have appeared."

"I truly hope you are speaking in jest, Cassandra. Do you believe that any of us spent time considering your appearance?" He was puzzled and obviously displeased with her assumption.

"Surely you understand what I mean, David."

"I most assuredly do not. Am I to presume that appearance is more important to you than health or life itself?"

She startled and stared at him, turning even more pale. "I do not deserve that."

He frowned and, not knowing what to do with his hands, brought his fists together.

"No, you do not deserve that...forgive me. Is there anything else you want to discuss, or should I let you rest now before I manage to ruin your spirits completely?"

"I was wondering..." He waited for her to continue — hopeful and fearful at the same time — but she remained silent. She appeared distressed and inhibited as never before.

"Cassandra, what is the matter?"

"You did nothing to stop the duel," she suddenly burst out furiously. "After everything I told you, it was still not enough for you to consider it."

"I am well aware that both you and Miss Bennet are angry with me for this incident. I do not wish to argue with you, nor do I want to distress you. I am only being honest. Nothing will change my opinion that Darcy behaved as any honourable man should in his situation. Of course I supported him."

"He — or you — could have been hurt, maybe murdered."

"No, indeed. We knew Markham to be a cowardly man, so we were prepared to confront him."

Cassandra remained angry and pale, and could no longer tolerate his gaze. She averted her eyes and turned to the fire in an attempt to dismiss him.

"Cassandra, I told you some time ago that it is a gentleman's duty to protect those he loves; that is simply how it is. No matter what occurs in the future — if you never speak to me again — I will still watch over you and do everything in my power to protect you."

Their eyes locked again and battled silently for a time — David, immovable in his determination, Cassandra, pale and powerless, lying against the pillows, biting her lower lip to conceal her turmoil.

"You are right; I should rest now. I am very tired," she finally said.

He rose to obey but barely took a few steps before she called his name. He stopped.

"David, thank you for your care."

He nodded, walked further, and then stopped again, looking down at her. To her surprise, he sat close to her bed.

"Cassandra, may I speak honestly? I do not wish to distress you even more, so please tell me if I should leave."

"We have always spoken honestly to each other, so please do," she whispered.

"Very well, then. I understand you must be uncomfortable with my presence here. However, I must stay for Darcy's wedding; I promised him as much."

"Please do not consider leaving because of me. You have more right to be here than I. You are Darcy's cousin."

"And you are his lifelong friend. He surely needs you as much. However, it is not a matter of rights. For me, your wishes are more important, so I would like you to put aside our differences and tell me what you want me to do." She turned her eyes to the fire, and then returned her gaze to him.

"I cannot offer you an answer now —"

"No, no, you misunderstand me! I am not insisting upon that subject any longer. In fact, that is precisely what I wanted to speak to you about: my insistence. I know everything happened unexpectedly — my confession, my proposal and everything that occurred afterwards — and now your accident. I have considered only my feelings and desires, but that will change from now on."

He paused a moment. His eyes still looked into hers, carefully searching her astonished expression.

"I shall not insist upon this matter any further. My feelings and wishes are not a secret to you, and they will never change. As for your own feelings — you must determine them. It is your decision whether I ever raise the subject between us again. I will not require an immediate answer; your health is all that matters for the moment. I can wait as long as necessary! Unless you tell me there is nothing to wait for…"

David looked at Cassandra hesitantly, fearing another harsh reply. She had told him frequently not to hope or wait. She would likely repeat her declaration — and then how would he dare continue?

"Thank you for your patience. I promise I shall give you an answer as soon as I am certain of one."

He was shocked in a pleasant way; his burning stare was the evidence. For a few moments, he could not find the words to respond. Her forced smile seemed finally to break his silence.

"Good…" was all he said and she smiled. He rose halfway and then sat again. She laughed lightly.

He seemed disconcerted for a moment and then smiled back at her. "Cassandra, I…I shall leave you now; you must rest. Georgiana said she would visit you later."

"Very well…"

He rose and hurried to the door; from there, he turned to look at her once more — and was gone.

Cassandra's eyes remained fixed on the door; she did not notice the tears coursing over her cheeks.

CAROLINE BINGLEY DID NOT LEAVE her room that morning. She was in the worst mood ever and could not abide the happy faces around her. Fortunately, Jane and Eliza Bennet had left the house the previous day. She could not tolerate them any longer! As for Lady Cassandra — although Caroline was not pleased to see her hurt, she was indeed relieved that she was confined to her room and would likely remain so until the wedding. What a torture to have Lady Cassandra around the house day after day!

On her little desk were spread the letters she had received from her friends, Miss Cardington and Lady Sophia. She finished her own missive to the latter and looked at it with great satisfaction. Yes, that was the best solution: she would accompany Lady Sophia on her tour! There was no better way to put behind her everything that had happened than an extended tour with a well-known member of the *ton*. There would certainly be many opportunities to meet desirable and worthy gentlemen — to be sure!

She had not said anything to Charles and did not plan to tell him yet. He did not deserve that much consideration after he had supported Eliza Bennet against his own sister!

MR. BENNET WAS CONTENT AT last! Following weeks of difficulties — the frightening incidents with his beloved Lizzy and later with Lady Cassandra, and day after day of complaints and cries from his wife — he was relaxing in the perfect solitude of his library with one of his favourite books.

Mrs. Bennet — together with Mary and Kitty — was calling on Lady Lucas, while Elizabeth and Jane were visiting at Netherfield. Mr. Bennet smiled to himself, feeling gratitude and affection. His elder daughters had been indeed fortunate in their choice of husbands. He knew for certain they would both be happy — though in different ways. Yes, Mr. Bennet was enormously content.

As he read, enjoying his favourite port, he could not but wonder at how blissful silence was. The day was perfect. Unfortunately, as with other happy moments in the past, the silence was short-lived. Less than two hours later, thunder fell upon the house in the form of an annoying, female voice. It took Mr. Bennet only an instant to determine that it was not his wife; Mrs. Bennet's tone — though frequently loud and tiresome — was ten times more agreeable, he thought.

He could hear "the voice" approaching and Hill's unsuccessful attempt to stop her with pleading requests to wait until she was announced to the master of the house.

"I shall not wait! Do not dare ask me to wait! I demand to speak with him this instant! Where is he?"

That was the last thing Mr. Bennet heard before his library door was unceremoniously thrown open, and a lady whose stature was as imposing as her voice barged in. She remained close to the door, peering around with unconcealed disdain and apparent concern for her own safety.

"I suppose you are Mr. Bennet! What a small, uncomfortable library you have here."

Mr. Bennet laid his book on the table and politely rose to greet his guest, a smile of satisfaction spreading over his face. What an incredible moment, worthy to be noted down and kept among the most treasured family mementos — close to Mr. Collins's memorable visit from last autumn. Yes, the day had enormous potential, and it would certainly prove more diverting than any book of farce.

"Yes, madam. I am Mr. Bennet and very honoured to receive your ladyship in my humble abode. Without any doubt, you must be Lady Catherine de Bourgh — the noble patroness of my cousin, Mr. Collins!"

"I am indeed, sir, but I have no time for civilities. I wish to speak to your daughter, Elizabeth."

"I am afraid that would be impossible, as none of my daughters is home at the moment. But may I take the liberty of asking your ladyship whether you left Mr. and Mrs. Collins in good health?"

"They were perfectly well."

"Does Mr. Collins still visit your ladyship daily? I understood the parsonage is quite close to Rosings."

"It is indeed, but that is not the purpose of my visit."

"Oh, I am sorry. May I ask the purpose of your visit, then?"

"To speak to your daughter. Where exactly is she?"

"I am afraid I have to inquire about the nature of your business with my daughter before answering further."

"Oh, you can be at no loss to understand the reason for my journey hither. A report of a most alarming nature reached me two days ago, and I came to insist that rumour be universally contradicted!"

"To what is your ladyship referring? I do not have the pleasure of understanding you."

"I am talking of the rumour that your daughter is engaged to my nephew! Though I know it must be a scandalous falsehood, I instantly resolved on setting off for this place, that I might make my sentiments known to you all."

"Lady Catherine, thank you for making your sentiments so well and clearly known, but I am still at a loss as to what I can do to help you. This rumour might be scandalous, but it is not at all a falsehood. The engagement was made public in front of a hundred people, and Mr. Darcy himself seemed unusually pleased with it."

"Of course he seemed pleased, as your daughter — with her arts and allurements — has made him forget his duty to his family! But I will tell you what you can do — what an honourable father should do — you should advise your daughter not to aspire to quit the sphere in which she has been brought up."

"Sphere? What sphere?" Mr. Bennet asked genuinely. In truth, he had not been so diverted in years.

"Your family's sphere!"

"I am afraid we do not have a sphere, Lady Catherine. Longbourn is nothing to Rosings, I know..."

Lady Catherine stared at him, her mouth gaping in shock.

"Mr. Bennet, you ought to know that I am not to be trifled with. Do you know who I am? I am Darcy's closest relative!"

"I do know that; you are also Mr. Collins's noble patroness, as I had the honour to be informed last autumn. I can see your ladyship is somehow displeased with my obtuseness, but I still do not understand how I may help you, as we now agree that we do not possess a sphere at Longbourn!"

"Mr. Bennet, I can see this marriage to be profitable for you all. You desire it because Mr. Collins will inherit the estate should your demise occur, and your wife and daughters will be homeless."

"Well, let us hope I survive a little longer."

"This marriage will never take place as Mr. Darcy is engaged to my daughter! What do you have to say now?"

"I am truly shocked, your ladyship! He is engaged to your daughter, too? When exactly did the event occur?"

"Their engagement is of a peculiar nature — it was the dearest wish of his mother and me since they were infants."

"Now I am truly puzzled, your ladyship. Mr. Darcy's engagement to my daughter is of a *common* nature, and it appeared to be *his* dearest wish — and hers. This seems a hopeless situation to me, and I see no satisfactory resolution to it. But let us sit and have some refreshments. Mr. Darcy will arrive soon as he spends most of his time here. That would be a good time to demand an explanation from him."

"I will certainly not stay and have refreshments with you, sir! I am most displeased with you, as I can see you are as unreasonable and inconsiderate as I remember your daughter to be last spring. But you must understand that I came here with the determined resolution of carrying out my purpose and will not be dissuaded from it."

"I am sorry to ask once more, but what is your purpose again? I am still not clear on that aspect —"

"I want this engagement to be broken and any understanding annulled! Are you clear now?"

"I am indeed. I thank you for your kind explanation. Should I call for those refreshments now? And perhaps a glass of wine? It does miracles for a lady's nerves; I can testify to that."

"I will leave this instant — and now I know what I have to do! Netherfield is close by, and once I find my nephew, I will make him see reason!"

"Netherfield is only three miles away, Lady Catherine. You may walk if you wish. It is a very pleasurable path, and your chances of meeting Mr. Darcy will increase, as he seems fond of walking lately."

"Walking? Preposterous!" she yelled as she exited the room like a whirlwind, unable to breathe from rage.

"Lady Catherine!" called Mr. Bennet with such a determination that she had to turn to him.

"Please send my best wishes to Mr. Collins when you see him."

Lady Catherine slammed the door so violently that the windows indeed trembled this time.

Mr. Bennet poured himself another glass of port and resumed his place in his favourite chair with his favourite book. He was suddenly almost content with his wife. He might have chosen much worse when he married — he could now see that clearly.

However, for only a ten-minute meeting, Lady Catherine was certainly the most amusing woman he had ever met — but only for ten minutes. *I pray Darcy inherited his character from his father's line.*

In her carriage, Lady Catherine could barely breathe. Rage was suffocating her, and her mind refused to accept what that ridiculous country gentleman had told her! Darcy could not be engaged to his daughter!

A few minutes later when the carriage stopped in front of Netherfield, she bounded from the vehicle and pushed the doorman away, demanding to be told where her nephew was. The poor man remained frozen in shock, not understanding who she was or who her nephew might be. When she repeated, "Where is Darcy?" a maid, who arrived in a hurry, managed to articulate that she had seen Mr. Darcy walking in the direction of the library.

Lady Catherine de Bourgh had no difficulty discovering the location of the library or in thrusting open its door until it pounded back against the wall. However, she had great difficulty in remaining on her feet when she observed her nephew, Mr. Darcy, intimately occupied with Miss Elizabeth Bennet. And it was clearly *his* own will — as well as *hers*.

Chapter 22

Lady Catherine had departed Netherfield hours earlier, but the effects of her visit were still evident.

The sight of her nephew embracing Miss Elizabeth Bennet had turned her ladyship quite wild, and the main recipient of her anger was *"that impertinent country nobody who uses her charms to defeat the respectability of honourable gentlemen."*

The preoccupied couple was utterly astonished by Lady Catherine's abrupt entrance — which neither of them noticed for a time — and could do nothing to interrupt the furious invective that followed.

Darcy attempted to greet his aunt politely and have a reasonable conversation; he even apologised for not informing her earlier of their engagement and expressed his wish that Lady Catherine would soon understand and accept his decision. At that, her storm of words continued with greater force against Elizabeth and Darcy.

Never in her life had Elizabeth been abused in such a way, and the offense she felt was even worse because of Darcy's presence. And never had she been more tempted to put aside any trace of civility in response to the attack. She cast a quick glance toward Darcy and saw his angry face darkening; instantly her hand slid into his and he entwined his fingers with hers. At that moment, she no longer cared about Lady Catherine's presence.

"You cannot possibly consider marrying this woman! Honour, decorum, prudence forbid it. She will never be noticed by your family or friends! She will be censured, slighted, and despised by everyone connected with you. Your alliance will be a disgrace; your name will never even be mentioned by any of us ever again! Do you not care about all that? What has she done to you to make you disrespect your mother's memory and wishes?"

"Lady Catherine, you will end this scandalous argument at once." Darcy's tone was icy and sharp. He took a step toward his aunt as though to protect Elizabeth from her abuse. "I shall not tolerate another word against Miss Bennet, so please allow me to accompany you to your carriage."

"To my carriage? I have no intention of leaving — I still have much to say about this subject."

"No, you have not! If it were not for our close family connection, this conversation would have been finished in a less civil way long ago. Come, Aunt, we have already exposed ourselves to ridicule with this scandalous debate. Let us maintain some slight appearance of civility!"

"Not so hasty, if you please. What about her sister's elopement with Wickham? Would you accept the son of your father's steward as your brother? Heaven and earth — of what are you thinking? Are the shades of Pemberley to be thus polluted? Has this woman's charms blinded you?"

"Lady Catherine!" he thundered, taking another step toward her.

"William?" Elizabeth's light voice fell like a summer breeze in the library and Darcy turned to her.

"If you have no objection to my family, Lady Catherine's opinion on this subject has no effect on me — so please do not allow her offensive words to affect you."

He looked at her, obviously surprised at her calm voice and cheery expression; her eyes sparkled with amusement, and he felt not only love but also admiration. "You are too kind and too wise. How could I object to your family when my own is so lacking in decorum?"

"I heard that, Darcy! Do not dare ignore me. I shall make my disapproval universally known in Town and —"

Elizabeth's lips twisted into a smile, ignoring her ladyship's presence as she continued speaking.

"Lady Catherine's obvious disapproval is a great misfortune indeed, and I am sure it will be painful to endure; however, I am also sure that, as your wife, I shall have such extraordinary sources of happiness that, upon the whole, I shall have no cause to repine."

Under Lady Catherine's shocked stare, Darcy lifted Elizabeth's hand and placed a soft kiss upon it.

"I shall leave you two now," Elizabeth continued. "Lady Catherine's situation seems quite pitiable at present, but unfortunately, I can offer no remedy for her distress, so I will beg you to excuse me."

She curtsied politely to Darcy and to a stone-faced, livid Lady Catherine and smiled sweetly to her.

"Lady Catherine, I hope we shall meet again soon. Please give my regards to the Collinses — in fact, I should write a letter to Charlotte. Would your ladyship be so kind as to deliver it?"

No coherent answer was forthcoming, and Elizabeth left the library with perfect composure, followed by Darcy's admiring gaze. In the hall, an entire gathering of servants apologised and disappeared instantly. Embarrassed, yet struggling to keep a light expression, Elizabeth was at least grateful that Jane and Mr. Bingley had not returned from their stroll, and Miss Bingley and the Hursts were still in their rooms. It was fortunate that only servants were present to witness Lady Catherine's openly expressed disapproval!

Elizabeth went directly to Cassandra's chamber, where she found Georgiana keeping her friend company; fortunately, it appeared the scandal had not reached that wing of the house.

"So — the old bat finally made her appearance. I wondered when this moment would come."

"Lady Catherine is here? Oh dear — that cannot be good," whispered Georgiana.

"Yes, she came to express her disapproval of my engagement to your brother."

"I imagine she was very displeased. I am so sorry, Elizabeth. Where is William? Does he know she is here?"

"William is in the library with Lady Catherine. And yes, she was displeased — more than displeased."

"Dearest Elizabeth." Georgiana took her hand and squeezed it warmly. "I can see you are distressed. Was it so bad? Did she offend you? I know sometimes my aunt can be very —"

Cassandra interrupted her. "I am sure she was more than displeased. She must have been as she always is: rude, impolite, inconsiderate and insufferable."

"There is no need to worry, Georgiana; I am perfectly able to handle Lady Catherine's displeasure." Then she turned to Cassandra with a meaningful look. "I see you know Lady Catherine very well."

"Indeed, I do. I first met her twenty years ago. As a small child, I was quite frightened by her, but by the time I was seven, she started to amuse me with her constant scolding of everyone and her pretensions of grandeur. I am sure you are amused, too, Elizabeth; you are too wise to allow yourself to be affected by Lady Catherine's reproaches."

"Well, I confess the entire situation was more embarrassing than amusing."

"But where did you meet Lady Catherine?" asked Georgiana.

"William and I were in the library when Lady Catherine entered."

Elizabeth's cheeks coloured slightly as she explained the situation, and Cassandra watched her with an amused twist of her lips. "I can only imagine what scandal Lady Catherine aroused. I wonder if there is a single servant left in the house who is not aware of her opinion. Did she happen to mention that Darcy must marry Anne?"

"She did."

"Poor Anne — her mother will never cease to expose her to ridicule with this hilarious nonsense. You know, when we were infants, *I* was the main recipient of Lady Catherine's anger, as she was certain I planned to steal Darcy from Anne and marry him myself. Of course, I was ten at the time, and though Darcy and I were inseparable, marriage was not among my priorities." Cassandra laughed.

"Cassandra, I truly do not understand how you can blithely dismiss all of this," said Georgiana. "It is very serious indeed. I wonder what Lady Catherine will do now."

"Come now, sweetie — I would say it is time to stop worrying about Lady Catherine. I feel pity for Anne; that is true. But otherwise, I am merely diverted by this woman who travels fifty miles to make a fool of herself and become the amusement and gossip of Meryton."

"Cassandra, I admit I am worried, too — not for me but for Georgiana and William. Lady Catherine insisted she will make her disapproval universally known in Town, and the rumours —"

"Elizabeth, Lady Catherine speaks a great deal, but fortunately, most people have the good sense to ignore her. As for her disapproval, the moment your engagement was made public, everybody acquainted with Lady Catherine must have guessed her disapproval; it will be no surprise to anyone."

"I surely hope so."

Their conversation was interrupted by the entrance of a troubled Darcy who almost ignored his sister and his friend and moved directly to Elizabeth. His countenance was still dark, and he avoided looking at Elizabeth. She rose from her seat and tried to meet his eyes.

"William? Is everything well? Where is Lady Catherine?" Georgiana inquired with no little distress.

"Lady Catherine has left. But no, everything is not well. Elizabeth, will you ever forgive me for what happened?"

He took her hand and held it while his apologising glance fixed on her face. Elizabeth smiled sweetly and, without considering the presence of the others, gently stroked his cheek.

"Surely you will not apologise for something that is not your fault, sir."

"It *is* my fault. I should not have allowed her to —"

"You know as well as I that nothing would have stopped Lady Catherine from expressing her opinion. Besides, I have a confession to make to you. There is something that makes me feel deeply ashamed of myself."

"What confession?" He sounded equally puzzled and worried.

"Last spring, when we were in Kent — when I first met Lady Catherine — I thought I saw a resemblance between you and your aunt." Her voice tried to be light and teasing, but she could not hide her embarrassment. "It was a time during which I had grossly misjudged many things...and many people," she whispered.

"Do not worry; you were not wrong." Cassandra's gleeful voice interrupted Elizabeth's confession. "I also can see some resemblance indeed. You do look like Lady Catherine sometimes, Darcy."

"We are not speaking to you, Cassandra, so please do not interfere," Darcy scolded her.

"Yes, I noticed you are not speaking to us, which is quite strange considering you are in my room," she replied, and Georgiana covered her mouth with her palm to prevent a peal of laughter.

Facing each other mere inches apart, one of her hands still in his, Elizabeth and Darcy continued to look at each other. Her cheeks coloured; she was embarrassed by the impropriety of her own behaviour, her eyes sparkling with emotion. Elizabeth daringly rose on her toes and placed a soft kiss on Darcy's cheek.

"You do not look like Lady Catherine at all," she whispered to him tenderly, and Georgiana chuckled while Cassandra burst out laughing.

"Yes he does, but love makes people blind, so you cannot see it," Cassandra concluded.

Darcy ignored her, and taking Elizabeth's hand, he lifted it to his lips, his eyes never leaving hers. "Cassandra?"

"Yes, Darcy?"

"You are very annoying."

"Thank you, Darcy; you are very kind...just like Lady Catherine." This time Georgiana could not hold back her laughter, and a moment later, both Darcy and Elizabeth had no choice but to return their attention to their companions and join them in their gaiety.

"Darcy?"

"Yes, Cassandra?"

"May I ask you one last question regarding Lady Catherine's visit?"

"Can I prevent your asking?"

"No, indeed."

"Then please do."

"In precisely what kind of *conversation* were the two of you engaged when Lady Catherine happened upon you in the library?"

THREE DAYS BEFORE THE WEDDING, a disaster happened at Longbourn. Just an hour before dinner, an accident took place in the kitchen and ruined two of the main dishes. Nobody knew exactly what occurred because Mrs. Bennet almost fainted from distress while she blamed first Hill and John, and then the entire staff and, finally, the whole world.

With great effort, Elizabeth and Jane persuaded their mother to rest in her chamber while Hill — tearful and apologising continuously — hurried to prepare a new meal.

"Oh Lizzy, I knew something would happen! What will Mr. Darcy say now? He will certainly believe I am not able to manage my own household and that I taught you nothing about these duties."

"Mama, I am certain Mr. Darcy has a good opinion of how well you are managing Longbourn; he has told me so many times. You have absolutely no reason to be distressed for such a small incident."

"Small incident? We have dinner guests and nothing for dinner!"

"Please calm yourself, Mama. Hill will surely prepare something for us shortly, and to tell you the truth, this delay is quite welcome as I was not hungry at all."

"Nor am I, Mama." Jane also attempted to console her mother.

"Oh, I am not worried about you, girls! I am concerned about Mr. Darcy and Mr. Bingley. They are hungry; I am sure of it."

"Well, I am certain they will survive another hour or so," laughed Elizabeth.

"Oh, vexing child, you like to torture me with your inconsiderate jokes! You would do better to find a way to keep your betrothed's attention before they leave!"

"Do not worry, Mama; I have serious doubts they will consider leaving for that reason."

"You should take them for a turn in the garden, Lizzy! I noticed Mr. Darcy is always willing to take a stroll with you — which is very strange if you ask me! But then again, Mr. Darcy has some unusual habits — very similar to yours, Lizzy."

"Thank you, Mama; I shall follow your advice immediately. I would very much like a walk in the garden. Jane, will you and Mr. Bingley accompany us?"

"Yes, I believe so…if mama does not need me any longer."

"Oh, of course I do not need you, silly child. Go and take care of your betrothed at once."

Elizabeth grabbed Jane's hand and hurried from the room. Mrs. Bennet continued complaining of her nerves and the lack of understanding from her family.

"Well, well — you are back. Is Mrs. Bennet well?" asked Mr. Bennet with obvious amusement.

"She is resting, Papa; I dare say all is well."

"What extraordinarily good news, Lizzy. So, gentlemen, should we retire to the library for another hour or so? My port is waiting for us."

Darcy cast a quick glance at Elizabeth while considering how to reply, and she blushed slightly but did not hesitate to intervene. "Papa, Jane and I were thinking that maybe a short walk in the garden would be beneficial…I mean, if Mr. Darcy and Mr. Bingley would agree to join us."

For a moment, Mr. Bennet was tempted to insist the gentlemen keep him company, but he quickly decided that having fun at the expense of his dearest daughters would have been too cruel.

"Of course you are right, Lizzy. A quick stroll before dinner would be more beneficial than an hour indoors — more beneficial indeed. And I have a book I intend to finish this evening."

Less than five minutes later, the couples were outside, each lady taking the arm of her betrothed.

"It is a very nice evening." Bingley started the conversation.

"Yes, very nice, though quite cold," Darcy agreed instantly, covering Elizabeth's hand with his palm. Their gloved fingers entwined and Jane, who did not fail to notice the gesture, blushed violently.

"Miss Bennet, Bingley — would you please excuse us for a few minutes? There is something of great importance about which I would like to speak privately with Elizabeth."

His request took the other couple by surprise, but Darcy did not wait for an answer before he directed Elizabeth to take an alternate path toward the back of the house.

Elizabeth started to laugh. "That was not very gentlemanlike of you, William — not to mention most improper. Poor Mr. Bingley looked quite shocked, and Jane was equally distressed."

"My dear, I finally have the chance to spend a few minutes alone with you and do not intend to waste them worrying about Bingley's state of mind. As for Miss Bennet, I am truly sorry if I offended her, but I hope Bingley will succeed in alleviating her distress."

Darcy took her hand and entwined his fingers with hers again while she leaned against him, and they continued to walk through the back garden. "Let us pause here."

"We would be completely unchaperoned here, sir. Not to mention that it is already dark, so our situation is even more improper," she said in mocking reproach.

"Yes, I am aware of that," he said as he sat and gently pulled her near him.

She laughed. "You seem to give little consideration to my reputation, sir."

"We are to be married in less than three days, madam. I dare say your reputation will be just fine."

"Well, it depends," she managed to reply before his lips captured hers in a tender, gentle kiss.

"You know," Elizabeth said some time later when she was able to breathe normally again, "Mama insisted I should distract your attention before dinner is ready. She was afraid you would be upset and leave."

"Well, I am prepared to report to Mrs. Bennet that you performed your duty admirably."

"Thank you sir," she whispered against his lips and then daringly engaged his attention once more.

"Elizabeth, I confess I can scarcely wait to be married and leave all this behind."

"I feel the same," she admitted, suddenly shy. "Is it difficult for you to handle my noisy family?"

"No, no I am not speaking of your family; not at all! But I would be grateful to be able to move to our home, with nobody around except you; I have to say, I am forever indebted to Bingley for hosting us at Netherfield all this time, but living with his sisters is difficult to bear despite Bingley's kindness."

"Oh, I am sorry." Elizabeth spoke sympathetically, but she could not help laughing.

"However, I am confident that you may compensate any unpleasant moments with other more pleasant company. You have Georgiana and Cassandra — and the colonel — to keep you entertained."

"Yes, very entertained, indeed. You should pity me, you know. I am grateful Cassandra is making a full recovery, but she has become more cruel than before. She finds the greatest enjoyment in having fun at my expense with David and my own sister joining her."

"Why would they make fun of you?"

"Well, it appears there is nothing more humorous than a single man awaiting his wedding day."

"I see," she said tenderly. "But at least they are making fun of Mr. Bingley, too, are they not?"

"No indeed — at least not as much. It seems I am the main beneficiary of their teasing. But the prospect of having you as my wife is worth any torture I have to endure," he said as she laughed.

"I have to say I am amazed, sir, seeing how much you have changed since we met last autumn. You are even more handsome when you smile, and you have become a true expert at teasing."

"Even more so in being teased," he admitted with amusement. He removed the glove from her hand, and his lips gently kissed her fingers. "I have changed, Elizabeth, because you were worthy of a better man."

"No, indeed! There is no better man than you are, and I am happy to say you did not change at all in essentials. You just smile more and are less proper and less restrained than I believed you to be."

His lips were still caressing her fingers and her other hand gently stroked his face. Their present position on the bench soon became uncomfortable and — to Elizabeth's astonishment — Darcy put his arms around her and lifted her, placing her on his lap. She withdrew from him briefly so their eyes could meet, and then her lips searched for his again, and her body pressed against him until she felt her breasts against the solid wall of his chest. Darcy pulled away a few inches, unbuttoned his coat, and embraced Elizabeth even more forcefully.

"I want to feel you as close to me as I can," he said a moment before their lips joined once more.

"William," she whispered breathlessly while his lips moved along her face. "Please unbutton my coat, too…"

For a moment, he was still, the assault of his daring kisses suspended, but before she had time to register the movement of his skilful hands, she felt herself crushed against him again, and this time the thin fabric of her dress allowed his warmth to burn her skin. She felt his fingers caress her neck and back, and then travel along her ribs until they rested upon her hips. They returned to her arms and shoulders, followed the line of her throat, tantalised the neckline of her dress and, finally, slid inside. She sighed, and he hastily covered her mouth with another kiss.

His caresses soon became less passionate; his lips released hers and gently covered her face, eyes and temples with countless, delicate kisses. They embraced so tightly, that each could hear the other's heart beating.

"We should return to the house," Darcy said, still kissing her temples.

"Yes," she agreed, but neither of them moved.

"This night will pass soon as will the next two — and then I will be allowed to hold you as long as I want." Her head rested on his shoulder and for some time they remained wrapped in blissful silence.

Then, to Elizabeth's shock, Darcy began to laugh, and she raised her head, staring at him.

"William, what is it? You startled me."

"I am sorry, my love...please forgive me. It is nothing. Let us return to the house."

Without rising from his lap, she looked at him with reproach. "Surely you cannot be serious, sir — to burst out with such levity and then tell me it is nothing. You absolutely must tell me the reason for your amusement."

"Elizabeth, I...I cannot. It is not a proper conversation to have with you."

Her eyebrow rose in astonishment. "Not proper? Mr. Darcy, we are in the back garden of my own home, you are holding me on your lap, risking being caught any moment, and you are concerned about the propriety of a conversation? You have a strange sense of proper behaviour, sir."

He playfully placed another kiss on her hair.

"Very well, but I warn you that you will be shocked, maybe even upset as it involves your sister."

"My sister? Jane? What reason might you have to laugh at Jane?"

"No, not at Miss Bennet...please forgive me. It is just that...well, last evening when I returned to Netherfield, I found a note from Cassandra, telling me she wished to speak to me. I hurried to her room, assuming something important had happened...instead..."

"Yes? Come sir; do not trifle with me. Now I am truly uncomfortable with this conversation."

"Well, I am too...and it was even worse last night when Cassandra demanded that I tell her — how *experienced* Bingley was." He chuckled as Elizabeth stared at him without comprehension.

"Experienced? In what way?" she asked, then her cheeks coloured highly, and she rose from Darcy's lap. "Ooooh," she whispered, while she hurried to button her coat.

"Elizabeth, I am sorry if I offended you..."

"You did not offend me. It is just that...I am not accustomed to such a conversation, especially between a gentleman and a lady, even if they are close friends."

"I am not accustomed either — trust me — and last night I was not at all inclined to laugh as I am now! It is true that Cassandra is like a sister to me, but that is not a discussion to have with a sister," he replied seriously, and Elizabeth's embarrassment was overcome by her own amusement.

"I can imagine...and may I dare ask how you replied to her?"

"I replied to her exactly the same: that I was shocked she could ask such a question that cannot possibly be answered. "But she said if I would not answer, she would ask Bingley directly!"

They had already started to walk toward the house, and Elizabeth burst out in peals of laughter so loud that she was certain they were heard from inside. "She would not dare!"

"I am afraid she would! Apparently, Miss Bennet is concerned about...various aspects following her wedding. Cassandra told me they had spent much time talking, and she somehow managed to comfort Miss Jane and assure her she had absolutely no reason for concern, as she will be the perfect mistress for Netherfield and the perfect wife for Bingley. However, Cassandra wanted to be certain everything truly would be fine with Miss Jane in every aspect of her marriage — starting with the wedding night."

"Now I see. Cassandra's care for my sister is wonderful and praiseworthy. And — ?"

"And what, Elizabeth?"

"Is Mr. Bingley *experienced*?"

"Elizabeth!"

"I am sorry, but if Cassandra is worried for my sister, how could I not be?"

"Miss Elizabeth," Darcy replied soundly and decidedly, "I shall not discuss any details about my friend either with you or Cassandra!"

He was so grave that Elizabeth covered her mouth in order to keep from laughing aloud again.

"As you wish, sir."

"And I will tell you exactly what I told Cassandra: I am absolutely certain that Miss Bennet's marriage with Bingley will be a happy one — in *every respect*!"

"Thank you for assuring me, sir."

"You are welcome."

Elizabeth could not hold her laughter any longer. "Cassandra is astonishing."

"She is indeed. Perhaps too astonishing at times," Darcy admitted.

"I understand she did not inquire about your *own* experience, did she? I wonder why —"

"No, she did not, perhaps because she did not seem concerned about *you* at all, Elizabeth. It may be that you did not appear to be frightened about *any aspect* of our future marriage," Darcy replied lightly.

"Or perhaps, being around you for so long, she already *knew* about your past experiences?"

The words came out before she was able to control them. Suddenly shy, she averted her eyes.

As they had almost reached the main entrance, Darcy stopped, and she was forced to do the same.

He leaned toward her so he could whisper in her ear. "Elizabeth, I have never loved another woman before, nor have I known the true meaning of passion and desire before meeting you."

She looked at him, and he lifted her hand to his lips. "As for our marriage, dearest Elizabeth, I heartily believe you are not frightened about its various facets, as we are to be the happiest couple in the world in every way!"

"I know that. I have known it from the first moment we became engaged — and maybe even before."

At that moment, Mrs. Bennet chose to call everyone to the house and finally allow poor Mr. Darcy and Mr. Bingley to have some nourishment before they fainted from hunger.

Bingley and Colonel Fitzwilliam were the only ones left in the Netherfield library. Darcy had retired a little earlier, and the colonel would have done the same, but to his utter surprise, Bingley had requested a private conversation with him, and the colonel accepted — puzzled and curious. However, a quarter of an hour passed and Bingley seemed more inclined to enjoy his brandy than to speak about the reason for his distress.

"Bingley, stop pacing the room. You are making me dizzy!"

"I am sorry, Colonel."

"Don't be sorry. Sit down and tell me what is happening to you. You are acting strangely, man!"

Bingley stared at him a moment then poured himself another glass of brandy.

"I don't know what to do. I need your advice, Colonel."

"About life in general or about a particular matter?'

"Please, I do not need your mocking tone right now."

"Forgive me, my friend, but you are quite amusing. What the hell is happening to you, man? You are to be married in three days. You should be the happiest man in the world."

"I am! And that is precisely what troubles me! That is the problem!"

"That? *That* as in…what?"

"The wedding, man! The wedding night — don't you understand?"

"Huh?" asked the colonel in the most ungentlemanlike manner. "Your wedding night is the problem? You mean you are not — You do not know? You never before —"

"Oh, hush, Colonel! Of course, I *have* and I *know*. Do not be ridiculous."

"Oh, good," the colonel replied, obviously relieved, and hurried to fill his glass once more. "Then what is bothering you?" He was certain their conversation could not get any worse.

"The problem is that it is not the same thing! It cannot be the same thing. Jane is so different, so wonderful, and so proper in everything she does. I could not possibly...you know..."

"Now I am completely lost," the colonel admitted. "Just ask away if you have a question. Do not torture me any longer."

"What should I do?" Bingley finally burst out. "I have never been in love with a woman to whom...you know. How could I do *that* without frightening Jane? I love her so much, and I desire her so much that sometimes I am afraid I will not be able to control myself. I feel I will lose my mind! You must know that, Colonel! You have already *been* with the woman you love."

Bingley looked more distressed than ever before, and his last words succeeded in shocking the colonel equally.

"Bingley, you are killing me!"

"I am sorry. I did not mean to be disrespectful. I only —"

"Don't worry about being disrespectful; that is my last worry. Let us sit down and talk calmly."

"As you say," Bingley obeyed.

"Bingley, you must know this is the strangest conversation I have ever had."

"I imagine so. I cannot apologise enough for placing you in this uncomfortable situation, but I thought you were the only one who could understand me and provide me with sound advice. I know how strong your affection is for Lady Cassandra and —"

"Bingley, what advice do you expect from me? I do not understand the reason for your distress, to be honest. I never thought of this before. Oh God, I need another drink," the colonel concluded.

"I can easily see why you do not understand and why you never worried about this. You are a man who always knows what he has to do in any circumstance. But I am a complete idiot who will surely disappoint the woman I love because I am unable to behave properly; it is as simple as that."

"Come now, Bingley — there are too many words and we have had too many glasses of brandy. You are not an idiot; you are only preoccupied with this matter. It will pass soon enough. As for your concern — let me assure you everything will be well. There is nothing to fear. You said it could not be the same as with any other woman. I will tell you: it is the same but completely different. It is more — much more. Have you not held Miss Bennet's hand? Have you not kissed her? No, no, don't answer me! Just think of that. I am certain you have experienced all these before with other women, and you surely noticed the holding of the hand or the kissing were the same...but not really the same."

Bingley stared at him with his eyes wide open. "Damn, you are such a clever man, Colonel. You said so little yet I finally understand everything."

"I am not clever, Bingley. It must be the result of those five glasses of brandy you just drank."

Bingley started to laugh so loudly that the colonel startled. "You should go to bed, Bingley."

"Yes, I should," he admitted without moving. "You may consider me a complete fool, Colonel, but I cannot help wondering. I hope she will be happy with me — that she will enjoy our marriage. I want everything to be perfect for her, but I already disappointed her last autumn. What if I disappoint her again. I failed so miserably to understand her feelings last year. Will I be able to recognise whether she truly enjoys being with me or only tolerates me because it is her duty to do so?"

"Bingley, from what I have seen, I doubt Miss Bennet is merely *tolerating* you. Indeed, she is a proper young lady — so no wonder she is restrained. But she seems to enjoy your company quite a lot."

"She does, does she not? I confess there were times when I felt that she would allow me to —"

"Bingley, let us stop this confession before the brandy makes you say things you will come to regret tomorrow. You must have faith in yourself. The mere fact that you are so concerned for Miss Bennet proves the depth of your affection for her. You want advice for your wedding night? Here it is: show her your affection and your care; be patient and considerate, and do not forget you said you want everything to be perfect for her."

"She is an angel," Bingley said dreamily, and the colonel patted him on his shoulder.

"Then, here is further advice — stop thinking about Miss Bennet as an angel; she is an exceptionally beautiful lady, but she is still a *woman*, not an *angel*, and I dare say that is most fortunate. Angels are not to be touched, and you surely would like to touch your wife. An angel is something for your fantasies. A *real*, beautiful woman who shares your affection and becomes your wife — that is something to experience every day for many years."

Bingley was staring at his companion wordlessly, dizzy from fatigue and the effects of the brandy, yet his mind was working frantically, considering everything he heard.

"You are a clever man, Colonel," he repeated.

"I know, I know — sometimes I astonish myself with my own cleverness, Bingley. Now let me take you to your room — and for God's sake, do not drink on your wedding night, or you will not be able to *perform* as well as you would wish."

Bingley stepped toward the door, but the last words turned him back to the colonel. "Thank you for telling me that, Colonel! Now I will have another reason to worry! How very considerate of you!"

Colonel Fitzwilliam could not control the burst of laughter any longer. Certainly that was the most diverting conversation he had had in quite a long time.

HAPPY FOR ALL HER MATERNAL feelings was the day on which Mrs. Bennet divested herself of her two most deserving daughters. It may be guessed with what delighted pride she watched them stand up in church next to their wealthy grooms, surrounded by illustrious guests and all twenty-four families from Meryton. Even Lady Cassandra was present with Colonel Fitzwilliam — what a handsome, amiable man! He took the trouble to carry her ladyship in his arms from the carriage into the church in order that she not miss the grand event.

The wedding breakfast was everything for which Mrs. Bennet had hoped. Lady Fitzwilliam praised the elegant arrangements and the choice of the dishes, and Lady Cassandra said she had not enjoyed herself so much in years.

Mrs. Bennet was utterly happy — and she did not worry about her nerves a single moment.

In a corner of the Netherfield ballroom, the newlywed couples were speaking to each other.

"I shall miss you, Lizzy; I shall write you every day," said a tearful Jane.

"I hope you will not have time to write me, dearest Jane. I shall miss you, too. But it is less than two months until we meet again at Pemberley for Christmas. Take care of yourself and your husband until then."

"I will do my best, Lizzy," Jane whispered as she cast a quick glance at her husband, who was engaged in a close conversation with Mr. Darcy.

"You surely do not have to leave so soon, Darcy; you are more than welcome to stay here…for tonight, I mean. Both Jane and I are delighted to have you and all our families as guests —"

"Bingley! You have finally married the woman you have loved for so long. I truly hope you will find delight in no one else's presence except that of your wife and will not welcome any guests into your home for at least a month! Stop being so kind and polite — it is time for you to be selfish."

Bingley smiled uncomfortably, and then he looked at his wife and met her timid glance.

"I cannot send people away," he replied with a low voice.

"Now you cannot," admitted Darcy, patting his shoulder sympathetically. "Fortunately they will leave — eventually. My uncle and aunt, together with Cassandra, Georgiana and David will depart for London shortly, so they will not give you much trouble."

"Trust me, Darcy; *they* never gave me any trouble."

"Yes, I believe that. Your troubles lie elsewhere," Darcy said, with a meaningful glance toward the Hursts and the Bennets. "My advice would be to ask for Mr. Bennet's help in the matter."

"I will — I certainly will. And you know, Caroline is determined to leave for a long tour around the country, and Louisa said they will return to London —"

"Yes, I have heard that. And Bingley — you will always be welcome at Pemberley, you know that."

"We shall come for Christmas."

"You may come sooner if you want. I can offer you and Mrs. Bingley the entire east wing, and I promise you — nobody will disturb you there."

"I shall take your offer into consideration, Darcy."

An hour later, after all the guests said their goodbyes to the Darcys, he handed his wife into the carriage and then closed and locked its door.

Inside the carriage, Elizabeth forced herself to smile while fighting the overwhelming emotion of departing Netherfield, their friends and families. As her trembling hands pressed together and her shimmering eyes locked on her husband's, Elizabeth managed a barely audible whisper.

"Finally we come to the end of this."

"No indeed, my love; it is not the end but the beginning. I am taking you home, Mrs. Darcy!"

Chapter 23

"Home..." she whispered, a timid smile fighting her emotions. Her eyes locked with his worried ones for a moment, and then she nestled into his chest. His arm encircled her shoulder in a loving gesture.

"Elizabeth, is anything wrong?"

"No... nothing is wrong. Quite the contrary. It is just that I still remember vividly the day I entered your home for the first time."

"I remember that day, too — every moment of it. I felt ripped apart; my joy and gratitude in meeting you again was countered by my fear that your feelings for me were still the same as in April. I feared Georgiana's insistence might distress you, yet I was grateful that she dared what I did not. I cherished every new moment in your company, though I was not certain whether you accepted the invitation with pleasure or a sense of obligation."

"Both, I imagine. I did not know what to do. I wondered how you felt about Georgiana inviting us. I was certain I did not deserve your attentions and was shocked when I received them. And when you asked me whether I wanted you to leave your own home, I was overwhelmed by your consideration and ashamed of my past behaviour toward you."

"You must not feel ashamed, Elizabeth. You were faultless; I fully deserved your harsh words and your rejection last spring!"

"You are too kind, my love," she smiled as her fingers tenderly caressed his face. "You have always been an exceptionally good man — the best man I have ever known — and, for a long time, I failed miserably to notice it."

"I had done nothing to deserve your good opinion when we first met, and my outrageous intervention in —"

"Oh, come now, Mr. Darcy! If we continue like this, we shall spend our entire wedding day and night arguing about the past. I used to have a marvellous philosophy, which could be quite useful to both of us in these circumstances. Unfortunately, I failed to follow it recently, so it might not be as good as I thought it to be."

Darcy placed a soft kiss in her palm. "You must not worry, my love. We will not spend our wedding night arguing, I promise you," he whispered, and his voice, together with the soft touch of his lips on her palm, made her shiver. "And now," he continued, still holding her hand, "will you not share your philosophy, Mrs. Darcy?"

"I certainly shall." She forced a smile as she fought the sudden lump in her throat. *"Think only of the past as its remembrance gives you pleasure."*

"A good philosophy indeed — especially for someone who has not much to be blamed for in the past. I am afraid that, in my case, it would not be —"

"Oh, this will never do." She stopped him, pressing her hand upon his mouth. Then she rose a little from her seat, just enough for her lips to replace her fingers and silence him in a most pleasant way.

If Darcy was surprised, he managed to conceal it successfully and handle the situation remarkably well; he needed only an instant to pull her upon his lap and tighten his arms around her waist. Elizabeth laughed shortly against his mouth. Their kiss was more a playful dance than a passionate urge — a tantalising tease of each other's lips and an expression of their delight in being together — finally.

"Elizabeth, I truly hate this bonnet," he said unexpectedly against her mouth, his fingers trying to slide beneath the object of his displeasure in an attempt to caress her hair. Her peals of laughter broke the kiss.

"I am sorry to hear that, sir. My mother warned me that you might also be displeased with the lack of lace."

"Lace? Of what lace are you speaking? What I meant is — I would rather have leave to admire your hair whenever I please. May I?" She nodded in agreement, still laughing, as he removed her bonnet.

"That is much better, would you not agree?"

"I certainly would," Elizabeth admitted, and he pressed a soft kiss on her temple, obviously content.

"So, dare I ask why your mother feared I might be displeased?"

"Well, because of the lack of lace on my gown, of course, dear sir."

"You are teasing me again, Mrs. Darcy. Surely, nobody believes a lack of lace can be the reason for someone's displeasure. In fact, I doubt I have ever noticed the presence or the absence of lace on anyone's gown."

"That is indeed a pity, sir, and I hope you are a singular case, because we — women — spend an excessive amount of time arranging ourselves in order to be noticed by you gentlemen," Elizabeth laughed. "Of course, some of us fail in the attempt and barely manage to appear *tolerable*; however, we are not to be easily discouraged."

Darcy's countenance changed, and as they were mere inches apart, Elizabeth could see her teasing disturbed him. She leaned closer as he started to apologise.

"Sir, I thought you had grown accustomed to my teasing by now and begun to enjoy it, but if you feel the need to apologise again for that evening, I must have been wrong in my estimation."

"You were not wrong. However, I cannot forgive myself as easily as you do, and my behaviour at the beginning of our acquaintance still troubles me. As for your teasing — I have always enjoyed it exceedingly, you know that."

"Always? Even when I was impertinent in my replies to you?"

"You were never impertinent; amusing and exceptionally bright, yes, but never impertinent."

"I am afraid you failed to notice it, sir, as you failed to notice the lace on our gowns," Elizabeth smiled. "Which is quite amazing, considering the fact that you are such a perceptive man."

"You give me too much credit, my dear wife. Where you were concerned, my perception betrayed me for a considerable time, or I would have seen your true feelings for me last spring."

She huffed and rolled her eyes in exasperation.

"You do plan to spend our wedding day arguing about the unpleasant things in our past, sir!"

"No, no indeed...forgive me." He placed butterfly kisses on her hair.

Elizabeth cuddled to his chest, sighing contentedly. "Much better indeed."

As she was resting on his lap, his left hand encircled her back as his right gently raised her face to his. She smiled, and his face was lit with delight before their lips joined and the past vanished.

As Darcy's caress became more daring and possessive, Elizabeth's restraint vanished; she was alone with her husband and they no longer need hide from others. For a moment, a sensible thought crossed her mind, telling her there were footmen outside the carriage, but his lips travelling along her throat and his fingers lowering the shoulder of her dress made her insensible of anything but her husband and the tingling shivers that overwhelmed her senses. She reclined in his embrace, and his kisses became more passionate. Some uncounted minutes later, Elizabeth felt herself pulled upright as gentle arms embraced her tenderly and lips rested lightly against her temple. She could feel Darcy's heart racing wildly and forced her own ragged breath to calm.

"We have two more hours until London, my love, and this will not help us pass the time," Darcy whispered. "Even more, though I praise my discipline and self-control, I fear my struggle will be in vain if you continue to encourage me in such a tempting manner," he added hoarsely.

Elizabeth blushed, suddenly mortified by her wanton behaviour. "You are correct, of course," she replied, trying to resume her position beside him.

His arms tightened around her. "Elizabeth, please look at me."

Her cheeks were crimson, and she was biting her lower lip as her eyes sparkled with unshed tears. "I am sorry, I…" She felt so deeply distressed while he seemed nothing but amused. Nervously, she averted her eyes and tried to rise again from his lap.

"For what would you be sorry, my love? For enjoying my kisses and caresses? I hope you are not truly sorry, just as I hope you will learn never to feel embarrassment from the pleasure and joy we will share in our marriage."

"I am sorry for making such an exhibition of myself. I do not know what is happening to me. I seem to act most irrationally when I am with you. I am quite aware of how I should behave, but unfortunately, I so forget all propriety and decorum on occasion that I must shock you. It is unacceptable that you — as a man — should be the sensible and considerate one who always puts an end to these…improper activities.

"Elizabeth, please stop…" She timidly raised her head, and he softly kissed her eyelids.

"Do I look shocked to you, my dear?" Can you not see that your behaviour is everything for which I have hoped? For more than a year, I have dreamt of the moment your love and passion would equal mine, though for a time I dared not think it would happen. You are the only woman to inhabit my dreams, Elizabeth, but you are more wonderful than any dream."

"More wanton, you mean," she replied, trying to defeat her emotions.

He laughed. "You say *'wanton'* — I say unrestrained, passionate, lively, and honest in expressing your feelings — exactly as you always have been!"

"I like your choice of words better than mine."

"What a relief to know that for once you approve my choice of words; I would say that is a great improvement over our first meeting," he replied, and she laughed tearfully.

"Yes, a great improvement, Mr. Darcy.

"Thank you, Mrs. Darcy. I am content that we clarified our little misunderstanding," he said with another soft kiss on the corner of her mouth. "Now, let us change the subject, shall we?"

She nodded, and then her head nestled on his shoulder in a peaceful silence,

"So, we were debating the importance of lace, I remember. Shall we continue?"

"As you wish, sir, but I insist you allow me to resume my place beside you. You cannot possibly keep me in your lap until we reach London."

"Are you uncomfortable with this arrangement?"

"Quite the contrary," she replied lightly, a quick blush colouring her cheeks, "but I imagine you are uncomfortable, as I know I am not such an easy charge —"

"Your concern is greatly appreciated, but please do not worry about my comfort," he assured her and gently tilted her head so their lips met again. The urgency of his kiss took Elizabeth by surprise — as they had just agreed they should stop that kind of activity; however, she hesitated only a moment before wisely determining it was her duty to obey her husband's wishes.

"Let us discuss lace," Darcy said breathlessly sometime later.

AT NETHERFIELD, CAROLINE BINGLEY HAD all her belongings arranged in the carriage and wanted nothing more than to be on her way as soon as possible. She could no longer tolerate Mrs. Bennet's smug grin, Charles's dumb smile or Jane's complacent countenance. Impatiently, she rolled her eyes in exasperation as Mr. Hurst indulged in yet another glass of wine and Charles expressed once again his regret for their early departure.

Finally, Louisa and her useless husband were settled in the carriage, and Caroline's journey commenced. She felt pleased, confident and full of anticipation for the tour she would start in a couple of days. For the next several months, she would be in Lady Sophia's select company — the company she deserved. This would be the perfect occasion to find an excellent husband — and she would sever forever any ties with the Bennets!

As for Mr. Fitzwilliam Darcy — if he could not recognise and appreciate her worthiness, it was his loss. From then on, he would be forced to bear Eliza Bennet and her family forever. He would surely come to regret her — she was certain of that — and this perspective kept Caroline Bingley cheerfully distracted for the remainder of their journey to London.

DRESSED IN HER NIGHTGOWN AND robe, her hair flowing over her shoulders, Elizabeth paced the room, brushing her fingers over the furnishings.

Darcy had accompanied her to her chambers an hour earlier and then left, promising he would return soon. She knew she needed privacy to prepare herself for what was to come, but she already missed his presence dearly.

Her maid helped her with her bath and prepared her for the night — and now, with everything arranged, Elizabeth was waiting alone in the large, silent, elegant room. Mrs. Darcy's chamber!

Her apartment was spectacular; it was not so much the grandeur or the richness that impressed her, but all the beauty around her and the thought that, from that day on, everything belonged to her — the former Elizabeth Bennet. For the first time in her life, Elizabeth felt intimidated.

She returned to the bed and stared at a box, elegantly wrapped. It was likely a present for her, but she did not open it, although she could hardly restrain her curiosity. Darcy had seemed to notice her interest, and she was certain she had seen him smiling mischievously, but he had departed before she could inquire further.

What could it be? It was clearly too large a box to contain jewels and too small for a gown or bonnet. Perhaps some books? But why would he offer her books so secretly on their wedding night? Surely, he did not intend to read, she thought as her cheeks burned. Oh, where was he?

JANE BINGLEY DID NOT DARE move — or breathe. She was completely undressed and her husband's arm held her tightly against his bare chest; her breasts were almost painfully crushed to him. Every movement — including their breathing or the beating of their hearts — caused their bodies to brush against each other. She felt exhausted and stunned as much as she was ashamed and incredulous at everything that had occurred between them.

Cassandra had told her that the experience of becoming a woman would be a pleasant one, but *pleasant* was hardly a proper word for what she had felt; in truth, she was too mortified even to contemplate everything her husband had done to her, but she vividly remembered it had been much more than pleasant. She would have never imagined Charles behaving in such a way — so unrestrained, so passionate — almost demanding in his insistence on defeating her embarrassment and modesty.

With shame and delight, happy that her red face could not be seen nor her thoughts read, she remembered how he had removed her nightgown while she struggled to keep her body hidden; how he impetuously covered her body with shocking, intoxicating kisses, how he kept asking her if she enjoyed what she was feeling. Oh, she did enjoy everything — she truly did. Her body was exhausted by her husband's passion, and the pain was still sharp inside her, yet — to her own astonishment — Jane hoped he would repeat his attentions very soon.

Cassandra had told her she would like being married to Charles — and Cassandra had been right again. *She is so smart, and she knows so many things!* Jane mused with gratitude, nestling to her husband's chest.

Charles Bingley was the happiest man in the world — and the proudest. All his fears and worries were now gone, and he was holding closely in his arms his beautiful Jane, the woman who had offered him everything that he had dreamed — and much more.

A trace of guilt shadowed his contentment, as he knew he had been ofttimes too impatient. But he was at least pleased to know that the only inconvenience she had suffered was embarrassment. She seemed ashamed most of the time — he knew that. She even begged him to allow her to cover herself with the sheets at one point, but he had silenced her with his kisses. And she did like being kissed — he had no doubts. How sweet she was in her complete abandon with him! And how incredibly beautiful she was as she took her pleasure — a pleasure he was giving her, and one he hoped he would be allowed to bestow on her again very soon.

The colonel was right — it was the same, yet so incredibly different from anything Charles had ever experienced. And his adored Jane was not an angel to dream of but a most beautiful woman to caress, to kiss, to pleasure, to love — and share a life.

Yes indeed — the colonel was right. *But again,* Charles mused, *he is always right. He is so damn smart and knows so much about everything!*

"I SEE YOU DID NOT open the box, Mrs. Darcy." Darcy's voice broke the silence, and Elizabeth startled and stepped away from the bed, as though she had been caught doing something improper.

"No, I did not. I…"

Elizabeth glanced at her husband and her eyes remained fixed on his intense gaze. Though she had seen him informally attired before, his appearance made her body shiver and her mouth turn dry.

Darcy smiled at her and stepped forward; she looked at him, mesmerised, and his every step made her tremble. She quivered and licked her lips; he smiled again. A moment later, he was so close that his scent intoxicated her.

"Do you not enjoy surprises, Mrs. Darcy?"

"Of course I do, but I was not certain whether I should open the box. I was not sure it belonged to me."

"And to whom could it possibly belong as it is on your own bed?"

"You should not tease me at moments like this, sir. I am quite nervous as it is."

A trace of concern passed over Darcy's face for a moment. "Are you truly worried, Elizabeth?"

"Indeed, I am," she whispered. Her eyes lowered to the floor, and his anxiety increased. "I cannot stop worrying about...what is in that box!" she continued and laughed. He breathed in relief and then suddenly lifted her in his arms, almost suffocating her against his chest.

"I see you find great delight in teasing me, Mrs. Darcy," he said, but she had no time to reply before he captured her lips. Her legs were not touching the floor, and her body was crushed against his, her arms entwined around his neck; she could not breathe, but she did not need air — she only needed his scent and his warmth.

After a while, he put her down, and she feared — and hoped — he would take her to the bed. Instead, he took her to the little settee in front of the fireplace and bade her sit. Still breathless, she looked at him in wonder.

"Do you not wish to know what is in that box?" he inquired, and for a moment she wanted to say *"no"*; indeed, she wanted to know nothing except what she knew must happen between her and her husband.

"I do," she whispered, and he seemed pleased.

In an instant, he brought her the present and sat beside her. A moment later the secret was revealed; an exquisitely carved box rested in Elizabeth's trembling hands, and its beauty left her breathless.

"Thank you..." she barely managed to say.

"No, do not thank me yet," he replied and opened the box.

The fascinating sounds of a waltz flowed from the music box, and Elizabeth's heart skipped a beat; tears glistened in her eyes as she stared at her husband in disbelief.

"Oh, William. A waltz? This is... I cannot believe that... It is so..."

"I sincerely hope these are grateful emotions," he teased, and she burst out laughing nervously as tears filled her eyes. With the music box in her arms, she daringly started to kiss him softly. The music stopped and then began once more. They smiled against each other's lips.

"Am I to understand you like my present?"

"Indeed I do like it. You are most unpredictable, sir. I never would have guessed the nature of your present."

"Well, I did promise you some private waltz lessons," he said, his fingers brushing her cheeks.

"So you did, but I never imagined it would happen tonight. I never imagined you were so fond of the waltz," she replied teasingly, her hands on the box still trembling slightly.

"I am not fond of dance, and the waltz would be a torture to me with any woman other than you."

"That is a pretty thing to say, sir. However, I could not help but notice you are truly proficient at it. You must have practiced a good deal," Elizabeth replied, and a little smile twisted his lips.

"No indeed, I practiced only a few times because Cassandra forced me. I do not need to practice too much in order to be proficient," he said with a laugh, and she narrowed her eyes, still incredulous.

"Elizabeth, I *never* danced the waltz in public except with you at the Netherfield Ball," he continued, more seriously.

"Truly?"

"Truly."

On the small settee, near the peaceful warmth of the fire, they took each other's hands and their fingers entwined in a tender caress; the box was in Elizabeth's lap, and still holding her hand, Darcy opened it again and the sound of music wrapped them anew. Her eyes sparkled with emotion and love.

"You know, William, that evening in London at Cassandra's ball, when you asked me to dance with you after you had just refused Cassandra..."

"Yes?" He turned to embrace her closely, his lips resting on her temple.

"Oh, nothing. Let us not speak of that now." She abandoned her idea, but he would not.

"You must tell me once you started, Elizabeth."

"I will...tomorrow," she replied and then turned her face so their lips almost touched. Darcy was tempted to insist, but the sweetness of her lips was too appealing — so he tasted them and forgot what he wanted to ask.

Her mouth parted with loving abandon while his hands travelled along her arms and lingered on her shoulders, then gently unfastened her night robe and removed it. She shivered — not from chill but from the touch of his burning fingers on her skin.

"Elizabeth?" he said breathlessly, their mouths unwilling to separate.

"Yes," she barely managed to speak as she struggled for air.

"Can we postpone the waltz lessons for another evening?"

Elizabeth laughed only a moment before his lips captured hers again; suddenly, the music box became an obstacle, and she put it down as gently as she could. As though that was the sign he waited for, she felt herself lowered to the settee, his weight almost crushing her and his kisses becoming more possessive. The settee was small, and he was so tall and heavy that Elizabeth was certain she would faint from lack of air. However, just as she was pondering this, she felt free, though her lips were still engaged with his. She slowly opened her eyes and saw him kneeling at her side.

Darcy withdrew from her enough for their eyes to meet; his fingers tenderly removed a lock of hair from her forehead and then brushed over her red, swollen lips; she caressed his face, and then her hands sneaked into his hair.

Slowly, he leaned closer to her again, but this time his mouth travelled down from her chin along her throat; each spot of her bare skin shivered under his intoxicating exploration while his hands carefully lowered the gown from her shoulders. She knew — she hoped for — what would follow, and the wait was unbearable.

Although she was anticipating it, the gentle, tentative touch of his fingers over her breasts startled her, and she moaned loudly as her back arched toward his touch. His caress, shy at first, became daring and more passionate, tracing torturous circles until his palms possessively cupped their roundness and rested there.

"You are so beautiful," he whispered, and she moaned again, turning her head in search of his lips. Yet, he avoided the kiss; instead, his mouth resumed its journey and one of his hands withdrew from its smooth captive, to allow his mouth to satiate its hunger. His lips traced a burning line over her skin, exploring and tasting with passionate urgency.

His hand was now free to conquer the last unrevealed parts of her body; the thin silk fabric of her gown was soft, and his fingers, strong yet gentle, stroked her legs and then travelled up, pressing gently against her skin. Instinctively, her thighs locked together, but his hand continued its conquest; with tender care, his strokes tantalised her legs and parted them daringly. Soon, no opposition remained and, to Elizabeth's shock, his hand moved a little higher. She could not suppress a cry, and shocked, she tried to clasp her thighs again. She heard him whispering her name and wished to understand his words but could not. His mouth hungrily captured her other breast and she exclaimed again as her entire body arched.

For Elizabeth, every sense was divided between the sweet torture of his lips on her skin and that most intimate part of her body, where his fingers began an intoxicating exploration. *This cannot be happening* — a vague notion — but an instant later, any reasonable thought vanished; she cried his name and her voice sounded so strange to her. Then, a few moments later, she heard nothing as waves of pleasure violently exploded in her body and everything turned dark around her.

It took some time before she could — and dared — open her eyes and was able to distinguish his face in the dim firelight. He was smiling, and she forced a smile in return; with mortification, she realised he was still kneeling beside her, one of his hands resting on her breast as the other gently caressed her inner thigh. She wanted to move, but he would not allow it; he covered her face with small kisses while she averted her eyes. Her mind told her that what happened was mortifyingly improper, while her senses confessed that nothing could possibly exist more blissfully pleasant than what she had just experienced.

"You are more beautiful than I have ever dreamed, Elizabeth," he whispered. "And you are all mine now…"

She looked at him puzzled, her cheeks flushed. "Is it… is it all done then?"

He laughed, and she averted her eyes again, even more embarrassed.

"No, my love, it has only begun. We should move to the bed now."

Her nightgown was discarded; she felt herself being lifted in his arms and carried across the room.

Darcy laid her on the bed, and she instantly nestled beneath the sheets to conceal herself from his intense stare. He slowly removed his nightshirt; her cheeks coloured as her eyes desperately tried not to look at his intimidating figure. His naked body protectively touched hers under the silky sheets and his arms enfolded her.

"What is wrong, my love?"

Her head cuddled on his chest and she sighed when she could hear his heart beating. Her hands moved to encircle his waist but his skin –so fully exposed to her touch — made her shy, and her hands dared go no further.

"Nothing is wrong. It is just…"

"Yes?"

"I never thought… Everything that happened was so…"

She struggled to find the words as she fought against her own embarrassment.

"My love, you worry me. Did I hurt you?"

"Oh, no! It is just that I never imagined you… It was so unexpected…"

"I see." His voiced changed instantly, and a warm whisper close to her ear made her shiver.

"So… may I dare presume you found it unexpected… in an enjoyable way?"

His tongue shamelessly tantalised her earlobe and she shivered with nervous delight.

"Oh please stop. I cannot possibly speak of that. It is so embarrassing!"

"This is quite astonishing, Mrs. Darcy. I used to believe you could speak easily on any subject, and I thought we clarified the matter of embarrassment earlier in the carriage, but it seems you have already forgotten our agreement. I am truly disappointed to discover that so soon after our wedding."

Darcy's voice could barely conceal his mirth as he scolded her with mocking sincerity. Elizabeth lifted her head slightly to meet his eyes and cast a sharp glance at him.

"You are a cruel man, sir, to trifle with me in such a way. I would not expect that of you. You should know this is not a proper time for teasing."

"I might be cruel sometimes, I will admit that. It is unfortunate, too, that you discovered my cruelty after the wedding."

"It is, indeed." She was forced to regain her spirit as their mocking argument continued.

"There is little either of us can do now, Mrs. Darcy, except to reconcile with our mutual disappointment and try to reach some sort of understanding. I will start by agreeing with you on one important point: this is not a proper time for teasing."

They were his last coherent words before he assaulted her with renewed passion and desire, and Elizabeth surrendered completely; every touch, every kiss, every stroke seemed even more irresistible, as this time she knew what they would bring. Her body seemed to possess a will of its own, and every reaction was a plea for more. For a while, she tried to keep the covers around her, but his greedy hands kept pushing them away.

"I want to see you, Elizabeth... please," he begged.

Her inner battle between reason and passion was won by the latter.

When his hand intimately stroked her thighs again, they parted with welcoming desire. His caresses climbed along her legs again, and she moaned loudly, imagining what would follow. Yet, what followed was not what she anticipated. In disbelief, she felt his lips travel down from her breasts to her flat stomach, amuse themselves with her navel, and continue until his mouth nipped lightly at her inner thigh. With shocked astonishment, her head spinning, she felt her legs parted, and his burning lips traced a line of fire along her thighs as his voice, hoarse with passion, said, "I want to taste every inch of you, Elizabeth." She was not certain of his meaning until his kisses moved closer and closer, and at that moment, she stopped breathing.

Her mind was screaming that he must stop whatever he was doing. Yet, the voice of her mind was a weak whisper compared to her body's demand for more. The sensations she felt when his mouth replaced his fingers were astonishing and the world collapsed around her. There was nothing except him and the storm of pleasure into which he threw her once more.

"My beautiful wife..." She barely understood the words of love tickling her ear as his weight suddenly took her breath away. "Please look at me."

She obeyed instantly, though her eyelashes felt heavy. He was lying upon her, their faces merely inches apart, and his warm breath bore the scent of her own passion.

"It will be painful," he said with soft concern; yet, what she saw in his dark eyes, more powerful than his obvious care for her, was a profound, barely restrained desire.

She knew it would be painful and had thought she would be afraid of that moment, but she was not. His expression changed again, and his eyes caressed her face with infinite tenderness. Elizabeth's soul melted in it as her body opened to him. With her own love and passion matching his, and with complete, unconditional trust in her husband, Elizabeth offered herself to him. Whatever was to come could not but be marvellous because it would come from him! And marvellous it was.

He entered her with a tender passion, causing the sharp pain that cut her body soon to be forgotten. He was inside her — inside her body as he had been inside her heart for so many months — and each of his moves tore through her in the most blissful, astonishing way — unbearable pleasure and unbearable pain. Her soul was full of love and her body full of passion — his passion and hers together.

A cry — his or hers? — waves of fulfilled desire shattering their bodies, her hands embracing him with desperation, his lips covering her face with innumerable kisses, the sound of their wildly racing breaths — and nothing more. Silence and blissful happiness.

HER HAIR SMELLED OF JASMINE and her body smelled of love — the most intoxicating blend of scents Darcy had ever experienced.

He was lying on the bed, spent and yet restless in his desire, holding Elizabeth tightly. Her back was turned against him and her long, silky hair was caressing his chest. He would like to read in her eyes — in her soul — everything she was feeling and thinking now that she was his wife, but she was turned to face the fire and seemed to avoid his gaze. Darcy was puzzled and worried.

His body was still unsatisfied in its need and urge for her, despite the fact that he had just experienced the most exhilarating explosions of pleasure. He still desired her and was angry with himself for this lack of control. He knew he had not been as patient as he should have been. He knew that his pleasure must have been a painful moment for her; he also knew he must have frightened her with his unbridled behaviour as he himself was amazed by some of his gestures. She had already been embarrassed by their earlier interlude, and he took her distress in jest. Instead of restraining his passion, he cared for no boundaries — no rules. To kiss her everywhere the way he did — it was something he had never considered before. Yet, touching Elizabeth, kissing her, caressing her seemed the most natural thing to do, and he did not hesitate for a single moment; he had simply been thirsty for her passion and impulsively slaked his thirst. Was she upset?

She did enjoy herself, he was certain of that, at least for some part of their...activities. He remembered vividly the expression of her beautiful face the moment she had reached the peak of her pleasure, and she was hurt too. He also remembered that moment very clearly. What was she feeling now? What was she thinking of him that very moment, lying naked in his arms, covered by bed sheets and her long, soft hair?

"Elizabeth?" He placed a kiss on her temple and felt her startling. "Please speak to me, my love."

Hesitantly, she turned in his arms so they faced each other. Her soft skin brushing his was a sweet, painful torture, which further aroused his desire.

"Do not worry; I am well," she assured him, still avoiding his gaze.

"You are not, my love. Were you well, I would see your sparkling eyes smiling at me. Was it *very* painful?"

She finally glanced at him, and her eyes were indeed sparkling — only with tears. "It is not that; do not distress yourself, I am well. I am just being silly; it is of no consequence. I shall be fine."

She nestled to his chest and they remained in silence for a time.

"You do not trust me enough to tell me what is upsetting you? I know you are not being '*silly*'."

"I am jealous," she burst out nervously. He felt her stiffen and stop breathing, awaiting his reaction.

"Pardon me?" inquired a shocked Darcy, wondering what on earth she could mean. "How can you be jealous?"

"Oh, I told you I am only being silly; you should not have forced me to speak of it!"

He turned her on her back and laid her against the pillows; his inquisitive stare — mere inches away — together with a severe expression and hands holding her possessively told Elizabeth clearly enough she ought not to trifle with him or attempt to escape without a full confession. She was not certain whether she should laugh or be angry at her own folly in raising such a preposterous subject in the middle of their wedding night.

"It is obvious that you are not...umm...inexperienced in this matter, and I cannot help wondering how many times you have done this before." Her voice was trembling slightly, her cheeks suddenly pale as she forced herself to keep her eyes on his.

He was speechless; his countenance changed visibly as his eyes averted from hers for a moment. His tried to say something, but he hesitated; his body moved from hers, and she felt suddenly cold. "William, please forgive me. I know I had no right to start such a conversation..."

Darcy's distress was obvious, so she easily understood she was right, and her aching heart sank.

"Elizabeth, it is true that this is a very improper conversation for a man to have with his wife, and I am at a loss as to what I should tell you. But I want to assure you that you have every right to ask me anything you want, though sometimes I might not be able to offer you the answers you expect."

"I understand." Elizabeth's voice was trembling, and her long lashes could not hide a tear in the corner of an eye. She tried to smile dejectedly.

"Do you truly want me to speak of this subject?"

"Yes... No... I do not know. We should perhaps sleep now." She turned her back to him again, facing the fire; a moment later, his arms embraced her with tender care. She remained motionless but did not reject his attention. More confidently, he pulled her to his chest, and his lips moved closer to her ear.

"I shall be as honest as possible, though I dread the thought of having this discussion." She did not reply; her breath became shallower.

"I will confess I am not...inexperienced as you said. I have had my share of knowledge as any man of my age I imagine — certainly less than some of them."

"I see. Thank you for your honest answer. I am aware I have no right to be interested in something that happened before you even knew me. But the mere thought of your holding another woman as you hold me was —"

"Elizabeth, I have *never* held any other woman as I hold *you*," he interrupted her.

He pulled her to him so fiercely that she felt suffocated in his embrace. One of his arms tightened its grip around her waist and the other was stroking her shoulder and neck; his warm lips caressed her ear while speaking, and his hoarse voice sent shivers along her body.

"I have never imagined I could touch or kiss a woman as I have you. What we shared this night was equally as new for me as it was for you, though I did know more of what was to come. You said that what we shared tonight was unexpected for you. I can say that for me it was more exquisite than anything I expected, than anything I dreamed during my lonely nights thinking of you."

He paused a moment, holding her tightly and searching for her hands; their fingers entwined, and now she was truly captive in his arms, her back crushed against his chest.

His voice was as tender as a caress. "Elizabeth, I have *known* other women before you, but I have never *loved* anyone except you — either with my heart or my body."

He felt her breath quicken and her heart beat wildly. She moved slightly in his embrace and turned her head so he could see her face. "Thank you."

"I love you, Elizabeth," he said, and again there was silence for a while. Darcy was certain she had fallen asleep, but he was proved wrong a few minutes later.

"It was painful but in a pleasant way," she confessed unexpectedly, and he startled.

"I am sorry," he said, somehow distressed, but she chuckled.

"Do not be sorry. Becoming your wife has mirrored our relationship from the moment we met until now."

"What do you mean?" he inquired, puzzled.

"I mean — quite painful at times, occasionally distressing, but in essentials exceptionally enjoyable. I confess I have no cause to repine."

She laughed, hiding her head against the pillows, and he breathed in relief. Finally, she was her usual self again. He could not see her, but he could *feel* her smile through every fibre of his body.

"I am very glad to hear that, Mrs. Darcy." There was another moment of silence before he continued.

"May I dare hope your distress is now gone and you will finally turn to look at me?" His voice was husky, and his lips were placing soft kisses along her ear; she shivered but remained still.

"My distress is gone indeed, but I would rather not turn."

"You would not? Are you still upset with me?" he asked, quite worried.

"No indeed, sir, quite the contrary. I would rather remain as we are only because I find it very pleasant being held like this," she admitted.

"Oh, now I see." He finally understood. His fingers removed the locks of her hair from her ear, baring her cheek and neck, and then continued to caress her soft skin tenderly.

"Then please do not turn around, Mrs. Darcy. I would by no means suspend any pleasure of yours."

Elizabeth laughed nervously, suppressing a moan as her skin quivered beneath his kisses. His hands started to move daringly along her body — so fully exposed to his passionate exploration. One hand encircled her waist, stroked her belly and then slid down to her thighs, while the other possessively cupped her breasts; his fingers traced tingling circles around each of them, teasing her nipples, which hardened with desire. Her body writhed and pushed against his, imprisoned by his possessive touches; his arms tightened their grip, pulling her closer to him and gently commanding her to obey his wishes. She felt his chest against her back, his strong legs entwined with hers and his thighs pressing against her bottom. She could feel his desire arousing again, and a sense of fear and passionate desire shattered her body.

"Allow me to make you a promise, Mrs. Darcy." She was not certain if he truly spoke or only the touch of his tongue made her dream it.

"Please do so, sir," she answered breathlessly. Her head turned a little so her dry lips could finally meet his.

"You said that *becoming* my wife had been sometimes painful and distressing…"

"And exceptionally enjoyable…"

"I promise that *being* my wife will never be painful — as long as it is in my power to prevent it."

"I do trust you in that, sir," she replied, and that shared promise seemed awkwardly serious considering the circumstances.

"And it will also be much more enjoyable than it has been so far — as long as it is in my power to accomplish it," he added more lightly, smiling mischievously against her lips, which he eventually captured with passion.

"I do not believe it can get *much* more enjoyable than what has already transpired between us."

"You must trust me in this too, my dearest wife," he said, barely able to speak as his lips were more agreeably engaged. "As I already said, this is quite a new experience for me as well. I can truthfully say that the more I practice, the more proficient I become. Would you not agree?"

She would laugh at his shameless promise, but she found herself crying her pleasure as his fingers daringly touched the warmth between her thighs. The strokes — long, gentle, and tantalisingly slow at first — turned into a wild torture. She finally turned in his arms to face him, but their eyes met only for a moment as his lips journeyed along her jaw line, briefly tasting her chin before moving to her throat until his hungry mouth reached the softness of her round breasts. His lips closed around her nipple and she cried again while passion conquered her once more. Moment by moment, the urge, the longing to feel him inside her again grew unbearable, defeating any remnants of fear or pain — and she pleaded with him, begged him until her longing was finally satisfied.

A brief, sharp pain and he entered her again with renewed, unleashed desire. As she was thrown into a storm of feelings, wondering how he could be so strong and large — yet fit so perfectly within her — possessive and almost wild in his thrusts, yet so tender and caring, a single thought crossed her mind: he was right again.

Now that she was his wife, everything was less painful and more blissfully enjoyable than ever before.

Chapter 24

The entire Town was covered with snow, and Elizabeth's eyes sparkled with delight as she walked the gleaming white paths on her husband's arm. Since the first morning of their married life five days earlier, they had taken long strolls in the same park where they had met in June. Apart from this meaningful digression, they preferred to stay home and enjoy their newly discovered marital bliss.

Though they received many invitations, they accepted none. Neither was disposed to entertain either strangers or friends; they had yet to see Cassandra and Georgiana or the colonel. A day earlier, the Gardiners had returned from Hertfordshire, and the newlyweds did call — briefly — in Gracechurch Street. However, they declined to remain for dinner, and wisely, Mrs. Gardiner did not insist.

Their time was spent mostly in the library or the music room, and with every passing day, their bond became stronger as they came to know each other more intimately — in every sense.

She was as lively as ever, whereas he was less restrained and less serious than before — a change quickly noticed by everyone around them, and with her naturally easy ways, Elizabeth became the favourite of the staff almost as soon as she entered the house.

Darcy was somewhat annoyed one morning when he overheard two maids gossiping about how fortunate they were that he had chosen a wife so different from him in disposition and manners. For a moment, he had considered dismissing them but then thought better of it. After all, they were right; he knew he was a fair master, and the servants were content with their lives in his home, but he had never been a joyful presence. Elizabeth, however, brought liveliness to his home — and to his life.

"We should return home," Darcy said, covering her gloved hand with his. "Your bonnet is covered with snow, and your cheeks are crimson. I am sure your feet and hands are frozen."

"I am not cold at all, quite the contrary. I have always enjoyed walking through snow. I feel very well, exceedingly well, I might say!" she laughed at him, and he felt an urge to kiss her red cheeks.

"Very well, we shall stay fifteen more minutes. Is that acceptable?"

"Am I allowed to negotiate, sir?"

"Not really, as you promised to obey me," he replied with mocking severity.

Thus began one of their little games during the last few days. They teased each other until their play turned into a minor skirmish. He loved to see her blush and then narrow her eyes in search of a sharp reply. Her lips twisted and her eyebrow raised in challenge reminded him of the beginning of their acquaintance and their lively conversations at Netherfield. The only difference was that now he could do what he was not allowed back then: whenever he felt she was about to win their arguments, he simply made use of his strength and silenced her with a kiss. She always accused him of improper behaviour, and of course, she was right.

"Be as you like, sir, I shall obey; besides, we have to prepare for dining at Cassandra's tonight."

"I am glad; I would not want you to catch a cold and be ill all the way to Pemberley."

"Will there be snow at Pemberley, do you think?"

"I hope so...for your sake."

He removed snow from her hair and briefly touched her face, but it was warm.

"I told you I am not cold," she whispered.

"So you did," he agreed. "I should have known that you are always as warm as a sunny day." With a short glance around, he placed a soft kiss on her cheek.

They returned home through snow that was now ankle-deep. Elizabeth's petticoat seemed frozen, yet she did not mind at all. She continued to chat with Darcy, and every time she looked at him, the snow falling from the sky tickled her face, and she laughed as she lost herself in her husband's loving gaze.

"Thank God you are home!" the housekeeper cried as soon as they entered, in a tone more proper for a mother. "You must be frozen — you should go upstairs immediately; your baths will be ready within minutes. A cup of hot tea will do wonders for your state," she added as she removed Elizabeth's bonnet.

"Thank you so much, Mrs. Abbot. You are a mind reader." Elizabeth smiled warmly. "Hot tea and a warm bath will be truly wonderful."

The efficiency of Darcy's staff was proven — again — less than a quarter hour later when the mistress and master of the house were each enjoying a cup of delicious tea inside their warm tubs.

As soon as the hot water enveloped her, Elizabeth felt drowsy and closed her eyes, sighing with contentment. Her body was heavy with fatigue, and her eyelids seemed unwilling to open. In fact, it was not quite fatigue, but more a lack of sleep. She had not slept an entire night in more than a month, first from apprehension before the wedding, and then...She felt her cheeks burning at the thought of their previous nights.

Her husband had shared her bed every night as he promised, and it was bliss to sleep in his arms. Well, actually, it was not quite sleeping as most of the night was spent in...certain activities. And afterward, it was difficult to fall asleep; his scent, his warmth, his arms confining her — every sensation was entirely new for her. Consequently, she usually slept only a few hours before the sun was up and she had to awaken.

Of course, she could have slept longer during the day, but that was unacceptable. How could she spend the first days of her marriage sleeping and abandoning her husband? That would not do — especially when she had the fortune to marry the most generous, kind and loving husband!

Indeed, Darcy was everything she had hoped for and so much more. Every day she spent with him was a chance to discover fresh, intimate details that only made her love him more.

Many of his former habits remained, of course — including the mask of severity that marred his countenance when he was displeased or preoccupied with something; but it was no wonder that he was frequently serious.

She understood only a smattering of his duties from the papers that constantly covered his desk.

There was a variety of people dependent upon him and numeous responsibilities to burden him; she invited him to share his worries, and he was as surprised — and pleased — with her interest as she was gratified by his confidence in her. He did not hesitate to answer any of her questions or to explain anything she wanted to know about his business. She felt treated not just with deep affection, but also with great consideration; he declared that he felt spoiled by her love and by her genuine interest in everything connected with him. What more could she want?

Then, when the evening came, they would retire to their apartments. There, he set aside all restraint, self-control, rules, and duties. There he was simply her husband.

One evening — the third day of their marriage — she pointed this out, and he replied while taking her in his arms, "I am your husband all the time, my dearest; here I am your lover." And so he was.

Though Elizabeth had known something of a wife's duties before her marriage, her knowledge was contradictory.

She had heard — from many whispers spread around — that those activities were unpleasant for a lady, and that most women tried to keep their husband's nightly visits as infrequent as possible. In fact, those *un*-pleasantries were the main reason many ladies accepted that their husbands kept mistresses. Elizabeth started to question the accuracy of this theory when she was about sixteen and had heard that some ladies of society kept lovers themselves. Why would a lady indulge in such activities, risking the ruin of her reputation, if those activities were abhorrent? She even dared to address that delicate question with her Aunt Gardiner, and the lady laughed for a time before she regained her composure enough to offer Elizabeth an answer — one that was honest, albeit 'dressed' in suitable language.

Elizabeth never doubted her aunt, so she trusted implicitly the revelation that, where there was affection and understanding between man and wife, and where the husband was concerned not only for his well being but for his wife's as well, the intimacy of marriage was nothing to be anxious about — quite the contrary.

Moreover, since the first moments she had admitted her feelings for Darcy, every time he touched her hand, danced with her, or merely smiled at her, the shivers that spread over her body were excellent indications that her aunt had been right in this — as always.

Of course, their engagement — as trying as it was — offered Elizabeth more reasons to feel confident and desirous of what would come in her marriage. However, everything she thought she knew proved to be pale in comparison to the reality of her wedding night.

That was not a duty to perform; it was the most intimate way of receiving her husband's love through his unleashed passion.

Of course, Elizabeth understood very well how fortunate she was among so many women who were less happy in their marriages. She knew that the exquisite pleasure her husband so generously offered her every night was something most precious. His soft, breathtaking kisses and tender caresses were proof of that care and consideration her aunt had spoken of so many years ago. In truth, she felt that Darcy was more concerned with her wishes than his and preoccupied with giving her pleasure long before he sought his own.

In those significant days since her wedding, Elizabeth learned that, for him as a man, the pleasure, the fulfilment came from the *act itself* — precisely that part of their lovemaking that was less pleasant for her as it was still a little painful and somewhat awkward.

She did enjoy being united with her husband — she liked it from the first time, despite the considerable pain she had to suffer on their wedding night. She liked to feel his weight upon her, to listen to his cries of pleasure, to feel his passionate thrusts inside her and that warmth spread in her body when *his* moment came.

Fortunately, the pain had diminished over time and become bearable; perhaps her body had managed to *accommodate* him, or perhaps it had become accustomed to the pain; regardless, her discomfort was less perceptible day by day. Still, for her, it was not so much her own pleasure, as it was a sense of happiness for sharing that complete intimacy with her beloved husband. It was the final proof that, regarding a wife's duties, both parts were correct: sharing a marriage bed could be a horribly unpleasant duty, something a woman should try to escape from as much as she could, or it could be an enjoyable affair, something to anticipate eagerly.

Elizabeth was certain their situation was special, as they were — unquestionably — the happiest couple in the world in every respect.

She laughed at her own musings, wondering what Darcy was doing and how long she had been in the tub, lost in her thoughts; she hoped she would have some time to rest a little before they left for Cassandra's dinner.

The maid helped her out, and then Elizabeth allowed her to retire. She looked at her bed, moved closer to the door and listened carefully. A moment later, she rolled her eyes in exasperation. What was this ridiculous behaviour? Surely, she could knock at her husband's door if she wanted to know what he was doing.

She did so, and his voice invited her in; he was at his desk, reading some letters.

"Come in, please," he said, hurrying to take her hand.

"I do not want to disturb you; I was only curious about what you were doing, but please return to your papers. I shall go and rest while you finish."

"My papers can wait," he replied. "They held my attention only while you were not here. I can do little when you are away, because I think of you all the time. You are dangerous for my business, Mrs. Darcy." He placed a long kiss in her palm and she shivered.

"Are you cold?" he inquired instantly.

"No…"

"But you shivered."

"Yes…"

Her voice turned more hesitant as his became graver; he stared at her and a smile twisted his lips.

"I see…" he said.

His thumb traced small circles in her palm where his lips had rested a moment before.

"This is why you shivered?" he inquired, and she felt she was melting. She forced a smile and nodded silently.

"Then we must do something about that shiver," he concluded and unexpectedly lifted her in his arms. She gasped and put her arms around his neck.

"Shall I take you to your room and allow you to rest? Or will you stay here with me?" he asked seriously, while his strong palm stroked her shoulder. Their eyes were locked, and she easily recognised that expression; his fingers were burning her through the thin fabric and his mouth was now dangerously close to hers.

"But it is the middle of the day," she managed to say just before their lips joined.

"Yes, I am well aware of that."

It seemed that he did not really need an answer as he laid her on the bed and moved to her side.

His lips travelled along her face, to her earlobe and down to her neck. When his mouth reached the edge of the gown, his hands abandoned hers and hurried to pull the fabric down; her skin was silkier than the gown and his hungry mouth only hesitated briefly before he tasted it.

She moaned and her back arched toward him; he lifted his eyes to look at her and kissed her lips gently. "Elizabeth, tell me if you want me to stop; if you really want to rest, I will leave you this instant," he whispered.

"The servant may enter," she replied breathlessly.

"That is not what I asked you, dearest." He smiled, kissing her once more. "No one will disturb us if that is your worry. My worry is what you wish me to do."

She swallowed the lump in her throat; it was full daylight and her husband was only a few inches from her, staring at her with a passion that made her tremble.

"Please cover me with the sheets," she said. He did so in an instant, as though he was afraid she would change her mind. Yet, there was no danger of that on her part.

By then, her mind and body were both prepared for what would come. She anticipated each touch, each caress, each kiss that followed on her neck, on her shoulders, on her breasts now free from the gown, and then her thighs opened just a moment before his hand travelled there, and she moaned loudly even before his daring fingers touched her. She heard him laughing briefly before he kissed her again. His mouth abandoned hers and started its journey down her body; Elizabeth wondered how it was possible that, though her head was spinning wildly, her mind was registering so vividly every sensation she experienced.

Several exquisite moments later, her body, already consumed by pleasure, started to burn inside, longing for him. Almost instantly, his kisses and caresses became more fervent, and he parted her legs; she felt him lying upon her, careful not to crush her, and she tensed, awaiting the usual pain to come — and to go. He entered her with some urgency, and the expectant cry escaped her lips, but this time her anticipation was wrong.

There was no pain at all. Her body remained still; he noticed and stopped moving. "Elizabeth?"

Still incredulous, she opened her eyes and met his — and she breathed deeply as she smiled at him.

For the first time in their marriage, her body started to move first, tentatively, then more and more confidently. She was not sure what was happening, nor did she dare to think of it too much. The rhythm of his thrusts soon became wilder and deeper, and she was certain that moment would come soon, and for the first time, she wished it would last longer. However, she was wrong again.

His movements slowed, and she felt his torso rising up from her; through her eyelashes, she saw him kneeling between her thighs, staring at her. She was completely exposed to his eyes now, the sheet long gone. He continued to move inside her slowly as his hands caressed her legs, her hips, her belly, and finally rested upon her breasts and cupped them with renewed possessiveness. She cried so loudly that he pressed a finger to her lips, and then leaned down to cover her mouth with his.

She could feel him pulsing inside her and thrusting harder. Her hips joined that pace, as eager as his were, and they moved together until, in desperate need of air, she broke their kiss.

She cried out again, shocked by another novelty: each of his thrusts built a fire inside her that spread and burned her very core, igniting every inch of her skin. Waves of pleasure shattered her body and she was certain she had fainted. She was proved wrong — again — when she felt that well-known warmth cooling the fire inside her and his weight falling upon her.

"Oh my God, Elizabeth…" he whispered, kissing her palm tenderly as they lay side by side.

Her fingers caressed his, but she did not look at him yet.

"What happened?" he inquired and held his breath.

"What do you mean?"

"I mean — it was…somehow different. You were different…"

He could not find the proper words, and only continued to caress her hand gently before pulling her to his chest. She sighed and remained silent, her fingers entwined with his.

"Elizabeth…? I know you were not comfortable to do *that* now in full daylight, but I hope you feel confident enough to tell me if my insistence upset you."

"You did not upset me; you know that, but I am not completely at ease yet. I mean — we never…during the day," she replied with obvious embarrassment. "On the other hand, you cannot expect me to become completely at ease with every aspect of marriage in less than a week, can you, sir?"

He laughed and kissed her other hand. "You are correct, of course, my dearest." He paused, and she felt him looking carefully at her while his voice betrayed his amusement.

"Perhaps if we were to practice daily, any uneasiness would pass very soon."

"You are insufferable, sir!" she censured him. His insinuating flirtation succeeded in easing her embarrassment, and his obvious good mood gave her the courage to confess her intimate secret.

"It was different than before, you were right…"

"In a good way?" he interrupted her, hesitantly, and she chuckled.

"In a very good way," she admitted, averting her eyes for a moment. "For the first time, there was no pain at all when you…you know…" She blushed.

To Elizabeth's surprise, instead of words of relief, a long silence followed. She could see the concern in his eyes, while a furrow of worry appeared between his eyebrows.

"Elizabeth, what are you saying? Do you mean that, until now, every time was painful for you?"

She tried to find the words to explain, but he continued, his face pale. "So all this time I hurt you?"

"William, you never hurt me. It is just that —"

"Please, my love, you know what I meant. Were you in pain each and every time?"

She nodded, suddenly regretting her unfortunate slip of words.

"Was I so demanding, so insistent that you could not resist me? Why did you not tell me?"

"Tell you what, William? I knew that, for a woman, it would be painful. I expected it to be so. I expected it to be even worse, but it is gone now. I confess that the intimacy of marriage is more... enjoyable than I expected and hoped it would be."

He seemed to pay attention more to his own thoughts than to her words as his torment grew. "I had no idea, no idea at all. In my selfishness, I was certain you enjoyed sharing your bed with me. I thought you welcomed my attentions."

"I do, William! Trust me, my husband; you have no reason to worry, and I have no reason to complain. The pain has diminished each time since our wedding night, and I became accustomed to it. Besides, how could I have refused you something that gave you so much pleasure when you have been so generous and caring with me every time? I enjoy being with you; I cannot and I do not want to resist you," she concluded with a loving glance.

He looked at her blankly, rose from the bed and hurried to pour himself a glass of wine; he gulped a little, threw the glass in the fire, and paced the room. She was startled.

"Good God, I shall never learn! Will I never be able to see your true feelings and wishes? I see only what I *want* to see! Again and again, it is all about my desires and— Oh heavens, I practically forced myself upon you."

"William, please come here," she demanded. She had to repeat her request before he tentatively stepped closer to the bed. She reached her hands to him, forcing him to stay there, and then encircled his neck with her arms.

"My dear Mr. Darcy, allow me to tell you how much I love and admire you, though sometimes you are such an utter and complete fool! Do you not know how I long for your kisses, for your caresses, for your warmth? How can you believe you forced me to accept you? Did I not tell you — did you not see yourself — how much joy, how much pleasure, how much bliss I find in your arms? You want to know if it was painful? Yes, it was; in truth, the first time was so painful that I thought my body was cut in two."

"Elizabeth —"

"Let me finish, please! However, I would gladly bear ten times that pain for the happiness of feeling you with me... inside me! How can you doubt that you have seen my true feelings and wishes? Can you not *feel* my regard for you? If not, that would truly hurt me!"

"Elizabeth..." he interrupted her again. His strong palms cupped her face, and he held her thus for a moment, speaking to her only with his eyes. He was still heavy-hearted, she could see that, and the emotions of the day almost overwhelmed her; soon she could not bear his stare any longer.

"I would like to rest a little," she said.

"Of course, my love." He expected her to retire to her room, but she simply leaned back on the pillow and closed her eyes. He covered her and then lay by her side; she started to breathe steadily and cuddle against his chest. After a while, he felt her moving in his arms.

"William, we are such fools. Why did we argue, after all? I mean…we should have been happy…you know…after…"

"We did not argue, my love. We just — It was my fault. I am the only fool here; you have to grant me that. A very happy fool, though," he admitted as she laughed, and then she sighed and finally fell asleep.

IT WAS QUITE DIFFICULT FOR Darcy to wake her an hour later. When he finally succeeded, she could barely open her eyes, so he offered her a little coffee.

"Hmmm…" She watched him carefully. "You seem in a good mood, sir. Have you slept as well?"

"No, I have not. I have employed my time much better."

"Oh, I see." She put her cup down and leaned closer to him. "And may I inquire as to what employment has made you so cheerful in such a short time?"

"It is no secret, madam. I stayed here and watched you while you slept."

She opened her eyes in surprise. "You watched me?"

He leaned toward her so they almost touched each other. "That I *admired* you would be a better choice of words. And I recollected some special moments…"

"Oh —" She found nothing more to say.

"Can you guess of what moments I am speaking?"

"I cannot, sir. And I have no time for these kinds of games; it is already very late. We must hurry." She felt uncomfortable as she tried to arrange her gown and climb out of bed, but he held her arm, and she was forced to look at him.

"You did enjoy yourself today, did you not?" he suddenly asked, and her cheeks instantly turned crimson. She did not expect that conversation to start once more; however, he continued as his thumb brushed over her lips. "It was the first time you took your pleasure at almost the same moment I did; am I right? God, you were so beautiful, my love, and I was so happy I could see you. I love seeing you in the full light of day."

"You are embarrassing me," she whispered against his fingers.

"I thought we decided you would never feel embarrassed with me."

"Truly sir, feeling embarrassed is not something I can control. I do not possess your self-discipline," she teased him. Her palm was still on his face, and he turned his head to kiss it.

"My discipline always evaded me in your presence. As for mortifying you — please forgive me. I will try to be less honest in my expressions if that would please you. "

He gently laid her against the pillow. "You must learn to tell me what pleases you, Mrs. Darcy."

She felt she was melting, incapable of replying as his fingers touched her lips and parted them slowly. His tantalising mouth abandoned her hand and moved to her neck. "Is this pleasant enough, Mrs. Darcy?"

She licked her lips and turned her head to face him; she longed for his kisses, and when his mouth finally captured hers, she moaned with satisfaction. His body brushed against hers, and she started moving beneath him. She knew they should stop immediately and prepare for dinner, yet she hoped that he would not remember their engagement. She was shocked to discover how much she desired his attention such a short while after their previous interlude, yet she could not help herself.

Her arms encircled his neck, and his weight crushed her against the sheets; she felt herself burning inside, and cold shivers travelled along her skin. She quivered, awaiting his touches.

And then he stopped and separated from her, struggling to breathe again. "We should start preparing for dinner, my love, or else we shall arrive when the others are leaving."

She closed her eyes, struggling for air and only nodded in agreement. She was unable to speak — or to think — and all she hoped for was to regain some composure before she returned to her room.

His gentle kiss on her forehead made her open her eyes, and she faced his joyful, mischievous gaze.

"Are you well, dearest? Shall I bring you some water? You look quite flushed."

He seemed amused and satisfied with himself, but Elizabeth was not pleased at all. Was he toying with her? He surely would not dare!

A sudden knock at the door startled her, and she hurried up from the bed, desperately trying to arrange her gown. In no rush, Darcy put on his robe and opened the door without allowing the servant to enter. In the meantime, Elizabeth brushed her gown and passed through the adjoining room to her chamber, disappearing before being seen in such a state. In the privacy of her room, she filled a glass with water, swallowed it instantly, and then poured another. Her thirst was difficult to slake.

As she began to breathe steadily again and prepared to call for her maid, Darcy appeared in the doorway.

"Why did you run?"

"Why? Surely I could not stay to be seen by your servant in such a state."

"But I already told you there is no need to worry; no servant will ever enter my bedroom without my permission. However, I imagine there will be times when he will see you in your indoor gowns as I hope you will visit my room quite often." He tried to tease her, but she was still uneasy

"You know very well that it was not about my indoor gown, but about my whole appearance. I looked as —"

"You looked as though you had just been passionately loved by your husband and were willing to be loved again," he said without even lowering his voice. "We can only hope that the next hours will pass quickly and we can return to continue what we started."

She blushed violently and did not have time to reply before he kissed her hand and left the room with the same mischievous smile on his face. He was indeed very pleased with himself; that was quite clear now.

She remembered those nights they spent together before being married; he told her she was torturing him with her caresses and with the power she had over him. Surely, that power was gone now — or was all in his hands. She blushed at her own choice of words — indeed it was all in his hands, in his kisses, in his — *Oh, this will not do! What is happening to me?*

Elizabeth narrowed her eyes and bit her lower lip. His self-confidence and her weakness in the face of his mischievous little games deserved an immediate, proper response.

She changed her gown for a new one and then covered herself with a robe as she rang for the maid. She brushed her hair and pulled it back tightly; a quick glance in the mirror showed that she looked proper enough.

Breathing deeply and fighting the voice of reason that whispered to abandon her plan, Elizabeth stepped to her husband's room. She knocked at the door and waited to be invited in. His servant was just shaving him, and Elizabeth remained disconcerted in front of them.

"May I be of some assistance to you, Mrs. Darcy?" asked the servant with perfect politeness.

"No…no, thank you," she replied tentatively.

"May *I* be of some assistance, Mrs. Darcy?" inquired Darcy with a mischievous voice and a meaningful glance. That was enough to raise her courage to follow through on her little revenge. "In fact, yes, you may, sir. I would like a word with you, only for a moment. There is a matter of some urgency I would like to discuss with you."

"Now?" he asked, puzzled; then, with a gesture, he dismissed the servant.

"Elizabeth, what has happened?" He sounded worried and she felt even more pleased with herself.

"Nothing really." She smiled and leaned her head near his, as he remained in the chair. She put one hand on his shoulder and the other, daringly, rested on his thigh. Her lips were almost touching his ear as she whispered, "I just wanted to say that you were right about what happened earlier; I did enjoy myself…very much…in a different way than before."

She looked at his image in the mirror and watched his expression change; she smiled and briefly brushed her lips over his cheek. He turned his head toward her, but she withdrew before his mouth could capture hers. Only her fingers touched his lips for a moment, and then she left. Just before she closed the door behind her, she cast a last, quick glance in the mirror, only to see an astonished Darcy staring incredulously at her reflection.

She knew she should feel ashamed for her wanton flirtation, but she felt quite pleased: whatever power her husband might have over her, her own power was no less. She entered her room laughing, wondering how it was possible that she, Elizabeth

Bennet, once a country girl not pretty enough to tempt Mr. Darcy to dance with her, made him tremble only by whispering a few words and kissing his cheek.

That was indeed extraordinary, and she enjoyed every minute of it!

CAROLINE BINGLEY WAS GONE FOR only five days, and she was happier than ever before. Her tour with Lady Sophia was the most enjoyable time she had had in years, and there were many long weeks ahead to anticipate.

Of course, Lady Sophia had not been entirely honest with her, but Caroline forgave her after her ladyship explained to her the reason for secrecy. After all, she was correct: Charles never would have allowed her to leave if he had known that Viscount Markham would be in Lady Sophia's group!

Caroline was shocked to see Markham on the second day of their trip, and for some time she was not inclined to talk to him. She felt betrayed and hurt by his abominable behaviour two months earlier.

However, Lord Markham proved to Caroline that his interest in her was still alive. He patiently allowed her time to recover from her anger; he continued to be polite with her without being too insistent, and she could not ignore his charming manners for long. Just the evening before, she allowed him the opportunity to explain what happened during that horrible night at Netherfield.

He admitted that he had imbibed an excess of brandy and did not remember exactly what occurred.

He did recollect that he went into the yard to take some fresh air and that Miss Bennet was there — but he was at a loss as to what happened next. He had some memory of somehow falling over a woman, and he suspected it was Miss Bennet, but the others pretended it was Lady Cassandra — so that was the best proof that, whatever he might have done that night, it was only the result of his state of confusion. As he was an honourable man, he had even offered to marry Miss Bennet in order to satisfy his duty, but Mr. Bennet refused his offer. So, the next morning when he awoke and learned about the incident, he felt so ashamed that he preferred to leave the house immediately without daring to see Caroline and beg her forgiveness. Even more, Lord Markham confessed that he had insisted Lady Sophia allow him to join their group, precisely because he wanted to meet Caroline once more and win back her friendship.

At such an open declaration, Caroline surrendered completely. Her forgiveness was granted instantly, and all her hopes for an advantageous marriage to a handsome future earl were renewed. And this time she had no doubts she was correct in her judgement as that very morning the viscount sent her flowers — a most personal gesture — which clearly proved his intentions.

However, she would not repeat the same errors; she would not acknowledge to anyone these unexpected developments until she had received a clear offer of marriage. Only after she accepted the offer would she notify her family. That way neither

Charles nor his friends would be able to interfere and ruin her future again!

ELIZABETH AND DARCY WERE IN the carriage, face-to-face, silently staring at each other. They had barely spoken three words since they left the house, and each was waiting for the other to take the first step. Both had hidden smiles in their eyes, and each tried to conceal it. Biting her lips in an attempt to control her mirth, Elizabeth turned her eyes to the carriage window and watched the snow.

"It is lovely weather," she said.

"Lovely indeed — though quite cold," he admitted with perfect composure.

"I cannot wait to see Georgiana and Cassandra; I have missed them so much. I even missed the colonel. Did you not miss them, sir?"

"In truth, I just separated from them five days ago, and I have not had much time to think of them lately. But I will be pleased to see my sister and my friends again."

"Are you upset, sir? You do not seem inclined to talk to me," she said, sweetly.

"I am not upset; I am only astonished to see how much you have changed so soon after our wedding, Mrs. Darcy. You were such a sweet young lady before, and now you are quite evil. It seems you find great pleasure in tormenting your husband — among other things."

Elizabeth burst out in laughter just as the carriage stopped in front of Cassandra's house. Darcy helped her out and directed her toward the main entrance, but she delayed him a moment.

"I do not deserve such censure, sir. I have never been a '*sweet lady,*' nor am I evil now. I may be called, perhaps, '*impertinent*' as I always have been, but I hoped you would be accustomed to it by now. As for tormenting my husband, I confess I enjoy doing it as much as he enjoys tormenting me. In this we are evenly matched."

Her eyebrow arched in challenge, and there was such a mixture of sharpness and joy in her voice that he could not restrain his laughter. Without considering the impropriety of his gesture, he pulled her to him and kissed her lips passionately. Fortunately for their reputations, it was snowing, and there were few people on the street.

Cassandra's butler opened the door and started coughing meaningfully until the couple finally noticed him.

"Good day, Simons, how are you?"

"Good day, Mr. Darcy, and welcome. I am very well indeed, thank you, sir."

"Have you met Mrs. Darcy before?"

Elizabeth smiled and the servant bowed to her. "I met the former Miss Bennet a few months ago. I am happy to meet you again, Mrs. Darcy. May I congratulate you on your marriage?"

"Thank you," she replied kindly and finally entered followed by her husband.

Simons was just taking their coats when Georgiana hurried to her and threw herself into Elizabeth's arms. Her new sister embraced her tightly, almost tearful at such an open display of affection.

"Elizabeth, I missed you so much! Let me look at you — you are so beautiful! You seem changed since we last met though it was only a week ago!"

"Dearest, I agree Elizabeth looks beautiful, but I doubt she has changed in a week," replied Darcy.

Georgiana turned to greet her brother, and he kissed her forehead tenderly.

"I have to say that I agree with Georgiana," the colonel intervened, approaching them and bowing to Elizabeth. "You look more beautiful than ever, Mrs. Darcy. And you, Cousin, are changed, too."

"Really?" Darcy replied while shaking his hand. "Do I also look *'more beautiful than ever'*?"

"Heaven forbid, Darcy. I have never considered a man to be beautiful; that is a word I use only for ladies."

"You look different, Brother," Georgiana said. "You look more… I cannot find the proper word."

"Perhaps more *'married'* would be the word?" Darcy replied, and all started to laugh.

"Or perhaps *'happy'* would be the proper word," Darcy whispered to Elizabeth, and she squeezed his arm, smiling lovingly.

"Oh, look who is finally here!" Cassandra exclaimed from the settee.

Elizabeth embraced her. "You look very well, indeed, Cassandra! I am so happy to see you!"

"And you look beautiful, my dear. I dare say that marriage suits you very well — better than any other young woman I have seen in a long time," Cassandra said with affection.

"That is because she wisely chose the proper husband," Darcy intervened, approaching his friend and kissing her hand. "You do look well, Cassandra; that is true."

"Thank you, *'Elizabeth's proper husband'*!" laughed Cassandra.

Their little chat continued until dinner was ready. A small table was arranged so that Cassandra could reach her plate. Elizabeth and Georgiana were seated on either side of Cassandra, and the two gentlemen were opposite them. Their small gathering was warm and friendly; they chatted, teased each other, and made plans — as much as it was possible. The dinner was a bittersweet affair.

The subject of the colonel's departure was discussed for some time, mostly among Darcy, Georgiana and the colonel himself. Though preoccupied with meeting her husband's glances as frequently as possible, Elizabeth did not fail to notice the behaviour of Cassandra and the colonel, nor their distress and their unsuccessful attempts to appear easy and joyful. They seemed to avoid facing each other, yet they forced their smiles all the time.

"When will you leave for Pemberley?" the colonel asked Darcy.

"The day after tomorrow."

"Will you take Georgiana with you?" the colonel continued, and all eyes were turned to Darcy, waiting for his answer. Elizabeth blushed, Cassandra smiled and Georgiana seemed worried.

"Oh, Brother, please allow me to stay with Cassandra until Christmas," the young girl pleaded to Darcy's utter relief. "We will come to Pemberley together in less than six weeks."

"Of course, I will allow you, dearest. I mean, if that is acceptable to Cassandra."

"Cassandra wants me to stay, do you not, Cassandra?"

"I certainly want you here, sweetie. It is settled, then; see, Georgie, I told you Darcy would not object to your staying in Town as you feared." Her mischievous smile made Darcy gulp some wine and Elizabeth stare at her plate.

"That sounds like a good arrangement," the colonel said gravely. "I think Georgiana's presence will be good for Cassandra, considering she is not yet fully recovered."

"I will take care of her, do not worry," Georgiana assured him.

The colonel smiled at her as he cast a quick glance toward Cassandra. "I do not worry, dearest. You are a very trustworthy young lady, Georgiana."

"I hope you will join us at Pemberley for Christmas, too, Colonel," said Elizabeth. "We do count on your presence, you know."

"You are very kind, Mrs. Darcy. I will try to be there; however, I cannot make a promise that I am not certain I will be able to keep. The army is not a place for making long term plans, you know."

"I know, sir; however, we will hope and pray to see you there."

"The entire Bennet family will be there." Darcy addressed his cousin. "And the Bingleys, the Hursts and maybe Caroline Bingley, too. I do count on your presence, you see," he added meaningfully, and Elizabeth looked at him with mocking reproach, while the others started to laugh.

Cassandra's face was pale, despite the smile on her lips, and she barely spoke at all for the rest of the evening. When Georgiana inquired about her lack of humour, she blamed her fatigue, and that was a sign for Darcy to announce their departure. Cassandra thanked them for their presence without attempting to delay them. Hesitantly, the colonel offered to remain a little longer in case his help was needed to take Cassandra to her room. She agreed and expressed her gratitude with distant politeness.

Darcy and Elizabeth said their goodbyes, and the colonel accompanied them outside. The snow continued to fall, steadily. All was whiteness and silence.

The carriage moved slowly. Darcy put his arm around Elizabeth's shoulders and tenderly caressed her face. "You spent quite some time watching the snow."

"I love when it snows." She leaned her head against him.

"Then you will love Pemberley in winter."

"I will love Pemberley anytime."

He took her hand and then suddenly chuckled. "I was at a loss for words when

David asked me if we would be bringing Georgiana with us!"

"I felt very embarrassed, too; we did not even talk about her! I hope she did not feel neglected."

"She would have felt more neglected if she had joined us as I plan to selfishly engage all your time, Elizabeth. I am not quite ready to share you with anyone."

She only smiled; he had expected more of a reaction.

"What is the matter, my dear? Your thoughts seem to be elsewhere. Or perhaps you are displeased with the prospect of being alone with me for more than a month?"

"Oh, that remark does not even deserve an answer," she replied with mocking severity. "It is about Cassandra."

"Cassandra? But she looked very well indeed. She has improved greatly in the last week."

"She did look well, but she is so sad, and so is the colonel. I cannot stand to see them like that."

"Oh, I understand. But Elizabeth, there is little we can do in this matter."

"I know, but I cannot help thinking of us — of our situation a few months ago."

"My dearest, things are completely different with them. There are no misunderstandings between them! The colonel declared his affection and his intention toward Cassandra openly and honestly. She is well aware of his feelings, and all she has to do is recognise her own wishes. David was a perfect gentleman when he decided to wait patiently for her decision. You know I am fond of Cassandra, but I cannot see any fault in David's behaviour toward her, and I do not believe she is in any danger from him. Would you not agree?"

"I do agree. Though I was quite upset with the colonel at times, I must admit that his devotion and care for Cassandra has been beyond reproach. It is just that they seem unable to speak to each other — to confess what they want. No, not both of them — only Cassandra."

"Cassandra is a courageous woman. Things will settle between them eventually. I am very confident."

Though her heart was still heavy with worry, Elizabeth accepted her husband's conclusions for the moment as they had just arrived home.

DAVID PLACED CASSANDRA ON HER bed and sat near her. As he had carried her from the dining room, her arms still encircled his neck, and he gently pulled his arm from behind her knees.

For a moment they remained still, their bodies touching with every breath, their eyes locked.

"I should leave," he said, but he did not move. "I am glad to know Georgiana will stay with you. You need someone to care for you." Cassandra smiled.

"There is no need to worry for my health; I have thirty servants to take care of me."

"You need someone to *care* for you," he repeated soundly.

"David, please be — be careful. I want nothing more than for you to return safely."

"Cassandra, I must be sincere with you. My hope is that you will want much more from me than to return safely. In the meantime, I give you my word that I will be cautious. I have no intention of letting myself be killed." He smiled, but her face darkened.

"David, please do not speak in jest about being killed. You promised you would allow me time to decide, and you kept your promise. And I will keep mine; when we next meet, I shall give you my final answer — if you are still interested in hearing it."

"Do you doubt that, Cassandra? Do you doubt the depth of my feelings?!"

"I do not doubt you, but I know the paths of the heart can take unexpected turns."

"My heart is not as unsteady as you think." He paused and looked at her intently. "Cassandra, I will confess something to you, but you must promise you will take it more like a jest. I would not want you to be upset with me, though I know my confession may sound highly improper."

"David, what are you trying to tell me?"

"I am trying to tell you about the first time I fell in love with you. I never told anyone, because I was deeply ashamed of my feelings, considering that I watched you growing up, almost like my sister; and even more, for a long time I was certain you would end up marrying Darcy."

"Oh come now," she laughed nervously. "Do not tell me you have loved me since I was ten."

"No, thank God — not since you were ten, but close," he replied as nervous as she was. "I first saw you not as my friend but as the most beautiful woman at your ball — when you were seventeen. I had not seen you in years, so when you appeared before me, I could not believe it was you — I simply could not take my eyes off you. I could not stand being apart from you, not even for a moment. It was the first time in my life that I felt my heart aching with desire to be close to a woman — to you. Please do not misunderstand me. Not for a second did I think of anything improper, but — I know it might sound ridiculous — I truly, deeply fell in love with you back then though you were almost still a child. I do not think you remember much of that ball, but for me it was a night of torture and delight. Do you remember you danced the first set with me? Your first *'official'* dance."

"Oh God, David," she whispered tearfully. "Of course I remember everything about that ball, and no, that evening I was not a child any longer. I remember vividly every moment of that night."

Cassandra seemed so distressed and her suffering so obvious that David looked at her disconcerted and regretful, furious with himself for that imprudent confession. How stupid he was! He took everything in jest, but for her, the recollection of the time when her parents were still alive was nothing but cause for more grief.

"Cassandra, I beg you to forgive me, I did not want to— I am such a fool! I hoped you would be amused, I hoped you would at least smile a bit, and instead I brought back only painful memories and made you cry. How could I be so thoughtless?"

He rose and bowed politely to her. "I had better leave; I should have left much earlier."

"David!"

She grabbed his arm and forced him to return to his place near her. Her lips opened to speak, but no words came out; instead, she looked at him with an expression he had never seen before.

Incredulous, David watched her as she leaned her head toward his and felt her lips approaching his face. His mouth ached with desire to feel hers, but her soft kiss rested on his cheek, and then her whisper burned his skin.

"Do not worry about my crying, David. Though you see tears, my heart does smile. And no, you did not bring back *only* painful memories. I truly thank you for remembering me at that ball. You surely are neither thoughtless nor a fool. Please do not apologise to me ever again."

An hour later in the carriage taking him to his regiment, Colonel Fitzwilliam remained incredulous about their last conversation. He could still feel the touch of Cassandra's lips on his face as he wondered how it was possible that his silly confession made her heart smile.

A FEW STREETS AWAY, STILL preoccupied with the situation of Cassandra and the colonel, Elizabeth was staring through the window, waiting for her husband. He had some important letters to finish for the next morning, and he was already an hour late; she became impatient and tired.

She lay on the bed, snuggling between the sheets. Surely, he would wake her when he came to bed. She closed her eyes, trying to find his scent in the pillows. But there was no trace of him there as a servant changed the bedclothes each evening. He would come soon; she knew it. He had slept with her every night since they were married. Would he continue this habit at Pemberley? Or were other rules to be followed there?

Suddenly, her mind was invaded by the memories of her first visit to Pemberley — the torment in her heart, the uncertainties, Cassandra's little jokes, the day in the grove, the storm when he held her on his horse, and that night when he entered her room and held her hand. Then there was the revelation of his lasting love, the happiness, the hopes and the news about Lydia shattering all her dreams. She remembered the sadness, the pain breaking her heart, and the rain falling upon Pemberley when she left unexpectedly without any hope of seeing him again.

She had almost lost him forever — not once, but twice: first, when she rejected him with all the power of her prejudiced anger and a desire to punish him, and second, when she ran away from him, the power of her love trying to protect him. How would life have been without him?

"William!" She jumped from the bed and promptly entered his room. Darcy was at his desk, reading some papers; his servant was preparing his belongings for their trip. Her entrance startled them both; the servant instantly exited the room as Darcy hurried to her.

"My love, what happened? You look so pale — and you are trembling. Are you ill?"

"Nothing happened, just hold me, please," she whispered, her arms tightening around his waist.

He wrapped her in his arms and took her to his bed, lying down with her. He covered her with the sheets, but she would not let go of his waist. He gently caressed her hair, her arms, and her back while his legs entwined with hers. Her toes were frozen, and she continued to tremble for a few minutes.

"Elizabeth, you worry me. Please talk to me, dearest."

"I missed you so much," she whispered, and he was astonished and even more worried.

"I missed you too, my beautiful wife." Lost for other words, he held her in silence, hoping she would recover soon and confess to him what happened. About a quarter of an hour later, when Darcy was certain she had fallen asleep, Elizabeth lifted her head and looked at him.

"So, will you tell me what happened? Besides the fact that you missed me, which is easy to understand, considering I am a man without fault and have ten thousand a year."

His teasing tone spread a smile on her face as tears appeared in the corners of her eyes.

"I really missed you; that was the reason. I waited for you, and I started thinking about the trip to Pemberley, and I remembered everything that passed in the last year and how close I came to losing you, and... Forgive me for interrupting you; I will let you continue now."

"Mrs. Darcy, you should never apologise for coming into my room. Besides that, I confess that I am truly disappointed with your confession. What has happened to your philosophy? Did you not teach me to *'think only of the past as its remembrance gives you pleasure'*? Did you betray your own conviction?"

"Yes, so it seems," she admitted, smiling through her tears.

"You must promise me you will be faithful to this philosophy from now on as I depend on you to remind me of it whenever I become trapped by unpleasant memories."

"I shall try, but it is not easy, you know."

"I trust my wife completely — since I was wise enough to choose the most perfect one."

"Do you remember our brief talk in the parsonage about Mr. Collins and his choice of a wife?" she inquired, trying to ease the conversation.

"I certainly do. And do you remember how ridiculous I was in my attempts to be near you? I hated the colonel for all the time he spent with you."

"You did not!"

"I most certainly did! I was so frightened that he would propose to you! That evening at Rosings, when you were playing and he was sitting next to you, I truly, deeply hated him in those moments."

She laughed, light-hearted, and moved to place small kisses over his neck.

"You know, Elizabeth, I thought about bringing a small piano here to your rooms," he whispered.

"As you wish sir," she replied as her lips travelled along his jaw line. "However, you must remember — I am not truly proficient at the instrument."

"I know perfectly well all your proficiencies, Mrs. Darcy. Still, I would dearly like you to perform only for me — with no strangers around." She paused in her attentions and looked at him in wonder.

"Do you remember everything we talked of in the past, sir?"

"I do, and it seems you do too, or else how could you recognise the words I remember?"

"That was a complicated phrase indeed, sir!" She laughed with all her heart, and their lips finally met in a passionate, long-lasting kiss.

"Shall we stay in my room for the night or return to yours?"

"As you wish, but what about your papers? Do you not have to finish them?"

"The papers are my last concern at the moment," he said and, to Elizabeth's surprise, disappeared behind the door. He returned some moments later. "I dismissed Gerald for the night."

"Gerard was in the hall this whole time?"

"Of course. He only left the room for discretion. He would not leave without my order."

"Oh my! What will he think of me?"

"I am not certain. Probably he will think the mistress is so much in love with the master that she has no respect for rules or propriety when she bursts into his rooms," he teased her.

She felt ashamed for a moment and then abandoned any attempt and sighed deeply. "Well, Gerald would be correct," she admitted, just before Darcy rolled her on her back. Her fingers slid into his hair; their faces almost touched, and their eyes, darkened by desire, stared into each other's.

"So, Mrs. Darcy, shall we continue from where we were interrupted this afternoon?"

Never averting his eyes from hers, he slowly removed his shirt; the candles were still burning, and she could see small drops of sweat on his bare shoulders. He gently pulled up her nightdress; she closed her eyes and arched her body so he could remove it completely. With her eyes still closed and her skin shivering from a chill, she felt his moves and knew what he was doing. A moment later, he pulled all the bedclothes away from her and lay upon her, covering her only with his naked body. His hands captured hers and trapped them at either side of her head; their fingers entwined instantly.

"Open your eyes," he whispered as he kissed her eyelashes. She obeyed and their gazes met again.

Slowly, his legs separated hers; she swallowed and licked her lips. He kissed her only briefly and then released her hands. She encircled his neck, but he kept his distance so he could see her face. His hands travelled down along her body, rested on her hips a moment, and then stroked her thighs. She moaned. He lifted her legs to encircle his waist and placed another soft kiss on her dry lips; she struggled to keep her eyes open and held her breath.

He entered her slowly, inch by inch, and a cry escaped her as her body tensed. He paused and then continued with gentle moves, his intense gaze never leaving her face. Her eyes closed of their own will as the sensations overwhelmed her. It was too slow, tortuously slow, and she tightened her legs around his waist to pull him closer. He kissed her again, and with a last thrust, their bodies were finally united; she sighed and then relaxed and opened her eyes to watch him.

Equally slowly, he began to move inside her, bare skin burning bare skin. He seemed infinitely patient, with no trace of the urgency that had driven his passion the previous nights. His hands took hers and held them over her head; his mouth captured her lips, and his tongue tasted them greedily. She wanted her hands free to touch him, to explore him — but she was a prisoner with no escape from his passion, and she adored the sensation of complete surrender to him. However, she could not remain trapped for long; she was eager and inpatient — eager not to be free but to be conquered even more. Her hips lifted toward his and she cried when she felt him deeper inside her. She started to move beneath him and against him, their bodies brushing one another.

His chest was painfully crushing her breasts, and she struggled to breathe under his weight. She broke their kiss in search of air; and then, without knowing what she was doing, she bit his shoulder. He moaned and his mouth sought hers, but she avoided it. Her tongue tasted his throat, sucked his skin then bit him again, gently. He cried her name and thrust inside her even harder — and she bit him again.

And then she felt a violent move and — with great surprise — discovered he had rolled on his back and she was now lying atop him. Their hands were still joined; her breasts crushed against his chest; her legs encircled his waist, trapped beneath him. She remained still for a moment, their faces mere inches apart, staring at each other without a word. She could feel him pulsing inside her and her hips moved instinctively. He lifted his body so she could free her legs, and his movement pushed him deeper inside her. Her moan was the sign he needed. His hands separated from hers and embraced her bare back, stroking her skin from her shoulders to her waist while his movements increased.

For a moment, she seemed to have lost her rhythm, but his strong palms lingered on her hips, squeezing gently, and then guided her body until it matched his pace. She learned quickly, and her renewed confidence made her even more daring. As much as she liked being trapped beneath him earlier, she enjoyed experiencing the novelty of being free from his weight, to discover she could breathe easily, she could move easily, and she could use this freedom to her benefit — and his. She slid her fingers into his hair and squeezed it as he was squeezing her thighs. He tried to laugh, but he groaned with pleasure instead. She lifted her body a moment, and her breasts brushed against the hair of his chest; the sensation sent shivers across her skin, and she instantly repeated the gesture.

"Oh God, Elizabeth," he cried, and his voice brought her as much pleasure as his long, deep moves, which turned wilder with every moment.

She managed to keep her body moving together with his while she leaned toward his ear. Her full breasts pressed against his chest and the short, curly hair tickled her swollen nipples. The sensation was unbearable and, impulsively, she bit his earlobe. "Is this pleasant enough, Mr. Darcy?"

"God, yes, yes!" he articulated breathlessly, and with the same violent move, he rolled her back against the pillow as he reclaimed his place upon her. She was surprised — again — but only for a second. Instantly, her legs entwined around him and her arms encircled his back, stroking his skin; he moved inside her stronger, harder and deeper, and his mouth captured hers once more in a kiss that was deep, possessive, impatient, and mirrored the rhythm of their bodies unleashed in their need for fulfilment. When the moment finally came, he broke the kiss and demanded she open her eyes again, so they could see each other as their faces transfigured into the most blissful pleasure and their swollen lips cried one another's names.

They remained united, silent and still; he only rolled their joined bodies to relieve her of the burden of his weight.

A couple of minutes later, Darcy covered her with a sheet and his hand stroked her long, silky hair, which was caressing his sweat-drenched skin. She chuckled and he became very intrigued. That was not the kind of reaction he was expecting.

"Is something the matter?" he asked.

"No, nothing really. It is just that...I am happy to be your wife."

She surprised him; he could not repress a deeply satisfied smile, which she *heard* in his voice.

"I see. And may I dare ask the reason for such a sudden confession at this particular time of night, Mrs. Darcy? Does it have anything to do with my income of ten thousand a year?"

Flustered and slightly embarrassed, her fingers touched his chin tentatively.

"You sound very pleased with yourself and quite impertinent, Mr. Darcy."

He took her hand and placed soft kisses on each of her fingers. "I am very pleased with myself; I have no reason to deny that. And I am waiting for you to tell me about your happiness."

He teased her, and he could see she was amused, so he expected a sharp reply.

"My happiness has nothing to do with your fortune or with other things you have in mind, sir."

He raised an eyebrow in disbelief, and she laughed while her cheeks coloured.

"Very well, I will admit it has to do with *some* of the things you have in mind."

His glance was a mixture of tenderness and teasing. "I can see you are happy, Mrs. Darcy — not just today, but every day since we married. I see your eyes sparkling with joy and your lips smiling; I can feel your happiness, Elizabeth. Your happiness as my wife is what pleases me."

"Then you should be very pleased with yourself, husband, for I am not just happy but grateful to be your wife. I am quite serious now, William. As I told you when I came to your room earlier, I cannot stop wondering about how fortunate I have been in marrying you."

"We were both fortunate — or better to say, we were both wise — in choosing whom we married," he replied, his lips still pressed against her fingers.

"You were wise in choosing your wife. A woman can hardly choose — she can only hope she will gain the affection of a worthy man whom she can respect and appreciate. Of course, a woman can accept or reject any man's attentions — but nothing more. It is a man's privilege to choose."

"Sometimes, a man's privilege of choosing means nothing when he does not know how to use that privilege properly or how to bestow his attentions upon the woman he has chosen."

"And sometimes a woman cannot see the worthiness of the man for whom she has waited and hoped her entire life! I know I have every reason to feel grateful and fortunate; my prejudice and my hasty, unwise estimation of your character almost made me lose the path to true happiness."

"May I dare hope I am your true happiness?"

"Yes you are. Do you know what I adore most in you, husband?"

"Besides my income and my situation in life?"

She laughed and nodded. "Yes, and despite being tall and uncommonly handsome."

"Hmm... Now you have made me even more curious to hear your praises, because if we put aside my wealth and my features, I doubt there is much to adore in me." He cast her a meaningful look, and she blushed instantly.

"I adore exactly what I hated when we first met: your behaviour toward me. I could not imagine a more considerate and kind husband —"

"Considerate and kind?" he interrupted her soundly. "Madam, of what are you talking? Something must be very wrong in this marriage if, after five days of intimacy, my young wife describes me in such brotherly terms."

She chuckled, but his frown remained, and she started to laugh heartily. "Allow me to finish, sir, before you become upset with me. So, as I said — you are kind and considerate"—she paused and moved further so her face was at the same level as his—"and gentle, and generous, and tender, and loving, and passionate."

A smile overspread her lips and her mouth moved closer to his.

"That is a much more comforting description, madam."

Her smile became tender, and her head rested on his chest again.

"We should sleep now, William; it must be very late." She sighed and brushed her cheek against his skin while her palm gently caressed him, and finally, she placed a soft, brief kiss over his heart.

His arm encircled her shoulders. "Sleep well, my love." She whispered something, while her hand continued to caress him. She was obviously very tired, and her breathing became more and more regular; however, her caresses seemed to increase too. Eventually, his hand stopped hers.

"Elizabeth, you should not continue to do that if you truly wish to sleep," he whispered.

She opened her eyes to him. "What did I do?"

"Nothing, but that your touch gives me shivers, and *sleep* is the last thing on my mind.

Elizabeth stared at him in disbelief. "Surely you cannot mean... We just finished... and it was the second time today." Her astonishment was a new reason for his amusement; he kissed her hand and embraced her more closely, trying to dissipate her worry.

"Do not be afraid, my love. I will never insist upon anything you do not want. And you may touch me as much as you like. I will gladly bear the torture of your caresses with the last remnants of my self-control," he teased her. "Now let us sleep."

"I am not afraid of anything you may do, William; I know you would never force me — with anything. And it is not that I do not *want* it. It is just I feel really exhausted now."

"My love, I know you are exhausted," he smiled and kissed her temple. "I also know you have not slept much lately; in fact, I wonder if you have slept enough a single night in the last couple of months."

A few more moments of silence followed. "William, may I ask —? How is it that, except for our wedding night, it only happened once every evening, and then we would sleep? Yet today we already — you know — twice, and you still do not seem tired."

Darcy embraced her tightly and removed a lock of hair from her ear. "I was not tired before either." He smiled. "I only struggled to balance my desires with my concern. I could not stay away from you, but I tried to take into consideration your lack of experience, your fears, and your discomfort. As you said earlier, I mostly exercised the '*kind and considerate*' side of my character."

"I see," she whispered, not knowing what to say.

"From now on, my dearest, loveliest wife, as you have proven that I no longer have reason to be concerned, I intend to fully exercise my loving, passionate side — as you described it."

His deep, flirtatious voice and the gentle touch of his fingers near her ear sent shivers across her skin, and she tried hard to smile as she felt her face and neck burning.

"I see," she repeated.

"That is why I would strongly advise you to stop any further conversation about this subject and try to sleep as soon as you can," he concluded with another soft kiss upon her lips.

"Good night, husband," she said, cuddling to his chest.

"Good night, my love," he replied, certain he could not possibly fall asleep with her warm body pressed to his. However, as she said, he was not tired at all. He would allow her to rest as much as she needed while he watched her beautiful face smiling in her dreams.

She was truly happy — of that, he had no doubt.

Chapter 25

Elizabeth awoke to the sound of wind rattling the window; it was dark, but the room was softly lit by the fire. She sighed in contentment as she moved closer to her sleeping husband, cuddling as she listened to the storm outside. Darcy pulled her closer and whispered something; she smiled.

A month had passed since they had returned home to Pemberley — a month spent in blissful happiness — and Elizabeth had been granted everything she had hoped for, including snow!

Moreover, as happened in London, they barely separated for a couple of hours each day, and only when his duties required urgent attention. Elizabeth used these times to become accustomed to her role as mistress, and Mrs. Reynolds often congratulated her on her efficiency and quickness in learning her responsibilities. What Mrs. Reynolds did not know — and Elizabeth blushed at the thought — was that she struggled to learn everything as quickly as possible for a very selfish reason: she wanted as much time as possible to share with her husband.

Elizabeth turned so she could face him; he moaned and tightened his arms around her. Elizabeth chuckled at his insistence; he seemed unable to sleep if he did not feel her close to him. If she was afraid that her husband would stop joining her in bed once at Pemberley, her fears vanished the very first day of their arrival. Truth be told, he did not come to her bed every night; at times *she* slept in *his* room as had happened that night.

She gently brushed her fingers along his handsome face; he looked peaceful as his chest moved steadily in his sleep. *He is tired,* she thought. Indeed, he had every reason to be tired as he slept little at night and awoke early each morning to attend his most urgent business. Almost every day he would go downstairs when she was still asleep and return a couple of hours later to wake her.

It became a daily routine for her to enjoy late morning deep sleep until her husband's caress came to rouse her body and her senses, just as it became an evening routine for her to go and fetch him when some business delayed him in his study longer than usual. She always respected his duties, and so at those times, she would simply enter his study and sit on a sofa nearby, waiting. He had placed an armchair by his desk so she might sit next to him. The first night of her sitting so close, he turned and kissed her unexpectedly once he finished his work, and before either could restrain their passion, they found themselves making love right there in the armchair. As embarrassing as the incident had been afterwards, it did not take long for them to repeat it another night.

Elizabeth never imagined that her husband would allow himself to be carried away by passion and desire so easily — and so often — but he did. To her surprise — and occasional mortification — the moments of shared love outside the privacy of their apartments were not rare. Darcy's only concern was to assure their absolute privacy, so he always locked the door of his study or the library. Elizabeth remembered — with a frisson — that they had even made love once in the music room and in the billiard room. Though she always surrendered to his *"loving initiative,"* she still felt somehow awkward afterward, fearing someone would enter and discover them or, at the very least, that the locked door would betray their activities. However, day by day, she became less distressed by these worries, as Darcy seemed to organise his staff's activities and his own appointments so efficiently that nobody ever disturbed them, not even with a knock on the door. He was always careful to attend to his duties, and the others were always careful not to interrupt him unexpectedly.

At least, that was how things had worked for the first five weeks of their marriage, but as Elizabeth anticipated — and feared — major changes began that same day. Her family's Christmas visit was expected in the afternoon. The entire Bennet family together with Bingley and Jane, the Gardiners and their children, and Georgiana and Cassandra would be *invading* Pemberley in less than 12 hours, and there would certainly be no time for rest or tranquillity for the next four weeks.

Elizabeth was eager to see her relatives as well as her new sister and her friend, but Darcy looked positively distressed at the prospect.

"My darling husband," she whispered. She cuddled closer to him and rested her head against his chest, feeling his heart racing. She could not restrain herself from placing a soft kiss over his heart. He immediately moaned, and though he was sleeping, his body tensed. Elizabeth smiled, wondering once more at the strong effect her mere touch had upon him. With a will of their own, her hands moved gently up his chest to his shoulders, down his arms and rested upon his waist. Slightly embarrassed, as though she were being caught doing something forbidden, she dared to watch him closely. For the first time, she saw his "arousal" while he was asleep and barely restrained a gasp. She had felt his *size* — she even touched him briefly during their lovemaking — but she had never been bold enough to *look* at it until now. She even put a little more distance between their bodies and continued to stare. That it looked somehow awkward was her first thought. Awkward and strangely large was her second thought. Then she heard him sighing in his sleep, and her eyes turned to his face and admired his handsome features for a few minutes. When her eyes travelled down along his body again, she could see his arousal was larger as though he could feel the caress of her gaze. Only this time, *it* did not look either awkward or strange to Elizabeth. It was not a *thing* but a part of him — of her beloved husband — a part of the man whose love brought her so much happiness.

Elizabeth pulled the covers off him; for the first time, she knelt near Darcy and closely perused every inch of her husband's body lit only by the fire's dim light. Soon, watching was not enough, and her fingers daringly followed the path of her eyes, stroking his skin. He moaned again and whispered her name in his dream; she removed her nightgown and, naked, leaned near him — against him. Her lips tantalised his neck, resting on his throat for an instant, and then moved up to his chin, along the line of his jaw. Her hand was now upon his waist and moved down to his hips; his body shivered, and though he was not awake yet, his arms trapped her. Her kisses increased, and she climbed upon him to reach his face; her breasts brushed against his chest, and she could not restrain a moan as deep as his. Shy and slightly embarrassed, with tender curiosity, her fingers finally dared to touch his manhood. The feeling was nothing she expected, and for a moment, she tensed and remained still, not knowing what to do; then she heard her name in his pleading whispers and briefly wondered if her touch was at least half as pleasant for him as his caresses were for her.

"Oh God, Elizabeth, please," he whispered again, and now she knew he was awake. She also understood that he was begging her to continue, so she did not hesitate any longer. With every moment, every stroke, and every moan coming from his dry lips, she realised that his body enjoyed and longed for exactly the same things as hers and that she could grant him the same pleasure he gave her.

Her hands and her mouth explored and tasted his skin for countless minutes, and as he begged her for more, her desire increased. She felt his body trembling violently, then he stopped her ministrations, rolled her over swiftly, and entered her before she realised what was happening. A few minutes later, his thrusts deepened inside her as he covered her face with his kisses. His hands were stroking her skin, and impulsively, she allowed her hand to slide between them until it reached the very point where their bodies were joined. Her fingers touched his manhood, and he cried her name while his thrusts increased for several long minutes until the pleasure overwhelmed and exhausted them both.

"Mrs. Darcy, what are you doing to me?" Darcy asked some time later, taking her hand in his.

"I am sorry for disturbing your rest, husband. I hope you are not upset with me."

He cupped her face and looked into her eyes. "Do I look upset, my wife?"

"No, you do not look upset at all." She chuckled. "I am very pleased to please you, husband."

He laughed, kissing her hand. "It is not just the pleasure, you little minx, though

I confess I am deeply amazed by the pleasure we share every time. What makes me so happy, my love, is that I feel each of your kisses, each of your caresses, each of your looks as proof of your love for me."

"And that is how you should feel them, my dear husband. However, I really hope you will remember my deep love for you when you become annoyed by the liveliness of my family," she teased him.

He removed a few locks of hair from her face. "Do not worry, my dearest; nothing will annoy me if I have your delightful company from time to time."

"Well, you will surely have my company at least during the night."

He sighed with resignation. "Yes, that is what I fear."

"Do not worry, my love; four weeks will pass in no time."

"No, they will not, unfortunately; four weeks is a long time. Thank heavens Pemberley is so large a house that one can easily find solitude in it."

"I challenge you to escape my mother's affectionate attention, Mr. Darcy."

"I am sorry to discover you still doubt my ability to have my way when I truly want it, madam."

"Indeed, you are mistaken, sir; I have long stopped doubting your abilities, husband."

"That is comforting to know." He covered them both with the sheet.

"It is very cold, and the wind sounds quite wild," he said, suddenly serious. "I hope they will all arrive safely."

"I am a little worried, too. However, I am trustful knowing they are all coming together from London, so even if there are some difficulties, my uncle, Papa and Mr. Bingley will take care of everyone in the party."

"Mr. Gardiner and Bingley are reliable gentlemen, and Mr. Bennet can offer them proper advice if needed; let us try to sleep a little more as we have much to accomplish before their arrival."

Elizabeth soon fell asleep, but Darcy remained awake, listening to the wind until the dawn arrived.

"OH, MY DEAR MR. BENNET, what beauty!! I cannot believe my eyes! My dear Lizzy, she was so clever to catch Mr. Darcy! Such a tall, handsome man — and what an estate. Do you not think she was clever?"

In one of the carriages, Mr. Bennet was gathered together with his wife, Kitty and Jane, along with Mr. Bingley; Mary was invited to join Miss Darcy and Lady Cassandra. Mr. Bennet felt horribly tired and dangerously annoyed after such a long journey in such a small, crowded place, and his only consolation was that Bingley looked more miserable than he did.

"Yes, she was very clever. Thank God we will arrive in a couple of minutes," he replied briefly.

"Oh Mama, I cannot wait to see my room," said Kitty. "Do you think they will have guests other than the family? I would love to see new faces — and maybe they will have a ball."

"Kitty dearest, I do not think they will have a ball," explained Jane, gently. "Lizzy did not mention anything like that. You know Mr. Darcy is not fond of dancing and gatherings. He likes his privacy, and I believe they planned a peaceful Christmas with the family — not a large social event."

Oh, I like my privacy too, only I am more stupid than Darcy, and I do not know to stand up for it, thought Bingley while staring outside the window.

"You cannot know that, Jane," Mrs. Bennet intervened. "You know Lizzy has always liked balls, so we must try to persuade her to have one. As for Mr. Darcy — if Lizzy was smart and artful enough to make him marry her, I am sure she will easily convince him to approve of a ball."

"Mama," cried Jane. "Lizzy was not artful and she did not *make* Mr. Darcy do anything. They married for the deepest love!" she insisted.

"Of course he married for love, why else would a man like him marry a wild, diso-bedient girl like Lizzy?" Mrs. Bennet replied, rolling her eyes. "That was precisely Lizzy's *'art'* — to make him fall in love with her. Oh, I cannot wait to see the house. I am so sorry Mrs. Long and Lady Lucas cannot see it. Kitty, pay attention girl, you have to be able to describe every detail of Pemberley when we return to Longbourn. Do you hear me?"

"Yes, Mama," the girl answered obediently.

In the front of the house, Mr. and Mrs. Darcy waited for the guests to exit their carriage. They required several long minutes until everyone was satisfied with ad-miring the exterior of the house among hugs and kisses — and finally decided to enter.

Darcy followed them with hesitant steps, suddenly grateful that he had enough servants to take care of each guest instantly. He did greet them all with proper po-liteness; however, he breathed deeply when the din diminished as everybody finally decided to settle in their rooms, accompanied by Elizabeth — who seemed both happy to see them all and perfectly at ease with her duties. He had decided to retire to his library when he was surprised to discover Mr. Bennet and Bingley standing quietly a few steps away.

"Mr. Bennet, Bingley, I did not see you. I thought you joined the others in your rooms."

"We can find the rooms later," Mr. Bennet said and Bingley nodded in agreement.

"Of course, as you wish. In the mean time, may I offer you something?"

"Your library and your brandy," Mr. Bennet answered, and Bingley, again, agreed wholeheartedly. Darcy hurried to comply with the gentlemen's wishes while ex-pressing his hope that the journey had not been too trying for them. Neither guest answered, nor did Darcy inquire further.

One hour and three glasses of brandy later, Mr. Bennet finally declared himself tired, and a servant was summoned to show him to his room. Once he left, Bingley hurried and filled his glass once more.

"Bingley, easy with the brandy, my friend." Bingley looked at Darcy and finally burst out, "They drove me out of my mind; I struggled not to jump from the carriage — can you believe that?"

Darcy patted his shoulder. "I am sorry to hear it, my friend. But why on earth did you and your wife not take a separate carriage? I dare say, that way the journey would have been quite enjoyable."

"Damn, Darcy," replied Bingley, with a furious glance. "Of course I wanted a separate carriage. I even bought this large, comfortable carriage to be sure my wife travelled in the best accommodation, but my mother-in-law liked the carriage so much that she insisted we would all fit in it, and it would be rather stupid to take a second one. And do not dare to laugh, Darcy!"

"Forgive me, Bingley; believe me that I truly understand your trouble."

"No, you do not understand, Darcy! You cannot understand it, as you never have to face this kind of trouble. You have been here all this time in complete silence and peace —"

"But why did you not come earlier? Did I not invite you to come as soon as possible?"

"I did not wish to disturb you, Darcy; no matter how generous your invitation was, it was not acceptable. Jane agreed with me that we could not bother you, and she was busy receiving guests, returning their calls, and rearranging the house. And, what is more, I am really worried for Caroline since she began her tour, I have received no news from her except a short note when she left the country. Louisa has received nothing either."

"That is reason for worry, indeed. Have you tried to discover her whereabouts? With whom is she on tour?"

Bingley waved his hand. "Oh, I did contact her friends' families; they all said she was most likely on a ship and would send me a note as soon as she could. I do not want to disturb you with Caroline's silliness. Let us have another drink, shall we? Then I will go and see if Jane needs my assistance."

"Bingley, I do not think you should drink more. I do agree with your other idea, though. I think you should go to your wife. Surely, her company will be more comforting than mine right now. We can talk more after dinner."

"Yes, you are right; I have barely had time to speak privately with my wife in the past few days, you know? Can you imagine that?" Bingley walked to the door without waiting for Darcy's answer.

"And we will have to go through this madness again when we leave."

Darcy could not restrain his laugh. "My friend, let us not worry about your departure right now. I am sure we will come up with a solution by then. Let me direct you to your rooms, shall we?"

Downstairs and along the halls, Bingley progressed, silently wondering about his rooms, as he had never visited that wing of the house before. They finally stopped, and Darcy shook his hand.

"Go rest, my friend. This wing is only for you and your wife — nobody will disturb you here."

"I have never been in this wing before," Bingley said.

"Well, you have never been married and in need of complete privacy before," Darcy smiled mischievously. "Oh, and I forgot to mention: as you are all so tired, we will have a late dinner tonight. So you have at least three hours to rest and to…speak privately with your wife. If you need something, you will have to ring the bell."

Bingley stared at him silently; just before Darcy turned to leave, he finally managed to reply.

"Darcy? I am forever in your debt, my friend!"

"Go to your wife, Bingley." *As I intend to go to mine.*

ELIZABETH WAS EXHAUSTED BUT SATISFIED. Each member of the party was settled properly, and now she lingered to talk a few minutes with Jane. Elizabeth felt a little worried as her sister looked pale and tired, but Jane blamed the trip and assured her sister that everything else was fine. Elizabeth did not insist as she could easily imagine how difficult the journey must have been. She inquired about how Jane felt as a married woman, and was content to see happiness lighting her sister's blue eyes; Jane's eyes always spoke more eloquently than her shy voice.

"Oh Lizzy, if I dare tell you… I am so happy — I could not imagine a better husband than Charles."

Surely, he cannot compare with my husband, was the first thought that crossed Elizabeth's mind, but she gave her sister the proper answer.

"I am very happy for you. I was always certain Mr. Bingley was worthy of your good heart."

"Lizzy, *he* is the good and kind one — and so patient. I know mother annoys him sometimes, but he bears everything with so much civility. Do you know he purchased this carriage for me? He said he wanted me to travel as a princess, and the carriage is indeed wonderful."

"It is wonderful but not large enough for five people for such a long distance and on winter roads."

"I know, but Mama insisted, and I begged Charles to agree. I know he was displeased, and I had no time to talk to him privately these two days. He was so silent all the time. I am so afraid he is upset with me."

Jane was tearful, and Elizabeth was half-worried, half-amused.

"Dearest, I have no right to give you any advice, as you are my elder and wiser sister, but you should not allow yourself to be persuaded by Mama's demands, risking the displeasure of your husband."

"I know... I know. But it is so hard to refuse Mama. If we were only a little further away..."

Elizabeth kissed her sister's cheeks. "My sweet Jane, let me assure you that, here in these rooms, you will be far away from everyone. Nobody will disturb you, and you can spend all the time you want in only your husband's company. I dare say, Mr. Bingley will enjoy that very much."

Jane laughed tearfully. "That sounds tempting though not easy to do. We cannot possibly isolate ourselves here, hiding from our family. After all, we are here to spend Christmas together."

"That is true, dearest. However, as you are so fatigued, it is very likely that you will suffer some slight headaches and will want to rest from time to time; also, if there are evenings you want to retire earlier or mornings you wake later, I am sure everyone will understand. And, in cases like these, it will be Mr. Bingley's duty as a loving husband to stay by your side. Do you not agree?"

"Lizzy! Are you teaching me to dissemble?"

"I am teaching you to do everything possible to enjoy your husband's company, my dear sister."

A moment later Mr. Bingley entered the room; he remained still, staring at his wife, almost oblivious to Elizabeth's presence. Jane blushed, her eyes fixed on those of her husband. Elizabeth was certain that, were Mr. Bingley indeed upset with Jane, he would quickly forgive her.

IT WAS ALREADY TWO O'CLOCK in the afternoon, and Elizabeth wondered where her husband was hiding. However, before going in search of him, she decided to inquire after Cassandra, as she was certain the journey had not been easy for her either. To her pleasant surprise, Cassandra was resting, but she appeared fully recovered.

"You look beautiful, Elizabeth," Cassandra said. "I imagine you are enjoying your marriage?"

"You know I am enjoying my marriage, Cassandra; however, I did not come to speak of my marriage, but of you. How are you feeling? I am happy to see you so well recovered."

"Well, you have already answered your questions. I am here, well and fully recovered."

"But how are you feeling?"

"How am I feeling about what, Elizabeth? Ask me what you want to know; do not play at politeness with me."

"If you do not play at rudeness with me, your ladyship, as I am not so easily impressed." Elizabeth playfully reprimanded Cassandra, never losing her smile.

"Please forgive me. I did not mean to be rude or disrespectful."

"Fine; be as you want. As long as you are well, I will not insist further. I surely do not want to force your confidence, just please tell me if I can help you in any way."

She prepared to leave, but Cassandra called her.

"Elizabeth, do you know if he will come for Christmas?"

"We do not know for certain. William received a letter a couple of weeks ago, and the colonel expressed his wishes to be with us, but his plans were not fixed at that time."

"He sent me no word — not a note, nothing."

"But did you... did you have any understanding? Did he promise he would write or anything?"

"No, of course not. I mean... I promised to give him an answer upon his return. But I do not know when that will happen or whether he will still want my answer by then."

"And do you have an answer?" Cassandra nodded silently. "I see."

"Elizabeth, may I ask you a favour? I know I am being childish, but can you please ask Darcy if he knows anything? Perhaps David mentioned something to him. I know it is silly to ask you —"

"Cassandra, I am happy to see you childish about this," she replied, and Cassandra blushed like a young girl.

"I will go and fetch William, and I will gather every piece of information from him before returning to tell you." They both sounded like young girls sharing a secret and laughed at their silliness.

"I will wait for you — assuming Darcy allows you to return any time soon. By the way, did he lock you in your room as I anticipated?" Elizabeth's cheeks turned crimson.

As she was walking toward the door, Elizabeth cast a quick mischievous glance at Cassandra.

"No, there was no need lock me in. I was more than pleased to stay inside of my own free will!"

A completely astonished Cassandra stared at her until Elizabeth exited the room; only then, did her ladyship recover and burst out laughing. "Mrs. Darcy, you are absolutely shameless," she said, and she could hear Elizabeth's laughter from the doorway.

CHRISTMAS WAS ONLY TWO DAYS away, and Pemberley was more animated than ever. The ladies spent their days in preparation and decorating while the gentlemen usually found occupation in the library. Mrs. Bennet never ceased to marvel at the courses and dishes, just as she never ceased to wonder at the greatness of the house. It was entirely fortunate that the bustle of daily activity seemed to be fatiguing for Mrs. Bennet, and she usually retired quite early after dinner, more so as she was quite content with her rooms and both maids who served her. She was so pleased with her son-in-law's treatment that she even dared to embrace him one evening when he inquired whether everything was to her liking.

Mr. Bennet would also retire early each evening after dinner — not to his room, but to the library; his only complaint was that he did not have time enough to enjoy all the treasures there. Mr. Bennet was content, though, as Darcy insisted that his father-in-law return to Pemberley whenever he wanted. He also offered to lend him any book he would like to take home to Longbourn.

Both Mr. and Mrs. Bennet were genuinely pleased with Elizabeth's choice of a husband, though for entirely different reasons.

For the Gardiners, the time spent at Pemberley was a wonderful opportunity, and they were equally grateful and delighted. They passed the days joining those at Pemberley or visiting friends and relatives in Lambton. Mrs. Gardiner was prouder than ever as she learned the favourable opinion of Mrs. Fitzwilliam Darcy in the neighbourhood. She was as satisfied with her niece's choice of a husband as she was with Darcy's choice of a wife; she hoped Lady Anne would have been pleased, too.

A recently discovered enjoyment for the newlywed couples and the younger members of the party was long sleigh rides around Pemberley's grounds. Usually there were three or four sleighs equipped with blankets to keep the riders warm — each of the conveyances spacious enough to accommodate at least four people. However, the Darcy and Bingley couples always took a separate sleigh each — at which Georgiana, Kitty and even Mary chuckled meaningfully. The other sleigh was for the three girls and Cassandra who joined them occasionally; the fourth was for the Gardiners and their children. Sometimes, Mr. Darcy was in the mood for an extended ride after dinner, and those times the only ones inclined to accompany him were his wife and the Bingleys — so, from time to time, two sleighs could be seen skimming along the snowy paths in the moonlight.

"I say, Bingley, if you are decided to find an estate here in Derbyshire, I would be happy to assist you," said Darcy during dinner. Their voices were low, so the others could barely hear them.

"Would you, Darcy? I mean…if I am able to convince Jane. I know she is happy here, but I wonder if she would agree to move so far from her family."

"Well, Bingley, you know best. On the other hand, she would be moving further from some members of her family and closer to her favourite sister — which I dare say would be an advantage."

"An advantage indeed," cried Bingley and everybody turned to look at him. Darcy laughed.

"Very well, my friend; in a fortnight we can start looking for an adequate place for you. It might take a few months to find it and accommodate it properly."

"A few months? Oh…but I will be back in Hertfordshire by then."

"Why is that? Do you have fixed plans? You are welcome to remain at Pemberley for as long as you need."

"No, I do not have any fixed plans. Perhaps Jane — I am not sure. Staying at Pemberley, you say? But I do not want to intrude. I know you like your privacy."

"That is nonsense. You see for yourself that Pemberley affords complete privacy to both our families."

"Yes, I noticed that, Darcy. Oh, that would be the best arrangement ever — to find an estate here and learn from you how to manage it. Jane would be so proud! But damn — what about the carriage? How will my in-laws return to Hertfordshire?" Darcy rolled his eyes in exasperation.

Bingley did not miss his friend's gesture and felt suddenly embarrassed. "I am absurd, am I not? Who cares about the carriage? They can have it for good. I dare hope you will loan me one until I am able to purchase another."

"Of course I will, Bingley — even two carriages if you need them. And no, you are not absurd; you only worry about insignificant details rather than focusing upon what is truly important to you."

"You are right, of course, Darcy. I will speak to Jane this evening and —"

A sudden din of voices from the main hall interrupted him. Before Darcy could identify the source of the disturbance, the door opened, and Colonel Fitzwilliam burst into the room.

Darcy and Georgiana rushed from their places to greet him; he looked well, though obviously tired and half frozen, but as joyful as ever. Elizabeth smiled at him and immediately glanced at Cassandra. Her cheeks were crimson, and her eyes fixed upon the colonel's face; Elizabeth wondered whether her ladyship was still breathing.

"Cousin, what an extraordinary surprise! Come and join us; you look as though you need a glass of brandy."

"I intended to surprise you, Darcy, but I am afraid the surprise is even greater than I intended. I left my regiment together with my friend Colonel Thomason and his family as they planned to reach London before Christmas, but their carriage had an accident ten miles back; we barely managed to ride a few more miles, and I am asking your assistance to host them here for the night. Please forgive me, I know I have no right to impose, it is just that —"

Elizabeth approached him with a warm smile. He kissed her hand and apologised again while Elizabeth, with a short glance at her husband, continued.

"Surely you must not apologise for bringing friends, especially as they were in such a dangerous situation. Please invite them in, and we will have their rooms ready in no time."

A few minutes later, Pemberley's dining room was filled with Colonel Thomason — a handsome gentleman in his late thirties — his wife and his two sisters. They were all embarrassed by the intrusion, but the colonel made the introductions with a perfect mix of politeness and friendliness. If Darcy seemed rather restrained in his expression, Elizabeth's warm manners and genuine welcome managed to dissipate the new guests' tension and embarrassment. Half an hour later, the newly arrived were shown to their rooms to refresh and prepare for dinner. The colonel joined them after he assured the others in the room that he would return as soon as possible.

As soon as they left the room, opinions about the new acquaintances were shared. Elizabeth looked at her husband and then at Cassandra, who was now ghostly pale; her eyes stared at the table while her hands were entwined to stop their trembling, and she appeared oblivious to everything around her. The colonel had not greeted her beyond the strictest civility.

"Thank you, my love," Darcy whispered to Elizabeth and she smiled back at him.

"You are quite welcome, though I do not know what for."

"For the way you handled this awkward situation; you never cease to amaze me. It is as though you always know what to do and what to say to make people comfortable."

"Well, I had little else to do. They seem such agreeable people — and even if they were not, how could we possibly leave them outside to freeze, especially as they are the colonel's friends."

"No, of course not — but still…"

"However, I am not sure what I can do to make *you* feel comfortable, as you are clearly not in the best disposition," she teased him.

"Well, I *could* tell you what you might do, but it is not possible with a thousand people in the house," he burst out in frustration, and she laughed heartily.

"You are not only highly improper, but also quite disagreeable and haughty, dear sir."

"I am glad you are so amused, because I really am not. I did understand David's reasons, but really — the last thing I needed was a new party of people here. And they did not even say clearly when they would leave! Their carriage could be fixed in two weeks or so; can you imagine that?"

Elizabeth placed a quick kiss on his chin. "Let us hope that will not be the case, my love."

The colonel's voice called out to make his presence known. Elizabeth blushed slightly.

"Mrs. Darcy, thank you for your hospitality. I am grateful to you, as are my friends."

"I am glad I could be of some help, sir. I hope they will be comfortable in their rooms."

"I am sure they will, but, Darcy, may I have a word with you?"

The colonel looked positively distressed and embarrassed as he spoke animatedly.

"I know I am already being impertinent with my demands, and I would never dare if it were not Christmas in only two days… What I mean is… Darcy, I beg you to loan them one of your carriages to take them to London tomorrow morning. I know I am asking too much, but —"

Elizabeth could hardly hold back her peals of laughter as she saw Darcy's face light with relief.

"Say no more, David! *Of course,* I will give them a carriage; in fact, I will loan them my best, largest one as we will not need it for the time being. I will send my coachman with you, and he can bring it back. Is that arrangement satisfactory, do you think?"

"Darcy, you are simply the best man," the colonel shook his hand. "I will go and inform Thomason. The poor fellow did not dare ask you such a favour. He will be so relieved!"

He left instantly, so he did not hear Darcy mumbling. "Not more relieved than *I* am."

AN HOUR LATER, THE ENTIRE party was assembled in the dining room again. Colonel Thomason seemed as amiable and pleasant as Colonel Fitzwilliam, and his wife and sisters were voluble, amusing and quite pretty. Mrs. Bennet did not forget to mention she had a daughter married to an officer, but Mr. Bingley quickly changed the subject so Wickham's name was avoided. Then there were questions about the balls in the North, and the young Misses Thomason seemed as willing to talk about dancing and officers as were Kitty and Mrs. Bennet.

Elizabeth smiled with indulgence the whole time, casting meaningful glances toward Georgiana and Darcy. It was also obvious that the Misses Thomason shared a deep admiration for Colonel Fitzwilliam and nearly competed for the favour of flirting with him. The colonel appeared to tolerate them with good humour and even winked at Colonel Thomason a few times.

Another thing Elizabeth noticed was Cassandra's unusual silence. She expected that Cassandra would be slightly uneasy at the colonel's sudden appearance; however, it was more than that. Cassandra's torment was so obvious that it was difficult for Elizabeth to see it without enquiring.

The gentlemen were invited to accompany Mr. Darcy to the library following dinner. Colonel Fitzwilliam remained a little behind and approached Cassandra, who was standing near the window.

"Lady Cassandra, I am very happy to see you finally. Please forgive me for not speaking to you more when we entered. It was such a situation —"

"Do not worry, sir; I noticed you were busy when you entered, as well as later during dinner. You cannot possibly neglect your friends; I understand that."

Her sharp voice and refusal to meet his gaze silenced David for a moment. "I hope you are well?"

"I am quite well, thank you."

"Well then... Darcy is waiting for me. Perhaps we could talk later?" He searched her face as she stared through the window.

"Whenever you can spare a moment," she replied coldly.

The colonel could find nothing more to say and hurried to catch the other gentlemen. As soon as he exited, Cassandra asked for a cup of tea and joined the ladies for a few minutes. A short while later, she excused herself as she was feeling unwell and wished to retire to her room. Everyone offered assistance and expressed regrets and hopes for her recovery. Cassandra could not bear the small talk any longer.

She hurried from the room and briefly met Elizabeth's eyes. She knew Elizabeth understood, but she was in no disposition to talk to anyone. All she wanted was the complete solitude of her chamber — and her thoughts.

IT WAS ALMOST MIDNIGHT, AND Colonel Fitzwilliam was pacing the room, his heart racing , trying to maintain his composure. What was happening with her — again? She promised she would have an answer for him once he returned, and in truth, their last meeting gave him every reason to hope for a happy conclusion.

Now things were even worse than before; she simply ignored him! She barely looked at him the entire evening and answered him coldly as though he meant nothing to her. Even more, when he returned from the library, she had long retired, apparently to avoid him. How could she be so deceitful, and how could he be so foolish as to allow her to hurt him repeatedly? He came all that way only to be with her for Christmas, and she cared nothing for him. So why should he remain? The only thing he could not bear was her indifference, and that was precisely what she was showing him after almost two months apart.

He opened his window, allowing the wind to blow in his face. It was still snowing, and the Pemberley grounds were covered in white. It was freezing cold, but that was nothing compared to the empty coldness in his heart. He leaned against the balcony and closed his eyes; he wanted to feel the snow falling upon his face in hopes that it would make the pain disappear.

When he opened his eyes again, he frowned, not from the cold, but from fear and disbelief. In the near wing on the upper floor, he could see Cassandra leaning against the balcony as he had done; her hair was down, and she was dressed only in her nightgown while the wind swirled around her. *Damn, she is completely out of her senses! She will catch her death, that insane woman.*

Without much consideration, angry at her insincerity, and worried for her careless behaviour, he pulled on his coat and shut the door behind him.

THE NIGHT WAS AS BEAUTIFUL as a fairy tale — as though fate wanted to laugh at her torment — and she deserved to be laughed at; Cassandra knew that. All her hopes deserved to be laughed at.

She had longed to see David again since the moment he had left, and now he had finally come. He was safe, for which she had prayed; he was healthy, as she wished, and obviously he had not much interest in her, as she should have anticipated. What could she expect from a man she had refused so harshly and decidedly — a man who had shown his affection and devotion for her honestly with no requite from her?

Six weeks had passed since he departed — since he rocked her heart once more with the confession about his first love. How was it possible? *She* was the one hopelessly in love with him back then when she was seventeen — *she* had lived with that bittersweet memory for all those years. The revelation that her love could have been shared — that her life could have been so different — made her feel angry and powerless.

Cassandra spent countless hours wondering whether she would have wanted her life to be different; perhaps she would have been happy with David from the beginning, and perhaps even her parents would have lived longer.

But then she never would have met Thomas or known his sweet love — never felt their child inside her. She had lost her parents; she had lost Thomas and their child; and she had been angry with the entire world and with God Himself. Still, God was so good to her when He offered her a second chance. God kept her alive, healed her, and then brought David back into her life — David and his love. She refused him, and from her own folly, she almost died; God was still there, next to her, as were David and his love.

One morning — about a week before their journey to Pemberley —Cassandra finally realised she had no reason to blame herself any longer for what she had lost if God was so merciful as to forgive her. She had no call to fear being happy if He was offering her the gift of happiness for the second time. She had no right to refuse what was so generously given to her twice when so many spent their lives looking for love and never finding it. She woke up that morning without the burden of suffering on her soul but with her heart full of hope and love — and gratitude.

Now David was there and Christmas was near. Where were her hopes now? He came with his friends and two young girls who competed for his favour. Had he already chosen, or were they merely distractions as were all the others? However, he surely would not trifle with them in front of their brother without having serious designs on one of them. How dare he be so cruel as to arrive with them? Was he trying to hurt her as she had hurt him?

The snow was falling on her face, melting in her tears. She leaned over the balcony to admire the surroundings, and then lifted her eyes to the moonlit sky. It was as enchanting as a fairy tale, but her soul lay in waste.

"Cassandra, what on earth are you doing? Are you out of your mind? Get inside immediately!"

She startled and almost lost her balance as her feet slipped on the snowy balcony. David grasped her arm and pulled her inside; his strong fingers hurt her, but she said nothing.

"Are you out of your senses?" he cried while she stared at him blankly.

"I am perfectly well; I just needed some fresh air."

"Fresh air? You are almost undressed outside on a freezing night."

He released her arm and watched as she moved away from him.

"I thank you for your worry, David, but as you see, I am fine. You should leave now."

"Yes, I should leave; forgive me for my intrusion."

"Be careful not to be seen on your way out. We would not want to upset the Thomasons with nasty rumours about your walking into a lady's room in the middle of the night, though both girls seem so charmed that I am sure they would forgive you anything."

"What — what did you say?" he asked unceremoniously, but she had turned her back and moved further away. She wanted him gone instantly, as she could not hold back her tears much longer.

"Cassandra, what is happening to you? Why are you acting like this?"

"Please leave," she begged, and he could hear her distress.

If only a moment ago he had been certain of her indifference, now her voice and behaviour puzzled him exceedingly. She was obviously crying and suffering. That could not be indifference. Even more, she talked such nonsense about —

David looked at her in complete shock, his mouth and eyes open wide in understanding. In two steps, he reached her and clutched her to him almost brutally; she did not resist, only her eyes remained lowered to the ground. "God, Cassandra! Are you jealous? Is that it? Are you jealous? Please tell me that is the reason — please," he begged her, as his hands caressed her hair and a broad smile spread over his face.

"You have no shame, sir," she replied furiously as she wiped her tears, her eyes like daggers of wounded rage cast at him. "You have no shame and no honour to come here with your *friends* and then question *my* behaviour. How dare you speak of jealousy? I am asking you to leave this moment; you have no right to be in my chamber."

Each of her angry words was a sweet balm for his previous distress. By the time she finished her tirade, he took her hands by force and kissed them tenderly, as she struggled to be free of his hold.

"I missed you so much." He spoke with such tenderness that she stilled. "I was so afraid of losing you, yet so hopeful when I left you; these weeks have been a torture for me. I counted the hours and the minutes until I would see you again. I was close to resigning from the army if they would not allow me to come."

Cassandra could not speak — could not move or breathe; even her heart was afraid to beat again, frightened that it was only a dream and any movement might awaken her.

"Do you know how hurt I felt when you ignored me all evening? I hoped you would come and greet me, smile at me, perhaps whisper your answer to me, and release my torment as soon as possible. Instead, I received only cold indifference —"

"Cold indifference? I almost cried when you entered the room, and then what did *you* do? Nothing! How could I whisper anything to you when those girls were almost in your lap?!"

He burst out laughing, and she turned her back to him again, trying to dry her cheeks. David encircled her with his arms, crushed her back against his chest, and then tilted her head so he could wipe away her tears with his lips.

"You were jealous of the young Thomason girls," he teased her, and she fought to break free from his arms. "You were jealous of two girls Georgiana's age," he continued as his lips covered her face with soft kisses.

"David, please stop. We have to talk seriously," she whispered, though her resistance became weaker.

"As you like," he continued between kisses. "Any wish of yours is my command, your ladyship," he said and, indeed, he stopped his caresses and turned her to him. She finally met his eyes.

"David, I do not find much amusement in this; I admit I was jealous. My turmoil all these weeks was no less than yours. And then when you arrived this evening, I was certain I had lost your interest in hearing my answer. Do you still want to hear my answer, David?"

"Not really," he teased her, and she frowned. "My beautiful Cassandra, I do not need words to confirm what your tears already tell me," he added tenderly as he softly kissed her lips. She tentatively responded to his kisses, trying to say something more, but he captured her lips gently.

"Why did you come to my room?" she asked, her lips only a few inches from his.

"I saw you on the balcony, and I was afraid for you."

"I was just thinking of you."

"And I of you as I was outside on my own balcony."

"I cannot believe everything has changed in only a few minutes, David."

"I cannot believe I was so stupid to waste all those minutes doubting you." He continued to kiss her with growing passion and suddenly lifted her in his arms, their lips still joined, as she cried and put her arms around his neck. After closing the window, he carried Cassandra to the bed, where they both reclined.

Only then did she withdraw her lips from his to whisper, "David, I still have so many things to tell you."

He briefly frowned. "There is only one thing I want to hear this moment, Cassandra. Will you allow me in your life — now and tomorrow and for a lifetime?"

"I will… I do," she said, as her fingers gently touched his face.

"Then anything else can wait." As she closed her eyes to receive his kisses, he rose from the bed.

"Are you leaving?" she inquired with surprise and no little concern.

He laughed, removed his clothes and threw himself next to her; she began to laugh, but he quickly captured her lips with unleashed urgency.

"Do you think I intend to leave?" he asked as his hands possessively removed her gown.

"Not anymore," she replied breathlessly.

"You know, madam, I am quite concerned about your lack of trust in me. First, you believed me capable of courting other women in your presence, and then you thought I would leave you with only a kiss. But we will talk about that later… while we rest…because we will have to rest from time to time, you know."

She laughed, but it turned into a deep moan as his body joined hers. He remained still inside her, and his eyes fixed on hers for a moment; she pulled his head closer and kissed him softly as he began to move.

"God, Cassandra, you cannot imagine how long I have waited for this moment."

"I can imagine, but I would like you to tell me nevertheless." She smiled against his lips.

"Or perhaps I should prove it to you?"

"That would be even better."

David paused once more and kissed her eyes to open them; with delight and utter happiness, he saw her green eyes glowing as never before while her hands tentatively caressed his back.

"Cassandra, did you miss me all this time?"

"You know I missed you, David. Do you want me to say it again?"

"No — I want you to show me. I want you to make me feel that you missed me."

"That would be even better," she agreed, smiling with passion.

They needed quite a long time to express everything they felt, to dissipate doubt and misunderstanding, and to satisfy their long-denied desire. In the end, however, their understanding was complete.

As much as he was incredulously happy about the passion they had shared, David was even more delighted about Cassandra's choice to remain nestled in his arms afterward. He still remembered vividly the first time they made love and how completely she had changed by morning. This time, however, it was different; he felt her fingers entwine with his and caress his hand — and that small gesture filled his heart.

"There is something I want to tell you too, Cassandra."

"What is it?" She turned her head to face him; her hair tickled him and he buried his face in it to reach her ear.

"I love you. As the months have passed since I proposed to you, I find that I love you more.

Cassandra looked at him silently. He waited for her reply, but it did not come; instead, she rose from the bed covered only in a sheet and unlocked a drawer of her dressing table. David watched her, puzzled and slightly worried. She returned and handed him an old notebook.

His confusion increased. "What is this?"

"It is my diary. I want you to read these pages. It was written after my coming-out ball."

Half an hour of deep silence followed as he read, looked at her with disbelief, and then read three more times, his expression gradually changing; finally, she took the book from his hands and silently cuddled up to his chest.

She could feel his heart racing and his body tense as his arms enveloped her. "You could have been mine all this time." He tightened his embrace until she could barely breathe. "All the pain could have been avoided if —"

"David?" He did not reply, only kissed her temple. "I spent years buried in regrets, sorrow and lost happiness, but now my tears are spent. I shall never forget my past, and part of my heart will always belong to Thomas. My future happiness will sometimes be shadowed by painful memories — that is true — but I do love you deeply; I love you with a seventeen-year-old's shattered dreams as well as a twenty-five-year-old's hopes. So if you are sure you want me, let us not waste any more time."

She nestled against him and stretched her hand to caress his face; she startled and rolled in his arms to look at him. "David, are you crying?" she asked incredulously, her green eyes smiling through her own tears.

"I certainly am not, madam," he replied soundly. "Who could imagine a colonel in His Majesty's army crying? That would be unacceptable."

"Unacceptable, indeed," she laughed and kissed his cheeks.

David held her hands and kissed them tenderly many times, and then his lips brushed hers.

"We still have many things to discuss, Cassandra. We have to decide what to do; tomorrow I shall speak to Darcy, and he will help me to apply for a special license. And you — to whom should I apply for your hand?"

"You already said these could wait until tomorrow. I am too exhausted and incoherent to speak now."

"I am sorry. Should I leave and allow you to sleep? I shall see you tomorrow morning; there is no hurry."

"I said I am too exhausted to speak," she repeated in a lower voice.

"Oh...I see," he smiled and kissed her hands again. "So am I to understand, that, if I do not require you to speak, I may stay longer?" he asked between kisses along her throat.

"You certainly may stay, Colonel, as long as you do not expect me to speak... coherently," she managed to say before his hands greedily explored her skin, banishing all her thoughts and words — the coherent ones.

Darcy had quite a stressful night; for the first time since their marriage, Elizabeth was already asleep by the time he entered their rooms, and she looked so tired that he had no heart to wake her only for his pleasure. So he allowed her to rest, which greatly affected his own.

He finally slept at dawn; when he awoke, Elizabeth was gone. His man informed him that the mistress left word she would be downstairs.

Darcy finally found her, but she begged him to wait for her in the breakfast room as she was occupied with making proper arrangements for their guests' journey to London. She promised she would join him for coffee in five minutes, and Darcy had no choice but to obey. He spent more than half an hour alone, reading newspapers and wondering whether he should buy Elizabeth a new watch as her old one did not accurately measure how long a minute was.

"Good morning, Darcy." He was greeted by a cheerful Cassandra.

"Look who is here so early in the morning! I cannot believe my eyes," he said, and was rather shocked when Cassandra placed a quick kiss on his cheek as she had not done since they were children.

"All right, that demands an explanation," he said soundly as she poured herself a large cup of coffee.

"I, too, would like an explanation about why you kissed my husband, Lady Cassandra." Elizabeth sat by Darcy, smiling, waiting for an answer. "I dare say you are feeling much better today. I imagine you slept quite well."

Cassandra replied in a lower voice, ignoring Darcy, "Your guess is only half correct, Elizabeth. Indeed, I feel better than I have felt in many years, but I did not sleep at all the entire night — and neither did David." Darcy promptly spilled his coffee on his coat.

He looked at them in disbelief, waiting for some sign of remorse from his friend or embarrassment from his wife. He saw none.

"I cannot deny that I am happy you reached an understanding with David, Cassandra; however I also cannot refrain from telling you that you are shameless to make such a public confession," he scolded her.

Cassandra smiled sweetly. "Thank you, Mr. Darcy; I learned that from your wife."

A lost Darcy witnessed Elizabeth and Cassandra laughing together. Elizabeth leaned over to him and covered his hand with hers.

"Forgive us, my love. It is a joke between Cassandra and me. I shall explain it to you later."

"By all means, my dear wife, do explain it to me. But a little later, as now I am going to have a word with David — if he is awake." He rose from his seat, but Cassandra stopped him with a mischievous smile.

"He is very much awake, but there is no need for you to go anywhere; he will be here soon."

"You *are* shameless, you know that," Darcy repeated to his friend, shaking his head in reprobation. Then his countenance softened, and a caring smile appeared on his lips. "I am pleased to see you happy, Cassandra."

"Thank you, Darcy. I shall always be indebted to you —"

"Oh, stop speaking nonsense; we have serious things to discuss," he interrupted her, while Elizabeth considered that neither Darcy nor Cassandra was comfortable receiving gratitude.

"So true, Darcy. We have many things to discuss," said the colonel, striding into the room.

"Good morning, Mrs. Darcy, Lady Cassandra," he said politely, but Cassandra laughed.

"No need to be polite. I already told them what happened," Cassandra confessed. "I hope you do not mind."

"Mind? No indeed, I am quite pleased."

"I am not pleased at all, David as somebody could hear her," said Darcy. "For heaven's sake, there are a thousand people in this house, not to mention the servants. We must be guarded. You would not want to ruin your reputation forever, would you?"

"I am sorry, Darcy. You are correct as usual. It is your home, and I have no right to disrespect your rules. I promise I will be more cautious from now on," Cassandra apologised, as did David, but Elizabeth began to laugh.

Neither Cassandra nor the colonel managed to discover why she was laughing. Darcy did not need to ask; he was only grateful that his wife chose not to betray his own occasional disregard for the rules.

"David, we must discuss your plans; considering the situation, I hope you will not long delay your wedding. I know I am not Cassandra's guardian; still I dare say I am responsible for her and —"

"Of course you are responsible for me, my dear elder brother," Cassandra replied. "And I would be more than grateful to you if you would take care of everything. I already told David he was to ask you for my hand, you know. Elizabeth, shall we go upstairs now? I want to talk to you privately."

"Gladly," Elizabeth said, and as she rose from her seat, she leaned and unexpectedly placed a soft kiss on Darcy's lips. He had no time to react — even less to scold her — as two servants and Colonel Thomason entered the room at that moment.

Darcy spent the next few minutes slightly embarrassed, wondering whether the others had noticed his wife's impulsive gesture; however, he could not deny that the taste of her lips was indeed delicious. He checked the clock to see how many hours remained until he could be alone with her again.

SUCH A JOYFUL CHRISTMAS EVE had not been seen at Pemberley for years, Darcy thought. He was deeply, completely happy — happier than he would have dared to dream a year earlier. There he was, surrounded by his dearest relatives and friends and wondering how a family dinner could be so perfect. He smiled at himself as he realised how pleased he was to have Elizabeth's family there, though his tranquillity was somewhat disturbed. And there were David and Cassandra; his beloved Georgiana, more lively and cheerful than he could remember; his old friend Bingley, completely charmed by his wife; and his dearest Elizabeth, glowing with happiness as she hosted their small party and frequently turned her sparkling eyes toward him.

The dinner ended, and Darcy invited the gentlemen to his library for a short drink, as they were all desirous to be reunited with the ladies as soon as possible. While they enjoyed their wine, their conversation was interrupted by Darcy's servant, entering with an express for Mr. Bingley.

"For me? Who would send me an express?" he wondered and broke the seal so hastily that he tore the paper.

A moment later, his face paled as his mouth opened in shock. The others put down their glasses and moved toward him as he was in evident need of support.

Finally, Bingley lifted his eyes to Darcy and then to David, and managed to articulate: "Caroline has left for the Continent. She married Markham a month ago."

Chapter 26

August — one year later.

The marriage between Lady Cassandra and David Fitzwilliam was not a discreet event in Town. The genuine happiness of the colonel's family, together with the rumours and wonderings of those who had never considered such an alliance before made it the talk of the *ton* for the entire season.

The wedding took place at the end of February at the Fitzwilliam residence, and though both the bride and groom expressed their request to have only the family invited, guests filled the large ballroom.

The only comfort of the newlyweds was that they shared the *ton's* curiosity with the Darcys. There were many who had been convinced for years that young Darcy would eventually marry Lady Cassandra; hence, the unexpected turn of events was difficult for them to understand. Mrs. Darcy was therefore carefully scrutinised and severely judged with respect to her looks, manners, behaviour and disposition; Elizabeth was declared pleasant enough, pretty enough, with a lively disposition and — most of all — exceedingly fortunate in securing Mr. Darcy for a husband. By what arts and allurements she managed to catch Mr. Darcy remained a mystery, still unsolved by summer when the couple returned to Pemberley.

The Bingleys found an estate only 30 miles from Pemberley, and Mr. Bingley offered it to his beloved wife precisely at the time she announced to him another more precious gift: the news that he would have an heir.

The only reason for distress tormenting Charles Bingley was the lack of news from his sister Caroline. Except for the brief note announcing her marriage to Markham, no word arrived for months.

As happened with their engagement, the Darcys shared the blessed secret of expecting a son or daughter a month later than the Bingleys, as they preferred to share the bliss of their future parenthood between themselves.

Mrs. Bennet's nerves barely survived such happy news; she expressed her desire to visit her daughters instantly, but Mr. Bennet disagreed with great determination. He insisted the weather was entirely too hot for such a long journey, and he forced his wife to delay the trip until some unfixed date in the future.

Instead, at Miss Darcy's invitation, Kitty and Mary were allowed to spend the summer at Pemberley. Understandably, Miss Darcy, being surrounded only by newlyweds she did not wish to disturb, could benefit from the company of two sisters-in-law of the same age, and Kitty and Mary could certainly benefit even more from Miss Georgiana's friendship.

In such a pleasant way June and July passed until, unexpectedly, Mrs. Bingley's state became a source of worry for her husband. Her health seemed much worse than did Elizabeth's though Jane was only a month nearer to her confinement.

While Elizabeth changed few of her habits, Jane was rarely able to leave her bed. A doctor was fetched from London and, upon thorough examination, declared Mrs. Bingley's pregnancy to be a reason for concern.

When Jane's state did not improve, Bingley decided they would go to London so Jane could be under the doctor's constant care. Even more, he hired a nurse to be with her day and night.

Of course, the Darcys could not stay away, so they returned to their town house only two days after the Bingleys. A week later, Cassandra and David followed them, so that only Georgiana and the two Miss Bennets remained at Pemberley to enjoy each other's company as nobody informed them about the gravity of Jane's state.

Bingley's despair was heartrending for his friends; day by day, his distress grew and was more difficult to handle. He had reached the point where he declared he cared for nothing but his wife's health. After many glasses of brandy, and tearful with worry and helpless torment, he swore to Darcy and the doctor that his wife would never be put in a similar situation because surely he would never touch her again and put her at such a risk.

The doctor, a proficient physician who had treated the Darcys for more than 30 years, patted Bingley's arm, assuring him he had seen many other ladies bear a difficult pregnancy with the first child, only to have easy, uneventful births later. Then, while having a glass of brandy himself, the doctor concluded it would be a pity for a man who was so much in love with his wife never to touch her again. To the shock of Darcy — who was assisting silently in the conversation — the doctor suggested to Bingley that he could offer him some medical advice about how to *"delay"* a new pregnancy, until the moment he and his wife would wish to have another child.

"DARCY, BE SO KIND AS to pour me a glass of wine," said David to his host, and Darcy hurried to fulfil his request.

"I have just come from the Bingleys, and I have to say I am very impressed. Bingley has been brave indeed — I grant him that. To have his son born a month earlier than expected after such a long labour when everyone feared the child would not survive — I would never imagine both Bingleys being so strong! I say, Mrs. Bingley has gained my deepest admiration. I saw her today, only a week after those horrible days and nights, smiling so serenely as if she had the most peaceful time of her life."

"Yes, she is remarkable indeed."

Darcy sipped some of his wine and then continued regretfully. "I still cannot forgive myself for how grossly I misjudged Jane last year. When I think that I could have ruined her happiness forever — and Bingley's — and mine too as Elizabeth never would have forgiven me."

"Now, Darcy, do not ruin my disposition. I am in such a good mood since Charles asked me to be the child's godfather!"

"Yes, I noticed that. I think it was a wise decision of Bingley. I cannot see a better godfather than you."

"As for Mrs. Jane Bingley — she is so kind that I am sure she forgave you a long time ago, so perhaps it is about time to forgive yourself, too."

"I truly hope so." He offered his guest another glass of wine.

"Darcy, did you see poor Bingley's face? He seemed lost in his own world as he looked at his son and his wife," the colonel laughed.

"Well, he has every reason to be proud and grateful to his wife. She gave him a strong, healthy boy. What more could a man wish for?"

Suddenly understanding the effect of his words, Darcy stopped and looked at David with regret. He tried to apologise, but David would not allow it.

"Do not worry for me, Darcy; I am perfectly happy as I am now — just Cassandra and me and hopefully a few godsons from both you and Bingley. Now, speaking of that Bingley boy — he will be a very spoilt child. Mark my words! Thank heaven your child will be born soon so the Bennet family attention will be split in two."

"Not quite so soon." Elizabeth still has two months until…you know."

"I know that — two more months. Just long enough for Mrs. Bennet to change her residence from the Bingleys, where she stays now, to your home, to be as close to your wife as she has been to her eldest daughter."

"Heaven forbid, David! Mr. Bennet indicated they will leave town in a month, not a single day later."

"Your father-in-law is a wise man."

"Well, he does his best, considering the circumstances. I know he has been of great support to poor Bingley all these weeks as Bingley's family seemed indifferent to his problems."

"By the way, do you have any news of Bingley's sisters?"

"Well, the Hursts are still at Brighton, and they sent a note that they will return next month. As for the present Lady Markham, not a single word."

"Damn, that stupid woman continues to torment poor Bingley with her silence. What is she thinking? Where the devil is Caroline, and how is it she has only written him twice in as many months?"

"Something is not right, David. Something has been wrong since the day

Markham decided to marry her. And this long, strange silence! Bingley visited the elder Markham, and not even he is aware of Caroline's whereabouts. He said he had not seen her since they married."

"That is indeed strange — especially considering we met Markham in town a month ago! Did he not allow her to contact her family? I do believe him capable of such cruelty. I am quite certain he is completely out of his mind. Do you remember what he said when we last met him in July?"

"That we finally are all a big family now, just as he always wanted? Of course I remember, but it was not only his words but his voice, the look in his eyes."

"Have you seen him since then? Did you get any news? I know you have hired some men to find his location."

"Nothing at all; he did not reside in any of their houses, and nobody — including his father — has seen him."

"Do you trust the earl to tell you the truth?"

"I do. The elder Lord Markham did misbehave in the past, in more than one situation. He always supported his sons in everything they did, and he trusted them implicitly, but he is also known as a reasonable man and an honest business partner. I am certain he understood Bingley's worry about his sister. If he knew something, he would have at least mentioned it."

"You are probably right. If we meet Markham again, we should force him to tell us where his wife is."

"I would rather not meet Markham anytime soon. I promised Elizabeth I would never allow him to provoke me again, and I intend to keep my promise; however, it would be very difficult were I to face that man. Elizabeth was distressed when I told her about our meeting, and I will do everything in my power not to upset her again during this time."

"I understand — you must be worried about your baby. You know, I might be selfish, but that is why I am somehow pleased that Cassandra will never... I do not think I could bear the worry, the fear that something might happen to her or to the child."

"David, are you out of your mind? Why are you telling me all this now, when you know perfectly well I hardly sleep a few hours a night? Is this your way of offering me support and comfort?"

"Blast! Please forgive me, my friend. I never thought that... I did not mean that... Damn, I am such an idiot!"

Half an hour later, David still had not succeeded in redirecting Darcy's attention to other subjects of conversation. Their discussion was rather dull and only served to make the time pass until the ladies' return.

An impromptu opening of the library door and a livid Bingley entering the room animated them — more than they would have wished.

"BINGLEY? WHAT HAPPENED?" BINGLEY EMPTIED a glass of wine in one swallow and then indicated for David to fill his glass again. Darcy took the glass from his hand before David could comply.

"Bingley, calm yourself and tell us what on earth is wrong with you? Did something happen to your wife or son? Elizabeth and Cassandra are there —"

Bingley interrupted him and barely managed to reply. "It is about Caroline — I got a note from her."

The other two gentlemen watched in silence as Bingley re-filled his own glass and started pacing the room while answering them.

"My steward said the note arrived quite late last night, but he did not know who brought it; of course, I did not open it until you left — a couple of hours ago. How could I have known it was an important letter? It was from Caroline; I barely recognised her handwriting. She sent word they have been in town for six weeks, but she was not allowed to speak to me. She begged me to come to see her, and I went, but Markham — he is out of his mind — he refused to allow me to speak to her. He demanded that I tell him how I discovered their whereabouts. I tried to enter by force, but I could not. I need to enter, even if I have to defy Markham. I will call him out if need be. He cannot keep my sister imprisoned, even if she is his wife — can he? I must see her immediately. She begged me to come to her, but Markham would not let me," Bingley repeated, moving desperately around the room, looking from Darcy to the colonel with a lost expression on his face.

"Bingley, come and sit down. Let us speak rationally." Darcy grabbed his arm and forced him to take a seat.

"I have no time to sit, Darcy — I must leave immediately."

"There is nowhere you can go for the moment, Bingley. You cannot enter Markham's house by force, and fighting with him would be a foolish thing to do. We will find a more reasonable way."

"You were not calm and reasonable when your *wife* was involved, Darcy," Bingley replied sharply. "You fought Markham yourself, remember?"

Darcy ignored the offensive tone. "I did fight Markham, but I did not have a wife and a newborn son at the time, Bingley. You cannot afford being hurt for behaving impulsively. Let us consider this situation wisely."

"I know neither of you care much about her, but she *is* my sister," Bingley whispered. "I have not forgotten how poorly she behaved in the past, but she is in a dangerous situation — I am certain of it. And I cannot abandon her — I simply cannot."

He handed the note to Darcy in a defeated gesture of helpless despair. Darcy glanced at it, looked at David, and finally turned to Bingley.

"So, it appears that Miss Bingley — I mean Lady Markham — is in town now. You are right to be worried, Bingley — such a pleading note is hardly her style. She must be quite desperate to send it."

"See? See? You agree with me!"

"I do . . . and do not worry; nobody will abandon your sister, Bingley. We will find a way to speak to her."

Darcy rang for his servant and sent him to fetch his attorney; in the meantime, he wrote a note to the elder Lord Markham, asking for an urgent audience. He also sent word to Mr. Gardiner, requesting his attendance, and then turned his attention back to his companions.

"We shall consider the situation carefully. Though I understand your sister's difficulties, we must not forget about Mrs. Bingley and Elizabeth — we cannot allow any of this to affect them. As for Cassandra — she probably will be overcome with anger."

"You are right Darcy — you are right, of course. I do not want Jane to discover anything. She would be devastated with worry," Bingley said while the colonel nodded in agreement, obviously agitated himself.

"Of course we must keep this private, but I cannot help saying it sounds more silly than dangerous to me," the colonel intervened. "It sounds like he is keeping her prisoner, but that is ridiculous. I mean no offence, Bingley, but why would a man like Markham keep your sister hidden? He has little to gain from her except her dowry, which I doubt is important enough to justify such a ruckus."

"I do not know, Colonel! I could not speak reasonably with him; I doubt he has any sense remaining in him. He kept saying I should bring Darcy and Fitzwilliam to beg him to see Caroline. It is as though he has become obsessed with you."

"The first thing we have to do is search for Markham's companions," Darcy directed. "He is not the sort of man to stay alone all these months. I also believe we should talk to the earl; I shall do that myself. If we are to speak to Markham, we should have his father with us. Perhaps he will make his son more reasonable."

"He has never been reasonable when it came to his sons. I doubt he will have much influence on that lunatic." The colonel was becoming more irritated with each passing moment.

"I shall speak to the earl; do not bother yourself. Now let us establish the details; we need a strategy for approaching Markham," said Darcy.

"I cannot believe we are planning *strategies* for Markham," the colonel burst out. "This is quite ludicrous! Here is *my* strategy: break the door down, put Markham on the floor, beat him senseless and take your sister out of the house; after that, let him come and search for her if he wants. If we are lucky, he will be so drunk that he will not remember what happened." Darcy looked at him with reproach, but Bingley's face lit slightly.

"Well, if there are not many servants around, we could try that approach. Colonel, Darcy, I am sorry to give you so much trouble. Perhaps I should go and solve it on my own."

"Oh shut up, Bingley," said the colonel. "That is not what I meant. It is not your fault. This stupid Markham has been an annoyance for years. We must do something about him."

"Yes we must." Darcy was serious and decided. "As I said, let us prepare our strategy."

IT WAS ALMOST DINNERTIME, AND Cassandra took a final look at her image in the mirror; she was pleased with her appearance and, with a smile, waited to see the approval in her husband's eyes — as usually happened. She wondered what was taking him so long to prepare himself. He returned home just minutes before, apologised briefly and went to change, promising he would join her presently. She was worried as his entire behaviour was changed, and his disposition, she had noticed, was quite poor. She was determined not to hesitate a moment before asking him about the nature of his unexpected business with Darcy, which had kept both of them out the entire afternoon. Something was not well; she could sense that.

A few moments later, David entered her room, took her hands and gently made her sit while he spoke softly. Despite his caring voice, each of his words threw her deeper and deeper into her nightmare.

"Surely you are mocking me, sir! You cannot seriously consider confronting Markham in order to see Caroline Bingley! You have no right to do that! You gave me your word! You promised me!"

"Cassandra, please calm yourself." He tried to embrace her, but she pulled away in a rage. "I promised I would never lie to you, that I would never keep anything from you. That is why I am here talking to you."

"You are twisting your own words, sir!"

"No, I am not, my dear."

"Do not dare patronise me, Colonel. You are not a man of your word; that is all I can say!"

"My love, I promise nothing bad will happen. We are only going to talk."

"How dare you do this. How dare you promise me again."

She fought so hard against her tears that her voice lost all its strength.

"I am making you this promise as I am certain I shall keep it. I shall return before you even know it."

She was pacing the room, and he stopped her, encircling her in his arms. Her fears and despair turned into rage, and she continued to accuse him of betraying her until she concluded she should not have married him at all. Her words were offensive and hurtful, but David gave them no consideration. He could feel her fear, and for a moment, he wondered whether it was fair to put others' troubles before his wife's peace of mind.

"I have never cared about Caroline Bingley, and I thought you felt the same, but apparently I was wrong. You clearly are more concerned with her than you are about me."

"My dear, that statement does not even deserve a reply; you know as well as I do how unfair it is. I am not concerned about Caroline either — why should I be? But

Bingley is deeply worried for her — she is his sister, after all. And Bingley will go and deal with Markham. What should I do, Cassandra? Should I hide to keep myself safe? Would that truly please you? Would I be worthy then of your affection? Bingley is my friend, and we were there for him as he worried about his wife and child. Should we then abandon him in this trying situation?"

"No, of course not! But Bingley should not expose himself either! What we should do is to hire 100 people to go with Bingley — perhaps from the army or the militia. He should wait outside while they bring Caroline out. *I* will pay for those 100 men. I will pay for anything necessary to help Bingley!"

She became more animated as she realised how unreasonable her ideas were; David smiled with gentle understanding as he kissed her hair. She was still resisting him and struggling to push him away.

"My love, you know only too well I have to go. You are the most courageous woman I know. I do understand your torment, but the past is gone — we cannot live our lives in fear of Markham. For heaven's sake — he is an idiot! I know he is a dangerous idiot though, and I promise I will be cautious. We will be at least four men there — none of us will be in real danger, you must see that. We are not going to war, for God's sake!"

"Then I shall come with you!" Cassandra declared and David burst out laughing so hard that he had tears in his eyes. He covered her face in kisses while she fought to escape his arms.

"That was the sweetest profession of love, my dearest, and I shall always be grateful to you for your care. Now I have to leave; the others are waiting for me. I shall return before you know it."

"Stop patronising me, Colonel Fitzwilliam. I intend to come, too, so do not treat me like a child!

"Then do not behave like a child, your ladyship. Surely you cannot imagine I would allow you to participate in a potentially dangerously situation. So you are worried for me and want to come — for what? If we are unable to handle him — four men — of what use could you be?"

"So you admit the danger for yourself!"

"No I do not. I only admit how delighted I am with your care for me. I will gladly continue this conversation as soon as I return — which I estimate will happen a little after midnight. Please have dinner and then try to find some sleep; you will awake in my arms tomorrow morning."

David placed a soft kiss upon her lips and then left; she heard the door shutting behind him. Her hands trembled and her heartbeat increased wildly with the sound of his retreating steps.

For a few moments she remained as stone in the middle of the room, and then she moved to the window only to see him enter the carriage. David cast a last quick glance to the window, and she thought she could see a smile on his face. Her heart seemed to stop, a cold shiver shattered her spine, and everything became dark around her.

IN THE PEACEFUL COMFORT OF their rooms, Elizabeth was sitting on the sofa close to the fire; Darcy had been speaking for quite a while but she could not — would not — accept the meaning of his words. Caroline always wanted to marry a title with considerable wealth; now that her dream had come true, why would she want to leave? That was preposterous, and she was certain it was only one of Caroline's schemes. She was likely just upset with Markham for not giving her enough pin money or something.

"Surely, you cannot consider going," she said bluntly.

"My love, you must understand why I have to go. We cannot leave this burden on Bingley alone!"

"Charles should be at home taking care of his wife and newborn son, not chasing Markham around town for one of Caroline's whims."

"Elizabeth, that is not fair. Everything indicates that Caroline is in a dangerous situation. And you know only too well that one cannot abandon one's sister, no matter how badly *that sister* behaves."

Elizabeth turned pale and averted her eyes. "Lydia was silly and impulsive, but she has never been as mean as Caroline. It is not a fair comparison."

"I know it was not fair; forgive me. I did not mean to compare them, only to sympathise with Bingley's worry. I understand why he cannot dismiss his sister's cry for help despite her past misbehaviour. Can you imagine his torment, his distress, his fatigue after all those sleepless nights of fear — and now this? How can I leave him alone in this trying moment? I am certain you understand Bingley cannot succeed in this without my help."

"I still do not understand why a woman would be unable to leave and visit her family? Why would she need an entire *regiment* to take her from her husband's house? This is all so strange!"

"I agree with you, and that is precisely why Bingley is so out of his mind with worry and why I know I have to go with him." She looked straight at him as tears rolled down her cheeks.

"William, I am so afraid."

"My love, do you trust me? Do you trust me when I tell you nothing is more important to me than you and our child? Do you trust that I will not do anything to put myself in danger — not for me, but for you? I give you my word that we will be exceptionally cautious; we have planned our strategy carefully."

"A strategy? What strategy?"

He explained it to her in every detail while holding her hand and caressing her fingers; she only nodded in silence. She could see the wisdom of their plan, despite the cold claw of fear that clenched her heart.

"And," Darcy concluded with a smile, "as an ultimate solution, if Markham proves unreasonable, David has proposed to beat him senseless and grab Caroline from the house."

Elizabeth's lips twisted and her eyes narrowed as she met her husband's curious gaze.

"Well, what can I say? Perhaps you should apply the colonel's solution first — after all he is an officer in His Majesty's army and familiar with the requirements of a successful strategy."

Darcy laughed, and she smiled with a heavy heart. Feeling their child kicking, she startled and took his palm to press it to her abdomen. She did trust him implicitly. She knew he would take care of himself, if only to be able to take care of her and their child. She could not ask him to stay idly by her side, abandoning their brother in time of need. He would not be Fitzwilliam Darcy if he accepted that, and she would not be worthy to be his wife if she continued to upset him with unreasonable pleas.

"Please be careful, my husband," she whispered as she wiped her tears and wondered why breathing had suddenly become so difficult.

FOUR MEN COULD BE SEEN entering the small cottage in which Markham had taken residence; two of them barely maintained their composure as distress shaded their faces darker than the night.

They had expected to be detained; however, surprisingly, a servant invited them in the moment they knocked at the front door. The earl attempted to inform the servant who he was but the man seemed completely indifferent to his words. The only remark was that his master was waiting in the main room — and then the servant withdrew down the hallway.

Though Bingley's story had given them some indication about the alteration of Markham's state, the latter's appearance took both Darcy and Fitzwilliam by surprise. He was drunk, but it was more than that; his cold laugh the moment he saw his visitors only confirmed the impression.

"Oh, you are finally here — Darcy and Cassandra's new husbands; what an honour for my humble abode! I expected you earlier. What took you so long? I have already started to drink alone, but I may offer you something. What would you like?"

"Son, what is happening to you? Are you unwell? You look very ill. What are you doing here in this house? I cannot believe you are in town and did not inform me." The earl moved toward his son, and the young Markham cast a quick glance at him.

"I have been very busy, Father. Do not start lecturing me; I am in no mood to listen to you."

The earl stared at his son, his eyes wide in disbelief, completely ignored in the middle of the room. Markham filled his glass once more and turned to his visitors with an inquiring look.

"Lord Markham, I apologise for interfering, and I hope it will not be a long interruption," said Bingley with perfect politeness. "I only wish to speak to my sister if that is convenient."

"In fact it is not convenient. I do not want you to speak to my wife. She is my wife — you know? I told you as much earlier, but I notice you brought reinforcements this time. I was certain you could not accomplish the job alone."

"Lord Markham, I shall not enter into an argument with you; I have a simple request, and you cannot deny me. Surely, you must see how strange is your refusal to allow me to meet with my sister. This is not acceptable, and I cannot understand how —"

"You cannot understand because you are an idiot, Bingley — as is your stupid sister. I am so tired of her that I will not speak of her any longer. Now — you two — may I be of some assistance to you?"

"Lord Markham!" Bingley burst out furiously, but Markham ignored him completely while he continued to smile at the others. Darcy cast a quick glance at the earl; clearly, he was of no help in solving the situation.

"Come Markham, stop fooling around. We are here to see Mr. Bingley's sister, and we will not leave without achieving our purpose. All we want is a few minutes with her; you cannot deny us this." Darcy took a step toward Markham, his countenance as decided as his words; he intended to put an end to the quarrel, and he would not be stopped.

"Of course I can deny it to you. I can do whatever I please regarding my wife; however, I might be tempted to exchange benefits. I will allow you to speak to my wife if you will allow me to speak to yours. How is that? That way, every party involved will be satisfied to some degree."

Darcy instantly turned pale and took another step forward; a moment later, he regained his composure. "You tread on dangerous ground, Markham. Be careful what you say."

"*You* are on dangerous ground, Darcy; you are in my home at my disposal, and now you upset me. Leave my home immediately! I will call on you if I want to speak to you again!"

"Charles…please do not leave me," sounded a weak voice, and everyone's eyes turned to the door where a woman dressed only in a nightgown and holding a small bundle tightly to her chest stepped tentatively into the room, supporting herself with the wall. "Please do not leave m —"

"Caroline?" cried Charles as he ran to her. Darcy and the colonel looked at each other in utter disbelief. The woman — so thin that it was a wonder she could walk, her hair cut off and in complete disorder, her face swollen, looking at them with fearful eyes — could not possibly be Caroline Bingley! Even Bingley seemed unsure of her identity but, as he moved closer to see her face, he ran to her, calling her name. A barely audible whine mixed with Bingley's voice and Markham's command.

"Stay away from her, Bingley, and you — go upstairs woman. How dare you leave your room?"

"Oh God, you have a child," Bingley cried as he supported his sister in his arms. "This is a child. Is it yours, Caroline?"

"A ch-child?" The earl, livid, looked at his son in utter disbelief. "You have a child? My grandchild?"

"Oh, do not be too enthusiastic, Father; I do not think he will live. The poor creature was born too soon and will likely die any minute; this woman was unable even to give me a worthy heir."

"It was not my fault," yelled Caroline, and both Darcy and David could recognise the determined, argumentative voice of Caroline Bingley. "You hit me that day, and I fell on the stairs. That is why James was born early. You almost killed your son, you cruel, heartless wretch!"

"James? His name is James?" asked the earl, still dazed by the unexpected news while Darcy and the colonel seemed uncertain as to what to do next.

"Who the hell knows his name? And you — go upstairs this instant, woman — I will speak to you later!"

"Son, did you hit your wife? This cannot be true; I cannot believe it. It surely was a mistake, was it not? Did you fetch a doctor to see the child? We must have a doctor immediately," the earl said tentatively with a hopeful look. He grabbed his son's arm, but the young Markham pulled away.

"Stop talking nonsense, Father. Leave me alone — all of you. This spectacle is over."

It only took a moment for Darcy and the colonel to join Bingley, who was holding Caroline close to him. The two men surrounded their friend while he walked tentatively to the door, supporting his sister and her child. Caroline seemed unable to walk; she struggled to move her feet while her arms held the infant tightly. With horror, Darcy could not take his eyes away from the bruises visible over her neck, face and wrists; some darkened impressions left by a merciless hand were visible on her nape as she bowed her head to watch her child.

"Where do you think you are going with my wife, Bingley?"

"I am taking my sister home; a doctor will take care of her without delay as it is obvious she will not find the care she needs in your house. You will not oppose me, or else, as God is my witness, I will kill you. Step aside."

"You will kill me? You? That is so amusing that I will laugh for days."

Markham moved in front of the small group but could not reach Bingley or Caroline, as Darcy and David moved before them.

"So that is your plan — stealing my family away? We will see about that; we will see if anyone would blame me for shooting thieves who tried to kidnap my child," Markham said with unleashed rage. He leaned near the fireplace, and a second later, a pistol appeared in his hand. Instantly, both Darcy and David ran to him, but it was the earl — only two feet away — who grabbed his son's arm first.

"Son, what are you doing? What is happening to you, my boy? Please let us sit and talk, nobody is stealing your family. Son, I am begging you."

By that time, Darcy and David had reached Markham and held him from behind but his father continued to plead with him, standing in front of him, holding his arm tightly. Markham fought violently to escape his captors, and in his struggle, he hit his father; the earl lost his balance and, searching for support, fell against his son.

The blast shattered the entire house; both the earl and his son grew limp and eventually their strangely entwined bodies slid slowly towards the floor. Darcy and David could do little but put Markham down; David was still holding him forcefully while Darcy moved in front of them to check what had happened. A moment of silence followed and then Darcy's grave voice.

"The pistol went off; he is badly injured."

MIDNIGHT HAD COME AND GONE, and he was still not there. He did not keep his promise, and despite her harsh words, which were still resonating in her own mind, Cassandra knew David was a man of his word. Therefore, if he did not keep his promise, something had happened. She moved around the room, stopping in front of the window, as she had a thousand times that night. She stared outside through the moonlight, hoping, praying, begging to see his carriage. The street remained empty.

She threw herself onto the bed, crying from helpless despair. She wanted to go after him but did not know where he was, and what if he should return and not find her there? She should go to the Darcys'; perhaps Elizabeth had received some news. Surely, Elizabeth would have informed her if she knew anything more. Still she should go. She would not disturb Elizabeth, only ask the servants whether Darcy was home. Yes, that is what she should do!

She took her coat and awakened her maid, sending her to fetch the coachman. The maid looked in shock at her mistress — dressed only in a nightgown, her hair down, barefoot — but obeyed silently. A moment later, however, Mrs. Spencer appeared in the doorway; Cassandra turned her back to her companion, but Mrs. Spencer ignored her dismissal. She took Cassandra's arm gently but decidedly.

"I cannot allow your ladyship to go anywhere. The master specifically told me to keep you in the house. He said he must find you here when he returns."

Cassandra turned red at that daring answer, and a sharp reply escaped her lips. Mrs. Spencer's countenance remained unchanged, and a loving smile lit her face as she gently directed Cassandra back to her room.

"I know he is late, but he will return, my child; I can feel it. You must learn to be confident in your husband and to trust the Lord."

"And you should learn to trust Mrs. Spencer," added David from the doorway; his voice made Cassandra gasp and she remained still while her husband moved slowly to her. Mrs. Spencer sighed and exited the room, hiding her tears.

Cassandra's eyes travelled along his body to confirm that he was unharmed, and then she looked at his face to find answers to the questions she did not dare to ask. "Darcy and Bingley are fine," he whispered.

His arms embraced her closely, and she crushed herself against him. His gaze, the expression of his face and his tensed body told her something had happened. However, as long as he was safe and her friends were safe — she selfishly chose not to ask more for the time being. The nightmare was over, and anything else mattered very little to her.

DARCY STOOD AT THE EDGE of Elizabeth's bed and watched her carefully while he related the tragic events to her, choosing his words carefully.

"So the earl killed his son?"

"No — no. It was an accident; the gun went off between them. The earl is still in shock. Despite the fact that his son's character was revealed tonight, I am sure the earl would prefer to have died himself to save his son. What a punishment for a father."

Elizabeth looked deeply into her husband's eyes and confessed with all her sincerity, "Lord, forgive me — I feel no regret that a man's life was taken. I feel no pity for either Markham or the earl. I know it sounds cruel, but that is how I feel. I am glad he is gone."

Darcy kissed her hand. "You must not trouble yourself any longer with any of them."

"I shall not — they both will be forgotten soon. Only poor Caroline likely will not be able to forget him."

Darcy shivered as he remembered Caroline's state. Elizabeth looked at him closely and took his hand.

"Is she so altered? Is that why you did not allow me to see her?"

He could not possibly tell Elizabeth the truth about Caroline's condition, not after all the emotions she had to bear that night. "The doctor is with her now, and you need to rest without delay. We will talk more tomorrow."

She hesitated a moment, obviously desirous to continue, but finally accepted his decision.

"Very well. William, I am pleased you decided to bring Caroline here."

"My dearest, I confess I am not at all pleased, as my first concern is your peace of mind, but I saw no other solution in the midst of that din. We thought of little else but keeping the entire story as private as possible — though I doubt there will be any secrecy after tomorrow. Bingley's house was already full of guests with your parents staying there."

"Oh, you could not possibly have exposed poor Jane to such distress — not now when she is still not recovered. As for Mama, only imagine her reaction when she discovers this abominable story."

"Precisely. Besides, we have an entire floor unoccupied, so Caroline can reside there without disturbing you at all. We shall offer her the best accommodations and hire some extra help to serve her and take care of her son until she... until she is strong enough to travel and return to her house."

He was not at all certain Caroline would recover enough to travel; even the doctor was shocked when he saw her and discreetly confessed to Darcy that he was sceptical about any improvement.

"William, can I at least see the child, please? Only a moment, then I shall return to bed — I promise."

Darcy hesitated; the child was as weak as his mother was, and his life was in God's hands. Could he allow Elizabeth to become attached to that poor infant? He knew he was selfish, but he could think of little else but his wife and his own child. For Caroline's child, he already arranged to hire a servant and a wet nurse — and the latter was found and fetched in only a few hours time. He would do anything in his power to offer the best care to both mother and child — anything except exposing Elizabeth to more worry and pain.

"Please, William — only a moment. My love, I understand your concern. I imagine the child cannot be strong and healthy when he was born early and his mother is so ill, but I will pray for him, and I will accept God's will — whatever that might be. May I see him, please? "

He smiled and, though his heart was still heavy, kissed her hand in acceptance. "You are the mistress of the house, Mrs. Darcy. You may do whatever you wish."

IT WAS DAYLIGHT, BUT THE room was obscured, and Elizabeth asked the maid to open the window. She touched Caroline's forehead briefly and then turned to Cassandra and Georgiana.

"I believe we have reason to hope. Her fever has not increased since this morning. Dr. Morrison said that is a good sign.

"Thank the Lord. She is so changed; I still cannot believe she is Caroline," whispered Cassandra.

Elizabeth never would have believed it possible, but she did greatly worry for Caroline and had spent many hours praying for her life and health. That was quite ironic — considering her past "friendship" with the former Miss Bingley. *Fate has a strange sense of humour*, Elizabeth mused.

"Elizabeth, I think she is awake," Cassandra said loudly.

Elizabeth sat at the edge of the bed as she touched Caroline's hand. The patient moaned and moved, trying to lift her head but it fell back on the pillow.

"Caroline, how are you?" No coherent answer came, only moans and the violent movements of a body half conscious. Elizabeth called for the servants, and two maids entered instantly, holding Caroline's hands as she struggled.

Finally, after more than a quarter of an hour, Caroline fell asleep again, but her head kept moving violently, and her hands grabbed the sheets in despair as if she were in a dark nightmare. After another long hour, she eventually calmed, her breathing became steady again, and she remained so until later that day.

An hour before dinner, Elizabeth came once again to check on Caroline. The nurse's report was satisfactory, and she had almost exited the room when she heard Caroline's weak voice calling for someone. Elizabeth hurried to the bed and called her name until Caroline finally opened her eyes and they faced each other. Elizabeth attempted to calm her obvious distress when suddenly Caroline grabbed her arms painfully.

"Where is my son? What happened to him? Where is my child?" Caroline kept crying while she tried to rise from the bed, pulling at Elizabeth's hand.

Elizabeth struggled to calm her with no success. Caroline's agitation became greater and her cries louder and louder until the servants interfered and freed Elizabeth's arm from Caroline's hands. Elizabeth moved away from the bed to the other side of the room.

"Caroline, he is here… do not cry, he is here…" Elizabeth repeated, almost yelling to cover Caroline's voice while she took the infant from his bed and moved closer to Caroline.

The patient needed a couple of minutes to hear and take in the meaning of Elizabeth's words. The child's soft cries seemed to bring Caroline back to reality, and she started sobbing with despair as she stretched her arms to take the child from Elizabeth.

"Careful, let me put him near you," Elizabeth said, smiling reassuringly while she put the small burden on the pillow so Caroline could see him. "You are too weak to sit, and we do not want to harm him, do we? He is such a beautiful boy. Here he is, close to his mother."

Caroline stared at Elizabeth in disbelief, and then her eyes rested upon her son and she cried again, covering her mouth with her palm while tears rolled down her cheeks.

"He looks so changed. He has grown so much, and he looks so healthy," she cried in wonder.

"He does look healthy and sweet." Elizabeth smiled with no little emotion. "And yes, he did grow a lot, though you have been in our home for only a fortnight —"

"A fortnight? We have been here a fortnight? But how —? Oh dear God, what happened with —? I had a horrible dream. Was it a dream? Is he dead? Or —?"

"Caroline, calm yourself. I will tell you everything if you promise to stop crying. Your son is asleep. We must stay quiet not to distress him."

"Yes, yes, I do not want to distress him. My little angel — you are so beautiful," she whispered as her fingers brushed against the baby's little hands. "Oh dear God, is my son really healthy? Will he live to grow up? He always said my child was unworthy of his name and was too weak to live. But now he looks so healthy — does he not look healthy?"

"Your child is as healthy as he is beautiful; the doctor confirmed that. He was indeed quite weak as he had been born before his time; he was hungry too as you were not strong enough to feed him adequately. But all is well now; we hired a wet nurse and a maid to take care of him, and he improved wonderfully. You should be proud of him! Dr. Morrison will come to visit you soon and will confirm it for himself. We should take good care of you now, Lady Markham —"

"Do not call me that," Caroline interrupted her brutally, and Elizabeth looked at her in surprise. "Do not call me Lady Markham, please. Call me anything you want except that," she insisted in a more subdued voice while her eyes pleaded to reinforce her request.

Elizabeth nodded silently, and an awkward silence fell upon the room.

As though he could sense it, the child started to sob in his sleep. Caroline caressed him gently, but he continued to wail. A couple of minutes later, uncertain whether her gesture would upset Caroline, Elizabeth hesitantly lifted the child in her arms and pulled him to her chest, whispering in his ear. Almost instantly, the baby's cries vanished, and he resumed his peaceful sleep; she sat on the bed near Caroline, gently cradling the child.

"He is comfortable in your arms. He appears to know you very well," Caroline noted with both sadness and disbelief. "Did you hold him before — by yourself?"

"Oh, of course I held him; in fact, we have become quite good friends lately. He is a very handsome, nice young gentleman, though a little spoiled," Elizabeth attempted to joke. "But now that you are well, I am sure he will be much more comfortable with his beloved mother."

Caroline's face was pale; she stretched her hand to touch the baby's small head and then looked at Elizabeth in surprise. "You are expecting too; you will have your own baby soon."

"Yes, I will, and Charles and Jane have a little boy. Did he mention that to you? Charles is so happy he will have two boys around," Elizabeth continued, smiling gently.

Caroline seemed to disregard that second bit of information, her eyes fixed upon Elizabeth.

"You are expecting, and still you took the trouble of taking care of me and my child. After everything I have done to you, after my unforgivable behaviour toward you and your family, after all my offences and meanness — my child found safety, comfort, and peace in your arms. You brought us to your home and put your own feelings aside for us when you easily could have chosen to stay far away from this horrid affair."

"Lady — pardon me, umm — Miss Bingley, I will speak openly since you brought up the matter. I will not even attempt to say you are not correct; your past behaviour to my family and me has been always unkind and ungenerous. However, my own behaviour has not been correct at all times, so we are rather even. We could talk about this matter again sometime, if you like, but for now we should put the past aside and talk instead about the present and the future," Elizabeth said, placing a soft kiss on the child's small hand.

"I have been wrong in so many ways . I have been at fault so many times with you, and you are so kind, so generous. I never thought that would be possible. No other woman in your place would —"

"Come, Miss Bingley, we are family now. Let us not argue about the past! Any fault you may have had, any offences and arguments were instantly forgotten and forgiven the moment I saw this beautiful little face. Anyone in my position would have done the same. How could one not take care of such an angel?" Elizabeth concluded with a warm, affectionate smile.

She put the baby on the pillow again and intended to retire in order to allow Caroline to enjoy his presence. She knew mother and son needed time to rebuild their bond, and the two maids sitting discreetly in the corner of the room were sufficient to offer any help or support needed without imposing on Caroline while she was relishing the private company of her child.

A moment later, she felt her hand imprisoned by Caroline, and before she could understand what was happening, Caroline placed a grateful, humble kiss upon it. Elizabeth startled and fought to pull her hand away while Caroline whispered, tearfully, "Thank you, Mrs. Darcy. Thank you."

A moment of curious silence passed — a brief hesitation — and then Elizabeth smiled, brushing Caroline's forehead with gentle fingers.

"You are quite welcome, Caroline — quite welcome indeed."

Chapter 27

A month passed by peacefully, and calm happiness returned to Darcy's home. The tragic events surrounding young Markham's death were often mentioned in Town despite the family's attempt to keep the matter private. In addition, there was no little talk about Caroline Bingley's great fortune in becoming a young and exceedingly wealthy widow.

Caroline and her child were still in Darcy's house at Elizabeth's special invitation. Caroline's condition continued to improve while little James became as healthy and strong as any infant his age. Caroline spent all her time in her apartments, most of the time holding her son and speaking to him or singing to him in a low voice. As Elizabeth predicted, the bond between mother and son was rapidly restored.

The relationship between Caroline and Lady Cassandra gradually became quite different than it was earlier in their acquaintance, and though they could not be called close friends, Cassandra's frequent visits and constant inquiries after the child's health became a daily habit.

Lord Markham had called every single day after his son's burial, asking about Caroline and his grandson's health, but Caroline never agreed to see him. He also expressed his regrets — with painful honesty — as he declared he alone was culpable for everything that occurred regarding his sons. Cassandra refused even to speak to him directly, but the Darcys, the Bingleys and Colonel Fitzwilliam accepted his apologies with wisdom and generous understanding in consideration of all he had endured.

The earl presented Bingley with a settlement on Caroline and her son: a house in Town in a fashionable neighbourhood and a generous allowance to afford them a comfortable life even without any other support. To everyone's shock, Caroline refused it instantly and declared she and her son would live with the Bingleys.

Mrs. Hurst censured her younger sister, insisting that she should be happy that her son would be the heir of Markham's name and enormous fortune. After that, Caroline also refused to see her sister and held on to her refusal for more than a fortnight.

Lord Markham left a copy of the settlement with Bingley. Even more, he insisted that his grandson would be his heir, and he expressed his deepest hope and ardent wish that, sometime in the future, Lady Caroline Markham would be able to forgive him and allow him to see his grandson.

THE END OF OCTOBER WAS a little cloudy but the weather was still fine. Elizabeth and Georgiana were enjoying a cup of tea and watching their companion. It was the first time Caroline had agreed to leave her room and join Elizabeth in the drawing room.

Her son was close to her on the settee, sleeping peacefully, as Caroline refused to go anywhere without him. Georgiana moved near to admire the infant's pretty face and attempted to take the child in her arms for a moment, but to her shock, Caroline turned instantly and pulled her hands away from her son. A moment later, red-faced and deeply embarrassed by her unwarranted reaction, Caroline begged for forgiveness and encouraged Georgiana to hold the child as much as she wanted as the boy was always pleased to be cradled.

It took some time before the tension vanished from the room; Elizabeth started to talk about the weather and then continued to chat amiably about the Bingleys and Caroline's return to her brother's home, which was expected soon as the Bennets had left town the day before. Mr. Darcy was out on some business and was expected to return before dinner, as were Lady Cassandra and her husband. Georgiana was still holding the child as Caroline stood up to fill Elizabeth's cup of tea once more, asking if she was comfortable enough on the couch.

"I am fine, thank you, Caroline. In fact, I am very well indeed except that I can barely move." Elizabeth smiled.

A moment later her smile faded, and she let go of the cup. A sharp pain made her bend over, and a cry escaped her lips; she tried to rise from the chair, but she fell to her knees when another spasm came over her. Caroline held her while Georgiana, pale and frightened, still carrying little James, called for the servants.

Two hours later, Darcy returned home; he was hungry, tired and worried about Elizabeth as he had been out for the entire day. At least he was content that he had finished all his business and could stay home with Elizabeth for the next few weeks in anticipation of their child's birth.

He had barely entered the house when he heard in the main hall far more voices than expected. He easily recognised the colonel, Cassandra, Bingley and — to his shock — his sister-in-law, Jane. Before he had time to wonder at such a sudden gathering, Bingley approached him nervously.

"Darcy, where on earth have you been? Your butler has been looking for you for at least an hour."

Darcy frowned as the sudden understanding fell over him; he noticed the doctor drying his hands and moving slowly down the stairs toward him.

"Where is my wife? Where is Elizabeth?"

"Mrs. Darcy is well, sir — as well as can be expected in her condition."

"You will excuse me; I need to see her this minute." Darcy pushed Bingley away, running to the stairs.

"Sir, you should wait another moment; the midwife is with her, preparing Mrs. Darcy and *your son* to receive your visit," the doctor said, obviously pleased with Darcy's shocked expression.

For only a moment, Darcy remained stone still before disappearing up the stairs, not even noticing his friends calling to him.

That night Mr. Darcy refused to leave his wife's apartment, though everyone — including Elizabeth — assured him there was no reason for worry. The servants retired but no further than Elizabeth's dressing room to be near their mistress. The midwife could not hide her disapproval of such behaviour. Did no one ever sleep in their own rooms in this house? Finally, she abandoned any attempt to argue with the master and his disobedient staff, and found a place to sleep on a sofa nearby in case she should be needed.

Darcy moved an armchair close to Elizabeth's bed and sat by her. She was more beautiful than ever — rather, she was beautiful in a different way than ever before — and he could not find the words to tell her everything that was in his heart. Her tender smile and her eyes sparkling with happiness proved to him that no words were needed — so he remained silent, smiling tearfully, wondering at the miracle brought to life by their love, while she finally fell asleep, her hand resting in his.

Four months later

THE DARCYS' CARRIAGE DROVE ALONG the white streets of a frozen London; inside the carriage it was also cold, and Elizabeth slid her frozen hands into her husband's to warm them. To her surprise, his fingers did not entwine with hers as she was used to.

"Thank you for taking the time to come for me, William," she said, a little disconcerted.

"There is no need to thank me. It is always a pleasure to accompany you; you know that. Besides, when I came home and learned you had just left to visit your sister, I saw no reason to remain inside alone. My only option was to come for you."

"Forgive me for not being there when you arrived. It was on very short notice, and I was certain you would be out on business until later in the afternoon. Cassandra came by to take me, as we wanted to plan together with Jane the last details about Christmas dinner. As I had just nursed little Will, I took the opportunity and joined her. Are you displeased? Has anything happened?" she inquired, puzzled by his obviously low spirits.

"Of course I am not displeased. Why should I be? No, nothing happened. It is just that…you should have stayed home and rested. I am afraid you are tiring yourself too much. Things have not been easy for you the last months: first, all the duties you had to learn at Pemberley, then the blessed news of our child, Jane's illness and then Caroline, the birth of our son ten weeks ago and your insistence on nursing him yourself. Now things are finally settling, everyone is well and safe, and our son is growing up wonderfully. You should use this time to rest more. Cassandra could have made plans with Jane first and shared them with you tomorrow."

"Oh, do not worry for me, dear husband. I confess I am so tired sometimes that I fear I might fall asleep on my feet." She laughed. "But I could not resist walking out of the house for a short time — especially as it snowed earlier; did you notice? You know I love snow."

"Yes, I did notice it snowed."

He was obviously upset, and Elizabeth could not understand the reason. Perhaps he received some distressing news and was unwilling to share it with her yet. She took his hand and continued, smiling.

"Jane was looking wonderful, do you not think so? And Caroline — I was so pleased to see her well recovered! Two beautiful, healthy boys in the Bingley's house — Mr. Bingley has every reason to be thrilled. And he seemed quite pleased to see you, too."

"I was pleased to see Jane again, and indeed I am content everything turned out quite well for Caroline's situation. As for Charles — trust me, I meet him every day, so I doubt he missed my presence since I saw him just this morning. I dare say I see Charles more often than I see you." His countenance turned grave as he ceased to conceal his poor disposition.

"I am not sure I understand you, William. We see each other every day, do we not?"

"We see each other every day indeed, but you are not looking at me any longer, Elizabeth — not the way you used to look at me."

"You are upset with me, and I cannot determine the reason. What have I done to displease you?"

"Forgive me, Elizabeth, you have done nothing. I should not have mentioned it. It is just that…things are changing. That is what displeases me, and I do not know what to do to avoid that."

"What is changing?"

"You are changing!"

"And pray tell me, what is this change that bothers you so much? Have I neglected some of my duties or —"

"You have neglected nothing, my dear; in truth, you have succeeded wonderfully in everything you have done, Elizabeth, and your efforts are indeed praiseworthy. My tenants and their families cherish you, my aunt and uncle have come to love you, and the servants adore you. As for Georgiana, Cassandra or your own family, there is no need to mention them. Yes, everyone around you seems to benefit from your generous efforts. Everyone seems to have a fair share of your attention — everyone but me."

"Everyone but you?" She startled and frowned, looking at him in disbelief.

"Or better said, I have become only one of your many duties, and that is not enough for me. You have time for everyone and everything, though until a few months ago you could not stay away more than a few hours without coming to see me, do you remember that? I did notice it snowed earlier. That is why I interrupted my meeting and hurried home to take you on a walk through the first snow in the Park. And you were out — visiting your sister."

"William..."

"I know I am being selfish, but that is how I am. I am afraid it will never change. I do understand your care for your sister — and for my sister, and for our friends, and for the others around us — but truly, it is enough for me to know they are all well. I have no wish to speak of other's troubles any longer, and I have become tired of company after the last months we spent in Town. I miss being alone with you. I miss your smiles directed only at me. I miss your teasing. I miss your sparkling eyes staring at me in front of the fireplace. I miss feeling you abandon yourself in my arms when we are alone. I miss seeing you blush and shiver when I touch you. I know it is not your fault, but — Is my presence no longer enough for you? What can I do to become as important to you as I once was? I know we have our son now; we are not only the two of us, but..."

Elizabeth watched him as she struggled to understand his words. From only a few inches away, the distress was so obvious on his face that she could not resist the urge to lean toward him and kiss his cheek. He did not turn to her but kept staring at a point in front of him, and Elizabeth could not decide whether she should be upset or amused by his stubbornness. She took off her glove and caressed his face.

"Dearest husband, how can you say that? How can you not know that my love is deeper and stronger than ever? I do love you and treasure you with all my heart, and no day passes without my thanking God for allowing me to be your wife. I miss being with you, too — I miss it so much! Today when I saw it was snowing, my first thought was of you — wondering whether you were in front of a window to see it — but I did not dare consider you would interrupt your business for this. Now that I know of the responsibilities that burden your shoulders and the people who rely on you, my small wishes and caprices seem so unimportant.

"Elizabeth, nothing is more important to me than your wishes. You should know that —"

She shook her head in disapproval.

"There are many other things more important than my wishes. Day by day, I understand how fortunate I have been, and I must do everything in my power to pay back my good fortune in some way. I have a marriage full of love and affection — the most wonderful, handsome and prosperous husband. I have a beautiful, healthy child. Even the birth of our son was easier for me than for other women. I have everything, and so many others have so little! I cannot allow myself to act only according to my own desires — if so, I would do nothing but abandon myself to your arms." She paused a moment, watching him carefully, and then laughed softly.

"Well, perhaps I would evade your arms from time to time, only to check upon our son and to nurse him; I hope that would not bother you too much."

"Do not laugh at me, Elizabeth. I do understand that our son is more important to you than I am; that is how it should be." He sounded offended but Elizabeth replied gently while her fingers stroked his jaw line.

"I must laugh at you, dear husband, or else I would have to become very angry with you. How can you even ask whether your presence is enough for me? How can you not feel my love? I would like nothing more than to be alone with you — day-by-day and night-by-night as we were before — but with everything that has happened these last few months, that could not be. Indeed, we have had little privacy since we left Pemberley — but understandably so. There were so many things to do, so many others needing me and so many others needing you. And there were all the engagements we had to keep — though I confess some of them were as tiresome for me as they were for you. I am not complaining; I know how important my status is as your wife and as the mother of your heir. As Lady Fitzwilliam rightfully said — I cannot and I would not neglect complying with my duties, especially considering we have to prepare for Georgiana's coming out ball next year. And —"

He unexpectedly silenced her when his mouth captured her lips; she released a small cry of surprise and had no time to breathe under his possessive attack. His lips withdrew from hers only an inch so he could whisper, "I could not care less about all those things — so be so kind as to stop talking about social nonsense."

"Well, I can hardly speak of anything right now," she laughed and a moment later was silenced once more.

It was fortunate for Darcy's good name that the carriage stopped in front of their house a couple of minutes later — before any permanent damage was done to their clothes and appearance.

When they entered the main door, Mrs. Darcy was still quite flushed, and the maid who helped take off her coat wondered whether the mistress was not — heaven forbid — a little feverish.

"It is time to nurse our son. I shall see you later." Elizabeth smiled as they climbed the stairs.

"Very well." He entered his room as he heard her loving voice asking the maid about little William.

Darcy remained there, staring at the door closed behind her, unable to move — or to think properly. What had just happened? How had she managed to dissipate all his worries and put an end to his torment in only a few minutes? Had he only been a fool all these months? Most likely so!

He threw himself into a chair and poured a glass of wine. Had he upset her with his unreasonable reproaches? It was true that she did not seem upset at the moment — but she was so right in her response! She had done everything she could to honour him and his name, and what was her reward: his careless words of reproach for not giving him enough of her time? Truly, does she have any time at all? With every moment of recollection, his heart raced increasingly until he became full of rage against himself.

The servant announced dinner was ready, and Darcy harshly dismissed him. After a lengthy period of agitated pacing around the room and muttering to himself, he finally regained some of his composure. Only then did he notice the hour and the servant waiting in silence in the doorway to help him prepare for dinner — and he finally decided what to do.

Elizabeth sank into the bathtub, lost in her thoughts.

She was tired, and her heart ached. They had argued — their first argument since they married — and though they had reached a truce quite soon, she could still taste the bitterness of it. The more she recollected their discussion, the more she agreed that he was right; she did not give him the proper consideration a husband like him deserved; she could easily see that. Certainly, they did spend much time together, but it was true they were rarely alone.

Even when they retired to their rooms, she was usually so tired that she fell asleep almost immediately, and though they began to share intimacies again about two months after their son was born, their lovemaking was somehow different — she could not deny that. She had become more restrained and a little uncomfortable, and truly, she felt she had lost the courage to do some of the things she used to do before. She had wondered many times whether it was proper — now that she was a mother — to behave as she did when she was a newly wedded wife, and her puzzlement increased as Darcy seemed more restrained too — less demanding and less insistent in his attentions toward her. Instead of trying to keep her roused, or awaking her when she fell asleep before he came to bed — as he did in the first months of their marriage — he now appeared more preoccupied in allowing her to rest. She feared that was a sign of his decreasing passion and desire for her — as happened to many men after they had an heir — but after his earlier outburst in the carriage, that seemed unlikely.

She laughed as she felt tears in her eyes, remembering his expression when he complained about her giving too much of her time to others. It was a little strange coming from someone who was always so generous to everyone within his sphere of influence.

"Please come and help me out of the bath," Elizabeth called to the maid. She had to prepare for dinner and look for him — immediately.

She startled when she saw the shadow of her husband along the wall.

"Did I frighten you?" he asked gently as he came closer. She instinctively crossed her arms over her chest.

"You did not frighten me. Well, yes you did a little, as I did not expect to see you." She smiled.

"Yet there was a time when you knew you would see me here every evening."

"It is true, but that was more than six months ago."

"Seven months," he replied. Elizabeth smiled again and blushed.

Darcy knelt near the tub; his dark gaze met her eyes in a silent search of her thoughts. She shivered. He took her wet hand, wiped it with his fingers and then placed a burning kiss in her palm. She shivered again.

"Are you cold? Should I bring you some hot water?" he asked.

"The water is fine," she replied. In fact, she did not much feel the water.

"Did you shiver because I kissed your hand?" he whispered, and she nodded, obviously uneasy.

"I am such a selfish, insensible idiot," he confessed unexpectedly, and she burst out in a nervous laugh.

"You are neither selfish nor insensible," she said moments later, staring at her fingers entwined with his.

"But I am an idiot, am I not?" he insisted, tipping her chin to meet his eyes. He leaned to reach her face, and his lips wiped her tears. "Please forgive me, Elizabeth."

"There is nothing to forgive. It is I who should apologise; you were right in everything you said."

"I was wrong and unfair, and I am surprised you are still speaking to me."

"Well, since I am imprisoned in this bathtub, I can do little else but speak with you," she teased him.

"That is true," Darcy admitted. "You are my prisoner and will be so for the next four hours at least."

"Hmm… I am afraid that will not be possible, sir. I shall have my rescue quite soon. Mary will be here any moment to help me prepare for dinner."

"I have dismissed Mary for tonight," he replied seriously. "As for dinner — it is prepared in my room."

He leaned closer so his lips brushed against hers. "Are you displeased?"

She withdrew a few inches to look at him; her arms encircled his neck and warm water fell all over his robe. "Do you think I am displeased, husband?"

His lips tasted hers for a short moment. "I hope not."

She returned the kiss, biting his lower lip — as she had not done in months.

"What should I do for you to become certain, sir? Perhaps invite you to join me in here?"

Darcy broke the kiss; his thumb brushed against her wet, red lips.

"I have long waited for such an invitation, my dearest."

"Then you have been a fool, sir. You should have known you needed no invitation to join me whenever and wherever you please."

"That is very dangerous encouragement, Mrs. Darcy, as it gives me the right to take advantage of you. Are you aware of that?" Her right eyebrow rose as a mischievous smile twisted the corners of her mouth.

"Truly, sir? I was not aware of the danger. Thank you for enlightening me," she replied in jest. Darcy laughed delightedly and kissed her hand.

"Let me help you out of the tub," he said and brought her a towel and her robe. She looked at him, puzzled and slightly embarrassed by his indirect refusal of her daring invitation.

He covered her in the robe and unexpectedly took her in his arms; her arms gathered around his neck, and she cast a quick glance at him, only to meet the smile of satisfaction in his eyes.

"You are disappointed I took you out of the water, are you not?"

"No, it is just that... You said you waited so long and I thought..."

They were already at the door to his room when he stopped to whisper close to her ear. "You thought correctly, my love. However, I decided to postpone accepting your invitation because the tub is not comfortable enough for the way I planned to spend these next few hours."

"Oh..." she whispered as he entered his bedchamber, holding her tightly.

He put her down on the settee near the fireplace. On a small table was a silver tray with some dishes, but she paid no attention to their contents. She felt her husband watching her closely; he sat near her and removed her robe, covered her in a dry one and then embraced her; she cuddled to his chest, and her hands took his.

"There is much more food in the dressing room... for later," he said and she could feel the amusement in his voice, mixed with all those signs of passion she knew so well.

"I am not so very hungry," she replied. "I am content just to stay here with you like this." One of her hands released his and moved up his torso. "Your robe is wet too, William. You should change before you get cold."

He gently pulled her aside. "My dear wife, if you are content just to stay *near* me, I am afraid you will be disappointed very soon. As for my wet robe — it is indeed uncomfortable."

His voice had become deep and grave, and each of his words made her quiver. His voice, his glances, his movements, and even his breathing were insinuating, flirtatious, passionate — and demanding.

She swallowed with some difficulty, trying to control her trembling — but with no success. She had not changed at all — and neither had he. He said she was his prisoner for the next few hours, but she knew very well that she was also a prisoner of her own love and passion — imprisoned for her entire life.

"Then you should remove your robe," she said, licking her suddenly dry lips while she struggled to hold his intense gaze. She untied his robe and pulled it from his shoulders; he wore nothing beneath it.

"I should go and get another one while we are eating."

"Yes you should — when we eat."

He moved closer to her and she leaned back against the settee.

"Are you not hungry, Elizabeth? When we were in the carriage, you said you were starving. I do not want to —"

She cupped his face and pressed her lips against his. "You do not want what, husband, or better said — what is it that you want? Are you hungry?"

The scent of his naked skin intoxicated her; he was almost atop her now and she closed her eyes to feel his weight on her but she suddenly felt herself lifted in his arms and carried to his bed.

He placed her against the pillows, and his strong palm caressed her face, as his tongue tasted her earlobe.

"I am hungry indeed. I have been starving for you for a long time."

"But why did you starve, my love?" She entered into his passionate game, moaning at his touches. "I have never rejected you, nor did I do anything to keep you away."

"I was afraid — afraid it might be too soon after Will's birth, afraid I might hurt you, afraid I might bother and tire you with my insistence —"

"You should have asked me if you had any doubts; you should have told me what you wished."

Breathing had become more difficult for her, and she was not certain whether she was still speaking coherently. Each of his caresses proved how much her skin had craved his touch.

"I shall tell you now, or perhaps I should better show you…" His lips brushed against hers one more time, and then his mouth followed his hands, travelling down to her throat, to her shoulders, resting a few moments upon her heart, and then lower, along her body, caressing, kissing, and tasting each spot of her silky skin.

"You have always been more eloquent with your gestures than with your words, husband."

"And what is it that you want, Elizabeth?" He stopped his caresses and looked at her; under his intense stare, she had to open her eyes and, searching for air, gained courage to speak the truth.

"What I want is to make all your doubts and worries vanish, to make you always certain of how much I love and desire you, to feel your love and passion upon and inside my body."

With each of her words, he leaned closer to her until his face was touching hers; her arms stroked his back while her legs opened for him and encircled his waist. Holding his gaze a little longer, she had to close her eyes when she felt him crushing her with his weight, and his mouth covered her moans the moment he slid inside her.

The time went by in the rhythm of their joined movements, and Elizabeth could not say for how long their restrained passion searched for its eventual fulfilment. All she noticed from time to time — as her body struggled to recover from the exhaustion of pleasure — was the fire that became less intense as the logs within the fireplace burned one by one. *It will be cold if the fire dies,* she thought, and then she returned her face to meet her husband's lips once more. She did not need the fire to keep her warm, as long as she could feel her husband's passion deep within her body and his love deep within her soul.

ELIZABETH, WRAPPED IN HER ROBE, watched her husband as he tried to remake the fire. A moment later, while he was preoccupied with his task, she silently exited the room, barefoot. When she returned a few minutes later, the fire was burning, and Darcy was filling her plate with food. He smiled at her.

"How is Will?"

"He is asleep; he sleeps so peacefully, my little treasure," she replied, her eyes glowing with tenderness.

"How many times a night do you check on him?"

She laughed. "Yes, I know I am being unreasonable; even Mrs. Taylor scolded me that I disturb the poor child, entering the nursery so many times. She even suggested that we hire two maids to watch him for nothing."

"Would you be more content if we were to hire three maids? Another one to watch the first two, and of course, Mrs. Taylor would watch the third maid to be sure she takes care in supervising the others."

"You are mocking me, sir, and enjoy laughing at me, but you are no better; I know how many times you check on Will yourself."

"It is not the same," Darcy replied. "I am the master of the house, and I may do whatever I want — just ask your mother."

"Oh, I have not the smallest doubt of that, sir," Elizabeth said, playfully. "You are twisting the rules however it pleases you."

"It is the advantage of my ten thousand a year, madam."

She laughed, and he sat near her, pulling the small table in front of them. Elizabeth started to eat, but he remained still, watching her. She looked at him, puzzled, her eyes still laughing from his last statement.

"Are you not hungry?"

"Not really. I feel quite satiated for the moment."

She laughed again, her cheeks crimson. "I was speaking about the food."

"As was I, madam. I feel content to have a glass of wine and watch you."

She found nothing to say for a few minutes and only continued to take small bites; finally, he decided to put some cold meat on his plate and join her. She cast a quick glance at him and suddenly began to laugh.

"You had a wonderful idea ordering dinner in your room; this way we did not waste any time in changing our garments and preparing for dinner."

"Indeed, we have employed our time much better."

"I am being very serious, William. I mean, if this is acceptable to you, we could have all of our dinners in one of our rooms every time we dine alone."

"Elizabeth — it is a splendid idea. Perhaps we can bring our son to stay with us for a couple of hours, just before you feed him and put him to bed."

"I would love that." She smiled lovingly.

"Of course, that would be possible only when we are at home for dinner and have no company."

"I trust we will succeed in rearranging our social engagements to our mutual satisfaction," she replied. "Besides, I have started to feel quite tired lately. Lady Fitzwilliam suggested I should rest more, so I plan to follow her advice."

"Are you unwell?"

"Not all the time, but I am sure I will be — quite often — especially during the evenings when we have visitors." Her eyebrow rose in challenge, and she leaned to whisper to him. "You seem surprised, husband. Perhaps you disapprove of my mischievous plan. I am ready to abandon it if it displeases you. I know only too well that disguise of every sort is your abhorrence."

He stared at her, and for a moment the shadow of that painful day in their past clouded his visage — but only for a moment as Elizabeth's smiling eyes were watching him closely, lightening any dark memory.

Darcy smiled and cupped her face. "Well, *'disguise'* is a relative term, and so is my abhorrence."

He paused a few moments, caressing her cheeks as their gazes locked.

"The only thing beyond any doubt or relativity is how ardently I admire and love you, Elizabeth."

Epilogue

Pemberley, six years later!

"This place always amazes me," Cassandra exclaimed with joy. "It seems to become lovelier with each passing year."

"I believe the same," said Elizabeth as they walked a grove together arm-in-arm. "Every time I come here, its beauty takes my breath away."

The grove was situated on one of the hills surrounding Pemberley House. It was railed by trees, arranged almost in a circle, and flowers of all colours were spread around, warmed by the late August sun. Behind the trees, a stream with clear water completed the brilliant picture of light and colour.

"This garden was made by Papa especially for Mama and for me," young William exclaimed with pride, his back straight, his expression serious. "It is only for our family and for Aunt Georgiana, but she married last month, and she is on a tour with my new uncle now," the boy continued to explain seriously, as if the Fitzwilliams were not aware of that news.

"We only allow very special guests here," he continued, forgetting that the Fitzwilliams had visited many times in the last few years.

"I see. And we are special guests?" Cassandra inquired.

"You are indeed."

"Thank you, young sir," Cassandra replied and then unexpectedly grabbed the boy in her arms and started kissing his face.

"Aunt Cassandra, put me down please! I am no longer a baby boy!" said the child of almost six years, trying to escape her arms.

She finally put him down, and with what remained of his dignity, he moved slowly but determinedly to the place where his father and his Uncle David were talking. He could not stay around ladies any longer. His Aunt Cassandra always treated him like a child, and one of these days he would became quite angry with her — quite angry indeed.

It was difficult to be angry with Cassandra though, because, besides his mother and Aunt Georgiana, young William loved his Aunt Cassandra the most — especially since she was his godmother too — but godmother or not, a lady should not take a grown-up boy in her arms to kiss him in public!

This thought of grown-up boys instantly made him think of his cousin James Markham, one of Will's best friends.

James had some rather big troubles, poor boy, caused by his own mother — Aunt Caroline. As James and his mother lived most of the time at the Bingleys' estate, Will had a chance to meet him as well as his Bingley cousins quite often. All the time — truly all the time! — whenever they ran out to play, James's mother would call him and check on him, and she always insisted on kissing him on his cheek even if they were in public! Moreover, she rarely allowed James to climb trees, to ride, or to swim in the stream, because she said he might hurt himself. That was not the right way to treat a growing boy either! And his grandfather, Lord Markham, whenever he came to visit them, instead of taking James's side — as Grandpa Bennet did with Will — seemed to agree with Lady Markham all the time. James had confessed to Will many times that his grandfather was very good to him but did not want to buy him a horse as he was afraid James might be injured in an accident. That was a strange notion, Will thought, considering James would be an earl some day. What kind of an earl would he be if he could not ride really well? However, he had to admit that James's mother and his grandfather were not so bad after all — outside of the fact that they did not allow James to play as he liked.

Of course, he was not allowed to play any time he wanted and any way he liked either, but in his case, it was different. His parents were always right; he had no doubt about that. He had the best father, the most beautiful and perfect mother and now he had a beautiful baby sister. He was lucky to have such a family; Mrs. Reynolds told him that many times — and Mrs. Reynolds was always right too. Even more, he had to admit he also had very nice relatives; he really liked all his cousins. He looked forward to the next Sunday when they would come to visit at Pemberley and would stay for a fortnight. The Bingleys, Aunt Caroline and James, Grandma and Grandpa Bennet, the Gardiners — not to mention his godparents who would surely be there too. That would be a crowded house, indeed — as his father said — and Will really liked to have many people around!

He sat near his father and his godfather, wondering why he was upset with his Aunt Cassandra after all.

"You should not treat the poor boy in that improper manner, Cassandra," laughed Elizabeth as they sat together on the blanket.

"I know, but I cannot help myself. I absolutely adore him, and he is so sweet when he tries to behave like an adult." Cassandra laughed. "He is aloof and haughty like Darcy, and I love teasing him."

"He does look like William; he is already quite handsome and has such dark, expressive eyes," Elizabeth said while her loving gaze rested upon her husband and her son. "However, I am not certain whether he has the same disposition as William or only tries to mirror him. He struggles so much to be exactly like his father! And, to be honest, you have to admit William is not that aloof or haughty, either."

"No, he is not...anymore," Cassandra admitted. "You had a very positive influence upon his improvement."

"William needed no improvement at all. He has always been the best of men," Elizabeth replied decidedly. Cassandra laughed again.

"Well, I do hope Darcy does not hate kisses as much as Will does."

Elizabeth blushed slightly and then laughed, too. "You must not worry about any of my gentlemen in that regard," she replied, looking toward the small group in front of them.

Among the three gentlemen — all appropriately dressed for a late summer day — a spot of colour was making a lively, noisy contrast: pale green ribbons and lace with reddish brown curls dancing on a girl no older than four. She took tight hold of young William's arm.

"May I kiss you, too?" she insisted, and the boy stepped backward.

"You most certainly may not! What a strange notion — to kiss me! That is the most unpleasant thing to do. Why would you want to kiss me?"

"Because you are my favourite cousin, and I like you very much."

Young William looked at her and remained silent for a moment, thinking of all his cousins. There were Charles, Ellen and Francis Bingley and James Markham and Peter and George Wickham. He had to admit that he, too, liked this cousin the most, though she was very annoying and quite demanding sometimes, not to mention her strange, silly ideas.

"I like you too; you are my favourite cousin too, but you still cannot kiss me," he replied. "Kisses are very unpleasant," he concluded, as if teaching his younger cousin a lesson.

"No, they are not unpleasant," the girl insisted. "Mama and Papa kiss me all the time and so do Aunt Georgiana, Aunt Lizzy and even Uncle Darcy. And more," she whispered, "Papa kissed Mama many times; I saw it."

Again the boy remained silent. He too had seen his father kissing his mother a few times, but he would not possibly admit it to anyone, and he did enjoy it when his mother and father kissed him good night or even during the day — but he would not admit this to his cousin either.

"Well, that is different — the rules are different when mothers and fathers are involved," he concluded, with a meaningful look to his father, who had told him so many times.

Darcy tried hard to conceal his smile while the colonel called the girl to him and whispered something to her. The girl's face lit instantly, and she suddenly turned to her cousin and said triumphantly, "When I grow up, you will *beg* me to allow you to kiss me, and I shall refuse you. And I shall not even dance with you unless you stop being so aloof and haughty!"

"I am not aloof or haughty; I am a very proper gentleman; Aunt Georgiana and Mrs. Reynolds have told me so many times," the boy defended himself. He would also like to say that Mrs. Reynolds told him he was even more handsome than his father was at his age, but that was not something to discuss with his younger cousin. "And," he continued, "I certainly will not beg you to kiss me or to dance with me; that cannot be true." He turned to his father hopefully, searching for support. "Will I, father?"

Darcy could not hide his smile while he patted his son's hair. "I cannot say for sure, son, but it might well be true — so you should be guarded with your words when you speak to young ladies around you."

The boy remained still, looking from his father to his cousin so seriously that neither Darcy nor David could repress their chortles. A moment later, David took the girl in his arms and rolled around in the grass with her; the girl laughed with all her heart while young William stood silently at a distance. David grabbed the boy's leg and pulled him to fall over them. The girl was thrilled and instantly climbed over her cousin, placing a quick kiss on his cheek. The boy wiped his face, torn between laughing along with the others and being upset for the mistreatment. Only when Darcy started to laugh, too, did the boy decide to imitate his father.

Elizabeth and Cassandra exchanged delighted smiles; the small burden on Elizabeth's lap yammered softly, and she lifted the infant in her arms.

"You are awake, my love," Elizabeth whispered and kissed the child's cheeks. Cassandra caressed the child's small hand and was rewarded with happy babbling.

In a moment, the girl left the men's group and hurried to the ladies; she stopped in front of them, her cheeks red from laughter and exertion, her curls spread around her face, her green eyes shining.

"Oh, you are awake, my sweet, darling, precious little Anne," she said while she knelt and kissed the infant's face. "I am sooooo happy you are a girl like me, and you are so beautiful, and you allow me to kiss you," she continued while the baby's fingers entwined in the girl's curls, and a mixture of laughter and babbling melted the two women's hearts.

A few minutes later, with a last kiss to her cousin and one to Cassandra and Elizabeth, the girl returned to young William.

"Cassie is adorable," Elizabeth said to her friend. "She is so beautiful, so sweet, and so good-humoured all the time."

"So spoiled, so outspoken, so daring, so disobedient," continued Cassandra looking after the little girl.

"So much like her mother. She does resemble you very much, Cassandra — both in spirit and in appearance. She is already a little beauty."

"She is beautiful, is she not?" Cassandra asked as if she needed confirmation. With a long glance toward the little group, Cassandra's voice became weaker and slightly trembling. "Elizabeth, I confess I do not care much about her beauty but just for her health. I cannot believe God has been so good to me as to complete my happiness with this precious gift. I did not dare hope I would have a child of my own — and here she is. I am happier than I ever dreamed, yet there are still times when the dream turns into a nightmare. After all these years, I am still not certain I deserve to be so happy. I know it is hard to understand me," Cassandra said, fighting her tears as she smiled at her daughter who was waving to them.

"My dearest friend — I do understand you, though I do not dare presume to know the depth of your grief. However, I do have a philosophy that I have used many times and it has accomplished miracles more than once. Did I not share it with you?"

"No, you did not — and I would be more than grateful for a miracle." Cassandra smiled tearfully.

"Then be prepared to be grateful, for here it is: think only of the past as —"

"— as its remembrance gives you pleasure," completed Darcy, who approached them, kissed Elizabeth's hand and then took his daughter in his arms. "I learned it from Elizabeth a long time ago, and I can testify to its wisdom," he explained to his friend while his eyes gazed adoringly upon his wife; she responded, laughing at him with sparkling eyes.

"It sounds very wise indeed," Cassandra admitted, a short laugh vanquishing the sadness on her face. "I shall try to follow your advice, Mrs. Darcy — as your advice has proved quite useful to me more than once."

Elizabeth reached for Cassandra's hand, and then she smiled at her friend.

"You should do that, Lady Cassandra. As for useful advice — we will not quarrel about the relative amount of wisdom in our conversations since we first met seven years ago, your ladyship. Let us just say that our shared advice is a part of the past that always gives us pleasure and can be remembered with joy, shall we?"

Cassandra squeezed Elizabeth's hand, and her face lit as she responded.

"I would not dare contradict you, Mrs. Darcy!"

A cool summer breeze stirred the fronds as the sun went down, and the master of Pemberley invited his guests to accompany him back to the house. Young William and little Cassie were the first to obey and hurried along the path. Elizabeth took her husband's arm, and he placed another tender kiss upon her hand while their daughter rested on his chest. Right behind them, Lady Cassandra and David shared a quick, gentle kiss of trust and understanding, following their friends.

Leaving behind their past and taking with them only its remembrance, the Darcys and Fitzwilliams stepped together toward the future, which was laughing happily before them through the joyful voices of their children.

THE END

CPSIA information can be obtained at www.ICGtesting.com
Printed in the USA
LVOW051818290712

292038LV00003B/2/P

9 781936 009107